D0119290

AUTHOR KIRBY M

CLASS AFG

TITLE Betrayal

WHALLEY

Betrayal

Betrayal

Margaret Kirby

PIATKUS

03660696

WHALLEY

Copyright © 1989 by Margaret Kirby

First published in Great Britain in 1989 by
Judy Piatkus (Publishers) Ltd of
5 Windmill Street, London W1

British Library Cataloguing in Publication Data

Kirby, Margaret, *1947–*
  Betrayal
  I. Title
  823'.914 [F]

  ISBN 0–86188–823–5

Phototypeset in 11/12pt Compugraphic Times by
Action Typesetting Limited, Gloucester
Printed and bound in Great Britain by
Billing & Sons Ltd, Worcester

For Jay C. and Roo,
Two very special people

Acknowledgements

No one can write a novel of this size without the co-operation of many people but I would particularly like to thank The National Autistic Society; my agent, Maggie Noach, who answered my questions and lifted my spirits with unceasing patience; and Christopher MacLehose, who believed in the book a long time ago.

Prologue

Together they stood beside the five foot high cake, hands clasped on the ivory-handled knife, and Lisa looked out at the sea of faces. None of them were friends, many were enemies.

She saw Toby again; Bishop and the girls; and the Italian, now leaning against a wall in order to minimise his height. Glancing quickly away from him, she smiled up at her husband as the flash-bulbs exploded.

As most people suspected, it was a one-sided love match, yet she was determined to be a good wife. Aware of her own emotional short-comings she believed that with her husband's understanding it would be a sound marriage. She was also certain that in Neal Gueras she had found the perfect solution to the problem of Jessica.

Her confidence on both counts was totally misplaced.

Chapter One

'You mean you're not really my mother?' asked seven-year-old Lisa Greene, her dark eyes incredulous in her pale face.

Stephanie Greene tried to take the leggy, rigid body of her adopted daughter on to her lap, but it was impossible. She finally gave up and contented herself with putting a small, plump hand on the child's dark hair. 'No. That is, I didn't actually give birth to you. I was luckier than most women, I was able to choose my own beautiful baby girl. Most women aren't that lucky, you know. Whatever they have, boy or girl, pretty or plain, they can't change them for nicer babies, can they?'

'You've always said I grew in your stomach,' said Lisa, thoroughly confused. 'Hasn't any baby ever grown there?'

Stephanie winced. The lack of children of her own could still give her pain. 'No, but we waited to tell you until you were old enough to understand everything. I expect you'd like to hear why your real mummy couldn't keep you, wouldn't you?'

'I . . . No, thank you.' Plainly shocked, the child's voice sounded remote.

Stephanie hesitated, fleetingly wishing that Simon was here, but as usual he was abroad looking for antiques for his shop. 'It doesn't change anything,' she continued. 'We're exactly the same people as we were before you know. And remember, I chose *you*.'

The stunned child thought she detected a note of regret. 'But why don't I remember choosing you?' she asked in obvious puzzlement.

'You were only three months old. Tiny babies can't choose things like that for themselves!'

'Then people shouldn't be allowed to adopt them until they're bigger.'

Nothing she'd read had prepared Stephanie for the awkwardness of the conversation. 'Do you mean you'd rather have grown up in a

3

children's home, without any of your pretty clothes and lovely toys?' she asked with a forced laugh.

'I don't know,' said Lisa, her mind still in turmoil.

Her childish candour was unfortunate. Stephanie, never a very secure woman, had tried for years to feign affection for her adopted daughter, knowing all the time that in reality the child aroused no vestige of maternal love in her. Now, seeing Lisa's bewilderment, she chose to interpret it as a rejection of all her own efforts and thankfully abandoned the deceit forever. 'You'd better go to your room,' she said sharply.

'What have I done?' asked Lisa in hurt surprise.

'You're an ungrateful girl and if you don't go I shall tell your father as much. He'll probably stop your ballet lessons.'

'But he likes me to go to ballet.' She was puzzled by the threat and her failure to be cowed infuriated Stephanie, kindling a dislike that would in time border on hatred.

'Get out, you little bastard!' she shouted, smacking the child sharply round the face. 'Go on, get out! You're nothing but a disappointment to us both anyway.'

Terrified, Lisa stood stock-still, her right hand covering her mouth to choke back her sobs. A second blow nearly sent her tumbling to the immaculate, constantly raked, pale lilac shag-pile carpet.

'Get out! Get out!' screamed Stephanie, and at last Lisa managed to make herself run blindly from the room. Sobbing, she ran straight past the astonished housekeeper, along the wood-panelled hall and up the curved stairs. She stopped for a moment on the landing, nursing the pain in her cheek, but when she heard Stephanie's shrill cries below she scampered to the safety of her bedroom.

For hours she lay there, nails digging into the palms of her hands, sobbing wildly until, finally exhausted, she slept.

Simon Greene returned unexpectedly a little before midnight. As usual he looked in on his sleeping daughter first, placed a beautifully wrapped present beside her pillow and then went − somewhat less enthusiastically − to his wife's room.

Stephanie was propped up against a mass of lacy pillows reading a new Catherine Cookson novel. Her only original claim to good looks had been her youth, but now − at forty-two − she had something better, money. With this she'd created a slightly corpulent but undeniably ultra-feminine image.

'I wasn't expecting you tonight, Simon.'

Her husband, equally corpulent but not in the least handsome and not particularly masculine in appearance, smiled ruefully. 'I was worried about Lisa.'

'Why?'

'I knew you were going to tell her today and I was afraid she might take it badly.'

Stephanie laughed gently. 'Why on earth should she do that? No, it went very well. She was surprised, of course, but she's an intelligent little thing and fully realised how lucky she'd been.'

'We've all been lucky.'

'Of course.'

'Did she ask about her real parents?'

'No,' said Stephanie, on safer ground at last. 'She wasn't in the least interested in them.'

Simon sat on the edge of his wife's bed until her frown drove him to the rocking chair in the corner of the room. 'Well, that's everything straight at last. Should I mention it too?'

'I think perhaps . . .'

'Better not make too much of it? No, quite right. I won't say anything. After all, she knows exactly how much we think of her, doesn't she? There can't be any doubt about that?'

'None at all.'

And indeed there wasn't.

'What would you like for your birthday, Lisa?' asked Simon. 'Choose something special. You'll be a teenager at last!'

'I don't really need anything.' Lisa's voice was placating. He could always pinpoint the moment when she'd changed from an outgoing, humorous and totally honest little girl into an over-anxious, withdrawn and secretive child. It was the day after she'd learnt that she was adopted.

In his ignorance he'd thought that the more things he and Stephanie bought her, the more lavish their displays of affection, the quicker she would recover. But Lisa would never recover. She'd learnt that being beautiful misled people, that being rich meant you could buy anything, even another human being, and that overt displays of love were not to be trusted.

'Isn't there anything you'd like?' he persisted.

How could she tell him that what she craved was a sense of belonging? That she no longer knew how to fit in and make Stephanie pleased with her again. Dumbly she shook her head.

'Well, your mother thought . . .'

'She isn't my mother.'

It was the first time she'd spoken of her knowledge to Simon and he was caught unawares. He loved Lisa too deeply, and fearing to lose her through discipline and arguments he lost her anyway because she

5

assumed his forever smiling expression to be as insincere as his wife's.

'That's biologically true of course but . . .'

'She doesn't really love me!' cried Lisa suddenly, tears filling her eyes. 'I try and try but she's always cross.'

Simon shifted uncomfortably from foot to foot. 'You're at a difficult age,' he said at last. 'Most young girls quarrel with their mothers.'

'It *isn't* just my age. She's always finding fault with me. Why Daddy?'

He wished that he could give her a satisfactory answer. As the years passed Stephanie became more and more difficult to live with and although he suspected it was his work that worried her, he knew that it was Lisa who suffered the most.

'You're two very different people,' he said slowly. 'I think it's an unfortunate clash of personalities, that's all. Deep down she loves you very much.'

They both knew it was a lie, and to Lisa, Simon's lie was yet another betrayal. 'I would rather like a puppy,' she confessed nervously. 'I'd take care of it myself and . . .'

'Sweetheart, Stephanie doesn't like animals,' Simon apologised gently. Lisa swallowed hard as he squeezed her hand in apology. There was nothing else to be said and in the event she was very pleased with the new ski suit they chose for her. After all, she'd known that a puppy was out of the question.

'Now that you're sixteen I suppose you ought to go on the pill,' said Stephanie to the quiet but beautiful girl opposite her at dinner. Light from the leaded windows shone on the polished table. Intently, Lisa studied the flecks of dust caught in the beam. 'I'm speaking to you, Lisa!'

'I don't need the pill, Stephanie.' She had stopped calling her mother two years earlier, at Stephanie's request.

'So you did know I was talking to you?'

'Yes.' Sometimes she wondered how much longer she could cope with Stephanie's unpleasantness.

'And you don't need the pill?'

'No, thank you, Stephanie.'

'Well, don't come whining to me when you find yourself pregnant.' Lisa kept her head lowered. 'Of course, you wouldn't,' she muttered to herself. 'You'd go to Simon, as usual.'

'Simon says I can go to finishing school in Switzerland after my "A" levels.'

'Let's hope the Swiss are ready for you.'

6

'At least I might get some pleasant conversation at meal times,' Lisa muttered defensively.

Stephanie leant forward. 'If you're not very careful your sharp tongue is going to impede any chance of a good marriage.'

'I'm not going to *get* married.'

Just then the door opened and Simon hurried in. 'I've brought a visitor home. If you've both finished perhaps ...?' He glanced enquiringly at his wife.

'We'll join you in the library,' she responded, rising a trifle heavily to her feet, having in the last couple of years put on rather too much weight.

'Who is it?' asked Lisa, relaxing slightly now that she and Stephanie were no longer alone.

'Neal Gueras, a business acquaintance. A very important business acquaintance.'

'How old is he?'

'Mid-forties, I'd say.'

She gave a sigh of relief. Not an eligible business acquaintance, for once.

Her adoptive father and the tall, heavily built man with thick brown hair swept back off a high forehead were suddenly silent as she entered the library. The visitor's unusually dark eyes looked steadily into hers. 'Mr Gueras, my daughter, Lisa,' said Simon quickly. 'Lisa ...'

'I'm Neal Gueras,' he said in a deep voice, 'I'm delighted to meet you at last. Your father is always talking about you. Now I can appreciate why.'

'Which won't make it any the less boring in the future!' she responded with a laugh. The dark eyes narrowed slightly, his expression changing from politely benign to surprised alertness. 'Possibly not!' he conceded.

'Mr Gueras became a father for the third time today,' gushed Simon, trying to stop the conversation.

'How exciting!' enthused Stephanie.

'Not really; a third daughter, and positively no chance of a son in the future. Not, in my opinion, in the least exciting.'

Until then, Lisa had rather liked him. He was so different from most of Simon's business acquaintances. His clothes, his manner of speaking, even his aftershave, all spoke of a different world from the one she was used to. However, his chauvinistic dismissal of a baby girl disappointed her so acutely that she turned sharply away from him.

'You disapprove?' He sounded amused.

'Of course she doesn't!' responded Stephanie. 'She ...'

7

'Let her speak for herself.'

Never in her life had Lisa heard anyone speak that way to Stephanie.

'Yes, I do,' she said with total honesty. 'Children should be loved for themselves. Not because of sex, appearance or temperament. They're human beings. I hate the way adults talk about children,' she added in a low voice.

'I apologise,' put in Simon quickly.

'It's quite all right,' said Neal quietly. 'Why do you feel so strongly about this, my dear?'

'Because I . . .' At the last moment she stopped. She couldn't tell him. She knew that she could never tell anyone how much she hated knowing that she'd been a disappointment. She'd only been adopted because she looked beautiful and misleadingly docile, and she spent hours thinking about the babies who stayed in institutions until they grew up. It made her feel both guilty and a fraud, because inside she wasn't docile, and neither to her eyes was she beautiful.

'Go on,' he prompted.

Her eyes lost their frankness, she bit on her bottom lip and shrugged casually. 'I don't.' She saw the disbelief in his eyes. 'I was just being controversial!' she added with a quick laugh, but it wasn't the laugh he would have expected from a carefree teenager.

When Neal was leaving, Simon attempted to apologise again. Neal started to brush the apology aside, it was of no importance. 'She's adopted you see,' explained Simon. 'It's as though . . .'

Adopted. Neal didn't hear the rest of the man's speech. He was busy working out the difference this made. The girl was going to be exceptionally beautiful, not in any conventional mould but definitely beautiful.

His only interest in life, apart from his work, was collecting uniquely beautiful things. But she was very young, and who knew what the future held for him? By the time her beauty was fully formed he might well be dead, but if alive he'd definitely be interested. He'd mention her to Bishop tonight. 'Forward Planner 4-year,' he thought wryly, smiling to himself.

'My dear Simon,' he said with deceptive casualness. 'She's both lovely and young enough to get away with almost anything! A very lovely girl. You must take good care of her.'

Simon knew an order when he heard one, and was grateful for the finishing school. She'd be safe enough there for a couple of years, or so he thought. She probably would have been, but for Toby Walker.

Chapter Two

Lisa glanced out of Simon's car and wondered why she never really felt happy anywhere any more. 'Is Stephanie home?' she asked.

'Of course. She wants to know what finishing school's doing for you.'

'It's rather boring,' said Lisa apologetically. Simon pretended that he hadn't heard her and as the car slid to a halt Stephanie hurried out to meet them. She kissed Lisa on the cheek before stepping back to survey her keenly. 'You don't look any different!' she exclaimed in disappointment.

'That's a relief!' laughed Lisa. 'I've spent all my time fighting to keep my own identity.'

With a sigh, Simon took Lisa's two leather suitcases out of the back of the car. A few months ago, French, the chauffeur and general handyman, would have done it but he was gone now. Things were not working out as well as Simon would have liked, and it was on Lisa that his hopes were pinned.

Stephanie felt like screaming at this tall, remote girl whose eyes were too old for her face and upon whom Simon's very survival depended. Unfortunately for her this made antagonising Lisa out of the question.

'We've been invited to a dinner party tonight,' she said abruptly. 'I hope you're not too tired to come?'

Lisa's spirits sank even lower. 'Stephanie, I've done nothing but study how to lay tables, arrange flowers and pick guests — or is it the other way round? — for the past term. Do I have to go?'

'No,' said Simon quietly, 'but there will be some young people there and it would be nice to have you with us again.'

She could tell that it was important to him and so reluctantly agreed. 'Where's French? Can't he carry those for you?' she added.

Simon shook his head. 'French isn't with us any more.'

9

Lisa's eyes clouded. She'd always liked French. 'Why not?'

'He found a better position.'

'But ...?' Simon glanced at her and she realised that he didn't want to talk about it in front of Stephanie.

'You're young,' said Stephanie icily. 'I suggest you carry your own cases. Simon has had chest pains for the last few weeks, he shouldn't do heavy lifting.' With that she turned and went back into the house.

'Is that true?' asked Lisa anxiously.

'It's probably only indigestion. The doctor says I should lose weight and give up smoking, but that's a difficult combination. When I don't smoke I eat more!'

Lisa realised that he didn't look well. He was pale and his hair had turned completely grey. 'I know everything there is to know about balanced diets and animal fats, I'll make sure you eat properly while I'm home,' she teased, picking up her cases and following Stephanie indoors.

An hour later she was sitting in the library when Simon came hesitantly into the room. 'You don't really dislike finishing school, do you, sweetheart? It's important that you get all you can out of it. Stephanie and I, we're self-made people. I want you to ...'

'All they teach you is how to be a good wife! We've got to be able to fold napkins into imitation boats, turn tomatoes into red water lilies, think of colour themes for our dinner parties, know how to make a shy guest feel comfortable – it's so trivial.'

'But ...'

'Oh, we do some work. Languages, history ... but they don't really count for much. It's certainly a finishing school. They're showing us how we'll finish up: rushing about playing at being a hostess while our wealthy husbands are off running their industries and making love to girls who learnt how to please men in bed rather than out of it!'

'Surely you want to make a good marriage?'

'I'm not sure what you mean by a good marriage,' replied Lisa softly.

They looked at one another and he was the first to glance away. 'I meant a wealthy one.'

'You're wealthy. Do you want me to have a marriage like yours?' she asked gently.

'I made my money after I'd married; that's quite different.'

'I really want to work with children,' she confided, her face suddenly more animated.

'But that's ideal! Lots of rich wives don't know what to do with their spare time. You could work for the N.S.P.C.C. or something like that.'

'I don't think I'd be able to make a living doing charity work!'

Simon cleared his throat. 'You'll never be poor, darling. I've put a lot of money into a trust fund for you. No matter what happens that will always be there.'

'I'm very grateful, but I do want to earn my own money.'

'You might not have time,' he said sadly.

Lisa stared at him. 'What do you mean?'

'Lisa, I have to talk to you during the holiday. Not now, but soon. Perhaps tomorrow night, when Stephanie's at her bridge evening.'

'If you don't hurry up and get ready the dinner will be half over before we even arrive!' said Stephanie indignantly as she walked in on the pair of them. Lisa stood up slowly and walked gracefully out of the room.

'You have to admit she's stunning,' whispered Simon.

'With her approach to life, she needs to be. I'm only thankful *he* isn't going to be there tonight. I'd expected the school to soften her ...'

'She's all right,' Simon said in a tired voice. 'I'm going to have a whisky before I shower. Do you want a drink?'

'The doctor said no alcohol.'

'Sod the doctor!' he snapped, and Stephanie left him. She knew that there were times when he was better alone. Especially these days, when things were going so horribly wrong.

Dinner was at the house of a Hatton Garden jeweller who'd done a lot of business with Simon over the years, not all of it legitimate. Simon had bought gifts for Stephanie from his shop, but outside office hours, in the small back room, other transactions had taken place. David Markoff either hadn't heard the rumours about Simon's current misfortunes or else he didn't care. Unlike many of the Greenes' so-called friends he hadn't severed all contact, and Simon was grateful. So grateful that he spent most of the evening chatting to David's wife, and missed the beginning of what was to be his greatest personal disaster.

Lisa, still hungry because the food had been good but not abundant, wandered off into the room where the drinks were being served and began to help herself to some dry roasted peanuts. The young boy behind the bar, his eyes constantly checking the guests for attractive men, was totally disinterested in her and simply refilled the crystal glass every time she emptied it.

When Toby Walker slid on to the stool next to her she was beginning to feel bored with the nuts and reached in front of him for some olives. To her surprise he put one large hand round her wrist and kept it lightly imprisoned.

11

'If you're that hungry, I suggest we go on somewhere else and have a proper meal!' he laughed. She turned to look at him. He was stunningly handsome with jet black hair, dark blue eyes and a fantastic tan that looked genuine. 'I'm Toby Walker,' he added as an afterthought, and then paused as though she ought to know the name.

'I'm Lisa Greene, and kindly let go of my wrist. I'm desperate for an olive.'

'Only an olive?'

'Possibly a heap of spaghetti bolognaise wouldn't come amiss.'

'I'm suitably crushed!'

'Why should you be? You weren't responsible for the extremely lean cuisine we've just finished, were you?'

'No! Are you here with anyone?' he added, his eyes lingering on her crossed legs which looked endless from where he was sitting.

'Only my parents.'

'Who are they?'

'Mr and Mrs Greene!'

'Very sharp! I meant which ones are they? Point them out so that I can see where your good looks come from.'

'That's my father over there, talking to Mrs Markoff, and my mother's the lady in the glittery dress.'

'You don't look like either of them.'

'That's probably because I'm adopted.' She wondered why she'd told him; it was something she usually kept to herself.

'A beautiful orphan, how romantic!' His eyes glinted with amusement.

'Sarcasm is more effective when it's done with subtlety,' she retorted, and wished she'd kept silent.

'I don't know anything about that. I'm an actor.'

'At least that's different. Are you resting at the moment? That's what actors usually do, isn't it?'

'No, I'm working. I've got a series running on television.'

'You mean you're the star?' she asked with a laugh. She was only flirting with him because he was so handsome and the youngest person in the room apart from herself. She didn't imagine he was really famous. All show-business people exaggerated, it was part of their nature.

'Yes,' he said slowly. 'I'm the star. Where have you been living? On the moon?'

'I'm at finishing school in Switzerland.'

'My, my! Daddy wants you to marry well, does he?'

'Yes. What's your programme called? I'll make sure I watch an episode.'

'*The Outsider*. I'm an undercover intelligence officer who rushes round saving the country every Monday night after the news.'

'I'm impressed. How did you get the part?'

He shrugged. 'I was lucky. In the right place at the right time, that sort of thing. I hadn't done much before. I took up acting rather late, having started out as a draughtsman.'

'Useful to have a trade to fall back on in the hard times.'

'There won't be any hard times after this, providing I'm sensible, of course.'

'And are you sensible?'

'Not always,' he said slowly.

'Good! I don't ever intend to be too sensible, not even when I'm old and grey.' Their eyes met and she was fascinated by his undoubted magnetism.

'Lisa, darling,' cooed Stephanie, 'I'd like you to meet ...' Toby turned round and smiled his most charming smile at her. He was amazed by the venom in her small, over made-up eyes and saw how quickly she reached out a fat hand to take hold of Lisa's arm. 'Lisa, I said ...'

'I'm talking to someone,' protested Lisa.

'Hasn't your school taught you about mixing?' hissed the older woman. 'You can't just sit here chatting away to some second-rate TV star, there are important people for you to meet.'

Toby, who could hear every word, had to turn away to conceal his annoyance. He didn't consider himself to be in the least second-rate.

'Stephanie, please!' protested Lisa under her breath. 'I'm enjoying myself. Toby, didn't you mention something about going out to eat?' and she slithered off the bar stool so that her dress got caught up, revealing shapely thighs and a tantalising glimpse of lace-trimmed french knickers.

Toby shrugged. He knew enough to remember that the Greenes were no longer people of any importance. However, he wasn't sure about Lisa. He fancied her, but then he usually fancied attractive girls. However, there was something about her that was refreshing and attractive, although she was a trifle too edgy for him to feel entirely comfortable with. Just the same, it would be interesting to find out what she was like between the sheets.

'Sure! Don't worry, Mrs Greene, I'll bring her safely home in the morning!'

'In the morning?' Stephanie was still standing with a look of shock and fear on her face when Simon finally joined her, by which time Toby and Lisa were speeding across London, laughing at everything and entirely innocent of the alarm their excursion was causing at the Markoff dinner party.

At three a.m., after a long walk along the Embankment, where Toby talked about his work and his ambitions while Lisa listened intently, they drove to an overnight café for long-distance lorry drivers.

She was intoxicated by the strangeness of it all. Toby himself came from the East End — when he forgot that he was an actor his speech lapsed into a heavy London accent — and the café and its occupants were quite outside anything she'd ever encountered.

There were wolf whistles and appreciative shouts as she walked in, her low-cut green silk dress ludicrously out of place; but it was obvious that the café-owners knew Toby well from the way they greeted him like an old friend.

Over an enormous fry-up of bacon, eggs, sausages, tomatoes, fried bread and chips, it was Lisa's turn to talk. Toby seemed fascinated by the finishing school, unable to believe the sheer banality of some of the classes.

'What about sex?' he asked.

'Sex?'

'Sure. What do they say about that? Isn't it part of the curriculum? I'd have thought it was pretty important, but perhaps not if you're expected to marry a peer of the realm!'

'The only thing they ever talk about is being careful not to squander ourselves on the wrong person. I suppose they're scared we'll get so frustrated we'll dash out and have it off with the first personable waiter we clap eyes on!'

'And do you?'

'Jump into bed with waiters? Certainly not!'

'Get frustrated?'

Lisa knew that she was going to blush and was furious with herself. She put a fork loaded high with chips into her mouth and then hoped he'd lose interest, but he didn't. 'What do you do?' he persisted. 'Mess around with each other?'

'No!' She was so startled that she began to choke.

'So, who keeps you happy?'

'Sex isn't the most important thing in the world,' she said, after taking a long drink of water. 'Most of us don't bother about it while we're there.'

This was totally untrue. The majority of the girls spent a lot of time and ingenuity fixing up assignations with men; returning in the early hours of the morning by climbing up ladders previously hidden by their co-conspirators. But Lisa and one or two other girls didn't take

14

part in any of this. At the back of her mind Lisa was nervous of an affair. She'd seen how involved and vulnerable it made the girls; watched them agonising over late periods and broken meetings, and decided that she didn't want that kind of pain. Sex could wait.

'For one awful moment there I thought you were going to tell me you were saving yourself for your husband!' he laughed.

'I'm saving myself for someone I really want.'

There was a long silence. Toby's face remained expressionless but inside he could hardly believe his luck. She was young, very nearly beautiful, and a virgin. It wasn't the kind of situation he was used to, but it was one he knew with certainty he was going to enjoy.

He'd already discovered how misleading obviously sexy and experienced girls were. They squirmed and moaned a lot, but deep down they were as cold as ice. It was the girls like Lisa who were the best. The ones who were cool and self-controlled on the surface. Once you got them going there was no stopping them.

Aware that he was becoming aroused by his own thoughts he decided to change the subject. 'Why do you hate your parents?' he asked softly.

'I don't!' she protested.

'I think you do.'

'I certainly don't hate Simon. He's a bit weak and can't control Stephanie but basically he's all right.'

'You do hate Stephanie?'

'Let's say we don't get on too well.' Her voice was tight, her eyes suddenly filled with pain.

'Why's that?'

She remembered that terrible scene when she was seven years old. The hatred that had burst from the previously loving Stephanie. The realisation that her life until then had been based on a lie, and the knowledge that although she'd been chosen she wasn't really loved. 'I don't think that's any of your business,' she said abruptly.

Toby lost interest. His erection had subsided and he could safely get up from the table. Conversation was no longer important. 'How about coming back to my place? It isn't exactly palatial but it's O.K. We'll have coffee and play some music. What do you say?'

She wasn't stupid. She knew that if she went back with him there might be coffee and music, but she'd also be expected to jump into his bed and she didn't want to. Not yet; perhaps later on, but not now. 'No thanks, Toby. I'd better get home.'

He wasn't expecting a refusal, not even from an upper class virgin who'd never seen his series. Normally his dark good looks were enough, and he'd thought that things were going well. He was annoyed, but clever enough not to let it show. 'Some other time then?'

'Yes, definitely some other time.'

'Always providing you're allowed to see me again.'

'I shan't ask their permission.' Despite her bravado she knew they could stop her if they found out.

'How about coming to a Boxing Day party with me? It doesn't start until nine and should go on all night. I could pick you up at seven and we'll have a few drinks first.'

Lisa thought quickly. He was outstandingly attractive and quite obviously experienced. She probably wouldn't find a better person to initiate her into all the secret delights that the girls at school talked about so endlessly. She was also flattered that he'd chosen her.

Unaware of quite how jaded and consequently perverted Toby Walker was becoming, she decided that he would be perfect for her first lover; and the fact that at last someone really seemed to like her made the decision all the more inevitable. 'Sounds fun! I'll write down my address for you.'

'I know where you live.'

'You do?' She was plainly astonished.

He cursed himself for the slip. 'I heard your mother talking about your house. Let's get going.'

He drove fast and badly, never dropping below 80 m.p.h. unless braking sharply and frequently, but Lisa found it all exhilarating. When he finally leant across to kiss her goodnight she was a little surprised to find his tongue half-way down her throat in the first few seconds, but quickly got caught up by his passion. Eventually he drew away and gave a low laugh. 'Roll on Boxing Day!'

She was still holding her fingers to her bruised lips when Simon turned on the hall lights. 'Where the hell have you been?' he shouted, his face flushed with rage.

'For a drive with Toby Walker; formerly a draughtsman and now, it would seem, the hero of every woman's dreams!'

'A drive?'

'And a walk.'

'Nothing else?' He could barely control his temper and a vein was throbbing in his left temple. Lisa was dismayed by his rage, it seemed so out of proportion.

'We had something to eat before we came back. Let's be honest, the Markoffs didn't exactly put on a banquet fit for a king!'

'You really expect me to believe that's all that happened?'

'It's the truth,' she protested defensively.

'You should take a look at yourself in the mirror!' he roared,

16

stepping closer to her as his flush subsided, leaving his skin the colour of putty. Automatically she glanced at the ornate mirror hanging over the telephone table. Her lips were swollen and there was a love bite just below her left ear. She didn't remember the love bite.

'He kissed me good night. That's not a crime.'

'He made quite a meal of it, didn't he?'

Lisa felt the excitement of the evening draining away. 'Did you expect me to go through life like a nun?' she asked, wishing he'd leave her alone with her thoughts.

'Yes!' he shouted, regardless of the fact that Stephanie was now standing behind him on the stairs. 'That's exactly what I expected. Why would I bankrupt myself on that fancy finishing school if it wasn't to keep you out of trouble? You're ...'

'I'm what?'

'Important to me,' he mumbled, turning his head away so that she couldn't see the expression of self-disgust in his eyes.

'What is all this? I'm not in line for a royal marriage! Besides, apart from future kings even royalty aren't expected to marry virgins. If they were, the line would soon die out.'

'You stupid little slut!' hissed Stephanie, pushing her husband to one side. 'If you've thrown everything away on that oversized male model I'll never forgive you. Don't you realise the sacrifices we've made to send you to Switzerland? Haven't you the faintest idea of why we're ...'

'Be quiet!' snapped Simon. For once his wife obeyed him. Lisa looked from one to the other in bewilderment. 'I don't like it in Switzerland. If money's a problem I'll be happy to come home. Besides, I really don't see what harm one evening out with an attractive man can possibly have done. I thought you wanted me to mix with the people at dinner. You both seemed keen for me to go.'

'Not for his benefit!' shrieked Stephanie, beside herself with temper. 'He isn't of any importance at all. He was only there to make up the numbers.'

Lisa decided they were behaving in the manner they believed expected of doting parents. Either that or they'd got her in mind for a friend's son and didn't want her soiling herself with anyone else. Well, for once she wasn't going to try and please them. Toby had liked her and Toby was fun. A little bit dangerous perhaps, but fun.

'Is he seeing you again?' demanded Simon.

'He ...' She stopped, taking in their wary expressions. In that split second she made her decision not to tell them the truth. She didn't know why, but there was something about the intensity of their distress that was out of key and she sensed that if she said yes they

17

might very well make it impossible for her to get to the party. 'He didn't suggest it,' she concluded. 'I think he can have his pick of women at the moment. I was just a momentary diversion; that's all, truly.'

Their relief showed her that she'd been right to keep silent about the party. Simon gave a weak smile. 'Sorry, precious. I guess we over-reacted but it is five in the morning. Anything could have happened to you. A car accident; a situation you couldn't handle; all sorts of things.'

'I'm all right, honestly.'

'Next time you want to go off with some handsome young man, please talk it over with us first, will you? There's a good girl!' He put an affectionate arm round her waist but she drew away. Everything he'd said tonight, apart from his fear, had been a lie, of that she was absolutely certain. She was beginning to think that he and Stephanie were well matched. Both lied fluently and both pretended to care for her well-being. It still hurt but at least she knew that neither of them could be trusted. She'd work out a way of getting to the party later on; right now all she wanted was her bed.

'I'm tired,' she said with a yawn. 'I'll skip breakfast if you don't mind. Perhaps you'd call me before lunch, Stephanie?'

After she'd gone Simon glanced at his wife. 'We've been lucky,' he said quietly, 'but it shows how careful we have to be. Finishing school's definitely the best solution.'

'I can't think what men see in her. She's almost plain at times,' said Stephanie acidly.

'Obviously men don't think so, and she is promised to ...'

'Let's hope he hasn't forgotten.'

'If he'd forgotten,' said Simon slowly, 'I'd be dead by now.'

Stephanie's eyes widened and she took hold of her husband's hand in a rare gesture of affection. 'But you're not,' she reassured him, 'and as long as madam upstairs doesn't repeat tonight's little caper then there's no reason for you to keep worrying.'

He was grateful for her sympathy, and when they went back to bed she let him into her room and allowed him to seek comfort from her familiar body. It wasn't entirely a selfless act; she knew that without Simon her life would be very different. But as long as they had Lisa they were safe.

Chapter Three

Lisa spent most of Christmas Day in the library reading. Since she'd been away both Simon and Stephanie had taken to drinking heavily and by mid-afternoon were incapable of making conversation. It gave her an opportunity to call Sabrina, asking her to ring up that evening inviting Lisa to a fictitious party.

'How thrilling!' enthused Sabrina, her voice huskier than usual because she was entertaining her latest boyfriend in her room and knew that a husky voice was what he expected of her. It signified smouldering sexual passion and kept the boredom well hidden. Sex was still boring for Sabrina but she spent a lot of time in pursuit of that elusive thrill.

'It is quite. He's rather a hunk.'

'Do I know him?'

Lisa hesitated. It seemed unlikely that Sabrina would watch a T.V. series considering that she claimed game shows over-taxed her, but she decided not to take the chance. 'No, just a man I met at a dinner party.'

'I expect to hear every detail in return for helping you out!'

'Naturally,' lied Lisa, who had learnt early on that it was safer to keep her feelings to herself.

'Super! I'll call them about seven, if they're still sober enough to take the information in by then.'

'They'll recognise your voice, that's all that matters. I'll do the same for you one day, Sabrina.'

'No need. My doting parents don't care what I do or who I do it with! William, stop it!' There was the sound of a light slap and a lot of giggling. Lisa put down the telephone and gave herself up to wondering what tomorrow evening would be like.

When Toby drove up to her front door the following day she ran from the house. Simon and Stephanie were upstairs dressing to go out but she didn't want them to see the low-slung Lotus that was a rather distinctive canary yellow.

'I thought you might have changed your mind,' said Toby casually. She looked at him in surprise.

'Why should I do that?'

'From what I hear I'm not exactly what your parents have in mind for you.'

'Where did you hear that?'

'I do have friends, you know.'

'Friends my parents talk to?'

Toby wished he'd kept quiet. 'Let's say I guessed it, then.'

'You guessed right!'

'Are you wearing those black french knickers again?'

She blushed. 'What do you mean by *again*?'

He laughed. 'I caught a glimpse of them when you were sitting at the Markoff's bar.'

'You'll have to wait and see, won't you?'

He began to relax. At least she knew that she wasn't just there for the party. In fact, if things went well they might not go to the party at all.

He had a maisonette in Battersea. Lisa was shocked by the street and the outside of the building, but inside it was spacious and made more so by white walls and the clever use of mirrors. The main room had three steps up into a dining area and kitchenette with two doors leading off.

'Not quite what you're used to?' queried Toby, putting a classical tape on his beloved music centre which had been a gift from an older woman who'd hoped to educate him in the arts. He turned the volume down low. Lisa didn't look nervous but you could never be sure and he wanted it to go well for her. After all, it was generally accepted that women never forgot their first lover and he wanted to be remembered as a success. 'Drink?'

She'd been looking at his book shelves, mostly Harold Robbins and Alistair Maclean, and when she turned to look at him she suddenly seemed much older than her years. A trick of the light made it appear that she was assessing him, although being relatively reasonable and totally sober he realised this couldn't possibly be true. Just the same it was disconcerting. 'Do you want a drink?' he repeated.

'A dry white wine would be nice.'

'Sorry, I've only got a rather vile red. How about whisky?'

'Vermouth?'

'Not in fashion at the moment.'

'Campari?'

He was getting annoyed. 'It's whisky, gin, vodka or beer, O.K?'

'Vodka and tonic with lots of ice – unless that's out of fashion too!' Her laugh was strained, betraying her tension.

'I think I can manage that,' he muttered, hoping that the ice box at the top of his fridge hadn't frozen solid. Fate was kind, and within five minutes Lisa was sitting next to him on the two-seater settee, drinking her vodka and fiddling with the clasp of her leather shoulder bag.

Toby put down his drink, removed the bag from her lap and put an arm round her shoulders. 'Any trouble getting out tonight?'

'No.'

He glanced at her empty glass. 'That was quick! Want another?'

Needing a little Dutch courage before actually going into the bedroom, she held out her glass. 'It hasn't got much taste.'

Toby laughed. 'True, but it's got a good kick in it. Tell me, why stay on at finishing school if you don't like it? Wouldn't you be happier doing all the usual things rich girls do? Lunching at fashionable restaurants with your friends, going to the theatre in the evening, doing the occasional charity fashion show!'

She shook her head, and immediately wished she hadn't as the room tilted alarmingly. 'No thanks, I want . . .'

'What?'

She sighed. 'I wish I knew. To be free of everything, I suppose.'

'You are free. This is as free as you get. Believe me, I know.' There was a touch of bitterness in his voice. 'Make the most of it. Life can be a bitch later on.'

She turned an enquiring face towards him, and he promptly forgot exactly what a bitch it was turning out to be for him and drew her closer, lowering his mouth to cover hers and delighted to find her tongue quickly slide inside his mouth, flickering lightly round his teeth and the inside of his lips.

After a few minutes he took her by the hand and they walked to the bedroom. Lisa felt that it would have been more romantic if he'd carried her, but although built like an athlete, Toby was so heavily insured against injury he scarcely dared lift anything heavier than his head in the ordinary way of things. There were some very strict penalty clauses in his contract should he become injured through his own stupidity. He often wondered what the television company would say if they knew the truth about his private life.

Once in the bedroom, Lisa had difficulty in breathing. She stood perfectly still and waited to see what was expected of her. Sabrina had never mentioned before or after, only during.

'Take your clothes off,' whispered Toby. 'Take them off slowly while I watch.'

21

It was amazing how she seemed to have acquired extra thumbs all of a sudden. She fumbled with her stockings, couldn't reach the zip at the back of the dress and tried to pull a full length slip down over her hips without first slipping off the shoulder straps. All the time, Toby stood there watching her while his dark blue eyes sparkled with desire, and something that she wasn't sophisticated enough to recognise as triumph.

She was beautiful, he realised as she worked her way through her clothes. Beautiful in the way that a highly-tuned racehorse is beautiful. She had marvellous bones, long elegant legs, a completely flat stomach and a face that was a devastating combination of complete naivety and inborn knowledge, as though she'd never been young. There was so much that he could teach her. So many things that he could do. It was almost more intoxicating than whisky. She might even be able to help him forget ...

Finally naked, Lisa stood by the bed. She was trembling slightly from head to toe, and when Toby reached out and ran a long finger carefully down her right side, lingering over the sensitive hip bone, she jerked at the sharp, almost painfully sweet sensation it caused.

It didn't take him long to strip off his clothes, and as he walked towards her she noticed that his penis was standing rigidly upright brushing his lower stomach, and quickly raised her eyes. His chest was covered with dark hair that also surrounded the base of the penis, but his stomach was smooth and hairless.

'Lie down,' he instructed, pushing her gently on the shoulder, and she obediently stretched herself out against the sheets. For a few moments he remained propped on one elbow, studying her carefully, his eyes unable to see enough. Then he put his arms beneath her and lifted her body against his, moving his right leg quickly between hers so that when he released her from his grasp he was able to put a hand between her thighs and start moving his fingers in soft, ceaseless circles that made her start to squirm against his hand even as other sensations flickered from breast to stomach as he sucked and licked on her small, light pink nipples that fascinated him by their almost childlike appearance.

At first she tried to push his head away, ashamed of her small breasts and certain that they must be a disappointment to him, but he ignored her and once the pleasure began she ceased being embarrassed and realised that obviously size didn't matter at all.

Toby took a long time. He licked her ears and neck; he drew feather-like patterns on her stomach and back and returned again and again to her immature breasts, but never once did he attempt to put his mouth lower than her stomach because he sensed — quite

22

correctly — that if he startled her this time she might never come back to him, and there was so much pleasure in store for them both that even Toby had the sense to exercise some discretion.

By the time he pressed himself against her entrance she was soaking wet, totally caught up in the pleasure, all fears dismissed. He entered slowly at first, hesitated at the slight restriction and then thrust hard, but her moan was more of surprise than pain and he felt free to carry on thrusting as hard as he liked.

She was tighter than any woman he'd ever had, even the occasional under-age virgin had usually been a technical virgin only, and this — coupled with the excitement of knowing that by simply being with her, making love to her and establishing a sexual hold, he was breaking the rules — made him incapable of lasting as long as usual.

Sometimes women begged him to finish but Lisa didn't because just as she began to tense, just as the feelings within her began to bunch up into a tight knot, Toby gave a groan of despair, shuddered and then slumped down on top of her.

Lisa stared at the back of his dark head in surprise. How could he let it end like that? she wondered. Surely there was more. There must be. All those writers couldn't be wrong. She felt frustrated, disillusioned and horribly vulnerable. Also, he was very heavy and she pushed at his chest.

'You're crushing me,' she murmured apologetically.

Aware of his failure, he rolled off her. 'I'm sorry. Just give me a few minutes and I'll make sure you're all right. You were too much for my self-control!' Taking a cigarette from the pack beside the bed he lit it. 'You don't mind, do you?'

'I'm afraid cigarette smoke makes me cough.' It was true but as soon as she'd spoken she knew it was a mistake.

His eyes darkened yet he kept his voice controlled. 'I always smoke after sex.'

'Then I think I'll have a shower if you've got one.'

'Sure, the bathroom's across the way.'

Above the sound of the water he suddenly heard the doorbell. Wondering who on earth could be calling on him at nine o'clock on Boxing Night, he pulled on his dark blue towelling robe and wandered down the steps and across to the side door.

At first he didn't recognise the man who stood outside. He was of average height with dark brown hair, wearing a dark blue overcoat with its collar turned up. It was only when he stepped across the threshold and Toby saw the light grey eyes and the mouth with its thin top lip that he realised who it was.

23

'What the hell are you doing here at Christmas time? Don't you ever enjoy yourself?'

'I leave that to you. You've got a girl here.' His voice was flat.

'True!'

'Lisa Greene.'

'It might be.'

'It is.'

'All right then, yes, it is. What's the matter? Fancy her yourself, do you? Well, I'm sorry, you'll have to wait your turn. She's mine right now. Completely mine, understand?'

'What a pity,' said the man slowly. 'You really ought to have checked first.'

'Checked out a date with you? You seem to forget who I am. I've got women hurling themselves at me all the time these days. T.V. has tremendous power. Surely you don't want me ringing you up every time I bring some over-excited groupie home?'

'Was Lisa Greene an over-excited groupie?' This time there was amusement in the voice.

Toby considered lying but there was something about this visitor that discouraged lying. 'Actually, no.'

'Quite.'

'Just the same, all's fair in love and war, and if it was her cherry you were after you're too late. Never mind, you can have her when I'm through. How's that for generosity?'

The visitor smiled. He actually smiled and Toby, despite his height advantage, instinctively took a step back. 'Your offer doesn't interest me. I'm not after her. I never have been after her. Surely you don't imagine she's my type.'

'Then who ...?'

'She was intended for Mr Gueras. Perhaps you'd care to call him and offer him your leavings? I could give you his holiday number if you like.'

Toby felt himself turning white. 'I didn't know!' he protested. 'How was I expected to know that? She isn't connected with him. Her family don't even move in the same circles.'

'You don't have to justify yourself to me, Walker. If I were you I'd make the most of her, and I'd be very careful to keep her happy too. For as long as you're allowed to keep her, that is. Goodnight, and a happy New Year!'

Toby slammed the door shut in fury. How he hated that man! He never brought anything but bad news. Bishop was a creep, and a psychopathic creep at that. But if what he'd said was true then it didn't bear thinking about, and so – as with everything else that

24

didn't bear thinking about — Toby pushed it to the back of his mind.

It had been a joke, he decided. Bishop's idea of a bit of Christmas fun. Well, it wasn't going to work. Lisa was still upstairs waiting for him, and this time he'd make sure she didn't have anything to complain about. As for Bishop, he could go to hell.

Almost dragging Lisa from the shower he proceeded to make love to her for the next two hours until she'd come to one screaming climax after another, and only when she was ready to fall asleep from exhaustion did he finally allow himself to come for the second time, and after that they fell asleep wrapped round each other. They made love once more after they woke and then Toby took her home. By that time, Bishop's warped sense of humour was completely forgotten.

On the morning of Wednesday 27th December, Lisa was woken by the sound of Stephanie crying. Not crying in her usual manner with temper or exasperation, but sobbing without restraint. Amazed, Lisa put on a robe and went out on to the upper landing.

The sobbing was louder now, but still coming from a considerable distance. She glanced down the well of the stairway. At the bottom, standing on the new green wool carpet that just failed to match the green fleck of the wallpaper she could see both Simon and Stephanie. They were not alone.

Her throat felt suddenly tight, as though some tension had made its way up the stairs and was closing in round her. Silently, her feet still bare, she crept down the first flight and crouched on the lower landing. By peeping through the banister rail she could just catch a glimpse of the visitor.

There was no obvious reason to feel afraid of him, or for Stephanie to be crying in such a heartbroken manner. He was only young, perhaps a little below average height and with a beautifully styled head of dark brown hair that fell forward over his forehead in a childlike cowlick. He was compactly built but not heavy, and his face was all angles; straight, thin-bridged nose, sharp cheekbones and a stubborn chin. She couldn't see his eyes clearly but his mouth was on the thin side, his complexion clear and pale. No, there was nothing frightening there, and his gloveless hands were held loosely at his sides without any hint of hostility. Yet she did feel afraid, and so obviously did Stephanie and Simon.

While Stephanie continued to sob noisily, Simon remained by her side. His head was shaking spasmodically and he seemed to be having trouble with his speech because there were long, halting pauses between his words. Although frightened, Lisa was also intrigued. She slipped back to her room, grabbed the nearest pair of slacks and a sweater off the back of her chair and then walked calmly downstairs as though unaware of anything unusual.

At the sound of her footsteps both Simon and Stephanie turned to look up at her. Stephanie's face was red and swollen with crying, but she managed to glare at Lisa with murderous rage. Simon on the other hand looked frightened; frightened not just for himself but also for her. He held up his right hand, gesturing for her to remain on the stairs, and she obeyed him instantly.

It was only then that she looked straight at their visitor. He'd been studying the older couple disinterestedly, but when he lifted his eyes to her a spark stirred in them. She was horrified at the coldness of the eyes. There was nothing behind them. No hint of passion or flicker of intelligence — they were like an X-ray machine, totally impersonal, and all the more terrifying as a result.

'What's the matter?' she asked nervously, aware that they were all looking at her as though she were in some way to blame for this strangely hostile scene.

'Where were you last night?' demanded Stephanie, blowing her nose as she spoke.

'I told you, at Sabrina's party.'

'Sabrina didn't have a party,' said Simon wearily. 'We've checked with her parents.'

Lisa glanced at their visitor. His eyes were moving from one to another of them without any visible emotion, yet she was quite sure that he was enjoying himself. She moistened her lips. 'I was with Toby Walker,' she admitted nervously. 'We were going on to a party but in the end we just listened to records and talked.'

'I see.' There was total resignation in Simon's voice. She'd obviously confirmed something he'd either suspected or been told and all at once he lost interest in her, turning away and glancing at the visitor. Stephanie, however, launched herself towards the stairs, screaming at the top of her voice.

'You stupid little tart! Do you realise what you've done? After all this time, after so much ...'

'Be quiet!' interrupted the visitor softly. To Lisa's amazement Stephanie obeyed him, walking back to stand by her husband, suddenly an old and defeated woman. 'Let's hope he was good!' For the first time there was a spark of animation in the stranger's voice.

'As a matter of fact, he was,' retorted Lisa, feeling more and more frightened but taking the initiative herself in an effort to push the terror away.

'Compared with whom?' he asked gently.

Her eyes met his and she realised that for some unknown reason he hated her. Not in the way that Stephanie hated her but enough to wish

26

her dead. For one fleeting second it was all there in his face, before he dropped his eyes and she was left standing on the stairs feeling sick and cold.

'She hasn't got anyone to compare him with,' said Simon quickly. 'I promise you she's ...'

'It isn't me who's interested. I don't care if she's fucked her way from here to Cornwall and back. I'm only here to tell you that as a result of last night, the generous oversight of your last business transaction no longer exists. The amnesty's over, Mr Greene. You owe us, and you've got three days to repay.'

'Three days! I can't find that sort of money in three months! For God's sake be reasonable, Bishop. You know how it is with me.'

'Indeed I do. You've been a fool and now you're going to pay the price. That's how it is with you. I see the same thing all the time. You're not special, in fact you're depressingly mundane; greedy and over-ambitious. A fitting epitaph perhaps. Simon Greene, beloved husband of etc., and then *Greedy and Ambitious* in beautiful Gothic script. Yes, very tasteful!' And he laughed without humour.

With a strangled shout, Simon stumbled forward, launching himself at Bishop with all the strength he possessed. Bishop stepped to one side while putting out a foot and sending Simon sprawling to the floor. He then bent over the fallen man and whispered in his ear.

Only after Bishop had vanished out of the front door did Lisa see the thin trickle of blood running from Simon's face on to the carpet. Ignoring the now hysterical Stephanie she ran and bent over him, crying out in horror when she saw that his nose had been slit along the bridge. A thin, clean line that could only have been made by a razor or very sharp knife. Dashing into the kitchen she picked up a fresh tea towel and then pressed it against the wound. Already the blood was only seeping; it had simply been a warning.

'You'll have to call the police,' she told a trembling Stephanie, but Stephanie, rapidly regaining her composure now they were alone, laughed bitterly. 'Call the police? You stupid girl! Do you think we can afford to have the police looking into our affairs? Open your eyes, Lisa. Look around you. Did you honestly think Simon paid for all this by selling his antiques?'

Until that moment she really had, and her face showed as much. 'Idiotic child!' continued Stephanie, not shouting now but sounding totally contemptuous of the tall, slim girl standing awkwardly in front of her. 'You think you know so much but really you don't know anything at all. You didn't even recognise your own value, did you?'

'I don't know what you mean. What kind of value?'

'You were wanted.'

27

'Wanted?'

'By a man, you silly bitch! He'd been waiting for you to finish your education before telling you, but you couldn't wait. You had to rush off and jump into bed with some second-rate gigolo who's not likely to give you anything except an illegitimate baby. If you only knew what you could have had, you'd weep! My God, when I think ...'

'But I don't know any men,' said Lisa, totally bewildered by the outburst. 'I've never met anyone who's showed the slightest interest in me before Toby.'

'You were too blind to see it, that's all, and of course you wouldn't listen to us. Oh no, you knew best. Well, look what's happened to Simon as a result of your piece of mindless bedhopping.'

'That's not my fault! It can't be. I haven't done anything,' she protested.

'You didn't have to. Your existence was enough. He was as misled by your looks as we were when we chose you, only we're the ones who have to pay the penalty for his mistake as well. And to think that I could have had that baby girl with the blonde curls in the cot next to yours!'

Lisa swallowed hard. She didn't know who this unknown man was, or why Simon was in so much trouble, but obviously it was her fault. Apparently even when you grew older it was appearances that mattered. This unknown man hadn't bothered to get to know her, had never made his interest known, but he'd been willing to make some kind of bargain with Simon on the strength of her.

'Did he want to marry me?' she asked slowly, 'because if that's what was meant to happen, nothing's changed. Don't you see that? I haven't married Toby, I've only slept with him.'

'Of course he didn't want to marry you!' shouted Stephanie. 'He wanted to be your protector, your ...'

Lisa was beginning to feel sick. 'Are you saying that you and Simon were trying to set me up as some man's mistress?'

'You'd have had a wonderful life. He badly needs someone, and he'd chosen you. He'd have made you very happy,' retorted Stephanie.

'That's the most revolting thing I've ever heard!' cried Lisa in disbelief. 'I'm only thankful that I found Toby in time. Perhaps he isn't rich and powerful, and perhaps he can't help Simon with his business affairs, but he chose me because he liked me, and I liked him as well. Surely I'm entitled to choose my own lover!'

'Choose!' Stephanie made a sound of contempt.

'Do you honestly value me so little that you were willing to give me away like an unwanted dog? Don't you feel anything for me,

Stephanie? Anything at all?' When Stephanie stayed silent it was as much as Lisa could do to hide her pain. Choking back tears she picked up the receiver. 'I'm going to ring Toby and ask him to let me move in. I can't stay here any longer.'

Stephanie followed Lisa to the phone. 'That's right, run out on us now that we're in trouble. You fool, do you think that a man like . . .'

'Stephanie!'

At the sound of Simon's voice, Stephanie fell silent. Lisa turned to look at this man she'd once believed cared for her. 'How could you?' she asked in disbelief. 'How could you have done it to me?'

'I had no choice.'

'But didn't you think about me at all? Surely you must have imagined how I'd feel?'

'Yes,' he murmured. 'I thought about you, but there was nothing I could do. Naturally you don't understand, and I'm truly sorry for that.'

'I can't listen to any more,' she cried, trying to hold back the hot tears. 'I trusted you, Simon. I believed you cared for me, but it was all a lie, wasn't it? You were the same as Stephanie, but I was too stupid to understand. Well, now I do, which is why I'm leaving here and never coming back. All I can say is that I wish I'd never met either of you.'

When Toby collected her forty minutes later there was a brief delay as he tried to put all her cases in the back of the Lotus, and he was so busy calming a distraught Lisa and wondering whether he was doing the right thing that he didn't hear the faint click of the camera, or see the teenager sitting high in the branches of the oak tree taking snap after snap of Lisa's hasty departure from her home.

Chapter Four

Toby deposited Lisa's suitcases on the floor of his living-room and stood looking at her. She was shivering with reaction and totally unaware that she wasn't as welcome as she'd automatically expected.

'Now what?' he asked at last. 'I hope you don't expect to live here?'

Flustered, she glanced around the small maisonette. 'I thought that just at first, until I get some money . . .'

'Where do you think that money will come from? Your loving father?'

Remembering what Simon had done, she flinched and shook her head.

'Well then?'

She hesitated. It was the first time she'd had to consider money, or the lack of it. 'I'll sell my fur coat and some of my jewellery. They should fetch a reasonable price so that I can get myself a flat. Until then I'll keep out of your way.'

He gave an exasperated laugh. 'And how exactly do you intend keeping out of my way? By hiding in the loo every time I bring someone home?'

'I'll stay in the bedroom reading.'

'I usually want the bedroom when I bring people back!'

She hadn't thought of that. 'You mean . . .?'

'You didn't think we were going to spend all our time together surely? Last night was great and I certainly intended repeating the experience, but I've got quite a lot of other girlfriends!'

'I didn't think,' she said quietly.

'What exactly happened this morning?'

After she'd told him he was very quiet. 'You're sure the man who came to see you was called Bishop?'

'Absolutely! He was horrible. To be honest, I was terrified.'

'Why on earth did you phone *me*?' he asked despairingly, uncom-

30

fortably aware of the danger in which she'd placed him.

'Because you're not a friend of Simon's! I couldn't go to Sabrina's – her parents and mine spend half their social lives together. You were the only person I could think of who wasn't involved, except through me.'

'Couldn't you go back once things have calmed down?'

'No! I can't face seeing them again. It wouldn't be the same. Surely you can see that?'

'The trouble is I do have to work.' He was beginning to sound impatient. 'When filming starts I have to be on set by seven and I'm often tied up until seven or eight at night.'

'I won't mind being on my own,' she assured him. 'Besides, it won't be for long.'

He had a nasty feeling that she was wrong about that but he didn't want to discourage her and kept his doubts to himself. They spent the rest of the day storing her luggage in cupboards and under any convenient table or shelf. In between work they made love twice, and he was amazed by her enthusiasm.

When they were drifting off to sleep that night he wondered if perhaps this was going to turn out all right. A grateful and willing bed partner on tap day and night was rather appealing, and he could always go to his other women's houses when he wanted a change.

His telephone rang at 4 a.m. Completely exhausted by the events of the day, Lisa didn't stir and it took Toby several minutes to locate the phone which was buried beneath two of her shoulder bags.

'Yeah?' he mumbled, fumbling for a cigarette.

'Bishop here.'

His stomach lurched and he dropped the unlit cigarette. 'Bishop?'

'Yes. You owe us, Walker. You owe us quite a debt.'

'I don't know what you mean.'

'We think you do. You'll be needed on 28th January from 7 p.m. on. Make sure you keep it clear.'

'But I might be working.'

'That's our intention!'

'At the studio, and they don't take too kindly to actors changing schedules.'

'If you don't do as we say you won't have any schedule to keep. Actors of your calibre are two a penny, as I'm sure you know. We got you the job and we can just as easily take it away. After all, you have something of a drink problem.'

'That's a bloody lie! I admit I used to knock it back a bit, but since I began this job I . . .'

'Once an alcoholic, always an alcoholic, Toby. Don't you

remember what they told you at your group meetings?'

'Sod off you fucking nuisance!'

'Remember, keep the 28th clear,' continued Bishop smoothly, totally oblivious to the insult. 'Incidentally, is she worth it?'

'I ...'

'I understand. Hard to say at this point in time, isn't it? After all, who knows what kind of a price you'll end up paying. One more thing. Make sure you look after her well.'

'That's none of your business.'

'I'm not the one who's telling you.'

'I'm sorry, I ...' The line went dead, and when Lisa awoke at 8 a.m. he still hadn't managed to go back to sleep.

She snuggled against him. 'How about breakfast in bed? Or would you prefer something else first?'

'Just coffee,' he growled, wishing he'd never set eyes on her. She looked surprised but went into the tiny kitchen and started the percolator going. She quite enjoyed playing house. It was much more fun doing it on a small scale than learning how to plan a banquet for forty or a business dinner for twelve.

When she took in his coffee he was reading through a script. She perched on the edge of the bed and looked over his shoulder. ' "It's better for both of us that you tell me now," ' she read aloud in a pseudo-American accent, ' "otherwise it will simply take longer and be far messier." I don't believe it! How on earth do you manage to make words like that sound convincing?'

'It's not that bad.'

'I suppose you've got to defend it! Aren't you going to drink your coffee?'

He had a momentary desire to fling it in her face but swallowed hard and picked up his cup. 'Lisa, I'd rather you didn't knock my work. It's difficult to suspend disbelief when someone's hooting with laughter in your ear.'

'Don't other people laugh?'

'Not to my face.'

'Then I'll let you play cops and robbers in peace. I wonder if I ought to ring Simon, make sure he's all right?'

'Do what you like but leave me alone. I'll come out when I've learnt this episode. Until then, just stay away from the bedroom!'

'Of course,' she agreed quickly.

'You are on the pill, I hope?'

'Actually, it gives me migraine.'

He had the feeling that this wasn't going to be one of his better days. 'Then get yourself fixed up as soon as clinics re-open after

Christmas. Until then you'd better leave it to me. When are you due?'

'Three days' time.'

'We should be OK then. Off you go now.'

Closing the door quietly behind her she wandered round the dining area. The telephone was on a small coffee table, and after glancing nervously at it once or twice she finally made herself lift the receiver and dial home. It was a man who answered; a man with a flat London accent who sounded totally indifferent until she said who she was and asked for Simon.

'You'd better come home, Miss Greene. Your father's dead.'

Lisa's fingers tightened convulsively round the receiver and she gave a small cry of disbelief. 'He can't be dead! I saw him yesterday and he was perfectly . . .' Her voice tailed off as she remembered the small trickle of blood, but the injury had been a minor one, it couldn't possibly have killed him.

'I'll fetch your mother,' said the man. Stephanie was sobbing hysterically, crying about a gun and not having known Simon owned one.

'You mean he killed himself?' Lisa still couldn't believe that she'd never see Simon again.

'Yes! How did he expect me to cope? The police keep asking so many questions and I don't know any of the answers. He shouldn't have done it. He knew that I . . .'

'I'll come right round,' she promised, and ran to the bedroom. Toby's face darkened. 'I thought I told you to stay out?'

'Simon's dead!' she sobbed. 'He shot himself, and the police are there asking Stephanie all sorts of questions that she can't answer.' He was already out of bed and dressing.

On the short drive there he did nothing but hurl instructions at her, instructions that made no sense at all. 'Don't mention anything about that jewellery he gave you; don't tell them that he owed money; and above all, don't mention Bishop's visit.'

She wasn't really taking it in until he said that, then she turned on him in astonishment. 'Of course I'll mention Bishop. It's all his fault. He must have frightened Simon so much that he couldn't go on.'

'I very much doubt if Simon killed himself,' said Toby softly. 'For once in your life trust somone and just keep quiet, for your own sake if not for Stephanie's.'

Lisa knew that it was going to be a very long time before she trusted anyone again. 'Why should I trust you?' she asked shakily.

He put a hand on her knee. 'Because I love you?'

She shook her head. 'You don't, and I'd rather you didn't pretend.'

'Most women like to hear it said.'

'I'm not most women.'

'You're certainly not. Most women don't bring as much trouble with them!'

'Oh, Toby, I'm so sorry, but it isn't my fault. Besides, you're not really involved. You needn't even come in with me if you don't want to.'

'I never had any intention of coming in.'

'So much for love,' she remarked sadly as she climbed out of the car.

What Lisa always remembered about the period following Simon's alleged suicide was the strange way people behaved. The police, particularly the ones present when she first arrived back, weren't in the least sympathetic or tactful. They acted as though Simon had committed a crime, not so much by his suicide – which was technically a felony – but by removing himself from their reach.

They asked endless questions about his antiques shop and his most recent trips abroad. They took away his passport and his desk diary; they bullied the two women endlessly for names of business contacts; and never once did they offer even a pretence of sympathy.

After one brief outburst of sobbing on Lisa's shoulder, Stephanie pulled herself together remarkably quickly. Although outwardly still prone to tears she proved surprisingly adept at handling their inquiries, pleading ignorance and a total inability to understand any aspect of her husband's business affairs.

No, she hadn't ever asked him about his work; no, she didn't entertain for him; no, they rarely went out, let alone mingled socially with anyone in the public eye. He was a hard working, self-employed businessman, and that was all she knew. Other women? How could they think of such a thing? She and Simon had been devoted to one other.

Lisa, nervously following Toby's advice, pretended that she'd been away on a visit when it happened, explaining that there hadn't been any argument about her leaving home since she was in any case due to return to finishing school in ten days' time.

The policeman assigned to Lisa asked why she'd taken so much luggage away for a few days. She smiled, telling him that she was quite hopeless over packing and always took enough clothes to last a year for an overnight stay. She wasn't a nightdress and toothbrush person, she explained with a laugh.

As the days passed the police became less polite. The presence of Simon's solicitor didn't deter them; they had their job to do and the

34

discovery that Simon Greene had left debts of over a quarter of a million pounds, while giving credibility to his apparent suicide, made them very interested indeed in his business and where the money had gone.

After a few days, Lisa lost all sense of time. She wished that Toby would ring but sensed that until the police left she wouldn't hear from him. She and Stephanie spent a lot of time together yet said little. Lisa knew Stephanie blamed her for the disaster but wouldn't say so aloud because there was always the fear of someone listening outside the door.

Finally, to their mutual horror, a senior officer from New Scotland Yard's Fraud Squad was appointed to the case. When he arrived – middle-aged, jaded but surprisingly polite – Lisa thought that now they would learn all about Simon's probably numerous indiscretions. She was totally wrong. Within forty-eight hours the police had finished and left. The Chief Superintendent apologised for all the harassment the family had undergone.

He explained that no one had thought to talk properly to the family doctor. Simon had been ill; a heart condition and blood disorder combined had dramatically shortened his life expectancy, and ahead lay only the prospect of illness with increasing pain. He'd decided to die quickly, and spare his family the long drawn out suffering. As for the money – well, everyone knew the antiques business was risky. His creditors had all come forward, but none of them had been pressing him for payment. He'd gone through bad times before and come through. No, it was his health that had been to blame and the Superintendent couldn't apologise enough for the innuendoes that had been appearing in the daily tabloids.

After the funeral, Toby rang. He didn't say anything about his long silence but asked Lisa if she wanted to go back to him. 'I'm not sure,' she said slowly. 'You didn't really want me there, did you? Perhaps it would be better if I stayed with Stephanie. There isn't any money for finishing school now so I ought to start thinking about a job.'

'I miss you!' he laughed. 'I didn't expect to, but I do. It was fun having you around. I'd like you to come back.'

She was surprised, not remembering a great deal of fun. 'How about your other women?'

'What other women?'

'Obviously you've found a way round the problem! If you're quite sure, then give me until Saturday. Stephanie's got a lot to do here. The house is on the market and we keep getting the most ghastly people looking round. They're not really interested in buying, they're just fascinated by Simon's death. People can be utterly revolting at times. Anyway, she needs some help. Her sister's coming at the weekend, I ought to stay until then.'

She told Stephanie that evening. The older woman shrugged. 'Go where you like. He's probably as good as the next man. I'm afraid your prospects aren't too rosy around here.'

'I'm only going to live with him for a while.'

'And after that?'

'Who knows? I'm going to take it a day at a time. Will you be all right?'

For the first time Stephanie's mask slipped. 'How should I know? Perhaps they want me dead too. You can't imagine what it's like sitting in this house, jumping every time the bell rings! Although they're not likely to ring before they enter, are they?' And she gave a strained laugh.

'Who could possibly want you dead? Simon obviously made a few enemies − he doesn't seem to have been the most successful of businessmen − but that's not your fault. Anyway, he killed himself because he was ill.'

'He was no more ill than I am.'

'You told me yourself he'd been having chest pains.'

'He had a hiatus hernia. No one kills themselves over a hiatus hernia!'

'That's what he told you, but the doctor said ...'

'Any fool can tell he was got at. How come he didn't tell the police about Simon's illness straight away? Why keep it until things were getting really difficult for us all?'

'I suppose he felt that it was confidential information.'

'He was bribed.'

'But who'd bribe Dr Morris?'

'The same people who killed Simon, of course.'

Lisa stared at her. 'The Superintendent said ...'

'Him! I knew we were all right as soon as he arrived. There are certain crimes that have very long tentacles, and those tentacles often reach out to some surprising places.'

'Isn't anything what it seems?' exclaimed Lisa. 'Aren't there any normal, honest people in the world? I can't believe all this.'

'Go to your televison star and enjoy yourself. If he hadn't come along those tentacles would be round your pretty neck as well. You've been lucky. Get out while you can.'

'But it was you and Simon who tried to involve me!'

Stephanie sighed. 'Yes, it was. I didn't care − after all, you weren't going to get hurt − but Simon cared. He wanted you to go off and live a normal life, even if it meant offending certain people. Then he

36

did something stupid and you were his only way out. He did love you though, and if his death's set you free then wherever he is he'll feel it was worthwhile. So go now, while you still can.'

'I told Toby I'd stay until Saturday,' said Lisa hesitantly.

'You're no help here,' said Stephanie bitterly. 'All you do is remind me of things I'd rather forget. Go tonight for all I care.'

'Do you really mean that?' asked Lisa quietly.

'Yes.'

'Then I will. I'm sorry I was a disappointment to you,' she murmured hesitantly.

Stephanie looked up at her. 'Be happy. I know you haven't been happy with us. Be happy with Toby instead.'

For a brief moment Lisa wanted to hug the older woman, explain how hurt she'd been all those years ago, and how ever since she'd been shielding herself against another possibly even greater hurt; but Stephanie wrapped her arms round herself and sat looking at the floor.

She obviously didn't want any emotional scene, and the sad truth was that they were two people with nothing in common at all and so, at eight o'clock that night, Lisa drove out of Stephanie's life forever.

For a time she *was* happy. For several months she and Toby thoroughly enjoyed themselves. They went to parties, took long walks and told each other everything they were willing to reveal. They also learnt to know each other's bodies off by heart.

For Toby too it was a particularly good time. His show was doing well; he drank sparingly; and with Lisa waiting at home no longer felt the need for endless conquests among the girls and women who pursued him. His life had a stability he'd fully expected to resent and in fact enjoyed.

When Lisa got herself a job at a small, exclusive kindergarten helping out with the under-fours he was even more delighted. Knowing that when he was busy working so was she, the slight unease, not great enough to be called jealousy, that he had previously felt when on set disappeared.

He couldn't pinpoint the exact moment when it began to go wrong, but the increasing number of times that Bishop rang him with night work was an irritant, while the work itself preyed on his mind, eating away at his nerves. Even then it only showed in small, petulant outbreaks of temper that never seemed to ruffle Lisa.

No, if there was one moment when he knew it couldn't last it was on the Friday night at the end of May when he arrived back at the maisonette, worn out by countless retakes and sudden script changes,

37

longing for a quick shower and bed and instead found Lisa dressed up in a black backless dress, the table set for an intimate dinner for two.

'What the hell's up?' he snapped. 'It isn't my birthday, is it?'

Realising that he was in a mood, Lisa didn't laugh. She'd already learnt that he didn't like being laughed at. 'Of course not. It's just that I've got something to tell you and I thought it would make a nice change if I cooked you a decent meal for once.'

'I fancy fish and chips,' he said churlishly, and slammed off to the bathroom.

When he emerged wearing his oldest pair of denims and a short-sleeved shirt with a hole in the back she realised that he wasn't going to go along with her plan. Sighing inwardly, she placed a stuffed pepper in front of him.

'What's this?'

'An hors d'oeuvre.'

'Why not just call it a starter, you stuck-up bitch?' he complained, reaching for the wine bottle lying in its wicker basket. 'I'll have a drink instead. How about you?'

'You know I don't drink red wine.'

'Bloody affectation. You can drink some tonight, can't you?'

Despite knowing that she'd end up with a migraine she decided she'd better placate him and held out her glass. 'Only a little, thanks.'

Filling it to the top, he smiled unpleasantly. 'Drink it all up!'

She wasn't quite sure how to handle his mood and felt uneasy. 'I will, later on,' she promised.

'Now!'

'Toby, I don't want it. I . . .'

Picking up the plate with the stuffed pepper still on it, he flung it across the room. 'Then I don't want your bloody pepper filled with dog meat!'

'Toby, please . . .'

'Toby, please!' he mimicked.

She went over to the stove and produced the Chinese-style steaks she'd prepared. He looked suspiciously at his. 'What the hell's all that stuff round the meat?'

'What on earth's the matter with you?' she snapped, losing her patience.

'I'm tired,' he said sullenly. 'I wanted a bit of peace and quiet, not all this fuss.'

'I'm very sorry but unfortunately I'm not psychic, and it so happens that I wanted to tell you something important tonight.'

'You're moving out? Hurrah!'

'I'm pregnant.'

'Oh, well, that's ... You're what?'

'Pregnant. Toby, I know it isn't what we intended but ...'

'Who's the father?' he asked softly.

She blinked in surprise. 'Don't be silly!'

'And don't talk to me like one of your kindergarten brats! Now answer the question, who's the father?' As he spoke he drank his third glass of wine and stood up to fetch a second bottle.

'You, of course.'

'Why of course? You spread your legs quickly enough for me, why not for other men as well?'

'But I'm living with you!'

'I thought you were taking precautions?'

'It must have been that night when I'd forgotten to put the diaphragm in and you didn't want to wait.'

'I see, so it's my fault, is it?'

'It isn't anyone's fault!' she shouted. 'This isn't a crime we're talking about.'

'No, just a hideous mistake. Well, you can bloody well get rid of it. I don't want any bawling babies messing up my life.'

'Get rid of it?'

'Sure, or get out. Suit yourself, so long as I don't ever have to visit you both. And there won't be any child support either. I shall deny paternity.'

'Haven't you had enough to drink?' said Lisa after watching him drain the second bottle of wine.

'Nothing like enough, and I see you haven't drunk anything at all.'

'I don't feel like drinking.'

'Nauseous already, are you? See what I mean. Babies are the biggest killjoys invented. I expect you'll go off sex as well.'

'I'm not nauseous but I don't like red wine.'

There was a brief, ominous moment of silence before he spoke again. 'Drink it or I'll pour it down your throat for you.'

Suddenly she was frightened, not only because he was drunk and the pregnancy announcement a disaster but also because of his sudden change of character. He was no longer the Toby she knew, and the fear showed in her eyes.

'I've managed to frighten you for once, haven't I?' he jeered. 'Miss High and Mighty doesn't know what to do. Drink it up, Lisa.'

She sat perfectly still, her hands in her lap, waiting tensely as he walked round the table and picked up her glass. 'Open your mouth and tip your head back,' he commanded softly.

Pressing her lips closely together she lowered her head, and for the first time ever, Toby hit her. He hit her hard with the flat of his hand

39

and she automatically opened her mouth to cry out. At once he put the other hand into her mouth, forcing her jaws wider apart and pushing back on her head, oblivious of her attempts to bite him. Her neck felt as though it was going to crack and then as he poured the wine down her throat she began to choke and splutter, so that half of it dribbled down her chin and on to the tablecloth.

'There's a good little baby!' he sneered, releasing her head because the glass was empty. 'Now, how about some nice steak.'

She was trembling all over and heard herself stammering. 'I'm not very h . . . h . . .'

'Hungry?' he put helpfully, absent-mindedly taking a swallow from the whisky bottle.

Lisa didn't answer him, hoping that he'd walk away and settle down with the whisky bottle. Trapped in a sudden nightmare, she longed to be left alone. 'Fine,' he said pleasantly. 'Then let's go to bed. I feel like some fun.'

'I thought you were tired,' she murmured.

'Not now. You may know more about most things than I do, but not what I'm feeling. Are you going to move or do I have to make you?'

She moved. Walking as upright as she could and determined not to let him see her fear, which she sensed would only encourage him, she sat on the bed and stared straight into his eyes. 'Well?'

'Take off your clothes,' he continued pleasantly and began to search through the chest of drawers. Within seconds she was undressed, anxious for it to be over so that he would fall asleep. It was only when she saw what he had in his hands that her fear increased. 'What are those for?' she asked warily, eyeing the pair of tights he was holding.

'I thought we'd try something different tonight. They say women like being tied down, it makes them feel they aren't responsible for enjoying sex. Takes away any deep-rooted guilt.'

'I've never felt guilty about sex,' she protested as he tied her legs to the corners of the bed. She sat up and began struggling with him when he tried to grab her left hand, but he bent her fingers back so savagely that she screamed and her arm went limp, allowing him to tie her left hand as well.

After that he turned of the main light and slowly began to take off his own clothes. 'Right, get started,' he instructed, standing in his already bulging Y-fronts. 'Start playing with yourself. Save me the trouble of getting you warmed up. That's why I left your right arm free!'

'I won't!' She said physically sick.

'I rather think you will, unless you want me to knock the shit out of you, and somehow I don't imagine that will be good for the baby you're so pleased about.'

'You wouldn't!' she cried in disbelief. 'Toby, you wouldn't do that. This is getting silly. Untie me and let's . . .'

He stepped closer and slapped her several times round the face. The slaps weren't hard but she could tell from the look in his eyes that he'd like to hit her harder. 'Believe me, I won't have any compunction at all about hitting you, pregnant or not. Now, do as I say. You women all think you're better at it than men, don't you? More sensitive, a more delicate touch. Well, let me see just how good you are.'

Her mouth was dry, her tongue sticking to the roof of her mouth, and she'd never felt less sexually aroused in her life. Tentatively she placed her right hand between her thighs and moved it aimlessly around, her eyes tightly closed.

'Open your eyes!' he shouted, still drinking from the whisky bottle, his voice thickening with excitement. She ignored him and the blow to her breasts came as such a shock that she caught her breath with astonishment and then, as the pain spread, cried out a little. 'I meant what I said,' he warned. 'Open your eyes.'

She looked at him standing at the foot of the bed, his eyes on her right hand although now and again he glanced at her face. 'I don't think you're very good at this,' he said after a few moments. 'I might have to punish you again.'

Despite herself she began to cry and he watched the silent tears with satisfaction. 'I see you're getting the message.'

'I can't,' she whispered desperately. 'I'm no good at it.'

'Of course you can. Just think of something exciting. Some wealthy father from the kindergarten touching you up for the price of a pair of ear-rings. Come on, Lisa, use your imagination.'

It was hopeless. She tried but the more he frightened her the more impossible her task became. Eventually he sat down on the bed. 'You're right, you're useless. Would you like me to help you?'

She lay quite still, not daring to answer because she didn't know what he had in mind. 'Answer me!' he said furiously, reaching out and pinching her left nipple.

'Yes,' she murmured faintly, lacking the courage to say no.

'Please?'

'Yes please.'

'There's a good girl!' He put the whisky bottle down on the floor and bent his head, moving her hand to one side and using his tongue instead. For ages sheer terror kept her from responding but finally to her own amazement and despair she found that she was building to a

41

climax and when she finally arched into the air, Toby plunged into her, laughing triumphantly.

Almost immediately he slumped semi-conscious on to her and because of the tights fastened round her ankles and left hand it was impossible to move him. She had to wait several hours before he surfaced into consciousness, and then he groaned and fumbled with the knots, apparently unaware of all that had gone on between them that night.

In the morning when she woke he'd already left for work but there was a note for her on the dining table. '*Sorry about last night, I suspect I got drunk. Can't remember much. Hope I didn't behave too badly. Have booked a table at Langan's Brasserie for 8 p.m. just in case I did. P.S. I love you.*'

Tearing up the note, she wondered where they went from here.

Chapter Five

Lisa slept for most of the day but awoke at four and decided to shower and choose a dress for their dinner. It seemed safer for them to go out. She was still nervous after last night, and if they were going to talk about what had happened she wanted plenty of people around to keep Toby under control.

Her face was bruised, although nothing that careful make-up wouldn't conceal, and her breasts still ached where he'd struck her, but apart from that all the damage was mental. He'd terrified and humiliated her when she was most vulnerable, and quite obviously she couldn't continue their affair because she'd never be able to let him make love to her again.

Placing a hand gently on her stomach she thought about the baby, and after whispering to it not to worry, she turned on the shower. Whatever happened she was going to love this baby with all her heart, with all the love she'd never been able to give to anyone else; it would grow up knowing that regardless of what it did she'd always be there. She'd be the most perfect mother any child could ask for. It wouldn't even miss it's father because they'd have such a wonderful life together.

Still daydreaming unrealistically, she wandered around applying makeup, perfume, a heated brush to her hair and all the other necessities for ensuring that she looked her best. Toby wasn't going to see how terrified she was, but he'd soon know that she was angry.

He was unusually quiet when he got home. Touching her bruised cheekbone lightly with one hand, he frowned but apart from that gave no indication that he remembered the night's violence. It was only when they were halfway through the main course in the restaurant that he plucked up the courage to speak.

'What happened?' he asked quietly. 'What did I do?'

'You got drunk.'

'I'm sorry, I should have warned you that I used to have a drink problem, but I thought it was cured. I went to one of those clinics and dried out. Since then I've been O.K.'

'Well, you weren't last night,' she said stonily.

'My head told me that! What happened?'

'Happened?'

'Yeah. Don't go all mysterious on me, Lisa. I know that when I drink I get violent, and despite your careful efforts with the foundation I can see that your face is bruised. Tell me exactly what I did.'

She told him everything, very quietly but in graphic detail, sparing him nothing. Only when she had finished did she look across the table at him, and was astounded to see that he was crying. 'I can't believe it,' he murmured. 'I mean, to you of all people. The first woman I've ...'

'Loved?'

'Yes!'

'Well you know what I think about that word.'

'But I do, Lisa, even if it's not what you want to hear.'

'You've got a funny way of showing it. Just coffee, please,' she added to a hovering waiter.

'What can I say?'

'Not a lot. I got the feeling you really hated me.'

'That's stupid! Sometimes I resent you. You're so much sharper than I am. You've always got a clever answer, you know about books and serious theatre, things I'm not even interested in, and sometimes that makes me feel a bit inadequate – but I don't hate you! As for the baby, well ...'

'You don't have to worry about the baby. I'll move out as soon as I can find somewhere else to live. I promise I won't turn up on your doorstep with a little bundle wrapped in a snow-white shawl; neither will I sell my story to a newspaper, however desperate I may be for money!'

'I don't want you to go. I want you to stay. In fact, I want us to get married.'

'No way, Toby. I don't trust you any more.'

'It won't happen again, you've got my word on that. I won't drink at all, not even a glass of wine. How's that? It's what I should have done before but I thought ... well, it's what all alcoholics think, isn't it?'

'How would I know? There aren't any in my family.'

He reached across the table and took hold of her hand. 'You've got every right to be annoyed with me, and frightened too I should think, but at least let me have another chance. We'll continue living together until the baby's born, and then if you feel that I'm O.K. perhaps we could marry later on. Surely I've got the right to one more try. It is my baby too.'

Lisa shook her head. 'Let's go back. I'm tired and I need to sleep.'

'Of course.'

Back at the maisonette, he tucked her carefully in bed and then lay by her side, watching her sleep. He didn't want to lose her, although he wasn't as pleased about the baby as he'd made out, but he was willing to put up with that as long as he kept Lisa.

In the middle of the night she had a nightmare, hitting out blindly at him when he tried to comfort her. He knew why, and hated himself for what he'd done. Never again, he vowed. He'd never strike her again.

Next morning Lisa sat down and considered her options. There weren't many. She could try and find herself a small flat using the money from her possessions to pay the rent, but that money wouldn't last very long and with the baby becoming more and more obvious the kindergarten were unlikely to keep her on.

She could also ask Stephanie about her trust fund. It seemed amazing that Simon had found the time to cancel out the fund between her leaving home and his death, yet according to the solicitor there was no mention of it.

She could also stay where she was. Toby had talked to her for over an hour before he left for work, promising yet again that he wouldn't touch alcohol any more. Assuring her it had been one isolated incident and entirely out of character.

The trouble was, she needed to believe him. She didn't want her baby to live in a small, badly heated room, growing up without any garden and with a mother out working most days. She wanted time to love the baby, enjoy seeing it grow, and above all to be with it. This baby would have everything she'd missed. Staying with Toby seemed the only practical solution for the moment.

When she told him that she'd give him one more chance, he was positively ecstatic, his relief seeming quite out of proportion. It was almost as though he were under pressure to keep her with him, except she knew that was impossible because she didn't have anyone left who cared.

They went out celebrating at Annabel's and had their photo taken, Toby even going so far as to tell the reporter that Lisa was expecting and hinting that marriage was imminent. She thought it amazing considering he was only drinking mineral water.

For several months it worked reasonably well. Toby's popularity

45

grew until it became difficult for them to eat out, since he was mobbed by hordes of young girls and a few not so young ones. At parties too he became the centre of attention for all the attractive models and small-part actresses anxious to be photographed on his arm. By now Lisa was bulky and preferred to stay in the background. Occasionally she saw women slip Toby their telephone numbers, or follow him out of a room, returning later with such a complacent look on their faces that she wondered if he'd given them the benefit of one of his quick performances that left her totally unaroused but were part of the new pattern of their lives.

She minded, but not as much as she should have done. It was humiliating to stand around on her own wondering what he was up to, trying to ignore the sympathetic glances of some of the other men, but if she'd truly loved him it would have been unbearable and she knew this. As it was, she simply pretended it wasn't happening.

Once or twice she challenged him, but he always denied anything had happened. 'You can't believe I'd be unfaithful upstairs while you were downstairs on your own!' he laughed, his blue eyes full of synthetic charm.

'I believe you're capable of it,' she said coolly.

'In that case, I'm surprised you don't make a scene.'

'They're not taking anything I want!' she retorted swiftly, and saw his face darken.

'No, they're bloody well not, are they? You don't like me near you any more. You're always too tired, or too nauseous. It's hardly surprising if I do ... It wouldn't be surprising if I did ...'

'If you keep practising,' said Lisa furiously, 'you might get it down to under three minutes.'

'What's that supposed to mean?'

'That I might be a great deal keener if you spent a little longer over our lovemaking. You obviously think that foreplay's going out of fashion.'

'I see,' he said slowly. 'So now I'm not even any good at that.'

'You don't do much for me any more; I assume it's quite nice from your point of view?'

'Have you looked at yourself lately?' he asked aggressively. 'It's hardly surprising I don't want to spend hours poring over your body, is it? Frankly, you're a bit of a turn-off.'

'This lump isn't due to over-eating!' she shouted. 'I can't help my shape. It's your baby in there, and I'm beginning to think its head is as large as yours.'

For a moment they glared at each other, then Toby lifted his right hand and hit her with a casual backhand flip across the mouth. Even as the salty blood from her split lip trickled into her mouth he turned and left the flat.

Lisa sank down on the settee, holding a handkerchief to her mouth. She knew that she was to blame. She'd deliberately taunted him, hitting out at any area where she felt he was vulnerable, and why? Because she didn't know why she was with him. Because the sexual chemistry which had brought them together, and the emotional elation that had kept their relationship charged up, had died on her. They had nothing in common left.

She couldn't talk to him. He wasn't interested in anything except his career and the frivolous side of showbusiness. He wouldn't even go to watch the R.S.C. or take her to the opera. Television was his god. It had make him famous and was the beginning and end of his world. He was also starting to believe his own publicity, losing his own identity in that of his character.

She understood all this and knew it wasn't uncommon, but it wasn't the kind of life she wanted. Yet she didn't know how to get out. Finally, she went to bed, swallowing one of Toby's sleeping pills as an afterthought.

When she awoke she felt muzzy headed. The room was still dark, but two of the corner lamps were on and the bedside clock said 4 a.m. The pill was making it impossible for her to wake up fully, but she was aware of Toby standing next to her.

'Awake?' he said politely.

'Not really. I took one of your pills and ...' She let her eyes close again.

He shook her by the shoulder. 'Wake up, I've got a surprise for you.'

She forced open her heavy lids and looked up at him. 'Can't it wait?' Someone in the room laughed, and it wasn't Toby. 'Who's that?' she asked nervously, pulling the duvet round her shoulders.

'Just a friend. We thought we'd see if we could satisfy you between us. I explained that I'm not enough of a man any more.'

'You're drunk again!'

'I've had a few, but I'm not drunk. You must remember Roger; he plays my partner.'

Now her brain was beginning to clear. 'Get him out of here,' she cried.

'That's not nice. Roger gave up a very attractive blonde to come and see you. He doesn't even mind about the baby. He rather likes big women, and you're certainly big, aren't you, Lisa!' As he spoke he pulled the duvet off the bed.

Lisa screamed and dived for a sweatshirt but Toby caught hold of

47

her round the waist. 'Naughty! Let Roger have a good look. Come on, Roger. See what a big girl Lisa's grown into!'

Roger advanced towards the bed. Slightly below six feet tall and with a baby face, he looked the picture of innocence until you studied his eyes, which were tired and old. At twenty-three, Roger had done it all, or so he'd thought until tonight. This was something different, and high on drugs and alcohol he was beginning to feel a tingle of excitement at last.

'Hi, Lisa! Nice to see you again.' He gave another giggle, and she shivered with terror as Toby settled himself behind her on the bed, holding her tightly so that she couldn't wrench away from Roger's touch.

'She likes a lot of foreplay,' explained Toby. 'She was complaining earlier about my speedy technique. Are you good at foreplay, Roger?'

He laughed, catching hold of both her legs before she could kick out, and with Toby holding her waist while Roger imprisoned her legs there was absolutely nothing that she could do.

It was like a nightmare. She wished that she hadn't taken the sleeping pill. It had slowed down her already dulled reflexes and made it impossible for her to think quickly enough. After what seemed hours, Roger lifted his head.

'I think she's ready!' he exclaimed, nearly falling across her body.

'Stop it!' she shouted, beginning to cry as she felt Roger's fingers on her. 'Please, please leave me alone. Just go away, both of you. Haven't you done enough? I can't ...'

Toby lifted his head. 'You're not very grateful, Lisa. We thought you liked all this.'

'You're an animal!' she screamed. 'You must be insane. I only wish your fans could see you now.'

'Castrating bitch,' he muttered as he lifted himself above her, thrusting into her so hard that she was terrified for the baby. As she twisted and turned, trying to protect her stomach, flash bulbs suddenly exploded relentlessly around her. She screamed again, but Roger only smiled.

'Don't worry. It's just a friend taking a few snaps in case you try and run out on poor Toby here, who wants you to marry him.'

'I wouldn't marry him if they paid me a million pounds!' she spat out furiously and then realised with despair that although Toby had finished, Roger was going to take his turn. The realisation was too much for her and she finally lost consciousness.

Without her hatred and terror the excitement died away for both men. Finally they stood by the bed, looking down at her tear-stained face, her eyes now closed, her hair matted with sweat, and abruptly Toby realised what he'd done.

'Christ, Roger, suppose we've damaged the baby?'

'Don't be stupid, we didn't hurt her. We only gave her a good workout, like you said she wanted. Besides, you needed the photos, didn't you?'

'Did I? I can't seem to remember . . .'

'You said she won't marry you, but if you threaten to have these published then she won't dare refuse and risk the publicity. That's what you told me. Because of her parents and some scandal they were in? You said she'd never be able to face that sort of thing.'

'Neither could I!'

Roger shrugged. 'Suit yourself, but I doubt if she'll think you'd mind. All grist to your sexual reputation! No, if she's the wife you want then I imagine you've got her. Thanks for the loan, I enjoyed it. Next time I'll have her first.'

'There won't be a next time.'

'Of course there will. Once you get a taste for this kind of thing there's no going back. I'll bring a bird along as well. Foursomes are good fun, especially if you get the women to work on each other. That's a great turn-on.'

'Sod off home,' said Toby wearily, and was asleep on the settee before Roger had shut the front door behind him. He was woken at six-thirty by the door bell, and knew who the visitor would be before he opened the door.

'You look fresh and bright!' said Bishop with the faintest hint of a smile round his mouth. 'A hard night, was it? Difficult to get the little lady to agree?'

'You could say that.'

'But she will marry you?'

'I think so.'

'That's not good enough, Toby.'

'All right, yes, she will.'

'Good, I'll pass the message on. Make it soon, he'll want to see a picture in the paper before the week's out. Special licence naturally.'

'Naturally,' said Toby, thankful that for once he'd managed to do the right thing.

'The arrogant bastard's gone and married her!' snarled Neal Gueras, hurling the *Daily Mail* across his office in a fury. 'Didn't you tell him what I said? Didn't you make my wishes clear?'

'Of course,' said Bishop smoothly, bending down to pick up the paper and noticing how drawn the bride looked, and how satisfied the groom.

'Then what the hell does he think he's playing at?'

Bishop shrugged. 'Perhaps she's the one who pushed him into it. From what I've heard she's pretty besotted.'

'That isn't what *I've* heard,' said Neal coldly. 'In my opinion he's done this deliberately, in order to show us that because he's going through a period of temporary fame, he's untouchable.'

'You could be right, but ...'

'He treats her badly,' said Neal abruptly. 'She isn't the type of girl who'd put up with that.'

'Maybe she enjoys it. Some do, you know!'

'I'm well aware of that, although you appear to have a monopoly on the supply. Now get out, you're beginning to annoy me. If I thought for one moment that my message hadn't been passed on ...'

'I assure you it was. Even though I did wonder if he was going to play ball.'

'A minute ago you were blaming her.'

'A mistake,' responded Bishop, knowing full well that it had been, and furious with the hapless Lisa for putting him even temporarily out of favour.

'Keep watching them,' ordered Neal as Bishop started to leave. 'If there's any trouble I want her out, understand?'

'Yes.'

'Good. Tell Mrs Watts to get me an up-date on the price of gold, and send Rose in for dictation.'

'Yes, sir. How's Mrs Gueras?' he added politely.

'Since when did you care? She's exactly the same of course. Now get on with your work.'

Lisa sat staring at her wedding ring, no longer able to twist it nervously round her finger because it was so swollen, but picking at it restlessly as she waited for her husband to come home.

She was scarcely recognisable. Her face was pinched and there were dark hollows beneath her eyes. Her right cheekbone was bruised, and above her right eye there was a fading yellow mark. Similar marks covered her upper arms and breasts, but since she'd stopped going to the ante-natal clinic she was spared the humiliation of people knowing that Toby was always knocking her about.

She'd never had any time for battered wives, believing in her youthful ignorance that no one needed to stay with a man who physically abused them. Now she knew better. Her fear of him was so great that she was more terrified of having him come after her and possibly kill her than she was of staying with him. At least he was out a great deal, working, drinking or laying some dollybird. She didn't care if it was the latter; it was only the drink that caused the trouble.

50

He was rarely sober any more, and she didn't know why that had happened either. There were rumours in the paper of his show being axed, but that didn't make any sense as it was high in the ratings. Toby refused to discuss what he called total fabrications in the gutter press he had once courted so assiduously.

She wondered if he was in debt because sometimes when she was alone at night, men would ring up, refusing to leave messages with her; men who sounded both dangerous and annoyed. Again Toby wouldn't talk about them, except to say that they were friends. They didn't sound particularly friendly to her.

Hearing his key in the lock, her stomach lurched and she began to tremble. She knew he was drunk because he was having so much trouble with the door, but she didn't dare go and help him because that would be wrong. Nearly everything she did these days was wrong.

She was amazed to realise he'd brought people back with him; amazed, and at first relieved, until she recognised Roger and his current girlfriend, an underage blonde nymphette called Candy.

'How's my little wife?' sneered Toby, nearly tripping over the edge of the rug.

'Fine.'

'That's what we like to hear, isn't it, Candy?' Candy gave a girlish squeal of laughter and stared adoringly at Toby. 'Like her?' he continued. 'Think you'd fancy her?' Again a squeal of laughter.

'What are you on about?' asked Lisa, keeping a wary eye on Roger who was blocking the only exit.

'We've come to keep you company. I've been neglecting you lately, so Roger and Candy are going to help me make up for my lapse.'

'No, they're not. I know what you're suggesting and I absolutely refuse. If you don't get those two out of this house, I'm calling the police.'

'I don't think so, sweetheart,' he laughed, and pulled the telephone cord out of its socket. She glanced round the room. Roger was still by the door, his eyes glinting. Candy stood by Toby, her cheeks flushed with excitement, while his blue eyes were cold and full of hate.

'Why did you marry me?' she whispered. 'Why force me to marry you when you don't like me any more than I like you?'

'But I do! I like you so much I want you to get to know all my friends personally. Into the bedroom, unless you want Roger to carry you, and he can be a little rough when he's high.'

'Get them out!' she hissed through clenched teeth.

Toby reached towards her and pulled her blouse off her shoulders. 'Now get the rest of your clothes off.'

She knew that this time she had to stand up for herself and the

51

baby. Toby was beyond all reason, set on some mad course of destruction intended to include her, and he wasn't going to succeed. She looked quickly round the room before turning docilely towards the bedroom door.

'Good girl, I knew you'd see sense!' he laughed, and then she turned, picking up the nearly empty whisky bottle lying on the telephone table and smashing it against the wall so that she was left holding the neck, extending the hideously jagged edge towards Toby.

'Get them out of here or I'll cut your face to ribbons, Toby Walker,' she said softly. Candy gave a scream of fright and started to move towards Roger. 'You too, Candy,' continued Lisa, never taking her eyes off the frozen Toby. 'If you don't get out of here I'll cut your face as well, and let's be honest, that's about all you've got going for you, isn't it!' With one final frightened squeak, Candy wisely fled. After a brief delay, Roger followed, leaving husband and wife alone.

'You wouldn't do that,' said Toby quietly. 'You haven't got the guts to cut me. I'd break your arm before you got near enough.'

'Try me.'

He looked at her face and tried a change of tactic. 'O.K. I'm sorry, I shouldn't have ...'

'Too right. I don't know why you married me, or why you're behaving like you are, but I've had enough. I'm leaving here and now, and nothing you do or say will stop me.'

'You can't leave me. People will ask questions!'

'What people? I don't know anyone who cares what happens to me, and I'm certainly not going to go round boasting about what's gone on in this house during the past few months. All I want is peace, and that's something I'm never going to get with you – you're insane! Now get out of my way.'

'You've made a big mistake, Lisa, and you're going to be sorry,' he snarled, and suddenly lunged towards her. Startled and terrified she jabbed the bottle forward and up, feeling the impact as it came into contact with his face, and hearing a dull tearing sound.

Maddened beyond any sense and shouting furiously, he began to pursue her round the room. She managed to cut him twice more before he cornered her, but eventually found herself trapped against the wall, and at the sight of the blood pouring from his torn face she lost her nerve and began to scream, a scream that turned to a shriek of terror as he caught hold of her arm and twisted it, forcing her to drop the bottle to the floor.

She heard a bone snap and felt a blinding flash of pain shoot up into her shoulder, but still she kicked out, trying desperately to keep him at a distance, certain that he was going to kill her and her unborn baby.

'You cow!' he whispered as he closed in. 'You're going to wish you'd never been born.'

She screamed again but there was no point because there wasn't anyone within earshot. As the first blow landed on her stomach, she felt certain that she and her baby were about to die.

After a few minutes she began to lose consciousness. She could no longer try and protect the baby and her screams started to die away as she slid slowly down the wall. Her soft whimpering only infuriated Toby more, and he was yelling obscenities at her as he picked up the broken bottle, holding its jagged edge lightly against the skin beneath her left eye.

'If you think you're leaving me, you're wrong,' he hissed furiously. 'I'm not giving up after everything I've been through for you. I'll make such a mess of your face that for the rest of your life you'll be grateful if a man's even kind enough to speak your name.'

'You haven't done anything for me!' she cried, attempting to twist her face away but finding it caught between the fingers of his left hand.

'Of course I have. Where do you think I went on all my evenings out? Pub crawling? Stupid bitch! I was ...'

'Get away from her, Walker,' said a quiet voice. Toby froze, the bottle still by her face but his expression suddenly one of fear. 'Step back slowly,' the voice continued. 'Any sudden moves might frighten me, and when I'm scared I tend to shoot first and see if I was right afterwards.'

For a second Toby hesitated. Lisa actually felt the glass prick her skin but was too terrified to utter a sound because the voice that had interrupted her nightmare was deadly despite its softness. Deadly and familiar. He was the man she'd seen in Simon's hall on Boxing Day.

'Don't make any more mistakes, Walker, you can't afford them. Step away from her.'

'I'll get you one day,' whispered Toby before backing off, turning away from her to look at the visitor.

'Now fetch her robe from the bedroom.'

'Why the hell ...?'

She needs medical attention. Even private hospitals might ask questions if we take her in looking like that.'

Lisa, unable to stop shaking and whimpering, realised that her blouse was torn to shreds and blood was dripping from the cut beneath her eye and landing on her cream skirt. Taking the robe from Toby's outstretched hands she tried to put it on, but the pain from her right arm made her scream aloud.

'Help her,' instructed Bishop.

'No! Don't let him near me, I'll do it. I just ...'

'Certainly not. Move aside, Walker, and sit down quietly in the corner.' Toby obeyed, all aggression suddenly gone, and now Bishop moved forward, glancing down at her. 'Didn't your mother tell you that rough games get out of hand? Too much excitement always ends in tears, you know.'

'It wasn't a game! He ...'

'Lost your sense of humour? I didn't honestly think it was a game. Neither of you looks as though you've had any fun at all! Come on, let's just drape it round that shoulder.'

She cringed inwardly at his touch, not because he hurt her − he was amazingly careful and caused no pain at all − but because he made her skin crawl. He'd saved her life, and hopefully the baby's too, yet she couldn't feel grateful. He was enjoying himself far too much for her to feel anything but increased dislike.

'Not even a thank you?' he queried, plucking a cordless phone out of his coat pocket. 'I might be quite hurt by that, if it weren't for the fact that you're obviously in a state of shock.'

'Why you?' she asked in confusion. 'Why is it always you?'

'Always? We scarcely know each other! Steve, bring the car round and take her to the hospital. They're expecting her. Ask for Dr Cooper and get him to have a gynaecologist come over too. There's a chance she might be losing our friend Toby's claim to immortality!'

'Who's Steve?' murmured Lisa, terrified it might be another friend of Toby's.

'A nice lad. He'll be very kind to you. He'll probably hold your hand if you ask him. I'd come myself but I want to talk to lover boy here. Walker, let Steve in when he arrives.'

The dull ache in Lisa's stomach was beginning to turn into a sharper, more ominous pain and she tried to wrap her arms round her abdomen until the injury brought her up short and she cried out again.

'Shoulder?' asked Bishop casually. 'Don't worry, they'll soon fix that up.'

'No, it's ...'

'The baby? Probably for the best, don't you think? Shouldn't imagine you want a permanent reminder of this marriage. I'm sure there'll be other children, unless you're irreparably damaged of course!' And he gave her a smile that was more frightening than any of Toby's blows.

'You bastard!' she cried. 'You're enjoying all this, aren't you?'

'Not at all, but I admit it's diverting. Ah, here comes the cavalry!'

Steve was tall, well built and extremely kind. He carried her out of the flat, laid her carefully on the back seat of the car, then got in beside her, letting her head rest on his knees while another man, silent and totally lacking in curiosity, drove them through the streets of Battersea and into London.

Now and again, Lisa couldn't help crying out. Her arm was on fire with pain and her stomach felt as though there were hot pokers sticking into it. Steve stroked her forehead as he murmured encouragement, and she would be forever grateful to him for helping her keep her self-control.

Once at the hospital things happened with lightning speed. A young, fresh-faced doctor, after one look at her, took out a needle. She tried to push him away, terrified of losing consciousness and probably the baby as well, but he gently held her down on the trolley and the last thing she heard was his voice telling her that she was going to be all right. She didn't believe him.

Chapter Six

For a few days it seemed that Lisa was right and the doctor wrong. But then, as she continued resting in the luxurious, deeply-carpeted private room with its pale lilac walls and snow-white curtains and bedspread, the bleeding stopped and finally the gynaecologist professed himself satisfied that the baby was safe and well.

'How can you be sure it isn't hurt?' asked Lisa anxiously. 'What if it's got brain damage?'

'Babies are well protected,' he assured her. 'Besides, we've done a scan. The baby's fine and so are you.'

'When can I go home?' she asked, and then wondered where home was.

'I'm afraid there's no question of you going anywhere at all until after the baby's born. You've been through a traumatic experience and need rest and quiet. As I understand it, you're homeless at the moment. Where could you possibly go that would offer you more peace than here?' He smiled his very expensive smile.

'Well, it's true that I . . .'

'Precisely! Now I must be on my way. I'll look in tomorrow if not before. Dr Cooper tells me the arm's coming along nicely too.'

'Mr Heywood, who's paying for me to stay here?'

'I understood it was a family friend. I'm afraid I don't . . .' He was obviously embarrassed.

'I'll speak to one of the nurses,' she said quickly.

'Just relax, Mrs Walker. Money is fortunately not one of your problems at the moment, but tranquillity is. Stop worrying and rest. The baby needs all the rest you can give it for these final few weeks.'

Of course he was right, but since she never had a visitor and up to now hadn't been allowed a television in the room in case she became over-stimulated, her mind had nothing better to do than worry away at the problem.

It wouldn't be Toby. He didn't have that kind of money. His own private treatment was paid for by the television company; and it certainly wasn't Stephanie, who hadn't so much as sent her a get well card. Who else was there? she wondered.

It bothered her, and at night she stayed awake worrying despite the mild sleeping pill they allowed her. After three sleepless nights, Dr Cooper came to see her. 'Sleeping badly I understand, Mrs Walker. Why's that? Pain from the arm?'

'No.'

'Worrying about the baby?'

'No, I ...'

'Afraid we might let your husband in to see you? We won't, you know, not under any circumstances, although he does ring up each morning.'

'Big deal! No, I ...'

'How about a psychiatrist to teach you to relax and forget all the trauma of the past months. Would you like that?'

'Not particularly. How much does a psychiatrist cost?'

'Cost?' He looked as horrified as if she'd sworn at him.

'Yes. I don't understand how I can afford to stay here. *That's* what's keeping me awake at nights. I don't need a psychiatrist, he'll only add to the worry! Why won't anyone tell me who's paying for all this?'

'You should have asked me before. It's your godfather.'

'My what?' She couldn't believe her ears.

'Godfather. I must say you're a lucky girl to have ... However, he's naturally anxious that you get the best treatment and ...'

'I don't have a godfather.'

'Everyone has a godfather!'

'Not if they haven't been christened.'

'You weren't christened?'

'Yes, of course I was. I was simply pointing out that not everyone does have a godfather.'

He gave a polite laugh. 'I see. Well, that's your worry solved. I'll prescribe a little sedative for tonight I think.'

'Look, my godfather died in a road accident when I was twelve.'

'Just to make sure you sleep properly,' he continued firmly, his face flushed.

'Who the hell is paying for all this?' shouted Lisa angrily, and before she knew what was happening, one of the nurses was holding her gently down and the doctor was injecting her. She was still asking the same question when she fell asleep.

It was three hours before she awoke, her mouth feeling thick and dry. She tried to sit up to reach her water jug but her arm stabbed a reminder of its injury and she gave an exclamation of pain. It was only then that the man waiting in the corner approached the bed. 'Did you want something?' he asked gently, his voice deep and calm. She recognised him from a long time back, but couldn't place when or put a name to him.

'A drink, please. They put me out and I'm very thirsty.'

He poured her some squash, holding the glass while she drank through a straw because her mouth still hurt from one of Toby's blows and a straw made it easier.

'You don't remember me, I assume?' said the man after a short but not awkward silence.

'Yes, you came to see Simon once. It was a long time ago.'

'Quite a long time, and a lot of water's flowed under the bridge since then, not all of it crystal clear either!'

She remembered Roger and her eyes shadowed. Immediately he wished the words unsaid. 'You were the man in the library,' she murmured. 'Your wife had just given you a third daughter and you weren't pleased.'

He raised his eyebrows. 'I wasn't? That must have been Rebekah. She's a quiet little thing, no trouble at all.'

'Still no sons?'

'I'm afraid not. I was sorry about your father.'

Lisa settled herself against the pillows. She didn't feel in the least tense in this man's company. There was something solid and comforting about him. His presence was strangely reassuring considering they scarcely knew each other. 'I didn't appreciate him when he was alive, but he was a good man.'

'I'm sure he was.'

'The police don't seem to think so.'

He chuckled. 'There's good and there's "good". The police have different interpretations of such matters. Do you remember my name?'

'I'm sorry, it seems to have vanished from my mind.'

'Neal Gueras.'

'Of course! You used to ring Simon up now and again. He often spoke about you.'

'Then you'll understand why I felt compelled to make sure you were properly looked after.'

Lisa looked thoughtfully at him. 'You mean *you're* paying for all this?'

'Yes.'

'How did you know that I was hurt?'

'It made some of our more sensational papers.'

'Not the instant it happened! I was brought straight here. I remember Bishop saying I was to be taken to a private hospital at once. Do you know Bishop?' she added, apparently casually.

'Certainly. Once he realised who you were he very sensibly took it upon himself to ensure you had the best treatment available.'

'Why was he there that night?'

'Business with your husband, I think.'

'That was lucky!'

'Quite. Presumably you'll want a divorce as quickly and quietly as possible?'

'Yes, but . . .'

'I'll get my solicitors on to it. You mustn't feel that this is done only because of Simon. I always understood that there was a provision for you in his will, a fund of some sort. Since this hasn't come to light I feel it's only right I should make some money available to you in compensation.'

'You didn't run off with the money, if there ever was any, that is?'

'I called in a debt. It's possible that he liquidised the money he'd invested for you in order to pay it off.'

'If he owed you money it was yours by right.'

'I want to help you,' he said quietly. 'I'd like to take care of you.'

She looked into his eyes and knew what he meant. 'I'm sorry but very soon baby will make two. I don't think you'll want to take care of us both!'

'You underestimate me. I shall make sure you both have a suitable little house ready and waiting when you leave here. After that, we'll just have to wait and see.'

'A house?' She was stunned, and felt tears in her eyes.

He touched her lightly on the cheek. 'You're overwrought at the moment. It won't be a mansion, and neither will it leave me penniless! Now I really must be going. Business calls, I'm afraid, but once I heard you were worrying about money I knew I had to set your mind at rest.'

'Will you come and see me again?'

'Would you like me to?'

She sensed it was an important question and hesitated. 'Of course,' she said at last. 'I never see anyone at the moment.'

'And even I'm better than no one?'

She smiled. 'That wasn't what I meant. I'm very grateful to you and feel better already.'

'Then I'll certainly come again. Just take care of yourself, and don't worry about anything, will you promise me that?' She nodded, and with a final smile he departed, leaving behind the same scent of expensive cologne that she'd noticed in the library so long ago.

Tranquilised, isolated and safe in her small room, she didn't question his motives as she would normally have done, and didn't think about any long-term relationship with him. All she did was look forward to his visits and nurture the baby she was longing to hold in her arms. Someone of her own at last.

On Friday 13th March, the baby was born. Lisa's labour was long and difficult but her daughter was beautiful and weighed a healthy 8lbs. She had a mass of dark hair, very smooth skin and an unusually mature look in her eyes. Lisa named her Jessica, and had never been so happy in her entire life. She remained happy for at least three hours, until it was time for Jessica's first feed.

The trouble was that Jessica didn't seem to understand what breasts were for. She simply lay in Lisa's arms, staring upwards and totally ignoring the nipples. Even when Lisa managed to insert one into the baby's mouth it was allowed to slip out again, and the problem was intensified by her broken arm which severely restricted her movements.

After a time one of the nurses came to see how Lisa was progressing. She found her tearfully imploring her daughter to try harder, and had to suppress a smile as she hurried to reassure this already over-anxious young woman.

'It doesn't matter if she's not hungry,' she smiled. 'I expect she's rather sleepy. Your milk will be through better tomorrow. She'll soon be as greedy as anyone could wish, just you wait and see.'

'I thought they suckled instinctively! She doesn't seem to understand what's going on.'

'We'll give her some glucose mixture from a bottle this time. It's done more these days for the first feed. The important thing is that you rest tonight. Tense mothers have tense babies, you know. They're very quick to sense if you're worrying, and it makes them anxious.'

'But I wasn't worrying, I was happy!'

'Come along, Jessica,' said the nurse briskly. 'How about some nice glucose while Mummy has a rest?'

'I want her sleeping here with me,' said Lisa quickly, 'not left in the nursery.'

'Are you sure? It's surprising how every little snuffle sounds like a train going by when you're first left with them!'

'I'm quite sure.'

'Then I'll bring her back when she's had the glucose. What a lucky girl you are, Jessica. Most of our mothers are very happy to get a few nights' peace and quiet.'

'I want her to know she's loved,' whispered Lisa. The nurse smiled, privately considering Lisa highly eccentric but trained to keep her thoughts to herself. When she returned, Lisa looked at her anxiously. 'Did she drink the glucose all right?'

'Like a lamb. She'll be fine tomorrow just as I said.'

It was true that her daughter's small sucking sounds and mewing noises kept Lisa awake, but she didn't care. At last she'd got what she wanted, and in any case she was too strung up to sleep. At six in the morning she put the baby confidently to her breast, but once again Jessica lay still and placid, showing no interest in the nipple.

'Come on, sweetheart!' urged Lisa. 'Don't be difficult, they'll think it's my fault. Have a drink for Mummy.'

After ten minutes she rang for a nurse. It was a new one who was quite used to first-time mothers having feeding problems. She swiftly moved Jessica around until, with her head tilted at what even the nurse acknowledged to be a strange angle, she finally began to suck. She sucked strongly and well, but after four minutes when she was moved to the other breast she reverted to placid indifference and not even the nurse could find a position where Jessica was willing to continue feeding.

'Obstinate!' she laughed. 'Don't worry, she must have had enough or she wouldn't stop. Remember to start on that breast next time.'

Lisa put her daughter back in the cot and looked carefully at her. It was true that she was beautiful, far more so than most wrinkled newborn babies, but for some reason she felt uneasy. Whilst she was experiencing the most incredible love for her child, she had the peculiar sensation that her love wasn't going to be returned.

That evening, Neal came to visit. She'd just finished feeding Jessica – on one side only again – and the baby was lying peacefully next to the bed. 'She's lovely,' he said appreciatively, glancing down at the child. 'Far more beautiful than any of mine were at that age. You look beautiful as well,' he added softly. 'Motherhood suits you.'

She was so pleased to have someone to talk to that she scarcely noticed the compliment, although the enormous bouquet of roses that he handed to her was impossible to overlook and she rang for a nurse to arrange the flowers straight away.

'Do you really think she's all right?' she asked anxiously.

'Of course. Don't you?'

'I suppose she looks fine, but somehow she doesn't seem to ... I don't know, respond I suppose you'd call it.'

He laughed, but kindly. 'What do you want? A conversation with her?'

'No! But I'd imagined that when you picked a baby up and cuddled

61

it, you sensed that it felt happy and secure. When I pick Jessica up she just lies there like a doll. And she's incredibly difficult to feed.'

'Let her have a bottle. That way you'll keep your figure better.'

'I'm not bothered about my figure!'

Neal was, but decided he couldn't really say so. Instead, he sat close to Lisa and took some papers out of his briefcase. 'I've had my solicitors working on your divorce. It will all be settled very discreetly. He won't deny either physical or mental cruelty, and he won't ask for any access to his daughter, although he's willing to pay a token amount of alimony if you want it.'

'I don't want it, but I might need it.'

'I think it's better to cut him right out of your life. If he pays maintenance and then at some future date decides he does want to visit Jessica, a judge might well feel he was entitled to do so.'

'Well, in that case I . . .'

'Fine, it's agreed he won't help maintain her.'

'Neal, I'll have to go out to work to support her if Toby doesn't pay me anything. I don't want her left with childminders.'

'Money won't be a problem. I've no intention of letting Simon's daughter live from hand to mouth.'

Lisa sank back on the pillows and looked thoughtfully at him. 'I didn't know you were that close to Simon.'

'I'm afraid you knew very little about him.'

'What's that supposed to mean?'

'I'm only saying that he didn't tell you every detail of his life, and anyway I rarely have personal contact with people who do business for me. I find it makes for a difficult situation should anything go wrong.'

'You mean he worked for you?'

'Sometimes. An antiques dealer works for a lot of people. If he was going to America and I happened to know of some particular painting that was coming on the market around that time, then I'd ask him to purchase it for me using his own name. It's better with a private art collection to maintain strict secrecy over purchases, otherwise theft can be quite a problem.'

'What exactly do you do?' she asked with interest.

'I'm a commodities dealer.'

'Copper, gold, that sort of thing?'

'Correct, but why are we talking business when I've brought some champagne to celebrate little Jessica's birth?'

He found some glasses in a cupboard beside her bed and together they toasted the sleeping baby's future. After two glasses, Lisa felt quite light-headed. 'Does your wife know you're here?' she asked with mock innocence, her front-fastening nightdress revealing rather more than she realised when she lay back.

Neal looked at the swollen creamy breasts and felt his mouth go dry. For some reason even the knowledge that she'd been Toby's didn't bother him any more. He still wanted her, and he was going to have her however much it cost him.

'Naomi never asks me about anything these days. She spends all her time at our house near Iver in Berkshire. It's quiet there. She doesn't like London life — entertaining, theatre, shopping — it's a nightmare for her. As long as I go home regularly, she's quite content.'

'Why doesn't she like London?'

'She grew up in a quiet village in Greece, and her family were very poor. I'm afraid she doesn't like the lifestyle of the wealthy.'

'Then she shouldn't have married you!' Lisa stated with the cruel logic of the young.

'I was poor then. It's the usual boring story. I've spent a lot of time making money, and while I've been busy with my work she's brought up the girls while remaining basically the same person I married. I, on the other hand, have changed out of all recognition. It isn't her fault.'

'But difficult for you both?'

'For me certainly. I need someone in town to act as hostess and companion. For her? Not really, as long as she's allowed to live as she wishes, she's quite content.' Neal's ability to lie through his teeth with apparent sincerity was notorious but Lisa believed him. She might not have done except for the champagne, but as it was she accepted all he said. She also realised that the price of her small house and raising Jessica might be paid for by acting as hostess and companion when Neal was in town. The prospect wasn't displeasing. Provided that sex wasn't involved, she'd be perfectly willing to accept if he asked her.

'So how do you manage?'

'I've got a very good friend, Kay Masters, who stands in for Naomi as necessary.'

Is Kay married?'

He laughed. 'Hardly! Not many husbands would be that complacent. No, Kay's totally free.'

Oh well, thought Lisa, wrong again. He didn't need her as a hostess. It was almost a disappointment. The sophisticated, powerful older man watched the emotions flicker across her face and was pleased. He'd sown the seed and then taken away the pressure. He'd return to the subject in time but leave now while she was relaxed and at ease. 'I've got a late night appointment and ought to be going. Is there anything you need at the moment? Mr Heywood says you can come out in another six days.'

'I'd like a good book. Something big but not too taxing on the brain. My concentration's gone at the moment, I keep looking at Jessica!'

'I'll drop in a few paperbacks. My wife's a romance fan, is that your genre?'

'No! Comedy or horror will do me nicely.'

'I'd have thought you'd had your fill of horror,' he said dryly, and then gave her the briefest of kisses on her forehead before leaving. That night she slept better than she had since Simon died.

The next morning, Steve arrived. She remembered how kind he'd been to her on the night Toby attacked her and tried to thank him but he brushed it aside. 'It wasn't anything, Mrs Walker. I was only doing my job.'

'You were marvellous. I'd have been in hysterics without your comforting presence.'

'Here are some books from Mr Gueras,' he said quickly, handing over a box that must have held at least twenty. 'If you don't like any of them he said he'd be ringing later and you could let him know.'

'Please thank him for me.' Her tone was cool now that she realised the young man no longer wished to be friendly.

'May I look at the baby?' he asked, sensing her change of mood and not wanting to offend.

'Of course, although she's probably asleep.'

'No, she's awake. Her eyes are wide open, she's obviously going to be very bright.'

'Unlike her father!'

He was surprised by the tartness of her tone. 'I suppose so. Good luck in the future.'

'Thanks. Oh, Steve?'

He turned, looking apprehensive. 'Yes, Mrs Walker?'

'Why don't you call me Lisa? I only wondered if you knew where this house of mine is going to be?'

'I'm afraid not.' She was sure he was lying, but guessed that Neal wanted to surprise her.

Turning her attention to the books she found them all excellent, and they kept her occupied during her spare time, which wasn't as much as she'd expected because for some reason bathing and dressing Jessica took a great deal longer then she'd anticipated.

'She's so passive!' she complained to Neal one evening as she struggled to put Jessica's limp legs into the babygrow.

'What did you think she'd do? Lift up her arms and put her hands down the holes?'

'No, but ...'

'Lisa, how many babies have you handled before Jessica?'

64

'None.'

'And how many have I handled?'

'Three.'

'Then let me assure you that Jessica is perfectly normal, and you are setting ridiculously high standards for a five-day-old baby! God knows what you'll be expecting her to do in a year's time. Compose a symphony or something?' She laughed, but deep down she still wasn't happy.

On the day that Neal collected her from hospital the paediatrician gave Jessica her final examination. He went over her from head to foot, checking and double checking because he'd been told about Lisa's worries. Finally he put the baby back in her cot and smiled. 'She's perfect in every way. Normal responses, excellent physical development, and if anything a little forward. You've nothing to worry about there, I assure you.'

'Why won't she let me move her from one breast to the other at feeding times?' demanded Lisa.

He shrugged. 'Perhaps she doesn't like change. Her weight gain's fine so it obviously doesn't matter.'

His first sentence was, if Lisa had but known it, a pointer to what was wrong, but it was to be a long time before the truth was revealed, and realising that to continue worrying against all advice was insane, Lisa finally accepted what everyone had been saying all along and told herself firmly that she was taking home a perfectly healthy, normal baby daughter.

At ten-thirty, Neal arrived with a case containing Lisa's clothes, all of them collected from Toby's flat, and a beautiful hand-crocheted shawl for Jessica.

The trio were escorted to the entrance porch where two nurses waited until the chauffeur had ushered them into the back of the car and settled himself behind the wheel before they gave a final wave and turned back to their duties.

Rebekah Geuras had been born in the same private hospital, but although both nurses remembered that, they made no comment, not even to each other. They knew how unwise it would be, and no other hospital offered such superb working conditions. In any case, Mr Gueras looked far more interested in this child – and its mother – then he had been in Rebekah, despite the fact that it was yet another girl.

Naturally they both thought he was the father of the child. This assumption was to be made by other people too, and wasn't discouraged by Neal until later, when the truth about Jessica finally came out.

'Where are we going?' Lisa asked, half-nervous and half-excited.

'To your new home.'

'But where is it?'

'Wait and see! Baby all right?'

Lisa hugged Jessica closer to her, telling herself that it was only natural for the tiny limbs to stiffen in protest against such sudden restriction. She was too young to realise it was a gesture of love and not aggression. 'She's fine. What did Toby say when he heard about her?'

'Who?'

'*Toby*! I just wondered ...'

As the car slid to a halt outside a beautiful Chelsea mews cottage, Neal Gueras turned to the slender, fine-boned girl beside him and put one well-manicured hand lightly on her wrist. 'He's gone, Lisa. He's no longer part of your life. Forget him. As far as I'm concerned, Toby Walker never existed.'

She felt a flicker of apprehension. 'But he's Jessica's father! I can't forget him. She's even got his hair.'

'Then I'd prefer it if you kept your memories to yourself.'

Lisa looked out at the enchanting little whitewashed house and then at the heavy-boned intelligent face of the man next to her. For a moment she wished that there was a choice; that she wasn't so totally dependent upon his good will. Then he smiled at her, his eyes kind, his voice deep and reassuring.

'It's for your own good, my dear. After the things that he did to you, it's only sensible to put him firmly out of your mind.'

'I wasn't intending to conjure up action replays of our fights, I'm not a masochist.'

'Lisa, this is the beginning of a new life for you and your daughter. That's all I'm trying to say. Toby doesn't belong in it any more.'

She nodded. He was right. Whatever lay ahead of her now it was quite obvious that Toby Walker wouldn't be a part of it, and for that she was extremely grateful. So grateful that she pushed the other worry, the worry over exactly what Neal would want from her in the future, to the back of her mind. He was a friend of Simon's and she had to stop thinking the worst of everyone.

If he wanted to help her, he could obviously afford it. For the moment, Jessica was her priority. With Neal's help she could spend as much time with Jessica as she liked, without any financial worries at all. It was an offer anyone in her position would find very hard to refuse. And so, holding her baby daughter in her arms, she climbed out of the sleek silver Rolls-Royce and up the two steps into the entrance hall of her new home, leaving Toby Walker behind her.

Not, however, forever.

Chapter Seven

The mews house was beautiful. The ground floor consisted of a large living-room with open plan stairs, plus a small kitchen where Lisa could eat but not entertain, while on the first floor there was a vast room with a door concealing two steps up into a tiny room in the roof where Jessica would eventually sleep.

It was carpeted throughout in cream wool with tiny flecks of beige. The beige had then been picked out as the base for all curtaining while the walls were a restful shade of leaf-green, with the exception of the kitchen which was wood-panelled, matching the wood of the folding table and two chairs in the furthest corner of the room.

Despite being small, the kitchen contained everything Lisa could possibly want, from a six-place-setting dishwasher to a microwave oven, which would make preparing Jessica's meals blissfully easy when that time came. A small fridge-freezer just fitted in by the sink, which was complete with waste disposal unit. The rest of the room had fitted cupboards and oven plus a small hob.

For the first few days she didn't really appreciate just how convenient and tasteful the house was because she spent nearly every moment of her time looking after Jessica, but as the baby settled into a reasonable sleep pattern she gradually took more notice of her surroundings.

She was both surprised and a little disappointed when Neal didn't come to see her within the first week. However, he sent a car round each day with some small gift, either for her or Jessica, plus the standard instruction for her to tell the chauffeur if there was anything she needed.

The chauffeurs varied. Most of them were young, unsmiling but highly respectful. The only trouble was they didn't ever want to talk. The exception to this was a cheerful, open-faced young man called Mike. He always had a smile for Lisa, and often consented to a cup of coffee in the kitchen where he would listen to her talking and admire the baby as though there was nothing else in the world he'd rather be doing.

After a week she asked Mike why Neal wasn't coming to see her himself. He stirred the sugar in his cup for an extra long time before giving a wry grin. 'Why do you think?' he queried.

'Is he busy at work?'

'He's always busy at work! Guess again.'

'He's waiting until I'm looking more presentable?'

'Don't fish for compliments! Talking of fishing ...'

'Yes?'

'If you want my honest opinion, he's playing a fisherman's game with you.'

'What on earth's a fisherman's game?'

'He's set out the bait, now he's waiting until he thinks it's been taken.'

She leant against one of the worktops and stared at Mike, unaware of how beautiful she was looking after the peace of the past few weeks and the joy of Jessica. 'You mean this house is bait?'

'That's only my opinion. Mind you, it's expensive bait; hardly your common or garden earth worm!'

'In that case I've already taken it. I am living here.'

'He's playing you very carefully. A clever fish can get away even after it's taken the bait. He doesn't want to take that risk.'

'Aren't *you* taking rather a risk, telling me all this?'

'Not really. I think you're intelligent enough to know better than to repeat any of it.'

'And trustworthy?'

'Of course — who else can you talk to?'

Her face clouded as she realised how alone she was. 'No one.'

'Hey, I didn't mean to upset you, it was a joke. I like you a lot, that's why I'm talking to you like this. I also assumed you'd already worked most of it out for yourself.'

'How many times has Neal done this before?'

'What?'

'Made women so grateful that they sleep with him.'

Mike laughed. 'He isn't the sort of man who has to make women grateful in order to get them into his bed; they leap in quite willingly. Money and power has that effect on the female sex!'

'He's quite attractive.'

'So am I, and beautifully groomed young women with designer label clothes don't fall over themselves to grace my bed! I'm younger too, so I think it's the money that makes the difference.'

68

'Do you want elegant women in designer label clothes?'

'Certainly not, I want them out of them! Christ, is that the time? I must go or he'll wonder what we've been doing and I could lose more than my job! How's Miss Pears today?'

'She's all right. I wish she'd look at me with a bit more interest though, she seems far more interested in her mobile than my loving face!'

'You've got enough people interested in your face, I should leave Jessica to her mobile! By the way, I shan't be round for the next few days. I'm off abroad. Should be back by next weekend. I'll bring a giant teddy for Jessica if there's room in my haversack.'

'Where are you going?'

'Amsterdam.'

'Simon used to go there a lot. He was in antiques.'

'He's the reason I'm going. He always did our work for us when he was alive.'

'What work?'

'Just remember how the elephant got its trunk, Mrs Walker! Take care now.'

After he'd gone, Lisa found it hard to settle to anything and wandered listlessly round the cottage. She was physically stronger now and Jessica slept a great deal of the time. No one knew where she was, and without Neal contacting her she felt very isolated indeed, yet for some reason she didn't like to call Sabrina or even Stephanie. Neal hadn't actually forbidden it, but she'd got the impression that she was meant to keep her new address a secret, certainly until her divorce was through.

After lunch she put Jessica in her pram and set off for a walk. She'd only got to the end of the cul-de-sac when she became aware of a very tall, heavily built man walking behind her. She slowed down, her nerve endings beginning to twitch as the memory of Toby and his beatings intruded on her previous calm. To her horror, the man slowed too.

Lisa then stopped, pretending to examine the heel of one shoe. As she did so, she glanced behind her and saw that the young man had stopped as well, apparently to light a cigarette. Her hands were clammy and her heart started beating far too fast. She walked more quickly, almost running as she turned into the main street and headed for the nearest shops. When she finally found a chemist and wheeled the pram in to buy some disposable nappies the man had gone, but when she came out he was on the opposite side of the road reading a newspaper.

Finally, Lisa gave in to her fear and turned back for home. It was only when she re-entered the mews that she lost him. He carried straight on past the end, walking briskly as though heading for some appointment, but she guessed that he was a friend of Toby's and was now so scared that she was grateful for the locks on the windows and the small spy-hole in the front door.

Fortunately Jessica continued to sleep because once she'd finished checking that the house was secure, Lisa sat shaking with terror and weeping silently. Only then, when she truly believed that Toby had found her did she finally ring the number Neal had left in case of emergency.

'Priority Commodities, good afternoon!' said a cheerful voice, not at all what Lisa was expecting.

'I need to speak to Mr Gueras,' she said abruptly.

'I'm sorry, Mr Gueras is in conference. If you leave your name and number I'll pass your message on,' was the unruffled reply.

'I need to speak to him now. He told me that I could always reach him on this number.'

'I'm sorry, Mr Gueras is . . .'

'I heard you the first time! Would you please tell him that I'm on the line? My name is Mrs Walker.'

'Mr Gueras cannot be disturbed in conference, Mrs Walker. Please leave your number and . . .'

'Forget it!' she cried as Jessica began to wail, and slammed down the phone. So much for his promise of instant support. She ran into the living room and found Jessica still wailing for no apparent reason. She changed her, offered her a feed, cuddled her and crooned to her but nothing worked. Jessica had decided to use her lungs.

At least the noise might deter any would-be prowler she thought as she tried to ignore the screaming. In sheer desperation she put on a recording of Von Karajan conducting *Aida* and turned the volume up. Amazingly, within the space of three minutes, Jessica was silent, lying staring at the ceiling with a look of absolute contentment on her previously enraged features.

Worn out by her fright and soothed by the familiar music, Lisa closed her eyes and drifted off to sleep. Her rest was abruptly disturbed by a frenzied hammering on the front door, and she struggled to rouse herself sufficiently to peer through the spy-hole, having first checked that the bolts were in place.

She was totally unprepared for the sight of Neal on the front step, his chauffeur only a couple of paces behind him. Fumbling with all the locks she finally managed to let him in.

'What the hell's been happening?' he demanded, grabbing her by the shoulders. 'First of all you ring me up saying it's an emergency, then you don't answer when I ring back, and now I come round here expecting God knows what disaster and can't make myself heard for that damned row.'

'I didn't hear you ring. I put the music on to drown Jessica's crying and must have fallen asleep.'

'Wonderful! I rush away from a conference and end up ruining your beauty sleep. I deserve to lose that contract. I assume it was Jessica's crying that constituted the emergency?'

'No, it wasn't!' shouted Lisa. 'How dare you come in here like some third-rate bully boy? You told me I could always contact you on the number you left, but I found myself fobbed off by a talking parrot. Then, when I finally manage to pull myself together and get some peace, you start throwing your weight around and complaining about me. Well, go back to your precious contract, and take that chauffeur with you. He gives me the creeps.'

'He isn't a chauffeur. Surely you remember Bishop?'

She did but knew that she'd managed to insult him and took a perverse pleasure in the knowledge. 'Sorry, Bishop. You all look alike in that uniform.'

'He happens to be wearing his own suit,' said Neal coldly.

'It must be lack of character that turns even a suit into a uniform!'

'Wait outside, Bishop,' said Neal quickly, and Lisa's brief moment of triumph faded at the look of dislike in Bishop's eyes. 'Now then,' he continued, 'perhaps you'd tell me what the emergency was.' And so, eventually, she did.

'It could have been anyone,' he said comfortingly as she wandered into the kitchen to make some tea.

'Why should he have followed me?'

'You're an attractive young woman.'

'It wasn't that kind of following! Why won't you listen to me? I tell you he was checking on where I came from and where I was going. I'm sure he's a friend of Toby's.'

'He sounds inept enough.'

'I'm sure I'm right, and if Toby knows where I am, what will he do?'

Neal put an arm loosely round her shoulders and was relieved to find that she didn't draw away. 'I've no idea, but I'll send someone round to see him and make sure he stays away, all right?'

'What makes you think he'll listen to you?'

'He will.'

'So you agree I might be right!'

'It's possible. Certainly I can understand your fright.'

He could, and he was also livid with the man who'd caused it. He was there to keep a discreet eye on Lisa and let Neal know where she went and anyone who called. Obviously he wasn't up to the job, but he'd made it doubly difficult for the next man to take over because now she was suspicious.

'How would you like to come out with me next week?' he asked casually. 'I've got to go to a business dinner and I thought you might enjoy the social side of the evening. You're looking much stronger now.'

'How many people will be there?'

'Less than eight; it's a very small group and they're not important people, I just thought ...'

'You make it sound like my starter for ten!' she laughed.

Neal stared blankly at her. 'I'm sorry?'

'You know, "University Challenge". It's the easy question that gets you in. I thought this dinner sounded like a gentle trial run, to see how I cope before I'm allowed to run amok at something more important!'

He smiled politely but she could tell that he wasn't really amused. 'Not at all. I thought that after the past few months and some of the undesirable publicity you've received, you'd be more comfortable at a small gathering.'

'What undesirable publicity?'

'I kept the papers from you at the time but there were stories about your final fight with Toby, and one or two lurid tales suggesting the kind of life you used to lead. Most of it total rubbish, of course, but ...'

She remembered Roger and the photographs. The reason for her marriage, obviously still in existence, and stared at Neal in total silence, all the animation and colour draining from her face. In the living-room the opera came to its conclusion and Jessica began to cry again, but for once her mother didn't notice.

'What's the matter?' Neal quickly moved to her side and put an arm beneath her right elbow as he guided her to the kitchen stool.

'Nothing, I ...'

'Is there something I don't know about? Some misguided behaviour on your part? If there is, I want to know about it.'

She shook her head. 'I don't think you do.'

Neal's mind began to race. He thought that he knew everything about the marriage. The drinking, the drugs, the violence – but none of that would account for the almost trance-like look of shock on her face at this moment. 'Lisa,' he said softly, 'I only want to help you. If there's something you want to talk about ...'

'There isn't. I never want to talk about it. Is that Jessica crying?'

72

It wasn't the first time that Neal had silently cursed Lisa's baby, but he managed to nod and followed her to the other room where they both stood looking down at Jessica.

She was still very beautiful and gaining weight rapidly, but whilst she stared intently at the ceiling he was surprised to notice that she took no interest whatsoever in her mother even when she was picked up. Not a very affectionate child, it appeared.

'She's already yelled her head off once today,' said Lisa anxiously. 'Do you think she's sickening for something?'

'No, babies like to cry. It exercises their lungs. Look, I've got to go. I'll call back tonight, although it might be late. About twelve-thirty or so.'

'I'm usually in bed by eleven.'

'Perhaps you could make tonight an exception?'

She gave him a very straight look. 'I suppose I haven't any choice.'

'What do you mean by that?'

'You own the house, and he who pays the piper ...'

'Calls the tune? My dear Lisa, I hope you don't think that ...'

'I'm not stupid, Neal. Naturally I'll wait up for you.'

'Because you want to?'

She gave a slight smile. 'You can't have it all ways. I'll stay up. That's what you wanted, isn't it?'

'Yes, but only if ...'

'I'll see you later. Do be quiet, Jessica. This isn't like you.'

It was impossible to give Lisa a kiss when she was holding Jessica up against her face so Neal contented himself with a light touch on the shoulder and a warm smile that vanished when he got into the car and slammed the passenger door shut behind him.

'That bloody child is more trouble than her father! I'm going to start hinting at the possibility of a nanny before long.'

'If you really want Mrs Walker to engage a nanny, you'd better start telling her that you're totally opposed to the entire concept. The way her mind works she'll automatically take the opposite view.'

'When I want your advice I'll ask for it!' he snapped, before closing the glass partition between himself and Bishop. He only wished that he knew what she'd remembered when they were in the kitchen because he couldn't afford to leave any loose ends around. By the time she was his, her past had to be snow-white; not because his contemporaries had high moral standards but because his enemies would be delighted should they stumble across anything offering a chance of blackmail. It was vital that whatever she was hiding was brought out into the open as soon as possible.

When he climbed the stairs to his top floor flat in Kensington he

73

was feeling tense and irritable, and for once neither Kay's culinary nor sexual skills brought him any relief.

When she finally fell asleep he looked at her face and saw the first few wrinkles round the eyes, the creases in the neck, and knew that she was beginning to show her age. Not that he had any particular obsession with youth, on the contrary it was usually callow and unskilled. No, age alone wasn't responsible for his dissatisfaction with his mistress. He no longer wanted her because she wasn't tall, slim, dark and elusive. In other words, she wasn't Lisa.

There had been many Kays over the years. Women in their early thirties with carefully styled blonde hair who were always elegant in their Chanel suits and their Jaeger casuals, and who would probably feel naked without their pearl necklaces and matching ear-rings. They were all the same. If you closed your eyes they were indistinguishable one from the other. They even talked alike with their crisp vowels and standard expressions of surprise and delight.

It was a pity, he thought, looking down at the blissfully unaware Kay, that he'd suddenly grown out of them. They now bored him almost as much as Naomi. He was sufficiently wealthy and famous to be acceptable everywhere without the help of any of these socialites who'd eased his entry into Henley, Glyndebourne, Wimbledon, shoots and even the Royal Enclosure. Now he was automatically invited in his own right. He'd been both philanthropic and highly reticent about his generosity, so that people accepted him without question.

The result was that he now wanted a woman by his side who would attract attention herself; someone other men wanted. He needed a woman who was different in both looks and personality, and in Lisa he sensed that he'd found her. She was not yet perfect, of course, but he could soon alter her to fit the exact image he had in mind.

Yes, the days of the Kays were over. He was grateful, but that was all. There had never been any question of love or emotional involvement on his side, although naturally he'd pretended that there was, and whilst Lisa aroused a great deal of compassion and protection in him there wasn't any question of love there either.

But there was desire. A stronger, more urgent desire than he'd ever felt for a woman before, and it was proving difficult to wait, to mark time until the perfect moment; but until that moment came he still needed Kay because she was always available and he was a man of strong sexual appetites which she both understood and shared.

Just the same she would have to go, and since she knew rather a lot about him that meant more than simply parting company. It would probably be a job for Bishop, who was practised and proficient in such matters.

74

Finally, his mind once again back with Lisa, he slept.

'You look wonderful!' enthused Neal as Lisa came slowly down the stairs. She had on a deceptively simple-looking navy wool dress that fitted tightly to the waist before flaring out into a calf-length skirt that was very full and had two shocking pink panels inserted into each side. She wore navy pumps, and her only jewellery was a pair of delicate silver ear-rings in the shape of tiny butterflies with transparent wings.

'You're sure it's suitable? I wondered if it was too plain.'

'It's perfect. Why are you still wearing your wedding ring?'

'Because as far as I know I'm still married. Besides, it's difficult to get off and it keeps the wolves at bay!'

'I'll keep the wolves at bay. I'd much prefer it if you took it off.'

'Why?'

He smiled. 'I don't usually go round with married women!'

'I hadn't thought of that. Give me a minute, I'll try and get it off with soap. Did you bring your secretary to babysit?'

'She's in the car. Is Jessica settled for the night?'

'As far as I can tell,' she called from the kitchen, struggling to ease Toby's wedding ring off with some Fairy liquid.

'Any luck?' he asked, wandering round the room and examining a half-written letter on the coffee table.

'Yes, it's off. I thought that ... Do you mind! You're reading a private letter.'

'Who are you sending it to?'

'You mean to whom am I sending it!' Neal flushed with annoyance and turned away to conceal the fact. 'Actually it's to Stephanie. I thought she ought to know of Jessica's existence. I might not post it, but it was something I needed to write. Look, can we leave a number for the sitter? If Jessica should play up ...'

'Of course. I'll write it down on the pad. She should be here in a minute. I came in ahead to make sure you were ready and there weren't any problems.'

Just then Miranda Grant entered. She was small, fair, and in her early forties. An efficient and trustworthy secretary, she'd also raised four children of her own and was delighted to help her employer out. She'd met Naomi several times and didn't blame him for liking the company of other women.

'Baby asleep?' she asked cheerfully.

'Yes, but if she should wake and start screaming there's a bottle in the fridge that just needs popping in the microwave. I usually feed her myself but quite honestly she seems to find a bottle easier! If she still screams then put on some classical music, that always shuts her up. We won't be late, will we, Neal?'

'About midnight.'

'Don't worry,' soothed Miranda. 'I can cope with almost anything babies throw at me. You go out and have a good time.'

'I've left supper in the kitchen and the T.V.'s on. I do hope she's good.'

'It doesn't matter if she isn't,' remarked Neal as they walked out of the front door. 'Miranda's only too happy to be helping out. In fact, she'll be in her element if Jessica does wake. She's very maternal.'

'So am I, but I don't find Jessica screaming her head off the most wonderful experience imaginable.'

'May I suggest we don't mention Jessica again until we get back? This is meant to be a change for you. About the other guests: Mr and Mrs Hopcraft are very quiet and not particularly important, but the Erskines are vital to a new contract so it's important that they have a good time.'

'What am I meant to do, dance a tango on the table top?'

'Hardly, he's a very conservative type. Just be nice to him. Use your considerable charm to good effect. He and I have been talking business all day, you're the final step in the game.'

'Really? And while I'm charming Mr Erskine, what will you be doing?'

'Talking to his wife and making sure she's suitable.'

'For whom? Mr Erskine? Or were you thinking of trying her out yourself?'

'Joke now by all means but please don't be flippant during dinner. If they'd wanted cheap entertainment they could have watched a game show.'

Stunned, she turned her head away and looked out of the window. All at once the excited anticipation drained away and she wished she was back in her own home, watching televison and knitting a jacket for Jessica. Perhaps it was boring, and possibly she was finding life dull, but she didn't need any instructions on how to behave at a dinner. How old did he think she was for God's sake, fifteen?'

'Here we are!' he said cheerfully, trying to ignore her sudden silence. 'You'll enjoy the food.'

'Better than the company by the sound of it!' she retorted. Mike — who was driving them that evening — had difficulty in hiding his smile as he held the door open for them both. She might have taken the bait but she wasn't going to be easy to land, he thought with amusement.

In fact the dinner went off perfectly. After a couple of glasses of wine, Lisa found herself enjoying meeting people again, and James Erskine was an elderly man of great olde worlde charm who was a pleasure to talk to. By contrast, George Hopcraft talked too loudly and even told a joke that Neal made plain wasn't acceptable in mixed company. This quietened him down, but since he wasn't important, Lisa was able to ignore his occasional double-entendres and concentrate on James Erskine.

They lingered over their coffee and brandies and she was astounded when Neal said it was two a.m. The Erskines invited Neal and Lisa to visit them in America if they were ever there and Neal accepted on their behalf, then George Hopcraft — who'd drunk a great deal and was feeling left out — asked if Naomi was keeping well. An awkward silence fell.

'Extremely well,' said Neal crisply. 'She still can't go out very much but she's considerably improved. Your concern is most touching,' he added in an aside that made Mrs Hopcraft flinch. George merely laughed and said that in that case America would presumably be too far for her to go.

For a moment Lisa felt awkward. Obviously the Erskines knew about Naomi, yet they'd invited her. This could only mean they imagined she and Neal were lovers. She supposed it was a reasonable assumption, especially since she'd removed her wedding ring, but she didn't like it.

James and Felicity departed, still smiling and friendly, and then it was time for George and his wife to climb in a taxi and go on their way. 'Ignorant fool!' snapped Neal. 'He scarcely knows Naomi.'

'I think he wanted to make us feel uncomfortable.'

'You perhaps, he'd know better than to imagine he'd distress me. I can't think what possessed him.'

'He probably felt the Erskines had monopolised the evening.'

'So I should hope. He and his singularly boring wife were only there to make up the numbers. Was he drinking heavily?'

Lisa laughed. 'That depends on what yardstick you use. Not by Toby's standards, but it did seem to be affecting him as the evening went on.'

'Let's forget them,' said Neal with a smile. 'You were wonderful! Did you enjoy it?'

'Yes, it was good fun. I'd expected there to be more business talk.'

'Not in front of the ladies!'

'Why's that?'

'Far too boring. Here's Mike with the car. He's always prompt.'

'You mean you knew all along how late we'd be?'

'I run my life by the clock, Lisa.'

77

'Then why tell the babysitter we'd be home by midnight?'

He coughed apologetically. 'That was for your benefit. Miranda knew how late we'd be, but I was worried you'd refuse to leave if I said three in the morning.'

'I don't like people lying to me,' said Lisa indignantly as she climbed into the back of the Daimler.

'That's understandable. I wouldn't have to lie if you weren't quite so neurotically possessive about that daughter of yours.'

'I thought we weren't meant to talk about her until I got home?'

'Touché! So, you enjoyed yourself?' He moved close to Lisa's side, putting one arm round her shoulders.

'Yes. Is this the way back?'

'It's the scenic route! What perfume are you wearing? I noticed it earlier.'

'Ma Griffe — Toby gave it to me early on, when he was still being nice!'

Neal gently pressed her head down on to his shoulder and stroked her hair. 'You make most men want to be nice to you, Lisa.'

'I haven't noticed!'

'Toby isn't typical of most men.'

'Sabrina said that all men were totally unreliable.'

'She sounds like a feminist to me.'

Lisa pulled herself upright. 'That's typical of a man. If you don't agree with something a woman says you claim she's a feminist, but what you really mean is that she's a closet lesbian.'

'My dear girl, that's totally untrue.'

'Don't patronise me. I'm not your dear girl and it is true.'

'If I've offended you, I apologise. You're very defensive, aren't you?'

'Only when I feel threatened.'

'You mean you feel threatened by me?'

'Not physically, but I get the feeling that you could take me over if I wasn't careful. Swallow me up so that I became nothing more than a part of you. It would be terribly easy to lose my own identity at the moment, and you make it even easier.'

'Nonsense!' He was secretly amazed at her perceptiveness.

'Perhaps, but it seems true to me.'

He moved over to her again, putting both arms round her waist. 'Why don't you relax a little? Make yourself comfortable.'

'I'll make myself comfortable once I get home. Please let go of me, Neal. I feel trapped in the back of this car.'

He released her at once and sat drumming his fingers on his knees until they reached her house. 'Wait here for Mrs Grant,' he instructed

78

Mike, who touched his cap in acknowledgement and looked out of his window to conceal his amusement.

'Everything all right?' asked Lisa, rushing into the living room and looking anxiously at the sleeping Jessica.

'She was as good as gold,' responded Miranda, deciding not to mention that she'd never had so much trouble getting a baby to drink from a bottle before. The child didn't seem to have a clue about the teat and ended up nearly upside down before she started sucking.

'Mike will run you home,' said Neal swiftly. 'He'll come back for me later. I'm sure your family needs you.'

Left alone with him, Lisa stood in the middle of the room and looked Neal straight in the eye. 'You might as well have gone with her. I'm exhausted.'

'I thought we'd have a nightcap. I know there's some brandy in the cabinet. I put it there when you were still in hospital, for medicinal purposes naturally!'

'I don't want any but help yourself. You bought it so you can drink it.'

'Aren't you going to sit down?'

'All right.' She sat opposite him on one of the easy chairs.

'Come and sit next to me.'

'I'm quite comfortable here, thank you.'

'This is silly. We've had a pleasant evening, surely you can bring yourself to sit beside me for ten minutes or so?'

Knowing that she was being both ungrateful and rude, Lisa tried to conquer the terrible sick feeling in her stomach and walked slowly over to sit beside him. When he slid an arm behind her and began to kiss the side of her neck she wanted to scream and pull away but gritted her teeth and sat perfectly still.

'I can tell you're enjoying this!' he said after a few moments, and turned her face towards him. 'I'm not Toby,' he said slowly, 'and I'm not going to do anything you don't want me to. Now, please, just relax.'

'When people tell me to relax it makes me even more tense. Do you think I enjoy feeling like this?'

'No, but give yourself a chance. Surely a goodnight kiss isn't too much to ask?'

'I'm sorry, I just don't ...'

Neal Gueras wasn't a patient man and he wasn't used to being held off. Despite his initial good intentions he found that sitting next to her, with her slender body close to his and her perfume drifting up to him, he simply couldn't wait. He had to kiss her, and so he gripped

79

her tightly by the shoulders, turned her body towards him and covered her mouth with his.

She instinctively went rigid, closing her lips against his tongue and pulling away, trying desperately to free herself. Images of Roger and Toby flashed through her mind, and she remembered how Toby would hold her by the shoulders before forcing her down on to the bed and doing things that he knew she hated for the sheer pleasure of hearing her scream.

Because he wasn't Toby, Neal had left her arms free and was totally unprepared when she slipped off one of her navy pumps and began hitting him round the head and shoulders with it.

'What the bloody hell ...?' he shouted, pushing her away and leaping to his feet. Then, looking down, he saw her crumpled up and sobbing uncontrollably, still clutching the shoe tightly in her right hand.

He sighed and turned away, knowing that it was his fault and he'd only made things worse. Lisa continued to cry, and the sound of her sobs woke Jessica who decided to join in so that when Mike tapped discreetly on the front door, Neal was highly relieved to see him.

'Carry that child upstairs and put it in the cot next to the bed,' he instructed. Mike, after one quick glance at the rumpled, tear-stained Lisa, did as he was told.

Neal sat down carefully next to her and gently removed the shoe from her hand. 'It's all right,' he said quietly. 'That was my fault and I'm sorry. I'm going to get a doctor to come and see you. He'll help you get over everything you've been through these past months. You won't mind that, will you?' She shrugged. All that she wanted was to be left alone, which was totally unrealistic, so she forced herself to shake her head.

'Good girl! I'll be off now but I'll ring in the morning. Have a long lie-in if you can. And, Lisa ...'

She glanced up at him. 'Yes?'

'I'm sorry.'

She bit her bottom lip. 'It's my fault. I'm the one who should be apologising. It was only that ...'

'I do understand. Now go upstairs and get some rest. Have you any sleeping pills?'

'One or two.'

'Then take one. Goodnight.'

She didn't answer but when Mike came downstairs she raised her head. 'Have you ever seen a crying fish before?' she asked wryly.

'There's always a first time. Actually, I'm fully expecting to find a tearful fisherman waiting out there!'

Despite her misery she couldn't suppress a smile at the thought, and then Mike gave one of his quick winks and hurried off into the night.

'Where's Kay tonight?' snapped Neal as the car started up.

'In the flat, sir.'

'Take me there.'

God help her if she didn't come up to the mark, thought Mike as they sped through the night. She was obviously going to be rather busy for her final few weeks, until Lisa capitulated. He wondered how she felt about it all, or if she even realised what was happening.

Chapter Eight

Kay was lying on top of the king-size bed pretending to read her book but in reality trying to think where she'd gone wrong. She thought she'd been the perfect mistress: never making a fuss when left alone for Christmas and Neal's long summer break, never running down Naomi but always willing to listen when Neal complained about her; and above all always being available to do whatever he wanted, whenever he chose.

For ten years now she'd been by his side. There'd been other women, she knew and understood that, but she was the one who appeared on his arm in public. She was the 'old friend' who stood in for his missing wife at public functions. But not for much longer.

Nothing had been said, nothing needed to be said. She knew because he rarely took her out any more. She was gradually slipping out of the social round. At the moment friends still rang her; she attended coffee mornings with other women and sat on the committee for underprivileged children, but eventually that too would stop.

It was hard for her to face up to it because over the years she'd made the mistake of falling in love with Neal Gueras. At first she'd found him different — exciting and powerful, but that was all. He'd enabled her to keep up the lifestyle she'd been used to prior to her father's death when crippling taxation depleted the family fortune, and that had been enough for her.

He was sexually demanding but did not go in for any show of affection. His manner could vary from punctiliously polite to gutter-born crudeness which shocked and occasionally frightened her. Also, he never said he loved her. She didn't know when her feelings had changed. Perhaps it was after she lost their love-child. He'd been so supportive and understanding then. Even her spell of depression that seemed to last forever, he tolerated with unusual gentleness.

Yes, it was probably then that she started to love him, which made

82

this particular turning point in her life extraordinarily difficult because she no longer had anyone of her own to turn to.

Her mother was dead now, her only sister married and living in Australia, while her friends were solely mutual friends. Neal had carefully weaned her away from the people she'd known from childhood and she wondered where she'd go when he finally turned her out of his London flat.

Perhaps he'd give her a little place of her own, she thought optimistically. After all, she did know rather a lot about him, and he wouldn't want her talking about the things she'd learnt. Not that she ever would, but he might be afraid to leave her homeless.

She shook her head. He'd never do such a thing; she was being unnecessarily morbid. Neal would look after her. It was in his own interest as well as hers, and in any case she hoped that in his own way he was still fond of her.

All at once there was the sound of his key in the door and his footsteps on the stairs. He'd made it plain he was unlikely to be calling tonight, and this change in plans lifted her spirits. She looked up at him, smiling warmly. 'How nice, you changed your mind!'

He didn't return the smile 'Where did you get that négligée set?' he asked quietly.

She frowned, puzzled by the question. 'It was part of the last Paris collection. Don't you remember? You particularly liked ...'

'Of course, the Paris collection. It was very expensive as I recall.'

She felt uneasy. Neal never discussed money; had never cared how much she spent or where as long as she did him credit. 'I suppose so.'

'Then I suggest that you start earning it,' he said curtly.

'Earning it?'

'Please don't turn coy about our relationship, Kay. Everyone knows exactly how you earn all the clothes you wear so appropriately on your back!' And he laughed unpleasantly.

'I'm sure no one ...'

'I didn't come here for a discussion, I came here for sexual satisfaction. Now provide it.'

Kay sat up and wrapped her arms round her knees to try and stop herself from trembling. He was a stranger. Nothing in their time together had prepared her for this and she didn't know what to do.

'Come along,' he said irritably. 'Even the £50 a time girls know how to get started, and God knows every fuck we've ever had has cost me a bloody sight more than that!'

'Don't!' she cried in anguish. 'Please don't talk about us like that.'

'I'll talk how I like. It might help if one of us removed our clothes.'

'You've still got your coat on,' she said stupidly. He took it off and threw it on the nearest chair.

'Better? Feeling more liberated now?'

'I don't know what you want me to do.'

'Bake me a cake! Just remove that stupid nightgown before I tear it off.'

She got up from the bed and eased the shoulder straps down her arms but the silken material clung too tightly for her to slip the gown over her hips and she had to lift it over her head instead. When she was finally naked he was looking at her with amused tolerance.

'Not a very professional performance! Fortunately I'm not in need of too much visual stimulation.' She moved back towards the bed but he stopped her with a quick movement of the hand, and she waited warily as he took off his own clothes and walked towards her.

He put out a hand and ran it round the circumference of her left breast. 'Not quite as firm as a few years ago, is it, Kay? Never mind, we're all growing older and I expect it still feels good. Does it still feel good, Kay?'

She nodded, too frightened to speak.

'I'm glad. I'd hate to feel you were always putting on a performance for me. I believe in total honesty in relationships, it's by far the best way.' As he talked he was running his hands all over her, resting them lightly on her hips before moving lower to grasp her by the buttocks and pull her closer to him.

Now he bent his head and nibbled lightly at the hollow at the base of her throat while his fingers worked their way between her thighs until she was soaking wet and moaning with anticipation. All at once he lifted her off her feet and then pulled her down on top of him, thrusting fiercely into her while still standing so that she had to clasp her legs round his waist while he turned until she could see herself in the floor-length mirror by the window.

He moved her up and down on him, slowly at first but then faster, and she could see her distorted face, her mouth opening as she gasped with shock and pleasure and then – just as she was on the verge of climaxing – he lifted her clear of his body, threw her face down on the bed and entered her from behind, lifting her hips high off the bed so that he could penetrate as deeply as possible.

The violence of his movements pushed her up the bed until she came to a stop against the pillows, and now she was screaming at the waves of pleasure washing over her and this time as she climaxed he did too and she felt him shuddering above her before he collapsed onto her back.

For a moment they lay in silence and then he rolled away and swung

84

himself off the bed. 'Good?' he asked casually.

She looked at him. He seemed perfectly normal, there was no sign of the strange mood he'd been in when he arrived. 'Fantastic!' she murmured. 'Better than ever.'

'I'm glad. Aren't you going to take a shower?'

'Not yet.'

'I'd like you to take a shower.'

'What's the matter with you tonight?'

'Just do as I ask,' he said coldly. After she'd gone he looked at himself in the mirror and hated what he saw. How could he have come here and made love to Kay when all the time he was picturing Lisa? It was a sign of weakness in him, and as such he'd eradicate it in the only practical way. If Kay weren't here then he wouldn't be tempted, so Kay must go a little earlier then he'd anticipated.

She came back a few minutes later and found her cases on top of the bed. 'Pack your things,' he instructed. 'We're finished. It's over.'

'You can't mean it; not after what we've just done!'

'That was a farewell gift to you. Now I want you to go.'

'Where on earth can I go at six in the morning with five suitcases and no money of my own?'

'You've got money. I've been paying you an allowance for years, and to the best of my knowledge you've never used any of it.'

'But ...'

'It's all arranged,' he continued smoothly, seeing the desperation on her face. 'You can stay at the cottage for a few weeks until we sort things out. I'm not unreasonable, you know.'

'You can't afford to be!' she said bitterly. 'Not after the things I've learnt about you.'

The look in his eyes told her only too clearly that she'd made a terrible mistake. 'I didn't mean that,' she said quickly. 'I was only joking, I ...'

'Of course you were. Excuse me a moment.' Abruptly he left the room. Kay looked at the cases, most of them empty, and shivered. She thought of making a run for it, but there was only one way out of the flat and that was through the dining-room where Neal was using the phone. He wasn't gone long and when he returned his smile told her better than any words that money wouldn't matter to her any more.

'Please don't hurt me!' she screamed, hurling herself at him and trying to hide her face in his chest. He pushed her off and pulled on a polo-necked cashmere sweater. 'I've no intention of hurting you. I employ other people to do that kind of thing.'

'I swear I'll never tell anyone anything. I'll go abroad. I can always begin again out there. Suppose I go to ...' The door opened, and when she looked up Kay's last hope died within her.

'Bishop, Kay hasn't finished packing but I don't think that matters. She wants a little break, somewhere to pull herself together and work out her future. I don't mind if you take her to your little place in Norfolk for a few days, as long as I'm not required to see her again.'

'*No!*' screamed Kay, totally hysterical at the thought. 'For God's sake, don't let him near me. What have I done to deserve Bishop?'

'You threatened me,' he said softly. 'That was a terrible mistake. Get her out of here, Bishop, and make sure no one sees you. I'll get one of the others to dispose of her belongings.'

As Bishop put a hand over Kay's mouth to muffle her screams she looked back despairingly at the man who'd been her lover and protector for the past ten years, and he looked back at her with total disinterest. For all the emotion on his face she might have been a complete stranger.

Three months later her mutilated body was washed up on the French coast. She was finally identified by a cousin twice removed. He told the authorities that she'd been determined to take her new boat across the Channel on her own, despite his warnings. The boat was found the following day and the cousin twice-removed returned to Scotland a wealthier man, who was fortunately far wiser than the unfortunate Kay.

It was Neal's first mistake. This perfect murder was to cost him a great deal of money.

Six months later he sat behind his heavy oak desk and looked enquiringly at the bespectacled man opposite him. 'How's the patient, Mr Oakleigh?'

Lewis Oakleigh, a top psychologist at one of the main London teaching hospitals whose unfortunate weakness for under-age girls had brought him into contact with Neal, moistened dry lips and cleared his throat. 'She's much better,' he said reassuringly.

'Perhaps you wouldn't mind going into a little more detail. Would you say she's ready for a proper relationship yet?'

'Given the right circumstances, the right approach, and naturally the right man, I'd say yes.'

Neal smiled pleasantly. 'You're quite certain? You don't want to hedge your bets even more?'

'It isn't a question of hedging my bets. She's been badly damaged emotionally from an early age. The incident with her husband was the

86

final straw. At only seven years of age she underwent the trauma of discovering ...'

'I want that woman, and I've been paying you a small fortune to make sure she's ready for me. Are you trying to say you've failed? That you need even more time to cure her?'

'I've done everything I can. It isn't like treating measles or a broken leg, you know.'

'Is she cured?' snapped Neal.

'She'll never be cured because we can't erase all her past life. Like the rest of us, she's the product of her experiences. What I *can* say is that she's now as ready as possible to embark on new relationships with men. In point of fact she shows no great desire to do so, but ...'

'I think you can safely leave me to arouse the necessary desire, Lewis. Your opinion in the case of any female over the age of fourteen is not, I would have thought, altogether reliable.'

Oakleigh flushed and once again wished he'd never been stupid enough to let these people find out. It meant he was constantly at their beck and call, accumulating knowledge that made it impossible for them to let him go. He was also acutely aware of the fact that should he ever refuse their work, or − as in the case of Lisa Walker − not make a totally satisfactory job of it, then they would remove him without conscience or hesitation. His stomach churned. 'I've done my best. You could always ask for a second opinion.'

'Totally unnecessary; I know you've done your best. I can see a difference in her already. Here's a cheque for the final month. We'll consider her cured as from today!'

'She'll never be cured, that's the whole point of my report!'

'As far as you're concerned, she's cured, Lewis.'

Oakleigh was a good psychologist and hated the fact that when working for Gueras he was rarely allowed to see a case through. As he stood up, he forced himself to speak out again. 'You should have someone examine her daughter.'

'All right, if it will stop Lisa worrying about her. You'd think she'd got enough on her plate without inventing difficulties.'

'She isn't inventing them. There's something wrong with the child.'

Neal raised his eyebrows. 'You sound very confident. Perhaps you could tell me what the problem is?'

'You need a child psychologist for that.'

'And naturally they don't let you near children! Fine, I'll get someone else. That's all, Oakleigh. Close the door behind you, I don't want any more interruptions.'

Once he was alone, Neal flipped through the notes and frowned. She wasn't going to be easy, but then nothing worth having was. He'd

87

once spent three years chasing a Reubens painting, three painstaking, expensive years, but now it hung on his dining-room wall and every time he looked at it the pleasure was just as great as when he first set eyes on it in someone else's house.

Naturally women weren't as satisfying as a good painting but he still felt sure that Lisa was worth a good deal of time and money. He decided to cancel his evening meeting with Bishop to pay a call on her. An unexpected call.

At seven-thirty, Lisa was trying to bathe the rigid Jessica in the kitchen sink because she hated the big bath and became even more difficult when that was used.

'What's the matter with you?' demanded Lisa tearfully. 'Most children enjoy bathtime. Why won't you ever smile at me? Jessica, look at Mummy!' But Jessica lay tense and apparently unhearing, staring intently at the strip lighting over the gleaming work surfaces.

Finally she was clean. Then came the nightmare of forcing her unbending limbs into the sleepsuit before cradling the resistant body in one arm while attempting to insert the teat into her disinterested mouth. Lisa hummed gently as she fiddled with the bottle, but if Jessica heard she didn't look at her mother in acknowledgement. Instead, she gazed unblinkingly at a pattern on the living-room wall formed by the light from the lampshade reflecting off the oval mirror above the fireplace. When she was eventually feeding she drank greedily, and after she'd finished did produce a smile − only it wasn't for Lisa, it was for the pattern on the wall.

'Why won't you love me, Jessica?' whispered Lisa, getting ready to take her daughter upstairs. 'What's the matter with you?' But Jessica merely arched herself against the loving arms and struggled to get free.

With her daughter finally in bed, Lisa changed out of her slacks and blouse and put on a mohair dress of pale blue that clung tightly to every curve. She liked it because it made her feel feminine again, as she used to feel before everything went wrong. Mr Oakleigh had made quite a point of the fact that she mustn't let herself go; that just because she'd had a bad experience with Toby she couldn't spend all her time in slacks and jeans in a rather childlike attempt to become undesirable.

Tonight, as she sprayed on the last of Toby's 'Ma Griffe', she realised he'd been right. She felt better already, and whilst she'd never admit it to anyone, Jessica's continuing strangeness made the evenings all the more precious because for a short time she could pretend that everything was all right, and it was a perfectly normal baby who lay sleeping in the attic room.

She knew it must be Neal as soon as he arrived, he was the only person who knocked on the door. Everyone else used the bell. 'Hello, stranger!' she smiled. 'I thought you must be abroad on business.'

'That's a lovely dress.'

'It's quite old but it always makes me feel good. According to London's answer to Freud, I have to spend a great deal of time making myself feel good!'

'I take it you missed me?'

'Of course I did. No one else ever comes to visit me!'

'A somewhat backhanded compliment.'

'It wasn't meant like that. Is that Corton-Charlemagne?' she added, glancing at the bottle in his hands.

'I understand it's your favourite?'

'It certainly is, what bliss!'

'Where's Jessica?' he added politely, going into the kitchen to find a corkscrew.

'Asleep upstairs.'

'Is she keeping well?'

Lisa hesitated. 'You don't really want me to say, do you? I know you get annoyed when I talk about her, and I'd hate to spoil the evening before it's begun.'

'If I hadn't wanted to know I wouldn't have asked. Glasses?'

'In the cabinet. Actually, I'm beginning to wonder if she's deaf. When I dropped a tray in the kitchen this morning, she never even blinked.'

'She hears music well enough but perhaps we ought to have her looked at by a paediatrician. Would you like that?'

Lisa stared at him, her eyes reflecting every conflicting emotion surging through her. 'I think she should be examined,' she said at last. 'The trouble is, I'm afraid of what they're going to find out.'

He filled the wine glasses and handed her one before puting an arm lightly round her waist. 'If there's something wrong, then the sooner we know the quicker we can do something about it. And if there isn't, you can stop worrying and get on with your life.'

'There is something wrong, Neal, and it isn't minor.'

'In which case she deserves a good specialist as soon as possible.'

She swallowed hard. 'Yes, of course, and I am grateful. Only, until today you've never seemed to take my worries seriously and now that you are I feel, I don't know, as though your belief makes them more real.'

'I can assure you it doesn't! I'll make the necessary arrangements to have her looked at and we won't talk about it for the rest of the evening. Is that fair?'

'Very fair! So tell me, where have you been these past weeks?'

He could hardly tell her the truth. Most of his time had been spent either dealing with the increasing difficulties within his organisation, disposing of his former mistress, or visiting his wife and daughters – while all the time wondering if Lisa was missing him and whether his plan of leaving her temporarily isolated would work in his favour. Instead, he shrugged. 'Work and domestic affairs. Very boring, but necessary.'

'Tell me about your family.'

'I married young, a girl from the same village in Greece. After a time I realised there was no future for me out there and moved to London to set up my own business. I started out in antiques, the same as Simon. However, I diversified along the way.'

'You certainly did! Surely Naomi must be very unhappy with the way things have worked out?'

'No,' he lied smoothly. 'She likes the money and the houses my success has brought her, but as you know, she finds socialising almost impossible. She also feels that she's failed me because we have no son.'

'You think she's failed you too,' interrupted Lisa. 'I remember ...'

'Nonsense! All right, I wanted a son to inherit everything I've worked for but it isn't a matter of life or death.'

'I should hope not! And what are your daughters like?'

'Louise, the oldest, is very pretty, selfish and empty-headed. Ruth, the middle one, is bright but quite plain and totally without Louise's social skills, while Rebekah is just a small girl who finds it difficult to make friends.'

'You make them sound a highly exciting trio! Really, what a way to talk about your own daughters!'

'You asked, I thought you genuinely wanted to know.'

'I did, I'm just a bit stunned by your critical appraisal. Where's all the paternal love?'

'I'm afraid I'm not a very good father. I've been too busy working to get to know them all that well. Naomi looked after Louise and Ruth. She hasn't been well since Rebekah was born, so Rebekah has a nanny, or rather an ever-changing succession of nannies.'

'What's wrong with Naomi?'

'She drinks,' he said bluntly. 'More wine?'

'Thanks. I drink.'

'Naomi has a drink problem. That's why she rarely comes to London.'

'There are clinics she could go to.'

'She doesn't believe she's got a problem. You can't help people who won't admit there's anything wrong.'

'So that's why you've got your mistress. Kay, I think you called her. What's she like?'

Neal smiled. 'I find your curiosity quite flattering.'

'I'm simply intrigued by the way you live.'

'In point of fact we no longer see each other. She got tired of waiting for me to divorce Naomi and started seeing other men. I understood her reasons but it changed the quality of our relationship.'

Lisa stared at him. 'That's a woman you've loved you're talking about. Don't you have any strong feelings for anybody?'

'Yes.'

She quickly looked away, knowing who he meant and not wanting him to say the words because then the evening would be ruined and all the tension she'd spent months overcoming would return.

'Are you any better?' he asked quietly. 'Can you honestly say that you've been warmer in your relationships? What about poor Simon and Stephanie? What kind of love did you give them?'

'Stephanie hated me, that's quite different.'

'And Simon?'

She stared down at her feet. 'I wasn't very kind to him,' she admitted reluctantly.

'Then there was Toby. I know that in the end he treated you appallingly, but did you ever love him? And if not, why did you marry him? Was that fair to either of you?'

'I didn't have any choice!' she shouted. 'Do you honestly think I wanted to marry him? I'm not that stupid. Of course I never loved him, and I never pretended to. I lusted after him at the beginning, and if I'm honest that was mostly because I knew Simon and Stephanie disapproved, although perhaps I'd have fancied him anyway. But love? No, I never loved him.'

'Then why the marriage?' pressed Neal, his brain racing as he tried to reconcile what he was hearing with what Bishop had implied at the time.

'He blackmailed me into it. I was expecting Jessica and he wanted us to be married before she was born. I didn't and so he . . . Well, let's say I didn't feel I had any choice.'

'What did he do?'

'Sorry, that's private. It's over now. In another six weeks I'm free of him.'

'And free of whatever it was he had on you that made you marry him?'

He regretted the words immediately. Lisa went chalk-white and seemed to shrink into herself, wrapping her arms round her body protectively. He wanted to take hold of her, carry her up to her bedroom and make love to her there and then. To blot out whatever she was thinking with his body; bind her to him with his lovemaking and his protection, but he knew that it wouldn't work. It was too soon.

Instead, he sat beside her and took one hand in his. 'Listen, Lisa, when you feel able to talk about it, make sure you talk to me. I can handle anything Toby Walker may have dreamt up to frighten you, and then you'll really be free. But until you're ready to trust me, just remember that I'm here. I'm extremely fond of you and I hope that in time you'll become equally fond of me.'

She knew that she never would. She was grateful to him and felt safe when he was around, as though nothing and no one could touch her while he was near. But at the same time, he himself made her uneasy. Whilst protecting her from the rest of the world he seemed to offer a threat of his own, a danger that she didn't understand and didn't want to. There were fleeting moments, on her own, when she wasn't even certain that she liked him, but in his presence that was always forgotten.

'Right,' he said briskly, sensing her change of mood, 'it's time for me to leave. I'll get in touch with someone at Great Ormond Street about Jessica in the morning. Incidentally, there's a charity ball next month in aid of the N.S.P.C.C. I'd like you to come with me if you would. Princess Margaret will be there.'

Lisa smiled. 'If I do come I'll practise my curtsy first.'

'It will do you good,' he urged. 'You haven't been having enough fun lately. Speaking of which, next time I see you we must discuss your shopping arrangements. A credit card in your name but charged to my account would be the best solution.'

'I'm not Kay,' said Lisa quietly. 'I don't want your credit cards.'

'Think of all the things you could buy Jessica at Pinky Blue's!' he reminded her, and for the first time saw a spark of interest in her eyes. Well, it didn't matter if she started with the child. She'd soon get hooked on buying for herself; they all did eventually.

Contenting himself with a light brush of his lips against hers, he hurried off to the waiting car, leaving Lisa with a great deal to think about.

Chapter Nine

Dr Phillips was middle-aged with fair hair turning grey and eyes that were kind but alert. Lisa, sitting down opposite him with Jessica on her lap, sensed that he would at least listen to her and was grateful to Neal for arranging the appointment so quickly.

For his part, Dr Phillips noticed how tense the young mother was and also registered that her eight-month-old daughter was sitting totally limp on her lap, like a bundle of clothing rather than a small child.

'Hello, Jessica!' he said kindly. The little girl's head stayed flopped on her chest and she gave no indication that she'd heard him. He glanced down at the notes before him, mostly from Lisa's own psychiatrist, and then back at Lisa.

'How long have you been worried about Jessica?' he asked gently.

'Since she was born.'

'Why was that?'

'Silly little things. She didn't know how to feed properly for one. In the end I gave up breast feeding and she did better with the bottle, although that still has to be held at very odd angles before she'll drink!' She stopped, waiting for him to tell her that this was common, but he didn't.

'Go on,' he encouraged.

'Also, she didn't like being cuddled. She never responded to my touch or the sound of my voice. And although her eyes were open virtually from birth, she never looked *at* me. She still doesn't. She'll look at bright lights or patterns but never at people.'

'She's very young,' he murmured, keeping his eyes on Jessica.

'I know, and it isn't that I want her to be talking or crawling or anything, but somehow she doesn't seem to be *with* me. It's as though she isn't part of what's going on around her. I suppose that sounds stupid to you.'

'Not at all. Is she always limp like this?'

'No, she's usually the complete opposite! If I want to change her ...'

He stood up and walked round behind Lisa's chair. 'In a moment we'll get you to change her nappy. Right now I'm going to drop a pile of books. Whatever happens, try not to jump, all right?' The books fell to the floor with a loud bang, but Jessica didn't react. 'Nothing?' asked the doctor.

'Nothing,' confirmed the nursing sister who'd placed herself so as to observe the child's reaction.

'Right, now if you'd pick her up and ...' As he spoke he gently rustled some papers on his desk and Jessica lifted her head, trying to trace the source of the sound.

'She heard that!' exclaimed Lisa in surprise. 'I'd begun to think she was partially deaf.'

'No, she certainly isn't deaf. Does she make any noises?'

'She cries!'

'When you talk to her, does she croon back, babble at you, or attempt her own kind of speech?'

'No, when I talk to her she refuses to look at me.'

'Let's see what happens when you change her, shall we?'

Lisa's heart sank. She was beginning to wonder if her own incompetence was responsible for Jessica's hatred of being changed but tried to keep relaxed as she took her over to the couch.

As soon as she tried to undo the stretch suit, Jessica went rigid from head to toe. Her limbs locked and although Lisa struggled to ease the tiny legs from the garment it was impossible because Jessica's knees were unyielding and she tried to kick her mother away without once letting her limbs relax.

'Don't worry, Mrs Walker, at least we can see what you mean!' said the doctor lightly. 'I'll try my luck while you have a rest.'

'She hates strangers,' said Lisa quickly. 'When people look in her pram, she screams and screams.'

'Does she now? And I suppose a lot of people look in the pram because she really is exceptionally beautiful, isn't she, Sister?'

'The most beautiful child I've ever seen,' said the nurse with total honesty.

'Now, let's have a proper look at you, Jessica,' murmured Dr Phillips as he tried to manipulate the tiny limbs. She went perfectly still and then started to scream. She screamed dementedly, going blue in the face from lack of oxygen, but he failed to undress her and change the nappy.

Eventually he walked over to the light with her in his arms, turning her lovely face towards his own. 'Hello, Jessica!' he repeated, watching as the huge deep-blue eyes with their sweeping black lashes slid away from his direction to stare off into the distance. He tickled her lightly under the chin. Immediately she arched her back and tried to pull away from his grip.

'I wondered if it was because she's only got me,' said Lisa hesitantly, worried by the silence in the room.

'I think not. Jessica, look at the rattle.' But Jessica wasn't interested in the rattle. Instead she twisted away and reached out for the catch on the window. The doctor moved closer so that she could grip it, and at once she smiled with pleasure, totally absorbed in the feel of the metal.

With an inward sigh the paediatrician tried to loosen her grip but she held on fast, screaming in fury when he finally managed to get her away and hand her back to Lisa. She continued screaming, pushing her hands at her mother's face as she attempted to get free.

'Please take her next door, Sister. Let her play with the sand and water,' he instructed.

'She won't play with anything,' said Lisa.

'Water might well interest her.'

As he began to write some notes, Lisa bit on her bottom lip. It was the first time anyone had shown the slightest bit of interest in Jessica's strange behaviour and now she was even more worried because she sensed that Dr Phillips was concerned too.

At last he looked up and cleared his throat. 'Mrs Walker, Jessica is very young and at this stage there are several disorders that may be causing her to behave in the manner we've witnessed. However, she is definitely showing signs of a disorder known as infant autism.'

'Infant what?'

'Autism. Autistic children are totally unable to forge emotional relationships in the normal manner and − like Jessica − are anxious to avoid direct eye contact, although it's been discovered that at a later stage they do look at people, but in swift sideways glances that are easily missed.'

'Do they grow out of it?' asked Lisa nervously.

'As I said, we know very little about the condition, and I wouldn't like to say for certain that this is Jessica's problem. However, if it is then the answer is no. They do not grow out of it.'

'You mean she'll *never* respond to me?'

'Autistic children seem totally unaware that other people exist,' he explained as gently as possible. 'They live in their own world, and it's one we can't penetrate. But you must remember that she may be suffering from some other form of mental disorder and . . .'

'You mean she's brain damaged?'

'Until your daughter is nearer the age of two we won't be absolutely certain of our diagnosis, but if she is autistic we can't ever tell you how or why it happened.

'Some specialists believe it's inborn, the result of brain damage or even a chromosomal abnormality; others think that it could be the result of life experience, some sort of trauma immediately after birth. Personally I don't think this is true. I'm quite sure that your daughter has been cherished from the moment she was born, and quite probably the damage occured in the womb ...'

She didn't hear any more. All she could think of was Toby kicking her, kicking his unborn daughter and turning her into a mentally handicapped child. 'But she looks so normal,' she blurted out. 'I mean, she's lovely. You said so yourself. If she was brain damaged, wouldn't it show?'

'That's another reason why I suspect infant autism. For some reason these children are outstandingly attractive. Indeed, as they grow older they can look exceptionally intelligent. It's totally misleading, of course, and somehow makes it much harder for people to accept the diagnosis.'

'But you're not sure, are you?' pressed Lisa, suddenly wishing she'd never made such a fuss about Jessica. If she'd waited the baby would probably have grown out of it all, and then she'd have been spared this nightmare of an examination.

'I'm not sure she's autistic but she is mentally handicapped. Her responses are totally wrong. You saw how she ignored the falling books but listened when paper rustled. That's not normal. You've been worrying about her since the day she was born, and you were right.'

'Surely she might get better? Perhaps she's just a little slow.'

'But she isn't slow. Physically, she's doing very well and she can sit up without support.'

'What happens when autistic babies grow older?'

'It varies according to the degree of autism. Unfortunately this term covers a vast range of difficulties. It isn't a text book disorder. No one can ever tell you how an autistic child will develop because they're all different.'

'Then how do you ever know you've made the correct diagnosis?'

'When Jessica's old enough she'll be tested against a standard set of nine criteria for diagnosing infant autism, two of which are common to all affected children.'

Lisa decided she didn't want to know what they were. 'Will she ever learn to walk and talk?' she asked desperately.

'She'll certainly walk. She might well have you running after her non-stop twenty-four hours a day if she's one of the hyperactive kind, but talk − well, not really. She'll probably speak but it won't make sense. She'll latch on to certain words or phrases and use them indiscriminately. She may echo your words in the wrong context, but she'll never progress beyond a fairly early form of communication.'

She listened to his words and felt tears rolling down her face but was unable to do anything about them. Dr Phillips pushed some tissues towards her, wishing he could offer comfort but unwilling to lie about a handicap that he found usually totally destroyed the life of the family concerned, until the child was finally sent away.

'Will she become more loving?' she asked, thinking that if she could only cuddle her child then she wouldn't mind everything else. It was the rejection that was so difficult to accept.

'No,' he said softly. 'They're always very aloof.'

'I hate him,' muttered Lisa after a short pause. 'It's all his fault. I'd like to kill him for what he's done to her.'

'Mrs Walker, no one's to blame.'

'What do you know about it?' she demanded. 'Jessica's father hit and kicked me only a few weeks before she was born. I nearly lost her then. Can you honestly sit there and tell me that he didn't do it?'

'Children like this are born to ...'

'I don't care about the others! We're talking about Jessica, and it's his fault. He damaged her before she was born; she's never had a chance and she never will!' She began to rock backwards and forwards in her misery, sobbing quietly to herself as the anger drained away until only despair at her new knowledge remained.

The doctor sighed and looked at his watch. 'I'm very sorry,' he told her gently. 'I'd like to see Jessica once a month from now on, just to see how she progresses. We'll send you a card with your next appointment on it.' She nodded, too choked by tears to answer. 'Is there anyone who could come and take you both home?' he continued anxiously.

She fumbled in her bag for Neal's number. 'If I could ring ...' Her voice tailed off as she began to weep again. 'See to that, Nurse,' he instructed, and the young probationer put her arm round the slight figure and led her through to where Jessica lay on her stomach, splashing her hands in a soggy pool of sand and water with obvious relish.

Her extremely vocal displeasure at having this pastime removed echoed down the corridors of the hospital as Lisa clutched her tightly to her chest and wondered what she'd do if Neal couldn't come and take them home. When he arrived half an hour later she was still crying. Jessica had gone limp again, which made it easier for Neal to take her in his arms and pass her across to Mike, who watched the distraught Lisa with sympathetic eyes.

She let Neal put an arm round her and turned her face against his chest, trying to muffle her sobs as she clutched at the lapels of his light grey suit. 'I'm afraid she's had a bad shock,' the sister explained, outlining what Dr Phillips suspected. Neal nodded and led Lisa out to the car before instructing Mike to take them all to his Chelsea flat.

She didn't take any notice of where they were going. She didn't even check on Jessica when Mike lifted the carrycot out and carried it up to the top floor, placing it carefully on the small single bed in the second bedroom.

'That's all,' Neal said curtly when Mike remained standing in the hallway.

'Will you be wanting me later?' His eyes were drawn again to the tear-stained Lisa.

'No, I'll do the rest of the driving myself. Bishop wants you.'

Only the sound of Bishop's name brought Lisa back to reality. She raised her head swiftly as though suddenly aware of a second man's presence and fearful it might be Bishop himself. When she saw Mike she smiled fleetingly, a smile noticed and resented by Neal who almost shut the door on Mike's foot.

'Feeling better?' he enquired, hearing Jessica start to scream and silently cursing her timing.

'Not really, but I don't suppose I will. Did they tell you what was wrong?'

'Sit down while I make some coffee,' he responded, wondering what was the best line to take over the child's disability.

Lisa followed him into the tiny but immaculate kitchen. 'It's Toby's fault,' she said dully. 'Dr Phillips said it can be caused by brain damage. I should think he kicked her enough times to damage more than her brain. I'd like to kill him myself,' she added.

'I doubt that. Besides, are they sure that's what caused all this?'

'They're not sure of anything!' she said bitterly. 'They won't even say with certainty that she's autistic, although they didn't offer any reassuring alternatives. No, they didn't say Toby caused it, but I know he did.'

'So what happens now?'

'Nothing! I take her along once a month while they watch her progress, or lack of it as the case may be.'

'And then?'

'He didn't say. I don't think he wanted to talk about what happens to autistic children. He probably thought I'd heard enough for one day. I tell you one thing, she isn't going into a home. She'd hate it.'

Neal thought that Jessica was unlikely to notice any difference in her surroundings wherever she was but didn't say as much. Instead he contented himself with pulling Lisa closer to him, while running one hand soothingly up and down her arm.

'Whatever happens, remember that I'm here. If you need a nanny or trained nurse to help you cope, I can make sure you get the best there is. And if a home should turn out to be the best thing for Jessica – if not for you – we'll find the finest one.'

'She isn't going anywhere. I've always despised people who rejected less than perfect children, and nothing I've seen or heard today has made me change my mind. All right, she might not show her appreciation, and perhaps she'll upset me and tire me out, but she's my daughter and I'm not going to let her be put in an institution where she's just another number and no one cares what happens to her.'

'I don't think it has to be like that,' he said softly.

'If you really want to help me,' said Lisa suddenly, 'I'd like you to find me a job.'

'A job?' He was so amazed that he released his soothing grip and Lisa quickly moved away from him.

'I know I can't go out to work but surely there are people who'd like work done at home; typing, translations, that sort of thing. I'm good at languages.'

'In that case it's possible I might be able to channel some work from one of my companies your way. There's a lot of paperwork involved.'

Lisa frowned. 'I didn't really want to work for you. You've done quite enough for me already.'

'You wouldn't be working for me. I'm not involved in every section of my business. You'd work for the director in charge of that particular company. At least let me have a word with him.'

'I suppose it would be sensible,' she conceded, knowing full well that outwork for a girl who hadn't ever done any proper work at all would normally be impossible to come by.

'Why do you want to work?' he asked curiously.

'I don't like being a kept woman.'

He laughed aloud. 'I don't think you qualify as a kept woman! They have to work for their keep you know, and not in offices either!'

'I need my own money. I've used up everything you got me for my furs and jewellery, and Jessica does need lots of mundane things like milk powder, baby powder ...'

'Lisa, she isn't going to get any easier, you know,' he said quietly.

99

She raised her head and now the despair was showing in her eyes.

'There's Christmas too,' she continued frantically. 'She ...'

'Darling, you can't run away from it. Jessica is going to be a terrible burden on you. At the moment she's immobile but ...'

'Dr Phillips said she'll probably walk normally.'

'Quite, but he didn't say her behaviour would improve at the same time, did he?'

'No, he didn't say much at all except that she wouldn't ever learn to speak very well. But I'm sure that with enough love ...'

'I agree,' said Neal quickly, suddenly remembering Bishop's advice. 'I'm sure mother-love can accomplish a lot. That's why a part-time nanny's out of the question. Otherwise I could find you a convenient office job in the export office with flexible working hours, but it wouldn't be right. It's a pity because then you'd really be independent.'

Lisa looked directly at him. 'I didn't say a part-time nanny wasn't acceptable. All I said was that I refused to part with Jessica. If by taking on some help I could earn a living for myself, then it would probably be the best solution. I'd always be fresh for Jessica and wouldn't feel beholden to you all the time.'

So Bishop was right, thought Neal with considerable amusement. Lisa automatically opposed suggestions. He was surprised, not by her behaviour — women had long since ceased to surprise him in that respect — but by Bishop's perspicacity. 'I'm not sure ...' He let his voice tail off.

'Not sure of what?'

'You'd be very busy, it might prove too much along with looking after Jessica. And of course you wouldn't have any time for a social life.'

'I'm not bothered about that, although if I did want to go somewhere — like the N.S.P.C.C. Ball — surely I could manage it?'

'If you had the energy.'

'I'm young! At my age you can keep going on very little sleep.'

'I'm sure Toby encouraged that,' he retorted, and saw her face close against him. He could have groaned in dismay, and wondered why the thought of Lisa and Toby in bed together had the power to make him seethe with fury when it was quite obvious that their good times hadn't lasted very long.

Once she was his, he told himself, it would be different. He wouldn't mind so much then because he would show her what loving meant and Toby would be obliterated from her mind.

'Is Jessica still crying?' she asked, suddenly aware of the screams coming from the small bedroom.

'I'm afraid so. Finish your coffee and I'll take you home.'

He was amazed when she dropped her head and began to cry. 'I don't want to take her home,' she sobbed. 'I don't want to be on my own with her tonight. Every time I look at her I remember what the doctor said and I simply can't bear it. She's too beautiful to be retarded; he must have made a mistake. Oh, Neal, why did this have to happen? I wanted a baby so much.'

He held her and stroked her, murmuring meaningless words of comfort and trying to soothe her by his presence. After a long time she wiped her eyes on the back of her hands, which he found strangely endearing.

'I'm sorry,' she muttered. 'You must think I'm very feeble.'

'On the contrary I think you're extremely brave. You were the one who knew she wasn't right. But for you this diagnosis would never have been made.'

'Is that supposed to cheer me up?'

'Lisa, isn't it better to know? Isn't that what you wanted? To find out if you were right or not?'

'But I wanted to be wrong!'

You poor child, he thought to himself, but he didn't say it. Instead he helped her to her feet and led her towards Jessica's room. 'I'll come back with you and if necessary I'll stay the night. I'll stay for as long as it takes you to come to terms with this – that's a promise.'

'I don't know what I'd have done without you today,' she remarked as they put the carrycot in the back of his sleek Jaguar. 'I don't think I could have coped alone.'

He knew then that it was only a matter of time, and had to look away from her to hide the light of victory that he knew must be showing in his eyes.

That night, Jessica went to sleep early. She'd been rigid during her bath, ignored the teat on the bottle for half an hour and then screamed non-stop when Lisa tried to nurse her, but once she was in her own cot again, staring up at the mobile she seemed to enjoy, she quickly fell asleep.

Neal, horrified by her unnatural behaviour, poured out two large brandies and handed one to Lisa. 'Is she always like this?'

'Tonight was rather extreme, but then her routine's been disturbed.'

He doubted if Jessica recognised a routine, but again perhaps she did. A quick telephone call to a psychologist friend while Lisa was struggling with her daughter had told him quite a lot about infant autism, and rigid order seemed to occupy a lot of their time as they grew up. Perhaps Jessica already needed it. He was rapidly becoming certain of one thing: if Lisa were to become his regular mistress, Jessica would have to go.

'Tired?' he murmured as Lisa rested her head on his shoulder.

'Yes, but my brain's buzzing. It's been such a traumatic day and now we're back here and everything's normal again and yet it isn't. It never will be normal again, will it? Not now that I know the truth.'

'Just relax,' he replied, and gradually − soothed by the rhythmic movements of his hands on her back and arms − she managed to let some of the tension drain out of her. Eventually her eyelids drooped and he knew by her breathing that she was asleep. Looking down at her he wondered how long he was going to have to wait before he could make her his. At that moment he didn't mind; it was enough that she'd begun to trust him.

When she awoke she cried out briefly, and he realised that she thought she was back with Toby. 'It's all right,' he said quickly. 'It's me, remember?'

She gave an embarrassed laugh. 'I'm not used to waking up next to strange men!'

'I understand. Shall I get a Chinese sent in?'

'Lovely! Didn't you have any engagements tonight?'

'Nothing I can't break,' he lied as he went to the phone, and Lisa was far too sleepy to hear that he made two calls instead of one, and that the second call caused him considerable annoyance.

'He can't come!' snapped Bishop, slamming the phone down in a fury.

'Wife trouble?' queried Steve, relieved that tonight he might get away in time to go to the pub and meet his friends.

'No, that bloody Walker girl.'

'If you mean Lisa,' said Mike, 'you'd better not swear about her in front of him. He's ...'

'Making a fucking fool of himself over her. I know that without your assistance, thank you very much!'

'Very concerned about her,' continued Mike, privately wondering why Bishop hated Lisa so much.

'Her and that damned daughter of Toby Walker's. If I had my way ...'

'Which you won't,' said an older man, listening to the young men as they discussed something that he too knew was important but didn't intend to talk about to anyone because with Neal Gueras you never knew where a tape might be hidden, recording your every word.

'Right,' continued Bishop briskly. 'We're to go ahead without him;

those were his instructions. There's only one question to be discussed, and that's the matter of the Bellini family.'

'Aren't they in banking?' asked Steve, glancing surreptitiously at his watch.

'They are. Were you anxious to get away?' Steve shook his head. 'I'm so glad. The Bellinis are, as you've astutely put it, in banking. They're very heavily into banking, amongst other things.'

'What other things?'

'Power,' said Bishop shortly. 'They're rapidly becoming more and more powerful in Europe, and we've heard that they're thinking of coming to London.'

'Who's behind them?' asked Mike.

'We think that it's P2.'

'I read a good book about them,' said Steve helpfully. *'In God's Name*, I think it was called. All about the Pope and ...'

'Yes, well, thankfully the Pope isn't coming here. He's got quite enough power from on high without wanting any of ours! No, what we need to do is find out exactly who does fund the Bellinis, and what areas are likely to interest them.'

'One thing,' said Mike. 'I happen to know for certain that it was a member of Bellini's group who first started the investigation into Kay's death after her body was washed up in France. You remember that the police there originally accepted it at face value and then got difficult? Apparently they only got difficult because of this forensic man. He seemed to be doing his job efficiently but was actually paid by the Bellinis to try and prove it couldn't have been an accident. Something about tides and that sort of thing.'

'Check that,' instructed Bishop. 'Find out all you can about who gave him the orders and how much he was paid. In the meantime we're all to find out everything possible about the entire Bellini family.'

The ten men seated round the table rose and left quietly until only Mike and Bishop were left. 'It's that bloody woman's fault!' snarled Bishop.

'Kay's?'

'Lisa Walker's! If she hadn't come along ...'

'Some other woman would have done. Let's have a drink down the road.'

Bishop sighed. 'O.K. And yes, some other woman would have done, but this girl's got trouble written all over her.'

As usual, Bishop was right.

103

Chapter Ten

'You're going then?' asked Mike cheerfully, carrying Lisa's shopping into the mews cottage.

'Going where?'

'To the Ball.'

'Yes, like Cinderella I *shall* go to the ball!'

'What about the little one?'

'Neal's arranged a baby-sitter. She's a trained nurse who looked after his wife for a while when she was unwell.'

'Nurse Clarke!' He laughed.

'What's so amusing about her? Put that box down on the table, would you?'

'I took her out once and then discovered she didn't fancy me at all.'

'I'm amazed you can laugh about it. I thought all men had fragile egos.'

'Not at all. Besides, I didn't really fancy *her*. It was just that Mr Gueras felt she needed a break. She was getting too involved with his wife – interfering, he called it. I was meant to take her mind off her job.'

'Coffee?'

'Thanks. Yeah, it was funny because by the end of the evening I'd discovered she was more likely to fancy Mrs Gueras than me!'

'You mean she's a lesbian?'

'You'll be quite safe. If Mrs Gueras is her type, then you won't be!'

'What is Mrs Gueras like?'

'Pretty ordinary. Short, on the plump side, dark hair that she usually wears up, and totally lacking in humour. She's kind-hearted though, or used to be. These days she's not quite so gentle, but I imagine she's had to harden herself to survive.'

'And the girls?'

'I'm not meant to gossip like this.'

'Don't worry, I shan't tell on you but I'm dying to know more about them and Neal won't tell me much.'

'The girls are a strange lot. Louise is a deep one; all curves and blatant sexuality but probably pretty cold underneath. Ruth's the nicest but she wants more than she's ever going to get from either of her parents. As for Rebekah, that poor kid's never had a chance and spends all her time plaguing the life out of the rest of the family just to get some attention.'

'They sound dreadful!'

He gave her a strange look. 'Don't start feeling sorry for Mr Gueras. He's got the family he deserves.'

'That's not a very loyal remark.'

'I'm a company man, and loyal when appropriate. Besides, I like you and it's something you should know.'

She wished he'd kept quiet. At the moment Neal was something of a hero to her. He'd been so supportive over Jessica, and seemed to understand instinctively both how she felt about the child and her fear of involvement with any man. He was always there when she needed him but never intrusive. In other words, he was just what she needed at that time, and she didn't want to hear about any negative aspects of his character.

'Well, who knows what goes on in families? Mine wasn't exactly the cosy unit people must have thought. Shall I show you what I'm wearing on Friday?'

Mike drank his coffee and shook his head. 'I'll be driving you there, I'll see it then. Right now I'm off. Heard any more about this job you wanted?'

'There are still one or two details to sort out.'

'Do you good to get out more. It's an unreal world, you can lose your sense of perspective cooped up here alone.'

She took his cup and put it in the dishwasher. 'Don't worry, I know what I'm doing, but I've got Jessica to think about.'

'Now and again just stop and think what you'd do if Jessica wasn't handicapped. Don't get so caught up protecting her that you throw away your entire life in the mistaken belief that then she'll be safe forever.'

'I think you'd better go,' said Lisa slowly. 'I'm quite capable of working things out for myself.'

'I've upset you and I'm sorry. It's only that you're too nice for . . .'

'For what?'

'For the sort of life you're being offered.'

'Lots of women go out to work.'

'It's not the work that concerns me! In any case, you don't truly believe you'll be doing an honest day's toil for an honest wage, do you? You're not that naive! Life with Toby must have scratched those rose-coloured spectacles of yours a little!'

'Get out.'

'But perhaps you're smarter than I realise. Perhaps you're angling for marriage? If so, I can tell you for nothing that it's not on. Plenty of women have made that mistake. Women may come and women may go, but Naomi goes on forever!'

She slammed the front door behind him, shaking with temper. How dare he talk to her like that? He was meant to be her friend. Well, perhaps not exactly a friend but he'd always been cheerful, almost admiring at times. Now he was making her out to be either a pea-brained Pollyanna or a scheming hussy with designs on an ageing woman's husband.

She wasn't either. She was far smarter than he realised, but she did know that he was right about one thing: life in the cottage was too isolated and safe. After the Ball, she'd press Neal for a job. That would be the best time. She quickly pushed the jibe about such work to the back of her mind. Mike didn't know everything. He was only a chauffeur, however intelligent and alert. No, the job would be genuine enough, she was sure of that.

'After the ball is over . . .' hummed Lisa cheerfully, lying back in the foam-filled bath, listening to the reassuring sound of Nurse Clarke bustling around the nursery.

She was surprised at how excited she felt. It wasn't only pleasure at going out again, it was a sense of reawakening, of feeling truly alive; of being a person in her own right. Not just the terrified wife of Toby or the anxious, guilt-ridden mother of Jessica, but herself, Lisa Walker. She resolved to revert to her maiden name as soon as the divorce was absolute, taking yet another step away from the nightmare.

Early that afternoon she'd taken Jessica along with her to Lazartigue's Hair Centre in St. James's Street. They'd examined her hair, exclaimed over its terrible condition and given her nearly three hours of treatment before pronouncing themselves satisfied. She'd come away with a bag full of their products, including a mud pack for her scalp, regulating jelly and body emulsion; all foul-smelling – but she had to admit that her hair felt better for their treatment – and all hideously expensive. So expensive that for the first time she'd used the charge card given to her by Neal. She only hoped he'd approve of what they'd accomplished.

106

She was just patting herself dry before applying her favourite Body Shop lotion when the bell rang. Quickly wrapping a long satin robe round herself, she went down and looked through the spy hole. 'Neal! You're not meant to be here until eight.'

'Don't worry, I'm not staying. I've brought you a small present for the evening. May I come in for a second?'

As he came in, he glanced at her hair. 'Like it?'

'Very nice.'

'That's lucky, I used your card to pay.'

He smiled. 'I told you it would come in useful. Here, I'd like you to wear this tonight.'

She opened the small box and looked inside. There, on a dark cushion, lay a bottle of Joy perfume. She continued to look at it for a few moments and then replaced the lid. 'You want me to wear that tonight?'

'If you would. It's my favourite perfume.'

'Then you wear it. I prefer something by Dior.'

His smile didn't waver. 'Perhaps you do, but I like my women to wear Joy.'

'All of them? Your wife, your mistresses and your casual girl-friends? Is that how you recognise them in the dark, by the smell of Joy?'

He frowned. 'Don't be ridiculous. Surely it isn't much to ask? Most women are delighted to wear it.'

'I am not most women. I'm sorry but I don't want it. Not only do I find it too heavy, I also object to wearing what is tantamount to a badge proclaiming to the world that I'm yours, when I'm not. I don't belong to anyone, and if the day ever comes when I find myself dressing, talking or thinking along lines dictated by you, then I'll move out.'

'Admirably independent! Where do you intend to go? Somewhere they'll look after Jessica when you want an evening on the town, I trust?'

Lisa thought for a moment and then handed back the box. 'Here you are; give it to my replacement. I'm not coming.'

'Not coming?'

'I'm sorry about the cost of the hair. I'll pay you back when you find me this elusive job. I hope you can get someone else at such short notice.'

Neal's first reaction was to take the perfume, turn her out of the cottage the next day and make quite sure no one in London gave her a job with a decent salary, thus forcing her to return to him on any terms he cared to make.

His second thought was wiser. He wanted her, and he wasn't ever going to get her by using those tactics. She'd probably rather starve than come back to him, however desperate she became. In any case, it made a change. No other woman had turned down the most expensive perfume in the world simply because it wasn't her personal favourite. In fact they were usually so overcome with delight that he came close to despising them for their greed. Lisa was different, and that was her attraction. Different to look at and different in behaviour. If he wanted a change from the Kays of the world, he'd simply have to accept her as she was ... but only for the moment.

'Don't be silly,' he said softly. 'If you don't want to wear it, fine, but please keep it. You can give it away as a Christmas present.'

Now that she'd won, Lisa felt guilty. 'I wasn't trying to be awkward, I honestly don't like it. Stephanie used to drown herself in the stuff; I couldn't wear it, there are too many memories attached.'

'Did Toby ever buy it for you?' he asked quickly.

'Of course not. If I don't want it from you then obviously I wouldn't want it from him either. Besides, he didn't give me anything as expensive as Joy. He was saving up for his old age!'

'Is the nurse all right?' he asked, sitting down for a moment and wondering if she was naked beneath her robe.

'She seems fine. Jessica was hideous but she coped.'

'Good. You look well,' he added. 'Less troubled.'

'I'm feeling better. Hadn't you better leave now? I've still got loads to do.'

'Did you get the ballgown you wanted?'

'I found it in my wardrobe. Whoever picked up my things from Toby's managed to put that in. I sent it to the cleaners and it looks marvellous, but you can't see it until later.'

'I look forward to that.'

When he'd gone, Lisa was surprised to find herself shaking and had to sit on the arm of the chair. It wasn't true that Stephanie had worn Joy, she'd made up the lie on the spur of the moment because she sensed that it would make it easier for Neal to accept her decision. The entire experience of turning down his gift had been highly unpleasant, but everything in her had rebelled at the thought of wearing a perfume that he gave to every woman in his life, regardless of whether or not it suited her.

All of Dior's range suited Lisa. She liked Diorissimo best, but Miss Dior was lovely too, and she alternated between them for formal functions. Joy seemed to her a perfume for the older woman, and she thought she was probably right because most of Neal's women were naturally older than her.

Unfortunately she wasn't yet mentally fit enough for an argument, however minor. It left her drained, bringing back memories of Stephanie as well as the terrible rows with Toby. Why couldn't life be peaceful? she wondered.

'Are you all right, Ms. Walker?' asked the nurse, suddenly coming into the room.

'Yes, thank you. Really, it was nothing.'

'Mr Gueras is a very forceful man,' she continued in a quiet voice. 'His poor wife is terrified of him. Everyone has to fit in with his ideas. He doesn't encourage individuals to express their own personality, especially not his women.'

'I don't think you should discuss him like this,' said Lisa coolly. 'You're also under a slight misapprehension. I'm not one of his women.'

'I apologise. Normally I only work in Mr Gueras's homes for his family and friends.'

'*I'm* a friend!' laughed Lisa quickly. 'I'm only saying that it isn't any more than that. Now I must get changed.'

'No more than that!' muttered the nurse to herself. 'I wonder who she thinks she's fooling? I've seen too many like her to be taken in by that story!'

In her room, Lisa peered in the magnifying mirror and wondered if every woman's skin looked terrible when enlarged. She applied a thin layer of moisturiser and sorted out her makeup brushes while she waited for it to be absorbed.

When she was finished she took out the floor-length, peach-coloured satin gown from its cover, laying it carefully on the bed. It was outstandingly elegant with wide shoulder straps ending in a bow in the middle of her back, and a skirt that hinted at the days of the bustle with its extra fullness, plus another larger velvet bow at the base of her spine.

When she slipped into it she shivered with delight at the feel of the material against her bare skin. All that she wore beneath it was sheer silk stockings and a wisp of suspender belt in matching peach. Finally she pulled on the elbow-length cream gloves, stepped into the dyed peach shoes and gave herself a final check in the full-length mirror.

Her confidence rose as she studied her reflection. She was still a trifle too thin but the shine in her hair lightened her expression and some of the lingering anxiety of the past months had gone. The bustle gave her extra shape, which she needed, and the colour of the gown set off her creamy skin and dark brown eyes.

Her only regret was that she'd had to sell her double strand of pearls. They were the one finishing touch the dress needed, but it was no use looking back. Feeling generally satisfied, she went downstairs just as Neal arrived.

He looked at her for a long time. 'Am I all right?' she asked, beginning to feel quite uncomfortable and annoyed that her self-confidence was so fragile.

'You look incredible,' he said slowly. 'You're quite perfect. I'll be the envy of every man in the room.'

'I doubt it, but thank you for the compliment. Shall we go?'

'I've brought you something else,' he said slowly. 'However, after the perfume I'm not sure if . . . But let's see. If you don't like it, I'm sure you'll tell me! Turn round and close your eyes.'

She did as he asked, although she hated closing her eyes and feeling his hands moving near her throat, just as Toby's hands had once closed round it, trying to choke . . .

'It's all right,' he soothed, feeling her trembling. 'I'm not going to hurt you. Now, how do you think that looks?'

Lisa opened her eyes and glanced down. There, quite unmistakably, nestled her very own double strand of pearls. She gave a squeal of excitement. 'I was just wishing I'd still got them! How on earth did you manage it?'

'I never sold them.'

'But you gave me money.'

'I sold most of the pieces,' he lied, 'but these were too good. I couldn't bring myself to part with them, even for you. I take it I did right for once?'

'Absolutely right! Oh Neal, thank you so much!' She gave him a light kiss on his cheek.

'The car's outside,' he said quickly, hoping she couldn't tell how much the gesture meant to him. 'It won't do to be late.'

Just as they arrived outside Grosvenor House he leant across and whispered, 'I like your perfume,' in her ear, so that she was smiling broadly when they descended from the car and photographer's flashlights exploded around them.

'Surely they're only here for the Princess?' she said in surprise.

'Not at all. Everyone who comes tonight expects to get their picture in *Tatler* or *Vogue*.'

'Why?'

'They want the whole country to know how generous they are with their money, purchasing expensive tickets for unfortunate children.'

'The whole country doesn't read those magazines. Besides, if they didn't have a ball but simply donated the money, then the N.S.P.C.C. would benefit even more. The food and decorations must cost a fortune.'

110

'My dear girl, you mustn't begrudge people their chief pleasure in life!'

'What's that?'

'Dressing up and meeting each other, of course.'

'All the time?'

'Most of the time. You wait, you'll find it an addictive pastime, and these Balls do a lot of good so I don't want you turning cynical during the meal. Some of my friends might not appreciate it.'

'I promise to be good!' she laughed, and once again a flashlight popped as one of the photographers realised that here for once was a genuine beauty who was also new on the social scene, and decided to try and get an exclusive shot of her.

There were twelve people seated at their table, including themselves, and all the other women were over thirty, with one or two nearer fifty. Lisa felt very young and gauche. The men all smiled warmly at her and made conversation but she knew from the very beginning that the women were deliberately excluding her.

They were too well bred to make it obvious, but they spoke of people she didn't know and country houses she'd never heard of. Only one of them, a brunette in her mid-thirties, was overtly hostile and she made her move early on.

Princess Margaret had arrived, surprisingly petite and with glorious eyes that still had the ability to dazzle people, and the meal had begun when Bunny — as her friends called her — leant across the table to Lisa.

'Your gown's beautiful, Lisa. It is Lisa, isn't it?' She nodded. 'I've never seen one quite like it before. Tell me, did you make it yourself?'

There was total silence. The men glanced at Neal, their faces frozen — particularly that of Bunny's husband — while even the women looked uneasy. Nevertheless they turned towards Lisa eagerly, awaiting her answer.

'Actually no,' she said calmly, hoping they couldn't hear the pounding of her heart or guess how horribly sick and unwanted she felt. 'It's a Victor Edelstein. I must tell him what you said. I'm sure he'll be terribly amused!'

'My dear, it was only a joke!' said Bunny quickly. 'Of course I recognised it as an Edelstein straight away. I've worn his gowns myself.'

'In that case I trust he sees the joke too!' said Neal with a distinctly chilly smile.

After that the hostility remained concealed, yet it was there all through the meal. The man on Lisa's left made valiant efforts at conversation but she found it difficult to respond. The watercress

111

soup, the perfectly cooked saddle of lamb and the fresh strawberry mousse all tasted like cardboard to her, and most of her concentration went on forcing the food down.

When the meal was finally over and the speeches finished the ladies withdrew to repair their faces before the dancing began. Lisa was forced to accompany them but they didn't attempt to talk to her.

It was only when she was re-applying her lipstick in front of the mirror and heard the name Kay that she really started to listen to what they were saying.

'Utterly mutilated, darling. I know it's true because Graham's uncle has a friend in Interpol and he actually saw the body himself. He told Graham's uncle that there simply weren't enough rocks in that area to account for the mutilation. She'd even . . .' The voice dropped and Lisa stared into the mirror. Kay. Did they mean the Kay that Neal had known, or was this another one? She doubted it, particularly when the oldest of the women present, Georgina Smythe, finally spoke directly to her.

'Did you know Kay?' she asked coldly.

'Kay who?'

'Neal Gueras's mistress.'

'I'm afraid not. Has something happened to her?'

The women raised their eyebrows and glanced knowingly at each other.

'I asked a civil question,' said Lisa forcefully. 'Obviously you intend to tell me something about her, so why don't you just get on with it instead of smirking and making half-audible remarks?'

Georgina was taken aback by the direct attack. 'Naturally we thought you knew,' she drawled.

'No you didn't, otherwise you wouldn't have bothered to start the conversation. She left Neal, didn't she?'

'She most certainly did! Her body was washed ashore in France a few weeks back. Didn't he tell you?'

'Why should he?'

'Surely you were interested in your predecessor's whereabouts?' asked Bunny aggressively. 'Or are you so bloody confident of yourself that you don't care? She'd been with him for years. We all thought that when Naomi finally . . . that is, if anything happened to Naomi, Kay and Neal would get married. But then you came along.'

'I'm afraid I don't see any connection between my friendship with Neal Gueras and Kay's death.'

'Then you're a great deal more stupid than you look!' snapped Georgina, and one or two women waiting their turn for the mirrors looked at her in surprise.

Lisa flushed and stood up. 'I take it Kay was a friend of yours?'

'She most certainly was.'

'Then I hope she'd have been proud of your behaviour tonight. Excuse me please,' and she swept out of the cloakroom.

Neal guessed something had gone wrong by Lisa's heightened colour but didn't question her. Instead he led her out on to the dance floor where couples were already enjoying the music. They danced well together. She was reasonably accomplished but Neal was very good. He was easy to follow, guiding her effortlessly round the room without holding her too tightly.

Some time later they slipped out on to one of the balconies surrounding the vast white oval ballroom and Lisa leant against the edge, her cheeks cooling in the night air. 'What happened to Kay?' she asked Neal abruptly.

He was standing just behind her but never even tensed. In fact, he put his hands lightly round her waist, while his voice was matter-of-fact and slightly regretful. 'She met with an accident shortly after she left me. I understand that she decided to take up sailing as a hobby, and contrary to all advice took a rather small boat across the Channel on a windy night. No one knows exactly what happened but she was finally washed up on the French coast a couple of weeks after she disappeared. I'm amazed she tried to do the trip alone, but you'd understand more about independent women than I would!'

'That's all there is to it?'

He bent and kissed the nape of her neck. 'What else could there be?'

'The women tonight said she'd been mutilated.'

'What a gruesome lot they are! Naturally she was mutilated. A body that's been thrown against rocks and debris for two weeks is bound to look disfigured. Victims of drowning don't reappear two weeks later in pristine condition.'

'You don't sound very upset!'

'I was, but there was nothing I could do, and it's all over now. What an unpleasant subject this is. Can't we change it?'

'I suppose so.'

'What did George Chapman talk about when you were dancing?'

Lisa gave a gurgle of laughter. 'The price of gold! He's worried over the South African situation.'

'He didn't tell you you were beautiful?'

'Of course not!'

'But Martin Grey did.'

'Yes, but as he's somewhat the worse for drink, that's hardly a compliment.'

113

'You are beautiful. The most beautiful woman here tonight.'

'Don't be silly!'

'I've already been approached by Patrick; he wants to take some studio portraits of you.'

'Patrick?'

'Never mind! Come closer and let me kiss you properly.'

Lisa pushed against his chest. 'Not here! Isn't it time we danced again?'

'If not here, then where?' he asked patiently.

'Back home.'

'Is that a promise?'

She laughed, elated by the wine and his belief in her beauty. 'Yes, it's a promise.'

'Once Princess Margaret's left, we'll go.'

At three a.m. the princess and her party left, and at three minutes past, Neal and Lisa, after he had exchanged a brief word with Georgina Smythe's husband who nodded nervously. Lisa didn't say goodnight to anyone, privately resolving never to have anything to do with any of them again.

'Was the evening a success, sir?' asked Mike, opening the car door for them.

'Excellent, thank you. We'll go to the mews.'

'They thought I'd made my own dress!' laughed Lisa. Mike turned his head away to hide his amusement.

'You don't need to tell him every detail, darling,' reproved Neal, but Lisa looked out of her window and pretended not to hear.

Back at the mews, Mike drove Nurse Clarke to her small town house, leaving Lisa alone with a distinctly affectionate Neal. She tried to keep up a stream of cheerful chatter while making the coffee. 'I didn't come for coffee,' he said quietly. 'I was promised a kiss, remember?'

'How about coffee first?'

'Lisa, do stop fidgeting around in the kitchen and come and sit down. Now, did you enjoy the evening?' As he spoke he manouvered her onto the settee and put an arm round the back of her neck.

'Not the women, but I enjoyed everything else. Why didn't they like me?'

'I don't imagine women are ever very keen on you!'

'I've always got on with other girls perfectly well. I had lots of friends at school.'

'This is real life, and these women are all fighting to keep their looks, their husband and their social position. A beautiful newcomer is hardly likely to be met with rapturous glee.'

114

'Why not? I don't want their grotty husbands, or their social position.'

'They don't know that.'

She felt his left hand wandering near her left breast and tried to ease away from him. 'That's not a kiss!'

'I can't kiss you when you keep turning your head away,' he protested.

Deciding that there were worse things than a kiss, and genuinely feeling affectionate towards him, Lisa turned her face up to his, but his kiss wasn't soft and caressing as she'd expected. Instead it was almost harsh, his mouth hard against hers, his tongue probing insistently between her lips until she finally opened her mouth to him.

After the first panic-filled seconds she found that it wasn't unpleasant to have a man's mouth on hers again, and even his hands on her breasts, slipping easily down the front of the ballgown and gently manipulating her nipples, weren't displeasing. In fact, provided that she let her mind roam free and didn't allow memories from the past to intrude, it was acceptably pleasant.

Only when she felt his right hand easing its way up her thigh did she resist, and he stopped at once. He expected to be stopped at that point; indeed he would probably have been disappointed if she'd allowed him to continue, and so he drew away from her as she straightened her clothing and ran her fingers through her hair.

'I'm very tired,' she apologised. 'Would you mind if I ...?'

He touched her lightly on the chin. 'Not at all. I should be going. I've got to visit Naomi and the girls this weekend and I'll need to be up early in the morning. It was a lovely evening, and I hope there'll be many more of them for us.'

'It was lovely to get out again. I'd forgotten what a real social life was.'

'About your working ...'

'Well?'

'I wonder if you'd mind thinking about this over the weekend. Now that Kay's gone I'm desperately in need of a hostess; someone to take to social events and to act as my partner when I give dinner parties. It takes a lot of time to do all that properly, and I'd really prefer it if you could take her place rather than going out to an office to earn your crust of bread!'

'You mean you'd pay me? Like a girl from an escort agency?' she said indignantly.

'Not at all, but I'd meet all your living expenses and put a little money into a bank account for you so that you weren't entirely dependent upon me. You must see that it would fit in with Jessica better than anything else. I'm not that difficult to be with, am I?'

'And who warms your bed?' she asked shortly.

He gave a brief smile. 'Don't worry, I'll see to all that for myself. You're quite safe; I don't expect you to undertake everything that Kay did!'

'I'll think about it,' she promised, suddenly desperately sleepy, and he was quite content with her answer.

Chapter Eleven

Paulo Bellini was as small as his son, Renato, was tall. He claimed to be 5′4″ to Renato's 6′4″ but very few people believed him. And yet he gave off a greater aura of power and authority than Renato.

Renato smiled frequently, eyes alight with intelligence and humour. Paulo never smiled and his eyes were cold and expressionless; there was none of the Italian expansiveness about him, which only made him stand out the more against his compatriots. That and his reputation.

Of the six men present at the meeting only Renato wore casual clothes, and only Renato's hair was carefully styled and worn long enough to cover his collar at the back. The rest of them were all in dark blue suits and wore their hair short and greased down – but then, they were bankers and businessmen, judged by their outward appearance.

'You say this woman's definitely taken Kay's place?' queried Renato, anxious to get the facts straight.

His father nodded, silently wishing that there was more of him in his son than he had so far been able to discover.

'But she isn't yet his mistress?' he continued, speaking in English because it was England they were discussing. It was customary for them to converse in the language of the country on the agenda.

'It is only a question of waiting,' his father responded. 'Six months is a long time for a man like Gueras to wait. His patience will snap.'

'It was highly regrettable about Kay,' commented one of the men. 'She provided us with a lot of useful information.'

'Perhaps that's why she died as she did!' said Renato dryly.

'She died as she did because that madman Bishop was responsible for her murder. Only he would have inflicted such torture on an innocent woman.'

Renato's teeth flashed in a smile. 'Scarcely innocent; a sexually sophisticated courtesan who was playing a double game. There was always the risk of such a death.'

His father banged his fist upon the mahogany table. 'But that is not why she died. She died to make way for this, this ...'

'Lisa Walker,' put in his secretary helpfully.

'And now Lisa Walker won't "put out", as they say in America. How very unfortunate for Gueras!'

'Renato, there is no cause for amusement. We were close to finding out where the money went. People talk about Spain and France, but nothing is known. Just a few months and we might have learned the truth. As it is ...'

'We write it off as a loss!'

'I am not happy,' said Paulo furiously. 'I did not build up my banks in order to be made a fool of by some second-rate criminal in London.'

'First-rate,' corrected his son with some amusement. 'I'm sure a second-rate criminal would not have managed to fight us like this.'

'You find this amusing, do you not? Excellent, we will see how amusing you find it when you are living in England with only your umbrella for company.'

A murmur went round the room and Renato sat up straight for the first time. 'You want me to live in England? For how long?'

'For as long as it takes to discover how he did it, where the money went and what else he is involved in. I am told that even now he is encroaching on the drugs market.'

'We don't dabble in drugs,' said Renato indifferently.

'He is still encroaching on our territory.'

'I imagine the Mafia are more concerned about that. Why not ask them to sort him out?'

'I wish to settle this debt myself, and so I send my son.'

Renato sighed inwardly and reflected that he would now have to give up his elegant mistress in Milan and start all over again in London, where such women were more difficult to find. Gabriela was intelligent, witty, and ran her own fashion house. She demanded nothing more of Renato than he did of her, and he'd miss her. She was very convenient.

'Well?' demanded his father.

'I apologise, I was thinking of something else.'

'Women, no doubt! I said that we are told this Lisa woman has been heard to say that she wouldn't marry Gueras even if he were free.'

Renato raised his eyebrows. 'Considering his wealth, that reflects very poorly upon his technique!' he mused. Two of the men laughed, Paulo did not.

'You are to go within the month. I wish you discreetly settled before Gueras realises one of our family has arrived. Then you must make it clear that you are there only to oversee the London branch of our bank, and to have a good time before looking around once again for a suitable second wife.'

'Luciano is to come with me,' said Renato curtly, the mention of a wife bringing the image of his young son to mind.

'Naturally. Women like a man who loves children.'

'In England no one loves children if what their papers say are true,' said Renato. There were general murmurs of agreement in which even Paulo Bellini joined in.

'Do we still have anyone inside Gueras's organisation?' asked Renato casually. His father shook his head and they went on to talk about their Swiss branch. After a time Renato left the room with the excuse that he had a lot of arrangements to make.

When he arrived at Gabriela's appartment she didn't look delighted to see him. 'I'm rather busy.' There was a hint of annoyance in her voice.

'Then you'll be relieved to hear that I'm leaving. I have to go to England for a time. I came to say goodbye.'

Her almond-shaped brown eyes widened and she held the door open. 'Come in.'

Raising himself to his full height, Renato looked down at her and shook his head. 'You've already said you're busy. Good luck with your next collection. I wish you happiness.'

'You will return?' she asked.

'To Italy, yes. To you, I think not. My father feels it is time I found myself a second wife. Once I return that will be my priority.'

She smiled invitingly. 'Your first wife didn't come between us.'

'We were both younger then,' he said harshly, and never looked back because he didn't want to see the pain in her eyes, and yet her first rejection of him had made him want to lash out and inflict just such a hurt. There were times when he regretted the speed of his reactions. Just occasionally it would, he knew, be better if he stopped and thought before speaking.

During the next two weeks, as he chivvied his staff to make all the necessary arrangements for his trip, he tried several times to speak to his father about an insider in the Gueras organisation, certain that the older man had lied at the meeting.

Only when they stood together in the departure lounge of Milan airport were his suspicions confirmed. 'We do have someone close to Gueras,' Paulo murmured as they embraced. 'It's better that you do not know who, and tell no one else that such a person even exists. You understand?'

119

'I understand. Come, Luciano, it is time to catch our plane.' The tiny boy and the huge man walked away together and Paulo felt his breath catch in his throat. The child looked so lonely. It was certainly time for Renato to start looking around again once this job was over. Paulo needed more grandsons to inherit the Bellini empire. One frail child was not enough.

He watched the plane until it was a mere speck in the sky and then turned away. He didn't know why he felt so emotional this morning. There was no risk attached to the job Renato had to do, and in any case his son could take very good care of himself, yet he did feel worried.

It was probably because of women, he told himself. They had been a constant source of trouble with Renato since the boy reached his fourteenth birthday, yet still – at thirty-six – he hadn't once fallen in love.

It left a dangerous void in his emotional life, and whatever else happened there must be no scandal attached to any member of the Bellini family. Somehow Paulo felt that London was going to be an unlucky place for them all.

Bishop could have told him why.

Louise and Ruth looked anxiously across the table at each other. It was Sunday evening and their father had spent the entire day with his family, a day full of such tension that Rebekah had become almost hysterical and was now fortunate enough to be eating with her nanny upstairs. They both envied her.

It was 8.45 p.m. and they and their father had been seated at the table since 8 o'clock, waiting for Naomi to come down. Neal's fingers drummed incessantly on the table top and he glanced frequently at his watch while his daughters looked down at their laps. They knew why their mother was late and dreaded the moment when she eventually appeared.

Just as Louise was about to offer to go and see if her mother was all right, the door opened and she came in. Her hair was carefully swept up and coiled into a neat bun; her makeup was over-stated but at least she'd used some, and her maroon-coloured velvet skirt with oyster pink satin blouse was smart, although the colours clashed hideously.

'Ready, my dear?' asked Neal softly.

Naomi looked round the room in puzzlement. 'Where is everyone?'

'We're all here, Mother,' said Ruth quickly. 'The party was yesterday.'

'How silly of me! I do hope I'm not late,' she added, glancing nervously at her husband.

120

'Only forty-five minutes! For God's sake sit down and ring for the soup.'

Naomi gave a strange laugh. 'He makes it sound as though the tureen will walk in! He means ring for the maid of course!' She continued giggling to herself as soup was served and the maid withdrew. Both girls began to eat carefully, aware that their father would be in a hyper-critical mood. He glared at Ruth. 'Must you crumble your roll like that? It looks as though you're planning to feed the birds.'

'Feed the birds – tuppence a bag!' sang Naomi, memories of Mary Poppins springing suddenly into her drink-sodden mind.

Neal groaned and wondered what Lisa was doing. He'd come so close to getting her into bed last week. She'd been in an excellent mood after her first visit to Ascot and, full of champagne and high spirits, had almost given in. Almost, but not quite. The story of the fifteen months since she'd left Toby. If only he had more time he thought, but now life was complicated by the presence of Renato Bellini in London , and if anything he had less time than ever to spare in pursuit of her.

Looking down the table at his wife, his eyes glittered with hate. She could have been sixty in the harsh overhead light, and her orange-tinged lipstick, fortunately being removed by the occasional spoonful of soup she swallowed, was so wrong for the outfit that he wondered briefly if she'd worn it to annoy him but then decided she was too drunk to think of such a thing.

After the soup they had roast beef, Yorkshire pudding, runner beans and tiny new potatoes from the vegetable garden. It was all perfectly cooked and tasted delicious but none of the women could enjoy it.

The girls were terrified that their mother would cause a scene and Naomi was plucking up the courage to do just that. Finally, after toying with her meat for a few moments, she cleared her throat.

'That girl you're with in *Tatler* again this month – what's her name?'

'Lisa Walker; Simon Greene's girl.'

'Simon Greene? I don't remember ...'

'Hardly surprising in your condition.'

'I suppose she's your new mistress?' she said loudly. Louise gripped her knife and fork more tightly while Ruth put hers down and swallowed hard, all appetite gone.

'Don't be ridiculous, Naomi! Pass me the horseradish sauce please, Louise.'

'What's ridiculous about it? Kay's gone. Someone must be giving you all this sexual satisfaction I keep reading about, and it isn't me.'

'Eat your dinner, dear,' said Neal softly, but his eyes held a threat visible even to Ruth.

'I want an answer!' shouted Naomi, lurching to her feet clutching a glass of claret.

'I've given you one. She is *not* my mistress. Now please sit down and remember the children are here.'

'Do you imagine that they don't know what you're like? Auntie Kay indeed! They knew all about her and her cool dis ... dis ... distemper!'

'I take it you mean disdain? Kay's dead, Naomi.'

'I know that. I do read the papers. Poor Kay, she didn't have any protection, did she? Not like me. Oh, you'd love to have me killed too, I don't doubt that for a moment, but you can't, can you? You can't afford the enquiries that would follow. I know too much about you, and it's all written down as well.'

Neal glanced up from his plate and stared at her. 'Indeed?'

She laughed. 'Surprised? Fancy stupid, drunken Naomi having the wit to leave anything with a solicitor, but I have and you don't even know which solicitor I've used!'

'You're talking nonsense. I had intended to stay overnight but I think I'll return to London after dinner. I've had enough of this house for the moment.'

'What about me?' she screamed, hurling her linen napkin to the floor and knocking over the gravy boat as she thumped the table with her hand. 'Do you think I like living here on my own, week after week? Don't you think I've got needs and feelings?'

'I'm sure everyone's aware of your needs, Naomi!'

'I only drink because ...' She frowned, losing her thread of thought.

'Because you can't afford cocaine every day?'

'Who started me off on that? It was you, wasn't it! Admit it, tell the children what kind of husband you are. "Try some of this, dear, it will make you feel much better." That's what you said. And you were clever because it did. It made me feel better but not for long enough. Never for long enough!' She began to weep.

She cried badly, her face turning red and blotchy while her nose ran and beads of sweat made their way through the caked makeup. Neal could scarcely bear to look at her but forced himself to get up from his chair and walk to the other end of the table.

'You're tired. Louise, ask Nurse Clarke to come and take your mother to bed.'

'That's right, pack me off to bed. But you won't be sharing it, will you? You'll be off to that trollop in London, rolling around in her ...'

'Shut up!' he said dispassionately, and twisting her right arm, forced her from the chair and towards the door. 'Do you honestly think any man would want to share your bed these days?'

'It's your fault!' she screamed, ignoring the appearance of Nurse Clarke hurrying down the wide staircase. 'You've made me what I am. Well, don't forget I've covered myself. If anything happens to me, you'll be in so much trouble you'll be lucky not to go down for twenty years or more. I've watched you these past few years; I've seen the people who've come and gone and ...'

'Get her to bed,' he ordered the nurse. 'Make sure she goes to sleep. I'm beginning to wonder if you're quite up to this job,' he added quietly, and Nurse Clarke turned away. Naomi was past help, but she wasn't going to lose her position by telling her employer that. Besides, she thought he probably knew.

When he strode back into the dining-room, Louise was crying softly into her handkerchief while Ruth sat, white-faced and straight-backed, her hands clenched into fists on her lap.

'You musn't get upset, Louise,' he said benignly. 'Your mother isn't well. She can't help herself.'

'Why?' asked Louise as rudely as she dared. 'Why's she like this? I can remember when she was quite different. She used to laugh a lot and loved playing with us.'

'She never got over Rebekah's birth. Her hormones were affected or something. I'm told it does happen.'

'Never mind Rebekah, what about Kay?' muttered Ruth.

'You were saying?' queried her father politely.

'Nothing.'

'I'm very glad to hear it.'

'What did she mean about prison?' continued Louise, her blue eyes challenging her father.

'I've no idea, she gets these delusions now and again. Alcoholics do. The worst thing I've ever done is drive at 100 m.p.h. on the M1 and I don't think you get twenty years for that!'

'But ...'

He sensed that Louise wasn't going to let up and went straight for her weakest point. 'The only person I know who might not want the police investigating his activities is your friend, Bishop. There's some very strange things go on in his Norfolk cottage. Yes, if the police were ever to investigate any of my companies I don't think Bishop would come out of it very well. Shall I ring for dessert?'

Ruth looked at her sister compassionately. Poor Louise loved their

123

mother but was also besotted with Bishop. Now she wouldn't know who to believe or what to do for the best. As for herself, she didn't care about their mother any more and she loathed Bishop. All she wanted was a little peace.

In Kensington Gardens five hours earlier, Lisa had been wanting peace as well. A day that had started out well had turned into a complete nightmare, all because of Jessica.

Alone together for the weekend they'd spent the first day indoors while Lisa painted the nursery light blue, a colour that seemed to soothe the little girl. While Lisa painted, Jessica — now on her feet — had dashed around the room grabbing at every tin or metal object she could find. She had a fixation for all shiny things and in the end the room had to be stripped bare, and even then Lisa spent a lot of time protecting the paint tin.

Even so, she'd enjoyed herself. Opera played loudly as background music made Jessica considerably easier; in fact she could hum the 'Seguidilla' from *Carmen* with remarkable accuracy. This peculiar skill, almost a musical gift, was entirely out of keeping with the rest of her behaviour, but Dr Phillips said it was common with autistic children, which stopped Lisa from hoping Jessica was simply a difficult musical prodigy.

On the Sunday the painting was finished and after a simple lunch, Lisa decided they'd go to the park; Mike dropped them off at Kensington Gardens before disappearing on an errand for Neal. Strapped in her pushchair, which she hated, Jessica began to scream the moment they left the car. She screamed and fought against the harness keeping her in, and when people stopped and said, 'Oh dear, what's the matter with you, beautiful?' or 'A lovely little girl like you shouldn't be crying!' and other inane comments, she responded by spitting. This was a new accomplishment and one which embarrassed Lisa as much as it delighted her daughter.

When she let Jessica out of the pushchair matters improved. Because the day was so lovely there were crowds of people there, but Jessica ignored them. She ran around on the grass, occasionally bumping into another child or a seated adult and bouncing off without even a glance. They smiled and forgave her because she was young and so beautiful.

To Lisa, sitting on a bench and trying to relax, it was at times like this that Jessica's disability became more obvious. True she was on her feet early, and confident on them, but other toddlers in the park acknowledged each other, looking seriously into their contemporaries' faces and reaching out to touch.

Not so Jessica. One little boy of about three was entranced by this tiny vision and ran up to give her a hug. He was treated to an ear-splitting scream as Jessica hurled herself to the ground, burying her face in her arms and kicking her feet in terror. The mother ran up and told her son off, ignoring Lisa's assurances that he hadn't hurt her daughter, but still Jessica screamed, curling herself into a ball as she tried to shut out the world.

Eventually she stopped yelling and with a few quick glances around her, stood up. Lisa called her name and waved but Jessica ignored her. Then her eyes were caught by something bright and shiny in the distance and at once she was off. She half-ran and half-walked to the edge of the Round Pond, looking out to the middle where a replica of a liner was being sailed by remote control.

For a few seconds she stood watching, then she simply continued walking straight into the water and out towards this wonderful shiny boat that she wanted to hold. If she realised that the water was gradually reaching her face she didn't care. All she wanted was the boat, and adults and children alike watched in disbelief as she went deeper and deeper into the water.

Lisa ran towards her, calling her name even though she knew it was pointless. There was no doubt that Jessica would drown in her quest for the boat unless Lisa were to wade straight in after her, not even pausing to take off her shoes. She just caught her as the water closed over Jessica's head.

Choking and terrified, she howled hysterically. She hit and kicked at her mother, still struggling to reach the boat she would have died for, and when the boy who owned it brought it to shore, she managed to break free and hurtle into the water again, tiny hands outstretched after the vanishing toy.

Shaking with fright, Lisa picked her up for the second time, gripped her as hard as she could and waded back to the grass where they both slumped to the ground in a soggy heap. The boy walked towards them, holding out his beautiful boat. 'Would she like a look?' he asked politely.

'I don't think . . .' began Lisa, but she was too late. Jessica had got her hands firmly round the desired object and was tugging with all of her strength.

'Just look at it,' explained the boy. 'It's not for playing with.'

Jessica turned brick-red and started to scream again, pulling furiously at the expensive model. The boy looked at Lisa. 'Would you ask her to let go, please?'

'I'm afraid she's . . . Yes, of course. Jessica, let go!' And Lisa wrenched the small hands off so that the boy could take his model boat safely home.

'She's too young to understand,' said Lisa feebly, beginning to shiver with cold.

'My sister's little but she understands about drowning. She wouldn't just walk out of her depth like that. Your little girl's very brave.'

Lisa smiled, trying to ignore the stares of the bystanders, aware that Jessica wasn't brave, she simply hadn't understood the danger. Even worse, she was oblivious to physical pain or discomfort, apparently unaware that she was now drenched to the skin. She began to yell at the top of her voice and Lisa shook her in desperation. 'Stop it!' she shouted. 'You're a very bad girl!'

Jessica went rigid and clapped her hands over her ears. While her own shrieks didn't bother her, she was becoming highly sensitive to noises made by other people or strange objects. Trains and cars terrified her, as did the sound of the telephone ringing.

'You want to keep a better eye on her,' said a woman in her early forties as Lisa, carrying a soaking Jessica, squelched back to the bench. 'They're all over the place once they're on their feet. You won't have time for daydreaming from now on.'

'She's retarded,' said Lisa shortly. 'There's nothing I can do to control her. Excuse me, I must get her in the pushchair.' The woman walked away, obviously not believing what she'd heard. Jessica looked so very normal, and the woman's expression said clearly that she knew Lisa was at fault.

'You little horror!' she murmured, rubbing ineffectually at the wet curls with a handful of tissues from her bag. 'Come on, we're going home.'

Jessica kicked out and caught Lisa on the nose. With a cry of pain she relaxed her hold and Jessica rolled out of her arms and on to the grass, immediately dashing off once more and heading straight back for the pond, Lisa's nose was bleeding heavily, her face ached and it was only when she heard the splash of water that she realised Jessica was already back in the pond. Shouting out, she began to run but this time someone came to her assistance and a man grabbed hold of Jessica before she was more than waist deep.

'Thank you so much!' she gasped, a stitch in her side adding to her discomfort. 'I didn't think ...' She tailed off as she recognised a rather damp Bishop. Jessica was lying stiffly in his arms, her eyes staring up at the sky, the brightness of the sun entrancing her so that the boat was finally forgotten.

'I ought to take a picture of you now!' he said disagreeably. ' "Ms Lisa Walker, the most beautiful young socialite on the scene at present, takes her equally beautiful daughter to one of London's parks for the day". I reckon I'd be well paid for something like that! You look like two drowned rats!'

She was too humilated to respond, and feeling tears prick the back of her eyes she turned away. 'Can you carry her to the pushchair for me?'

'I *can*, but will I?'

'Don't be so damned pedantic. Will you carry ...?'

'My pleasure. They'd put a dog down if it was as mad as her, you know. I once had a collie-cross that used to lie on the bars of the electric fire. It didn't have any sense or feeling either. They put that down without a murmur.'

'I'm surprised you didn't kill it yourself.'

He smiled. 'That's better, far more your usual style! Right, Jessica, in you go.' He bent down to put her in her pushchair and she went completely limp, lolling in the chair like a wet rag doll, staring at a point over his shoulder, lost once again in her own world.

'I'll take her home,' said Lisa, checking the straps.

'I'll walk with you.'

'No thanks. Mike's meeting us at the park gate.'

'Then I'll walk with you to the car. Mr Gueras wouldn't expect me to leave you alone dripping blood and pond water everywhere. People might talk, and he doesn't like people talking about him or his friends.'

Jessica started to make grunting noises as she wriggled her fingers in front of her face. She kept that up for hours some days, as though the movement hypnotised her.

'Is that speech?' he asked in amusement.

'She's only fifteen months old.'

'Doesn't she coo or blow raspberries?'

'She's very good at spitting!' snapped Lisa, wishing Jessica had done it to Bishop when he'd bent over the pushchair.

'Probably inherited that from you.'

'This wretched nose!' she exclaimed, ignoring the remark.

He handed her a large handkerchief. 'Use that and pinch the bridge. I'd put ice cubes down your back but it doesn't actually achieve anything except added discomfort! Incidentally, I've ruined my shoes wading in that damned pond.'

'What were you doing in the park?'

'Just taking a stroll. Relaxing in the sun.'

'You weren't by any chance watching me?'

'Of course I was. Everyone was watching you and Jessica. It was better than listening to the band!'

'That's not what I meant.'

127

'I didn't really think it was! You enjoyed Ascot?' he added casually.

'It was lovely. All those hats!'

'Horses, too, I hear.'

'I was more interested in the clothes.'

'You do have some normal feminine traits then?'

'Look,' she said wearily, her skirt dripping water on the pavement, 'I'm grateful for your help but I can manage now. I'll tell Neal what you did for me.'

Bishop glanced at Mike hurrying towards them and then looked back at the limp, bedraggled child.

'The sooner you resign yourself to having her put away the better,' he said softly. 'You won't be able to keep them both, you know.'

'Go away!' she shouted, and Jessica began to scream once more. As Mike coped with the pushchair and her daughter, Lisa climbed into the passenger seat, buried her head in her hands and wept. Sometimes she wondered if she was ever going to have any peace again, but she'd never part with Jessica. Never.

Chapter Twelve

The two men met at Brown's over afternoon tea. Neal thought that Renato Bellini might be fascinated by the ritual, and Renato accepted because he knew that at Brown's he was unlikely to be seen by anyone he knew and he wanted this meeting to be secret.

'So your father's worried about the bank?' queried Neal, eating his tiny toasted teacake.

'Not perhaps worried, but suspicious. I'm here to watch the director. As an observer only, you understand.'

'You've found somewhere to live?'

Renato nodded but didn't give any details.

Looking at the younger man with his mass of dark hair, deep set oval eyes and typical roman nose, Neal wondered about women. Might it be possible for them to trap a Bellini by using one of their agency girls? They were all first class, most of them from titled but impoverished families, and all more than willing to do anything they were asked if the price was right. With this man they probably wouldn't mind if they weren't paid, but would he do anything with them that could be useful? It was difficult to say.

'Your business prospers?' Bellini asked, knowing full well that it did, and a great deal of that at the expense of P2's coffers.

'It fluctuates but on the whole I'm satisfied. Another sandwich?'

The minute triangle looked ridiculous in Renato's enormous hand. He was certainly big, thought Neal in surprise, remembering the size of Paulo Bellini. It wasn't just the height, he was big-boned as well, and heavily muscled without an inch of fat. A fit man. He looked at the mouth, its full lower lip at odds with the thinner top one. A very mobile mouth, and definitely that of a sensualist – but a pervert? Disappointingly, he thought not. Certainly there'd never been any hint of the Italian vice, as Neal always considered it. No, boys wouldn't interest Bellini.

'You must come to Berkshire and have a weekend with us,' he said casually. 'I'm sure you'd like a break from London.'

'My young son is with me. He is only four.'

'My youngest daughter's only six. He'll be fine. It will make a change to have a boy around the place.'

Renato smiled, revealing a small cleft in his chin. 'Still no son? You must keep trying. A son is so important.'

Neal knew that the Bellinis were aware of Naomi's condition and had to be confident that there never would be a son but he nodded pleasantly 'I never give up,' he said smoothly, and remembering the new girlfriend, Renato realised that he hadn't, although an illegitimate son was scarcely the same, should the girlfriend ever allow him near enough to father one. The thought amused him and his smile widened, showing the white, uneven teeth that could turn any woman's stomach upside down with longing.

'How long will you be staying?' asked Neal, reaching out for a cake even as Renato declined, indicating his waistline and making Neal feel gluttonous.

He gave a typically Continental shrug. 'Who knows? However long it takes to assess what is going on here.'

'At the bank?'

The smile vanished and the face tightened. 'But of course! Where else? Are there other things that I should know of?'

'I doubt it,' said Neal, rising to his feet. 'I'm sorry but I'm already late for an appointment. I'll get my secretary to ring you about a weekend in Berkshire, and do give my regards to your father when you next speak to him.'

'We talk only of pleasant things at the moment.'

There was a sudden silence.

'And I won't be included in pleasant matters?'

Renato smiled again, his eyes mocking. 'Why ever not? I meant that naturally I would pass on your message, along with other pleasant matters of the day. Perhaps my English is not yet sufficiently accomplished for me to make myself clear?'

'Your English is extremely good. It's nice to have you here in London, even if it is only for a short time.'

They shook hands and parted but it was Neal who left in a temper. Renato Bellini felt very satisfied with the way things had gone. Now he must return to his apartment, play with Luciano, shower, change, and meet Bishop at the Ritz for dinner. He would be more careful with Bishop. Psychopaths should not be mocked.

It was 8 a.m. on the Tuesday morning. Neal had risen at six, spent an

130

hour at the gymnasium, had a working breakfast with two members of Scotland Yard's Flying Squad and then decided that he'd like to pay Lisa a surprise visit.

He succeeded. She didn't hear him ring the doorbell because of Jessica's screams and it was only by tapping on the front window that he managed to attract her attention. She opened the door and dashed away again, back to the kitchen and her hysterical daughter.

Slightly piqued by this lack of welcome he followed her, but stopped in the doorway in disbelief as a bowl of runny cereal was hurled across the room, coming to land only a few inches from his perfectly polished shoes. He stared around him. There was food everywhere; on the table, the floor and on the walls, while a plastic bowl of food was upside down on Jessica's head.

Lisa, wearing an old towelling robe and slippers, bore no resemblance to the fashionable young woman he was used to escorting round London, and her harrassed expression aged her several years. He felt his dislike for the child mount but kept his voice calm. 'What's going on here?'

Lisa wasn't deceived; she could hear the edge to his voice and snapped back in a mixture of shame and temper. 'She's not hungry, and if you don't like watching, go away. I didn't ask you to come.'

'I wanted to surprise you.'

'I imagine you're the one who's surprised. What did you think it was like here in the mornings? Did you imagine me lying in bed all sleepy and tousled, anxious for company as I stretched langourously beneath the duvet?'

'Something like that, I suppose. Does she always throw her food around?'

'Yes. The trouble is that unless I keep on she simply won't eat. She'd probably starve to death, because she hasn't got any sense of survival.'

'I gathered that from Bishop.'

She turned just in time to catch one of Jessica's flying fists in her face. 'Ouch! He told you about the park?'

'He certainly did.'

'Oh, Jessica, that hurt! I'm going to put you down, we're not getting anywhere at the moment. Let me unstrap you.'

But Jessica started to spit and scream until Lisa was nearly in tears. Neal watched impassively, wondering how much longer it would be before she agreed that Jessica needed to go into a home.

Eventually the child was on the floor and at once fell silent. She glanced obliquely at the visitor and then grabbed hold of one of the spoons that had gone flying in the struggle and began to hit herself over the head with it with intense concentration, totally oblivious of the pain, while rocking gently all the time.

'When does she go back to hospital?' asked Neal.

'This afternoon.'

'What do you think he'll say?'

'Nothing much, except an assurance that she's showing more and more signs of autism, as though he expects that to give me some kind of pleasure.'

'Has he talked about her future?'

'She hasn't got one, has she! She's so isolated I could cry, and yet occasionally I catch a look in her eyes that makes me feel she knows and that if only I could find the key to unlock the door, she'd be free. I don't believe she can't be helped. All I know is that Dr Phillips doesn't know the way.'

'Do you want a second opinion?'

She looked at her daughter, her beautiful raven-black curls full of Ready-Brek, her huge eyes ringed with dried egg yolk, and wondered if she could stand hearing the same depressing prognosis from another specialist. But she had to try; she owed it to Jessica.

'I suppose so, but this time I want to see someone who specialises solely in autistic children.'

'I'll find out who's best. Can she be left for a moment?'

Jessica had now picked up a small metal car and was spinning the wheels round and round in silent fascination. 'Yes, she'll do that for hours.'

'Hours?'

'Yes, literally hours. It seems as though while she's spinning the wheels her mind goes off on some journey of its own. She's really quite happy at times like this.'

He was tempted to ask Lisa what mind she was talking about, but didn't. The specialist must be the one to open her eyes to the finality of Jessica's condition. 'Come on then,' he urged. 'I wanted to talk to you about Wimbledon.'

Lisa ran her fingers through her hair and wished she'd washed and dressed before getting Jessica up but there hadn't seemed any point. At the moment all meal times ended up with her needing a bath and an old dressing gown was sensible, except when someone came visiting.

'I'm sorry I'm such a mess!'

'My fault for arriving unannounced. Besides, you look enchanting just as you are.'

'What was this about Wimbledon?'

'I've got tickets for Men's Finals Day. Would you like to come?

I've seats in the Royal Box – near the back, but it's still pleasant.'
'I like tennis. When is it?'
'A week next Sunday.'
'What about Jessica?'
'Nurse Clarke can look after her.'
'She doesn't like changes to her routine,' protested Lisa half-heartedly. 'I've noticed that although to outsiders we don't seem to have a routine, she gets very distressed if things are done differently. You know, silly things like washing her hands before her face or ...'
'What kind of a routine do you call that?' he asked, pointing at the kitchen.
'Because she throws her food around, it doesn't mean she's unhappy. At the moment she enjoys throwing food about, it's just a phase. She's very good in some ways, she ...'
'Yes?' She looked away from him. 'In what ways?' he persisted.
'All right, there aren't any,' she admitted, twisting her hands in her lap. 'But she honestly does like a routine.'
'I'm sure the nurse can follow any routine if you write it down. You can't let that child ruin your entire life. I've only suggested a day at Wimbledon, not a month in New York.'
'I've been out a lot lately and it's making her worse. She was dreadful after Ascot. It took me three days to get her back to normal.'
'What's normal?'
'Stop it!' she shouted, jumping to her feet. 'Don't keep on about her. Do you think I'm enjoying all this? Do I look as though I've had a lot of fun this morning?'
'I'm sorry,' he murmured, standing up and letting her lean against him. 'I know it's difficult and I understand how much she means to you, but that's because you won't let anyone else into your life. You're putting all your love and emotion into a tiny child who's never going to be able to appreciate it if she lives to be a hundred. Why won't you open yourself up? Surely you know how I feel about you? If you'd give me one-tenth of the affection you lavish on Jessica, I'd be a happy man.'
She sighed. She was so exhausted that it was wonderful to rest against him, let him put his arms round her and hold her. Life with Jessica was becoming a nightmare. Day after day it was a constant battle to keep her looking half-human as she sat hitting her head against the wall or uttered strange guttural sounds punctuated with screams and meaningless giggles. And all the time, every moment of their life together, Lisa was trying to get through to her daughter. But her belief that love alone would be enough was beginning to fade and she didn't know what to do next.

133

'It isn't just Jessica that makes me cautious about you,' she confessed as they sat side by side on the sofa. 'I can't get Toby out of my mind. When you kiss me I like it at first, then I freeze inside and just want to escape. I don't have normal feelings any more.'

'Of course you do, but under your present conditions they're not likely to show themselves. I had no idea what life was like here when you were alone. If you've no objection, I'm going to try and get you some full-time help. You'll wear yourself out otherwise, particularly with all the late nights we have.'

'I was wondering if I ought to stop seeing you,' she admitted. 'I enjoy it but I have to get up at 5 a.m. and I don't get any free time until we're off the following night. I'm burning myself out.'

'Right, first of all I fix you up with an appointment with a specialist then I get you some daily help, even if it's only with the cleaning. If I do all that, can you manage Wimbledon?'

'I should think so.'

'Wonderful! Also, I hate to remind you but there is a dinner party at my Chelsea house tomorrow night.'

'I know. I've arranged for Schaverien to do the catering; Pulbrook & Gould will do the flower arrangements and I was just going to check the wine list with you before ringing Grant's. Everything's covered, except I don't know what to wear!'

'I shan't suggest anything,' he said with a smile. 'You'll only say I'm being dogmatic again!'

'You won't forget the perfume in a hurry, will you? If you like a particular dress then tell me. I'm too tired to make any decisions right now.'

'How about the strapless jade taffeta. You know, the one with the straight skirt and matching jacket.'

'Fine. By the way, Bishop told me your wife wasn't well. Is she any better yet?'

'Yes, although it takes her time to get over her attacks. It's asthma, brought on this time by the cat getting indoors. She's allergic to lots of things: feather pillows, long grass, cats, birds ... Sometimes I wonder if it's all psychosomatic. A good excuse for staying indoors.'

'Don't be so unsympathetic. Isn't it time you went to work?' she added as his hands strayed down the front of her robe. He cupped one of her breasts and lightly stroked the nipple until it was erect.

'If you want me to go ...?'

'I'd rather you did,' she admitted.

He shrugged. 'Never mind, I'll put my faith in body language! Until tomorrow evening then. Mike will pick you up.' After he'd gone she felt very lonely.

*   *   *

134

When Bishop arrived at the Ritz, Renato Bellini was already waiting for him. He was sitting at a window table reading the wine list while all the women in the restaurant glanced at him as they wondered who he was and whether he was available.

He rose to his full 6' 4" and nodded pleasantly to Bishop. However, he didn't hold out his hand, which was a pity because Bishop had been prepared to ignore it and felt deprived of scoring the first point.

'It is pleasant to see you again,' smiled Renato, but his eyes said otherwise.

'Indeed it is. Paris last Spring, wasn't it?'

'Around that time. Are you still looking for girls?'

'No, we've got enough. You, I imagine, have them to spare!'

'The type of women I know wouldn't suit your purposes. My father was distressed to hear of Kay Marshall's death. He met her here several years ago and thought her a pleasant and cultured woman.'

'Is that when they met? I don't suppose the sea knows the difference between an aristocrat and a peasant! Well, appearances can be misleading; as can women.'

'Naturally, but no one in our position would ever be foolish enough to place our trust in one, would we?' And the teeth flashed in a cynical smile.

'She worked for you,' said Bishop quietly, realising that Bellini wanted it out in the open. 'What did your father expect? Marriage to Mr Gueras?'

'I don't think my father would make Neal Gueras a very good wife!'

'Highly amusing. How long had she worked for you?'

Renato shrugged. 'I've no idea. All the time, I suppose. Why?'

'We didn't know,' muttered Bishop through clenched teeth. 'We never knew until just before she died. If we had ...'

'Her death would not have been an accident! How fortunate she drowned as she did, then.'

'Why are you here, Bellini?'

'To check on our London director.'

'Bullshit!'

'To see the sights; to taste the wonderful British food and the even more wonderful women! Why do you think I'm here?'

'Because we're getting in your way!'

Bellini shook his head. 'No, that is not why. It is because we are worried about your organisation. It is, shall we say, less efficient than it was once. The control is looser. You are allowing yourselves to move into areas unacceptable to us it is true, but mostly we are worried about the lack of control.'

135

'There's room for us all.'

A waiter arrived and took their order but Bellini scarcely seemed to be interested in what he chose. 'Theoretically that is true, but firm direction from the top would be necessary and we feel this is lacking.'

'Of course you know why?'

Again a quick smile, this one almost menacing. 'It is a woman. A woman he wants and cannot have!'

'Incredible, isn't it? One stuck-up, razor-tongued, stick-insect of a girl has him running round in circles. I don't know why he doesn't just rape her and get it over with.'

'You are undoubtedly a ladies' man, Bishop, I can tell by your approach! Ah, the food.'

'He'll get over it,' said Bishop, toying with the duck.

'You think so? When?'

'Either when she puts out or when he gets fed up with chasing her.'

'You don't think she might be holding out for marriage?'

'No, she's not very keen on him. She had a brief disaster of a marriage to an actor that's left her with a retarded daughter and a lot of emotional hangups. I don't think she wants marriage at all.'

'What kind of mental trouble affects her daughter?'

'She's autistic; an absolute savage and totally untrainable.'

'There have been encouraging results achieved with such children,' murmured Bellini thoughtfully.

'Never mind the bloody child, it's her mother who's causing all the trouble.'

'On the contrary, it's your employer who's causing the trouble. Should he continue to be distracted from his work, allowing the situation to worsen, then we might feel it necessary to move in and straighten out the demarcation lines.'

'But not if someone else took over. Suppose Mr Gueras were to be superceded, then there would still be room for us both.'

'My friend,' said the Italian softly, 'we know of no one in your organisation whom we would trust to take over the running of day to day affairs. No one at all.'

The blood drained from Bishop's face as he sat opposite this powerful foreigner and was obliged to swallow the insult, politely delivered but so utterly final. He looked down at his food and found that the sight of it made him feel ill. Consumed by fury, he knew if he remained he'd say or do something utterly unforgivable and so he stood up and forced a bleak smile to his face.

'I don't think there's any point in discussing matters further. You've made your feelings quite clear and I'd prefer to eat alone.'

'Alone?' Renato's voice was amused. 'You are offended by

something I have said, I assume, but what? Surely it cannot be that you yourself were contemplating betraying your own employer? That you were seriously considering removing him and taking over the reins of his empire? No! You are far too loyal to have thought of such a thing, so how have I offended you?'

'Naturally under normal circumstances I'm loyal,' said Bishop stiffly, recognising too late the trap which Bellini had set for him, 'but these are not normal circumstances. If a man can't control the women in his life what chance does he have with the men? Gueras is losing respect, hence the chaos your secret society has already noticed.'

'We are not a secret society. We are a firm of bankers.'

'I'm not a natural Judas,' Bishop continued, ignoring the interruption, 'but there are times when personal loyalty has to be set aside.'

'An ambitious lieutenent is more dangerous than the most ruthless opponent,' mused the Italian. 'That is why in my country we prefer to keep things within the family. It avoids such power struggles. Since I now know that you would − albeit unwillingly − be prepared to take on the responsibilities currently undertaken by Gueras, then naturally my original comment no longer applies. I would say that today you have made quite clear to me exactly where your priorities lie.'

Bishop waited for the smile but it didn't come. The dark eyes opposite him were wide and innocent, yet he wasn't deceived. They were two very good poker players who concealed their feelings perfectly. The lack of a smile did tell Bishop one thing: Bellini disliked him. The games were over; he'd probed and tested until he'd discovered what he'd come to learn before forming his judgement and finding Bishop wanting. Not, possibly, as a businessman but as a human being.

'Things are different here,' Bishop said at last, still standing by the table. 'In our organisation the best man usually finds his way to the top of the pile.'

'Gueras has money, status, a shrewd brain, and moves in the best circles. You have nothing except your brain. A better one, I admit, but it is not enough. Your women are kept hidden, your background is unknown, you are not popular, and worst of all you have no sense of humour. You are not front man material and you never will be. A drawback, yes?'

'Yes.'

'You have a solution?'

'I'd have to marry well.'

Bellini laughed. 'You sound like St Paul − better to marry than to burn! Who among today's society women would be willing to marry you, I wonder?'

'Louise Gueras.'

There was a silence. 'Indeed? Well, perhaps you will manage after all. Naturally she would not marry you *after* you'd removed her father!'

'I'd marry her first.'

'Very wise. Would he approve of the marriage?'

'Possibly not, but he'd agree if she was pregnant.'

'A wife and a child! Perhaps also a cottage with climbing roses over the door?'

'I'm telling you what I can do. What's your opinion?'

'You must decide for yourself. I am only here to look round. Naturally I'm interested but that is all. I am more concerned with the whereabouts of the bullion that went missing in that bank raid six months ago.' Now he did smile, but only his bottom teeth were revealed and there was a hint of challenge in his eyes.

'I hope,' said Bishop at last, 'that nothing we've discussed comes about. In my opinion it's the girl who should die.'

'Be careful,' said Renato softly. 'If he thinks he's in love with her, and she should come to any harm, *you* might end up taking a trip across the Channel in a boat that isn't seaworthy. I don't think the French police are ready for yet another body on their shore!'

'I'll be in touch,' said Bishop curtly, before walking away.

Bellini nodded to himself and settled down to eat. It had gone very well. The more caught up they were in quarrelling amongst themselves the less time they'd have to notice where he went or what he did. But he sensed that Bishop shouldn't be underestimated, particularly if he had one of the Gueras girls hanging around after him.

Now he wanted to take a look at Lisa Walker and her small daughter. He would find out where she went with the child and observe them from a distance. It would be fascinating to see the woman who'd got Neal Gueras in such a state simply by keeping him out of her bed. She was probably very clever and totally self-centred, but just the same he wanted to see for himself. Both he and Gueras loved beautiful things, and flaws in temperament didn't matter if all you were going to do was look.

Thinking of Bishop, he smiled and drank the last of the wine. A very dangerous opponent but a decidedly worse ally. He didn't have an ounce of humanity in him, and that made him very dangerous indeed.

Chapter Thirteen

Men's Finals Day at Wimbledon marked the beginning of a new stage in Lisa and Neal's relationship. Much to her surprise, she found that after some initial nervousness she thoroughly enjoyed herself. It was exciting sitting a few rows behind the charming Duchess of Kent with an uninterrupted view of the tennis. On her two previous visits as a schoolgirl, she'd queued for returns at the gate during the first week, and although it had been fun at the time it couldn't compare with the luxury of the Royal Box.

Even the champagne with their strawberries and cream – things she'd affected to despise when younger – fitted in perfectly with the day, and Neal's obvious pride in her made her feel confident and self-assured.

When the tennis ended they went out to dinner before returning to Chelsea, and she was ashamed to find that when she stepped inside her home her stomach tightened in anticipation of Jessica's screams.

In fact it was peaceful, but Nurse Clarke looked flushed and admitted that the little girl had been difficult, a statement fully endorsed by the red lump above her left eyebrow where Jessica's foot had made contact during a frantic screaming struggle that had lasted for over an hour.

Lisa's shoulders began to sag as the nurse continued her report until Neal cut her short. 'What did you expect?' he asked sharply. 'You knew the child was handicapped.'

'I hadn't realised ...'

'Realised what?' he demanded, furious that the animated shine was already fading from Lisa's eyes.

'How bad her condition was. Or that she was utterly undisciplined.'

Lisa turned furiously on the nurse. 'My daughter's ill. She can't help the way she behaves, she's terrified by everything that happens to

139

her. What kind of discipline do you think I should exercise? A good thrashing now and again?'

'Perhaps if you ignored her temper tantrums? I can't believe she's totally unaware of what she's doing. She looks very intelligent.'

'I thought you knew she was autistic!'

'In my opinion autistic is a label they give to children whose parents lose control of them.'

'Get out,' said Neal. He spoke so quietly that at first neither woman thought they'd heard him properly. 'I said get out,' he repeated patiently. 'You've said quite enough. I shan't be requiring your services again, either here or in Berkshire. You'll leave before the week's out. I'll find someone new for my wife.'

'No!' protested Nurse Clarke vigorously. 'I don't mind about this job, I'm not a specialist with children, but your wife's used to me. I'm the only person she trusts and I help her. Without me she'll be totally lost.'

'It's a pity you didn't think of that before you spoke your mind.'

'You're being most unfair!' She was almost in tears and Lisa opened her mouth to speak but remained silent when Neal glanced warningly at her.

'In my opinion you're bad for my wife,' he continued calmly. 'I'm certain that a fresh face is just what she needs. Someone who won't pander to her as you do.'

'The poor woman needs someone. For all the interest you take in her, she might as well be dead.'

The genuine anguish on the nurse's face was terrible and Lisa turned away. She closed her eyes and tried to recapture some of her pleasure in the day that was rapidly becoming little more than a distant memory.

'Your loyalty's very touching,' sneered Neal. 'However, it does seem to me that such attachment to my wife isn't entirely healthy and precludes any chance of a dispassionate approach to her case. She'll be better off without you even if it's hard for her at first.'

Nurse Clarke was ashen, aware of the enormity of her mistake. She swallowed hard. 'I'm sorry about my earlier remark,' she began. 'I suppose I sounded unsympathetic but ...'

'Just go.' Neal's voice was casual. 'If you want a good reference I suggest you don't make any kind of scene when you return to collect your personal possessions. If you're right about the strength of my wife's feelings for you, then you should be able to help her make the transition to a new nurse more easily.'

Lisa saw the nurse's hands trembling and she was having trouble keeping back tears as she collected her bag and coat. 'I'm sorry' said

140

Lisa impulsively. 'I never meant ...'

The nurse glanced round and saw her employer was standing outside the front door talking to his chauffuer. 'You cunning little bitch!' she hissed. 'I can see what you're doing: playing the innocent and keeping him waiting. He won't marry you, you know. He can't, not so long as his wife's alive, and there's nothing wrong with her physical health. She could easily outlive him the way things are going, and then where will you be?'

'It isn't like that!'

'And the moon's made of green cheese, I take it? You all make me sick! None of you consider her feelings. That poor woman. I'm all she had, and now you've taken even me away. I only hope you can live with yourself.'

'Ready?' enquired Neal, and stood to one side as he let her out. 'I'm not sorry to see her go!' he continued cheerfully, turning back to Lisa. 'I've been waiting for an excuse to ... What's the matter? What did she say to you?'

'Nothing,' murmured Lisa, sitting down on the nearest chair. 'I'm a bit tired, that's all.' But she wasn't, she was suddenly seeing herself through the eyes of the nurse and she didn't like what she saw one little bit.

Neal took out his diary. 'Right, let's get organised. There's an important dinner on Saturday night that we ought to attend. Formal, your blue silk would be about right. Then on Sunday ...'

'I can't come,' she said tightly. 'You've just sacked the nurse and Jessica can't be left with an untrained babysitter these days.'

'I'll get someone who knows what autistic means by Saturday. Now, on Sunday ...'

'What about your wife?'

'Naomi?'

'Unless you've got others I don't know about.'

'Lisa, calm down.'

'I didn't like what Nurse Clarke said.'

'I thought she'd said something to you. One minute you were fine and the next you looked as though you'd just discovered there was no such person as Father Christmas.'

'Perhaps I did. She made me realise what I look like to other people. I didn't stop to think before. I'd assumed that when you said Naomi didn't like doing the social round with you, that was true.'

'It is.'

'Have you asked her to anything lately?'

'No.'

'Then for all you know, she's changed. Also, I don't like thinking of myself as just another number in a long line of women you've taken around.'

'You're not!' he protested.

'Nurse Clarke implied otherwise.'

'I'd just sacked the bloody woman, she wasn't likely to sing my praises! Use your common sense.'

'I suppose I've been naive not thinking about what it must look like to other people. We know we're only friends but ...'

'What I feel for you is far deeper than friendship. The only reason I haven't made it more obvious is because I know you're not over your disastrous marriage, but I'm not taking you around with me as an act of charity. All my contributions to charity are strictly tax-deductible!' He gave a short laugh.

Lisa sighed. 'She's spoilt it, hasn't she? I had such a lovely day as well.'

'I'm going,' he said abruptly. 'You're over-tired and not thinking straight. What does it matter if some people don't approve of you? You can't go through life pleasing everyone, and she was only an employee of mine. I could understand your attitude more if you'd been snubbed socially, but that's not going to happen. In all the years Kay and I were together it never happened to her, and I promise it won't happen to you either.'

'You don't understand what I'm talking about, but I suppose it's always different for the man.'

'It will work out all right. Just put Nurse Clarke out of your mind.'

She nodded, knowing full well that she couldn't but not wanting to spoil their day any more than she had done already. 'Do I have to wear the blue silk on Saturday?' she asked lightly.

'Of course not! Wear what you like. Why not go out and buy something new. I know a very good woman who's just starting her own business off Bond Street. She's going to be very popular, but at the moment she'll have time to work out a style that's uniquely you. I've got a card of hers somewhere.' And he began to go through his wallet.

Lisa kissed him lightly on his left cheek. 'You're very sweet. I don't know what I'd do without you at the moment.'

As he handed over the card, he smiled. 'I'll always be here,' he assured her. She thought it strange that such a reassuring remark should make the hairs at the back of her neck prickle, and as though her unease was contagious, Jessica chose that moment to begin crying.

With her awake, Neal quickly left. 'I'll let you know about a new nurse,' he promised, hurrying away. 'You could interview a couple if you like. Choose the one you feel comfortable with.'

He thought of everything, she reflected; everything to make her secure. He was also intelligent, and exuded an aura of confidence and power that was undeniably attractive. Then why, she wondered, was she so hesitant about their relationship?

During the next two hours, as she struggled to get Jessica back to sleep, she pushed the problem away. Sometimes she thought she was deliberately punishing herself by resisting becoming his mistress. As though as long as she didn't let him make love to her she wasn't harming Naomi or his children. That was the only logical way to explain her fear of total commitment to a man who obviously thought highly of her, and who could save her from having to cope alone with Jessica.

'You could have been a model!' exclaimed Carol in delight as she slipped the tape measure around Lisa's hips. 'I must thank Mr Gueras for sending you here. We'll really set them talking between us. Dramatic colours but no frills, that's how we'll do it. Of course you'd look good in a sack, but that wouldn't get me any attention! You do like clothes, I hope?' she added, breaking off a monologue that had started the moment Lisa walked in the door of the tiny shop tucked away behind Bond Street.

'I suppose so. I like to look good for special things, but the rest of the time I usually wear slacks.'

'What does Mr Gueras say about that?'

'Nothing. It isn't really his business.'

Carol pulled a small face. 'Don't tell me you think that would stop him! I was a friend of Kay's — don't worry, she was bound to get the elbow one day, it wasn't your fault — and I know he absolutely forbade her to wear slacks. You say you've got an important dinner this weekend? Well, I've got a lovely red and black number in shot silk that would probably ...'

'Kay left Neal,' interrupted Lisa.

'Sorry?'

'You said she was bound to get the elbow, but she left him. Apparently she wanted to settle down and find herself a husband.'

Carol flushed slightly. 'Very probably. I never saw her after they split up. She died before I had a chance to talk to her. Naturally I assumed ... Still, Mr Gueras should know.'

'Are you surprised that she'd leave?'

'It's nothing to do with me,' said Carol quickly. 'She always seemed potty about him, but she was getting older and perhaps ... Anyway, let's talk about something more cheeerful — like clothes!'

In a relatively short space of time, Lisa chose three evening dresses,

143

two day dresses that would be made up for her, and a selection of vivid casual clothes suitable for wearing around the house. Before she left, Carol brought her a cup of coffee and invited her into her small office. 'If you like I could work on an Autumn collection just for you. I've got the time and it would help both of us. What do you think?'

'That's the best idea I've heard for ages. Neal wanted me to go to the big fashion shows but ...'

'You'll have to go to them as well. He'll expect you to wear designer clothes most of the time, but if I do the specials and people like them I'll be made!'

'Will you really?'

'Of course. That's how it works. You've got a little girl, haven't you? How about one or two matching dresses for her. I know it's rather twee but it's still an attention grabber, and all girls like dressing up.'

Lisa shook her head. 'I don't think so.'

'Why not? I bet she's as beautiful as you, you'd look fantastic together.'

'She is beautiful,' said Lisa slowly, 'but she's also handicapped.'

Carol looked down at the floor. 'I'm sorry, I didn't realise. I'd heard Mr Gueras mention your beautiful daughter and ...'

'He did what!'

'At least *he* isn't bothered by her handicap. It was at a meeting I went to. I was trying to raise capital. He was there and said he might be able to put some custom my way and that his ... that he knew this attractive young woman with a beautiful daughter who'd be perfect for my style of clothes.'

'He must think that since people are bound to see her eventually it's better to talk about her than ignore her, which is what he does when he visits.'

'What's wrong with her?'

'She's autistic.'

'What does that mean?'

Lisa sighed. 'Unfortunately that's what most people ask. I can't explain but there's no way she could be dressed up in clothes like yours. Neal's invested in your business, has he?'

'Along with a few other people, but he's the main backer.'

'Did Kay ever wear your clothes?'

'No, she went for the town and country, Jaeger look. Besides, until recently I only designed for myself. I worked as a fashion editor for a woman's magazine − that was really tacky.'

'I hope you do well,' smiled Lisa, finishing her coffee. It was only when she was in the shop doorway that she managed to catch Carol off guard. 'How long had Kay been interested in boats?' she asked abruptly, and Carol's expression told her the answer.

Back home there were two women waiting outside the front door. The younger of them automatically took a step back when she followed Lisa indoors and saw Jessica standing naked in a corner of the room, banging her head rhythmically against the wall while a defeated-looking Mike sat in the middle of the settee, watching her.

The older woman's reactions were more reassuring. 'Poor little thing,' she said gently. 'It's difficult to understand why they're so self-destructive, isn't it? You must be frantic with worry.'

'I am,' admitted Lisa, murmuring her thanks to Mike as he slipped away. She talked to both women but it was the older of the two that she chose after discovering she'd spent three years with another autistic child, until he finally went into a home.

'I never want Jessica to go away,' said Lisa firmly. 'You see, I think that if I only spend enough time with her I might be able to break through in some way. I've got to try or I'll never know. If I sent her away and she got worse, I'd always blame myself. Is that silly?'

'Very commendable. Mind you, never is a very long time.'

'That's why I need help.'

'We'll work out a routine,' said Nurse Anthony calmly. 'Then the little one won't notice the difference when you're not here.'

'Except that it will be you and not me who's seeing to her!'

'It's the routine that matters most to them.'

'Is it?' asked Lisa despairingly. 'Don't you think people matter to her at all?'

'They might,' the nurse responded cheerfully. 'Who knows? But as long as I'm a familiar face as well as you, it should be all right. When would you like me to start?'

'Would Friday be convenient?'

'Certainly, and don't worry, Mrs Walker. We'll take care of her between us.'

When Nurse Anthony had gone, Lisa walked over to Jessica, now sitting down and making complicated patterns with her fingers. 'Time to put some clothes on,' she said quietly as she crouched in front of her daughter. For a brief moment their eyes met and immediately Jessica stiffened and her eyes slid away as she tried to scamper off on all fours. Lisa reached out but wasn't quick enough. She watched as the little girl went sideways round the room like a small crab, making huge detours past a chair and a coffee table that blocked her path. Jessica uttered harsh guttural sounds as she moved, keeping her head tilted so that it was impossible for her mother to catch her eye again.

When it became obvious that the child would continue scuttling

145

round the room until she dropped, Lisa was forced to make a lunge for her and carry her, rigid and kicking, to the settee where she began trying to put back the clothes torn off in her absence.

'To think you were offered exclusive dresses!' she said ruefully. 'Oh, Jessica, what's going to become of you?' Suddenly, Jessica lay still, staring unblinkingly at the ceiling. 'I love you,' whispered Lisa, bending down close to her daughter's ear. 'I love you more than anything on earth, do you know that? I want you to know it, Jessica. I love you, and I always will.'

Jessica didn't move, not even when tears from her mother's eyes plopped on to her upturned face. It was as though Lisa didn't exist.

By the time the Henley Regatta came round, Lisa and Neal were an established couple on the social circuit. Nurse Janice Anthony had helped Lisa find a routine that suited Jessica and she no longer had to worry about her daughter when she was out. She often thought that because she had an exciting life outside the home she was better able to cope when she was there, and coping was becoming more of a challenge as time went by.

The weather for the Regatta was perfect; warm, sunny and dry. Lisa looked wonderful. Carol had designed her a calf-length dress of floating chiffon in palest ivory, its tightly gathered waist accentuated by a wide sash in deep pink. Round the bottom of the skirt there was a generous scattering of matching rosebuds and when Lisa moved they seemed to sway in a gentle breeze. The final touch that made the dress truly outstanding was in the sleeves. These were long and shaped like an inverted 'V' inlaid with lace, ending just below the middle fingers of both hands. They were kept in place by tiny mother-of-pearl rings that fitted over the middle fingers.

Her hair was slightly longer now, curling gently to just below her ears, and although her face appeared devoid of makeup it had actually taken her over an hour in front of her makeup mirror to get such a natural look.

The amount of time and effort that had gone into her appearance brought due reward to Carol, Lisa and Neal. Lisa's photographs dominated not only the fashion magazines the following month but also some of the national papers, and so many women asked her where she'd bought her dress that Carol was swamped with orders for something similar, although she refused to duplicate what Lisa had worn, knowing that it had been right only for her.

Neal was delighted by Lisa's success. She was beginning to blossom into the kind of woman he'd always felt she could become, and if she was still restrained and diffident in company that was all to the good.

146

The last thing he wanted was a pushy woman seeking the limelight for herself.

As for Lisa, social success gave her confidence in herself. She realised that providing she looked good no one would bother to search any deeper and find out if she felt as confident as she appeared. As long as she smiled pleasantly and stayed with Neal she was perfectly safe and always had an enjoyable time. For the moment that was enough.

She was beginning to realise just how lucky she was to have him. Wherever they went, women made it obvious they found him attractive, sometimes becoming aggressive in their attempts to gain his interest. When she looked at him dispassionately she could understand it. He was young-looking for his age; fit and well built, with the self-assurance and air of authority that only money and power can bring, and he had an abundance of both. Watching him talk to some of the women in their party during the day, Lisa decided that he looked like a man who'd be a good lover — the complete antithesis of Toby.

One divorcee called Rowena spent most of the day talking to him, and kept touching him on the arm or brushing imaginary specks of fluff from his shoulders. He took her attentions patiently, but now and again he'd catch Lisa's eye and smile, so that it was obvious where his interest lay.

At the end of the day they wandered hand-in-hand back to the car. Mike was standing close by and hurried across to open the doors. Neal shook his head. 'I'll drive us home. You can take the train.'

Mike glanced at Lisa and back to his employer, his face suddenly expressionless. 'Very good, sir.'

'Have a day off tomorrow,' continued Neal expansively. 'I shouldn't need you again until Monday morning.'

'Thank you.'

Lisa smiled at him but he looked away, suddenly absorbed by the litter scattered over the grass. She slid into the passenger seat and slipped off her white satin shoes. 'That's nice! They were beginning to pinch.'

'I thought we'd go back to my flat and finish the day off with a quiet dinner at home, all right?'

She knew then that he was tired of waiting. He'd been very patient but time had run out. She either became his mistress or she'd lose him, and after watching women near him today she couldn't really complain. At least the thought didn't repulse her. She too was drawn by his self-assurance and almost old-world courtesy, and he had been extraordinarily kind to her.

'That sounds like a good idea,' she murmured.

Letting out a small sigh of relief, Neal started the engine. He talked most of the way back to London, discussing some of the people they'd met and laughing about Rowena. Lisa put in the occasional remark but as they approached London her nerve gave way and she fell silent.

'Nearly there,' he said cheerfully. 'I expect you're pretty tired.'

'Not too bad, but my feet ache!'

'You'd better lie on the sofa while I see what Mrs Howard's left in the freezer. Thank God for the microwave.'

'I'm not really all that hungry.'

'I'm sure we could both do with a drink.'

'We've been drinking all day!'

'I don't call a couple of glasses of wine drinking all day.'

'I had far more than that.'

'I'm sure a whisky would still be acceptable.'

'Very,' she responded dutifully, hoping that it would help her relax because the back of her neck felt as though it was trapped in a vice and a tight band round her forehead was threatening to turn into a bad headache.

Once inside the flat she felt even worse. Her stomach churned and she could feel that the palms of her hands were damp with perspiration. Suddenly she didn't seem able to concentrate on Neal; all she could think about was Toby. Toby hitting her while she was pinned beneath his body. Toby and Roger abusing her until she'd wished she could die from sheer shame. She even heard Toby's laughter in her ears.

'Sit on the sofa,' murmured Neal. 'You look exhausted.'

'I've got a bit of a headache,' she confessed, and waited for the look of annoyance to appear on his face.

'Don't worry, just lie down and try to rest. I won't be long.'

She closed her eyes, sank into the deeply cushioned sofa and put a spare cushion beneath her head. She moved her shoulders around in an attempt to ease the tension but instead felt sharp stabs of pain shoot up the back of her neck. Even her legs felt tense, and when Neal sat down next to her her eyes flew open and she looked at him in terror. 'I'm sorry,' she muttered. 'I can't.'

'Can't what?' he asked gently, smoothing some hair off her aching forehead.

'Sleep with you.' She'd finally said it. Now he could begin to ease her out of his life, and the thought made her want to cry.

'Not ever?'

'I don't know, but not today. I thought I could but I can't. You've

148

got every right to be annoyed. I honestly thought I could. I wanted to but ...'

'It isn't compulsory!' he teased, massaging her aching temples. 'What made you think this was exam time?'

She gave a small smile. 'Did I make it sound that bad?'

'Just about. Roll on your side and I'll massage your shoulders for you. Now, why the sudden panic?'

'It just seemed logical that after a lovely day like today, when you've had women chasing you non-stop, you'd bound to want ...'

'I didn't find Rowena in the least attractive, and since I always want you, why should I suddenly decide to start exerting emotional pressure today?'

'I don't know. That's nice! I can feel it doing me good. I suppose it was partly because I wanted to as well.'

'Good.'

'But now I don't.'

'Then we won't. Was this shoulder ever damaged? You seem to have some lesions round the joint.'

'I hurt it when Toby knocked me down once. I didn't go to the doctor because it seemed to clear up. You're very good at this,' she added as his thumbs rotated on one of the pressure points.

'Another of my hidden talents. Let's see if the lasagne's ready. I thought we'd eat off trays in here.' Swinging her legs down to the ground, Lisa was amazed to find that she not only felt better, she also felt disappointed. Contrary woman, she thought, smiling at her lack of logic.

After they'd eaten they sat together on the sofa drinking Napoleon brandy from green brandy glasses. 'Carol's dress was a great success,' he commented, running one tanned hand lightly down her arm. 'Particularly the sleeves.'

'She got the idea from Anne Boleyn. She had an extra finger on one hand and all her dresses were designed to disguise that.'

'You haven't got an extra finger, have you?'

'Certainly not!'

'I thought I'd have noticed before today! How on earth did you manage to get all these tiny pearl buttons done up?' And he ran a finger caressingly down her spine. She shivered, but with a sense of excitement.

'Carol came over and helped me dress.'

'Will she be there to undress you?'

'I doubt it!'

'How difficult are they?' he teased, and then she felt his fingers moving deftly until the back of her dress opened and he was able to

149

run his hand over her naked back. His touch was extraordinarily light, the resulting sensation highly stimulating. She wriggled slightly beneath his hand. 'Are you still attached to the sleeves by those nifty little rings?'

Quickly, she slipped them off her fingers. 'Not now.'

Neal took the brandy glass from her and then slipped off his jacket and loosened his tie. 'That's better. We might as well both be comfortable.' As he spoke he peeled the bodice of the dress down over her arms so that she was naked to the waist. He touched her carefully on the shoulder, easing her back against the cushions. When she looked into his eyes she knew that if she wanted to stop him she could, and that knowledge was enough to relax her. Lying back, she let his hands gently stroke her neck, shoulders and breasts.

After a time he put an arm beneath her legs and swung them on to the sofa, releasing the pink sash at the same time and then pulling the dress down over her hips and easing it past her thighs until she moved her legs so that he could drop the dress to the floor, leaving Lisa in sheer silk stockings and skin coloured satin french knickers.

For several minutes he sat looking at her, only his hands moving reassuringly over her upper body as he took in the full beauty of her. The porcelain skin, unmarred by any stretch marks, and the long slender legs that he'd spent so many nights imagining wrapped round him in passion.

Even now he knew that she might start to panic and so he refused to hurry but instead murmured reassuringly as he took off his clothes and lay next to her, feeling the slight tremor that was running through her whole body.

His hands wandered a little lower and when he touched her stomach she caught her breath as her flesh jumped in anticipation. Moving so that he was lying half on her and half on the settee, he put his mouth against the hollow of her neck, kissing the small pulse that was beating rapidly there. His right hand continued down, slipping beneath the waistband of her satin underwear until at last he found the soft, warm centre of her being that he'd dreamt of for so long.

Lisa gave a moan and arched slightly against the pressure of his hand. Pleased, he swiftly removed the delicate satin garment, leaving her naked except for the suspender belt and silk stockings, an erotic touch that he found highly stimulating at a time when he didn't need any further stimulus.

His searching fingers told him that she was partly ready and all at once he couldn't wait any longer but moved on top of her, gripping her tightly by the shoulders as he parted her legs with his thigh before

150

entering with a thrust as controlled as he could manage under the circumstances.

It was only then that Lisa felt a moment of terror. The weight of his body reminded her of Toby, and she tried to move back up the sofa, away from his suddenly urgent body. He wouldn't let her. His hands tightened, but he lowered his mouth to her ear and whispered his love for her, trying to calm her and take her with him as his passion mounted and he knew that he wouldn't be able to last as long as he'd hoped.

His voice soothed her. She relaxed beneath him, taking pleasure in his pleasure, enjoying the feel of a man inside her moving so urgently. Her affection for him had never been so great as at the moment he climaxed and shouted aloud before his body shuddered and trembled and he almost fell against her, murmuring her name again and again.

After a few seconds he put his arms round her, enclosing her in a safe circle while he poured out words of love that astonished her even as they made her feel cherished for the first time in her life. She herself said nothing, but felt immense gratitude for the way in which he'd helped her to make love again. She never considered her own lack of fulfilment, being thankful simply to have enjoyed his lovemaking.

Far more ominous was the fact that Neal didn't consider it either.

Chapter Fourteen

Exactly a month after becoming Neal Gueras's mistress, Lisa met Renato Bellini for the first time. Far from losing interest once he'd possessed her, Neal – much to Bishop's annoyance – was more obsessed than ever. He showered her with jewellery and clothes, but never perfume. Not after his one mistake. He was a man who'd survived because he never made the same mistake twice. He also wanted her with him whenever possible. If it hadn't been for Jessica, he'd have spent more time in the week at the small mews cottage, but Jessica was too much for him and so weekdays were Lisa's alone.

She was grateful because it gave her the time she needed to devote to her daughter. The older Jessica grew, the more obvious her handicap became and the greater the strain on Lisa. From being a withdrawn, anti-social child who threw the occasional tantrum, Jessica had become a child who was permanently angry. She was either busy demolishing items in the home or inflicting physical damage on herself. Oblivious to pain, she would bang her head against walls, tear out sections of her hair until the scalp bled, jump all the way down the stairs, run full tilt into doors, or sometimes sit silently scratching at her skin until it was red raw.

Lisa was at her wit's end. Only the knowledge that the following month she had an appointment with a top expert on autism kept her going. She followed Jessica everywhere, forever catching her when she jumped, restraining her when she tried to hit her head and trying to divert her attention, channel the ceaseless energy into more useful outlets. This was impossible. Jessica seemed determined to maim herself, regarding all Lisa's attempts to save her as infuriating interference.

Music still pleased her but no longer had the ability to keep her silent. Instead she would hum or sing along with the sounds even as she tugged at her hair. One afternoon when it was raining, Lisa took

Jessica on her lap and tried to read to her. Her daughter's terror at being held was pitiful. She screamed and kicked, all her joints locked with fear or hatred. She didn't seem to mind being read to, but only once she was safely off Lisa's lap and sitting in a corner facing the wall, secure in her self-inflicted isolation.

She also became difficult over food, refusing to eat anything solid. All her food had to be put through the blender unless it was Farex. Because of this, Lisa took to giving her bottles again. At least that way she knew exactly how much milk Jessica had taken, and could be certain that she'd had the vitamin drops her strange diet made necessary.

On the rare occasions when Jessica became absorbed in dismantling a toy or watching her hands move in front of her face, her outstanding good looks made the situation seem even more tragic. She had the face of a serene beauty and yet lived out her days in frantic terror and torment.

On the Saturday that she was to meet Bellini, Lisa endured a particularly difficult day, made worse both by Janice Anthony having the day off and a terrible feeling of lethargy that left her utterly drained. From five in the morning until seven at night she'd coped with everything Jessica quite literally threw at her, and when Janice arrived back she found her employer almost on her knees with exhaustion.

'Why not go to bed,' she said sympathetically. 'I'll bring you up a light supper after Jessica's asleep. You look all in.'

'I can't,' said Lisa regretfully. 'I've got to go out tonight. It's a business dinner and Neal particularly wants me there. Apparently someone important's come to live in London and I'm to be introduced!'

'Then you'd better rest for half an hour. He won't want you looking like a washed out rag.'

'I'll put on some eye gel while I rest, that might improve me a bit! At least I've got all Barbara Daly's beauty tips. According to her, make-up can conceal anything you want. In this case, the whole face!'

Janice shook her head. She worried about Lisa. She was more wrapped up in her child than any mother Jancie had met and was also trying to be the perfect partner to an important man with no time for Jessica. As a result she couldn't ever complain about how she felt.

'One of them will have to go,' she muttered, opening a jar of baby food meant for a child half Jessica's age. 'She can't go on like this.'

She was amazed by Lisa's appearance when she finally came downstairs an hour later. All signs of strain were gone. Her hair had been set on heated rollers and framed her face in soft curls. She wore a long, figure-hugging dress in dark grey silk with vivid slashes of turquoise and black cutting diagonally across the bodice and skirt.

'I don't know how you do it!' she exclaimed admiringly.

'Nor do I! What's more, I don't think I can for much longer.'

'Something will crack,' Janice agreed.

'Undoubtedly me! Listen, there's the car. See you in the morning.'

'Will you be back tonight?'

Lisa hesitated. 'I hope so but I'm not sure.'

'As long as you enjoy yourself.'

'Let's hope I do.'

She opened the door before Neal had time to ring the bell, walking quickly to the car. She didn't want him to see the chaos in the downstairs room, or the mark on the kitchen door where Jessica had hurled a bottle of blackcurrant juice. By tomorrow Janice would have it all cleared up and he need never know.

'You look wonderful!' he greeted her. 'I'm sure you get more beautiful every day.'

'You say that to all the ladies! Now, what do I need to know about tonight's guests?'

As the car rolled smoothly away from the kerb, Neal closed the partition between them and the driver. 'There's only one person who matters tonight, and that's the Italian, Renato Bellini. I'm very anxious that he should feel welcome, and it's important to my business that nothing spoils his visit. We'll be seeing him again, of course, but first impressions are very important.'

'What's his wife like?'

'I don't think there is one. She died or he divorced her, I'm not sure which.'

'There's quite a difference!'

'It isn't important,' he said irritably, and Lisa quickly suppressed her smile.

'How nice should I be to him?' she enquired with mock innocence.

'As nice as possible, of course.' He glanced at her questioning expression. 'Not *that* nice, but . . .'

'It's all right, I know what you mean! Is he easy to get on with or am I going to find the evening a bit difficult?' She hoped not; the day had been bad enough. She didn't fancy spending the evening pandering to a difficult adult.

'He likes women, you'll be fine.'

'If he liked men we were both in trouble! All right,' she added quickly, 'no more jokes, I promise!'

When Renato Bellini's red Ferrari drew up outside the Chelsea flat he felt curiously excited. He'd heard so much about this new woman of Neal's that he was eager to see her for himself. He was the last of the six guests to arrive but when he walked into the room all conversation stopped.

His eyes swept the room until they came to rest on the woman he'd been waiting to see. The woman who, according to all reports, had caused Neal Gueras to lose his business grip. His first thought was that she was as far removed from his vision of a *femme fatale* as it was possible to be. Tall, slim and fragile-looking, he received no immediate message of sexuality from her. Instead he experienced an overwhelming desire to protect her from the complicated web of intrigue and deceit in which she was now involved. A desire as futile as it was alien to his nature. He knew he was already too late.

Only when the other guests began to murmur among themselves did he realise he'd been staring at her for too long. Immediately he walked with long, smooth strides across the room and shook hands with Neal, giving him the briefest smile possible. 'I am late it appears. My apologies,' he said politely.

'Not at all,' responded Neal, who'd noticed the attention given to Lisa and felt flattered that his choice of woman was so appreciated. 'I don't believe you've met Lisa. Lisa, my dear, this is Renato Bellini, one of the Italian banking family.'

Lisa held out her hand, faintly overwhelmed by the size of the man. He was considerably taller than anyone else in the room, and with his large shoulders and leonine head, topped by a mass of wavy, unruly hair, was the most unlikely Italian imaginable.

Bending over her hand he lifted it to his mouth, allowing his lips to brush lightly against her skin. A shiver ran up her arm and she found her eyes caught by his. For a brief moment they might have been the only two people in the room. 'I've heard a lot about you,' she said quietly.

'And I you. You are not at all what I expected.'

'In what way?'

He smiled with all of his charm but his eyes were solemn. 'You are far more beautiful, and far too young for my friend, Neal!'

Lisa laughed lightly, well aware that Neal wasn't in the least amused. 'How kind of you. I must admit that you're not at all what I expected either.'

'In what way is that?'

'I thought all Italians were small and dark.'

'It appears we are both a grave disappointment to each other!' he retorted, but his eyes said otherwise, and Lisa was astonished by the thrill of pleasure simply talking to him was giving her. She felt like a twelve-year-old girl in the presence of her favourite pop star. It was

155

both ridiculous and yet in a strange way a relief because now she knew for certain that Toby hadn't made it impossible for her to react strongly to a man. Immediately she realised how disloyal to Neal her behaviour was and her reply to Bellini was more a rebuke to herself than to him.

'Not at all. I've learnt never to expect too much and so I usually manage to avoid disappointment.'

'I am put firmly in my place,' he said quietly, but he never took his amazing copper-coloured eyes from hers.

Neal drew in his breath sharply. 'That sounded rather impolite, Lisa.'

'I'm sorry, it wasn't meant to. Well, since Mr Bellini has finally arrived, may I suggest we all go in to dinner?'

As he'd hoped, Renato found himself seated next to his hostess but was sorry to find that she seemed uneasy in his presence. He resolved to set about putting matters right between them. He wanted her to like him. One day she might need a powerful friend.

'How old is your daughter?' he asked, aware that the quickest way to many women's hearts was through their children. He was surprised to see Lisa flush slightly and when she picked up her wine glass her hand was trembling.

'Nearly two.'

'A very demanding age. What's her name?'

'Jessica.' Her voice was so low he couldn't catch what she'd said.

'Phillipa?'

'No, Jessica.' This time she spoke more loudly. By chance it was during a brief lull in general conversation and Neal heard. He looked down the table and frowned at her. Renato, apparently busy with his pâté, caught the look and wondered at its cause.

'I too have a child,' he said quickly. 'A little boy of four, Luciano. I have a picture somewhere if you'd like to see it?'

'Yes please.'

Taking his wallet from his inside pocket he handed her a colour snap taken at Christmas when his son had been given his first pony. He was standing by it, grinning broadly, and Lisa instinctively smiled in response. 'He's very handsome, and happy too by the look of it.'

'He can be shy but generally he's happy, yes. Do you have a photo of your little girl? She is undoubtedly beautiful if her mother is anything to go by.'

'Don't bother trying to charm me, Mr Bellini. I'm distrustful of too much charm. Experience has taught me it can't be relied upon.'

He raised his eyebrows. 'How sad. A little flirtation is fun for everyone. Perhaps you take things too seriously?'

'Perhaps.'

'And you have no photo?'

She sighed. Was the wretched man never going to give up talking about children? she wondered. 'No, no photographs. My daughter's handicapped.'

'In what way?'

If he hadn't been important to Neal she would have told him to mind his own business. It was soul destroying when people looked blank every time she explained about Jessica, but she realised that it was the only way to stop Bellini. 'She's autistic,' she murmured, hoping Neal couldn't hear her.

'An interesting condition but tragic for the people concerned. You have my sympathy. I take it that Neal doesn't like you talking about her?'

She hesitated, torn between loyalty to Neal and a desire to explain to the first person ever to show genuine understanding, exactly what it was like for her these days. Bellini kept his eyes fixed on her in a steady appraisal that she found unnerving.

'No,' she admitted. 'He finds Jessica's condition rather distasteful I think, and he certainly wouldn't want me telling you about her. I try not to burden him with details because I know how angry it makes him.'

'Angry?' His raised one eyebrow. 'Angry with you?'

'Yes, he thinks she should go into a home.'

'And you don't?'

'No, I . . .' She glanced round the table and realised that people were looking at them. 'You can't be interested,' she said quickly. 'Did I introduce you to Felicity Whitehead? She spent a year in Italy doing art. You should have a lot to talk about.'

Renato glanced briefly at the woman on his right then back to Lisa. 'I'd rather continue talking to you.'

'Well, you can't.' She wished her heart would stop pounding so hard. 'It's impolite.'

'Then I will try and talk about art, but we will continue our discussion some other time, yes?'

She gave him the briefest of smiles, her eyes straying nervously back to Neal. 'Perhaps.'

When dinner finally ended and the men were alone with the port, Neal and Renato stood together in a corner of the room. For the first time there was a distinct hint of antagonism between them, although only Neal's face revealed this. Renato's expression was agreeable; he was apparently oblivious of any undertones in the conversation.

'You seemed to enjoy the dinner,' said Neal tightly.

157

'You have a good chef. I rarely manage to eat well in England. Everything is over-cooked and lacking in taste.'

'Perhaps the conversation helped.'

'You are certainly a fortunate man. My hostess is an exceptionally lovely young woman.'

'I thought all Italian men liked voluptuous women!' Neal's smile was strained.

'And we Italians believe that all Englishmen are bad lovers. I am quite sure such generalisations are ludicrous!'

Neal blinked in surprise. There was a look in Bellini's eyes that he didn't care for, and the insult was no less blatant for being disguised as a joke. He counted silently to ten, remembering that the Italian wouldn't always be in England but while he was he had to be treated civilly.

'Of course,' he managed at last. 'How are things in the banking world?'

'In the world in general, very good. For us personally, not quite so wonderful. I have much to do here. It is possible that our director is not entirely honest.'

'You were robbed a while back, weren't you?'

'That is my father's affair. I deal with more mundane matters.'

Like hell you do, thought Neal to himself. Not only was Renato physically big and fit, it was plain that his mind was razor sharp. This was no playboy on a trip to England to justify his income.

'How is your good wife?' asked Renato casually.

'Being good in the heart of the country.'

The Italian's eyes were appraising. 'We heard she was unwell.'

'She's asthmatic but that's under control. No, the truth is, Naomi doesn't care for the bright lights of London. She's a home bird at heart.'

'How fortunate then that you have the lovely Lisa to deputise for her.'

'Yes.'

'A beautiful companion and an understanding wife. Your life is well organised. Such a pity about Kay Masters.'

Neal stared at him. 'Did you know her?'

'We were acquainted.'

'I didn't know.'

Renato shrugged. 'It was nothing. Ships that pass in the night, yes? Now, perhaps we should join the ladies? I would like to talk to the young woman who spent a year studying art in my country and speaks only of the men she met there!'

'Felicity's talked of nothing but Italians since she got back.'

'Living proof that an empty head does not mean an empty bed. Personally, I prefer a woman of some intelligence.'

'You do?'

'Certainly! And you?'

'There can be disadvantages.'

'I suppose so.'

The conversation irritated Neal out of all proportion. Even when Bellini left with Felicity he continued to feel annoyed, and once all the guests had gone he vented his ill-humour on Lisa.

'When I asked you to be nice to Bellini, I didn't mean you had to monopolise him during the entire meal.'

Utterly exhausted, Lisa was sitting slumped on the very sofa where they had first become lovers. 'I couldn't stop him talking.'

'He must have been bowled over by your I.Q. He's keen on intelligent women.'

'Then he's in for a shock tonight. Felicity only reads strip cartoons.'

'You liked him, didn't you?' demanded Neal, standing in front of her and looking down on her bent head.

'I'm not too keen on such practised charm but he was pleasant enough.'

'Come now, you were head to head during dinner! What did you talk about if he wasn't charming you all the time?'

'His son,' she said wearily, unaware that Neal was both annoyed and jealous.

'I'd have thought a man of his education would have better things to talk about than a four-year-old child.'

'Perhaps he thought I wouldn't understand the intricacies of banking. Look, I'm tired and I'd imagined things went well tonight. If you aren't pleased, I'm sorry, but right now I want to go home.'

'I thought that was coming. You aren't exactly eager for love-making, are you?'

'Not tonight.'

'Not any night.'

She looked at him in surprise. 'That's not true. I enjoy it, but ...'

'I don't think you do enjoy it.'

Lisa felt like screaming at him to shut up. She was so tired she could scarcely concentrate on what he was saying. She knew that for the first time he was annoyed with her, but she didn't know what she'd done. 'I thought I'd made it plain enough.'

'You say the right things but you never climax, do you?'

'Look, this isn't really the right time ...'

'Why not? I've already heard what rotten lovers Englishmen are

159

once this evening. You could make it a double.'

She swallowed hard. He sounded so aggressive it was like going back in time. Surely she couldn't be making a second mistake? she thought frantically. 'Don't do this!' she shouted at last. 'I can't help it. If I'm not satisfactory you'd better find someone else but don't start picking a quarrel with me because I can't stand it, not again.' She burst into tears.

All the annoyance drained out of Neal and he looked at her shaking shoulders in consternation. How could he have been so stupid? he wondered. He'd let the Italian get under his skin and then risked losing Lisa simply because he hadn't been able to vent his annoyance on Bellini himself. Feeling ashamed he put a hand gently on the back of her neck.

'I'm sorry, darling. I can't think what got into me. I didn't mean it.'

'You did!' she sobbed. 'I know I'm not very good in bed yet, but I thought you understood. You seemed to, and I do like you making love to me. It's only that tonight I'm too tired.'

He sat next to her and pulled her against him, making soothing noises as he ran his fingers through her hair. 'It's all right,' he whispered. 'It was my fault not yours. I was jealous of the attention Bellini paid you.'

'Jealous?' She lifted her head in astonishment. 'Jealous of a business colleague?'

'I'm afraid so. He was sitting talking to you and I wasn't. Ludicrous, isn't it!'

She rested her face against his. 'I only talked to him because you asked me to.'

'You didn't find him attractive?'

She thought of the shiver of excitement that had gone through her when he'd kissed her hand and remembered the compassion she'd seen in his expressive eyes when she was talking about Jessica. 'No,' she lied. 'He isn't my type at all.'

He held her for a few more minutes and then took hold of her hand. 'I'll get you home. I suppose it's Jessica wearing you out again?'

'Not entirely. I've felt off colour all day.'

'Spend some time in bed tomorrow. On your own, of course!'

They both laughed and Lisa tried not to imagine what it might be like to lie next to the tall Italian, with the long-fingered, sensitive hands, who'd wanted to talk to her again. She didn't dare to think about him. Not now, when she was just beginning to believe that in Neal she had everything she could possibly want. No, this was no time for adolescent daydreams.

* * *

As dinner parties went this wasn't going to be a particularly exciting one, thought Renato Bellini ruefully as he struggled with his bow tie. He wouldn't have bothered to go if it weren't for the fact that their banking director had organised it especially in his honour. Refusal would have been insulting.

He glanced at his diary to see who he was taking with him before remembering that Giovanni had offered to supply an extra woman. Had, in fact, been most anxious to supply an extra woman. It didn't bother Renato; he would be charming and never see her again. His life was full of such women. Sometimes he wondered if they found it embarrassing. In their place, he would.

Before leaving, he looked in on his son. He was the complete opposite of his father, who worshipped him even more as a result. Renato lightly touched the sleeping boy's head and murmured a prayer for his safety. Of his mother, the gentle French girl, Hélène, who had killed herself during post-natal depression, Renato thought not at all. The marriage had been good for business but she had never touched his heart. Only their child had managed that.

As he left the room, Luciano turned and murmured in his sleep. Did he think of his mother? wondered Renato. Was it possible that he could remember her? He'd only been ten months old when she died but there was the studio portrait by his bed that he always kissed at night, and probably there were fantasies that had assumed the stamp of reality over the years. He needed a mother, but Renato would never marry again without love. His marriage was the only time in his life that he'd felt lonely, an experience he had no wish to repeat.

His host and hostess greeted him effusively. There was a touch of anxiety in Giovanni Muti's eyes, but he hid it behind a spate of rapid Italian in which he gave Renato information on some of the guests before leading him to a small group of five, including the girl who was quite obviously the extra women.

'This is Deborah Sinclair,' said Giovanni with a note of pride. Renato wondered why being the third daughter of a minor Scottish earl should be considered any great achievement but plainly Giovanni was impressed by her. He took her hand, raised it to his lips and kissed the air above it; a token gesture that charmed whilst being meaningless.

Deborah, who'd seen Bellini several times in Italy and France without ever having been introduced, felt her pulse race but she kept her light blue eyes cool and smiled, her head tilted becomingly to the left because Terry O'Neill had once told her it gave her a kittenish charm.

Renato's dark eyes swept over her in swift appraisal. She was a little

161

over average height, and her dark blonde hair was swept up into a complicated french pleat that would probably be quite difficult to release should he so wish.

She had a lovely complexion, but he'd noticed that this was true of most British women, and was certainly very attractive if not quite beautiful. He moved slightly closer to her, not close enough for their bodies to touch but close enough for her to think that they might, and smiled carefully.

'Giovanni tells me you work,' he said smoothly, wondering why he was bothering to soften his voice when she really didn't interest him at all.

'Not exactly. I've set up my own bureau in London. I put people in touch with other people who work!'

'I do not understand.'

'Well, *I* don't actually do anything. I don't design clothes or help in a nursery school or cook meals for people's parties, but I know loads of people who actually do these things and I give their names and numbers to other people who want a dress by a new designer or ...'

'Or a child from a nursery school?' he queried, half-turning his body towards her and thus effectively isolating them from the rest of the group. She managed a flicker of a smile but he decided that humour wasn't her style.

'You do get paid?' he asked, wondering if her dress was a Saint Laurent. It was a fuchsia pink velvet with a plunging neckline, crossing over at mid-thigh and caught up by a black bow beneath her left breast. This meant that he could see the top of her breasts, virtually all of her legs — which were shapely and attractive — but none of her arms or hands because it was long-sleeved and she wore matching wrist-length gloves with three buttons on the side. He thought he'd enjoy peeling off the gloves.

'I get some commission if that's what you mean.' She was plainly embarrassed. 'The main thing is, it makes me feel useful,' she rushed on. 'I got so tired of doing nothing all day. Sometimes I used to go off to Paris on a spending spree because I was utterly bored. That can't be right, can it? Not when children are starving in Ethiopia.'

'I doubt if they'd begrudge you your Parisian wardrobe. They're more interested in food than clothes!'

'Now you're teasing me!' She gave a little giggle that could have come from the mouth of Fiona, Isabella, Alexandra or any of the other girls he'd met in London recently.

'Just a little,' he agreed, putting a hand lightly on her left wrist and drawing her away from the group. 'Let's find ourselves another drink

162

and some space,' he suggested, feeling guilty because he was being totally irrational tonight.

Deborah was probably a very nice girl, and she was typical of all the women he met these days. These were people he was used to, the type of women he'd always enjoyed. Until yesterday night when he saw Neal Gueras's girlfriend. He glanced down at Deborah's upturned face and saw that her mouth was soft and moist. He might take her home with him after all. He could hardly start leading the life of a monk because of a woman he didn't really know.

'What do you think of him?' Eleanor Muti asked Deborah as they went in to dinner.

'Divine! He's so exciting. And those eyes! I feel as though he's looking right through me and knows everything I'm thinking!'

'He's single!' laughed Eleanor. 'What a catch he'd be. He's incredibly rich, you know. Italian bankers always are.'

'Giovanni's an Italian banker.'

'He only works for Renato's family. He doesn't own any bank. I wish he did.'

'You're not exactly poor, darling!' responded Deborah a trifle tartly.

'Heaven forbid, but there's money and there's money! Come along, Julia St Clair's been watching you both like a hawk. She's obviously longing to get herself introduced to Renato, and you know what she's like once she's got a foot in the door.'

'I haven't heard anything about her feet!' laughed Deborah, and the two women went into the dining-room together.

Renato ate the salmon mousse, the poached turbot, the pink roast beef and the strawberry shortcake automatically, but afterwards he couldn't have said what he'd eaten. His attention had been caught by a young woman further down the table. She had titian hair that fell in carefully controlled ringlets to her exposed shoulders, and her black taffeta dress rustled every time she moved, making him think of silk underwear and creamy skin that a man could bury himself in.

Once or twice he glanced sideways at her and when their eyes met she was always the one to look away from his unblinking appraisal, but there was the suggestion of a smile round her lips and he noticed that when she curled her fingers round the stem of her wine glass, she ran her thumb lightly down the side in a gesture plainly intended for him.

After dinner the women withdrew while the men began to talk of share prices, shooting parties and horses. Only the horses interested Renato and once he'd discovered that none of the men really knew anything about horseflesh he sat silently, curled up in a vast leather

163

armchair, wondering about the girl with the titian hair.

'We'd better rejoin the ladies,' said Giovanni at last, noticing his guest's silence.

'I wonder what they talk about?' mused one middle-aged man.

'Us!' laughed Giovanni.

'How to catch us if they're single and how to keep us away from them if they're married to us!' retorted a cynical-looking man in his late thirties.

'Do you think that's true, Renato?' asked Giovanni, wishing his guest of honour wasn't so quiet. It made him wonder if the auditor had spotted some error in the bank's accounts.

'Undoubtedly, but I don't hold them to blame. If we're so desirable early on then it's our duty to remain so!'

'Wait until you're married!' retorted the cynic. 'You can try every trick in the book but they'll still spend their lives with headaches and female problems.'

'Then find a mistress. If she too becomes unwell, you might perhaps begin to wonder where the blame lies!' smiled Renato, but the smile was too sharp, the eyes too challenging, for his companion to object as he normally would. This man wasn't to be trifled with, they all knew that, and so he swallowed the insult and gave a light laugh.

'You may be right, but probably Italian women are naturally more sensuous. All that hot weather, I expect!'

Ignorant pig! thought Renato, smiling again and standing back until only he and Giovanni were left. 'The auburn-haired woman in the black dress, Gianni. Is she alone?'

'Not exactly. She came with James Hatherley-West, but he's not really interested in her. She's just one of the women he uses as a cover. He needs to marry and it's vital that no one . . .'

'Quite. Is she married?'

'Widowed once and divorced once. She's . . .'

'Yes?'

'Very friendly.'

Renato was genuinely amused. 'I wasn't looking for a virgin!'

'You don't like Deborah?'

'She's a very nice girl and therefore not my type at all! No, seriously, I do like her which is why I couldn't possibly get involved. She'd cling, Gianni. I imagine she's like ivy − very difficult to prise loose!'

'She's a friend of Eleanor's.'

'Enough said! I shall naturally take her home to her little flat but I might, I think, arrange for this Julia to go to my house later on. You

164

may inform her escort of my intentions. He could be pleased to have a night to visit his boyfriend.'

Julia felt a thrill of excitement run through her when Bellini approached. She knew exactly what was coming and hadn't been as excited for several years. He was unbelievably attractive and she'd watched him moving round the room with a panther-like grace that told her he'd be a wonderful lover.

As for his eyes, they were so full of experience and promise she could barely control herself when he looked her way. There was no point in being coy when he finally approached her. He wasn't the kind of man to want her to play games. They were certainly two of a kind when it came to sex.

'I have to take someone home, Julia' he said quietly. She was surprised that he knew her name. 'I've called a cab to take you to my apartment so that you'll be there when I return. I trust this suits you?'

'Very nice,' she said diffidently, but her eyes sparkled with anticipation.

He reached out and ran one finger lightly down the side of her neck. 'You have wonderful skin.'

'It bruises easily.'

'I'll remember that. Until later then.' Much to her surprise he turned away without even a token kiss of her hand. She was almost shaking with desire and as soon as he left with Deborah Sinclair – a born loser, if ever she'd seen one – she collected her wrap and said goodnight to the Mutis. Eleanor's smile was fixed, her eyes cold with annoyance, while Gianni gave a non-committal shrug as though he were no longer surprised by anything she managed to do.

Julia didn't care. She'd wanted Bellini's hands on her body from the moment she first saw him lunching in the marble courtyard of the Georges Cinque in Paris two summers ago, but she'd been married then and he'd been with a group of dark-suited, hard-talking business men. Tonight was her first sight of him since, and she'd certainly managed to make the most of it. The car that took her to Eaton Square was no normal cab. When it halted, the driver carefully escorted her into the ground floor apartment which occupied the width of two adjoining buildings.

'The Signor will be here soon,' he assured her, opening the door into a double reception room. It had a pale grey carpet, cool blue settees and armchairs. They were littered with huge grey scatter cushions that looked as though a small child had been playing with them, as indeed Luciano had on his visit earlier in the day.

'The visitor's bathroom is off to your left,' the driver told her.

'And the bedrooms?'

'The Signor will show you those. Goodnight, signora.'

She was allowed to bathe but not to slip between the sheets, she thought with amusement, but deciding against a bath sank down in one of the chairs, having first removed the cushions and thrown them into a corner of the room.

On the glass-topped coffee table in the middle of the room was the usual collection of magazines. It was only when she finally felt too tense to sit doing nothing that she picked one up and very nearly dropped it as she found herself looking at some of the most erotic pornographic photographs she'd ever seen in her decidedly unsheltered life.

She was so deeply engrossed in them that she failed to hear him enter the room, nor did she see the satisfied yet faintly contemptuous expression on his face as he saw what she was reading and knew that once again he'd been right and they would have a marvellous night.

'Come,' he said harshly. 'We've wasted too much time.'

Julia had never been propelled out of a room so firmly, nor had she ever been before held tightly by one wrist while a man unlocked a bedroom door and then almost flung her inside. Nursing her bruised wrist, she stared about her.

There were mirrors everywhere. Floor-length mirrors on every cupboard door, a mirror above the headboard of the super-king-sized bed, with a mirror directly overhead taking up most of the ceiling.

'I need to shave closely,' said Renato with a smile. 'The mirrors assist.'

'Who did that?' enquired Julia, pointing at a painting on the wall depicting a man and a woman closely entwined, the woman's mouth open in ecstasy as the man entered her from an impossible angle with a disproportionately large male organ.

'I've no idea. He must have been a keep-fit fanatic!'

'I meant who painted it?'

'As a matter of fact, I did.'

'You?'

'You're surprised? I have many talents, but not all of them will interest you.'

She began to slide the side zip of her dress down but he put out a hand to stop her. 'I will do it in time. You liked the photographs in the other room?'

Julia knew the game – the prolonged teasing, the extensive foreplay – and normally she loved it, but this time she simply wanted to feel him penetrate her. She wanted him inside her body, she wanted ...

'Of what do you think, Julia?' he enquired calmly, smiling inwardly at the light flush staining her magnolia skin.

'I was thinking that I wanted you.'

'Perhaps a drink first? A brandy or ...'

'I've had enough bloody drink at that boring party.'

He shook his head. 'Swearing is only attractive in women once their clothes are off! Besides, a connoisseur in love such as yourself must surely enjoy the preliminaries?'

'Usually, yes.'

'Good. I will pour us some brandy.'

Julia watched the way he walked with a measured stride to the concealed drinks cabinet, and wished he'd take off his jacket so that she could see the muscles across his shoulders.

'In the day there is a lovely view of the square from here,' he informed her, as though he genuinely thought she'd care. 'Here, your drink.'

He never took his eyes off her as she once again ran her thumb down the stem of the glass before tilting it and swallowing the brandy, her exposed throat moving as the liquid passed down it.

Renato took off his jacket and tie and undid the top buttons of his shirt before removing the glass from Julia's hand while pressing her back towards the bed. He eased her shoes off her feet and then turned his attention to the zip of the dress which he quickly slid from her body.

All she wore beneath the dress was a suspender belt and stockings and he smiled his approval. She was full-breasted with a small waist but rounded hips and thighs. In time she would become fat, but not yet. At this moment in time she was almost perfect. It wouldn't last much longer, she was a rose at its moment of absolute beauty, and he appreciated the fact as he knelt down beside the bed and buried his mouth between her breasts.

He enjoyed the feel of her creamy skin, the fullness of her buttocks that he cupped in his hands as he lifted her slightly in order to move his mouth between her thighs. She tried to keep him there by gripping them together but his hands moved up and held her so that she had no control over when he stopped.

He kept her trembling deliciously on the edge of her first orgasm for what seemed an eternity, moving hands and mouth from her head to her toes until every nerve end was screaming out for release. Finally, he moved fully over her, his huge body poised above her, and for one brief moment she wondered if she could possibly take him inside her. He saw the doubt in her eyes, but was used to that and murmuring assurances he began to ease his way inside her, enveloped by the moist warmth that he'd known she would possess.

As he began to thrust she began to moan, her head moving from side to side, and she gripped his shoulders in desperation, urging him on. Using all the words he'd expected and some that he hadn't.

It was then, at the very moment when he normally felt the greatest pleasure, just as Julia's body began to arch in an uncontrollable spasm of relief, that he lost all his desire for her. She wasn't perfect, she was over-ripe. There was too much creamy flesh, too much expertise in the way she touched him and in the words she uttered.

She wasn't what he wanted. He wanted a tall, slim, dark-haired girl with a finely honed beauty that would never turn to fleshy opulence, and whose touch would be more hesitant but instinctive.

Julia didn't notice any change. Renato's desire turned in seconds to dislike bordering on hatred, and it was this hatred that carried him through. He thrust into her savagely, ignoring her screams of ecstasy − genuine or assumed − pounding his fury with himself into her until her screams were tinged with pain and she tried to loosen his huge hands from where they were gripping her breasts, but he wasn't to be moved and continued thrusting into her long after she'd climaxed until finally, with a shout of despair that Julia mistook for pleasure, he ejaculated violently and then almost threw himself off her, turning on his side so that he didn't have to look at her face.

For five minutes or more she lay quietly, feeling somewhat sore but definitely satisfied. Eventually she touched him lightly on the shoulder but he shrugged her hand away. She sighed to herself. So many men were like that once it was over, but for some reason she'd expected better from him.

At last he got himself under control and turned to her, putting one hand beneath her chin and kissing her lightly on the cheek.

'You were wonderful, *cara*. You are made for love.'

'For sex,' she corrected him dryly.

'Most of us are made for sex, love is usually the more acceptable word.'

'Not to me.'

He was relieved that he'd chosen her. His behaviour would have hurt and bewildered little Deborah, who worked without working and wanted a husband.

'We must get dressed and leave,' he said slowly. 'I shall return to my son tonight.'

'Where does he live?'

'In another of my London apartments. This one is for beautiful women, the other for my work and my son!'

'How practical. No wife?'

'She died.'

'Perhaps you would get someone to drive me home?' she asked as she slipped on the crumpled black taffeta dress.

'I myself will take you.'

'No thank you. A driver will be fine.'

She had noticed, he thought regretfully. A pity, it wasn't her fault. 'As you wish.'

'Tell me, Renato, since we won't be meeting again – at least let me know one thing. Are you looking for love any more, or have you given up as I have?'

He smiled a half-smile and his amazing eyes stared thoughtfully into the distance. 'I look for nothing, but I think that one day I might find something by mistake.'

'Lucky girl!' said Julia with feeling. He pressed a bell and knew that she'd be taken home safely. An unusual woman but an honest one, which made a change.

Chapter Fifteen

That weekend, Neal was due to go home to his family again. He apologised profusely but Lisa was secretly grateful to have some time to herself. These days she was permanently tired, and the thought of three evenings free was bliss, although she knew she'd miss his company. It was just that sometimes she wished their entire life didn't revolve round social functions. They had so little time to themselves, and when they were alone all that Neal wanted to do was take her to bed.

However, by the Sunday afternoon she'd decided that life without him wasn't so desirable. Thirty-six hours of Jessica seemed like thirty-six weeks. There was no longer any doubt her behaviour was deteriorating. She was impossible to toilet train, squatting down whenever the mood took her whether she was out in the shops, playing in the secluded garden area or sitting on her mother's bed. She also hated wearing clothes, and was forever tearing them off, taking great delight in the feel of various textures on her bare skin.

'How about the park?' suggested Lisa after lunch. Jessica stared at the floor. 'Remember the park? You liked it there. We saw a boat, didn't we?'

For an instant she thought something stirred behind Jessica's eyes, but then it was gone and her daughter looked away as she scuttled into a corner and began to gnaw on her thumb.

'Park,' reiterated Lisa. 'Let's get a jacket on you. It's beginning to turn cooler in the afternoons.'

An hour later, and wondering if it had been worth the effort, Lisa finally managed to strap her daughter into the pushchair and set off. The park was crowded with children making the most of a sunny September afternoon. Jessica tried to twist round and hide her face in the back of her pushchair, making mewing sounds of fright and clawing at the striped canvas. Lisa sat on a bench and gently pushed her to and fro until the sounds stopped and she settled herself into a bunched heap with her chin down on her chest.

She recognised him the moment he came through the park gates. His height alone made him stand out, but the thick windswept hair and the distinctly Roman nose were what caught her eye. That and the athletic way in which he moved. He was very light on his feet for such a big man.

Coming directly across to her, he sat down so close that she felt she ought to move away but was terrified of disturbing Jessica.

'How pleasant, Mrs Walker. I'd hoped to find you here,' he said cheerfully.

'It's only our second visit.'

'I am very fortunate. And this is your daughter?'

She was glad he didn't attempt to touch Jessica. 'Yes.'

'You look worried.'

'I'm terrified of what she's going to do. She's been very difficult today.'

'It's a lovely day.'

'Yes.' She wondered how she could carry on such an inane conversation when her stomach was churning and her hands shaking simply because he was sitting next to her, his left leg touching hers.

'What's the matter?' he asked gently. 'Is it me you're afraid of, or what I'll think of your daughter?'

You, she thought despairingly. I'm afraid of you because you make me realise that I'm not like I thought, and at the moment I'm cheating Neal and cheating myself because he doesn't make me feel like this and he should. 'Neither,' she lied.

'I wonder what life must be like for her?' he mused, letting his hand rest on top of the pushchair. 'It is hard enough for ordinary people. No wonder some children opt out straight away.'

'Is that what you think autistic children do?'

'It's one theory, and seems to make sense. Perhaps they're exceptionally sensitive children who can't cope with ordinary childhood experiences, therefore they cut themselves off; pretend the rest of us aren't here. I can think of many people I'd prefer to obliterate from my mind!'

'Me too! It seems such a waste. I know I'm being stupid but sometimes it seems Jessica knows far more than I think and I wonder, if I could find the magic key to unlock the barriers she's put round herself, whether she'd be perfectly normal? I know she desperately needs my love, yet she totally rejects it. She can't bear to be touched or held. Even dressing her's a job for two people. I wish ...'

'What?'

171

'That I had someone else to help me, I suppose.'

'Her father?'

'No!'

He was taken aback by the vehemence of her denial. 'Not the right man?'

'He wouldn't understand. He's too wrapped up in himself. Anyway, sometimes I think it's all his fault.'

'But you're not alone,' he pointed out, keeping his eyes on Jessica as she started to sit up and take fleeting glances around her.

'No, I'm very lucky. Not many men would be interested in a woman with an autistic child.'

'Then why are you worried?'

Lisa looked at the back of his head, noticing how his hair curled upwards on the nape of his neck. As she looked he turned his face towards her and when their eyes met it was as though he could see right through her. See through the façade that she, Neal and Carol had created between them and know with absolute certainty what she was really like. Know all her anxieties and fears, and understand.

Look away! she told herself urgently. Don't get involved. He's only here for a few months and you'd just be another conquest. Look away. 'The problem is that he's not interested in Jessica!' she blurted out, then covered her mouth in horror. For all she knew, he might repeat what she'd said and let Neal hear of it. 'I didn't mean that,' she added quickly. 'I'm being unfair. Why, only next week I'm taking her to see a specialist from Switzerland. Neal arranged all that for me, and he pays for a nurse to help. He's wonderful about that side of things, it's simply that he finds coping with her difficult. But then, she isn't his child.'

'Quite.' It was impossible to tell from his voice exactly what he meant, but he gave her a quizzical look as though he wondered precisely who she was trying to fool.

'I'm far better off than most women in my position,' she continued, untying Jessica's harness. The child wanted to get out and roll on the grass. 'It must be dreadful to worry about money as well.'

'Yes.'

'I was coping quite nicely until recently. Now I'm so tired all the time that I just want to crawl into bed and sleep the days away. Perhaps it's emotional exhaustion!'

He watched Jessica start to pull handfuls of grass out of the ground before stuffing them in her mouth and then chewing enthusiastically, and all the time she darted short glances at him, watching him so furtively that unless he'd kept his eyes constantly on her he'd have sworn she was ignoring him.

172

'Of course you're tired,' he murmured while Jessica began hitting her head against the toe of his shoe. 'Weren't you tired when you were carrying this little one? I remember that my wife ...'

His voice faded a long way away until it had no meaning. The world tilted and turned black and Lisa gave an inarticulate cry before toppling on to the grass next to her daughter. Unperturbed, Jessica continued to bang her head.

Renato swiftly bent down and gathered her in his arms. He put her tenderly back on the seat and began to rub her hands as he murmured her name.

The moment she regained consciousness, Lisa snatched her hands away from him and began a mad scramble to push Jessica back into her pushchair. Infuriated, Jessica screamed and kicked out, spitting when her mother got too near.

'Please stop!' The Italian was appalled by her distress. He stood up and caught hold of her arms. 'Leave Jessica alone and wait a moment. Obviously I've made a mistake. Naturally I'd assumed that ... You look exactly as my wife did and I simply thought you were again pregnant. I didn't mean to offend you.'

'I'm not!' she shouted. 'I can't be. I won't, not again. What would I do? No, you're wrong, totally wrong.'

'I'm sorry,' he repeated helplessly. 'Of course you know best. It was a foolish error.'

'What right have you got to march up to me and start telling me how to look after my daughter before insinuating that I'm pregnant again? Who the hell do you think you are!'

He saw the tears brimming over in her eyes and wished that he could take away some of her pain. He was right, they both knew that, but he'd have given anything not to have been the person who made her face the fact.

Her distress affected Jessica who began hitting her chin against the leg of the park seat with ruthless determination, as though only through pain could she shut out her mother's emotional turmoil.

Renato picked the little girl up and put her in her pushchair. He didn't look at her or speak to her and she went limp, flopping helplessly while he did up the straps.

'I'm going home.' Lisa's voice was strained. 'I hope you enjoy the rest of the afternoon.'

'Let me walk back with you.'

'Even if I wanted you to, which I most certainly don't, Bishop or some other hanger-on would see us and then I'd have that to cope with. I'm beginning to think you're nothing but trouble.'

'What else have I done to you?'

'Only caused Neal and me to have our first quarrel.'

'For that I am not sorry.'

'If what you say is true, I certainly can't afford any more of them. Good day, Mr Bellini.'

He didn't reply but she was aware that he watched her as she left the park, and her ridiculous desire to turn round and rush back to him for some kind of reassurance that he couldn't possibly give made her all the more furious with herself.

Now that she knew the truth, something that she would certainly have worked out for herself had it not been for the fact that she'd been irregular ever since Jessica's birth, there was no room for anyone else, even if the handsome Italian had been as interested in her as he appeared.

All she could do was hope that she hadn't been mistaken in Neal and that he'd stay with her once he found out about the child. Until now she'd never doubted his feelings, but a pregnant mistress was a mile away from a young, fashionably dressed one whom he was proud to escort round London.

As she remembered only too well from Toby, pregnant women were not the epitome of most men's dreams, and the prospect of telling Neal the news was the most daunting challenge she'd had to face since leaving Toby.

It was Tuesday night before he contacted her again, by which time she'd gone through so many imaginary conversations in her mind that she was totally exhausted. He sounded slightly offhand over the phone but said that he had tickets for a surprise treat the following Thursday and he'd collect her at six-thirty.

She was ready half an hour early, totally disinterested in their destination because all she could think about was when she'd get the chance to tell him about the baby, and what he'd have to say.

'Guessed where we're going?' he queried when she opened the front door.

'No.'

'Where's all the legendary female curiosity?'

'I thought that was cats!' she said shortly. He looked considerably taken aback. 'We're going to the opera, darling.' They were always going to the opera and although she loved it she couldn't think why this visit should be particularly exciting.

'I've got tickets for *Chenier*.'

'Was it difficult?'

'It certainly was! Didn't you read the reviews? They say it's stunning.'

'I haven't looked at a paper for days. Is it Domingo?'

174

'It's your favourite, Carreras.'

For a brief moment she forgot her dilemma. 'How fantastic, I've never heard him sing live!'

'Let's hope he's as good as they say.'

He was. He was so good that he broke Lisa's fragile composure with the sheer beauty and poignancy of his voice. From his rendition of *Un di all'azzuro spazio* she was lost. Totally caught up in the world of the idealistic poet who believed in love and the power of the human spirit. When he sang the beautiful *Comme un bel di maggio* shortly before his death, Lisa began to cry. By the time he and his lover, Madeleine, went to their execution together, their voices soaring as they proclaimed their love, she could no longer see for tears.

As the audience rose to its feet in recognition of the skill of the artists, Lisa looked at the slender Spaniard and wondered if he realised what pain his gift could bring to people. Tonight he'd forced her to face the fact that true love, the burning, consuming passion that he and Rosalind Plowright had portrayed so vividly, did exist. She knew that. It was possible to love deeply and intensely, and she was carrying the child of a man she liked and respected, but now — after this evening — she knew that wasn't enough. She cried not only for the doomed lovers but also for herself.

'An expensive way of making you miserable!' joked Neal when they were on their way home. 'You've cried non-stop tonight. Presumably that means you enjoyed it?'

Her head was throbbing and her eyes felt hot and swollen. 'Yes, it was ... I can't describe it, but I'll never forget tonight, never.'

'He's certainly improved. I don't usually care for him. Too much passion and not the best actor on the opera circuit. Mind you, he excelled tonight. I doubt if anyone could have done it better. I'll find out when he'll be here again.'

'No!'

He turned to her in surprise. 'No?'

'Nothing could be like tonight. Besides, I'd rather not. He makes me feel things too intensely.'

'Fine, I'm a Pavorotti man myself. Now if you'd heard him sing Rodolfo ...'

She stopped listening. She was still with the lovers. What must it feel like to love a man so much you wanted to die with him? she wondered. She'd never choose to die with Neal. In fact, she couldn't imagine wanting to die with anyone she knew, but she could imagine what it would be like to love intensely. She would be alive.

'We're here,' said Neal. 'It was only a story, you know. The magic of the theatre. You don't get many singing poets in real life! I took you because I thought it would give you a lift, not to sink you into total depression. We'll go up and get ourselves a drink. You can go now, Mike. I'll drive Mrs Walker home.'

'Very good, sir. Goodnight.'

'Do you like opera, Mike?' she asked as she walked past him.

'No. A lot of overweight people running round the stage singing words I don't understand isn't my idea of pleasure!'

'It wasn't like that,' she said slowly. 'It wasn't like that at all.'

Mike watched her go into his employer's flat and shook his head sadly. There was no room in Neal's life for idealists, whatever their sex, and no doubt Lisa would eventually discover that. He wished she'd never met the man. He felt that was a far greater tragedy than anything she might see on the stage.

Once inside the flat some of the magic of the performance began to die away as Lisa realised that now was the moment when she'd actually got to tell Neal. She couldn't put it off any longer because she needed to know where she stood and what arrangements she must make for her future.

'Whisky?' He was already taking down two glasses.

'I'm not in the mood for a drink. I have to talk to you.'

'Talk away. I wonder if ...'

'It's very important.'

He put his glass down and turned slowly to face her. 'I'm listening,' he said softly, but his expression was watchful, his eyes alert.

'I don't think you're going to be very pleased about this. In fact, I'm sure you're not, but ...'

'Get to the point,' he said tersely.

'This isn't easy for me! You see ...'

'Is it another man?'

'No, nothing like that!'

Crossing the room he sat down beside her. 'In that case I don't think you need worry. I'm quite sure I can cope with any other emotional crisis you may have dreamt up.'

'I haven't dreamt this up! she said irritably, disliking his patronising tone. 'Actually, I'm pregnant.'

His face showed nothing. He looked at her for a moment or two and then stood up and went to collect his drink. When he returned there was a faint smile round his lips and a look that she could almost believe to be triumph in his eyes.

'You don't mind?'

'Mind?' Now he was smiling broadly, putting his right arm round her with such exaggerated care she wondered if he thought she was carrying the child on her back. 'Darling Lisa, I'm overjoyed! This is wonderful news. I may have a son at last. I can't tell you what this means to me. I'm a very lucky man.'

Anyone would think they were a normal married couple, she thought in astonishment. He hadn't mentioned his wife or his family, hadn't suggested that she might have to hide herself away once the baby began to show. All he'd done was congratulate her and look exceedingly pleased with himself. She should have been highly relieved but instead she was faintly uneasy.

'What about Naomi? Won't this make things awkward at home?'

'Naomi?'

She might as well have named his pet dog he looked so puzzled. 'Your wife!'

He laughed softly. 'Don't worry about Naomi. She isn't important. *You're* important. You and the baby. I don't want you overdoing things. You'll have to let Janice do more for Jessica because until the baby's born I'm not having you wrestling with that little animal, trying to carry her around while she kicks you in the face.'

Lisa flinched at his words but swallowed down her resentment as she forced herself to come out with her second worry. 'What if our baby's the same as Jessica?'

'Don't be ridiculous! As though you and I would produce anything like that. No, Jessica's her father's child. He's totally insane with his vile temper and perverse pleasures. You don't need to worry about that. I'm sure the specialist will put your mind at rest on that point.'

'Jessica isn't insane,' she said tightly, unable to keep silent any longer. 'She's sick. It's an illness. I thought you understood that.'

'The end result's the same.'

'I don't like it when you talk about her like that. I love her.'

'Highly commendable. You'll love our child even more.'

'I won't! I'll love it exactly the same.'

'I'm not going to quarrel over Jessica at a moment like this. Just remember that this one's my child, too, and I don't want your daughter causing a miscarriage.'

'I'm glad you're pleased,' she said, wondering why she was disturbed by his reaction. 'Exactly where do we go from here?'

'What do you mean?'

'I'm not going to feel quite so lively for our non-stop social whirl in the future. What will you do?'

'Go on my own.'

'While I stay in the mews cottage?'

He frowned. 'What on earth did you think would happen? You surely didn't imagine I was going to turn you out in order to put in a replacement? I love you, Lisa. You as a person, not just you as an attractive appendage. You obviously don't realise how much you mean to me. I thought I'd made it plain enough; perhaps I'm not very good with words.'

'Yes you are,' she acknowledged, moving closer to him so that she could rest her head on his shoulders. 'You're very good with words, but I don't always believe them. People mean such different things when they talk about love, and I didn't think your definition included a fat pregnant woman.'

'I shall enjoy your new curvaceous figure! Seriously, I'm very proud and absolutely certain that this time it will be a boy.'

'Even if it is, you won't be spending much time with him. What with your work, your family and your social life, when will you get to see him? Friday afternoons from three to five?'

'Why are you so uptight about this?' he asked, pulling her on to his lap.

'Because I'm afraid. Afraid it will be like Jessica; afraid I won't be able to cope on my own; and afraid that eventually I'll lose you.'

'Now it's my turn to ask you something. Do you love me?'

She could easily have lied. It would have been so simple to have given him the answer he wanted and known that she was consequently totally secure, but she couldn't do it. Perhaps it was because of the opera, perhaps she was being unrealistic, but knowing that their entire future might be based on her reply she had to be totally honest, and with a sudden and inexplicable memory of Renato Bellini picking Jessica up at the park she found herself unable to lie.

'No, Neal. I don't think I do.'

He tightened his grip on her. 'I don't think you do either, but I don't mind. You'll come to love me in time, and I'm perfectly willing to wait. What *do* you feel for me?' he added casually.

'I'm very fond of you, and I admire the way you're always so organised and confident.'

'And sexually?'

'I enjoy our lovemaking.'

'Is that all?'

'I don't think the earth will ever move for me again! Toby destroyed something in me when he ... It's good between us, Neal.'

'You've been brutally frank!' he said wryly. 'Not many women in your position would have been that honest.'

'Would you rather I'd lied?'

'Certainly not. I already knew the truth. I think you're very brave, but since I'm totally obsessed by you I'm not in the least discouraged. My ego doesn't allow me to admit defeat. All you need is time, and we've got plenty of that.'

'I don't deserve you.'

Neal took a sip of his drink. 'I only wish we could get married, but divorce is out of the question. Naomi and I go back a long way.'

'I never thought about marriage,' she said quickly and with absolute truth. 'I know how fond you are of Naomi. I wouldn't dream of ...'

'I can't stand the sight of her,' he said dispassionately. 'However, let's not talk about that. We must work out what gynaecologist you're going to use and where you'll live once the baby's born. This place won't be big enough for four and I don't suppose you're willing to consider putting Jessica ...'

'No!'

'Well, there's plenty of time to get the details sorted out. Now, how about a kiss to celebrate?'

It was very late indeed before Lisa left the flat.

Three weeks later, two days after Jessica's second birthday, she took her to see Dr Weissler in London. He was generally accepted as the up and coming specialist on autistic children but as far as Lisa could gather this was the first time he'd actually seen a patient while in England for a series of lectures. She was too thankful and nervous to stop and ask herself how Neal could influence such a man, accepting his usual explanation of money. Renato Bellini could have told her that Dr Weissler wasn't in need of money, but he was in need of assistance to cover up the unfortunate scandals that had dogged his career. Scandals involving close friendships with highly expensive call-girls in most of the capital cities of the world.

Although he was there under duress, Dr Weissler was charm itself, with a calming manner and a pleasantly dry sense of humour that appealed to Lisa. He discussed Jessica's birth and the weeks preceding it at some length before asking numerous questions, and only after that did he actually seem to pay any attention to the child herself. In reality he'd been watching her all the time. He'd seen how she refused Lisa's attempts to pick her up or nurse her, and watched the way she flattened herself against the wall as she undertook a never-ending circular journey round the room like a hamster on a wheel.

'Did she start to walk on time?' he queried, calling Jessica's name softly and noting the lack of reaction.

'She was on her feet at twelve months. I was amazed.'

'And her speech?'

'She doesn't talk.'

179

'No attempts at communication?'

'She makes noises but they're just sounds. Like a very small baby might make.'

'No speech at the present?' he repeated.

Lisa took a deep breath. 'Sometimes she does say words, but at the wrong time. I always say, "No, hot!" to stop her burning herself on the stove − not that she takes any notice − and sometimes now when I say "No" she says "hot" although she isn't very good with the letter "H" so it comes out as " 'ot". But obviously she thinks "No hot" is one word.'

'Does she connect it with the stove or any other equipment where hot is applicable?'

'Definitely not.'

'Anything else?'

'She says, "Kettle on".'

'Why do you think she says that?'

'She likes the sound of it. I often say, "I think I'll put the kettle on", and she seems to like the last couple of words.'

'Tell me, is she particularly attached to anything or anyone?'

'Certainly not anyone but she's obsessed with that box she's clutching now. It's strange. Originally it contained a beautiful pair of ear-rings, but when I opened it up she wasn't interested in the shiny ear-rings themselves, just the box. Now it goes everywhere with her. She likes the iron door-stop in our living-room as well, but thank heavens that's too heavy for her to carry around!'

'How does she cope with pain? For example, when she falls?'

'I don't think she knows the meaning of pain. She'll bang her head against things until she's covered with bruises unless I stop her.'

'I'd better take a look at her. Jessica, would you come here a moment?'

Lisa never forgot the next twenty minutes as Jessica hurled every possible object off the specialist's desk, kicked him in the face, spat at his nurse, screamed on one piercing note until Lisa's ears were hurting and then arched and rolled her rigid body as though in a fit, even biting Dr Weissler's hand when it came close to her mouth.

Eventually he finished and Jessica scuttled under his desk and began to chew on her thumb while crooning the 'Toreador Song' from *Carmen*, rocking to and fro as she did so.

'She likes music?' he asked, apparently unperturbed by all she'd done.

'Yes. She only has to hear anything once and that's enough.'

'These children quite frequently have what we term islets of exceptional skill in the midst of their apparently unco-ordinated lives.

'I don't think there's any doubt at all that Jessica is suffering from infant autism. She's quite severely affected as is demonstrated by her total rejection of all emotional relationships. They disturb her and she blocks them out. Her speech is virtually non-existent, and clearly she has no grasp of the meaning of words. Mind you, there have been times when older autistic children have learnt to write, and even if speech is still beyond their reach their grasp of the language is shown to be average or even higher for their age. A great puzzle to us all.'

'You can't tell me what her prospects are?'

'I'd be lying to you if I pretended that she had any. It's very rare for an autistic child to function at even the most basic level required if they're to fit into the community.'

'And there's no treatment?'

'There are pills, sedatives, drugs to quieten her down.' He didn't sound as though he approved, and neither did she.

'Is there something that I can do? I often feel that she's waiting just out of reach; waiting for me to make contact.'

'That could be maternal optimism. But there is a school of thought that believes in an interesting form of therapy, and has had one or two startlingly good results with it. Unfortunately, trained counsellors are rare. They're also very expensive because they have to devote hours to both the child and its mother.'

'Its mother?'

'Yes. The therapy is based entirely upon touch. Holding, to be more precise. You would have to be willing to hold Jessica for up to two hours a day every day of the week, month after month. Obviously at the beginning at least this would be against her will. It's an exhausting and time-consuming exercise that doesn't always work. Indeed, one or two children have gone backwards, been driven even deeper into themselves by such forced and intense confrontation with their own fears.'

Lisa felt sick. It took all of her strength and skill to keep Jessica still long enough to be dressed or bathed. The thought of holding her for hours at a time was so terrible that for one tiny moment she wavered, but then she looked down at her lovely child, now patiently watching her fingers as she waved them in front of her eyes, and knew that she had to try. If it held out even the slimmest hope then it had to be done.

'How could I find out more about this?'

Dr Weissler leant across the desk. 'Mrs Walker, do you really think that under the present circumstances, with another child on the way and as I understand it a move in the near future, this is something you *can* do? You'll need a lot of support. It's hard for married couples to cope. It often splits families up. Are you strong enough to do it alone? Are you able to do it alone? The cost is somewhat prohibitive.'

'I couldn't do it without help, but Neal ...' She stopped at the expression on the specialist's face. 'You don't think he'll help?'

'How can I say? You're close to him, what do you think?'

'He wouldn't mind the expense, he's always said that he didn't mind how much it cost to ...'

'Yes?'

'To put Jessica away,' she whispered.

'A very different thing from paying for you to spend most of your day shut away with your daughter, expending all your emotional energy on her while he and the new baby are left out in the cold.'

He didn't need to say any more. She knew that he was right. Neal would never agree to such a thing. He'd pay a fortune to keep Jessica out of their lives but she doubted if he'd part with a penny to keep her in it, especially once their own child was born. Utterly defeated she stood up, her face white are drawn. 'Thank you for your time, Doctor. You've been very honest and understanding.'

'I wish I could offer you more hope but sometimes it's better to be brutally honest at the beginning. You'll have other children, perfect children, and for all we know, Jessica's quite happy as she is.'

'You don't believe that!' accused Lisa.

'I can't know for certain. None of us knows what's going on in their minds. She *might* be happy as she is.'

'It's all right, I'm a realist. I'll just have to go away and think about things for a time. Can I contact you if I need to?'

He spread his hands regretfully. 'I'm afraid this consultation was a favour for a friend. I'm so busy that I can't possibly promise another appointment.'

'Could you give me an address where someone could help?'

'Mrs Walker, I can, but I'm not sure that I should.'

He saw a flicker of contempt in her eyes. 'He might be paying your fee but does that mean you're not allowed to do what's best for Jessica? If it does, then I don't know how you can live with yourself.'

With difficulty, he thought, looking at the determined young woman who understood nothing about the father of her unborn child. 'Very well,' he conceded. 'I'll give you an address.'

'I won't say that you did,' she promised. 'After all, we're both trying to help Jessica; that's what this appointment was about.'

Having been instructed to urge Jessica's admittance to a home once he'd verified her condition, Dr Weissler didn't feel that Neal would agree but he nodded. If he knew Mr Gueras half as well as he thought then this lovely young woman in front of him wouldn't have any time left for her autistic daughter once her second child was born. No damage would be done, but he would have salved his own conscience.

As he watched Lisa leave he remembered a time when he'd been young and idealistic, and could have wept for his own moral frailty that had allowed him to become trapped by a man like Neal Gueras.

Chapter Sixteen

Bishop stood in front of Neal Gueras's large leather desk and waited impassively for him to speak. He knew he'd been taking one or two risks lately. Issuing instructions without getting permission. Countermanding orders when the situation necessitated. And, of course, meeting Bellini had been a risk; but whatever the reason for this appointment he wasn't going to be the first to speak. He always preferred to stay silent for as long as possible.

Neal cleared his throat and put down the stilleto-shaped paperknife he'd been tapping on the desk top. 'I'm going away to Paris, Saturday week. I'll be gone five days.'

'Paris in November?'

'Lisa needs a break.'

Bishop's eyes narrowed. If he had his way the only break she'd get would involve her neck. 'Really?'

'Yes, she's pregnant.'

If possible, Bishop's pale face went even more white and his mouth tightened. 'I didn't know.'

'No one knew except me. I'm quite certain it's a boy.'

'Has she had a scan?'

'She's against them, but I'm positive it's a boy.'

'Did you just want me to make a note of your absence Saturday week?'

'Not exactly. Sit down, this is going to take some time.'

Bishop lowered himself into an armchair in the corner of the room, making sure that his face was in shadow. He didn't want to show any flicker of emotion during the coming discussion. Neal Gueras was an expert at reading men's faces.

'I want to marry her, Bishop. I have to marry her.'

He was grateful for the shadows. 'Why not wait until you're sure it's a boy? Rather a pity to marry for another daughter, I'd have thought.'

'It so happens that I don't want your advice. Even if it is a girl it could be a boy next time, or the time after.'

'I didn't realise she was so fond of children. Talking of which, suppose this one turns out to be an idiot too?'

'Listen!' snapped an infuriated Neal. 'We're leaving London late Friday night and won't return until the Wednesday morning. I do not wish my wife to be alive on my return.'

The silence was like a heavy weight pressing down on both men. Bishop was aghast. He'd never considered Lisa a candidate for marriage. There'd been so many women, all in his opinion far more suitable companions for his employer, and yet marriage had never been mentioned. Naomi was Neal's wife and Naomi knew everything. She'd probably got letters lodged with her solicitors in case of any eventuality such as this. They stood to lose everything if Neal pressed ahead. It was unbelievable.

'Well?' snapped Neal again. 'Is it beyond you?'

'Hardly, I merely wondered ...'

'Yes?'

'Suppose Mrs Gueras has protected herself in some way? There may be papers somewhere, affidavits lodged with ...'

'I've seen to all that. There were papers but they no longer exist. What kind of an idiot do you take me for?'

A prize one, thought Bishop. 'I was only checking,' he said aloud. 'In that case, it shouldn't be too difficult.'

'Her new nurse is useless. She'll agree with any verdict a doctor brings in so that's another worry out of the way. Just make sure there aren't any suspicious circumstances.'

'Aside from the fact that it's a murder.'

'In a minute I shall begin to think you don't want to do this.'

'It's all the same to me. If you're quite sure?'

'I am.'

'Anything else?'

'Just be very, very careful. We can't afford any hint of scandal right now.'

'I'm well aware of that,' said Bishop shortly, and left the room.

Once back in his annexe he hit the wall with his fist. A blow that would have broken most men's knuckles. 'The bitch!' he muttered. 'The scheming, conniving little bitch!' But he knew there was nothing he could do except obey. Naturally he'd record his disapproval in his own minutes to cover himself, but he'd also do as he was asked and wait. Women miscarried their babies all the time. A dead Naomi didn't bother him, was probably in fact better dead than alive with her drink problem. No, it was the idea of Lisa replacing her that really enraged him, but perhaps fate, possibly assisted by Bishop, would make sure that she didn't. With that comforting thought, he settled down to make his plans.

'I can't go to Paris!' exclaimed Lisa. 'What about Jessica?'

Neal refrained from saying what he thought about Jessica and put an arm round Lisa's waist. 'She'll be all right. That's what the nurse is for. You need a break. Not only are you tired, you're also worrying quite needlessly that our baby won't be normal. You've been to three specialists, they've all told you autism isn't hereditary but you won't listen. In my opinion you've got to get away and put things into perspective. I'm quite sure you're not good for Jessica while you're like this.'

It was true. She wasn't nearly as patient and caring as she should be, and Jessica felt it. That was why she was totally uncontrollable these days. 'You're right,' she admitted. 'And I would like to see Paris.'

'I thought we'd leave on Friday evening and come back the following Wednesday.'

'You said a long weekend!'

'Isn't it long enough? I might be able to fit in a couple more days.'

'It's too long. I thought you meant Friday to Monday. Jessica might think I've deserted her.'

'Nonsense! You've got the baby to think about as well as Jessica, and right now you're not being fair to either of them.'

Lisa looked at his broad, reassuring figure in its immaculate charcoal grey suit and knew he was right. She was fortunate to have him looking after her. It was impossible to envisage any situation that he wouldn't be able to cope with, and his confidence and power was beginning to have an effect on her. He fascinated her; she only wished that the power he wielded acted as the aphrodisiac it was meant to be. In bed she was proving a sad disappointment, although he never complained. In fact he took more and more care over his lovemaking, but she simply couldn't let herself go.

'Don't bother to pack much,' he added as he left. 'I thought you'd enjoy buying some French clothes. They make wonderful lingerie!' he added with a smile. She was relieved he wasn't planning to spend all their time in bed.

The Saturday after they left was a cold, damp day with a high wind. Louise, Ruth and Rebekah all felt on edge without knowing why. As a result, Louise picked on Rebekah, Ruth shut herself away in the library and tried to lose herself in *Jane Eyre*, and Rebekah alternately cried because Louise was being unkind or giggled uncontrollably at mildly humorous television programmes.

After tea, Louise's spirits lifted when Bishop arrived unexpectedly. For once he invited himself into the house and was positively agreeable. He even played a game of draughts with Rebekah and kept silent when she cheated.

After Rebekah went to bed he remained with the older girls. Ruth, who felt uncomfortable in his presence, decided to have an early night and leave Louise to enjoy Bishop's undivided attention. 'I only hope I can sleep,' she commented as she said goodnight. 'The wind in the tree by my window's making a terrible row. If you hear a crash in the night I'm probably lying pinned to my bed by a giant oak!'

'I'm not likely to hear the crash,' said Louise, smiling amiably now that she had Bishop to herself. 'You can't hear much in my room on a normal night, let alone in this gale.'

'I'll dash to your rescue,' promised Bishop dryly.

'You'd probably cut off my legs below the knees and then say you did it for my own good.'

'What an astute judge of character your sister is,' commented Bishop as the door closed behind Ruth.

'She's been in a bad mood all day. Daddy promised to take her to look at some horses this weekend, she needs a new one, and then he cancelled at the last minute for business reason. We all know what that means!'

'Really?' He'd actually put a hand on Louise's shoulder as she sat curled up at his feet and she could scarcely speak for excitement.

'He's tied up with that Lisa girl, of course. Their picture's in the papers often enough.'

'Sounds quite exciting!'

'I didn't mean literally.'

'How's your mother taking it all?' he added casually, letting his fingers drift up Louise's neck and tugging gently at her fair curls.

'In her usual way. She appeared briefly during the morning but I think she's spent most of the day in her room drinking. This new nurse isn't nearly as good as the last one. She isn't as strict, and Mother doesn't like her either which is a pity. Nurse Clarke was more of a friend and Mother must need one. I've never understood why Nurse Clarke left.'

'Probaby got a chance to travel. This isn't the most exciting of places to work.'

'But she was fond of Mother.'

'Has the new nurse got the same room?'

Louise wriggled as he pulled rather too tightly on her hair. 'Probably not. I think Mother said she didn't want a spy right next to her bedroom.'

'Can't you keep still?' he asked mildly.

'You're hurting me!'

'Don't you like it?'

'No I do not!'

'Pity.' He hesitated, but then remembered Lisa and her unborn child. Louise was probably his best chance of keeping alive his hopes of inheriting Neal's empire. 'Turn round,' he commanded, and then bent his head and began to kiss her trembling mouth.

Half an hour later, thoroughly bored but satisfied that Louise didn't realise it, he stood up and stretched. 'Time for bed, I think. If I stay here much longer I won't be answerable for my actions!'

Louise flushed with pleasure and gave a quick giggle. 'Perhaps I don't mind if you forget yourself.'

'Your father most certainly would.'

'Why should I care about him?' Her mouth turned down in a most unattractive expression, slightly reminiscent of her mother. 'He doesn't bother me.'

'Maybe not, but I do. You're still at school, Louise. I can wait,' he added with what was almost a smile.

Wildly elated, Louise watched him leave by the front door and only when the lights came on in the annexe did she finally go up to bed. She quickly fell asleep, dreaming of his hard mouth on hers and the way his teeth had nibbled at the soft skin at the base of her throat. For the first time she began to believe that marriage to Bishop was possible. After all, hadn't he said he was willing to wait?

Even as she slept he was waiting. Standing in complete darkness in his own bedroom, watching as the lights in the main house were slowly extinguished until only Naomi's remained. In a large cardboard box at his feet lay his weapon. 'Soon,' he murmured softly to himself. 'Very soon.'

Naomi couldn't sleep. Despite all the whisky she'd drunk and the tranquillizers prescribed by the doctor, sleep eluded her. She hadn't taken her sleeping pills because she knew it might be dangerous, but usually whisky and valium were enough to ensure a brief period of oblivion. Not tonight. Tonight something – the wind, the rain on her window or just pure, unadulterated misery – was keeping her awake.

She lay on her pillows, an overweight, prematurely aged woman with swollen fingers and a mottled complexion, and remembered the days when she'd first met her husband. She recalled how tall and well-built he was, and how his eyes had shone when he saw her. She remembered the first time they made love, the hardness of his body on hers, the sudden thrust and the brief moment of pain that was soon obliterated by waves of pleasure. A pleasure he'd always been able to give her for as long as she'd held his interest. They'd been happy together at first. Then he'd begun to work long hours while she'd spent endless months, miserable and sick, as she produced daughters for him. Daughters that he didn't want and blamed her for. It was then that she'd lost him.

He'd changed as well, she thought with sudden clarity. He'd become harder. Gradually most of the humanity seemed to ebb out of him until she found herself in bed with a harsh uncaring husband who ignored her pleasure and found his own release with greater and greater speed. Then, after Rebekah, he didn't bother to come to her bed at all.

If only they'd stayed in Greece, she thought fretfully. True, they'd never have become as rich and he wouldn't have been so important, but in the end what had they gained? For her part, very little, and she wept for the time so long ago when her heart had leapt with excitement every time she saw him, and his strong arms had seemed to promise her eternal love and safety. What a fool she'd been. Everyone knew nothing was forever.

It was small comfort to know she'd always be his wife, although there were times when she felt triumphant because he couldn't discard her. If she couldn't give him legitimate sons then he'd have to do without them, and she took satisfaction from that. She knew so much. In the days before drink and drugs clouded her judgement, she'd quickly realised that the men who stood in her husband's way on his upward climb usually died. Then, on a day etched forever in her memory, she'd actually seen her husband kill.

He'd taken an important visitor out to the stables. The man wanted to try out one of Neal's horses. She'd been on the middle landing looking out of a window and saw quite clearly that the horse her husband brought out was a notoriously evil-tempered one, due to be sold. Even as she frowned, her husband slipped a hand casually beneath the animal's saddle before helping the visitor to mount. The horse had come back alone, foaming at the mouth, eyes rolling wildly, and Neal had shot it there and then in the stable yard.

A search party went out and found the visitor lying with a broken neck beneath an avenue of trees. When everyone was fussing round the body, Naomi had slipped away to the stable block and drawn back the tarpaulin sheet covering the dead horse. On its back – right where the saddle had been – she found tiny holes flecked with blood. The poor creature had been driven mad by pain and Naomi knew how it had been done.

That night she started to write things down, and it was that very incident that she'd hurled in her husband's face over four years ago when he'd suggested a divorce. She was safe but it was cold comfort when she was a wife in name only, and the years dragged by in a fog of drink and broken dreams.

Lost in her thoughts, she didn't hear her door open. It wasn't until Bishop was actually in the room that she saw him and gave a small cry of fright. 'You startled me! What on earth do you mean by . . .? What do you want? My husband isn't here.'

'Your husband's never here,' he said cruelly.

Naomi shivered. She hated the man. 'What do you want?' she repeated.

'I saw your light was on and wondered if you needed something to help you sleep.'

'No thank you. I only have to press my bell and the nurse is here in minutes,' she added quickly.

Bishop smiled and Naomi felt her stomach tighten with fear. 'I think not, Mrs Gueras. It's been disconnected.'

She stabbed frantically at the bell push and waited. No door opened across the corridor. The nurse slept on.

'Like I said, I thought you'd need help sleeping. Here, take some of these,' and he held out his hand. She took the bottle and glanced at the label. 'Secanol? I'm not taking those; I've been drinking all day.'

'You'd certainly sleep, wouldn't you!'

'I'd never wake up.'

'That's right, Naomi. You'd never wake up.'

She looked at him in silence. So that was why he was there. To remove her. Another obstacle to Neal's desires was to be killed. But he couldn't do that; it was too dangerous. She tried to moisten her suddenly dry lips. 'You're making a mistake, Bishop. You might think this is what my husband wants but you're wrong. I've got papers . . .'

'Not any more.'

'He can't afford a murder inquiry, none of you can. The police are only waiting for an excuse to look into his affairs.'

'I'm doing what he asked. He wants you dead, and what your husband wants he gets.'

'You can't make me take them,' she gabbled, pulling the duvet up round her chin as though that could protect her.

'I think I can. Alternatively I could force them down your throat, but that might leave a mark and marks wouldn't fit in with the verdict we want. You'll have to take them yourself, along with a little more scotch, I think.' With gloved hands he picked up the bottle on her bedside table.

Naomi closed her mouth tightly and shook her head.

'Then I'll just have to persuade you,' he said softly, and placed a large cardboard box on her bed. A box that held things which scrabbled against the sides. Things that wanted to get out.

'What is it?' Her eyes were wide with fear but he knew that she still hadn't guessed.

'There's more than one there, Naomi.'

'What are they?' She was whispering now, as though afraid of enraging them.

'Don't worry, some people keep them as pets. You wouldn't,' he continued pleasantly. 'You wouldn't go near them or any of their relations. Can't you guess? Are you too drunk even to make a guess?'

'Get out!' She was almost pleading now. 'Get out and I won't mention this to anyone. If you don't, I'm going to start screaming.'

'Listen to the wind.' His voice seemed to caress her and his eyes gleamed. She'd never seen him so animated. 'No one will hear, Naomi. No one will come and help you. Now, take the tablets and wash them down with a little drink. It shouldn't be difficult, you've done it often enough before.'

'No!'

'I can't say I'm sorry. It would be a pity to bring these little creatures to see you and then keep them shut up. Shall we open the box? as they used to say on television. Shall we see what I've brought you?'

Naomi didn't move. She was so petrified that she couldn't even nod her head.

'I'll take your silence for assent. Out you come, my fine fellow.' And with his left hand he deftly loosened the lid of the box and just managed to catch one striped, furry tarantula spider as it began to climb on to the duvet.

'*No!*' Terror tightened her throat so that the scream was little more than a whisper and her eyes were bulging with fear. 'Please, Bishop, put it back. I ...'

With his free hand he placed the tablets next to her. 'Swallow one,' he said harshly. 'Now!'

She shook her head and watched in anguish as he lifted the tarantula above her head, hesitated for one fleeting second and then dropped it on to the back of her nightdress.

All her life she'd had a phobia about spiders, even money spiders. Now she could feel the tarantula scampering up to her shoulders and then saw its legs as it began descending down her right arm.

Bishop watched her gibbering and moaning and his expression hardened. He'd expected her to crumble quicker. Louise – stupid as ever – had over-estimated how drunk her mother was. 'Take the bloody tablets!' he snarled.

Naomi, scrambling round the bed with her nightdress riding above her flaccid, blue-veined thighs, was begging and pleading like a tiny child, but she still found the courage to knock the bottle of tablets to the floor.

Bishop, worried that the wind might drop and the nurse hear the moans and cries coming from Naomi, lost patience. He picked up the box and tipped all the contents on to the terrified woman's head. Five more huge, remorseless spiders dropped around her. One got caught up in her hair net and she flung her head from side to side, trying desperately to remove it.

They were all over her now. Wandering up her legs, marching over her bare feet – to Naomi it seemed like an army of them. Even when she rolled on top of one and squashed it, it seemed to her terrified brain that even more appeared to take its place.

With a despairing cry she lunged for the edge of the bed, hoping that she could make the floor and leave most of them behind on the bed, but Bishop put one hand contemptuously in the middle of her flabby breasts and watched her topple backwards, hearing her beginning to wheeze asthmatically.

When she fell, he picked up one of the tarantulas and dropped it into the middle of her face. It was then that the pain started. In her confusion she thought she'd been bitten and tried to shake her left arm free but the pain continued to spread like a red hot poker down into her hand and right up to her shoulder.

She groaned aloud and then felt a slight discomfort in her chest. A discomfort that swelled and surged until she screamed with the agony, her hands flying to the centre of the pain. The wind screamed with her, the two sounds indistinguishable.

Mouth agape, she began gasping for breath. It was an effort to keep her lungs functioning and she was shaking from head to foot with the shock of the pain. The tarantulas were meaningless now. There was only the pain in her chest.

'Help me!' she gasped, not to Bishop who was standing at the foot of the bed studying her as though she were an interesting specimen in a laboratory, but to everyone else in the house. Her nurse, her children, her housekeeper, anyone who might hear. 'Please, somebody help!' But her breathless gasps had no force and no one came.

Suddenly, for one blissful moment, the pain seemed to ebb away and she gazed at Bishop, still motionless at the foot of the bed. What now? she thought, trying to still the shaking of her body as he moved towards the bed, but he was only gathering up the spiders and putting them carefully back in the cardboard box. She continued to watch as he picked up the pills, put them into his pocket and at the same time carefully replaced the bottle of whisky from which he'd urged her to drink.

She thought it strange that he seemed to have given up. Then, without any warning, the pain exploded again and her entire body arched as though from an electric shock. A terrible moan issued from her mouth and finally, with shocking abruptness, it was over.

Bishop's eyes swept the room. It had turned out even better than he could have hoped but he had to double check. Everything must look right. The state of the bed didn't matter, in fact everyone would feel guilty that she'd been thrashing around with an asthma attack while they slept soundly.

Finally, when he was absolutely certain that there was no sign he'd ever been there, he took one last look at the dead woman. Her eyes were wide with terror and shock, her mouth twisted in one last, hideous grimace, and her mouth was slack with a trickle of saliva running down her chin.

Death, he reflected to himself, was rarely flattering to the victim and Naomi hadn't been an attractive sight alive. Smiling at the thought, he moved swiftly and silently down the back stairs and into his own annexe. Once there he killed the spiders, wrapped them in a pedal bin liner and put them in the dustbin. He flushed the Secanol down the lavatory and made himself a cup of tea before going to bed and sleeping the sleep of the innocent. After all, he'd only been carrying out orders, and there was always satisfaction in a job well done.

When their plane touched down at Heathrow, Lisa realised that Neal had been right. She felt both physically and mentally stronger, and their time together in Paris had increased her feelings for him.

They'd stayed at L'Hôtel, their room furnished entirely with antiques including an antique cupboard that concealed a fridge kept constantly filled with champagne. Their bed was a huge four-poster with green drapes and their bathroom had mirrors fitted all round the walls and even on the ceiling. The cuisine was excellent but occasionally they'd eaten out, wandering down small back streets that Neal seemed to know. Here the food was less lavishly presented but still superbly cooked, putting London's smaller restaurants to shame.

Then there had been the usual tourist attractions. The Eiffel Tower, the Louvre, even a trip to the Palace of Versailles where she'd marvelled at the ornate glory of the Sun King's reign. She'd also shopped in the Rue Faubourg St Honoré, buying three tailored suits in sharp bright colours, their style and finish the epitome of French chic.

Now, with her head resting on Neal's shoulder, she was still thinking about it all. Even though the nights didn't quite match the days, Neal had assured her he didn't mind. He understood her fear of losing control, promising her that in time it would come right, but once or twice she'd caught a look of thoughtful assessment in his eyes that made her wonder whether he was quite as content as he claimed.

'Happy?' he asked, handing her the travelling bag from the set of Louis Vuitton luggage he'd bought her while in Paris.

'Very happy. I feel like a new woman!'

He smiled kindly. 'It was good. I've been to Paris so often I'd ceased looking at it properly. You made me see it through new eyes.'

After customs they walked hand-in-hand to the entrance lobby and were talking intently when Bishop suddenly stepped in front of them. Lisa glanced at his expression and wondered if he ever smiled.

'I'm sorry to intrude, Mr Gueras,' he murmured, looking anything but sorry. 'I've got some very bad news for you.' She shrank closer to Neal's side. All she could think of was Jessica. I should never have left her, she thought wildly, and clutched hold of Neal's arm.

'Can't it wait?' he asked mildly. 'I'd like to get Lisa home.'

'I'm afraid not. It's about your wife.'

Lisa's grip loosened and she stood up straight, her heart thudding. 'What about her?' Neal sounded as irritated as Lisa felt.

'She's dead.'

'No!' Her hand flew to her mouth in horror as she stared at Neal. His face was blank with shock and he blinked rapidly once or twice. 'Dead? But how? What happened and when?'

'She was found dead in bed. Heart attack, the doctor thinks. They say there'll have to be an autopsy.'

'I didn't know there was anything wrong with her heart.' Neal's bewilderment was genuine.

'I don't think anyone did.'

'How are the girls?' asked Lisa. Bishop glanced at her insolently.

'Not too well. They were particularly upset that their father hadn't left any details as to where he could be contacted.'

'I'm so sorry,' whispered Lisa.

Neal squeezed her hand. 'I'll have to get someone else to take you home, darling. I think I ought to go straight to Beckett Lodge with Bishop.'

'Of course, don't worry about me. Poor Rebekah, she's still young enough to need her mother.'

'She hasn't had a proper one for the past seven years. I don't suppose she'll fall apart,' muttered Neal. 'Bishop, ring Mike and get him to bring a car here for Lisa. We'll leave straight away.'

194

Giving her a brief kiss on the cheek he strode out of the terminal, his face pale beneath its tan. She waited until both men were out of sight before sinking down on a chair, her legs trembling with delayed reaction.

She knew that heart attacks could happen at any time, and that logically it was probably Naomi's long history of alcohol abuse that had brought it about, but it was dreadful to think that she and Neal had spent so many hours making love while his wife was dying alone and probably in agony. She almost felt as if she'd caused the death herself.

'Come on, sunshine! I've been looking everywhere for you.' Looking up into Mike's smiling face she wondered exactly how long she'd been sitting there, feeling sick with guilt.

'I didn't know where to wait. Neal had to rush off.'

'I know. Is that your only case?'

'Neal took all the big ones with him.'

'Probably putting them away in Naomi's cupboards this very minute. Come on, let's get you home.'

'How dare you talk about him like that!' Mike turned to her in amazement. 'You make it sound as though he's already making plans to put me in her place. That's a vile lie. He was stunned by the news; for a moment I thought he was going to pass out.'

'Is that a fact? He should have been on the stage! Come on duchess.'

'Don't you like him?' she demanded once they were on their way.

'He's my employer, not a friend.'

'You're not a very loyal employee.'

Mike glanced in his driving mirror and saw how flushed she was. She looked very beautiful today. Pregnancy was suiting her, and probably she'd had a good time in Paris as well. He liked her and so he took a chance.

'Let's be honest about this. Naomi was a sick, unattractive and ageing woman who couldn't be called a wife in any real sense of the word. You're fit, beautiful, young and, even more important, pregnant. Now do you truly believe that Neal Gueras is going to spend very long grieving over being a widower? Not on your life. After all, now he's free to marry you. Who's a lucky girl?'

She reached forward and slammed the partition shut. For the first time she hated Mike. Hated him because he'd made her realise something she hadn't considered with the shock of the announcement: Neal was free. In the past, when he'd become too possessive or dogmatic, she'd been able to remind him that he already had a wife and she was a relatively free agent. Now her safety net had gone.

She realised that she didn't want to marry him. Didn't want to become his wife. She didn't ever want to marry again; Toby had been enough. No, she definitely didn't want to belong to Neal — yet how could she refuse if he asked her to be his wife?

She was pregnant with his child, reliant upon both his emotional and financial support. What possible reason could she give for turning him down? And why did she want to? Why was she afraid of marriage when she'd just spent five glorious days in his company? She didn't know. She only knew that she was.

When they drew up outside the mews cottage she stayed in her seat, not wanting to leave the car. She dreaded hearing how Jessica had been or what everyday disasters had struck in her absence. She only wanted to be left alone.

'Come on, princess, out you get!' Mike's voice was still cheerful as he opened the door.

'I was a duchess back at the airport!' she joked weakly.

'Sure, but you're the quickest social climber I know. In a few short months you've seen off Kay Masters and Naomi Gueras. That's no mean feat when you consider how long they'd both been around. You ought to patent your formula for success and sell it. You'd soon be a millionairess.'

She looked into his bright blue eyes, the intelligence that was usually masked by his smile for once plainly evident. 'I didn't want them out of the way,' she whispered. 'I never wanted this to happen.'

'I know that, but not many people will believe you so you'd better keep your feelings to yourself. Besides, you sound like an innocent victim and that's hardly the case, is it?'

'Isn't it?' All at once she was truly frightened.

He looked at her anxious expression, remembered the child she was carrying and gave a quick laugh. 'Of course not. Why, you're all set for the land of milk and honey from now on. Enjoy it, most girls would! Be seeing you.'

As he drove away she was touched by a fleeting moment of fear that his apparently encouraging remarks did nothing at all to dispel.

Chapter Seventeen

For over a week she stayed alone in the cottage. Jessica's behaviour had deteriorated even further since her absence but she left the nurse to cope as she waited constantly for the phone to ring. Janice brought in all the papers each morning and she read every single item of news about the death. Her own name featured prominently several times as Neal Gueras's 'constant companion' of the past few months, but she didn't mind that. She was looking for something more sinister, some hint that the death hadn't been quite as straightforward as Bishop had made it sound, but there was never any suggestion of foul play.

Finally there was the inquest. That was reported in the *Evening Standard* the same day, and on the front page there was a photo of a strained, unsmiling Neal arriving at the court room. The evidence was entirely innocuous. The deceased had died of a massive coronary brought on by the strain of a severe asthmatic attack. She'd suffered from an enlarged liver and hardening of the arteries more usually found in far older women. In other words, she'd been a physical wreck and her death would probably have occurred within the next two years in any case. The coroner commiserated with the widower and it was all over.

Late that night, when Jessica and Janice were asleep and Lisa in the living-room reading a book, Neal finally arrived. He'd lost weight and looked tired but once his arms were round her, his exhaustion vanished and despite her protests he began removing her clothes, his hands busy with zips and buttons until she was naked.

Terrified that Janice might waken, Lisa kept silent, realising that in some way Neal needed the comfort of her body. He too was silent. His mouth suckled greedily at her nipples and his hands moved quickly between her thighs as he went through the motions of arousing her, but very soon he was parting her legs and thrusting into her with a groan of pleasure.

197

Grasping her shoulder in a vice-like grip he thrust forcefully, almost as though he was annoyed at his own lack of control. Very soon his breathing quickened and with a shout that Lisa muffled with her hand he finally climaxed, wrapping his arms round her as he rolled off the sofa and they both fell on to the soft rug on the floor beneath.

For several minutes they lay there, until his breathing slowed and he lifted his head to look at her. 'I'm sorry. I didn't come here intending to hurl myself on you straight away. It was just . . . It's been difficult staying away this past week. All I could think about was you, and when I saw you again I couldn't wait.'

'It doesn't matter,' she lied, secretly feeling that he'd used her to obliterate the memory of Naomi.

'You're so beautiful,' he murmured, running a hand down the curve of her waist and hips. 'No one would guess you were pregnant.'

'Well, I am. I'd like to get dressed now, I'm a bit chilly.'

She pulled her skirt and silk blouse back on, then went into the kitchen to make coffee. When she returned with the tray, Neal was sitting in one of the armchairs looking as though he'd just come from a board meeting, all trace of passion gone.

'I want you to meet the girls,' he said abruptly.

Lisa swallowed a hot mouthful of coffee and felt it burning its way down her throat and chest. 'Already?'

'We haven't got that long. Our son isn't going to wait forever to be born.'

'Our *baby* isn't the issue here. We're talking about your daughters. I should think the last thing they want to do is meet their father's pregnant mistress.'

'They'll do exactly as I say.'

'Perhaps they will, but how do you know I'm willing to come?'

'Why on earth not? It's only a matter of time before we're married.'

Lisa stood up and looked directly down into his eyes. 'Neal, you haven't yet asked me to marry you, and even when you do I'm not sure what my answer will be. I don't like your trying to bulldoze me into marriage without having time to think about it. I'm not one of your employees who has to do as you say. I'm free, and sometimes I think I want to stay that way.'

At that moment he could willingly have strangled her. Bishop had done a marvellous job. Naomi was dead and everyone felt sympathy for him because he'd spent so many years with a woman most men would have discarded long ago. Now was the right moment to re-marry, and suddenly this slip of a girl was actually suggesting she

198

might not want marriage when he'd had two people murdered just for her, and she was possibly carrying his first legitimate heir!

He forced a smile to his face. 'I'm sorry, you're quite right. As usual I'm handling things all wrong. Come and spend a Sunday with us next month and we'll talk about our future afterwards. How does that sound?'

'Very acceptable.'

'As acceptable as the clothes from Paris?' He couldn't resist the remark but when colour flared in her face he wished he'd kept quiet.

'Keep your bloody clothes, Neal. I never asked you to buy them for me, and I certainly didn't realise they were a form of currency. One commitment for life in exchange for three tailored suits! Is that how it works? If so, keep them. Give them to Oxfam.'

'I didn't mean ...'

'I don't want them!' she shouted, forgetting Jessica and the nurse. 'I never want to see them again. Just get rid of them, and here's your charge card too.' She flung her wallet across the room.

He looked down at it and swallowed back his fury. He couldn't understand why the evening was going disastrously wrong. 'Don't be silly, darling.'

'I'm not silly. In fact I'm quite clever. Do you think I don't realise what's happening? Isn't it rather amazing that ...' She stopped. Upstairs, Jessica had begun to cry and all at once she remembered just how dependent on this man she was. The expression on Neal's face made her bite back the accusation.

'Yes?' His voice was terrifyingly gentle.

'I don't know what I was going to say,' she murmured lamely. 'I'm sorry, this has been a difficult time for me too. I've been alone here day after day, worrying about you, wondering how you were coping, and then when you finally arrive you throw yourself on me as though I'm some second-rate hooker before hurling a marriage proposal at me! It's hardly surprising I'm confused!' Then, to her own secret contempt, she deliberately burst into tears.

She knew at once that her strategy had worked. There was an immediate lessening of the tension as Neal started to murmur an apology for his behaviour and reassure her of his love.

He was as relieved as Lisa that the scene was over. For one terrible moment he'd thought she actually suspected him of having Naomi murdered. If that had been the case then she would have been a threat to him, but he realised it was only another example of her highly-strung state. Even her blunt comments about marriage he was able to dismiss as nerves. Everything would work out in the end; he simply had to have more patience.

199

When he finally left they'd fixed a date for her visit to meet the girls. 'They've got another three weeks to get over things,' was his final comment. 'If they're not ready to meet you by then, they never will be.'

She smiled, waved goodbye, closed the door and then collapsed against it, resting her back on the solid mahogany. Three weeks to get over the death of their mother! she thought incredulously. How could any man be so insensitive? But then again, Naomi had spent most days in her room so perhaps she was being unfair to him. Perhaps the girls weren't mourning their mother as much as she thought. She didn't really know. All she knew was that for one brief moment she'd unwittingly laid bare a side of Neal that she hadn't known existed. Despite his undoubted love for her and the influence he exerted over all she did she began to wonder if she wasn't making another mistake.

Next day, despite the lingering frost and cold easterly wind, Lisa left Jessica and Janice and walked briskly to the park. She needed time and fresh air. Time to think and fresh air to clear the nagging headache last night had brought on.

On her second circuit she was forced to stop abruptly as a small, dark-haired boy dashed in front of her, chasing a very large football. He threw his entire body on it and then looked up at Lisa with a wonderful smile. 'My ball!' he explained proudly. 'Papa give me an English football.'

'It's nearly as big as you!' she laughed, charmed by his obvious sweetness and glowing pride in his possession.

'*Si,* but I grow; the ball will not.'

'That's very true!'

He stood up and began kicking it back on to the grass. 'You play?' he asked at the last moment, his appeal almost wistful.

'I'm no good at football.' Lisa genuinely wished that she was.

'Luciano, come here at once! Leave the lady alone. She isn't interested in you ... Why, we meet again, Mrs Walker!'

Lisa's chest tightened but she tried to look calm as she glanced up at the handsome Italian. He was the last person she wanted to see just when she was persuading herself that marrying Neal was the right thing to do.

'Amazing!' she agreed with a smile. 'This must be your son.'

'Yes. Your daughter is not with you?'

'She's more difficult these days, and I wanted a chance to have a quiet think.'

'Then we will leave you alone.'

Luciano had spotted a playful labrador puppy and was running off to see if he could pat it. Renato and Lisa stood very close. She could

200

smell the tang of his aftershave. 'There is something worrying you?' he queried softly, taking her cold, ungloved hands in his own.

'I've got to make a decision and I'm not sure what to do. I'm really making a mountain out of a molehill.'

'I don't understand.'

'I'm making it a bigger problem than is necessary.'

He raised one eyebrow and her stomach lurched. She wondered what it would feel like to rest her head against his massive chest and have his arms round her. Would she still feel like trying to break free as she always did with Neal? Or would she feel protected rather than trapped? She thought she might. Presumably it all came down to sexual chemistry, she thought wryly. She couldn't ask for a more patient lover than Neal, so why should she think that with this man she'd be able to relax? It was far more likely that he'd discard her after one attempt. If all she'd heard about him was true, he was sexually so sophisticated that her pathetic performance would send him to sleep!

'To marry or not to marry?' he queried, keeping her right hand in his left as they walked over the grass.

'Yes.'

'You have others beside yourself to consider. Little Jessica; the baby that is so important to your lover. Refusal is a luxury you cannot afford.'

She snatched her hand free. 'How dare you speak to me like that? What the hell do you know about what I can or can't afford? If I don't love him, and I don't, how can I go ahead and marry him? It isn't fair to Neal. He deserves better than that.'

Bellini caught hold of her wrist, his fingers digging into her skin. 'I speak to you like that because no one else will, and because I know it is the truth. I will repeat it once more before we part. After that you can think what you like about me because I shall not attempt to counsel you again. You have to marry him. If you do not, you will die. It is as simple as that. Also, do not feel sorry for him. It is you who deserves better; but life is not always fair and so you must – what is the expression – make the best of things?'

'Die?' Her eyes were huge.

'But of course. Did you think he would let you go?'

'You're mad! Of course he'd let me go. What kind of a man do you think he is?'

Bellini gave a slight shrug of his huge shoulders and glanced around for his son. 'I know what kind of a man he is. Obviously you do not. And now we part. I will take Luciano home and you will go back to Neal and tell him how much you want to be his wife. That is the way it must be.'

201

'He hates Jessica,' she whispered.

'He loves you more. Give him a son, and after that anything you need for Jessica will be yours. If you love your daughter as much as you say, then fight for her. Neal Gueras can afford any treatment she needs. Remember that when you hesitate.'

'He isn't the only wealthy man in the world!'

'He is the father of your unborn child. I cannot think of any other wealthy man who would take his child as well as Jessica, can you?'

She shook her head. He was right. Also, her life would be comfortable and well cushioned so she was actually doubly fortunate. Except that she didn't love Neal; didn't feel any overwhelming desire to touch and be touched when she was with him. She hadn't minded that until she met this man with his devastating eyes, flexible mouth and the chiselled perfection of face common to Italian aristocrats. But now she had, it was hard to put all chance of any such relationship with a man behind her forever.

Finally she looked at him, her eyes full of unshed tears. 'No, I can't. But there's nothing to say I can't cope on my own.'

'He can help Jessica.'

'No one can help Jessica.'

'You do not know that.'

'I suppose not.'

He stopped walking and his fingers closed caressingly round her wrist. 'You are already lovers, he must be able to make you happy in that way. Why do you hang back?' The words were almost spat out through clenched teeth and suddenly there was anger in his eyes. Lisa went hot all over and stepped back so quickly that she tripped. Bellini put out an arm and pulled her against him, staring down at her flushed face.

For a moment they stayed quite still, their bodies just touching. She imagined she could feel his heat through her clothes. Abruptly he released her, his breathing ragged. 'I can understand why he would risk so much to possess you,' he said at last. 'I only wish that we had met sooner. Perhaps you will invite me to your wedding?' Then he raised her hand to his mouth, brushed it lightly with his lips and strode swiftly away across the grass. Never before had she felt so lonely.

When she got home she rang the number Dr Weissler had given her and began making enquiries about the holding technique for autistic children, and how much time and money was involved. When she finally replaced the receiver she knew that Bellini was right. If her visit to Berkshire went well, she would accept Neal's proposal, provided he accepted her conditions for Jessica's future.

Despite the Italian's forthright warning she still didn't understand anything at all about this man who wanted to marry her.

Beckett Lodge was invisible from the road. It wasn't until Neal swung the car sharply right into the concealed entrance that Lisa realised they'd arrived, and even then there was a long, tree-lined drive to negotiate before the house came into sight.

It was a large, three-storey, redbrick house with small leaded windows reminiscent of a Norman castle. An extra wing had recently been added, while to the right there was a stable block behind which she could see a wide stretch of grass sloping away to a considerable area of parkland.

The front door was white, matching the ornate iron grilles covering all the downstairs windows. As they approached, Lisa's eye was caught by a movement from a circular window set above the entrance porch. She glimpsed a girl's face looking out at her but when she looked closer it had vanished.

A tall, military-looking man wearing a dark suit and white shirt opened the door, and for a moment Lisa thought he was a business colleague. 'Darling, this is Wakefield, our butler. Wakefield, I'd like you to meet Mrs Walker who will be staying here for the weekend.'

The faded blue eyes were polite enough but there was no warmth in them. 'I hope your stay will be pleasant, madam,' he said stiffly, gesturing for a young lad of about sixteen wearing a lighter coloured suit to step forward. Without a glance at either Neal or Lisa, he darted out to the car and began unloading their suitcases.

'That's Michaels,' explained Neal. 'He's slightly backward but a very willing lad once he understands what's expected of him. Tell him to put Mrs Walker's cases in the blue room, Wakefield.'

'Very good, sir.'

'Where are the girls?' added Neal, a note of irritation in his voice.

Lisa, busy looking about her at the mahogany panelled walls and immaculately polished parquet floor with its beautiful Persian rugs, didn't hear him and was quite surprised when one of the numerous doors leading off the hall opened and a rather plain girl with brown hair emerged, holding a book protectively in front of her.

'Ruth, I wondered where you all were! This is Lisa Walker. Lisa, my middle daughter, Ruth.'

'I'm very pleased to meet you, Ruth.' Lisa smiled and put out her hand.

Ruth responded with a limp handshake and then hung her head as she muttered what Lisa assumed to be a welcome.

'Where are your sisters?' asked Neal sharply. Ruth's pale face flushed. 'I told you all to be waiting for us.'

'Louise is studying,' she murmured, still looking down at the floor.

'For goodness' sake hold your head up! Go and fetch Louise, please.'

Lisa watched Ruth walk heavily up the wide, curving staircase with its shining oak banister, her fears of a difficult weekend already confirmed.

'Sorry about the girls!' Neal gave a reassuring smile. 'Don't take it personally. They're never very sociable. Ah, here comes Rebekah!' The thin, dark-haired child coming down the stairs in front of them looked both shy and ill-tempered. She glanced defiantly at Lisa, as though daring her to speak.

'Rebekah, this is Lisa Walker,' smiled Neal.

'I didn't think it was the Easter Bunny.'

Her father drew his brows together in astonishment. 'We all know who she is,' the little girl continued, almost stammering in her anxiety to get the words out before she was stopped. 'We've seen her picture in the papers often enough. Mummy used to show it to us.'

'Hello, Rebekah,' said Lisa swiftly, stifling Neal's imminent outburst of rage.

'You're not as pretty as I expected,' continued Rebekah rudely. 'You aren't even wearing nail polish.'

'That's because I've got a little girl of my own and I'm forever doing her washing which makes all the varnish peel off.'

'You've got a little girl?' Suddenly there was a spark of interest in the child's eyes.

'Yes, she's ...'

'Never mind that!' exclaimed Neal quickly. 'Go and fetch Louise. I can't imagine what she and Ruth are doing. I thought Louise would be anxious to meet Lisa.'

'She's already seen her from the porthole window. She said she looked like a tart. What's a tart?'

'Something you eat for tea!' said Lisa, attempting to keep smiling.

'How can a person look like a cake?'

'Go and get Louise!' muttered Neal. Rebekah's mouth set in a tight line but she did as she was told while her father guided Lisa into an enormous drawing room, at least forty feet long with a high white ceiling and a vast picture window overlooking a walled garden. Cream drapes were tied back with thick cream cords while two comfortable chairs and a footstool upholstered in matching fabric were angled to look out at the view. By the far wall, dark-brown, high-backed velvet chairs were set round a low coffee table while at the far end a matching pair of early nineteenth century mahogany drum tables inset with green hide were covered with trailing plants in green and white cachepots. With its light aubergine carpet and attractive gold-framed hunting prints, the room's overall effect was both airy and clutter free, but Lisa felt a central focal point would give it a more welcoming air.

'I'm sorry about the girls,' Neal said stiffly.

'I warned you.'

'Frankly, I'm both astounded and displeased.'

'Don't get annoyed; just give them time.' Before he could answer, Louise drifted into the room. Lisa thought she was a very pretty girl but with a regrettably sulky mouth.

'Where the hell have you been?' snapped Neal.

Louise's eyes were innocent. 'Doing homework. You're always complaining I don't work hard enough at school. I thought you'd be pleased.'

'Not when I've brought Lisa down to meet you all.'

'Hi!' said Louise indifferently, her gaze fixed on Lisa's stomach, which mercifully was still amazingly flat. 'Rebekah says you've got a daughter of your own. I suppose she's been dumped with relatives while you're here?'

'No, she's stayed with her nurse.'

'Do you mean a nanny?'

'I mean a nurse. You see, Jessica's . . .'

'Right,' Neal interrupted, 'I think it would be nice to show Lisa round the grounds before it gets dark. We'll meet up by the stables in fifteen minutes. Does that give you enough time to freshen up, darling?'

'If someone would show me where my bedroom is?'

'I'm sure Daddy can do that!' Louise smirked, and despite herself, Lisa felt a blush spreading up her neck.

'Of course I'll show you,' said Neal courteously, but he shot a threatening look at his eldest daughter.

'How many rooms are there?' asked Lisa, relieved to find that she was on the first floor as her back was beginning to ache.

'On this floor there are three bedroom suites and three double rooms; the top floor has staff accommodation but only Wakefield sleeps there, which leaves the left wing deserted. Downstairs there's the drawing room that you saw, a dining-room, study, small drawing-room, kitchen and a vast utility room that houses everything without a proper home!'

'What's the new part of the house used for?'

'It isn't really part of this house, although there is a connecting door from my study. It's where my security men live.'

'Security men?'

'I'm afraid if you've got any money these days you have to protect your property very thoroughly. They're good men and well trained. One of them's an ex-SAS officer.'

'Simon never took precautions like that! Are you afraid of being burgled?'

'Not really, it's a more personal form of danger I'm afraid of. There's always kidnapping; the girls are targets for that, and there've been one or two threats against me.'

'If you were royalty or a pop star I could understand it, but ...'

'I assure you it's necessary.'

'Obviously you think so but I can't imagine ...'

'Bishop uses it as a base as well,' added Neal, knowing that any mention of his name would divert Lisa's attention.

'He doesn't come into the house, does he? Even the sight of him turns me cold.'

'He joins us occasionally. Louise has quite a crush on him. Not that I'd allow her to get involved but it's amazing to watch her flirt when he's around!'

'What does Bishop think of that?'

'He probably sees her as his entrance ticket into the family! Seriously, I haven't a clue what he thinks. He isn't one to give anything away. I'll meet you downstairs in ten minutes.'

Alone, Lisa looked carefully round her. The room was certainly blue, the shades varying from the very palest ice-blue of the curtains to the deep cobalt of the wool carpet. The bed had stunning light-blue parachute silk draped over the four posts, the white duvet and pillows trimmed with the same colour. Bluey-grey tapestries covered three walls, while the fourth had a vast walk-in wardrobe in light oak. The ceiling was covered mainly with white tiles but an occasional blue rose continued the colour theme. A vase of peacock feathers stood on a glass table by the window while the door to the stark, ice-blue bathroom had an overhead canopy and drapes matching those over the bed.

Once in the bathroom, she shivered. The large mirror over the basin showed her looking deathly white and she wondered who'd chosen such a cold theme. It wasn't friendly and was decidedly unflattering. She was relieved that she wouldn't be staying for long.

Her clothes had already been unpacked and she quickly took out a pair of rust-coloured slacks and matching jersey, then pulled on a multi-coloured mohair jacket that reached to just above her knees. It was one of Carol's own designs that helped disguise the small amount of weight she now carried. She was downstairs before Neal but Ruth was already waiting, dressed in scruffy jeans and what looked like a man's parka. 'Don't you ride?' she asked.

'To tell the truth I'm rather afraid of horses.'

'I adore them. I need a new horse but Daddy keeps cancelling every time we're due to go and look at one. We've got some good bloodstock here. It's a hobby for Daddy, but like everything he does it makes money as well.'

'You sound as though you think that's wrong.'

'I didn't mean to. You'd better not wear those shoes,' she added, looking at Lisa's flat Charles Jourdan pumps. 'Didn't you bring any wellies?'

'No.'

'We keep some spare ones in the utility room. There might be some your size. Go to the end of the hall, then turn right through the swing doors and along the little passageway.'

Lisa hurried down the hall and through the doors but stopped at the entrance to the kitchen as she heard her name mentioned.

'. . . young enough to be his daughter,' Wakefield was saying. 'Bold as brass too. You'd think she'd feel guilty coming here so soon after Mrs Gueras passed away.'

'Mind what you say,' cautioned a woman. 'If he was to hear, you'd be out without a reference.'

'If I got out at all.' Wakefield sounded suddenly gloomy.

Despite herself, Lisa couldn't stop listening.

'It's only natural,' continued the woman. 'They say she's pregnant which doesn't give him long to get her introduced to the family and safely married. Besides, Mrs Gueras wasn't a proper wife to him as you very well know.'

'She doesn't look pregnant to me.' Wakefield's antagonism towards Lisa wouldn't be appeased. 'She's rather thin and hasn't got a scrap of makeup on her face. Her hair's all over the place too.'

'It's the Masters' woman I miss,' confided the woman. 'When I think . . .'

Her heart thumping against her ribs, Lisa forced herself on to the utility room where she grabbed the first pair of boots that looked suitable and almost ran back to the hall. She'd expected the girls to be against her, but not the staff.

'We thought you'd got lost,' said Louise, fiddling with her small Cartier watch. 'Daddy was just about to come and find you.'

'I . . .'

'What size are those?' interrupted Neal.

'About a six, I think.'

He turned them upside down. 'They're an eight! Really, darling!'

207

'If we don't hurry up it will be too dark even to see a horse, let alone the grounds,' said Ruth anxiously.

In fact the horses were less frightening than Lisa had expected, and Neal didn't attempt to get her to touch any of them, accepting her fear with tolerance.

'I don't like horses either,' said Rebekah, moving closer to Lisa's side as they watched Ruth feeding an enormous mare some sugar lumps. 'I'm afraid of horses, storms and spiders. Are you afraid of spiders?'

'A bit. I don't mind small ones but I wouldn't fancy dealing with one of those enormous foreign ones that come over in banana crates!'

'Are they big and furry with yellowy stripes?' Rebekah seemed curiously troubled.

'Yes, they're called tarantulas.' Rebekah stared blankly into the distance. 'They don't live here,' Lisa said reassuringly, realising that the little girl was trembling.

Rebekah's head turned slowly towards her. 'Don't they? I thought ...'

'What?'

'I don't know.' She sounded confused. 'I thought I'd seen some once, but I can't remember when. It must have been a dream, I suppose. I do get bad dreams and I walk in my sleep.'

'Who puts you back to bed?'

'Nanny does if she finds me, but I often go back myself. It's only in the morning when I find my slippers in the wrong place or something like that, that I know I've done it.'

'She's loopy!' jeered Louise. 'Completely round the twist. Tarantulas indeed!'

'Shut up!' shouted Rebekah. 'I said it was a dream. Besides, you're frightened of things too.'

'I am not.'

'Yes you are. You're frightened Daddy won't let you marry that disgusting Bishop!'

With a scream of fury, Louise grabbed Rebekah's long hair and tugged viciously at it. 'Shut up, pest! Why can't you go away to boarding school like Mummy wanted, then we wouldn't have to put up with your spying on us all the time. You're vile!'

Surprised by the noise, Neal swung round and saw the girls fighting. He grabbed Louise by the shoulders and pulled her away. 'Leave the child alone, Louise. Aren't you a little too old for playground scraps?'

Louise went scarlet with humiliation but kept silent, her look daring Lisa to repeat what she'd heard. 'Come on,' continued Neal wearily. 'We'll go down to the parkland.'

Although it was nearly dark, Lisa had time to take in the extent of the grounds. All the lawns were immaculate, the park and woods large enough for exercising horses. There was a beautiful rose garden with a wooden pergola that would be glorious in mid-summer, and a covered swimming pool by the large patio, situated in the best place to trap the sun. Unfortunately, Lisa realised that anyone in the annexe had a good view of people in the pool, and she didn't care for the thought of Bishop watching her swim. But then she probably wasn't going to be living here anyway.

For dinner she changed into a dark blue empire-line St Laurent dress that hung in soft pleats to mid-calf length, studded with diamanté inserts across the bodice and round the wrists. After carefully doing her face and putting a heated brush through her hair she went down to the dining-room, hoping that Neal would be pleased with the way she looked.

She hesitated at the door. The girls' voices were raised in argument and all at once she didn't want to go in. She felt ridiculously afraid of facing them, especially without Neal. The sudden touch of his hand on her arm made her jump. 'Sorry, darling, I didn't mean to creep up on you. How about a drink before dinner? It isn't quite eight o'clock.'

'Perhaps we should join the girls? The weekend is for me to get to know them.'

'I wanted you to meet them but I've no intention of letting them monopolise you. I saw how Rebekah clung to your hand while we were outside.'

'Weren't you pleased? I thought it was nice that she wanted to be friendly, and it's obvious that with a little more attention she'd ...'

'She's got a prefectly adequate nanny. I'm the one who needs your attention!' Although he smiled, Lisa knew he meant what he said. Her heart sank. If he was jealous of his own daughters, what on earth would he be like with Jessica?

'In that case, a small dry sherry please.'

Taking hold of her elbow he guided her into his study. 'We won't be disturbed here. No one comes in without an invitation.'

'You make it sound like a Royal Garden Party!'

He took her in his arms and began to kiss her. 'I'll be glad when it's time to go to bed. Oh, Lisa, if only you knew how much you meant to me.' And his kisses deepened, his tongue thrusting into her mouth as his hands began fondling her breasts.

Horribly aware of the proximity of the girls, she tried to relax against him, feeling his hardness pressing against her body. Then he started to lower her to the small sofa, and this time she managed to wriggle free, laughing nervously. 'Not now! I thought we came in for a drink?'

'I'm afraid I got carried away. Perhaps you should carry an addiction warning!'

'Louise isn't very enamoured of me. I'm surprised I haven't already dropped dead from one of her looks! Was she very close to Naomi?'

'No, she's just trying to annoy me. Louise resents the fact that I've spent so much of her childhood away from home. She doesn't seem to appreciate that money has to be earned.'

'Maybe she isn't obsessed with money.'

'She's certainly good at spending it. The man who marries her is in for a shock. She spends more in one visit to Harrods than you've spent in all the time I've known you.'

Privately Lisa thought this was the girl's way of getting something from her father. If she couldn't have affection, and it didn't look as though she could, then she obviously used his money as a substitute, but Neal wasn't the type of man to understand her motives. To him money was the most important currency. She felt very sorry for the girls, growing up with an invalid mother and a father they scarcely saw.

'That sounds like the gong,' said Neal, finishing his whisky in one quick swallow. 'We'd better go through. I'm afraid I've crumpled your skirt at the back.'

'Never mind, I'll soon be sitting down so it won't show.'

'Not nervous, are you?' he asked as she slipped a cool hand into his.

'A little. They're so antagonistic. Not Rebekah, but ...'

'Bugger the children!' he said shortly. 'If they can't be civil they'll be sent away to boarding school. Remember, you're not on trial, darling, they are.' Horrified, Lisa's thoughts flew once again to Jessica.

The girls were already seated when they entered the room. Ruth gave them a half-smile, Rebekah an eager glance, but Louise's gaze swept over Lisa's dress and she raised her eyebrows slightly.

'Is something wrong, Louise?'

'No, Daddy. I only wondered why Lisa was wearing dark blue. It doesn't really suit her.'

There was complete silence. The young maid who was bringing in the soup stood frozen in the doorway and waited. Neal reached for a roll from the basket in front of him and broke it as though it were

Louise's neck. 'Such appalling manners certainly don't suit you, Louise. I'd prefer it if you were to leave us now. I don't wish to see you again until tomorrow morning.'

'I thought I was supposed to be getting to know Lisa.' Louise was nervous but apparently hell-bent on destruction.

'No, Lisa is here to get to know you. I imagine she now has your measure and your presence is therefore superfluous. We will see you at breakfast. Goodnight.'

Ruth and Rebekah had their heads bent. Rebekah was having difficulty in restraining her tears while Ruth's head shook spasmodically in a nervous tic.

'*I hate you!*' shouted Louise, all pretence at composure gone. 'How can you bring that *thing* here when Mummy's only just died? Don't you realise how horrible it is for us having to look at her, sitting in Mummy's seat, trying to be nice to us all when ...'

'I don't imagine she'll bother with you any more. Now get out!' He was no longer calm and his face was filled with such contempt that Louise burst into tears.

'I hope you know what he's like!' she shouted, turning to Lisa and almost spitting out the words. 'He can't love anyone except himself. Mummy could have told you that, or Kay. But they're both dead now. Isn't that jolly lucky for you!'

Before anyone could reply she'd rushed from the room, banging the door behind her so that the family portraits hanging round the room swung slightly on their hooks.

'Better than *Dallas*,' murmured Neal lightly, and Lisa gave him a watery smile. She was acutely shocked both by Louise's distress and also by the force of her dislike. Ruth and Rebekah seemed as though they'd respond to normal kindness but Louise was plainly going to be an enemy should Lisa ever consent to marry her father. And Louise was in love with Bishop. Lisa shuddered at the thought of their combined hatred.

'You may serve the soup now, Ann,' instructed Neal. Looking at the wide-eyed maid Lisa wondered what Wakefield would say when he heard about the scene.

The rest of the meal passed off quite well. When they'd finished they all went into the small drawing-room and played bridge on a beautiful mahogany Pembroke table with an inlaid satinwood board. At nine, Rebekah was collected by her nanny, an elderly, hard-faced woman, and an hour later Ruth made her excuses and went to bed. Only when they'd finally gone did Lisa realise how tense she'd been. She slumped back in her chair with a small sigh.

'Tired?' Neal gave her a sympathetic smile. 'It's been rather a baptism of fire! Still, we're alone at last. How about a nightcap?'

'I don't think the baby likes alcohol!'

'You don't mind if I do?'

'Carry on.' She watched as he opened the drinks cabinet and took out the Napoleon brandy. He was so much more at home here than in his London flat. He suited the large house, the stables and the estate. His air of authority and power was still very obvious but even more attractive, and she knew that there must be a lot of women who envied her. Sitting with him now, she too was attracted yet knew that once they began making love the attraction would vanish and he'd seem like a stranger touching her.

'I've asked some friends round for drinks tomorrow morning. Only one or two neighbours. I thought you might like to meet them.'

'Did they know Naomi well?'

'Scarcely at all. I suppose she was round once or twice when we first came here. After that she took to staying in her room when we had company.'

'It must have made things very difficult for you.'

'A little. Lisa, have you thought any more about marrying me?' She didn't answer him. 'I realise I took you by surprise the other night but you've had plenty of time to consider it since then and quite honestly, darling, I don't want to wait any longer than necessary. I promise I'll do everything in my power to make you happy.'

'Perhaps I will have a drink,' she murmured, and then wrapped her hands round the glass. 'I'll be absolutely honest. I have thought about marriage and I appreciate how much you love me, but it simply wouldn't be fair to you if I accepted.'

'Why?'

'Because I don't love you. I like you and enjoy being with you but I don't love you. I don't think I've ever loved anyone. Perhaps there's something wrong with me and I can't, but what I feel for you isn't enough.'

'Enough for whom?' he asked quietly.

'For you!'

'Is it enough for you? I appreciate that in some respects our relationship isn't perfect but we can talk to each other. We share several interests and I want you as my wife even if you don't love me. If it's enough for you then don't hesitate to accept, but it isn't enough, is it?'

She thought of Renato Bellini in the park. Remembered his hand grasping hers and pictured the smile on his face as he played with his small son. She knew instinctively that if he were asking her to marry him she'd feel quite differently about the question, and because she was honest she regretfully shook her head.

'No, I don't think it is.'

Neal didn't move. He stayed in the shadowed corner of the room. 'What about our child?' he asked quietly.

'You'll see it as often as you like.'

'But he couldn't take over from me when he grew up. He wouldn't be my legitimate heir. I've always wanted a son.'

'It may be another girl,' she reminded him gently.

'What about Jessica?'

'To be honest, I can't see Jessica fitting into our marriage at all. You resent spending time on your own daughters, all perfectly normal girls. Don't tell me you'd welcome Jessica with open arms. She's another very good reason for us to let things remain the way they are.'

'I could pay for special treatment,' he said at last. 'I understand this touch therapy's had good results. Wouldn't you like Jessica to be given a chance to try that?'

'Of course I would!'

'Isn't it expensive?'

'Very!'

'I could give her that chance, Lisa.'

'When?' she asked sharply.

'After you'd given me a son.'

It was then that she knew his desire to make her his wife wasn't based solely on overwhelming desire. He too had a reason for choosing her. She was young, attractive, of child-bearing age and obviously fertile. Much as he might love her, he wouldn't have offered marriage without all those advantages. Suddenly, marrying him to give Jessica hope didn't seem nearly so bad.

'I'm beginning to think we understand one another,' she murmured. 'You want something I can give you, and I want ...'

'I love you!' he interrupted. 'Of course I want a son, most men do, but I've known other women who could just as easily have given me one and I didn't marry them.'

'You couldn't, Naomi was alive.'

'Yes, but she could easily have been ...'

Lisa sat upright. 'Been what?'

'Dead, of course. She might have died years ago.'

'But she didn't. She only died once I was pregnant.'

'A fact which I admit gave me great pleasure. It's probably the first time she's done anything right for the past ten years, but all I was saying was ...'

She stopped listening because at the back of her mind was the terrible suspicion that he'd nearly made a mistake and said 'killed', as though her death would always have come at the most convenient time for him. If that were true then it wasn't very likely that she'd died of natural causes, whatever the inquest said.

Jessica! she reminded herself fiercely. He's rich, he's anxious to please me, I like him and he can give Jessica every possible assistance. If there are things about him that are dark and secret, I don't want to know. I have to think of Jessica.

'Lisa, have you been listening to me?'

She smiled up at him. 'I really am very tired. Could I give you my answer tomorrow night, when the weekend's over?'

'As long as it's yes!'

'And about Jessica,' she added as he helped her out of her chair. 'Whereabouts in the house would she live?'

'Once I've got my heir she can have the empty wing on the top floor. It's virtually soundproof and no one will bump into her by mistake. She'd have plenty of space to run around, and there's a bedroom and bathroom for her nurse as well.'

'She isn't a monster! People don't run screaming when they see her, you know.'

'Just the same, I'd prefer her up there. For her own sake,' he added unconvincingly.

'Where do you want her until the baby's born?'

'Until we have a son, I don't want her in this house at all. She can stay on in Chelsea with her nurse or she can go into a top-class home, but she's not wearing you out with her screaming and refusal to sleep until we've got a son and heir.'

'That could take years!'

'Darling, this is for your own good. Jessica is ruining your looks and your health. A break will do wonders for you; and let's be honest, she won't even know you've gone.'

'She will! She knows far more than people realise.'

'Lisa, you're tired. We can discuss this another time, when you're feeling more rational. Let me take you up to bed.'

She was grateful that he didn't attempt to come into her room. His earlier ardour had either been dissipated by the scene at dinner or else he sensed how far removed from desire she felt. As it was, she lay awake most of the night trying to decide what to do for the best. As a result she was pale and heavy-eyed next morning, and wondered how she could hope to be lively for their visitors.

Neal didn't come down to breakfast. 'He's in the annexe with Bishop,' explained Ruth.

'When did he arrive?'

'I don't know. He's one of those people who's suddenly with you.

214

I saw his light on when I went to the bathroom at three o'clock this morning.'

'Have you any idea why your father's with him?'

'Daddy never discusses business with any of us. He doesn't like being questioned about his movements either. Mummy knew that.'

'He'd better be here when his friends arrive,' said Lisa with feeling.

'Don't worry, he won't want to miss showing you off.'

'I feel so washed out I think I'll see what a shower and some makeup can do for me!'

Just then Rebekah joined them. She too looked pale and picked at her toast listlessly. 'Not hungry?' asked Ruth, taking a second helping of scrambled eggs from one of the silver dishes on the sideboard.

'No. I had a horrible dream last night.'

'You keep having horrible dreams. It's because you eat too much at night.'

'It is not. I never had them until Mummy died.'

'It's a normal reaction, Rebekah,' said Lisa gently. 'You're bound to miss her and when you're asleep your sadness comes out as bad dreams.'

'I don't miss her. She hated me. Why should I care if she's dead?'

'Rebekah!' Ruth was horrified. 'How can you talk about her like that?'

'Why shouldn't I? You know it's true.'

Lisa wished they'd keep quiet. She was beginning to get a headache, and although her sympathies were with Rebekah she wasn't up to a full psychological discussion.

'I'm dreaming because of those taran ... you know, the big spiders,' said Rebekah defiantly.

'Why should tarantulas keep you awake? They aren't in this country, you silly ninny!' responded Ruth.

'They are!' Rebekah threw her uneaten toast at her sister as she jumped to her feet. 'I saw them, I know I did. They were running around on the bed and ...'

'Which bed?'

Rebekah's face fell. 'I can't remember. I keep thinking and thinking but I can't remember.'

'You imagined it, or dreamt it. How many were there? Hundreds?'

'Of course not, stupid, but there were lots. They were running round over ...' Her eyes widened suddenly and she looked as though she was going to be sick.

'All over what, Miss Fib?'

Rebekah sat down again and Lisa saw that the child's hands were clenched tightly in her lap. 'Nothing.'

'I can't think why you've suddenly got this obsession with spiders,' continued Ruth. 'You never used to mind them; now you won't even wash a small one down the sink. You're as bad as Mummy was.'

'Didn't she like them either?' asked Lisa, wondering what had frightened Rebekah into silence.

'They absolutely terrified her. It wasn't an ordinary fear — I suppose it was a phobia. She used to scream her head off if a money spider so much as dropped on her arm. I can't think how she managed when she and Daddy lived in Greece.'

'I should try not to think about them, Rebekah,' suggested Lisa. 'I promise you they don't live in houses like this.'

Rebekah stared stonily at her. 'What's wrong with your little girl?'

'What do you mean?'

'I heard Daddy talking to Bishop outside my window this morning. He called her your idiot child.'

'Your father said that?' Lisa was furious.

'No, Bishop did! Daddy told him to shut up. Is she an idiot?'

Seeing how upset Lisa was, Ruth hurried to her rescue. 'She can't be a bigger one than you! Isn't it time you got ready for swimming? Natalie's mother will soon be here.'

'Blast!' muttered Rebekah, but she dawdled out of the room, her head bent as though she was weighed down with problems.

'Bishop's always foul,' said Ruth cheerfully. 'He tells me I've got legs like an elephant. Don't let what Rebekah heard upset you. It's when he starts to be nice that you need to worry! Louise is potty about him.'

'Does he like her?'

'I don't think so. Sometimes he's incredibly rude to her, but that only makes her more besotted. I think she must be a masochist. Are you worried about meeting our neighbours?' she added.

'I'm a bit nervous.'

'They're all right. Amanda Wichell's pretty poisonous but the rest are O.K. She's heavily into drugs. Do you take coke?'

'No.'

'You'll find Amanda's always rushing off to the loo for her fix. She tried heroin once but her husband had her put in a hospital. After that she settled for coke. Most people round here use it at parties, even the girls in my year at school, but Amanda uses it all the time.'

'Do you take it?'

'Not likely! I saw what drink and drugs did to Mummy. I don't think Daddy uses it either but he doesn't mind if other people do. May I ask you something?'

Lisa hoped it wasn't about Jessica again. 'Sure.'

216

'Are you going to marry Daddy?'

She put down her coffee cup. 'How would you feel about it if I did?'

'I wouldn't mind. You're much nicer than any of his other women and he'd probably be quite pleasant to us all for a time, expecially if you gave him some sons! I'd quite like it, but Louise wouldn't.'

'Why not?'

'I think she wants Daddy to lavish all his love on us. She doesn't realise he hasn't got much to lavish.'

'Well,' said Lisa carefully, 'it's possible I might but right now I'm not absolutely sure.'

'Don't let Louise put you off. That's what she's trying to do. Besides, Rebekah likes you and it would be good for her to have someone cheerful around. Not that Daddy would let you spend much time with her, although when he was away you could. She needs some loving.'

'I can see that. You've all been a little . . .'

'Deprived? Yes, we have. It's too late for Louise and me but you're still in time for Rebekah. Heavens, look at the clock! I must get to the stables.' She ran from the room just as Neal entered.

'What's up with her?' he asked mildly, giving Lisa a kiss on the forehead.

'She's off to her horses!'

'Sorry I missed breakfast. I had work to do. Were the girls all right?'

'I didn't see Louise. The other two were fine, quite chatty.'

His eyes sharpened. 'What did you talk about?'

'Nothing special, female gossip. Clothes, makeup, men!'

'I'm amazed Ruth knows anything about clothes. She's happiest wearing jeans and mucking out the stables.'

'I'd better get changed,' said Lisa quickly. 'I thought I'd wear the red Caroline Charles. That's not too dressy.'

'Won't your lump show?'

'I haven't got a lump!'

'I'm beginning to wonder where you're keeping that baby. If I didn't know how good Atkins was, I'd be worrried about it.'

She bent and kissed the top of his head. 'It's all right, I'm taking very good care of her.'

'Her?'

'Or him!' she laughed, failing to see the frown on his face. Neal didn't care to be teased.

By eleven-thirty the drawing room was crowded with couples, everyone talking loudly about people Lisa didn't know and places she'd never been.

217

'. . . and when I saw her at Badminton, I scarcely recognised her. She's so thin, darling, you wouldn't believe it. I asked her . . .'

'Went to Gloucester but honestly the cold! You'd think they'd be able to afford to run the heating. I mean, they are . . .'

'. . . and so I've decided to join the Belvoir Hunt. They're far more . . .'

'. . . I could have died. Imagine falling flat on your face on the *piste* right in front of Princess Caroline! She's changed since her mother died, gone quite staid. As for Stephanie, God knows what's going to become of her!'

'Laura didn't enjoy it one bit. Turns out she gets seasick. I'm going again next year though. It was Peter who got me interested. He's been going to Cowes for years, and last May he asked me if I'd . . .'

'Ghastly, isn't it?' murmured a voice in Lisa's ear. 'I don't suppose they've even bothered to talk to you apart from, "Hello, darling"?'

Lisa looked into the slightly haunted but undoubtedly lovely face of a woman who could have been anywhere between thirty-five and forty-five, and guessed by her glittering eyes that she was Amanda. 'Not really,' she admitted. 'Luckily, they all seem to be enjoying themselves.'

'Of course they are. Most of them haven't been invited here for years. They're positively preening their feathers. And they're all watching you carefully, take my word for it.'

'I can't think why. Did you want another drink?'

'After I've dashed to the loo. Weak bladder!' laughed Amanda. She obviously didn't expect to be believed. 'By the way, how did you manage to snare the gorgeous Neal? I've been after him for years without success. At least, that's to say, I never felt I was anything but a diversion! See you soon!' and with another giggle she disappeared.

'You look absolutely fantastic!' boomed a short, plump man whose few remaining strands of hair were spread across his scalp. 'Neal's a lucky devil. Don't know how he does it. All that charm, I suppose! My wife tells me he's the perfect gentleman. What she means is he's very rich and I'm not, but if I'd got his polish I could be. Absolute rubbish, of course. I mean, there *are* ethics. Still, he's done well for himself and there's nothing to stop people flying close to the wind, as I'm sure you know!'

'I've no idea what you're talking about,' said Lisa coldly, looking round for Neal.

'A woman of the world like you? Come now!'

'Why, if it isn't the malicious Mr Grey,' said Bishop, his voice cutting through the conversation like a knife. 'What poison are you pouring into this young lady's ear?'

'Just telling her how lovely she looks. No harm in that!' blustered Grey, backing slowly away.

'No harm at all. Of very little interest to you either if what I hear about your choir practices is true!'

'That's a damned lie! You should watch what you say. Law of slander and all that.' Still muttering he retreated, and Lisa was unable to suppress a gurgle of laughter.

Bishop's mouth turned up at the corners. 'He's a revolting toad,' he said casually. 'What was he trying to do? Touch you up?'

'Hardly! No, he was on about moral scruples, or business ethics, something like that. Does he really like boys?'

'Shouldn't think so but it shut him up! He's one of life's failures and his wife never lets him forget it. She married an up and coming insurance broker, and he stopped both going up and coming rather too soon for her liking!'

Lisa laughed again. 'You're in very good spirits.'

'Why not? Naomi's in heaven and all's right with the world. I'm going to find a drink.'

'Lisa, I'm so sorry, darling,' said Neal, walking up behind her and putting an arm possessively round her waist. 'I'm afraid I was called away to the phone, long-distance business call.'

'That's all right.' She was acutely aware that now he was with her his guests' voices had dropped. They were being eyed unobtrusively from all sides.

'Have you met everyone?'

'Only a woman called Amanda, whom I gather was once one of your conquests, and a Mr Grey who was singularly unattractive. Bishop saw him off.'

'Good. Have you thought any more about what we were discussing last night?'

'Yes, I ...'

'Neal, wonderful to see you again. Sorry about Naomi naturally but perhaps under the circumstances ...'

'Quite. Lisa, this is Dr Sutherland. He looked after Naomi.'

She smiled. 'It's nice to meet you. Do you live near here?'

'Just along the lane. Only a small place but quite large enough for me and my menagerie.'

'Ian's a bachelor with a fondness for stray animals,' explained Neal. 'He's wonderful with them. I think he ought to have been a vet.'

'I'm sure you're just as wonderful with people!' laughed Lisa.

'Oh, he is. So wonderful he attracts all the addicts for miles around. A very generous man, isn't that true, Ian?'

The doctor's smile was strained. 'I do what I can to help.'

219

'Just so. If you'll excuse us ...'

'That was rather rude,' said Lisa in surprise. 'You made it sound as though he was a poor doctor.'

'He is.'

'Then why did you let him look after Naomi?'

'She had a drug abuse problem. He's good at those.'

'Not if he's one of those doctors who allow endless repeat prescriptions.'

'Naomi couldn't have coped with total withdrawal. I was kind to be cruel,' he added wryly.

After that she met an assortment of bankers, stockbrokers, solicitors and publishers, but none of them made much impression on her. After they'd gone she was left with the distinct impression that she hadn't turned out to be at all what any of them expected.

She and Neal took a light lunch alone in his study. 'What was Kay like?' she asked, picking at her salad.

'Smart, blonde, conventional and quiet. Everything about her was quiet from her choice of clothes to her speaking voice. She would have made some man the prefect wife.'

'But not you?'

'Logically I'd have to say yes, but emotionally, definitely not. I used to think I wanted a docile woman. Once I met you, I changed my mind.'

'One of the girls said something which made me think you'd brought Kay here.'

'Occasionally I did. Naomi sometimes went into a clinic and then I'd bring Kay down if there was a dinner party.'

'So the people here this morning knew her?'

'Some of them. Why?'

'I got the feeling I wasn't quite up to the mark. I should have worn my grey wool dress with the white collar and cuffs!'

'I find that very sexy, it's like undressing a nun! Lisa, about marriage ...' She didn't speak. 'You said you'd thought about it.'

'So I have, all night to be accurate.'

'And?' He stopped eating and was unable to look at her face as he waited for an answer.

'If you honestly don't mind that I'm not in love with you, then yes, I'd like us to be married.'

Relief flooded his features as he stood up and took her in his arms. 'You'll never know how happy you've made me. I only hope you'll never have cause to regret it. I promise I'll do everything possible to make sure you don't.'

She leant her head against his chest and felt his heart racing. 'I'm sure I won't. I can have Jessica here and try the holding therapy once we've got a son?'

'Yes.'

'But she can't come before that?'

'Darling, we've been through this and . . .'

'In that case I'd like her to stay in the mews cottage. She's used to living there with Nurse Anthony and she'll be fine.' She tried not to dwell on the fact that she wouldn't be able to see that for herself. 'I can always visit her when I'm in town, can't I?' she added quickly. She felt his arms tighten for a second. 'Surely you're not trying to cut me off from her entirely? If you are then I can't possibly marry you.'

'I was just surprised, that's all. Obviously it would work out very well. Once the baby's nearly here you won't be going to town very often in any case.'

'I don't intend languishing here alone,' she retorted.

'I can't imagine you languishing anywhere alone, darling. There'll always be someone anxious to keep you company. Even that Italian spent an entire evening monopolising you!'

'Don't tell the girls until I've gone,' she said, suddenly anxious to change the subject.

'Why ever not?'

'Because I don't think it would be right.'

'Very well. Now I'm going to ring for some champagne.'

She could never remember how they passed the afternoon. All she knew was that now she was totally committed and there could never be any turning back.

They drove to London after tea and he made love to her in his Chelsea flat before taking her back to the cottage. Afterwards, as he slept silently beside her, she stared at the ceiling, her breasts slightly sore from his enthusiastic lovemaking, and prayed that she was doing the right thing and could make Neal as happy as he deserved. But most of all she prayed that Jessica would be helped, because it was on her that Lisa lavished her true love and affection.

Chapter Eighteen

Having made her decision, Lisa fully expected to feel relieved but instead found she felt guiltier than ever over Jessica because she'd agreed temporarily to abandon her. Every time she watched her climbing on to furniture and diving head first off – her latest obsession was with climbing – or studied the way she walked on tiptoe, her arms spread out like a tightrope walker, Lisa began to cry.

It was as though Jessica's world was becoming increasingly bizarre, and all these rituals were designed to make it more bearable. Jessica had also learnt to laugh, but at the most inappropriate things. Once started she couldn't stop and would giggle wildly until distracted by the sight of some silver paper, the glint of sunlight on a mirror, or similar trivia.

Neal was going to Sicily for a week and it was agreed that when he returned their engagement would be formally anounced. After that they would only wait another two months before the marriage because now the baby was beginning to show.

'Take care,' he cautioned as he kissed Lisa goodbye at the airport. 'Try and get plenty of rest. Janice says you're still doing too much for Jessica. That's not your job, darling.'

'Soon she won't have me around. I want to do all I can while I'm still there.'

'You've got two children to think about. This isn't fair to anyone. Won't Jessica miss you more if you don't start to let go now?'

'She's my daughter and I want her to know that I love her.'

Bishop, who was accompanying Neal on his flight, gave a thin smile.

'What's so funny?' she demanded.

'Nothing at all; it's admirable the way you rush to claim responsibility for her!'

'That's enough!' snapped Neal. Bishop walked away. He couldn't think what his employer saw in the girl. If he'd ever been stupid enough to marry and his wife had produced an imbecile like Jessica, he'd have packed her off out of sight straight away. Animals knew best, he reflected sourly. They deliberately killed any deformed offspring.

Lisa clung to Neal for a moment. 'I'll miss you,' she murmured.

His eyes softened. 'It won't be for long. Once I'm back and the engagement's announced we won't have to be parted again. You can even come on business trips, if you like, although they're pretty boring.'

'Ring me when you arrive. I'll want to know you're safe.'

'I will. Mike's going to take you back. He'll be around keeping an eye on you while I'm gone, just in case you need any help.' Giving her one last, lingering kiss, he turned quickly away. Lisa could guess how Bishop would be smirking if he were watching them.

'Back to Chelsea?' asked Mike cheerfully when she returned to the car.

'Yes please.' She wondered why she suddenly felt so lost and when she'd become dependent upon Neal's presence.

'You know the number to ring if you need help?'

'I can't imagine what kind of help I'm likely to need, unless it's with changing Jessica's nappies, and that can't be what you all mean!'

'Any odd phone calls, strangers at your door, that sort of thing.'

'I've never had any strange phone calls before!'

'Mr Gueras hasn't been away before.'

'Who would want to . . .?'

'Forget it! Just ring day or night if you want me for anything at all; even Jessica's nappies!'

Back in the cottage it was blessedly peaceful. Janice was busy preparing a moussaka for supper while Jessica slept on the floor in an untidy heap. She slept so badly that Lisa never tried to move her. She was left to sleep wherever she dropped off they were so grateful for any respite from her frantic energy.

It was the nurse's free evening. She offered to stay in but Lisa refused. 'I can cope perfectly well. This cold of hers is acting like a sedative. Have a good time.'

She was quite genuine in her assurances but when Jessica suddenly woke and began screaming and kicking the wall, she realised that she no longer knew how to handle her own child. The frustrated tantrum was so violent it was impossible to approach her to try and find out what she wanted.

'Would you like a drink?' asked Lisa. The screams continued. 'Are you hungry?' Jessica turned her head. 'Hungry?' she repeated,

223

miming eating with a spoon. This plainly didn't mean anything and Jessica began kicking at the emulsioned walls, then scratching with her finger nails so that flakes of paint dropped off.

'Stop it!' shouted Lisa. Immediately Jessica howled louder, her hands clasped over her ears. 'Are you hungry?' she repeated slowly.

Jessica stopped kicking and turned her body towards her mother. 'Are you hungry?' she said clearly.

'I'm not, but are you?' persisted Lisa, shaking with excitement.

'Are you hungry?' demanded Jessica again, then she grabbed Lisa's hand and led her towards the kitchen door.

'You are!' Lisa couldn't believe it. For the first time, Jessica had managed to communicate. 'Clever girl!' she said proudly. 'Jessica very clever girl.'

'Clever girl,' she echoed, tugging her mother towards the fridge. Lisa opened its door and Jessica grabbed a lump of cheese and began to chew on the entire slab. She'd now let go of Lisa and wasn't even looking in her direction but she'd succeeded in getting what she wanted and Lisa was so excited she didn't know what to do.

She needed to tell someone but there wasn't anyone to tell. She also wanted to know what this meant. Perhaps by some miracle Jessica was improving, or possibly this was a normal step forward in autistic children. It could, of course, just be a one-off occasion to which she was over-reacting. If only Janice were here, she thought. Significantly she didn't wish Neal were in England, knowing very well that he wouldn't have been in the least interested.

Leaving Jessica with the cheese, she went and poured herself a drink, and had just sat down when the doorbell rang. She remembered Mike's warning about strangers at the door. It was nearly nine o'clock and no one ever visited her in the evenings except Neal.

The bell went again, urgent and insistent. Slowly she walked across the room and looked through the spyhole. The tall figure of the Italian almost blocked her vision but his silk suit was unmistakable.

'What do you want?' she demanded.

'Quickly, let me in,' he whispered. 'I should not be here.'

She knew that; knew very well how furious Neal would be should he ever get to hear of it, but with a pounding heart she fumbled with the safety chain and then stepped back as he hurried through the doorway.

He glanced round the small living-room, taking note of the expensive velvet curtains and the collection of Meissen figures on the shelf over the fireplace. 'Very nice. I hope Jessica appreciates such luxury!'

'What do you want?' She was pleased to discover her voice sounded quite calm.

'One last chance to talk to you. I hear that you are soon to be married.'

'Who told you?'

'Your husband-to-be of course.'

'He told me no one was to know before the engagement announcement.'

'But I am different. I am a business colleague, the rules are not the same in all the games your lover plays.'

'I assume you're pleased?'

'Pleased for you, yes. It is what I suggested.'

'You were quite right.'

'For myself ...' He shrugged and raised an eyebrow. 'Let me say that for myself, I am not too happy.'

'I can't imagine why not,' she lied.

Reaching out he ran one finger lightly down the side of her face. 'Then you underestimate your powers of attraction. If things had been different here I would ...'

'Have added me to you list of conquests? No thanks. I'm afraid Jessica needs a stable background, not flying visits from strangers.'

'Always you retreat behind your daughter. You too need stability and that, I think, I could have given you. However ...' He smiled ruefully. 'It was not meant to be.'

As he spoke he moved towards her. Abruptly she was overwhelmed by terror. He was too big, far too similar to Toby, and all at once the room seemed to shrink in size. His features blurred and changed so that she was again backing away from her former husband, terrified of what torment lay ahead of her this time. When she backed up against the sofa she realised that this powerful man was almost on top of her and her scream tore through the room as her face twisted with terror.

Renato Bellini couldn't believe his eyes. One moment he was walking casually into the room and the next Lisa had disintegrated from a polished, elegant hostess into a terrified child, now whimpering senselessly as she stared blankly at his face.

Without hesitation he reached gently for her, pulling her effortlessly against him and keeping his arms around her, murmuring the words he usually reserved for little Luciano after a nightmare. Soothing her with his soft voice and hands. For a brief moment she resisted, as rigid as steel in his arms, then she seemed to crumple, her legs sagging and her head falling against his chest as she began to sob.

When the sobbing ceased he placed her gently on the sofa and sat beside her. 'What is it? What made you this way? I would never hurt you. Did you imagine . . . ?'

She felt utterly ashamed. What must he think of her? she wondered. Where was all the sophistication and polish now? In a few minutes he'd be gone, grateful he hadn't tried to make such a neurotic woman his mistress and probably pitying Neal as well.

'I'm sorry,' she said at last, pulling away from the blissful reassurance of his body. 'It was ridiculous. I'm afraid I once had a bad experience and for some reason it all came rushing back to me. You're built like a man I once knew.'

'What did this man do to you?'

She shivered. 'I don't want to talk about it. You really ought to go. I appreciate your calling but Neal wouldn't.'

'Does he know how frightened you still are? Has he found help for you?' The Italian was shaken by the intensity of her fear.

'I'm not like this with him!' She managed a shaky laugh. 'He did get me some psychiatric help, but it didn't do a lot of good. Just the same, he understands. He must do, otherwise he wouldn't be willing to marry me.'

For a son, thought Renato cynically, Neal would be willing to marry a psychotic, but this girl needed help. Before he could discover any more her daughter came into the room. Her eyes were huge and thick lashes brushed her cheeks when she looked down at the floor. Dark hair curled round her head and her skin was creamy white with a delicate pink flush on her cheeks. She looked utterly exquisite.

Disturbed by Lisa's screams, Jessica moved sideways towards the sofa, still walking on her toes with her arms outstretched and her hands flapping strangely in the air as though impersonating a bird. When she got near her mother she stopped. Having shot a brief sideways glance at Bellini and registered his presence, she wasn't quite sure what to do.

Renato sat perfectly still, ignoring her entirely. He fixed his gaze on a point half-way up the wall and studied it intently. This reassured Jessica who edged nearer to him, reached out and made a grab for the large watch on his wrist. When she failed to remove it she spat at him, kicked his shins and then scurried away on all fours into the corner of the room where she started pulling off her clothes.

'Neal's taking on quite a lot, isn't he!' said Lisa, still shivering from a mixture of shock and the strange excitement that his touch had caused over her entire body. An excitement that Neal never managed to arouse.

'He has agreed to take on this little one?'

'Once I've given him a son,' she said with a note of embarrasment.

226

'Ah, yes. Once that is done then doubtless you can blackmail him into keeping his word.'

'I won't have to blackmail him, he's already promised.'

Renato stood up, the sudden pain he was feeling proving too much for him to control. There'd been many women, many sexually sophisticated and stimulating women, but he'd never wanted any of them except in his bed. It was a terrible irony that it should be the prospective wife of his family's enemy who brought to the surface emotions of tenderness and protectiveness previously engendered only by his young son.

He knew that he had to leave quickly before he gave himself away and made her future marriage harder for them both. 'I forgot!' he said with a smile. 'He has promised, and being a gentleman his word is his bond, is it not? Then you are doubly blessed. Now I will go. I look forward to seeing you at your wedding. No doubt it will be one of the social events of the year.'

'I sincerely hope not,' she exclaimed, wondering why she felt so peculiarly alive. 'I want a quiet register office service.'

'If you succeed in that I shall know you will be wearing the trousers in your marriage, which I think is most unlikely! I wish you health and luck, Lisa.'

'Not happiness?'

He hesitated, lifting her hand to his lips. 'Why should I wish you that? You are quite confident of your happiness, are you not?'

'It's still usual to say it.'

'I am a foreigner, I do not know these things!'

'You do now.' Suddenly it was imperative that he said it.

'I will remember this. Your daughter is very beautiful, even more so than when I last saw her. If happiness should elude you, always remember that you are doing it for her.'

'Plus the lifestyle he can offer me!'

'If that is sufficient to help, then remember that too.'

She shivered. 'I'm going to be blissfully happy, Renato. I can't think why you're being so pessimistic.'

'Because he found you first and I am consumed by jealousy!' His tone was light. They both laughed, but didn't look each other in the eye and when he left they were careful to keep their bodies well apart.

Outside the mews cottage, Renato pulled the collar of his fur-lined suede coat up round his neck and slid into the Ferrari. As he reversed out into the main road he was aware of a small red Mini parked on the corner and knew that he'd been spotted.

He cursed fluently in both Italian and English. It had been stupid to come, a terrible error of judgement, and should his father learn of

227

it he'd probably recall him at once. But he'd had to see her once more, to prove to himself that she wasn't special at all and that his advice to her to marry Neal had been right.

He'd failed on both counts, and possibly put them both into danger as well. Altogether a very poor night's work. He decided to call in on the Honourable Melissa Fitzroy who gave the best head he'd found in England and never attempted to make conversation either before or after. It wouldn't help repair the damage he'd done but it might make him feel better physically.

Inside the red Mini, Mike watched the Ferrari speed away into the night and glanced at the dashboard clock. The Italian hadn't stayed long. For all Mike knew he hadn't even called on Lisa. One front door looked very like another in the mews. He didn't log the incident and quite deliberately saved both Lisa and Bellini from reprisals while inadvertently opening the door for the terrible bloodbath that their meeting was destined to set underway.

If when Neal returned from Sicily he was surprised by the warmth of Lisa's welcome, he put it down to her newfound sense of security and congratulated himself on having had Naomi murdered. At last he was going to have a wife who did him credit and appreciated the lifestyle he had to offer her. He didn't delude himself into thinking she loved him, but with the arrogance of all men who've succeeded in life he was certain that this would only be a matter of time.

On the day that their engagement was announced in *The Times*, Lisa was astonished to discover that her telephone never stopped ringing. Reporters asked questions about the date, venue and guest list for the wedding, and more personal ones about rumours that she was expecting Neal's child.

Eventually, on Neal's advice, she took the phone off the hook and waited for the end of the day when it had been decided that she would move into the Grosvenor House and stay until she was finally Neal's wife.

Unfortunately, as a result of being frustrated by the removal of the phone, reporters and photographers then descended on the mews. Lisa, peeping out from behind her bedroom curtains, was amazed by the number of people gathered outside her tiny cottage, and for the first time began to understand that Neal was more important than she'd realised.

She didn't answer the door and instructed Janice to keep all curtains closed, but when the nurse had to take in milk, Jessica — disturbed by the noise from outside and her mother's unrest — managed to dash out through the opening and ran straight through the assembled members of the press corps.

Totally unaware of the existence of any child, let alone a handicapped one, the press were at first delighted by this beautiful little girl and took endless photos as the women among them tried to talk to her. Panic-stricken, Jessica began to scream. Then she spun round and round, chanting, 'Bloody hell! Bloody hell!' at the top of her voice before noticing that she was still trapped. Driven to absolute frenzy by the noise and the flashlights she ran to the nearest puddle, threw herself down in it, splashed the water around and began to strip. Then, entirely nude and covered in filthy rainwater, she started laughing madly.

By the time Nurse Anthony got to her it was too late and the following day it was Jessica's photograph that was on the front of several of the tabloids, along with so-called expert's guesses on what was the matter with her and whether her behaviour had been caused by maternal neglect due to Lisa's active social life.

Stunned by the cruelty of the allegations, she rang Neal at home. She expected understanding and support; instead she got a tirade of abuse directed at her and Janice, and when she became tearful he shouted at her to shut up before finally promising to call in before he began work.

When he arrived he had himself under better control, but the sight of the photographers and the reality of Jessica climbing on to the mantelpiece and diving headlong off it onto the floor, stimulated a fresh outburst. 'I won't have it!' he shouted at a shaking Lisa. 'Look at her! She's like an animal. I thought you were providing structured discipline?' he continued, turning his fury on Janice.

'She doesn't understand about social behaviour, sir.'

'Then she damned well isn't going to live in society until she does! Lisa, this has to stop. I know you wanted her to stay here but it's out of the question now the press has found her. She has to go into a home. I'll find a good one and we'll take her there ourselves.'

'I don't want her in a home! I've told you and told you that. She'll regress without proper care.'

'You think she can get worse than this?'

Lisa's head was pounding. The baby she was carrying seemed suddenly to have doubled its weight and she was no longer able to pretend she wasn't pregnant. 'Don't talk about her like that! I thought you understood.'

'The only thing I understand is that she's caused enough gossip to ruin our wedding day. One of my P.R. men will issue a statement explaining that she's autistic and has been awaiting a vacancy in a

229

special home. He'll stress how hard you've tried to keep her with you but add that in view of the forthcoming child...'

'I didn't think we were going to mention that.'

'Jessica's forced me to change my plans. I think an unborn baby will provide a very legitimate reason for her going away without its reflecting badly on us. If you could manage a few tears when we take her, so much the better.'

'*You bastard*!' she screamed, picking up one of the Meissen figures and hurling it at his head. 'This isn't some Walt Disney weepie, you know, this is Jessica's life we're talking about. How dare you suggest that I cry to order? What kind of a man are you anyway? Autism isn't leprosy. She isn't contagious or dangerous, she's just a very bewildered little girl who can't cope with real life.'

'Which is why she has to be removed from it. Look, darling,' his voice softened. 'I know what this must be like for you but do you really want her turned into some kind of freak show? That's what would happen, you know. The Press never give up. They'll keep people hanging around here, hoping for a dramatic picture of a tantrum or panic. Don't you think it's kinder to let her go and live with other children who are like her?'

'No, I don't. Anyway, it isn't easy to find places for autistic children.'

'I don't think I'll find that a problem.'

'I want her to stay here.'

'I thought you wanted to marry me.' His voice was dangerously low.

'I do.'

'Then I think you might consider me a little.'

'She isn't your child. Why should her behaviour reflect on you?'

'You're her mother, you're also carrying my child. They might wonder at my choice.'

'Well, bloody well let them! If that's what's worrying you, don't bother marrying me. If you're so worried about what the gutter press have to say ...'

'I am marrying you and that child is going into a home.' Lisa had never heard him use that tone of voice before and she felt a flicker of fear, especially when she saw the set of his features and the total absence of feeling in his eyes. 'Now get some things together and I'll take you to the Grosvenor House. You were meant to go there last night. We'll return for Jessica as soon as I've made suitable arrangements for her, but I think it's better if you make the initial break now.'

'Let me stay until she has to leave!'

230

'You're getting far too upset. It's bad for the baby.'

'I'm not!' she shouted, and promptly burst into tears. Unlike Renato Bellini, Neal didn't attempt to comfort her. Instead he issued instructions to the nurse before standing by the door, watching his future wife sob uncontrollably.

When Janice came back with an overnight case, Lisa felt as though her chest was going to burst from the force of the emotion she was feeling but she swallowed hard and walked over to Jessica, trying to kiss the rigid little figure goodbye. Jessica turned her head away and put out both hands as though to ward her mother off.

'It isn't for long,' whispered Lisa. 'I'm only going now so that I can give you a real chance later on.' She didn't think for one moment that Jessica understood; she only hoped that the tone of her voice would offer some reassurance.

'Let's go,' said Neal, glancing quickly outside to make sure Bishop had kept the mews clear of newsmen. Lisa kissed Janice, whose eyes were also full of tears, and then quickly walked out of the cottage.

'It really is for the best, darling,' Neal assured her as they drove through London. 'I had to be firm for your own good.'

'That's all right,' said Lisa calmly. 'After all, it isn't for long.'

'What do you mean?'

'You gave me your word that she could come home once we had a son, remember?'

'I don't think ...'

'Yes you did, Neal. I've told a lot of people about your generous offer. They all think you're wonderful,' she lied.

His face relaxed slightly. 'Of course! The upstairs floor, wasn't it?'

'That's right.'

'Now,' he said softly, putting an arm round her shoulders. 'Now we'd better start talking about our wedding plans.'

They were married, just as Bellini had predicted, at Chelsea Register Office, followed by a blessing at Chelsea Old Church. At the Claridges reception the guests drifted around, the elegant Chanel, Dior and St Laurent dresses competing with the bold Bruce Oldfields, Emanuels and Anouska Hempels.

The women were so busy smiling their practised smiles, heads lifted and tilted at the most becoming angles, that none of them even realised the bride and groom were no longer there. The men, less plastic then their wives or mistresses because in men of their social standing signs of maturity were both necessary and attractive, being mistakenly taken for indications of intelligence and wealth, did notice; they envied the groom. Naturally none of them voiced their

231

envy for fear their comments might get back to him.

Lisa lay naked on the vast circular bed of their suite and watched her husband undressing, noticing with frightening detachment that his body was still firm and well-muscled, aided by regular sessions in a gymnasium. He looked at least twelve years younger than his fifty-four.

As he moved naked towards the bed she felt one brief moment of panic, acutely aware that now there could be no going back. She was committed to this man, literally until death. Death. Naomi. Kay. The words and images ran together in her mind and her panic increased.

Only when he lay beside her, twisting her round to face him, did the panic ease. Slowly he closed one hand over her left breast. His thumb rotated lightly round the nipple while his other hand strayed down his wife's rib cage, over her hip bones and then gently but insistently between her thighs.

As he lowered his mouth to her right breast and grazed his teeth across the swollen and sensitive surface, Lisa wondered if she would ever learn to respond to him as he deserved. The touch of his thumb on her nipple was beginning to irritate her and when she did open herself to his hand she knew that she was dry and totally unaroused.

Naturally Neal knew too, but he had anticipated his wife's usual inability to relax during lovemaking and was confident that in time she would allow herself pleasure again. Until she did he would make the best of the situation. After all, she was his and that was what he'd wanted. That and an heir.

He began to kiss her throat and ears, his tongue insistently probing and licking around the most sensitive areas until he felt her begin to move, her body gradually becoming more restless on the silk sheets. His right hand tightened on her breasts, but that was a mistake and she stiffened. At once he loosened his grip. There were so many things he couldn't do; so many things that still brought panic into her eyes, that sometimes he despaired of ever getting it right.

Lisa, her eyes wide open and her body refusing to relax, wished that he'd get on with it. She didn't mind that her pleasure was only slight. He was the one who had the right to physical satisfaction. That had been part of the bargain. Unspoken, and left out of the long, complicated pre-nuptial agreement but clearly understood. She shifted her body, trying to indicate that he should enter her.

Neal felt a twinge of irritation. This was their wedding day. He could get unreciprocated satisfaction from numerous women, and for years had been getting it from his late wife. He didn't want to repeat that pattern today of all days.

Finally he moved, his mouth travelling the length of her body until his tongue moved expertly between her parted legs. Lisa moved up the bed, her hands trying to push him away, but he ignored her. He thought that once he'd begun she would relax, become moist and receptive so that he felt less like an unwelcome intruder into her body.

Her eyes now shut, Lisa felt the rough dampness of his tongue as it began its invasion. Once she had enjoyed it when Toby did this for her. Once she had been totally abandoned to such pleasure. Once. A long time ago.

Then she felt a slight tingle beginning deep inside her, an increasing tightness, a sense of something building within her, and her husband – sensing it too – circled his tongue carefully around her clitoris before drawing the swollen bud into his mouth.

She had never been so wet for him before and to his dismay he realised that her arousal could prove his undoing. Just as Lisa's hips began to twitch of their own volition, he slid reluctantly up her body and entered her. Her eyes were widening in shock but then she realised that it was nearly over and closed them so that she couldn't see her husband's face when he finally spilled his seed into her. She couldn't bear to see the triumph in his eyes, nor face the knowledge that for a moment he had almost brought her to her first climax since ...

With a groan, he covered her mouth with his and it was over. She was glad, she told herself fiercely. She didn't want physical passion any more. Especially not from this strange, decidedly business-like marriage where the list of advantages she could expect had never been intended to include sexual satisfaction.

She continued to lie there, her thoughts drifting away to the past and all the events that had led up to this moment. As Neal swung himself out of bed and began dressing again, she sighed softly. She was loved, protected and rich yet she sighed, and Neal – who understood everyone better than they understood themselves – committed it to memory.

At last Lisa sat up. 'I'm starving!' she laughed, shaking off the melancholy mood that had threatened moments before. 'If I go down and devour everything in sight, will they guess what we've been doing?'

'Possibly.'

'Does it matter?' It was a purely rhetorical question.

'Not really,' he said slowly, watching as she stepped into the tiny satin briefs that were the only kind it was possible for her to wear at present.

'Don't look, I know I'm huge!' she protested.

Her movements were languid, her skin pale yet glowing, and he could have taken her again if there'd been time but consoled himself with the thought that from now on she was his whenever he wanted.

Lisa finished doing up her cream silk dress, cleverly designed by Carol to conceal her condition, and stared blindly out of the window, suddenly remembering her daughter. Poor little Jessica, trapped eternally in her nightmare world, surrounded by excellent nurses, lacking for nothing except acceptance. Acceptance and unlimited, indiscriminating love. At the moment. But soon, if fate was kind, all that would be changed.

'Lisa?'

She turned to face him, her eyes shadowed.

'It's time to go down,' he said kindly. Together they walked along the heavily carpeted corridor, her arm linked through his. They paused in the doorway and immeditely Lisa's eye was caught by Renato Bellini, standing alone at the bar.

She looked at his mass of wavy greying hair, the surprisingly sensitive mouth and wide-apart soft brown eyes that might have weakened his face were it not for the heavy lids that added to the over-all impression of an intelligent and determined sensualist. She felt a terrible desire to weep.

He murmured a greeting as they approached, taking her hand, raising it to his lips before brushing his tongue against the sensitive skin. Blushing, she withdrew it. Fortunately Neal hadn't noticed and the two men began conversing in rapid Italian.

Suddenly weary, Lisa sat on a stool and glanced around the room. She saw her two eldest step-daughters standing talking to Bishop, and gave a shudder. There was danger there. Her eyes moved on. So many men and women. Laughing; talking of nothing; flirting; quarrelling – they filled the air with the sound of their voices. And Toby! Unbelievably, she noticed him, standing with a new wife but watching her steadily, with an almost desperate message in his eyes that she couldn't begin to understand.

Suddenly Bellini spoke directly to her, his expression unfathomable. Neal laughed and started to lead her away from the bar. The Italian repeated his remark and despite the pressure of her husband's hand, Lisa turned back to him. 'I'm afraid I don't speak Italian.' She hoped she sounded sufficiently remote.

He smiled, but not pleasantly, his eyes glittering. 'I wished you a son.'

She laughed nervously. 'Thank you. I wish for one as well.'

An elderly woman began speaking to Neal and Renato moved surprisingly quickly to her side. 'Should it be a girl, I wish you luck,' he continued, the smile never wavering, his eyes holding hers. 'A girl would after all make everything a very expensive mistake, and your

234

husband cannot afford more mistakes.'

'Stop it!' she hissed. 'You were the one who told me I was doing the right thing.'

'Maybe I made a mistake,' he murmured, and she shivered.

'Darling, it's time to cut the cake,' said Neal, unaware of the small interlude that had just taken place. She went smiling to his side, hoping that it would soon be over and they could leave the crowded room that was already making her feel queasy and faint. Neal, noticing her pallor, made sure that they left as soon as was acceptable.

Until the child was born, he intended to take very good care of her.

Chapter Nineteen

'How did the wedding go?' asked Gemma Kingston. Renato Bellini shrugged elegantly. 'Well enough. He's married and he believes that he has an heir on the way. He was naturally at his most charming.'

She slid naked from the bed and knelt down in front of her lover, deftly releasing him from his clothing and closing her small, skilful mouth round his rapidly hardening organ.

'She is unusual — his wife,' he added, seemingly oblivious of her dexterity. Gemma swirled her tongue round the sensitive ridge at the top and his hands reached down and caught hold of her auburn hair. 'Very beautiful, but not what I would call particularly sophisticated. She intrigues me.'

Gemma wished he'd stop talking. She felt rather ridiculous. Like a professional masseuse or worse. Yet this was one of the few times when she could normally count on having his full attention. She moved her mouth more rapidly, applying suction. Renato caught his breath, closed his eyes and gave himself over to the pleasure.

When he'd finished he glanced down into the adoring eyes of his latest conquest and raised an eyebrow, silently querying such selfless behaviour. 'I think,' he told her warmly, 'that I would very much like to find out what she is like in bed!'

It was in this way that Gemma Kingston discovered, as countless other women had discovered before her, that for Renato Bellini she barely existed except to give him pleasure.

'Now she's finally made it, I hope she's satisfied!' said Louise spitefully.

Ruth shook her head. 'Don't be stupid. She's only just begun.'

'What else can she do? Thanks to her, Mother's dead, you and I are off to boarding school in Paris, and Father no longer listens to anyone, not even Bishop. Isn't that true, Bishop?'

Bishop's grey eyes glinted but his expression was bland. 'I've only ever advised your father.'

'You're the one person he's always taken notice of, except *her*.'

Ruth frowned. She found her sister's attempts at ingratiating herself with a man so patently disinterested as Bishop quite grotesque. It was strange that so many young men fell in love with Louise yet it was remote, emotionless Bishop whom she wanted.

'You don't care, Ruth!' shouted Louise. 'I think you actually like Lisa.'

That was true but she was saved from replying by the arrival of Rebekah. Small, unwanted Rebekah who'd loathed her mother, hated her sisters, worshipped her father and now feared Bishop without knowing why. Bishop — who guessed why — watched her constantly, terrified that she might bring about his downfall. 'Enjoy the wedding?' he asked sardonically.

'What's a honeymoon?' she demanded, having discovered that countering one question with another was the best way out of awkward moments.

'A period of time spent in the land of milk and honey!'

'Where's that?'

'Anywhere you choose. Egypt; Greece; Italy; even America, if your taste is so inclined.' Louise gave a gurgle of laughter and he wondered if he could ever bring himself to marry her, however advantageous such a marriage would be. He tried to picture her at his cottage in Norfolk, tearful and pleading as Annabelle had been last night. She'd probably try and laugh even then, he thought coldly.

She was pathetically eager to please. Not like her step-mother. Lisa didn't seem to care whether she pleased or not. He still had difficulty in believing she was now the second Mrs Gueras, despite having been there himself and watched the marriage ceremony.

'Have you ever been on a honeymoon, Bishop?' persisted Rebekah.

'No.'

'Is that because no one's ever wanted to marry you?'

'Yes.'

'Louise will, won't you, Lou?' she jeered.

'Bugger off, you horrid toad!' snapped Louise. Rebekah ran out of the room, well pleased with what she'd said. She hated Louise almost as much as she hated Bishop and knew that her shot about marriage had gone home.

'She didn't look all that special to me!' commented Toby Walker's second wife. 'She's very thin — apart from the obvious bulge, that is!'

'She was always slim.'

'I said thin. Neal Gueras is rather old for her.'

'She's thirty years younger than him.'

'Didn't you mind her leaving you for a geriatric? Or did your perpetual virility wear her out?'

'She went off me, all right? End of subject.'

'What very poor taste she must have. Imagine trading you in for such an old model. Mind you, he is disgustingly rich!' Toby nodded, remembering very well that it hadn't been like that at all, and wondering if he'd ever manage to lose his permanent burden of guilt.

On the day that Lisa and Neal returned to Beckett Lodge from their honeymoon on the beautiful, tiny Caribbean island of Aruba, Louise took to her bed with a cough, Ruth went out to look at a neighbour's horses and Rebekah locked herself in the schoolroom and refused to come out. Feeling thoroughly rested and extremely content, Lisa entered her new home in excellent spirits. Within two hours she knew that for everyone's sake the girls must leave earlier than had been planned.

Neal, similarly relaxed and elated, had no patience with them. Lisa suggested allowing them a couple more days to settle down but he refused. Louise and Ruth were to go to their uncle in Dover while Rebekah's nanny was sacked.

'She simply needs to mix more with children her own age,' explained Lisa, worried that Rebekah too might be banished if she didn't speak up in her defence. 'I'll look at local private schools.'

'Very well, but any more trouble from her and she's going away. I will not have you upset.'

That night, in the privacy of their king-size bed he reached for her yet again as he had done every night of their honeymoon. Lisa understood he was trying to prove to himself that he could give her as much satisfaction as she gave him but wished he wouldn't try so hard. Now that the baby was larger lovemaking was awkward, and the more her husband tried the more she tensed up.

When it was over he lay on his back, staring at the ceiling. 'I don't understand it,' he complained. 'I've never had this trouble with other women.'

'You know why it is, and I honestly don't mind. I enjoy our lovemaking. I don't feel frustrated or deprived, so can't you just accept that?'

'I regard it as a personal insult. I am your husband now. Surely it's about time you started to relax and take a more active part? I'm not asking you to swing from chandeliers, just make a little bit of effort.'

'I think junior is taking too active a part for my liking!'

Neal put an arm round her. 'I suppose that is a bit offputting for you. Let's hope things pick up once he's born.'

Lisa was disconcerted by the speed with which he was willing to vocalise his discontent. After all, he'd known what she was like in bed before and sworn it didn't matter. Apparently that wasn't true. She only hoped this didn't apply to everything else he'd said. 'I'm sorry,' she whispered. 'I'm going to try and be the best wife in the world for you.'

'So I should hope!' he joked, turning over to go to sleep. 'After all, that's why I chose you.'

When Lisa went down to breakfast next morning, the two older girls' cases were in the hall. They themselves were sitting silently round the long mahogany dining-table, their plates of kedgeree virtually untouched.

'What's your uncle like, Ruth?' Lisa asked.

'Like Daddy only more interested in us. We'll probably have quite a good time, although they haven't got their own horses.'

'Who cares about bloody horses!' snapped Louise, glaring sullenly at her stepmother. 'It's not an animal I'm going to miss.'

'Yes it is, it's Bishop!' teased Ruth.

'You can shut up too. What's it like, Lisa, coming home and turning your stepchildren straight out? Does it make you feel good? I'd have thought our going to boarding school in Paris next term was early enough to have the place to yourself, but apparently not. To be fair, you were just as quick to get rid of your own brat. What's wrong with her anyway, she looks weird!'

'She's autistic, and as soon as this baby's born I'm having her brought back here.'

'Only if it's a boy.'

'How do you know that?'

'Bishop told me. He said we were lucky to be going away. Apparently your daughter's utterly revolting. She and Rebekah should get on well together.'

'Shut up, Lou,' remonstrated Ruth. 'It isn't kind to talk about Lisa's daughter like that.'

'It isn't very kind to send us away from home either.'

'Daddy did that. You know full well nothing happens unless *he* wants it.'

Lisa pushed aside her scrambled eggs, wishing that she was back in her cottage. Although Jessica had been noisy and tiring, she'd been totally without malice. The hatred emanating from Louise made her feel physically sick.

239

'There's the car!' shouted Ruth, spilling her coffee all over the damask tablecloth. 'Come on, you know what Steve's like about being kept waiting.'

'Tough, he's only a servant. Not that I want to hang around here,' Louise added pointedly. Neither girl said goodbye before they left.

When a pale and subdued Rebekah slid into her place a little later, Lisa hardly noticed. She was wondering if the girls had been right and she should have stood up for them more, but they were Neal's children and she was afraid to interfere too much in case he started interfering in Jessica's upbringing. Life, she realised, was going to be a tricky balancing act for a time.

She didn't see Neal until mid-morning, and even then he was preoccupied. Murmuring something about work and needing to spend time with Bishop, he drank a cup of coffee with her and then went off to the annexe, leaving her to familiarise herself with the house and servants.

By the end of the day she knew that the household ran impeccably. Wakefield, the cook and the housekeeper had their set routine and were loath to make changes. She'd cast an eye over the accounts and found them to be in order, and studied the menus for the next week, including a dinner party on the Friday evening.

'I'm allergic to venison,' she told Cook, pointing to the planned dinner menu.

'What would you prefer as an alternative?'

'Perhaps pheasant?'

'Certainly. The first Mrs Gueras left everything to me but if you wish to discuss the meals ...?'

'I definitely do wish to discuss them. Every morning when I'm here, and at least a week in advance when we have guests coming. The first Mrs Gueras wasn't a fit woman. I am, and I intend to have a great deal more say in the running of things than she did.'

Cook didn't show any sign of resentment, but Lisa suspected she was merely too well-trained to show it. 'About the annexe,' she continued. 'There seems to be a tremendous amount of food and drink sent there. Why's that?'

'Your husband often has people staying there. I take my instructions from him.'

'I thought it was only Bishop and security men who stayed there?'

'I really couldn't say, madam.'

'I'll discuss it with my husband. One more thing,' she added. 'I'd prefer coffee to tea on my morning tray.'

'I'll instruct Ann.'

Lisa then wandered round the grounds and noticed Rebekah swinging listlessly on a rope ladder, near the start of the parkland. 'Why don't you show me round the park?' she called, and was pleased to see how her step-daughter's face brightened.

'I'll show you some of the secret walks!' she said excitedly. 'I'm the only one who knows how to find my way through them!'

In the annexe things were not going so well for Neal. He sat at the head of the table listening to the people around him, fingers tapping his notepad.

'There's no doubt they're bringing some of the stuff in,' said a thin-faced man called Keith. 'It's not as pure as ours and it's got a lower street value but it does limit our potential.'

'Are the Bellinis behind this?'

'They steer well clear of drugs. All Renato seems interested in is the bank.'

'And women!' laughed Mike.

Neal frowned at him. 'What about the casinos?'

'They've applied for a couple of licences but we can always try and have them turned down.'

'It isn't a question of trying. I don't want those licences issued and I'm leaving it to you, Bishop, to make sure they're not.'

'It'll cost us.'

'How much?'

'Less than a wedding reception at Claridges.'

Neal was too experienced to rise to the bait. 'In that case money won't be a problem. See to it.'

'There's protection,' continued Bishop. 'Presumably you want your new wife to have a minder?'

'Not an obvious one. She's a complete innocent. The last thing I want is to arouse her curiosity. On the other hand. . .'

'She's an obvious target for P2 if they want to muscle in. They're well aware that she'd make a more valuable hostage than Naomi.'

'Had you anyone in mind?' asked Neal icily, suddenly picturing Lisa kidnapped, tortured and half-starved, just as he'd once had the wife of a thriving loan merchant abused until the man agreed to hand over his list of clients and leave the country.

'I thought Mike could do it. He's been training and he's used to Mrs Gueras. She won't suspect anything if he's the one who drives her around. He's even practised getting out of road blocks on the police skid pan, haven't you, Mike?'

'Yep! Passed with flying colours too.'

'You might have to die for her!' said Neal softly. 'I'd expect

241

nothing less. In fact, should she be killed and you survive, I'd rectify matters personally.'

'No problem.'

Bishop gave a sigh of relief. Mike wasn't his idea of a perfect body-guard, but if things went wrong, Neal himself had made the final decision.

'Anything else?' Neal was anxious to get back to his new wife.

'Apart from the next big job, which still needs a lot of groundwork done, there's only the problem of Renato Bellini.'

'What problem's that?'

'We think he's here to get back the gold we took from his bank.'

Neal smiled. 'Of course he is! Did you think he'd come to enjoy our winter weather? Don't worry. A few more dinner parties, a couple of discreet meetings, maybe a very small concession in some area and he'll be off. You can safely leave Bellini to me.'

'And your good wife,' murmured Bishop.

'What did you say?' All the men sat very still.

'I was merely remarking on the wonderful way your wife has with him. They seem to have such a lot to talk about when they meet up.'

'That's one of the reasons I married her!' snapped Neal, colour flooding his face because he knew that Bishop was deliberately trying to make him jealous, and – even worse – succeeding. 'She's a wonderful hostess.'

'And so say all of us!' exclaimed Bishop when he and Mike were alone in the room.

Mike smiled. 'She's all right, there's no side to her. I like her.'

'Then you'll die content, won't you? I'm getting back to London. Derren tells me we've got trouble with some of the girls at the casinos. They're providing extra services out of working hours.'

'Life's just one problem after another!'

Ignoring Mike's amusement, Bishop gathered up his papers and left. In his opinion not enough had been done about Bellini, and if Neal wasn't going to take the Italian seriously it might pay him to keep in touch with the man himself. It wouldn't be the first time he'd run with the hares and hunted with the hounds.

At three-fifteen p.m. on the 22nd March, in a private room at Queen Mary's, Paddington, Lisa finally gave birth to the baby on whom Neal had gambled so much. For sixteen hours he had paced the floor of the waiting room, refusing to go in to the delivery room with his wife or to leave the hospital. He knew very well the risks he'd taken in order to make Lisa his wife and knew the trouble that could be caused should the marriage fail, as it very well might if the baby was a girl.

At three-twenty the consultant obstetrician, wiping sweat from his forehead, hurried into the waiting room. When a man paid as much as Neal Gueras for attention, he didn't expect to have a nurse break the news to him.

'Well?' He was braced for disappointment.

'You have a fine healthy son, Mr Gueras. He weighs 9lbs and is already crying lustily. Your wife is rather tired but ...'

'A son!' His face lit up and he found himself shaking with reaction. After three bitter disappointments and so many risks he'd finally got what he wanted. 'I have to see him,' he said, brushing the specialist to one side.

'Your wife is very tired but I'm sure she'd like to see you for a few minutes.'

'If she's too tired I'll just see my son.'

'They're together!' He couldn't keep the note of disapproval out of his voice, having seen Lisa struggle to produce such a large baby without the use of any painkillers in case they damaged the child.

Neal realised he wasn't behaving in the way expected of him and managed an apologetic smile. 'I'm sorry, you must think me very selfish. How is Lisa? I thought that as she'd already had one child ...'

'It was a bit of a struggle. Her pelvis seems to have become tilted and that made the last stage very difficult. However, she's as excited as you are at the end result!'

He went quietly into the room where Lisa and his son were resting. She looked tired but there was a flush of triumph in her cheeks and her eyes were shining with excitement. 'Isn't he gorgeous!' she exclaimed, holding out the dark-haired, red-faced baby for him to admire.

'He's certainly big! I can't believe it, darling. This is the happiest day of my life.'

'I'm pretty excited too. He's so perfect, not a bit like ...'

'Didn't I tell you he'd be fine? You should have more faith in me! The doctor said it was pretty painful for you.'

'Not really, more like hard work. They asked me what we'd decided to call him and I explained we hadn't dared to choose in case he turned out to be a girl.'

'I want him called Alexi,' said Neal firmly.

'Alexi James?'

'If you like. I can't believe it!' he repeated, putting one tanned finger gently against the baby's hand. 'Now then, tell me what you'd like as a reward? You can have anything in the world, anything at all.'

Bellini had been right, thought Lisa. For this one brief moment she

243

could ask for anything. The chance might never come again because already she was learning how quickly her husband tired of things once he'd obtained them. 'There's only one thing I really want,' she said slowly.

'Name it, darling, and I promise you it's yours.'

She raised her eyes to his and was stunned by the emotion in them as he gazed at his newborn son and heir. 'I want Jessica to come home to Berkshire.' Her voice was soft and for a moment he didn't seem to have heard. Then all the adoration vanished from his eyes and he stared at her in disbelief.

'I thought you'd got over that!' he exclaimed. 'When I said you could have anything, I meant diamonds, rubies, emeralds, jewellery of some kind, not ...'

'Jessica's all I want.'

'But ...'

'I want my daughter back.' She surprised herself by the hardness of her tone.

'Darling, I ...'

'I've given you your son, now let me have my daughter.'

'Very well!' He took the baby from her and walked across the room to the window so that he could stare hungrily down at the tiny features. 'Have her back,' he snarled, 'but don't think I'll forget this.'

'It was always intended that she'd come to Berkshire. You said she could have the top floor.'

'I'd have promised you the moon in order to make my son legitimate, but I wouldn't have gone out and got it after he was born.'

Another point to the Italian, she thought with dismay. He'd made it clear that Neal's promises weren't usually honoured. 'I'm staying here ten days,' she said calmly. 'By the time Alexi and I get home, I want Jessica and Nurse Antony in their rooms at Beckett Lodge.'

'And if they're not?'

'I shall tell everyone how you broke your word twice over.'

Neal remained with his back to her, his features twisted with fury, and it wasn't until he had himself under control again that he turned to her with a valiant attempt at a smile. 'I can't imagine why we're quarrelling like this, darling. Of course Jessica can come to live with us. As long as I'm not expected to see her and she isn't allowed near Alexi.'

'I'll see to that.'

'You don't want anything else as well? Not even an eternity ring?'

She thought an eternity ring would be highly inappropriate. 'No thank you. I really am very tired now.'

'I'll be back tonight with some flowers. I assume flowers are acceptable?' And he bent over to give her a kiss. She lowered her face but he lifted her chin with his right hand and kissed her full on the mouth.

'You're mine!' he whispered triumphantly. 'My very own wife, mine forever. I think an eternity ring would be very suitable.'

Fighting back a desire to pull away she allowed his tongue to dart into her mouth for a moment before he stood up and began to re-button his jacket. 'Only another six weeks to wait!' he murmured. She was grateful he was going to give her any time at all.

When he'd gone, leaving her alone with Alexi, she looked ruefully at their son's elongated head. 'They are not long, the days of wine and roses!' she quoted, knowing full well that the honeymoon was truly over and hoping that somehow she'd find the strength to be the kind of wife that he was going to expect from now on.

Ten days later a proud Neal escorted her out of the hospital and into the waiting car. There were one or two photographers waiting to take their picture and Neal smiled broadly for them. Lisa kept her eyes fixed on little Alexi and tried to quell her excitement at the thought of seeing Jessica again.

'Congratulations, Mrs Gueras,' said Bishop smoothly from the driving seat.

'Thank you, and thank you for the flowers too.'

'She was snowed under by flowers!' laughed Neal. 'Bellini sent the largest bouquet I've ever seen.'

'Really? What was the message?'

'Lisa lost the card, didn't you, darling.'

She nodded, knowing that Bishop wouldn't believe her but relieved that her husband had. '*Now you're safe*' was hardly the sort of message she could wave around.

All the staff were lined up in the hall to greet the new heir to the estate. Alexi slept through the proceedings, a great relief to Lisa who found his loud cries for milk the moment he woke rather wearing. But she was relieved by his exceptionally healthy appetite and the speed with which he'd first fastened on to her nipples. No Jessica-type problems for this baby.

Neal had installed a day nurse and a night nurse for Alexi, plus a young girl straight from school to help out with the tasks that didn't involve physical contact with his son. Lisa, who hadn't wanted any-one let alone three people, had to greet them pleasantly and quickly lay down the ground rules for the way she wanted him brought up.

She sensed that the day nurse wanted a strict routine but even the faintest hint of an orphanage-style regime made her sick to her stomach. She insisted that whenever she was around she was to have full and uninterrupted access to her own child, and that she must always be consulted if he seemed unwell.

The nurse, used to young socialites who intended to be perfect mothers but soon lost interest, gave in graciously and without any fears that the initial enthusiasm over the child would last. She might not have been so optimistic if she'd known about Jessica.

Lisa carefully controlled her impatience to see her daughter. She rested in the bedroom for an hour after lunch, then spent the afternoon quietly with Neal, discussing the forthcoming social season and where they intended to be throughout the year. Neal was unable to keep his eyes and hands off his wife now she was home, remaining with her when she fed Alexi. She had a feeling that he even resented his precious son when he lay suckling at her breast.

At six o'clock, Lisa decided she'd waited long enough. 'I think I'd like to see Jessica now,' she remarked casually.

'Of course,' agreed Neal, having decided that he'd handled the situation all wrong after Alexi's birth and determined to make amends. 'I'll go for a ride for an hour. Will you be eating dinner with me or would you prefer it in your room?'

'I'd like to eat with you.'

He nodded his acknowledgement of the game that was to become so familiar over the next few months. Every concession over Jessica would be rewarded with some open sign of gratitude, but neither of them would ever speak of what was happening. He only wished Naomi had been as quick to understand how he liked things to be.

Lisa was trembling with anticipation when she reached the upper floor and almost fell into Janice's arms. 'How is she?' she asked, her eyes searching the room. 'Did the home set her back a lot?'

The nurse's eyes were sympathetic. 'Quite a bit, but I'm sure she'll get over it. Naturally even here things have been strange, and when you remember how much she needed a fixed routine it isn't surprising if she's a bit disturbed.'

'Where is she?'

'Probably on her bed. She spends a lot of time there at the moment.'

'I thought she'd be crashing around on all this furniture. It's such a lovely big room.'

Janice didn't reply and Lisa went into the bedroom. Jessica was huddled into a ball on top of the duvet, a piece of tea towel clutched in one hand and what looked like a snooker ball in the other. She was sucking on the cloth and rolling the ball against her face as she hummed tunelessly to herself, her eyes fixed blankly on the opposite wall.

246

'Jessica!' Lisa's voice was soothing. 'It's Mummy, darling. Everything's going to be all right now.' Bending down she put her arms round the apparently limp figure.

For a brief moment nothing happened, then Jessica erupted into a kicking, screaming bundle of rage and she hurled the snooker ball at her mother's face. Lisa tried to dodge, but the ball caught her on the cheekbone and split the skin.

Janice gasped and hurried off for a damp cloth while Jessica continued tearing round her bedroom, screaming and banging herself against every hard object she could find. Then she stopped, stood on tiptoe for a moment and studied her hands carefully before turning her finger nails on herself and carving ten long gouges out of her own cheeks. Then she began to laugh.

Lisa covered her mouth, terrified that she was going to be sick. She couldn't stay in the bedroom any longer but ran from it, slamming the door shut behind her. 'What on earth's she doing?' she cried, dabbing ineffectually at the stream of blood and aware of a lump forming on her cheekbone.

'I don't know. She hasn't been that bad before, but she does have these terrible temper tantrums that erupt from nowhere. In between times she's like you first saw her, almost too docile.'

'She attacked me because I sent her away.'

'She can't reason things out like that: I expect you frightened her.'

'I think she does reason things out, in which case I can't blame her for resenting what's been done to her. Oh, God! I hope I've done the right thing.'

'Of course you have. I rung the therapist as you asked me and they're sending someone round in a couple of weeks.'

'Can't they come sooner? I'm afraid that my husband might want me in London by then and ...'

'I couldn't tell them that. They were adamant that you must be going to be here for at least three hours every day, so how could I explain?'

'Three hours every *day*?' Lisa was horrified. If Neal could feel jealous of Alexi, he wasn't going to be very understanding about Jessica keeping her tied to the house.

'I shall have to make my own arrangements once I've met the therapist,' she said at last. 'How does my face look now?'

'Rather a mess!'

'I'd better say her head caught me when she ran to greet me. If he thought she'd thrown that ball thing, he'd go mad. What on earth is it anyway?'

247

'It looks like a billiard ball. She was clutching it when I collected her.'

Lisa glanced at her watch. 'Look at the time! Neal will be back soon. I must go and get changed. I'll have a long bath. I don't want him to think ...'

The nurse watched Lisa thoughtfully. Obviously Neal the husband wasn't quite so malleable as Neal the lover. 'How's the baby?' she asked, trying to cheer Lisa up.

'He's fantastic! A bit noisy, but very alert and it's wonderful to have a baby I can actually cuddle. The first time I picked him up I waited for him to go rigid or loll about. When he didn't I could have cried. I can't tell you what a relief it is. Not that he helps poor Jessica, but it's nice for me to be able to give some love without having it rejected.'

'Better make sure your husband gets his love too,' cautioned Janice.

'I know, and he doesn't want his rejected either! It's lovely to have you around again. The staff here don't care for me. Well, I must get ready for dinner. I'll come tomorrow but I can't say when.'

After Lisa had gone, Janice looked at Jessica who was busy picking an old trainer to pieces. 'I hope it all proves worthwhile,' she murmured to herself. 'Your mother's taken quite a risk for you, my girl.'

Jessica, totally oblivious, continued with her destruction of the shoe.

Chapter Twenty

It proved difficult for Lisa to spend an hour a day with Jessica during her first week home. Neal, who seemed to be taking a rest from business except for long talks on the telephone, wanted her attention whenever Alexi left her free. Certain that he was testing her – possibly even hoping for a chance to complain that her daughter was monopolising her – Lisa was very cautious. Her solution was to spend the time when she was meant to be resting in bed, with her daughter.

After ten days, Neal suggested that they left Alexi with his nanny for four days since he had urgent meetings in London and this would give Lisa an opportunity to look round the shops. Realising she'd be away when the touch therapist called, Lisa hesitated.

'Surely you'd like some new outfits?' Neal was amazed. 'After those ghastly maternity clothes I'd imagined you were longing to get into something more exciting.'

'I'm still not back to my proper shape. I think I ought to wait until I've shed a few more pounds.'

'Really, Lisa! When you've shed a few more pounds you can buy more clothes!'

She still couldn't get used to the way he liked her to spend his money, and actually found it difficult to spend as much as he would have liked. This wasn't due to lack of interest in clothes but rather to her acute awareness that this area was his side of the marriage bargain. Every new dress, every hat, put her more deeply in his debt.

'What about the dinner party Saturday week? Surely I ought to stay here and get that organised? We do have thirty guests, ten of them staying the whole weekend. It would be dreadful if anything went wrong.'

'Be honest,' said Neal. 'You're not really ready to leave Alexi, are you?'

She gave a sigh of relief and smiled, 'I'm afraid not!'

'As long as you don't make a habit of staying here. That's how it began with Naomi.'

'I promise I won't. Do you have to stay away four days?' she continued, knowing such reassurances of her affection mattered to him.

'Unfortunately yes, but it's nice to know you'll miss me.'

Feeling that for once fate was on her side, Lisa was therefore on her own when the therapist came to visit and assess Jessica. A pleasant-looking woman in her middle thirties with a very calm and reassuring manner, she spent an hour watching Jessica and the same amount of time discussing Lisa's own childhood.

'So your adoptive mother wasn't physically demonstrative?'

'No, but that only made me all the more determined to show my own children love. It was dreadful when Jessica first rejected me, before I understood her condition. I wondered if I was totally unlovable myself.'

'At least you didn't repeat your mother's mistakes, that's the usual pattern. You do realise that sitting for an hour at a time and holding your daughter against her will will prove tremendously difficult, both physically and emotionally?'

'Yes.'

'Once you start this treatment it's vital that you persevere. If you do it half-heartedly or start missing days, Jessica won't understand. She might even regress. Unfortunately some children regress anyway. The confrontation with their fears is too much for them and they retreat even more. If that started to happen, we'd have to stop the treatment.'

'If it does help and she starts to improve, how much better will she get?'

'We don't know. All autistic children are different; there's no cut and dried answer.'

'Will she ever be cured?'

Mrs Honeywood felt sorry for this sad-eyed young woman who so patently adored her daughter. 'It would be wrong of me to say yes. There are reports of children going on to attend normal school after treatment, and they appear to fit in very well, but we don't yet know the long-term prognosis. To date, incidence of previously autistic children becoming normal adults is very rare, and when it has happened we can't be sure that the individual was truly autistic to begin with. Diagnosis is difficult even for experts.'

'In other words, I mustn't expect too much from this?'

'You must believe in what you're doing, just don't set your sights too high. Wouldn't it be reward enough to find that Jessica no longer

250

shunned human company? To be able to hold and talk to her like any other child?'

'If only people knew more about this!' Lisa burst out. 'No one's ever able to give proper answers to my questions. Everything is so confused, no wonder the children are muddled!'

'I know. It's such a rare and anti-social condition that the public don't seem interested. Other disabled children fare far better. These are truly the lost children; lost in their own world and in ours.'

'It isn't fair!' said Lisa fiercely. 'I'm going to fight for Jessica, and for other children like her.'

Mrs Honeywood's spirits lifted. 'You mean your husband would be willing to put his name to our charitable efforts? It would make a tremendous difference.'

'No, I didn't mean that. My husband isn't at all interested in autistic children in general, or Jessica in particular. I'll be quite frank with you − everything that we do with Jessica will have to be fitted round his absences. I promise that I won't miss a day but I can't promise I'll always know the exact time when I'll be able to sit with her. Often it will mean a special journey from London and back.'

'It's a very draining experience emotionally. You may not feel like going to London after a session with Jessica.'

'I can believe that, but unless I do, Jessica will suffer. As you've pointed out, it's vital that therapy is continuous.'

Mrs Honeywood nodded. 'I ought to be here the first couple of times just to help you through it. After that Jessica's nurse can probably provide all the support you need. When would you like to start?'

Lisa flipped through her social diary. The pages were full of hair appointments, dress fittings, social events, dinners, lunches − the time-consuming trivia that was intended to fill her days.

'We've got a dinner party next Saturday. Some of the guests don't leave until Sunday afternoon. I can easily say I'm tired and stay here on Monday, although I'm meant to be in town. Shall we say Monday at eleven a.m?'

'That would be splendid. If this proves too much for you, Mrs Gueras, you musn't feel that you've failed. I've known many women who gave up because of lack of support from their partners. On top of which, you've got a new baby to care for.'

'Don't worry about Alexi. He's got more attendants than the Princess of Wales! I shan't give up. I can't, otherwise all this was for nothing.'

The therapist didn't know what Lisa meant but she could feel the pain behind the words. 'With your approach we should do very well,' she encouraged, but secretly she had her doubts.

At six-thirty on the evening of the dinner party, Lisa was in the master suite letting her stylist from Jean-Louis David put the finishing touches to her new style. How Neal had managed to persuade such a busy man to come to Berkshire she couldn't imagine, but he was very cheerful and full of admiration for his own handiwork.

'Wonderful!' he enthused. 'Such a good idea to take some of the curl out. Far more sophisticated.'

'I feel as though half my hair's been pulled out in the process!'

'Did you want some touches of glitter on the top?'

She glanced at the black and gold Valentino creation lying on the bed. 'Perhaps a little. I don't want to overdo it though.'

When he finally left she stared at herself in the mirror. Her face was definitely too thin at the moment but it accentuated her eyes, and she knew that Neal admired her increasingly fragile beauty. She was about to step into her dress when he came out of the dressing-room, fiddling with his cuff links. 'Wait a moment!' he instructed, walking up to her, his hand reaching out to caress her left breast. She tried to pull away but he was too quick and she didn't want it to turn into a struggle.

Running his finger round the exposed nipple, he watched as it hardened into a tight peak. Then his hand cupped the breast, lifting it slightly so that he could lower his mouth to the creamy flesh.

'Neal, please let go. People will be arriving in a minute and I've just had my face and hair done.'

'I'm nowhere near your face and hair. I can't wait much longer, Lisa. Every time I see you like this I want you. Don't you want me too?'

In a way she did. She missed the comforting feel of his body against hers and the attentive care his lovemaking demonstrated. 'Yes,' she admitted.

'Then why keep me waiting?'

'I . . .'

'I'm moving back tonight,' he said firmly. 'We'll take it from there. Let's see what that dress looks like.'

It fitted her like a glove, nipping tightly in at the waist and then out over her slim hips, accentuating every tiny curve. Cream lace frothed at the top of the bodice, just covering her breasts, but its off-the-shoulder neckline created an illusion of nakedness, emphasised by the way the back plunged to the waist in a deeply slashed V.

Neal ran a finger down her spine. 'Quite exquisite! Just by chance

I think I have the very thing to set it off to perfection.' From his pocket he took a long, slim box. When he opened it she gasped at the gleaming gold necklace studied with huge emeralds that shimmered in the overhead light. 'Let me put it on,' he murmured, his fingers brushing the nape of her neck as he fastened the clasp.

Once again she stared into the mirror. The necklace looked heavy against her fragile bones and she knew that she now looked even more frail and exotic, and that every woman in the room would envy her. 'How did you know what to buy? I tried to keep the dress a secret.'

'A little bribe in the right place can obtain secrets far more important than those of fashion, Lisa.'

'I'd better remember that,' she said slowly. For a moment their eyes met in the mirror and neither of them was smiling. Then she lifted her face to kiss him and her brief moment of disquiet vanished.

When they finally descended the stairs she knew she'd never looked better and that Neal had never been so proud of her before. Once their guests began to arrive they were separated but he rarely took his eyes off her for more than a few minutes, as though watching added to his anticipation of the coming night.

She was talking to a Dutch jeweller who remembered Simon when she suddenly felt the lightest of touches on her back, right at the base of the cut-away V, and without looking she knew at once that it was Renato Bellini. With a final smile at the Dutchman she turned round and glanced up at him, grateful that he couldn't tell how fast her heart was racing.

'Bravo!' he enthused, bending his head over her hand. 'You look every inch the model wife.'

'And you look every inch the dashing Italian!' she countered, wondering how many men could have got away with the wine-coloured evening suit he was wearing to such devastating effect.

'How well we play our roles! I will talk to you later. Right now I think I should go to your husband who is watching me very closely.'

'I hope you've brought a partner.'

'But naturally; another Sarah, Elizabeth, Caroline or Jane. I will recognise her by her laugh!'

She watched him cross the room to Neal and hoped she wasn't looking as flustered as she felt. It was demeaning to find that he could still affect her now she was a married mother of two with a husband who lavished gems on her and constantly desired her.

But of course there was the other side to Neal. The side that surfaced when Alexi was born and they'd battled over Jessica. He hadn't behaved like a man in love then. Nor would he if she refused him tonight. No, Neal's love was conditional. Sometimes, Lisa wondered if any other kind existed.

She wasn't seated next to Bellini at dinner. The man on her left was young and amusing, while on her right she had the kindly Dutch jeweller, and the meal passed pleasantly. After coffee she glanced at Neal to see if he wanted the women to withdraw but he shook his head slightly. Surprised, she remained in her seat, treating herself to a small brandy and hoping it wouldn't make Alexi drunk when she next fed him. He was starting to be weaned on to the bottle but she usually gave him his six a.m. feed, enjoying the lovely baby smell of his chubby body when he snuggled against her.

She was so lost in her thoughts that she didn't realise people were walking away from the table, drinks in hand, and over to a small cabinet from which Neal had just taken a silver bowl with a tightly fitting lid. Placing the lid on one side he put a smaller silver spoon into the bowl and then walked away, quickly becoming immersed in what looked like a business conversation.

Both her dinner companions had left the table and were over by the bowl; in fact, scarcely anyone was left seated. She was quite relieved to see Bellini lounging back, dwarfing even the large Queen Anne dining-chair, eyes fixed on his fellow guests as they chatted and giggled on the other side of the room. When he realised that Lisa was alone he came to sit by her, eyebrows raised. 'Not your scene?'

'What?'

'Why, the coke your husband's so generously supplied.'

Astonished, she studied their visitors again and saw that they were busy spooning white powder into the thin lines, eyes sparkling with excitement. 'I didn't realise. I thought Neal was against drugs.'

'For himself and his family, undoubtedly yes. But for others – I very much doubt it. It is a highly lucrative business these days.'

'He's not a drug peddlar!'

'I didn't mean that he walked the streets of London handing his packages over in shop doorways.'

'Presumably he felt everyone expected it. There aren't many parties in London where it isn't available.'

'Have you ever tried it?'

'I'm very boring, Renato. I'm not into any kind of experiments. I don't like losing control of myself.'

'Wise where drugs are concerned, but in other circumstances I would like to see you lose control.'

'Don't!' She could feel herself blushing.

'What did I say?' His eyes were suddenly wide and innocent and she had to laugh because only moments earlier he'd been watching everyone in the room with a hawk-like intensity that wasn't in the least innocent.

'Never mind! I wonder if they'd notice if I filled the bowl up with Beechams powders one day?'

He laughed aloud. 'Probably not! It might even become the latest craze. Most people here are so bored they'd be grateful for anything new.'

'You despise them, don't you?'

'Not at all. To me they are not important. But you, I think, despise them.'

'I don't. It's just that sometimes I'm frightened by their lack of purpose. It's easy to see how it happens. Neal thinks I'm silly because I don't have every minute of my days filled with female things, but when I listen to some of the women I know that I can't be like them. I'm all wrong for their sort of life and there's no point in trying to pretend otherwise.'

'Your husband chose you because you were different.'

'Now we're married he'd rather I conformed.'

'A pity; do not let him succeed. Tell me, how is your little girl?'

Finding that he was genuinely interested in Jessica's new treatment, Lisa committed the cardinal sin of forgetting she was the hostess and remained engrossed in conversation with the Italian far longer than was acceptable. Surprisingly, it was Bishop who put a stop to their conversation before Neal became too enraged. He did this not to protect Lisa – in fact, the more mistakes she made the happier he was – but to protect the Italian whom he thought he might need.

'Mrs Gueras,' he said with cold courtesy, 'I don't think we've exchanged a single word this evening. Perhaps you'd care to come into the other room with me! They've begun dancing, and since your husband's occupied you might allow me the honour of the first dance.'

Bellini was quicker than Lisa to grasp the situation. Without a word he stood up and strode away from her side, quickly finding his Caroline – now high on excellent cocaine – and taking her off to the dancing without a backward glance.

Flustered, Lisa hesitated. 'Your husband's watching you,' said Bishop.

'But we were only ... Thank you, Bishop. I'd like to dance.'

He was very light on his feet and although she was taller than him she found dancing with him enjoyable. Three dances later she partnered the Dutchman and then her younger dinner partner, until an hour had passed and Neal was finally free to take her in his arms. He steered her through the packed floor and out into the cooler hallway.

255

'Enjoying yourself?'

She smiled, her face animated. 'Yes, a lot.'

'Remind me not to take you to Italy for a holiday.'

'Neal, Renato was asking me about Jessica. He was interested in her new . . .'

'Don't be such a cretin! He's no more interested in Jessica than I am. He just enjoys having your undivided attention as you smile and flirt with him in front of everyone.'

'I did not flirt with him!'

Neal's grip tightened on her wrist. 'That's not how it looked to me.'

'You're crazy. Why would I want to flirt with him?'

'Because you fancy him. I don't suppose he'd have to wait very long before he was allowed back into your bed. You'd probably have been knocking on his door after two nights. Let me remind you of something, Lisa. You're my wife and that's how it's going to be until death us do part, remember? And should I ever discover that you'd been unfaithful to me . . .'

'This conversation is unbelievable!'

'. . . I wouldn't hesitate,' he continued calmly, 'to put that idiot daughter of yours away in an institution and make certain you never set eyes on her again. As for your partner in any liaison, don't imagine he'd ever get the opportunity to make a fool of any other husband.'

Terrified by his simmering fury, she knew that further argument would be disastrous. Instead she dropped her eyes. 'I'm sorry,' she said quietly. 'I honestly didn't realise how long we'd been talking. If it looked impolite then I've let you down and that's the last thing I intended. He was simply someone to talk to, nothing more.'

'Next time choose someone who speaks English better, that might make your excuse more convincing!' But he smiled as he spoke and she knew that, provided she was careful for the rest of the evening, the crisis had been averted.

'I wish they'd go,' he said suddenly. 'All I want now is you.'

If Lisa had her way the guests would have stayed until dawn but naturally they didn't and at four a.m. she found herself alone in the bedroom with her husband. Before she could finish removing her makeup he was behind her, his hands possessively on her shoulders. 'Leave that,' he murmured, 'I want to undress you.'

Exhausted by the swings of emotion she'd experienced during the evening and shaken by her attraction to the Italian, Lisa felt it only fair to acquiesce with as much grace as possible. It wasn't her husband's fault that she didn't respond to his particular type of sexuality; a sexuality she could both recognise and understand even while remaining unmoved by it.

His hands were shaking as he unzipped the back of the satin dress and slid it off her shoulders. Then he laid her on the bed, hooking his thumbs into the sides of her silk french knickers and easing them slowly down her long legs, leaving her in her silk stockings.

Picking her up he moved her higher up the bed before stripping off his own clothes and lying next to her, his eyes travelling the length of her body again and again before he put out a hand and stroked her lightly across her hip bones. Her muscles jumped instinctively and all at once he wasn't able to spend as long as he'd intended arousing her. He quickly moved down the bed, parted her legs with firm hands and placed his right leg between them to prevent her from closing herself against him.

Lisa shut her eyes and tried to enjoy his touch. It was good to feel desired and feminine after pregnancy and giving birth, and she thought that if he'd only give her time it would be better than before Alexi's birth. But Neal was treating time as his enemy.

His fingers found her clitoris and he quickly rotated his thumb until he could see for himself the involuntary movements of her hips as she became aroused. Quickly he inserted two fingers into her, moving them in and out in an imitation of what was to come. When Lisa tried to stop him he forgot that he might be bringing back unpleasant memories and thought only in terms of personal rejection. As a result he increased the speed of the movement until she actually cried out.

Aware that it was all going wrong, and with the vision of her beautiful, adoring face close to Bellini's before him, he withdrew his fingers and thrust savagely inside her, no longer caring about what she felt but simply relishing the tight warmth of her and the wonderful sensation of conquest as he took her without any tenderness, in the primitive sexual pride of power and possession.

For Lisa the first tiny stirrings of feeling, the elusive flickers of promised pleasure, quickly died away, and after that all she was aware of was his intruding fingers and intrusive penis that made her feel dry and sore, a legacy of Alexi's long and difficult birth.

She tried to feel something more. She desperately wanted to please him because she knew he was searching for a response and that most women would have been able to give him one. Eventually she was reduced to moving herself up to meet him and tightening her muscles in an attempt to force him to climax quickly.

In this at least she succeeded. All at once he groaned with pleasure and then collapsed heavily against her, one hand still reaching out for her breasts. All the time he lay recovering, his fingers continued to

257

knead them until some of her breast milk began to leak. Thinking he'd be disgusted she tried to draw away but when he opened his eyes and saw what had happened he rolled across her and licked at the liquid, a gesture that Lisa found distasteful but which so aroused her husband that within ten minutes he was taking her again, with the vigour of a man half his age.

Finally, exhausted and content, he lay beside her, holding her body tenderly against him. 'Still no good?' he murmured, but with no idea of just how far from good it had been.

'I enjoyed it,' she lied. 'It's been a long time.'

'You make me feel young again,' he smiled, then fell deeply asleep.

Lisa, lying awake until dawn, felt very old. She tried to tell herself that she was still suffering slight post-natal blues and that everything would soon look better, but then she would start imagining how it might have been with the Italian until disgust at her betrayal of Neal cancelled out even that innocuous pleasure.

She spent most of the following day in bed, pleading exhaustion, and Neal − happy again now he'd resumed his marital rights − was more than content to let her rest. He even suggested that she didn't try and join him in London for a couple of days, and she realised she'd be safely alone for Mrs Honeywood's first visit.

It was only that thought that helped her cope with Neal's even more amorous attentions on the Sunday night and again on the Monday morning before he left for town. By then he was becoming irritated by her lack of pleasure and suggested a visit to her gynaecologist while in London. She agreed and he finally left with Bishop, leaving Mike to bring her to town on the Wednesday for a charity film gala.

As soon as he'd gone Lisa switched her mind to her daughter and the importance of the forthcoming day. It was now even more vital that Jessica gained from her marriage since it was increasingly clear that neither Lisa nor Neal was likely to remain satisfied with this partnership they'd entered into with such differing expectations.

Mrs Honeywood noticed that Lisa looked elated when it was time to go up to Jessica. She could have voiced all sorts of warnings but didn't, thinking it kinder to let Lisa find out for herself.

Jessica was sitting in the corner playing with an old alarm clock. She didn't look at the adults and so Lisa went and picked her up. With a scream of terror, Jessica began to kick furiously, her hands hitting Lisa round the face and ears. The therapist watched Lisa struggling to keep her balance until finally she and her daughter toppled on to the deep two-seater sofa brought from the mews cottage.

Following instructions, she turned the little girl round to face her, but Jessica twisted and turned like an eel. Eventually, Lisa managed to wrap one trousered leg across her daughter's thighs so that she lay on her stomach. She then took the tiny face between her hands, forcing her to look up into her eyes.

The terror on Jessica's face was unbelievable. Opening her mouth wide she howled in fear and confusion, frantically moving her head in an attempt to get free. Finding that she was truly pinioned with no hope of escape she closed her eyes and began to wail despairingly. It was the sound of someone without any hope.

Drenched in sweat and shaking with physical effort, Lisa looked to the therapist for guidance. 'Now talk to her,' she urged. 'Tell her you understand her fear. Explain that it doesn't matter that she's angry, explain you know what she's feeling, that it's all right for her to be this way. Keep talking her through it, repeating all the time how much you love her.'

'But she's hating it! I've never seen her so distressed.'

'Keep talking and don't let her get away from you. The touching is further reassurance of your love.'

Almost in tears herself, Lisa began to talk. She told Jessica how much she'd wanted her, and how happy she was to have a little girl. She promised her that no one would hurt her, that as her mother she'd always look after her, encouraging her to release her anger. All the time, Jessica cried and cried, tears pouring down her white face, her body trembling with confusion and terror.

For a seemingly endless hour they sat there, Lisa and Jessica, now both locked in the child's world. Never once did it seem to Lisa that her daughter was gaining anything at all. By the end of the time she was still fighting with all her force, spitting occasionally and screaming dementedly. If their eyes met she'd become even more terrified, once shouting, 'No, hot! No, hot!' as she tried to turn away.

After the hour, Janice arrived and Jessica's first lesson was over. Once released she scrambled from Lisa's lap, crawling away like a wounded animal into the furthest corner. There she sat, her back to the adults, arms across her chest, shoulders hunched and head down; shutting them all out as she began to hum *Tosca's 'Vissi d'arte'* aria with incredible accuracy.

'I have lived for art, I have lived for love!' said Lisa bitterly. 'That poor child. What have I done to her? She's never been so frightened in her life. How can it possibly do her any good? I thought ...'

'Come along,' said Mrs Honeywood sympathetically. 'Let's go and have a cup of tea and we'll discuss it.'

Once they were settled in the small drawing-room that had once been Naomi's, Mrs Honeywood realised that the worst was over for the younger woman. Many mothers turned almost hysterical themselves after the first session; obviously Mrs Gueras was tougher than she appeared.

'I'm afraid I was rather naive,' confessed Lisa, drinking China tea from a delicate bone-china cup. 'I hadn't thought it through properly. You did warn me but for some reason I still expected Jessica would begin to relax after a time, not fight me all the way.'

'She could fight you for weeks yet, but you handled her very well. The main thing is that you're sincere, that what she hears you saying – and, believe me, she does hear you – is the truth. It won't be easy for either of you, and it's often two steps forward and one step back.'

Lisa finished her tea, glanced at her watch and quickly stood up. 'I'm sorry but I'll have to go now. I'm due in London this evening.'

'What time tomorrow will you be with Jessica?'

'I thought about two-thirty.'

'Would you like me here again?'

She nodded; the thought of going through all that emotion unsupported was quite intolerable. She needed Mrs Honeywood's assurance that Jessica wasn't being harmed.

Chapter Twenty-One

An hour later she was in the car with Mike driving her through the winding Berkshire lanes and up to London. 'How's the little one?' he asked.

'Alexi? He's thriving.'

'I meant Jessica.'

'She's not too good right now. Those weeks spent in a home upset her, and I'm trying a therapy that's meant to have spectacular results, but all it succeeded in doing today was throwing her into a blue fit and leaving me feeling like something the cat brought in.'

'Perhaps the film will cheer you up.'

'What I'd really like is twelve hours' sleep! I don't even know what the film's about.'

'A doomed love affair. It's historical: Lady Jane Grey and her token reign. Not my cup of tea at all.'

'Well, at least it's in a good cause. Leukaemia research and cystic fibrosis, I think.'

'There's always something. Children dying here; children dying in Africa; cats dying in Venice. Makes you wonder where to draw the line!'

Despite her weariness, Lisa laughed. 'I think I'd pass if it was for cats in Venice!'

For a time they drove in silence. Then Mike, after keeping his eye on a car that had been following them for the past twenty minutes, told Lisa to put her seat belt on. 'In the back of the car? Whatever for?'

'I think we've got company. I'm going to try and shake it off.'

'Company?'

'We're being tailed. Don't panic this is what I'm trained for!'

'Why would anyone tail us?'

'Your husband's a wealthy man and he adores you. With me so far?'

'Yes.'

'Okay. Now, what better way to get some money than by taking this much loved wife and holding her to ransom?'

'You really mean I could be in danger?' She felt sick with shock.

'I really mean it. Hold on, there's a tight bend here. I'm going to drive through it and off to the right. With any luck they'll go straight on without realising they've lost us. Even if they twig what's happened, we'll have gained enough time to get free. Of course, if the driver's perfectly innocent he'll think I'm a total madman who shouldn't be allowed on the road! Here we go.'

The next few seconds were a complete blur to Lisa. The car picked up speed, tyres screeched, trees and fields spun crazily round and she was flung against the car door until the belt locked tightly. Then she held her breath in terror as a tree loomed in front of them.

Mike swore, spun the wheel again and this time they made it round the sharp right turn and were off along the winding lane, making short work of a stray chicken.

'No time to go back and collect it,' he said with a smile. 'Let's hope your London cupboard's not bare.' Lisa's teeth were chattering too much for her to reply and she kept glancing back over her shoulder to see who was behind them. Only when they reached the motorway did she begin to feel safe.

'Were you wrong?' she asked hopefully.

He considered lying and decided against it. 'No, I was right. Their reactions were too quick. I caught a glimpse of them when we nearly embraced that damned tree. They were attempting to turn as well. I don't think your average rep is going to try and imitate a rally driver, do you?'

She thought of her children. Of little Alexi, still a helpless baby, and Jessica. Jessica who, if Lisa had died, would have been banished once again to a home, all hope gone. 'I could have died,' she murmured in disbelief.

'Not likely; you wouldn't be much use as a hostage if you were dead.'

'But after they'd been paid . . .'

'You could drop dead of a brain haemorrhage tomorrow. No use looking on the black side. Anyway, nothing happened did it?'

'I still don't understand why they'd want me. I know Neal's wealthy but so are plenty of other people. It can't only be because of his money. Has he got enemies? I don't understand commodity broking but I suppose you do make enemies in big business.'

Mike began whistling, hoping she'd stop turning the problem over in her mind because if she didn't let it go she might eventually stumble across the truth.

'Other brokers wouldn't resort to kidnapping,' she continued, her fear receding as she grappled with the problem. 'I thought it was only criminals who did that kind of thing to each other. It's more like an American Mafia-type crime!'

Suddenly she thought of Simon. He'd been crooked. She didn't know how crooked or in what way but he'd worked outside the law. And he'd known Neal. Neal had known him well enough to extend help to Lisa when Simon died. Had it really been because of friendship? Or was it because there were things he didn't want her to find out? Things that Stephanie might have told her.

Then there was Bishop. Bishop, who'd called on Simon and Stephanie just before Simon died. Coincidence? Her mind was in total confusion, memories flashing through her brain. Bishop had known Toby as well; had turned up just in time to save Lisa's life. Coincidence *again*?

As they arrived at the flat, Lisa was remembering the fortunate way in which Kay and Naomi had died just as she came on the scene. Remembering too the antagonism of Kay's friends. Had they suspected something? Even worse, had they thought that she'd known Kay hadn't died by accident?

By this time she was picturing Neal with a violin case in one hand and a fat cigar in the other, and when he came beaming down the steps to help her from the car she was so relieved at how normal he looked that she fell into his arms and promptly burst into tears.

'What on earth's the matter?' he asked, throwing a questioning glance at Mike over her head.

'Bit of trouble on the way here, sir. We were followed and had to shake them off. Your wife's upset.'

'That's terrible! Did you get the number of the car?' Mike nodded. 'Come along, darling,' continued Neal tenderly. 'Come upstairs and you can have a rest. I'll talk to you tomorrow,' he added in a quiet aside. Mike, aware that the incident had set the new Mrs Gueras thinking along dangerous lines, only hoped she'd have the sense to keep her fears to herself.

In fact part of Lisa's distress was reaction to her hour with Jessica. The incident in the car coming straight on top of that, when she was already feeling jagged with nerves, had proved too much but it was a relief to be able to cry for Jessica without Neal knowing. Now that she was with him again her thoughts in the car seemed the product of an over-active imagination. He was so obviously the perfect businessman, with the constant sound of the ticker-tape coming from his machine in the corner of the tiny study, that her stereotyped image of a crook would not allow her to imagine him involved in anything underhand.

He was kind, reassuring and supportive, all the things she most needed, and by the time they left for the première she had almost succeeded in dismissing her fears from her mind. The tiny niggling doubt that remained she pushed to the background. She couldn't really afford to be right, and her sense of self-preservation was strong. Now she understood why Jessica closed her eyes to shut out the world. If you couldn't see it then it didn't exist. All the same, the first doubt had been sown.

'I've arranged for you to see Sanders,' said Neal as Lisa sank thankfully into bed at two a.m. after one of the longest historical films she'd ever sat through.

'Who's he?'

'Only one of the top gynaecologists in London!'

'I haven't had my post-natal check up yet. Why have I got to see a new man?'

'Because,' he said patiently, sliding naked into bed beside her and pulling her against him, 'I'm tired of having a non-responsive wife.'

'I'm exhausted,' she murmured.

'You've been in bed in Berkshire nearly all day!'

'I think it was the fright travelling here.'

'I'll soon take your mind off that.'

'Please don't. I honestly can't keep my eyes open.'

He suddenly snapped on the overhead light and sat up. 'Did you wear yourself out trying to communicate with that daughter of yours today?'

'No!'

'Because if you did, I'll be bloody annoyed. The whole idea of leaving you behind was so that you could rest.'

'I did,' she lied, hoping against hope that none of the staff would give her away.

'Good. At least let me hold you. If you don't want me to make love to you I won't but . . .'

'For God's sake, leave me alone!' she shouted and then – horrified by the expression on his face – burst into tears again.

'I think I'll come with you to see Sanders,' he said coldly. Lisa didn't reply; there was nothing she could say.

'Well, Mrs Gueras, everything seems all right,' said Dr Sanders, helping her down from the couch. 'There is the suggestion of an erosion but it's early days yet.'

'Try telling that to my husband,' she muttered, still seething over Neal's presence in the doctor's office.

'I most certainly will. Please join us when you're dressed.'

Behind his desk again, Dr Sanders looked at Neal Gueras and wondered why it was that men who professed devotion to their wives were frequently the most sexually selfish ones. 'Did you find anything?' asked Neal, already checking his watch because he was late for a meeting.

'A slight erosion which probably makes her sore. In addition, she's far from fully fit. She's at least twenty pounds underweight and probably anaemic. Your own doctor should be able to help there. Also, she's very tense. Any sort of pressure is bad for her right now. Childbirth isn't the easy matter many people like to make out. She needs a little more time and then you should take things gradually. Some women take months to regain their normal sexual drive after having a baby.'

'I'm expected to pay you for telling me that?'

'There isn't any magic pill. Your wife needs time and affection − non-sexual affection.'

'Send the bill to my office. Lisa, the doctor was just telling me that all's well but you need to put on some weight. You must have a word with Cook.'

Glancing contemptuously at the doctor, she followed Neal out of the room. So much for men, she thought wryly. A fat lot of explaining he'd done!

'Are you going shopping, darling,' he asked glancing again at his watch.

'I thought I'd have Mike drive me back to Berkshire to see Alexi.'

'Not Jessica?'

'Her too, of course, but Alexi's only tiny. After missing all the normal baby stages with Jessica this time with Alexi is all the more precious.'

He couldn't really argue with her sentiments, but being unable to get to Berkshire himself that night didn't want her absent from his bed. She had to learn that as her husband he had certain basic rights, mainly sexual. Unfortunately in his mind sex was rapidly becoming a battleground. 'I want you here tonight. Tomorrow you're at that N.S.P.C.C. lunch at the Mayfair. If you sleep here overnight you can lie-in tomorrow morning.'

She'd forgotten the lunch, but Princess Michael was going and she couldn't miss it. Neal was more delighted than she when the invitation came. With an inward sigh she realised she must go to Berkshire now, returning to London after Jessica's treatment, attempt a rest in the morning then go back to Berkshire later the following afternoon for further therapy.

265

'I'll be back by seven,' she promised.

'Wait in my car while we call up Mike,' suggested Neal, all good humour now he'd got his own way. 'Incidentally, weren't you going to arrange some therapy for Jessica? Wasn't that part of our prenuptial agreement!'

'I've started making the right contacts,' she said vaguely. Her husband smiled to himself. If everything went as he intended she'd never have time to spend long with her daughter. He genuinely considered that what little spare time she did have should be devoted to Alexi.

Lisa kissed him on the cheek before hurrying off to where Mike had just stopped the Mercedes. 'Where to today, princess? New Bond Street? Harrods?'

'Berkshire and Jessica, then back to London by seven. We'll both be worn out before very long!' She certainly would, he thought, noting her pallor and the dark circles beneath her eyes.

Today she didn't approach her time with Jessica with any expectations. But for Mrs Honeywood's presence she'd probably have let Jessica free the moment she began to scream because it was obvious that memories of the day before were increasing her distress.

After an hour she was released and again retreated to her favourite corner still sobbing quietly with her hands clapped over her ears in case Lisa continued talking to her.

'Well done!' said the therapist brightly as they left the room.

Lisa's hair clung limply to her forehead and the nape of her neck while the palms of her hands were damp with sweat. Shivering, she sat down on the bottom stair as they left Jessica's attic floor. 'Is it always like this?'

'Usually.'

'For how long?'

'For as long as it takes to break through to your daughter.'

'I'm totally exhausted. I didn't realise how draining it was going to be.'

'Is it the same time tomorrow?'

'I'm afraid not. It will have to be late afternoon. I'm tied up in London until about three. Could you possibly come around six?'

'That's too late for me but it doesn't matter. You know what you're doing. The nurse can keep you company. You do have to begin on your own one day.'

'I'm not ready yet. This isn't a good time for me.'

'There's never a good time. I think you are ready. You have my phone number. If there are any problems, ring me. I'll call in next week to watch another session. You'd better let me know later which day would be convenient.'

Lisa nodded. At that moment she couldn't think of a single thing she'd gained from this marriage except Alexi, and he would always have been hers.

After a shower she pulled on a cream and navy wool dress from Alistair Blair, ran the heated brush through her hair and peeped into the nursery. Alexi was sound asleep in his crib, the nanny sitting quietly by the open fire knitting a matinée jacket. 'Here's Mummy, how nice!' She smiled as she stood up.

'I only wanted to check everything was all right. I'm off to London again now and my husband will want to know.'

'He's gained three pounds this week, and he's sleeping through from ten to six.'

'I didn't imagine he was going to be placid!'

'Not placid, Mummy. Quite vocal when he's awake but a lovely baby. Shall I pick him up?'

'No, I'll come and see him tomorrow. He might be awake then.'

'The little girl upstairs sounded rather upset.' The nanny's expression was curious.

'I'm afraid she was. She doesn't like her therapy. Does she wake Alexi?'

'No, madam.'

'Then I'd rather you didn't mention it to my husband.'

'Certainly, madam. We wouldn't want Mummy to get into trouble.'

Wondering when she'd become mother to the nanny as well, Lisa went down the stairs and into the kitchen where she'd told Mike to have a cup of tea while waiting for her. 'Sorry I'm late, I ...'

'That's all right,' said Bishop, moving forward from the corner of the room. 'We're here to fit in with you. Who was the visitor?'

'Where's Mike?'

'Called away urgently. Don't worry, I've passed my driving test.'

'We'd better set off,' she said curtly.

'Spend a few hours with the baby did you?'

'Mind your own business,' she retorted, and didn't speak to him again for the entire journey. It was six minutes past seven when she walked into the flat, Bishop close behind her.

Neal looked up from his book and smiled. 'You're late!'

'Blame the traffic. Are we eating out?'

'I've booked a table at Le Meridien, and then I thought an early night. Yes, Bishop?'

'What are the arrangements for tomorrow?'

'I'll let you know in the morning,' said Neal irritably.

'Your wife had a visitor at Beckett Lodge,' Bishop put in casually, and only stayed long enough to see Lisa's colour change.

'Who was that?' A slight frown creased Neal's forehead. She hesitated, knowing that Bishop had intended to get her into trouble but also suspecting that Neal had sent him to Berkshire to check up on her movements. She decided to be honest.

'Jessica's therapist. I told you I'd got in touch with the right people and they sent Mrs Honeywood round.'

'Was today her first visit?'

She remembered that Bishop had been waiting in the kitchen and the cook didn't like her. 'No, she's been before, twice to be exact.'

'So you lied to me this morning?'

'Yes.'

'Why was that?'

'I thought you'd object.'

'Indeed I do. I'm the one who has to put up with the headaches and the doctor telling me that my wife is over-stressed and misunderstood.'

'I thought he told you I was fine?'

'Obviously we both tell lies!'

Sitting down she accepted a glass of chilled La Ina from her husband. 'Neal, before we got married you agreed Jessica could have this treatment. You knew that I'd be involved, and since I'm making quite sure that my time with her doesn't intrude on our life together ...'

'Except in bed.'

'She isn't the reason I'm not what you want in bed. I've never been any different, but suddenly you seem to expect something more of me – and at a time when I'm still getting over Alexi's birth.'

'To return to Jessica!' he said smoothly. 'I don't want you running round in circles pretending she isn't monopolising your time when she is. I think we should go through our diaries, mark down her treatment times and re-organise other areas of our life where necessary. I assume this course of treatment does have a measured time-span? You won't still be hot-footing it to Berkshire this time next year?'

'I hope not but ...'

'You can have six months. If there's no improvement by then you'll obviously admit defeat. Hopefully we'll be having other children and there is a physical limit to what you can do in a day.'

'Did you send Bishop to spy on me?' she asked angrily.

'Not exactly, darling, but you see I was beginning to wonder if there was another man.'

'God, one's quite enough for me, thank you.'

'This sexual antagonism wasn't evident before our marriage, Lisa. I agree you were a little shy and not as totally abandoned as I'd have liked but I understood that. What hurts is that now we're married with a perfectly healthy child and you're free to buy anything you like or go anywhere in the world, you suddenly seem to find my touch positively repellent. Is it surprising I'm not content.'

He was right. She did feel repelled by him and she didn't know why. Perhaps it had begun the day Alexi was born, when he demonstrated a totally ruthless and unloving streak that had shaken her self-confidence. Or perhaps it was because she kept thinking about Renato Bellini, mentally comparing the two men and retreating behind some schoolgirl crush when Neal tried to arouse her.

'I'm sorry, I'll try harder. It's all so new right now. Not the sex but the way of life. Also, there are things that get me confused.'

'What things?'

'Like that car following us yesterday, and for some reason I keep thinking about Naomi. I feel guilty about Ruth and Louise, and guilty because I'm not spending time with Rebekah. I just can't get everything done.'

'All you have to do is to be a good wife to me both in public and private. I don't hold you responsible for my daughters' happiness. Louise and Ruth are probably having the time of their lives. As for Rebekah, you've already shown her more affection than her real mother did in eight years! You aren't a child psychologist you know. Why not learn to enjoy yourself more. Most women would.'

'You don't want me too involved with the children, do you?'

'I want you involved with me!'

'What about Alexi?'

'We'll both see plenty of him as soon as he's half-human. Right now anyone will do provided they keep him fed and dry. Now, let's start the good life. Dress up and go out for dinner.'

She put her arms round his waist, trying not to feel resentful of the way he was dismissing their tiny son upon whom he'd previously set so much store. She didn't like anything he'd said but with Jessica's treatment just beginning, now was not the time to argue. She pretended to capitulate. 'Right, and I promise to order the most expensive dishes!'

'Only if you like them!' he laughed. That, she realised, was what lay at the root of all her problems. The things she truly liked weren't the things he wanted to provide. A £2,000 dress didn't compensate for the touch of a man you couldn't love. Only progress by Jessica could help with that, and all at once the hope of such progress seemed a very frail straw at which to clutch.

They had a table in a secluded corner of the Oak Room. Neal was suddenly the charmingly attentive suitor again, all smiles and compliments, and Lisa slowly relaxed.

The food was delicious. They ate pâté followed by wild duck with cherries, and after coffee and liqueurs lingered on, chatting about dinner parties to come, Alexi's progress, where Lisa wanted to spend their summer vacation and even, for a brief time, Rebekah.

Feeling better than for many months, Lisa sparkled. Neal was delighted to see several men he knew openly envying him his beautiful young wife. This was how he had envisaged their marriage. It was only when Lisa failed to comply with his vision that he became irritated. At the moment she was still new enough to hold his attention, and the knowledge that other men – such as Bellini – desired her, ensured his continuing interest. No other man had envied him Naomi.

Finally they went back to the flat and this time their lovemaking was more successful. Lisa was relaxed, Neal less impatient, and he sensed that at last there was some genuine response from her. Altogether a most successful end to the day.

'Will you have time to look at some clothes before you go back?' he asked pleasantly over breakfast next morning.

'I'm calling in on Carol to see if she's got any new ideas, then I might try Anouska Hempel's before I go home. Subdued colours are in but I don't want greys and dark blues, they turn my complexion to mud.'

'Remember me to Carol,' said Neal distantly. It was some time since he'd invested in her work and so far the returns were poor. It was true that she designed good clothes for Lisa but other less slender women found them difficult to wear. He was beginning to think she wasn't going to succeed. She'd also borrowed privately from him twice and unless her work picked up he thought he'd probably call in the loan. She wouldn't be able to pay but Bishop had expressed an interest in her and she'd turned him down. With money as the lever, Neal could make sure she accepted his deputy's invitations to one or two social occasions. There were times when it was wise to keep Bishop as happy as his nature allowed.

'I hope the therapy goes well,' he added, and with that astonishing statement kissed her gently, put on his heavy sheepskin jacket and left. If only life could always be like this, thought Lisa, but she knew that given their differing temperaments and sexual incompatability it wasn't very likely.

Chapter Twenty-Two

At first she thought Carol's shop was closed. There was no sign of life inside and the door wouldn't open. She hammered impatiently on the glass until Carol emerged from the back of the shop. 'Lisa, how nice! I was working on some new designs.'

'Where are your assistants? Last time I came you'd got two girls in the shop.'

'I had to let them go. Business isn't booming, I'm afraid. Didn't your husband tell you?'

'Why should he?'

'He is a shareholder, I only thought ... Come in anyway. Is this a social or business call?'

'Mainly business. I want some summer clothes in bright clear colours, not those ghastly beiges and greys that are in fashion.'

'Any special occasions?'

'I'd like you to do my Leukaemia Research Fund Ball dress for April and a choice of outfits for Ladies Day at Ascot. One for a real summer's day and the other for the more usual windy, rainy one!'

'How about Wimbledon?'

'I think I'll look at some other collections before I decide on that. Neal doesn't want me tied to one designer, not even you!'

'Fair enough. I had a friend of yours in here last week, Amanda Wichell. She's got quite a good figure and wanted a black outfit for a funeral of all things! She bought off the peg but she was most peculiar, kept trotting off to the loo in between trying things on. Is she pregnant?'

'Just high. She's been hospitalised for drug abuse once already. I quite like her, she's amusing and not a bit stuffy.'

'Has she got many friends? I could do with more custom.'

'Is it going that badly?'

'Not as well as I'd hoped. Perhaps if I produce a stunning ball gown things will pick up. Come through and look at some of my materials. By the way, what's Bishop like?'

Lisa began to turn over the samples of taffeta, silk, Swiss cotton and satin. 'He's vile, a real toad! I don't think he's human. This is nice,' she added, fingering a piece of emerald silk shot with silver thread.

'Yes, an oriental style would look lovely in that. Does he have many girl friends?'

'Quite a few but they don't last long. My eldest step-daughter's got a crush on him. I can't think why, he treats her like dirt. Could I get away with a mandarin collar and splits up the side in a ball gown?'

'No, but you could at Ascot. It ought to be quite short, say to the top of the knee. He's asked me out several times and I was wondering whether to go or not.'

'Damn! I wanted the green for a ball gown. What colour do you call this?' she added, feeling a sample of satin.

'Cerise. I think it would be too much on a ball gown. What should I do?'

'Carol, I'm trying to choose clothes, not your boyfriends! If you enjoy reading the Marquis de Sade then go ahead with Bishop. If not, find yourself a nice normal man. If the emerald silk and the cerise satin are out, how about this orange chiffon?'

'It's called dark apricot! Yes, that would make a lovely ball gown. I think I might go out with him. He keeps asking and I'm sure your husband ...'

'I don't want to hear another word about Bishop. That man haunts me. He's always hovering around when I least expect it, and spying on me in my own home. He hates me. I'm sure he's hoping to find me in the arms of some man. I can just imagine how he'd enjoy telling Neal that! All right, dark apricot it is. What about design? I don't want full skirts and a frothy bodice. I'm about a foot taller than Jane Seymour and however gorgeous she may look in that sort of thing, I don't intend to compete. Simplicity – that's our key word, isn't it?'

'I wouldn't call Jane Seymour's clothes the height of simplicity!'

'Carol, what's the matter with you? That's precisely what I said! No wonder you're not doing well. Let's start again.'

When she left, Lisa felt thoroughly dissatisfied. Her friend seemed to have lost all the enthusiasm and energy she'd shown when she first set up the business, and the questions about Bishop had been both boring and intrusive. Fortunately she didn't have any trouble with the better known designers.

Back at Beckett Lodge she just had time to shower and change before hurrying to Jessica. Feeling very nervous she walked into the playroom. It was all very different without Mrs Honeywood's support.

Initially, Jessica behaved in the same way but after about fifteen minutes stopped holding herself so rigidly upright and slumped in her mother's lap. She didn't respond to Lisa but her resistance was weaker and when she was allowed to climb down she stood staring at her mother's skirt for moment, put out a hand and then lightly stroked the woollen material before twirling away out of reach.

Janice who'd sat watching silently, was as pleased as Lisa. 'At the end it looked as though she'd enjoyed sitting with you,' she said with delight.

'It's early days.' Lisa was cautious. She didn't want to raise any false hopes but certainly today had been less of an ordeal. 'Tomorrow I can come in the morning because Neal will be joining me here during the afternoon. We've got twelve people to dinner at eight. Business, but wives will be here too, which means I've got to keep them talking after dinner. Still, that's why he married me!'

On her way down she looked in on her six-week-old son. Alexi was awake, lying on his back staring at the mobile that hung over his crib. He had Neal's slightly olive skin tone and Lisa's dark brown hair, his eyes already darkening from their original baby blue.

'Hello, sweetheart!' she murmured, picking him up and walking to the window while his nanny followed protectively a few steps behind. 'It's all right, you can go and have a cup of tea,' said Lisa briskly. 'I'd like some time alone with my son.'

As soon as the older woman had gone, she sat on the deep window seat and balanced Alexi on her knee. His head wobbled against her arm but his fingers closed round her hands as he made tiny baby sounds. She held him even closer. 'Who's a very special little boy? You are, did you know that?' He made small sucking sounds while his mouth opened and shut. 'It's true,' she laughed. 'You've changed a lot of lives simply by existing!' She put her cheek next to his and he nestled against her. It was all so different from poor Jessica, and helped to calm her after the therapy.

At least here in Alexi's small section of the house everything was normal. There were no tensions and no problems. He was simply an ordinary, healthy baby boy whom she could love without reservation. Slowly she rocked to and fro, her thoughts back with the lonely little girl she'd always been after Stephanie's outburst had destroyed her confidence. She could see herself so clearly, and the pain was still there if she allowed herself to think about it.

'Mummy, it's time for Alexi's feed!' said the nanny quietly. She'd spent an anxious fifty minutes in the adjoining room, wondering why her employer was suddenly spending so long with her son and hoping this wasn't going to be a new pattern. In her opinion babies were better off if they weren't handled too much. Fresh air, food and sleep were all they required in the early days.

'He's quite happy,' said Lisa dreamily. 'Mind you I ought to go and find Rebekah. Here you are, precious, back to Nanny.'

She found Rebekah teasing one of the three cats that roamed around the house. The only dogs around were two Rotweillers who patrolled the grounds at night. 'Come and tell me about your day,' Lisa called cheerfully.

'It was all right. When am I going to a proper school?'

'After Easter. Heathlands private school for girls. You'll have to sit an entrance test but Mrs Woodward says you're well ahead for your age.'

'They'd let me in anyway if Daddy offered them enough money.'

'Money doesn't buy everything in life!'

'Tell me something it can't buy,' the little girl challenged.

'Health and happiness.'

'That's silly! I meant proper things.'

'Believe me, they are proper things. How about having your tea with me?'

'Why?' Rebekah looked highly suspicious.

'Because I'd like some company.'

'If you want me to then I will. I thought you were just doing it to make me happy.'

'Would that be wrong?'

'Yes, because I might enjoy it very much and then you wouldn't offer to have tea with me again and I'd miss it, which would be worse than if you hadn't been nice at all.'

'Is that what people do to you?'

'Often. Mummy used to promise we'd always go for afternoon walks and things like that, but after we'd been out for one or two she'd forget or say she wasn't well. Then once, Daddy said he'd teach me to swim on Saturday afternoons but after three lessons he kept staying in town and swimming ended too. It hurts when that happens,' she added flatly.

'I'm sure it does. When I promise you something, Rebekah, then believe me I shall try and keep that promise if at all possible.'

Rebekah looked closely at her. 'Daddy might stop you. He wants all your attention doesn't he?'

'In a way, but there's not much I can do about your daddy.'

'Okay, I won't count Daddy. You'll always keep your promises unless Daddy stops you. That's fair. Daddy can stop anything. May we have tea in Mummy's old drawing-room? I'd like to eat there.'

'Fine. You'd better go and tell Cook.'

'What shall we have?'

'You choose, but nothing too heavy. Soups and sandwiches, something like that.'

They were still eating when the door burst open and the housekeeper stood in front of them, her face rigid with disapproval. 'How dare you . . .?' She tailed off when she saw Lisa sitting on the Louis XVI gilded canapé covered in silk damask, a tray on her lap.

'How dare I what, Mrs Sutton?'

'This room isn't for mealtimes, madam. It's always been kept as a quiet room. A place where the first Mrs Gueras could rest.'

'She doesn't need it any more and it's a warm comfortable room, not as large as the others. I think it's sensible to use it when Rebekah and I are on our own.'

'You know your mother cherished this room,' the housekeeper said to an open-mouthed Rebekah. 'How do you think she feels looking down and watching you both?'

Rebekah looked ready to burst into tears and Lisa stood up, furious with the woman for ruining the child's pleasure. 'That will do,' she said icily. 'I shall speak to my husband about this. It's obvious you're not happy working here any more. I think it might be better for everyone if you found employment elsewhere. Kindly leave the room at once.'

Rebekahs eyes were like saucers. 'Can Mummy see us?' she whispered.

'I don't know, but even if she can why should she mind? Wouldn't she want to see you having a nice time?'

'Not likely! I spoilt everything for her. I was meant to be the boy, you see, and when I was a girl and took such a long time being born that Mummy couldn't have any more children, Daddy stopped sharing Mummy's room and started having mistresses.'

'Who told you that?'

'Mummy and Louise.'

'They shouldn't have discussed it with you. It wasn't your fault that things went wrong between your parents.'

'How do you know?'

'Your father is far too intelligent to be affected by a tiny baby!'

'He went off Mummy because she couldn't be a proper wife to him. That's quite sensible when you think about it.'

'Let's finish our tea,' said Lisa quietly. 'I'd rather not discuss it any more.'

'Wait until Mrs Sutton tells Daddy what you said!'

'I shall speak to him about her. I don't think a housekeeper is more important than a wife!'

'She jolly well is. Who's going to run things if she goes? You won't have time and Daddy hates taking on new staff. You'll probably have to apologise to her,' she added.

'I most certainly won't! Now, how about a game of cards before you have your bath?'

'I'm quite certain I'm right,' said Renato Bellini into the telephone, wishing that even from this distance his father didn't have the ability to make him feel unsure of his own judgement. No one else ever had that effect on him.

'When you return,' concluded his father, 'I have found a highly suitable wife for you. She is young, attractive and from an excellent family. Do you remember . . . ?'

'I think I may have found someone over here,' murmured Renato, knowing full well that nothing could incense his father more.

'An English girl?'

'There are quite a lot of them around!'

'Catholic? Virgin?'

'Doubtful on both counts!'

'Renato, you know very well . . .'

'I do not wish to have a wife,' said Bellini harshly, his sense of humour suddenly deserting him as he thought of Neal Gueras' wife. 'You may instruct me about the gold and our position here in London but not, I think, about my marrying again.'

'Luciano needs . . .'

'I must go, there is someone at the door,' Renato lied and quickly replaced the receiver. Luciano was playing at his feet, pushing a Lego car around on the carpet and making quiet noises.

'Park?' he asked, standing up and putting a hand on his father's knee.

'Not today, I have to go away for the night. Tomorrow afternoon perhaps.'

'*Si, Papa.*'

He accepts things too easily, thought Renato. A man needs to be more determined, to have a stronger will. But Luciano was a loving child, and if it was his nature to be gentle then what right had his father to try and change him? 'Do you like England?' he asked the boy.

'Is very cold. Brrr!' He pretended to shiver.

'It's certainly brrr! Now, I must set off for my dinner party.'

'Are you taking a pretty lady?'

'No, but I'm going to see one.'

'I like pretty ladies who smell nice.'

276

Perhaps he'd grow up all right! thought Renato with a smile. He picked the boy up, kissed him warmly and then rang for the nurse. He wondered what Neal and Lisa's son was like, and what kind of a character he would develop in the next four years. Somehow he doubted if he'd be quite as gentle as Luciano.

While he was packing, Lisa was making herself as attractive as possible for Neal's return. She knew that she was deliberately trying to get him on her side before the housekeeper complained and despised herself for it, but since this was the best way to handle Neal it was only sensible to take advantage of her slight power over him.

Certainly when he arrived and found her waiting in the front porch, wearing tight fitting slacks and a low-necked angora top, the weariness vanished from his face and he put his arms tightly round her. 'You smell delicious!' he murmured.

'Let's go upstairs,' she responded. 'I want to show you some of the clothes I bought yesterday.'

Mrs Sutton came briskly out of the kitchen area. 'I wonder if I might have a word with you, Mr Gueras?'

'Later,' he said brusquely. 'I've only just arrived home.'

'Couldn't wait to get her into bed!' the housekeeper reported indignantly to the cook. 'After all these years of looking after the house, he behaved as though I was some new maid.'

In their bedroom, Lisa was modelling underwear she'd bought from a shop off New Bond Street specialising in La Perla, the Italian lingerie.

It was too much for Neal, and when she smiled agreement at the unspoken question in his eyes he immediately stripped off and pulled her down on top of him, his hands rapidly unclasping the sheer satin bra that concealed very little indeed, and then his mouth was on her breasts and to his surprise she was actually sitting astride him, far more the aggressor than ever before.

Much later he left her lying resting in bed and went down to the study to make some urgent phone calls before getting ready for dinner. It looked as though Lisa was now recovered from childbirth and he was delighted with her, although irritatingly aware that he still failed to bring her to a true climax.

After his calls he remembered Mrs Sutton and rang the bell for her. She was there at once, hands clenched in front of her. 'Is there some problem about tonight?' he asked, privately wondering when she was going to accept that it was to Lisa she should now address all her queries.

'No, sir. I thought you ought to know that the late Mrs Gueras's drawing-room has been turned into a second dining-room. Rebekah was having tea there yesterday.'

'On her own?'

'No, your . . . wife was with her.' The pause was infinitesimal but Neal heard it and his eyes hardened.

'In that case I fail to see how it concerns you. If my wife chooses to take meals in the hall, she's entitled to do so! I expect all the staff to respect her wishes as they respected my first wife's.'

'But . . .'

'Naomi is dead,' he said coldly. 'Much as you may regret this fact it cannot be altered. If you feel unable to continue as housekeeper, I'm sure I could make other arrangements for you.'

Not another post, she noticed with alarm, other arrangements. It sounded ominous. 'I'm very happy here, sir,' she said quickly. 'However, your wife seems to feel that I don't suit her.'

'Then I suggest that you learn to suit her, otherwise other arrangements will have to be made whether you wish it or not.'

Mrs Sutton had seen many things, heard many secrets and been paid handsomely both for her skill at her job and her utter discretion. All of that plainly counted for nothing when balanced against the attractions of a new wife who'd had the good fortune to produce a male child at her first attempt. She was almost incoherent with fury, but knew better than to show it. Either she swallowed her pride and bent to Lisa's will or the alternative didn't bear thinking about.

'I'll do my best,' she responded.

'I'm sure you will. I think we understand each other very well.'

After she'd gone he gave a sigh. The last thing he'd thought about when taking Lisa as his wife was domestic trouble. He'd underestimated the average unattractive, middle-aged spinster's antipathy towards such a vivacious and healthy new mistress after years of Naomi's reign. Well, if Kay and Naomi could die, one unattached housekeeper wouldn't prove any trouble. It was surprising how very easy successive thoughts of murder became.

After he'd changed for dinner he went into Lisa's dressing room to fill her in on their guests. She was wearing a full-length skirt of plum-coloured velvet with a high-necked white blouse whose puritan appearance was at odds with that elusive hint of submerged sensuality that Neal was still striving in vain to release in her.

'Has Mrs Sutton seen you yet?' His voice was casual.

'She seemed to think you weren't satisfied with her performance.'

'She gave an excellent performance of a modern-day Mrs Danvers last night! I think she expected me to end up begging forgiveness for taking tea in what I'd failed to realise was Naomi's quiet room.'

'No doubt you made her mistake plain!'

278

'Not plain enough if she complained to you. Can't we get rid of her? She'll never like me.'

'We can get rid of her,' he said slowly, 'but I'm not quite sure what kind of a reference I'd be able to give.'

'Why on earth not? Naomi was very pleased with all she did, surely that's enough?'

'I dislike staff changes. I don't relish the thought of members of my household moving on and gossiping about anything they may have seen or heard while working here.'

'Because of Naomi's drinking? Now she's dead surely that doesn't matter?'

'It isn't only that. There are things ...' He deliberately didn't finish his sentence but their eyes met in the dressing table mirror.

'You mean you'd prefer her to retire rather than take on a new job?'

'You could put it that way.'

'Can she afford to retire?'

'I'm sure I can find her somewhere cheap to live,' he said pleasantly. Instantly, for no logical reason, Lisa had a vision of a churchyard full of old grey headstones with one fresh white one, its lettering clear and unweathered.

'Perhaps it's only fair to give her a little longer to get used to me,' she said at last.

'That's very good of you, darling. Now, if you've finished doing your hair, I thought we should go through the guest list together.' All that Lisa took in was that Renato Bellini was going to be present.

Since the dinner party was informal the men wore lounge suits and the women cocktail dresses. It constantly amazed Lisa that the wealthier women became, the more they seemed to dress in a uniform of black cocktail dresses, silver or gold ball gowns and autumnal shades of brown for their casual wear. Presumably all the dresses had different designer labels on them but they were so similar in appearance they could easily have been bought from a chain store. It was the same with their shoes and hairstyles.

Glancing round the table she reflected that if the women played musical chairs, when the music finally stopped most of the men present would be hard-pressed to know if they'd ended up with the same wife or not. She felt strangely disconcerted by the thought.

The food was good – nothing less would have been tolerated – but scarcely exciting, catering as it did for the low-salt, lean-meat, health-conscious businessmen. Personally she found eating steamed broccoli an excellent example of something which might not make you live longer but would certainly make you feel you had.

The talk flowed around her and she knew that she must be responding properly because now and again Neal would beam down the table at her and she would smile back, well aware that he wanted the guests to see them as a perfect couple. The only incident of interest had occurred when Bishop arrived with Carol. Admittedly he wasn't unattractive and Carol might also have been interested in seeing Lisa's Berkshire home, but considering their conversation only the day before it was still surprising to see them together.

Renato Bellini had come alone. This had ruined the seating arrangements and disconcerted Neal but Lisa was pleased. She only wished he was sitting nearer her. However, he was at Neal's end of the table and deep in conversation with the man opposite him.

After a dessert of fresh fruit salad topped by meringue and cream, Lisa suddenly saw the door at the far end of the room swing slowly open, and to her horror, Jessica's head appeared round it, wide-eyed with surprise.

That morning's therapy had been the same as the previous day's, a quieter but still miserable hour for both of them. Now, to see her daughter walking into a room full of strangers, was as astonishing as it was unwelcome. Neal had his back to Jessica; the first that he knew of her presence was when the woman on his left said, 'What a beautiful little girl,' and his head swung sharply round because he knew very well that she couldn't mean Rebekah.

Slowly, Lisa stood up and began walking quietly round the table towards her daughter. Jessica was now gazing round the room, her eyes flickering from one object to another but never settling on any of the guests. Then she held out the skirts of her white cotton Victorian nightdress and began to sing. Again it was her favourite aria from *Tosca* and everyone remained riveted to their seats. Even Lisa, standing frozen half-way down the room, was deeply touched by the purity of her daughter's voice.

When the aria ended, Jessica glanced round her again. She would probably have been all right if some of the guests hadn't taken it into their heads to applaud her singing. The sudden shattering of the silence jolted her into awareness of people, and then they began to call out to her: urging her to sing again; asking her to sit on their laps. People with loud voices intruding into her secret happiness.

At once she changed – from a beautiful, almost enchanted child into a terrified animal, yelling at the top of her no longer musical voice and hurling herself round the room, hitting her head against walls and furniture in her fear. Grabbing a priceless porcelain figure of a clown she threw it to the ground, where it smashed to pieces in the marble hearth. The noise delighted her so she immediately seized a gold carriage clock and hurled that on to the marble as well.

With a roar of fury, Neal leapt to his feet. 'Stop that at once, you wicked girl! Stop it, do you hear me?' And he reached out for the tiny figure.

'Don't!' cried Lisa. 'Leave her alone, you're frightening her.'

Jessica whimpered and sank on to all fours, scrabbling around on the carpet, searching for a corner in which to hide. Failing that, she grabbed her nightdress and pulled the skirt up over her head. Then, feeling slightly safer, she started screaming again.

Unable to contain himself, Neal took two steps across the room and lifted his stepdaughter off the ground with his left hand as he swung his right hand back to strike her. Lisa's screams halted him for a brief second, and in that short space of time Renato Bellini had sprung from his chair and was level with Neal. Without a word, he grasped Jessica firmly round the waist and pulled her away from her step-father's grasp, before handing her carefully back to her terrified mother.

Lisa was so near to tears she couldn't even thank him. All she could do was wrap her arms round her daughter and run from the room with her, murmuring softly as she went, trying to ease the rigidity of the child's body.

In the dining-room everyone was silent. Bellini sat down in his chair and immediately recommenced his conversation with the man opposite. Taking their cue from him, all the guests promptly started to talk again, not daring to look at their host who was staring at the shattered remains of the clock and the clown and whose face was set in such an expression of fury that Carol, one of the few women in a position to see him, actually felt afraid for Lisa and her daughter.

'Enchanting little thing, isn't she?' said Bishop sardonically. 'I hadn't realised Lisa's influence was so great that Jessica was now compulsory viewing for visitors!'

'Don't be so vile!' snapped Carol. 'That poor little girl must have been out of her mind with fear.'

'She's out of her mind, all right.'

'She's so pretty too.'

'I don't think that compensates for her mental defects. If Neal's got any sense he'll have her put away after this, and a bloody good job too.'

'You've obviously got a keen understanding of the mentally handi-capped,' said Carol, wishing she'd never been talked into keeping Bishop company tonight.

He gave her a long, appraising look. 'Very spirited. Let's hope you don't disappoint me later on.'

'I don't intend to give you any opportunity to be disappointed.'

Just then Neal returned to the table, his smiling, courteous mask firmly back in place. 'I apologise for my step-daughter. She isn't responsible for her actions and doesn't normally come into this part of the house. I do hope no one was too distressed.'

Bellini watched a small muscle jumping in the corner of Neal's jaw and knew that Lisa was going to pay for what had happened. He pictured the look of anguish on her face as she took Jessica from him, and for the first time he actually hated Neal Gueras.

It was a good twenty minutes before Lisa returned and by then Neal was waiting impatiently for the women to leave the room. Bellini noticed with interest that Gueras now had himself well under control, going over to his wife, putting an arm gently round her shoulders. He also noticed how tense she was and that her automatic reaction, quickly smothered, was to draw away.

'Is Jessica better now, darling?' Neal asked courteously. Lisa nodded. 'Good! Perhaps ...'

She stared blankly at him and the mask slipped slightly. 'The other room!' he hissed.

For a second, Bellini thought she was going to walk out again, but then she made a tremendous effort and gave a brief nod. 'Shall we go into the drawing-room, ladies?' she suggested quietly, and they went far more rapidly than usual. Doubtless hoping, thought the Italian cynically, that the unfortunate Lisa would give them intimate details about her tragic child.

'Right, gentlemen.' At last Neal could be himself and his speaking voice took on a harsher tone than was usually heard by ordinary acquaintances. 'I think it's time we discussed the new casinos in London. I'm sure *none* of us here,' and he gave Bellini a swift glance, 'wishes the Americans to regain a position of power.'

'Certainly not,' endorsed a small balding man, better known as a caring left-wing M.P. 'From what I hear they're not going to stop at the casinos either. There's always the question of drugs and ...'

'Prostitution,' put in Bellini helpfully, and had the satisfaction of seeing the man flush scarlet. As the regular client of the assortment of rent boys run by Bishop on Neal's behalf, the politician was personally beneath contempt but naturally Neal used him. A tame politician was always useful.

Normally Lisa found the small-talk when the women were alone excruciatingly boring, but tonight she hoped they'd all be content with gossiping about the latest hairstyles or an earl's daughter who'd run off with the milkman. Naturally they weren't; she was inundated with questions about her 'lovely little girl'. Questions that were made all the more painful by the voracious appetite of the women for as many details as possible to pass on to assorted friends.

'She's autistic,' said Lisa briefly. 'It's a rare condition and very little's known about it. I'm sorry if she spoilt your meal. Somehow she slipped past her nurse and wandered downstairs by mistake. She's really very shy.'

'Is your little boy all right?' asked a raddled-looking woman wearing a low-cut dress.

'It isn't hereditary. Alexi is fine.'

'She sang beautifully,' said Carol, almost as upset as Lisa by what had happened. 'Can't that be used to help her?'

'It doesn't lead to anything. Lots of autistic children have one outstanding talent. She won't ever be normal enough to train as an opera singer, I'm afraid.'

'How good of your husband to let her stay here,' said the wife of the M.P. who liked young boys. 'He's obviously devoted to you.' She'd always liked Neal Gueras.

'I'm very lucky,' agreed Lisa, secretly wondering what Neal was going to say in the privacy of their bedroom.

'Isn't there any cure?' asked another woman.

Lisa was beginning to understand how Jessica must feel when surrounded by people. 'No, there is treatment but it takes a long time before you know if it's helping. Does anyone know what the Royal Ballet are performing next month? I'd like to take my youngest step-daughter for her birthday treat.' After that, no one had the nerve to return to the subject of Jessica. By the time the men rejoined them, Lisa had almost recovered her composure.

Bishop came across to her side. 'That's the first time your husband's provided a cabaret during the meal!' he sniped. 'Did the women want to know if they could hire her?'

'No, but one or two expressed interest in the clown who'd brought Carol along. I think it was for their children's parties.'

A sharp intake of breath was reward enough for Lisa, who'd decided that she couldn't possibly make Bishop hate her more than he did already and was practising defending both herself and Jessica against any further attacks from Neal.

As the guests mingled and some of the men gathered round the television to watch a video the MP had brought back from Frankfurt, Bellini moved smoothly to Lisa's side.

'Are you all right?' he asked softly.

'I'm fine.'

'And little Tosca?'

'She was in a terrible state when I left. I just can't thank you enough

283

for the way you took hold of her. Neal was so livid that . . .'

'It was nothing. How is the treatment going?'

'There is a change in her,' said Lisa slowly. 'Not exactly an improvement but at least she isn't fighting against me so hard. She's used to sitting on my lap and letting me hold her. Instead of screaming with fury, she looks pathetic and cries quietly.'

'You must be exhausted after such sessions.'

'Fortunately life with Neal doesn't give me much time to think about myself! He wouldn't like it if I kept saying how tired I was, and by convincing him I'm all right I fool myself as well. Rather like that song from *The King and I*!'

'You cannot fool your body. Eventually you will have to sleep.'

'I'm fine, honestly.' She lifted her face to smile an assurance. It was a terrible mistake. In his eyes she saw such an expression of affection mixed with desire that she began to move closer to him as her heart raced and her legs felt weak. He too remained frozen, realising that for the first time in his life he was face to face with a woman whom he wanted not only for lovemaking but also to cherish and protect. Here was a woman he might have considered marrying and he couldn't have her.

His mouth softened and the lines that ran from the side of his nose down to the corners of his mouth smoothed away as he very slowly began to lift a hand to caress her cheek. Fortunately for them both, the MP suddenly let out a shout of excited laughter and in the ensuing outburst of sexual innuendo the spell was broken.

Bellini's hand returned to his side while his face assumed its more usual cynical expression, only the softness in his eyes remaining as proof that Lisa hadn't imagined it all. She moved away from him, half-turning towards the television but averting her eyes when she saw two naked girls rolling round on a circular bed together.

Most people were staring avidly at the action but Bishop stood apart from the crowd. He'd been watching Lisa and Bellini from the moment they came together and had seen the tell-tale signs of the Italian's feelings. Inside he smiled to himself. It was now possible that, given sufficient rope, Lisa would hang herself; although the fact that it was Bellini who was involved made it more complicated because Bellini couldn't possibly be made to suffer, whatever his actions. Even so, it was nice to know the man had a weakness.

Carol tugging at his arm brought Bishop back to reality. 'I don't think I want to watch any more of this,' she said coldly. 'Perhaps you'd take me back. I have to be up early tomorrow.'

His mind went through the known facts about her. Single, no family, up to her neck in debt, dependent upon Neal Gueras to keep

284

her shop going. He was quite safe; she couldn't make a fuss whatever happened. 'Fine,' he said casually. 'We'll have a quick nightcap in my annexe and then we'll set off for London. I must admit I prefer action to watching this kind of simulated sex.'

Disturbed, Carol tried to enlist Lisa's help in making other arrangements for getting home. Lisa, however, was anxious not to antagonise Neal any further and since Carol had chosen to come with Bishop, she couldn't imagine why he wasn't entitled to take her home.

It was 3 a.m. before the last guest left, with the exception of Bellini who was staying overnight. He wished his hostess goodnight and then followed Wakefield up the stairs to the main guest room, acutely aware of Neal's eyes on his back.

Neal and Lisa went upstairs in silence but once inside their bedroom, Neal spun round to face his wife and all his submerged fury erupted. 'How the hell did that daughter of yours manage to get away from her nurse? Isn't it enough that she lives under my roof, and that I have to watch while you half-kill yourself in some pathetic pursuit of a cure that every sane person knows doesn't exist? Do you have any idea how I felt when she started throwing one of her tantrums? Can you imagine what people are going to say? Can you?'

Lisa held her hands out in despair. 'I'm sorry, darling, I really am. I've no idea how it happened or why she chose to come into a room full of people but obviously it won't happen again. I'll make sure of that.'

'It most certainly won't because she isn't going to stay here. Enough is enough. She's going into a home.'

'No she is not!' shouted Lisa. 'You gave me your word, and if you send her away I'm going too; and what's more I'm taking Alexi with me.'

He stared blankly at her for a moment and then – to her astonishment – burst out laughing. 'You cannot be serious! Really, Lisa, you're incredibly naive; it's almost touching! Do you seriously imagine for one moment that I'd let you take my son out of this house?'

She frowned as he continued to laugh. 'I admire your spirit,' he said at last. 'And yes, I did give you my word, but since Nurse Anthony can't control her I shall find someone who can.'

'No! Janice and I are the people doing the therapy; if we don't continue it will do irreparable harm. She wasn't being naughty tonight, she got frightened.'

'Have you any idea of the value of that clown she broke?'

'It's insured, isn't it?'

'No, you stupid girl, it isn't. How can I insure something I'm not supposed to have!'

'I don't ...'

'I could have broken her bloody neck!' he continued, savagely tugging at his cuff links.

'You would have done if Renato hadn't taken her away from you.'

Neal sat down on the bottom of the bed. 'Yes, the handsome Italian. Don't think that I'm not aware of his feelings towards you, and yours towards him.'

'He's just a friend!'

'That's not what it looked like tonight. Not that I blame him for wanting you, but I trust you know better than to encourage anything more than a light-hearted flirtation?'

'I don't flirt.'

'No,' he said slowly. 'I suppose you don't. Perhaps it might help if I told him you were frigid. It's true, and from what I've heard he'd soon lose interest once he knew that.'

'I am not frigid!' She was shaking with anger; tired of his repeated accusation which she knew was totally untrue.

'Really?' He stepped closer to her.

'Perhaps it's not me that's to blame!' she shouted, throwing discretion to the winds.

'You mean it's my fault?'

'We're the only two concerned so ...'

'It has to be me?' He smiled.

'It's possible; maybe if you weren't always in such a hurry I could relax more. Do you think I enjoy knowing you're getting impatient? How would you like it if ...'

He wasn't like Toby. His face never changed and he didn't give her any warning. One minute he was standing smiling at her and the next the palm of his left hand hit her right cheek with a crack and her head jerked to one side.

'You selfish bitch,' he said quietly. 'I'm beginning to think Toby had some provocation.'

Stunned and in pain, Lisa stood in front of him, not realising that she'd begun to weep.

'I'll show you just how impatient I can be,' he added, and ten minutes later she was lying still fully-clothed on the floor as he looked down on her. 'Next time I'd think carefully before calling me an impatient lover,' he said softly. 'Believe me, I can be a great deal less patient than this as well. I'm very disappointed in you tonight, Lisa. Very disappointed indeed.'

The slap he'd administered had been very mild but the damage it had done to their relationship was immeasurable.

Chapter Twenty-Three

Next morning Lisa awoke early. She had to give Jessica her therapy before leaving with Neal for London where they were due to spend the next four days, and was beginning to wonder if the treatment could work when – except for the therapy – she was so rarely with her daughter. Fortunately Janice was always there, and the situation was the best compromise she could manage.

Surprisingly, Bellini was still at breakfast. He glanced up over his cup then rose politely to his feet. He was actually on his third cup of typically English coffee but it had been worth it to see her again. 'You rise early!' he exclaimed in mock surprise. 'I imagined that society hostesses never left their beds before noon.'

'I've got Jessica to see to and then we go back to London. We're at the theatre tonight, a Help the Aged dinner tomorrow and Felicity someone's twenty-first birthday party the following evening. I shall be whizzing from London to Berkshire faster than anything British Rail can offer!'

'You come to see your daughter every day?'

'I have to or everything we've achieved so far will be lost.'

'I too must rush, but we will see each other at the party. Your husband and I both know Felicity's father.'

She felt a surge of pleasure. 'I expect you're anxious to get back to your son?'

'Naturally, but then I must get to work at the bank. Please say my farewells to your husband for me, and thank you again for a delightful dinner party.' He took her right hand in his and lightly stroked the top of her wrist. His fingers were long and slender, their touch featherlight, and suddenly she found it difficult to breathe.

He'd never behave like Neal, she thought bitterly. She'd stake everything she had on that. Realising he'd held her hand too long she suddenly withdrew it, feeling a physical ache at the breaking of contact. 'I'm glad you enjoyed yourself. Did you know the man opposite you?'

'A business acquaintance.' He sounded brusque, almost remote, as though she'd spoken out of turn.

'I didn't mean to pry,' she said quickly.

He gave a wry smile. 'I apologise, but you see ... Well, business is business and sometimes it can lead to minor annoyances which have to be dealt with.'

'I understand. Have a safe trip back.'

She didn't understand, he thought, following Michael as the boy carried his suitcase out to the car. He didn't understand himself. From what Stephen Holdsworth had told him during dinner it sounded as though P2, the masonic lodge to which his family had belonged since its inception, was now involved with things that he personally didn't wish to be associated with. Drugs and the laundering of money were best left to criminals like Neal's organisation in London. If P2 were becoming as corrupt as Stephen had indicated, then he didn't want any part of it. It was a large and unwelcome problem, and as soon as he'd played with Luciano he would telephone his father for advice.

Tipping the hovering boy he slid into the Ferrari and drove swiftly and efficiently away. Despite his business worries all he could see was the slim figure of Neal's wife as she'd looked last night, holding her terrified child in her arms as she tried to protect her from her husband. For the first time in many years he wanted to both love and protect a woman, and her fear and vulnerability were etched indelibly in his mind.

Lisa had another miserable hour with Jessica. The child kept sobbing softly, trying to hang her head while Lisa firmly forced it up again, all the time ignoring the bewilderment on Jessica's face. It didn't seem as if any of her mother's reassurances even reached her. But at least she now sat passively and Janice said that her behaviour in the day was less frantic and she was eating better.

After that, Lisa went straight to the nursery and was surprised to find Neal sitting there with Alexi on his knee. He was all smiles this morning, the distasteful scene of the previous night apparently forgotten. She assumed she was expected to forget it too.

'Isn't he doing well!' he exclaimed. 'I'd forgotten how quickly they grow. He's so alert. A proper little Gueras, aren't you, my boy?' Alexi obediently bestowed a windy smile on his adoring father and murmured contentedly to himself. 'Where have you been?' continued Neal. 'I hoped you'd have a rest this morning.'

'I've been with Jessica.'

His smile vanished. 'Of course, we mustn't forget Jessica. Did she throw anything of value this morning?'

'You know perfectly well there isn't anything of value in her rooms. She's definitely improving, she doesn't ...'

'I don't want to hear about her. Have you had breakfast?'

'Yes. Renato was still here. He asked me to pass on his farewells.'

'I'm surprised you didn't run off with him. I'm sure he'd have taken you if you'd played the battered wife.'

'What play are we seeing tonight?' she asked, determined to change the subject before she said something she'd regret.

'The new R.S.C. production at the Barbican. A modern play, I think.'

'How many of us are going?'

'Six, I'm afraid your handsome Italian isn't among them.'

She put a hand on his arm. 'Please don't keep on about Bellini. *You're* my husband. I'm not interested in other men. I've got you, Alexi, Jessica, two lovely homes ... what more could I want?'

He gave her a long, level look. 'I wish I knew, Lisa.'

'I'm a disappointment to you, aren't I?' she whispered, taking Alexi and holding him against her shoulder.

'I suppose so, but perhaps it isn't your fault. You're a good hostess, a good mother and, in public, an excellent wife. Also, to be fair, you always said you didn't love me. I suppose that's why things aren't so perfect behind the bedroom door.'

'That isn't why. I still can't shake off the memories of Toby, he's always there. Whenever I'm close to letting go I start remembering all the things he did to me and I just freeze, but I'm very fond of you, you must know that.'

'I'm sorry I hit you.' The words came out jerkily. Apologies were unfamiliar to Neal Gueras.

'I understand; I just wish I was better for you.'

'I behaved abominably. I don't know, following Jessica's ...'

'And I'm sorry about her,' said Lisa quickly. 'I realise it was a disaster.'

Suddenly he stood up and it was as if the conversation had never begun. 'Time to go,' he announced, and promptly left the room.

Lisa laid Alexi down in his cot. Immediately he started screaming in disgust and the nanny hurried in, looked accusingly at Lisa and picked the baby up, checking for a wet nappy or a loose pin. 'My husband's been holding him,' said Lisa shortly. 'There's nothing wrong except he didn't want to be put down.'

'Although why I should apologise to his nanny,' she remarked to Neal as they drove away from the house, 'I simply can't imagine. I do so hate leaving him with her.'

'You're a wife first and a mother second, darling. That's the way I like it to be. We'll see more of him when he's older.' She wondered if that was true.

Back at the flat, Neal checked his answerphone while Lisa went through the post. There were the usual numerous invitiations and requests for money plus one large brown envelope for Neal marked 'Confidential'.

Placing that on his desk she went into the bedroom to change. When Neal joined her she knew that he wanted to make amends for the previous night. This time he was careful and considerate but if anything their quarrel had increased Lisa's inability to respond and she could tell how disappointed he was when it was over and she was lying in his arms.

'I'd better ring for Bishop,' he said reluctantly. 'I'll need him for the rest of the day. If you want to go shopping, take Mike.'

'I rather wanted to see Carol. She's meant to be designing something for Ascot and I'd like to have an idea of what she's planning.'

'I'm not sure Carol's going to stay in business much longer.' He sounded totally indifferent despite his financial interest.

'Why?'

'I've no idea. Women simply haven't taken to her designs. It's all a matter of luck in the fashion game. Still, go and see her by all means.'

He had ten minutes to wait before Bishop arrived and picked up the brown envelope, glanced at the London postmark and wondered what it was. It felt stiff, like an invitation, but that wouldn't come in a cheap brown envelope. When the photo first fell out he glanced briefly at it, wondered why anyone should bother to send him such a tawdry picture and went to throw it away. It was only when he reached the kitchen, where the light was sharper, that he was actually able to see the face of the threesome so busily engaged in their work.

Blinking rapidly he held it closer to his eyes unable to believe what he saw, but there was no doubt about it. It was Lisa, with her eyes wide open, her lips parted in what could possibly be ecstasy, and her body taut beneath the ministrations of two men. One he recognised instantly as Toby Walker but the other one was a total stranger to him.

His hand began to shake and a vein throbbed in his temple. He still wanted to throw it away, forget its very existence, but he was drawn again and again to his wife's face. She was unrecognisable from the passive sexual partner he knew. All at once sheer, murderous rage made him shout her name as he crashed back into the bedroom where she was about to take a shower.

Lisa, poised naked by the cubicle, stared at him, quite forgetting her lack of clothing.

'You lying bitch!' he growled, walking slowly towards her with his hands stretched out in front of him. 'Toby Walker put you off sex, did he? Turned you into a frigid wife for me to cope with? That was the story, I believe?' Shaking with fright, all she could do was nod.

'To think I believed you! I actually apologised for last night! If only I'd known, I'd have invited a friend to join us. Perhaps that would have been more pleasurable for you, Lisa. Well?'

'I don't know what you're talking about.' Her voice was shrill with fright.

'I'm talking about this!' he shouted, throwing the glossy black and white photograph across the room so that it landed at her feet. She looked down and at the very moment she recognised herself the door-bell rang. 'That's Bishop,' snapped Neal curtly. 'I'll tell him to wait downstairs. Or shall I ask him to make up a threesome?'

Trembling, Lisa bent down and picked up the picture. At once it all came back to her. Roger, high on drugs, doing everything that Toby told him while she could only struggle and fight, too dazed with sleep to put up any real resistance against the two men, both of whom were big and fit.

Bishop, waiting several minutes outside the door, smiled to himself. When his employer finally opened it and snapped at him to wait in the car, he smiled even more broadly. He'd had a job prising the photo away from Toby but obviously it had been worth it. If Neal's face was anything to go by, Lisa wouldn't be quite so popular any more.

He'd totally misjudged both Neal and Lisa. Neal, far too intelligent to remain in the red-hot fury for long, had already begun to query one or two things in his mind and when he got back to the bedroom and found Lisa being sick in the hand basin he knew that his guess had been right. It wasn't ecstasy on her face in the photo, it was terror. The kind of terror that had made her what she was today. He no longer wanted to kill Lisa; now it was Toby Walker on whom his fury was focused.

When he put a hand on the back of Lisa's neck she screamed, almost falling over as she tried to get away from him. Quickly he took hold of her arms and pulled her down on to his lap. 'I'm sorry,' he apologised, realising it was the second apology in one day. 'I didn't stop and think. I was so shocked I totally lost control.'

'I hated it!' she sobbed, slumping against him. 'It was horrible, revolting! That pig of a man, and Toby urging him on all the time. You can't imagine what it was like. I still have nightmares about it.'

He pulled a towelling robe round her shaking body and ran his hands through her hair, soothing her as he would a horse or child, and all the time he was trying to work out who'd sent him the photograph, why, and where the negatives were.

When she calmed down a little he told her to rest before going out, then telephoned for Mike to wait outside the door of the flat until he was needed. Finally, reluctantly, he left her alone because he was already late for his meeting and today they had a very important visitor. He was the key to Neal's entire plan, and much as he wanted to stay with his wife he knew it was impossible.

Slipping the photo into his briefcase, he gave her one final embrace and left. Bishop, fully expecting his employer to be in a towering rage and probably less than sharp for the meeting, was disappointed by the iron control and apparent lack of concern he displayed.

Only when they walked towards the meeting room did Neal mention the photograph, and then he didn't say what Bishop expected. 'Find out about this,' he instructed, pushing the envelope into Bishop's hand. 'I want to know who sent it, where they got it from, and most important of all, where the negatives are. I also want to see Toby Walker.'

'He's on set,' said Bishop quickly.

'Then get him off the set! I want him here, in my office, after lunch today.'

He'd talk, thought Bishop. Toby wasn't a man to stay silent where his own safety was concerned. He'd say that it was Bishop who'd forced him to hand the photo over and Bishop who'd got the negatives. After that there wouldn't be anywhere on earth for Bishop to hide. 'What if he makes trouble?'

'Remove him.'

At least the older man was sufficiently rattled to make one mistake, thought Bishop with relief. Only one, but enough to save Bishop. One thing was certain: Toby Walker *would* make trouble, and by lunch-time he'd be well and truly removed. Without a flicker of expression, Bishop took his place next to Neal and began to set up the tape beneath the table top. Taking notes could make people nervous. Neal preferred the hidden tape recorder to jotting down official minutes. So did Bishop. Tapes could be doctored.

It took Lisa over an hour to pull herself together enough to go out but once she saw Mike her spirits lifted slightly. He was always so cheerful it was impossible not to like him, and she knew that he liked her as well.

He tugged at his wavy hair in mock-servility. 'Where to?'

'Carol's shop please, Mike.'

He hesitated. 'I don't think she's opening today.'

'Why not?'

'Bit of a heavy night by all accounts.'

'How do you know that?'

'Bishop told me. Weren't they together?'

'Yes, but she didn't seem very keen on him. She wanted someone else to take her home.'

'Obviously she changed her mind.'

It was hard to believe but if Mike had heard it from Bishop, it was presumably true.

'Anywhere else you fancy?'

'Not really. I know, I'll call at her flat over the shop. I'd like to hear what happened to change her mind!'

'I don't think ...'

'Come on, Mike!'

'Just remember, you were warned.'

She knocked on the flat door for ages before Carol opened it, and one look at her friend's swollen eyes and split bottom lip told her exactly what had gone on the previous eveing. She hugged her friend. 'Carol, I'm so sorry. Why did he do it?'

'Because I wouldn't play his nasty little games. Christ, Lisa, he's a perverted bastard, and he hates you too. I've never met a man so full of hate. He'd do anything to destroy your marriage, anything at all.'

'I know he hates me. I don't think he likes anyone very much! As for my marriage, well, there isn't much he can do.'

'Don't you believe it!' Carol took down two mugs and plugged in the percolator. 'He was laughing last night about some surprise he'd got planned for you and Neal.'

The photo, thought Lisa. It hadn't been Toby as she'd thought. It had been Bishop. Not that Neal would believe her, especially if the only proof was the word of a woman with every reason to bear his deputy a grudge. 'I think we've survived his surprise.'

'I shouldn't have gone with him last night,' Carol admitted when they were drinking their coffee. 'It was really a sort of bargain. He said that if I went with him, I needn't worry about all the money I'd borrowed from your husband. That he'd see to it for me.'

'Why didn't you tell Neal you were worried about the loan? He'd never have pressed you for repayment until things were going better.'

Carol knew it was more than her life was worth to tell Lisa that Neal *had* called in the loan, and then endorsed Bishop's promise of a longer repayment term provided she went along to the dinner. She'd known when she used him as a backer what kind of a man he was. She wasn't an innocent like Lisa, but she'd made the mistake of thinking she could use him and not pay any price for it, because she'd been totally confident of her business success.

She still didn't understand why business hadn't flourished. All she knew was that she owed Neal Gueras a vast sum of money and in order to repay it was going to have to join his select group of upper class young women who entertained foreign visitors whenever requested. This morning even that seemed preferable to any more evenings with Bishop.

'Why didn't you come to me?' pressed Lisa.

'I never thought of it,' lied Carol.

'I only wish Louise could see you. She's Neal's oldest daughter and besotted with Bishop. Which reminds me, they'll soon be home for Easter. I hope Louise has got over her resentment towards me. I could do with a few more friends at home. Only Rebekah and Mike are friendly, and Mike doesn't count because he's usually out chauffering.'

'That Italian likes you. I watched him last night. He kept looking your way, and when poor Jessica was crying he looked as though he wanted to take you in his arms instead of her!'

'Don't!' said Lisa quickly. 'Don't even joke about it. Neal already hates him because he thinks he admires me. If he heard someone else saying the same thing he'd blame me for flirting.'

'You didn't do anything. You didn't have to!' Carol added ruefully. 'I wish he'd fancy me. I think he's fantastic; incredibly handsome and so smouldering with passion you can almost feel it!'

'Perhaps he'd smoulder for you if he could hear you now!'

'No, I'm short, plump and fair. Obviously not at all his type.'

'Do you want me to talk to Neal about your loan?' Lisa still felt guilty over her friend's ordeal.

'Honestly, Lisa, it's all right. I'll speak to him myself. He won't want you dabbling in his business affairs.'

'You're a personal friend!'

'Please, Lisa, promise me you won't?'

She hesitated. 'All right,' she conceded, 'but if you ever change your mind just ring me up.'

'I will. Your chauffeur seems to want you. He keeps looking at his watch out there.'

'Heavens, I've got a hair appointment in ten minutes! You need something on that face, I'll ring in a couple of days to see how you are.'

'Thanks,' said Carol quietly. She watched her friend leave, knowing full well that within a couple of days she'd be installed in a different, far more spacious flat but without her dreams of becoming a second Zandra Rhodes. Carol Blades was yet another casualty in the shadowy world inhabited by Neal and his organisation, a world she'd been stupid enough to think she could take on and use without paying any price.

'Dead? What the hell do you mean, dead?'

'He made a fuss about coming so I did what you said.'

'I never told you to have him killed. He's no use to me dead!' Neal was beside himself with fury.

'I asked you what to do if he made trouble and you said remove him.'

'I meant from the television studio, not the bloody earth!'

'I'm very sorry,' said Bishop calmly. 'I misunderstood you.'

Neal's eyes narrowed. 'That's most unlike you, John.'

The use of the christian name was a warning and Bishop heeded it. 'I thought you'd like him dead, all things considered.'

'Meaning?'

'That your wife might be happier knowing he wasn't around any more.'

'Is there any particular reason for you to think that?'

'Of course, the photograph.'

'Yes, the photograph, the negative of which I shall probably never recover, thanks to you. Neither shall I ever find out who sent me the original.'

'I assumed it was Walker.'

'Did you, John? I'm not certain about that. You see, I can't imagine what he had to gain by it. As long as he kept quiet about his life with her and continued to work for us when needed, he had a good life. No, I don't think it was Walker himself, and now he can't tell me who it was. That's a great pity. I prefer to know my enemies.'

'It could have been Bellini.'

'He's never had any contact with Walker. Besides, he's too infatuated with my wife to get mixed up in anything like this. No, definitely not Bellini.'

Bishop shrugged. 'Another of life's great mysteries then.'

'Yes. How did he die?'

'Fell down the stairs at his flat and broke his neck. Drunk, of course. He hasn't been found yet.'

'How did you get him to his flat if you couldn't get him to my office?'

'We went there first. He said he needed to pick up some things to show you. Then, when I tried to hurry him, he refused and drew a gun.'

'You weren't quick enough to stop him?'

'I probably could have done, but as I've said I thought you were quite happy to have him killed.'

Neal studied Bishop carefully. It was impossible to read anything from that cold-eyed mask but he was sure he was lying. The thought disturbed him. 'How do you think this morning's meeting went?' he demanded, deciding to let him off the hook for now.

'Very well. With his inside knowledge, we should be home and dry.'

'Don't forget he'll be just as likely to betray *us* for the right money.'

'That's the trouble with traitors, you simply can't trust them!'

'When it's over you can remove him; after a suitable period of time, of course. And I do mean remove, as in permanently remove.'

'I don't think we should give him too long to think about this either. Six weeks maximum.'

'Six weeks?' Neal thought for a moment. 'Well, we could be ready by then but it will mean burning some midnight oil in Berkshire.'

'What about your wife?'

'What about her?'

'I only meant that when Naomi was alive she didn't notice the comings and goings but the present Mrs Gueras is far more alert. If you start disappearing to midnight meetings, I'm sure she'll miss you.'

Neal smiled pleasantly. 'It's kind of you to be concerned, John. I think I can deal with my own domestic affairs.'

'I'm very pleased to hear it.'

This was the nearest Bishop had ever come to insolence and Neal wondered whether to react openly or not. Finally deciding against it he waved a hand in dismissal and sent his secretary out for the evening papers. He wanted to see if there was any mention of Toby Walker's death.

Refreshed by a massage and facial, Lisa rested during the afternoon, had a light tea at Fortnums and then prepared for the trip to the theatre. After considerable thought she settled on a light, floral-patterned jersey two-piece. The top had a scoop neckline and was drop-waisted while the skirt had a mid-calf dipping hemline. It was one of Carol's originals and very comfortable to wear.

Neal arrived home late and harassed. He took Lisa's diamond necklace and ear-rings out of the wall safe without even glancing at her outfit. Then, muttering something about a terrible day, disappeared into his study and spent over thirty minutes on the phone.

As a result they arrived late at the Barbican, and the rest of their party were standing waiting in the foyer. They only just managed to find their seats before the lights went down and Lisa realised that her husband hadn't spoken more than a dozen words to her since they met up. Concerned about Carol and Neal, she found it difficult to concentrate and the play's plot proved totally incomprehensible. During the interval she was relieved to find it was incomprehensible to everyone else as well.

Amanda, fresh from a trip to the ladies', was the most animated of the somewhat quiet group but even she seemed slightly subdued, and while the others were discussing the actors' performances she steered Lisa into a quiet corner of the room. 'It must have been a dreadful shock to you,' she murmured, fixing her glittering eyes on Lisa's face.

'Not really, I didn't expect to enjoy it.'

'Not the play, darling! I meant the news about your first husband.'

'Toby? What's happened to him?'

'Didn't Neal tell you? It's in all the evening papers, he ...'

'Lisa, darling, I don't think you've met Donald and Natalie Chambers, have you? Excuse us, Amanda, but I'd like to introduce them to my wife.' With one swift movement Neal moved her back into the group.

She shook hands with Donald and Natalie — neither of whom had a word to say for themselves — and then tried to take her husband to one side but he stood solidly next to an American couple and ignored her. When they were taking their seats for the second act, she grabbed him by the arm. 'What's happened to Toby?'

'I can't tell you now!'

'Amanda said he was in all the evening papers. What's he done?'

'Be quiet!' he hissed, and for the rest of the performance she sat silently wondering what Neal was keeping from her. They returned to the flat at midnight and as soon as the door closed behind them, Lisa repeated her question. Neal turned away and poured himself a brandy. 'I didn't tell you earlier because I didn't want to spoil your evening. Toby's dead.'

'Dead?'

'He fell down the stairs of his maisonette and broke his neck. Presumably he was drunk.'

Lisa stared at his broad back and felt a terrible coldness in the pit of her stomach. 'You killed him,' she whispered. 'You killed him because of the photo.'

'Don't be silly, darling. I've been tied up in meetings all day, how could I possibly have killed him? In any case, I'm not in the habit of murdering everyone who annoys me!'

'I don't believe you.'

'It's true. Be grateful, otherwise your precious Jessica wouldn't be around today!'

'Neal, please look at me.' She was amazed at how calm she sounded. Slowly he turned towards her but she couldn't tell anything from his face. It was as much a mask as Bishop's, and that alone was enough to convince her she was on the right track. Pull back, she warned herself. Don't turn yourself into an enemy. 'You really didn't have anything to do with it?' She forced a note of doubt into her voice.

'No, I didn't. I'm bloody annoyed he's dead because I don't know how to lay my hands on the negative of that photograph.'

'So his death was an accident?'

'Unless he knocked some other wretched girl around and she pushed him. In that case I imagine she'd have your fullest sympathy.'

'I'm not sorry he's dead,' said Lisa slowly. 'I was always afraid he might come after me one day. Now I can really put him out of my mind.'

'I'm relieved to hear it. Did you enjoy the play?'

'I didn't understand a single word. Why don't they stick to Shakespeare?'

'Because he's stopped writing good plays! Now, if you don't mind, sweetheart, I've got to go out again. I'll be very late back so I'll probably sleep on the couch. It's business.'

'At this hour of the night?'

'Lisa, if I say it's business then it's business.'

'I see.'

'No you don't! It really is business but I can't give you any details. I thought you'd be grateful for a full night's sleep!'

She turned and went into the bedroom, well aware that no matter how strange it seemed, Neal wasn't likely to be blatantly visiting a mistress at this hour of the night. It was far more probable he was dealing with something shady, in which case she certainly didn't want to know about it.

'I'm off to Beckett Lodge in the morning,' she called as he pulled on his coat. 'I might not get back until mid-afternoon.'

'Remember it's the Help the Aged Ball and we're on the top table.'

'I'm not likely to forget,' she muttered before sliding gratefully between the dark blue satin sheets and falling asleep.

The alarm woke her at seven and she breakfasted alone. Neal hadn't slept on the couch and he didn't ring to apologise. She wasn't too worried. Perhaps he was feeling more relaxed about their relationship, in which case she too would have more freedom when they weren't together. Freedom that would enable her to see more of her two children.

She asked Mike to buy all the popular newspapers and then read them during the drive home. Toby was on the front pages and there were plenty of stories about his heavy drinking and high-handed dealings with the television company who produced his show. Amazingly there wasn't one mention of Lisa. Not a single article mentioned their marriage. She was relieved, but also puzzled.

'Sorry about your ex,' remarked Mike when she put down the last paper. 'I know he treated you badly but he just wasn't bright enough to cope with it all, was he?'

'I suppose not. He was nice once, when we first met. Do you think his death was an accident?'

'I'm not paid to think! If the press and police say it was an accident then that's fine by me.'

'I'm only worried because it was a very convenient death.'

'Makes everyone's life tidier then, doesn't it? If I were you I'd just be grateful. Going to send flowers?'

'I shouldn't think so.'

'Probably best. Your husband won't want people reminded that you were Toby's first.'

No, she thought, he wouldn't. But was he powerful enough to have stopped all the papers from digging up the dirt on their marriage and divorce? Let alone Jessica who'd once made the headlines herself.

Perhaps he was. The thought wasn't in the least comforting.

Chapter Twenty-Four

In Berkshire the staff were preparing Louise and Ruth's rooms and bustling around cheerfully until Lisa appeared. After that they glided silently round, all cheerfulness gone. Realising it was her presence that ruined their good humour, she reluctantly climbed the stairs to her daughter's room. She was pleasantly surprised to find her sitting with some paper and crayons, and even more surprised when Jessica actually looked up at her for a moment, her eyes lingering longer than usual before darting away.

Janice was doing some sewing and smiled at Lisa. 'I wanted you to see how much she's improving. She likes to sit and draw now, don't you, Jessica?'

Jessica sidled towards the two women. 'Don't you!' she echoed, then took hold of Lisa's hand and tugged her towards the paper. 'You drew that!' she told her mother proudly.

'You did it, darling.'

'You did it,' she repeated. Lisa remembered that the personal pronoun meant nothing to autistic children and Jessica was trying to explain that she herself had done it.

'It's beautiful, Jessica!' Her daughter grabbed the paper and pushed it in Lisa's face. 'Give it to me,' she said clearly and Lisa took it, placing it carefully inside her handbag.

'How about our little cuddle time?' she suggested brightly. The small hands clenched for a moment and then when Lisa sat down, Jessica obediently began to climb on to her lap. Both women held their breath but once she was safely on, Lisa smiled and kissed her fingers before putting them on Jessica's mouth.

This was new, yet the little girl obviously understood the significance because all at once she smiled. At that moment she looked so beautiful and so completely normal that it was unbearable when, within seconds, she reverted to a grizzling, fighting toddler who didn't want any physical contact.

Eventually she calmed down again and the last ten minutes were spent going through the finger-kissing routine again, this time making Jessica laugh aloud as she tried to kiss her own fingers and put them on Lisa's mouth.

When the hour was up she was rewarded with a bowl of her favourite ice cream while Lisa stayed on the settee, exhausted but also elated by what had happened. 'I must ring Mrs Honeywood,' she exclaimed. 'I'm sure this is a breakthrough, although there's still a long way to go.'

'We knew it was going to take months. You should be over the moon to see any improvement so quickly.'

'I am really. It's just that with Alexi growing so fast I suddenly want Jessica to be more normal to keep pace with him.'

'You musn't try and rush her. I'm sorry about Mr Walker,' she added.

'It is sad. I'm staying until after lunch. I thought I might take Jessica out for a walk in about half an hour if you'd get her ready.'

After checking on Alexi in the nursery, Lisa went to Rebekah's schoolroom and found Mrs Woodward, Rebekah's governess, sitting drinking a cup of tea. 'Where's Rebekah?' she demanded.

'She's ... Actually she's being punished. She refused to do her geography and threw her book at me. I'll fetch her for you.'

'Is she in her bedroom?'

'No, she's ...'

Lisa had already guessed where Rebekah was and ran on to the landing, wrenching open the door to the cupboard where cleaning materials were stored. It was large, dark and − she imagined − highly popular with spiders. It was an almost catatonic Rebekah whom she led out and held gently against her, waiting for the child to start crying and release some of her terror.

When she realised it was Lisa holding her she sobbed and sobbed, gabbling about spiders and her mother, saying that she was sure they'd all come from that cupboard and were they in her hair? All the time she talked she was brushing at her clothes and her bare legs as though she could feel the creatures on her.

'There's nothing there,' soothed Lisa. 'Come and lie on your bed, and when you're feeling better you can come out for a walk with me. I'm taking Jessica and ...'

'I don't want you to leave me!' shouted Rebekah. 'They'll come after me and run all over my bed, just like they did Mummy's.'

'Mummy never had spiders on her bed, Rebekah. You must have had a bad dream without realising it.'

'She did! They were great big tarantulas. They were crawling over everything and she was trying to knock them away, and then I saw ...' She stopped and frowned.

'Saw what?'

'I can't remember! I know I saw something else but whenever I get to that part I can't remember!' She started crying again.

'Look, wash your face and hands, change into some jeans and we'll go out for that walk. I promise there aren't any tarantulas in this house. As for your governess, she's going today. Why didn't you tell me what she was like?'

'You'd have said it wasn't true, like the spiders. They're just as true as that horrible Mrs Woodward.'

They certainly were to the overwrought Rebekah, Lisa realised as she marched back into the schoolroom and told Mrs Woodward to pack her things. The governess didn't argue and didn't mention a reference. Lisa assumed she'd complain to Neal later but even he wouldn't want to employ such a totally insensitive woman.

Finally she took both children down the back stairs, across the lawn and over the stile into the wooded fields where Ruth liked to ride her horses. Jessica refused to walk properly, choosing to twist and turn with her hands stretched in front of her, but apart from that she behaved well, making excited noises when a bird caught her eye.

'I thought she was mad,' said Rebekah. 'She isn't though, is she?'

'Not at all. She's afraid of a lot of things and that's stopped her from developing properly.'

'I'm afraid of a lot of things too. Perhaps she'd like me to go and see her when you're not here.'

'She might but she often ignores visitors. She lives in her own world and doesn't want to let other people in.'

'I know how she feels! There are lots of people I don't want in my world. I wish I was autistic.'

'No you don't! Jessica will never be able to go to school or make friends. She won't marry or have a job. She'll never grow up properly.'

'She might. You're trying to help her, aren't you?'

'Even with help, I've got to accept that she has limits. She may learn to mix more but ...'

'I'll teach her,' said Rebekah, her own terror forgotten. 'I'll help turn her into a proper little girl but we won't tell Daddy. He'd only stop me, because really and truly he doesn't like Jessica very much, does he?'

'I'm afraid not.'

'He didn't like Mummy either and he doesn't like me. Is it nice to

302

be you and have him loving you such a lot?'

Lisa hesitated. 'Of course it is. We all want to be loved.'

'You often look sad about it.'

'That's because of Jessica, not your father.'

'Louise says he'll tire of you. What will you do then?'

This time, Lisa didn't have an answer.

When she rushed into the Chelsea flat at ten to five she was both surprised and pleased to find Neal already there. He was wearing a sports jacket and slacks and she wondered if he'd been to work at all. After last night however she decided not to ask. If he wanted to be secretive about his movements it suited her very well.

'You're late!' he snapped, looking pointedly at the antique clock.

'I don't need three hours to make myself beautiful!'

He raised his eyebrows. 'In a good mood?'

'Why not?'

'I imagined you'd be annoyed at my overnight absence.'

'Not at all. I only hope you managed to get some sleep!' With another cheerful smile she went through to the bedroom. Neal followed her.

'What do you mean by that last remark?'

'Exactly what I said.'

'Are you insinuating that I spent the night with another woman?'

'No! Did you?'

'I did not, but if I had I wouldn't expect you to complain. It isn't as though you're falling over yourself to keep me contented in that area, is it?'

Lisa could feel all her good humour draining away. 'Look, if you're in a bad mood about something please don't take it out on me. I've had a busy but very productive time at home and I'm looking forward to tonight, so could you either talk pleasantly or keep silent?'

He studied her with slight amusement. 'That's how I first remember you. A spirited girl, that's what I thought you were.'

'So I was. Unfortunately life has a way of knocking the spirit out of people.'

'Not entirely, it appears! Why the pleasure over the Ball? Is the Italian going?'

'No, but I've got a super new Victor Edelstein gown that I'm longing to wear.'

He seemed to relax. 'I see. What went so productively at Berkshire?'

'I sacked Mrs Woodward. She'd locked Rebekah up over some childish piece of defiance and was sitting drinking tea when I walked

303

in on her. She'd shut your daughter in the landing cupboard, knowing full well she's terrified of dark places because she loathes spiders.'

'What had she done to be punished like that?'

'I don't think that's important. No child should be shut up in the dark. She's already convinced she saw tarantulas in her mother's room the night Naomi died. Heavens only knows what she'll start imagining if ...'

'She what?' Neal's eyes were sharp.

'I've told you before. For some reason she thinks Naomi died because a plague of tarantulas invaded her room. Where they disappeared to even she can't imagine but nothing I say can shake her firm conviction that she saw these horrible hairy things crawling all over the cover of Naomi's bed.'

'You were probably right to sack the woman. Rebekah starts at Heathlands after Easter, I dare say a few weeks off will help her get over her strange ideas. She's always been highly imaginative.'

'She's very affectionate, Neal. If you could find more time ...'

'Is that all that happened?'

'No, for the very first time, Jessica ...'

'I thought I'd made it clear to you,' he said slowly, 'that I do not wish to know *anything at all* about what goes on at your sessions with that child.'

Lisa's head drooped. 'I'm sorry. You asked and I just forgot.'

He tilted her head with his hand. 'Please don't forget again. And while we're on the subject, please don't bore our friends with accounts of her progress either. They may pretend an interest, but I assure you that a half-witted toddler is not gripping conversation.'

'You're determined to be hurtful tonight, aren't you? What's the matter? Has someone upset you or is it just plain ill humour?'

'I'm in a very good humour,' he lied, grateful that she didn't know how he'd spent his day searching for the negative of the photo only to discover more photos, two of them considerably worse than the one he'd already been sent.

'I'd better get changed,' she said shortly. He went back to the dining-room, remembering how Carol had looked last night when he and Bishop had shown her the London apartment from which she would now work and set out details of the agreement. She hadn't been quite so confident any more. He'd be interested to learn how she got on with their friend from New York tonight. From what he remembered of Glen, she'd certainly earn her share of their fee.

When they set off, Neal had to admit that his wife looked stunning. Her gown was of flame-coloured satin with two thin shoulder straps, a tightly ruched bodice, close fitting over the hips then flaring out into

304

a dipping Bo-Peep skirt that was split in the front to open as she walked, showing a tantalising glimpse of long, slender legs. With her dark hair and carefully applied makeup she looked almost exotic in her slender beauty.

Sitting beside her in the car, with the scent of her Dior perfume rising from her warm flesh, he was overwhelmed with desire for her. It was driving him mad this continued desire for possession that, no matter how hard he tried, always ended in disappointment. Even when she faked a response, he knew the deception. More than anything else he wanted to see her writhing with passion beneath him, knowing she was truly his. But even now she was his wife and had given him a son he didn't feel he truly owned her. She was no more his than in the days before they'd become lovers. In fact, he sometimes felt that she was less his because their differences were rapidly becoming more apparent.

As they climbed out of the car and the flashbulbs exploded he knew that there were many men envying him, but couldn't help feeling bitter at the knowledge that they wouldn't if they knew the truth about their relationship and that as a lover he failed to satisfy his young wife.

He still found this hard to understand. At their table tonight there were at least three women whom he knew would willingly go to bed with him, and would undoubtedly have a wonderful time and try to keep the relationship going as long as possible. He knew this because it had always been that way for him. Until now, with his own wife.

Lisa put her arm through his and smiled at him. 'I guessed as much. Nearly all the gowns are black, gold or both! That's why I chose this one. You didn't want me to look like everyone else, did you?' she added when he didn't respond.

'No, I certainly didn't. I like you to stand out in a crowd.'

At least she managed to please him in public, she thought with relief. Then they were swept away into a chattering group and she was busy listening to tales of broken marriages, vanishing nannies, unreliable housekeepers, and all the similar difficulties encountered by wealthy women who were too busy to cope with such mundane matters.

'We're very lucky,' she said brightly. 'Neal never seems to have any difficulty in keeping staff.' Afterwards she wondered why there'd been such an awkward silence. After all, it was remarkable, although possibly due to their high wages. Certainly there was no reason for people to look embarrassed.

Late that night when Neal was peeling the magnificent gown from her body and laying her carefully on the bed, as his hands started to

305

touch her she looked up at him and for a brief moment he looked like a stranger. He was concentrating so hard on what he was doing that his features looked quite different, less cultured and more ruthless. She shivered slightly and he quickly looked into her eyes. 'You're mine,' he whispered, his fingers moving between her thighs, 'Mine and nobody else's. Nothing can alter that.'

Wishing that she could feel more passion, Lisa moved uncomfortably beneath his touch and wondered why she resented his pride of possession. Hadn't she always wanted to be loved? Hadn't she longed for someone who wanted her for what she really was?

Yes, she thought with a flash of clarity as he thrust into her, that was what she'd wanted but it wasn't what she'd got. Neal didn't want her for what she was. He wanted her to be his idea of the perfect wife, and at the times when she didn't fit the picture he became far from loving.

Perhaps, she thought, as he continued thrusting at her already aching body, no one ever did accept you for what you were. Perhaps everyone had to pretend just a little all the time. She hoped not. It was such a depressing thought.

With a groan he climaxed, but when she reached out to embrace him he pushed her away. 'Don't bother to show how grateful you are that I've finally finished! What's wrong with you?' he added beneath his breath. 'What is it you want?'

She couldn't tell him because she still didn't know. She only knew that whatever it was, Neal wasn't the man who was going to be able to provide it.

'We have heard that another robbery is planned.'

Bellini stared at Giovanni Muti in astonishment. 'They plan to hit us again?'

'So I believe.'

'You hear this from a reliable source?'

'Utterly reliable.'

'Then it is to be a deliberate slap in the face for me. They intend that I return to Rome with my tail between my legs.'

Giovanni shrugged apologetically. 'Who knows how their minds work?'

'I do. Tell me, what do you know about the laundering of our funds?'

Giovanni smiled uneasily. 'These rumours abound since the unfortunate affair of Roberto Calvi. For myself, I know nothing of it.'

'The term "God's banker" means nothing either?'

'I have heard it, of course. We have all heard it. It is a media term that has caught the attention of the public. So emotive with its religious connotations. Here in England they still wish to discredit Catholics.'

'I'm beginning to think we do not need their help!'

'You are at a party tonight, Renato. Could you not discuss this with someone then?'

'Everyone there is connected with the Gueras organisation. I would simply alert them to our suspicions and shorten my own life span!'

'Get close to the woman. It is said that all is not well within the marriage. Perhaps she could help you.'

He thought of Lisa's fragility, the danger he could place her in, and shuddered mentally. 'I do not use women,' he said shortly. 'Not where business is concerned.'

'Who will you take to the party?'

'Camilla Foxby. She and I understand each other.'

'How fortunate for you,' said Giovanni dryly.

At the same time as Renato Bellini was organising his affairs, Lisa was holding a screaming Jessica in her arms, wondering what had gone wrong. They'd been progressing so well and then this morning out of the blue she'd regressed to the terrified child of their first sessions. Now it was as much as Lisa could do to keep her on her lap.

'What's the matter?' she murmured, trying to keep her eyes on her child's face. 'Please, Jessica, tell me what's wrong.' Jessica's eyes were screwed tightly shut as she kicked and punched, swinging arms and legs wildly at her mother who had obviously become the enemy again.

After thirty minutes Lisa gave up. Regardless of what Mrs Honeywood said, she felt certain that today she wasn't helping her daughter. She was making her worse. Until she knew what had caused the set-back, she didn't intend to persist.

Once released, Jessica curled into a ball on the floor and rocked fiercely as though trying to banish her fears by the sheer force of her movements. After ten minutes she stood up, walked on the tips of her toes to the bookshelf and started hurling books all around the room until the shelf was bare. Then she grabbed hold of the shelf and swung on it until the brackets came away from the wall and she tumbled to the ground, the shelf crashing down within inches of her head. Apparently unperturbed by either the noise or the danger she gave a squeal of satisfaction and began investigating the brackets, running her fingers over the smooth metal as though it was a much-loved doll.

Lisa looked across to Janice whose eyes were full of tears. 'What's happened to her?' she asked. 'Yesterday she was so good. I even took her for a walk with Rebekah. Now she's as bad as she's ever been. When did it start?'

'Yesterday tea-time.'

'Do you know why?'

'No, madam.'

'You do! You've never called me "madam" before. We're friends, we've been together for over a year now and I'm asking you, as a friend, what's happened to my daughter?'

'Mrs Gueras, I'm so sorry,' the nurse was barely able to speak coherently. 'She escaped again and I lost her. I thought she might have gone to look at the baby so I checked there, then I asked Rebekah to try and help me find her, but by the time we'd got down to the bottom floor it was too late.'

'What had happened?'

'I don't know exactly. I heard her screaming, you see. Really terrified screams, not just shouts. Rebekah realised where she was and ran into the dining-room ahead of me. By the time I got there he'd let her go but ...'

'Who had?'

'Mr Bishop. He was in there with Miss Louise and they were both in a fine temper. They said terrible things about poor Jessica, and Mr Bishop threatened to cut her throat if I didn't keep her upstairs where she belonged. He'd been holding her, there were bruises on her wrists, little blue smudges. Since then I haven't been able to do anything with her.'

'I'll kill him!' Lisa was white with fury. 'How dare he touch my daughter? Is he still here?'

'He went back to London early this morning. I think he spent the night in Miss Louise's room.'

'I don't believe it!'

'That's what the new maid told me.'

Lisa suddenly felt very tired. It was as though she was continually fighting against enemies who kept creeping up on her when she least expected it. Together, Louise and Bishop would make a formidable partnership, and with Neal already discontented could well succeed in driving him further away from her. She couldn't afford that. She needed Neal because of Jessica. And also, although she scarcely dared acknowledge it to herself, because she was now aware that no one walked away from her husband. They simply died.

'What can I do?' She sounded as frightened as Janice had felt on encountering Bishop's cold grey eyes across the dining-room the night before and listening to his brutal description of what he'd like to do to Jessica; a description she would never repeat to Lisa.

308

'I don't know.'

'I can't let him get away with it. Jessica needs a tranquil atmosphere and people she can trust. How could you let her get out again?' she added distractedly. 'You're the one person here I can normally rely on.'

The nurse didn't reply because she knew Lisa was right. It had been her fault, and she didn't like to explain that Jessica could be very cunning. She'd taken the nurse into the kitchen then run away, banging the main door shut behind her and triggering the automatic lock. By the time she'd got free, Jessica was far away.

'I'll speak to my husband,' said Lisa at last. 'Not about Jessica, I'm afraid he wouldn't listen, but about Bishop and Louise. I'm sure that will take care of the problem because if he's got any sense at all he'll banish Bishop from the house.'

But would he? she asked herself as she went downstairs. These days she was never certain how he'd react to anything she told him. Certainly it wasn't the right time to tell him when they met up before Felicity Manningham's twenty-first party. He was decidedly short-tempered and when he saw her new Bruce Oldfield dress and jacket in turquoise silk with a thigh-length split at one side, asked if she was planning to turn pornographic pictures into a full-time career.

Without a word, Lisa returned to the bedroom and changed into a high-necked black jersey dress with a diagonal pattern of silver sequins running from the right shoulder and a skirt that ended just below the knee. She only needed a veil to be allowed into a harem, she thought, and enjoyed the expression of disbelief on her husband's face.

'Where on earth did you get that?'

'Just a little something that was on the bargain rail in Harrods sale!'

'I hope they paid you to take it off their hands. I've never seen you wear anything so boringly conventional.'

'At least no one will take me for a soft-porn actress.'

'I didn't mean ...'

'We'll be late,' she said shortly. 'Besides, it would be bad form to outshine Felicity, and God knows that wouldn't be difficult, so probably this is best for everyone.'

'I'm surprised you're willing to wear it when your most ardent admirer will be there to see you.'

'If he's that keen he won't mind what I'm wearing,' she murmured sweetly as she slid into the back of the silver Mercedes.

'Since he's a Catholic,' retorted Neal, his brow furrowed with displeasure, 'I suppose he might find a perverted pleasure in lusting after a nun-like figure.'

'Why isn't Mike driving us?'

'He's at a class – self-defence or something like that.'

'And Bishop?'

'Bishop, my dear, has been invited to the party as a guest.'

'I thought the Manninghams were particular about the company they kept. Who's he taking with him?'

Neal shrugged, totally indifferent, and Lisa wondered what he'd do if his own daughter turned up on Bishop's arm. She suppressed a smile at the thought. Even Bishop wouldn't dare go that far, but it would have been nice to see Neal coping with the situation. 'After tonight we won't be in London for a time,' he told her as they drove up to Claridges.

'Why not?'

'I think you should be spending more time with Alexi. I've also got several people coming to stay for a night or two at a time. It's easier if I'm in Berkshire because they can use the annexe.'

'Why the annexe? We've got plenty of rooms in the house.'

'Because I say so.'

No, she thought, emerging from the car with her automatic social smile for the cameramen, this was definitely not the right time to tell him anything about Bishop and Louise.

She felt Neal's hand on her arm and realised that now the acting had to begin again. They must look like the perfect couple. Moving closer to his side she wished it was true. They could have been, if she'd been able to respond to him as he deserved and he'd given her more time before revealing some of his less pleasant characteristics. As it was she no longer trusted him and he was tiring of her. But not in public. Not yet.

It was a very loud party. Normally she enjoyed being with people nearer her own age but tonight she realised that no matter what her birth certificate said, she was no longer young in the way these people were. For the first time she found their behaviour irritating, their laughter and high-spirited pranks juvenile, and their propensity for throwing food and drink over each other seemed nothing more than bad manners.

Neal was in a side room playing backgammon, supposedly for charity, and the floor of the ballroom was packed so she wandered off into a smaller room where some young people were already spread-eagled on the chairs and the floor, overcome by high spirits, drink, drugs or all three. 'I'm getting old,' she murmured, wishing she was back in Berkshire with her children.

Just then she saw Renato Bellini standing in the doorway. He had a statuesque young woman on his arm. She was wearing a dark green

310

taffeta skirt with a basque-style top that showed precisely how well built she was. After a moment's hesitation he bent and murmured in her ear. She nodded and walked away.

Lisa, a glass of champagne in her right hand, watched him cross the room towards her and was overwhelmed by the desire to tell him everything that was happening to her. How frightened she was of Bishop and Louise. How difficult it was to help Jessica, and, worst of all, how she now distrusted her own husband. Instead she tilted up her chin and gave him a brief smile. 'We always seem to meet over food!'

'Indeed! Last time it was breakfast, this time it's dinner. What a pity that we are not together between the courses!'

'Most of the food's in the next room. I only came in here because I was feeling old! The sight of people my own age spraying each other with coloured foam and putting ice cubes down people's backs was somehow terribly depressing.'

'A sign of maturity, not old age. In my country even seven-year-olds do not put ice down each other's backs. It would be considered extremely bad behaviour.'

'It is, but somehow it all seemed worse tonight.'

'Your dress is horrible,' he said bluntly.

'I know. I wish I hadn't worn it now! I only put it on to annoy Neal, but since he's taken himself off to the gambling room I might just as well have worn my first choice.'

'What was that?'

'Apparently a tarty little number more suited to a racy actress than the wife of an up-and-coming tycoon!'

'Why so modest? Surely he's an up and coming ... what is the expression? Knight of the realm?'

She giggled. 'I think you mean a peer of the realm, but Neal's background isn't likely to elevate him to that status.'

'He hasn't said that he is in line for a knighthood?'

'No. Why should he get a knighthood?'

'For his charitable work and contributions to party funds, or so I am told.'

'That's ridiculous! Why he's ...'

Bellini's eyes sharpened, and he no longer looked lazy and disinterested. 'He is what?'

'I don't know, he's just not ... I thought most business tycoons took risks now and again, risks that might not be absolutely acceptable to people in high places.'

She knew something, he thought with surprise. She realised that her husband wasn't all he seemed, but did she know anything else? Did she have any idea of just how far his dubious empire stretched? Did

311

she know about the high class call girls? The crooked casinos? The drugs that were flooding the streets of London? Above all, did she know about the carefully organised robberies that provided his funds?

'He talks to you of such things?'

'Heavens, no! He'd have a fit if he even knew I thought about them. As far as Neal's concerned I'm purely decorative, plus a reliable mother for his son and a good hostess when called upon to fill that role. He never discusses his work with me.'

Bellini was relieved. It made her position safer and saved him the unpleasant task of trying to prise information out of a woman he desired, in the full knowledge that by getting her to talk he would probably be signing her death warrant. He would have done it, but now there was no need and his relief was intense.

'Tell me, how is Jessica?' he asked with a smile. Lisa, forgetful of Neal's instructions, told him.

They were still talking about children in general and autistic ones in particular when he came looking for his wife. For a few moments he stood unnoticed in the doorway. He saw the flush on his wife's cheeks, a flush that made her face even more animated than usual, and noticed how close her arm was to the Italian's. But most of all he noticed the expression on Bellini's face. He recognised the softening of the features, the relaxing of the tight mouth and the warmth and interest in the eyes. Eyes that were normally mocking or indolent but looked upon Neal's wife with what anyone could recognise instantly as love.

His first instinct was to make a speedy exit with Lisa, but then he checked himself. Bellini was becoming a nuisance; perhaps they could use his feelings for Lisa. A few months earlier he wouldn't have considered such action, but he no longer worshipped his wife so blindly. She was turning out too intelligent, too purposeful, and too cold. It was still a difficult decision to make but easier than it would once have been. Finally he walked quietly back to the ballroom and sat talking to a friend for another half hour. Only when he saw the Italian rejoin his girlfriend on the dance floor did he go and fetch his wife. She was delighted that his earlier ill-humour seemed to have entirely disappeared.

Chapter Twenty-Five

They returned to Berkshire next morning, driven again by Steve. Lisa missed Mike's cheerful smile. She was very surprised to find him waiting for them in the grounds of Beckett Lodge, but Neal was plainly expecting him because he left Lisa standing beside their suitcases while he talked lengthily with Mike, who kept glancing across at Lisa during the discussion.

Eventually he returned, asked icily whether or not Steve intended Lisa to carry the cases, then took her by the arm and led her to where Mike stood waiting. 'Darling, I wasn't going to tell you but Mike feels we're more likely to get your full co-operation if we tell you the truth. I'm afraid I've been receiving one or two rather unpleasant threatening letters recently, and the threats are directed against you.'

'Me?'

'Indirectly, of course. I'm the one they're trying to worry, you're simply the lever they're using.'

'Very comforting!'

'Anyway, Mike's been on a refresher course in martial arts and he's going to shadow you from now on. Everywhere you go, he'll go too.'

'What about the ladies' room in Harrods?'

'I'll take my handbag,' said Mike solemnly. She giggled.

'This isn't something to joke about,' said Neal. 'If you do have to use a room where Mike can't see you, then always make sure you note any possible avenues of escape. Windows, fire escapes, that sort of thing.'

'You've been watching the wrong movies!' she quipped, but inside she felt distinctly nervous.

'Better safe than sorry. Now, I wonder where Bishop is?'

He didn't have to wonder for long. No sooner were they inside the front door than Louise came running out of the drawing-room, flinging her arms round her father's neck in an embarrassingly one-sided embrace while Bishop followed a few paces behind.

'It's horrible abroad!' she complained when Neal finally managed to free himself. 'I can't believe it's only Easter, we seem to have been away for years! I even miss Rebekah,' she added. Lisa saw Bishop smile.

'She didn't miss you!' she told her step-daughter tartly. 'She's a far happier little girl without you constantly picking away at her self-confidence. She starts at Heathlands after Easter, so please don't start telling her horror stories about girls you know who went there.'

'As though I would!' Louise's baby blue eyes were wide with indignation.

'Alexi's very well, thank you for asking,' said Neal, brushing past his daughter on his way upstairs. She flushed, glancing at Bishop who averted his gaze.

'How is Wonderboy?' she asked Lisa.

'Very well.'

'You're looking thin,' she continued. 'I'm surprised Daddy hasn't said anything. He doesn't like scrawny women.'

'Perhaps, unlike some people I could mention, his taste is maturing.'

Bishop shot her a glance of dislike, immediately masked when Rebekah came running in, only to slow as she saw Louise and Bishop with her stepmother.

Lisa held out her arms. 'I wondered where you were. Daddy and I are back for two or three weeks this time.'

'Great! I've been up with Jessica and ...'

'You've been where?' Louise's face was twisted with distaste.

'With Jessica. She's very nice if you don't shout at her or touch her. She likes me.'

'Hardly a compliment!' laughed Bishop, and Lisa glared at him.

'I'm well aware of your feelings about Jessica,' she said quietly, her arms round Rebekah's shoulders. 'But if you ever lay a finger on her again, I promise you that I'll ...'

'You'll what?' he interrupted. 'Get me thrown out of here? I doubt that very much! Tell your husband? By all means try. He might wonder what she was doing in the dining-room *again* and dismiss the nurse. So, what will you do, I wonder?'

'I ...'

'You see you really have very little power, Mrs Gueras. You might be wise to remember that before you start threatening me again. I have to go now, Louise, there's a meeting in the annexe. I'll pick you up at nine.'

Lisa decided she'd never hated anyone quite so much as Bishop. Even Toby had been preferable to this cold, calculating man who cared for no one but himself and had an uncanny knack of homing in

314

on people's weak spots. 'You must be mad to go out with him,' she told Louise shortly. 'He's a psychopath, ask Carol Blades.'

'Who's she?' demanded Louise, but Lisa had already started up the stairs and her stepdaughter was left to wonder.

During the next week, Lisa was surprised that Neal spent most of his time in the annexe with Bishop, Steve, and assorted visitors who came and went both day and night. If she hadn't been so grateful for the time this gave her to spend with the children she might have queried it more. Instead, she asked no questions and enjoyed herself with Rebekah, Jessica and Alexi.

It was a happy week for Rebekah too. For the first time in her life she had a mother-figure and she responded by becoming far more cheerful and outgoing. Alexi, now just over a year old, was almost on his feet and his smiles and clutching hands were compensation for the unexpected difficulties Lisa was encountering in her marriage.

Jessica's was a different story. Mrs Honeywood was delighted at her progress, and certainly she had improved. She rarely wrecked her surroundings, her vocabulary was increasing and she seemed more able to cope with visits from adults she knew. Regrettably there were new aspects of her behaviour that seemed to Lisa even more bizarre.

She'd taken such a dislike to any noise that even the washing machine sent her screaming to her corner, and when the kettle boiled she covered her ears, whimpering like a puppy. She also objected to wearing clothes and was only happy entirely naked, clutching a soft jumper or skirt against her face as a security blanket. While unclothed she would relentlessly seek out water and then splash it happily all over her, laughing aloud at the feel of the liquid on her bare skin.

Janice was losing weight trying to cope with the new problem. Not only did she have to follow Jessica closely all day, but even at night the child had to be watched because she needed so little sleep. For the first time, Lisa was grateful she didn't have to spend all her time with her daughter. She began to understand why so many autistic children went into homes, however unproductive the end result. If she'd been an ordinary mother with two or three other children to look after, life with Jessica would have been impossible.

Eventually, when she and Neal had a rare couple of hours together one afternoon, she asked for extra nursing care at night to let the hard-pressed Janice catch up on her sleep. Neal, his mind full of far more pressing problems, frowned. 'I thought she'd already got you, Rebekah, and Mrs Moneybags to help her. Nurse Anthony's paid enough.'

'It's Mrs Honeywood, and I don't think money comes into this. If Janice is tired then she can't cope with Jessica in the day. As for Rebekah, she's scarcely trained help, although she is marvellous with Jessica. Why ...'

'Very well, but I warn you, my patience is running out. At the rate your daughter's going she'll soon need a house of her own.'

'If she lived in the annexe, perhaps you'd bring your friends into the house and I'd see a little more of you.'

'They're not friends, they're business acquaintances. As for seeing more of me, it's certainly time you saw more of me at night. I don't want Alexi to be an only child. Another son would be most welcome.'

'And worth what?' asked Lisa coldly, well aware that once again Jessica was to be used as blackmail.

He gave a brief and not entirely pleasant smile. 'An extension of time for the treatment? Say another twelve months? I'm sure you'd like her to have a better chance of partial recovery?'

'Suppose I have a daughter?'

'I won't have your head chopped off! Mind you, I don't think I'll extend Jessica's treatment either.'

'Are you serious? I get pregnant but Jessica only benefits if I give you another son? That's not fair.'

'Whoever said anything about fair? I'm not running a boy scout troop!'

Lisa swallowed hard but kept silent. She had no intention of getting pregnant again and thought thankfully of her diaphragm tucked neatly in its plastic box in her bathroom cabinet. At least there were some areas of her life that Neal couldn't control.

At the end of the week all the visitors left and Neal again had time for his family. It rapidly became apparent that the family was both extended and different. Extended because everywhere that Louise went, Bishop went too. Different because Rebekah was cheerful and communicative and even her father responded to her. Only with Bishop was she still sullen. Lisa noticed that she not only refused to speak to him, she also made quite sure that they were never alone in a room together.

When he thought himself unobserved, Bishop's eyes continually followed the child and there was a hint of worry in his expression, although Lisa couldn't believe he cared if one eight-year-old girl didn't like him. He didn't. What he wanted to know was why, and if it put him in danger.

Ruth was much the same as ever. Every spare minute was spent on horseback. She was polite and pleasant to Lisa when they met but not effusive. Neither was she effusive with her father. Lisa thought that in some respects Ruth resented him more now than before, although she didn't know why.

Louise was happy. Happy that at last she had Bishop's attention. Proud of the fact that he admired her looks and her jokes. She never seemed to notice the boredom on his face when she giggled, or the slight twitch of his mouth when she argued with a total lack of logic.

On the Sunday morning, Lisa woke to find herself in her husband's arms and it was obvious what he intended. Having gone to bed late the night before she hadn't bothered to put in the diaphragm and she tried to struggle free but the weight of his right arm across her chest kept her pinned to the bed.

'Why the struggle?' he murmured. 'Surely you like being wanted? I thought you might think I'd neglected you this past week.'

'I need to go to the bathroom.'

'I don't think you do. I think you're after that piece of plastic you keep hidden in your cabinet.'

She went stiff with shock and he laughed deep in his chest. 'Surprised? I thought you'd have learnt by now that very little escapes my notice.'

'You've no right to go through my cupboards.'

'I have every right! As a matter of fact I found out by ringing your gynaecologist.'

'How could you? What I tell him is strictly in confidence. He isn't allowed to . . .'

'I pay his bills and he's sensible enough to know it. Now shut up.'

There was no point in fighting him, she knew that. Instead she lay totally inert and let him carry on alone. It was the biggest insult she could offer and she took some satisfaction from his obvious humiliation. Afterwards he rolled away from her and reached for a cigarette. 'Don't ever do that to me again.'

'What?'

'You know perfectly well. I warn you, Lisa, if you ever do, I shall take steps to make you more animated. I've seen for myself how animated you can be!'

'Even you wouldn't bring another man into our sex life.'

'Not even me — that's an interesting remark!'

'I'm getting dressed,' she said and quickly ran a bath as hot as she could bear, hoping to wash away his touch. It hadn't been a rape but she felt as soiled as if he'd been a stranger for there'd been no trace of love or affection. No pretence of either this time. It had simply been sex; sex for a son.

Later she went to look for Rebekah in the garden. As she rounded the corner by the annexe, she bumped into a middle-aged man with

317

greying hair and a tiny white scar on his left cheekbone. He jumped as much as she did and apologised profusely.

'I'm so sorry! I was meant to leave yesterday. Unfortunately it was a case of too much whisky so ...'

'You're still here! Did you want to see my husband?'

'You mean you're Mrs Gueras?'

'Yes.'

He went pale. 'No, no really I don't think ... I'd rather he didn't know I was here this morning. Not very professional to overstay my welcome!'

It was all the same to her. She didn't have to manage the catering for the annexe but since the man was so worried she promised not to mention their meeting and hurried away. Up in the top window of the annexe, Bishop stood motionless by the glass and wondered if fate had suddenly decided to be kind to him. He hoped that for once he was right.

Eventually Lisa found Rebekah with Ruth at the stables. They were both in riding clothes and looked at Lisa's skirt and jersey in surprise. 'We're all going riding before lunch,' said Ruth. 'Didn't Daddy tell you? That Italian's coming to lunch and he likes to ride.'

'Renato Bellini's coming?'

'Yes,' said Ruth, blushing slightly. 'Daddy told him he could have his pick of the horses. He's got a very good seat,' she added with a laugh.

'How do you know?'

'He nearly made the Italian riding team for the last Olympics.'

'Well, I shan't come with you. I'm terrified of horses. I shall stay with Alexi and enjoy the sun.'

'Darling,' said Neal, having walked silently up behind her, 'that's not very sociable of you. If we're going to spend more time in the country you ought to learn to enjoy riding. I think today's the best day for you to start. Your friend's already here, he's just gone to change. Let me see, I wonder what horse would suit you?'

She cringed, knowing that Neal didn't give a damn whether or not she learnt to enjoy riding. All he wanted was to humiliate her in front of Bellini, and that he was most certainly going to do. 'Get changed then!' He gave her a gentle push in the small of her back. 'We'll wait for you,' he added, and the palms of her hands felt damp as she went back to the house.

She and Bellini met in the front porch. He looked immaculate in his jodhpurs and riding boots, a small whip in his left hand and his riding hat dangling by its strap from his right, but for once she was too frightened to appreciate him.

318

He smiled. 'Good morning!'

'I'm sorry. Neal didn't tell me you were coming otherwise I'd have made myself a bit more presentable,' she murmured.

'It is of no matter. Always you look beautiful!'

'Not today. I'm terrified of horses but Neal thinks I must learn to get over it. I'll be with you shortly.'

He could almost scent her fear and realised, as she had done earlier, that she was being publicly punished, under the disguise of concern, for the interest she'd shown in him. He felt anger at Gueras rising in him again but pushed it down. For the moment there was nothing he could do except wait. Reaching out he touched her lightly on the arm. 'It is quite safe. Even my son rides, and he is very timid.'

'I don't suppose you made him learn in front of a crowd of competent riders, including his stepchildren.'

'That would be difficult!'

'Just don't laugh at me,' she muttered. He'd never felt less like laughing in his life.

Neal watched the Italian striding purposefully towards him and gave an inward smile. He was looking forward to the next half hour. It would be interesting to see how well controlled this representative of the Bellini family really was. This was of considerable interest to his organisation, and using Lisa as part of the test had only been a last minute idea brought on by her insulting reaction to him earlier.

Renato's face looked thinner and harder than Neal remembered it and his mouth was set in a tight line emphasising the two grooves running from the side of his nose to the corners of his mouth. Lines that women thought of as laughter lines but there certainly wasn't any laughter on his face this morning. His eyes were gleaming beneath the heavy brows, but when he greeted his host he sounded calm and relaxed. Neal introduced Ruth and Rebekah then glanced ostentatiously at his watch.

'My wife's taking a long time to get ready. She's got this ridiculous fear of horses, but I'm sure it's nothing that can't be cured. Ruth's chosen her a horse I think she'll like.'

Ruth's mouth opened in astonishment. She certainly wouldn't have chosen the tender-mouthed Snowball for a nervous rider, but one look at her father's face kept her silent.

Neal tapped his riding whip irritably against the side of his leg and Snowball rolled her eyes. Bellini glanced at the horse and decided that even if Lisa managed to get on it, she'd have great difficulty staying in the saddle. After another ten minutes she appeared. She looked even more fragile in her black riding outfit and her face had lost every trace of colour.

Rebekah ran over to her and took her by the hand. 'It's all right,' she whispered. 'I don't like riding either but it doesn't hurt. Just pretend you're sitting on a bike.'

Lisa moistened her lips and looked at her husband. 'Which one's mine?'

'You haven't said hello to our guest, darling.'

'We met by the front door. Which one's mine?'

'This one.' He prodded Snowball tightly and she tossed her head. Lisa promptly took two hasty steps backwards. Neal laughed. 'For goodness sake, don't be so jumpy. You'll end up making the horses nervous!'

Bastard! thought Bellini, but he looked on impassively, only the whitening of his knuckles revealing his emotion.

'She's too big!' protested Lisa.

'With legs as long as yours I can hardly put you on a pony! Let me give you a hand up.'

'I'll get on myself, thank you.'

'Right, go ahead. We're waiting.'

She looked round the yard. 'Why is everyone watching me?'

'We're interested in your technique!' He laughed and it was echoed by Bishop and Louise who were standing by the stable gates, Louise's arm linked through Bishop's.

She thought she was going to be sick. It was obvious that the horse was highly strung and equally obvious that it sensed her fear. Grabbing hold of the reins she tried to put one foot in the stirrup but couldn't reach and only made Snowball whinny her disapproval.

'I said you'd need help,' smiled Neal. Bending down he cupped his hands together. No sooner was her foot resting in them than she found herself being thrown forcefully in the air. She clutched at Snowball's mane, missed and slid ungracefully down her other side onto the cobbles. The fall jarred her hip and leg and she felt her breakfast rising in her throat.

'Bravo!' called Bishop laconically. 'I've only ever seen that happen in films before today. Come along, Louise, we'd better take that walk and leave your stepmother to enjoy herself.'

Lisa walked round to where Neal was standing. 'You did that on purpose!' she said in a low voice.

'How was I to know you were going to throw yourself in the air with such enthusiasm! Come along, we're still waiting!'

'I am not getting on that creature's back, Neal. I don't care if you all hang around here until the sun goes down. I absolutely refuse to go riding.'

Neal took hold of her right wrist and pulled her against him. 'If you want a second nurse for that bloody child of yours, you'll get on that horse and join us for the ride.'

Breathing suddenly seemed difficult, as though there was a con-striction round her chest, and Lisa swallowed hard to keep the tears away. Turning back to Snowball she found the Italian standing between her and the horse. 'Allow me,' he said gently, bending low to take the weight of her foot. For a moment her legs were shaking too much for her to move, but at last she managed to lift her right foot in the air and this time the hands stayed rock steady and she was able, somewhat inelegantly, to mount.

Bellini darted a look of contempt at Neal and then turned back to his own horse. His opinion of the man was sinking with every second that passed. He failed utterly to understand such petty cruelty.

They moved sedately down the track that led to the fields, then Snowball balked at the avenue of branches that had to be passed through before they reached open ground. The girls had gone on ahead and Bellini quickly reigned his horse in, forcing Neal to go ahead of his wife.

As Snowball's head went back for the second time, Bellini moved his mount alongside and spoke quietly in the nervous animal's ear. He tried to ignore Lisa's tightly clenched hands gripping the reins as though they were a lifeline, resisting the temptation to tell her to relax, realising full well that she couldn't. Instead he soothed her horse, and after a few moments Snowball consented to move under the branches and out into the April sunshine.

Neal, irritated by the Italian's manoeuvrings, was waiting for Snowball to emerge and with a laughing, 'Let's race to the other side,' he touched the nervous animal's neck with a stinging flick of his whip. Bellini's eyes widened with shock as he saw Snowball take off at a gallop, shaking Lisa around like a sack of potatoes as she tried desperately to hang on.

'Not too elegant on horseback, I'm afraid!' said Neal calmly.

Renato looked him straight in the eye and smiled. 'One day I shall kill you,' he said pleasantly, then turned his horse back towards the stables. 'All at once I find riding is not to my liking.'

'I must say I'm surprised,' responded Neal, smiling despite the threat. 'I'm sure your father would have expected you to exercise more control.'

'My father has never had to deal with a man such as yourself. He is used to gentlemen.'

Neal looked thoughtfully at the rapidly disappearing broad back of the Italian and it was only when Rebekah's horse came thundering to his side that he realised something was wrong.

Not unexpectedly, Lisa had fallen again. This time she'd thrown

321

out an arm to save herself, and it was obvious that her arm and shoulder were both damaged. For Lisa, doubled over with the pain and still shocked by the sudden bolting of her horse, the sight of her husband hurrying to her was not a reassuring one. She turned her back on him, keeping her injuries to herself.

'Lisa, I'm sorry,' he said quickly. 'I didn't mean you to get hurt. I only wanted . . .'

'I know what you wanted!' she spat at him. 'I'm not stupid. You wanted to humiliate me in front of Bellini, and you've probably managed that. My only consolation is that you've shown yourself up as well.'

'I didn't intend anything of the kind. I . . .'

'Liar!' she shouted, uncaring of the frightened girls. 'You're a bully and a liar. I only hope you've just cost yourself all this morning's efforts to get a second son. Don't touch me!'she continued when he tried to get nearer to her. 'If you do I shall scream.'

'You need help back to the house. You can't walk.'

'Send Mike to get me. I'm not letting you near me again after this. I could have been killed!' she added, her voice rising. 'Is that what you wanted? Another dead wife, like poor Naomi?'

'Stop it! You're obviously hysterical, and if you want Mike to take you back to the house then Mike it shall be, but stop talking about dead wives.'

'Why? Do you think your daughters don't know how much you wanted their mother dead? And do you think they imagined you were really trying to help me today. They're bright girls, Neal. They've got eyes in their heads.'

'*Be quiet!*' he roared. 'Ruth, Rebekah, go and tell Mike he's needed. He can take Lisa back with him. He's quite used to riding Snowball.'

'I want to stay with Lisa,' said Rebekah stubbornly.

'Get back to the house or else Heathlands might become a dream. I know plenty of good boarding schools you could attend, young lady.'

When the girls had gone, husband and wife were left looking at each other. Lisa's moment of rage had passed, now she was left with only pain, shock, and the memory of her fear in the stable yard.

'I'm sorry,' muttered Neal.

'So am I.'

'I didn't mean you to hurt yourself . . . I'll send Bishop for a doctor,' he added as he saw Mike running across the field towards them.

'You'll have to find him first.'

'They were going for a walk.'

322

She gave a hard laugh. 'Don't you believe it! If you want Bishop, I suggest you try your daughter's bedroom.' The darkening of his complexion told her that her shot had gone home, and she nursed that pleasure while Mike put her gently on Snowball's back before sitting behind her and slowly taking the animal back to the stables.

Once there he and Bellini helped her down, Bellini making sure that it was Mike who carried her into the house. He knew someone was bound to be watching the stable yard, and much as he longed to carry Lisa himself common sense stopped him. One day he promised himself he'd have the right to carry her whenever he wished but unfortunately it wasn't yet.

'Broken in two places,' said the doctor. 'I've set it and given her something to make her sleep. That arm's been broken before. She ought not to ride again or she could end up with a permanent weakness.'

With a pang of conscience, Neal remembered all his promises about their marriage giving Lisa protection. Protection against injuries like those inflicted by Toby Walker. Quickly he pushed the thought aside. It wasn't his fault she'd fallen, he'd only intended to show Lisa in a less flattering light to Bellini, while also demonstrating his ownership and total control of her life. It seemed probable that the point had been made. Now he'd make it up to her. He wished she was more materialistic; women who collected clothes and jewellery were far easier to placate than a woman like Lisa.

'Fine,' he murmured distractedly. 'How long will the plaster have to stay on?'

'Six to eight weeks. I'll call in tomorrow, check she's over the shock.'

Her shock, thought Neal bitterly, was nothing when compared to his when he discovered Bishop and Louise entwined on her single bed, both of them totally oblivious of his presence. He'd waited for a few seconds and then moved quietly away. There was nothing to be gained from open confrontation but he'd make sure that from now on Louise wasn't out of his sight when Bishop was around. He had far better plans for his oldest daughter than marriage to a psychotic gangster, however intelligent. Besides, Bishop in the family would be a threat to Alexi's inheritance and that was one thing Neal would never allow.

Bellini left straight after lunch, refusing to intrude longer upon their hospitality when Lisa was unwell. That was what his mouth said; his eyes said other things. Things that were best unspoken.

At dinner that night, a dinner from which Bishop was pointedly excluded, Neal casually mentioned to Louise that during the summer holiday she would be going to Holland to stay with some friends of his. 'They've got a son and daughter around your age. I think you'll enjoy yourself,' he said smoothly. 'They're very wealthy, you won't miss the comforts of home!'

'I don't want to go to Holland. I want to stay here.' She sounded like a petulant child but it was no petulant child he'd seen on the bed with Bishop.

'What you want doesn't come into it, Louise. I say you're going to Holland.'

'What about Ruth?'

'Ruth can stay here with her horses.'

'And Rebekah can stay with her precious stepmother, so as usual I'm the one being singled out.'

'Not just by me!' he said icily. Louise went very quiet. She couldn't believe that her father knew how far she and Bishop had gone but there was something in his voice that told her to tread warily.

'I'll come back like a lardball. All the Dutch are gross.'

'You're a lardball now!' said Rebekah pertly.

'Shut up, brat!'

'*Be quiet*!' thundered Neal. 'Remember that Lisa is trying to sleep upstairs.'

It was a pity he hadn't shown concern for his wife earlier, thought Ruth but she kept quiet. Unlike her older sister, she was rapidly learning the art of survival in this household, which was to keep yourself out of the way and never offer an opinion on anything. She was also beginning to understand why her mother had turned into such a total non-person. Neal didn't encourage any other sort, which made his choice of Lisa as a wife all the more extraordinary.

Late that night Neal walked through the concealed door in his study and emerged in a book-lined room of the annexe. There were a few high-backed chairs, a telephone on a shelf and a small nest of tables but nothing else except for the huge video screen set up at one end of the room.

'Well?' he demanded.

'She didn't do very well,' said Bishop laconically. 'Not that Graves actually complained but he made it clear she wasn't very lively. Shall we have a look?'

'I suppose so. What did you give her beforehand?'

'Only some coke. I thought we'd save the hard stuff for later.'

For fifteen minutes the two men watched the flickering screen in silence until Neal called for the lights again. 'If he was as bored as I felt then he *was* cheated. Obviously not a natural.'

'Worth keeping?' enquired Bishop, who'd privately pencilled Carol Blades off.

'I think so. She does owe me a great deal of money, and by the time she's hooked on drugs as well, she'll work for years before she's able to pay me back. There's nothing like motivation for keeping this sort on their toes.'

'So what do you suggest?'

Neal yawned. It had been a long day and all he wanted to do was sleep, preferably beside his wife. Perhaps he could offer some kind of comfort, she might even welcome his physical closeness for once he thought optimistically.

'I said, what do you suggest?'

He quickly thought back to other girls with similar problems when they started out. Some had become highly proficient but somehow he didn't think Carol was going to be one of those.

'Find her a companion, let her work as one of a pair. She's a typical English rose so probably a dark-haired girl, possibly mixed blood, would be best. And make it someone experienced. She'd better move into Carol's flat and give her a few lessons before they start work. Be sure the other girl isn't into drugs. I don't want them both stoned out of their minds when they're wanted for work.'

'How about Ayeesha?'

Neal smiled. He'd once been with Ayeesha himself. 'Excellent! She'll know precisely what to do. You're a good judge of women, Bishop. At least, when it comes to choosing them for other men!'

With that parting shot he returned to the house, leaving his deputy in no doubt at all that if he intended to marry Louise he'd have to move very quickly. Well, he did intend to marry her, and when it came to moving fast there wasn't anyone else in his league. Just the same, it was a pity he'd got to rush things.

A pity too that Louise was so incredibly boring, he thought as he packed away the tape. She was Naomi's daughter all right – an unintelligent blob. Still, a man couldn't have everything. At least, not all at once.

During the six weeks that her arm was in plaster, Lisa saw very little of Neal. There were no more dinner parties at home and no more trips to London. His visitors never came to the house and he never came to their bed, choosing instead to sleep in his dressing-room. They met occasionally for meals when he would talk politely of general matters but it was as if they were strangers.

At first she'd been afraid her injuries would interrupt Jessica's therapy but now that her daughter was quieter it usually proved possible to continue. However, on a bad day Jessica was impossible to hold with only one arm and had to be released.

325

Upon realising that she no longer had to sit on Lisa's lap, Jessica often chose to stay there. She began reaching out and touching her mother's face, tracing each individual feature with her fingertips like a blind child, smiling to herself as she became familiar with Lisa's expressions during her exploration.

She was still very beautiful. Her earlier chubbiness had been replaced by a more slender appearance but her eyes glowed with apparent intelligence even when she was talking nonsense. Regrettably she was increasingly obsessed with rituals. If Janice didn't always lay the table in the right order, sometimes placing Jessica's spoon on the cloth before her fork, then the child would scream and refuse to sit down until it had all been done again. Nothing could break these obsessions. Even Mrs Honeywood, normally optimistic and cheerful, admitted that they would probably stay with Jessica all her life.

'Which rather rules out dining at the Ritz!' joked Lisa one particularly trying day. 'The waiters might not understand!'

'If she ends up beautiful and rich enough they won't turn a hair. You're expected to be eccentric then.'

'She'll be beautiful enough but not very rich. I can't see my husband leaving her any of his fortune and a good marriage is out of the question. Any marriage is out of the question.'

'Some people might think that a blessing.'

'You've got a point!' concurred Lisa. Nevertheless, she regretted the limitations imposed on her child. When she'd first married Neal she'd genuinely believed that through hard work and will power she'd find a way to break through to Jessica so that within a few years her daughter could lead a relatively normal life. Experience and exhaustion combined had changed her mind. Now she was only aiming for slight improvements, sufficient to allow her to take her child out and about more. Sometimes she regretted her loss of faith but nowadays she couldn't ignore the severity of Jessica's handicap. Not since she'd given birth to Alexi.

At one year he was taking a keen interest in everything. A sturdy, big-boned boy, he looked older than his age and was both placid and affectionate. It would have been easy to underestimate his intelligence but for the fact that his nanny said he was passing all his milestones ahead of his age.

Milestones meant nothing to Lisa. She remembered looking up what was normal for small children when Jessica had first given real cause for concern but she couldn't recall anything she'd read. Most experts had told her there was no such thing as an average baby and that reading books was futile. Even so, she believed the nanny, who

326

was not a woman given to over-enthusing about any of her charges.

'I thought Daddy would play with Alexi a lot,' remarked Rebekah one morning as she held her half-brother on her knee. 'I'd expected to feel pea-green with jealousy but he doesn't take any more notice of him than if he were a girl. He never comes to kiss him goodnight or play with him. He wanted a boy for years but he still ignores him.'

'He's very busy,' said Lisa without much conviction. She suspected that Neal was the same about everything he wanted, ranging from a painting to a wife or son. It was the search and initial possession that gave him the greatest thrill. Once he had them they were far less interesting. Naturally Alexi would always be important because he would inherit most of his father's wealth, but as a person he counted for very little. As did she, thought Lisa ruefully. That was undeniably partly her fault, but she sensed that he would have tired of her quite quickly anyway. The thrill of possession soon dies when no deeper emotions are involved.

'He's so busy that he doesn't see what's under his nose!' retorted Rebekah, putting Alexi on the floor.

'What do you mean by that?'

'Haven't you noticed how fat Louise is getting?'

'She's always been plump. I think I'd like a swim today, it's quite warm enough. What do you think?'

'We're not allowed to use the pool when Daddy's got visitors in the annexe. Louise isn't just plump, Lisa. She's fat. F.A.T., *fat*!'

'No one told me I couldn't use it.'

'I just did!'

'I'll pretend you didn't.'

Rebekah pulled a face. 'I'm not coming with you. Daddy will be livid.'

'All right, I'll take Jessica and stay in the shallow end. She loves water and that way I'm not really swimming, am I?'

'I'm glad Daddy married you but he made a big mistake because he likes what he calls docile women. You're not docile, are you?'

'No!' She gave Rebekah a quick hug. 'You're too mature for your age. If you're not coming swimming, how about doing some of that homework your new school's so keen on?'

'I think Saturdays ought to be free days.'

'Once you've finished your maths it will be. Run along quickly, otherwise you'll see me going to the pool and then I can't plead ignorance of the law!'

Half an hour later, Lisa and Jessica were in the shallow end of the outdoor pool, Jessica splashing the top of the water with her hands and shrieking with laughter while her mother floated lazily on her back.

Inside the annexe, Neal reminded himself to tell Lisa the pool was out of bounds when he was working and then returned with renewed concentration to the large plan spread out before him. This was their final chance to go over the details and he didn't want to make any mistakes. Nothing must be missed or the Italian would retaliate. Aware of the growing power of the P2 Lodge in general if not the Bellini family itself, he realised this couldn't be allowed.

When the plan was finally rolled up, the man with the scar on his cheek took his leave and hurried away from the building. A worried man, he turned right instead of left and nearly fell into the pool. Jessica's scream of fright alerted Lisa to his presence but when she recognised him she gave a quick smile. 'Here again? What a keen lot you commodity brokers are, beavering away on weekends!'

He muttered something non-committal before turning away and hastily climbing into his battered Ford Escort. Providing everything went well the following Wednesday, he wouldn't be driving it much longer. He could have almost any car he chose, but not immediately. Preferably not even in this country according to Mr Gueras, but he didn't see how he could get Mary to go abroad when she spent all her free time with her mother who lived three houses away from them. Of course, he could always go without Mary. That realisation brought a smile to his face, especially when he remembered the slender limbs of Neal Gueras's young wife.

By eight that night all the cars that had been parked in the block of double garages concealed behind the stables had gone. Only Bishop's silver Mercedes and Mike's red Triumph Stag remained, and Neal — tired but satisfied that nothing had been left to chance — went into his wife's bedroom to see if she wanted to go out for dinner.

'When did the plaster come off?' he asked in surprise. She was blow-drying her hair in front of the full-length mirror that gave him a tantalising glimpse of her full breasts, all the more erotic for being on such a slight frame.

'Two days ago. You weren't around at the time.'

'I've been busy with work but I'm free tonight. How about going out to dinner? I hear the new Chinese place, the Lotus House, is excellent. Wear your exotic green silk with the mandarin collar — highly appropriate!'

Things were returning to normal, she thought. He was once again interested in what she wore, how she looked and sex. She'd recognised the look in his eyes when he'd stood behind her. Well, it was part of the bargain. She only wished it didn't always end in arguments.

328

Chapter Twenty-Six

The restaurant was crowded but Neal and Lisa were found a table in a secluded corner of the room. They were served swiftly and efficiently, which was more than could be said for most of the diners. As usual, Neal seemed able to command the best from everyone, and again Lisa wondered why.

Looking at her sitting opposite him, Neal felt his body stir in anticipation of taking her to bed that night. He almost wished that she no longer had that power over him. However much he wanted her, and however patient and careful he was, he never elicited the right response and the intensely sensual anticipation he was experiencing tonight would again disappear in a confused outburst of frustrated irritation, leaving him with a feeling of anticlimax that might linger for days. He knew now that she wouldn't ever be his in the way he wanted, but as yet the knowledge didn't mean he was willing to discard her. Just as she was persevering with Jessica so he was persevering with her, but in both cases the expectations were rapidly decreasing.

'Am I wearing odd ear-rings?' asked Lisa, feeling uncomfortable under his scrutiny.

'I was just thinking how lovely you looked. I'm beginning to wish we'd eaten at home!'

'Alexi's very forward for his age,' she said brightly, hoping to steer him off the subject of tonight.

'I wouldn't expect our child to be anything other than intelligent.'

'Intelligent enough to recognise a father he never sees?'

'This is meant to be a pleasant evening for two, remember?'

'I thought you might like to catch up on some family news.'

'Not particularly.'

'Rebekah says Louise is positively fat. Perhaps you ought to have a word with Cook. She will feed the girls up while they're home, as though they're half-starved at school or something.'

'The reason Louise is fat,' he said as the waiter served them their spare ribs in barbecue sauce, 'is because she's pregnant.'

'Pregnant?'

'I'm afraid so. It appears I'm not the only one who hasn't been watching the family as closely as I should.'

'Is it Bishop?'

'Unfortunately, yes. They'll marry by special licence within the next four weeks. That's why Louise hasn't returned to school. At least I'm spared the expense of a lavish wedding.'

'Doesn't she realise how foul he is?'

'Apparently not. It isn't his nature that worries me, it's the waste of Louise as a negotiable asset. I had two prospective husbands lined up for her. Now I'll have to wait for Ruth, and she isn't exactly Helen of Troy.'

'Simon wanted to decide who I married. I felt that was a betrayal of our relationship, using me for his own ends. Surely you don't intend doing the same with your children?'

He had a job to stop himself from smiling. 'It was me your father wanted you to marry!'

She stared blankly across the table at him, suddenly noticing how the shadows from the candle flickering in its glass bowl made him appear sinister and unapproachable. 'It can't have been you!'

'I assure you it was.'

'But he said I'd ruined everything for him when I went off to live with Toby. Even Stephanie said that his death was my fault.'

'She always over-dramatised things.'

'Was Simon telling the truth? Were you annoyed?'

'Yes, at the time.'

She pushed her untouched food to one side. 'That doesn't make any sense.'

'Why?'

'Because you married me anyway.'

'Which just shows how right Simon's original choice was! And I'm just as capable of choosing well for my daughters.'

'I'm not interested in your daughters. I want to know if you were responsible for Simon's death.'

'My dear Lisa, he killed himself!'

'Because someone had called in a loan and he didn't have the money to repay it. Who called it in?'

'I really couldn't say.'

'You mean it wasn't you?'

'I'm not a moneylender, Lisa.'

'You lent money to Carol Blades.'

His eyes narrowed. 'Who told you that?'

'She did. She was terribly upset because Bishop was threatening her. She only went out with him so that he'd put in a good word for her. I wanted to talk to you but she stopped me.'

'Very wise.'

'You'd have given her more time if I'd asked, wouldn't you?'

'Possibly not; she wasn't a very good businesswoman. However, this isn't really connected with Simon, is it?'

'Yes! You said you weren't a moneylender, but you are.'

'I invested in her business, which is an entirely different matter.'

'So you weren't responsible for Simon's death?'

'No more than you,' he said quietly.

And then she knew. Knew that indirectly he *had* been responsible for Simon's death. Knew too that Neal had obviously stalked her all through her time with Toby, possibly even using his influence to ensure the relationship didn't last. Bishop's arrival when she'd been injured hadn't been coincidental. Neither had Neal's interest ever been in the least paternal or connected to his relationship with Simon. It had all been done for one reason only: possession of Lisa herself. She lowered her eyes to her plate and knew that she had to hide her knowledge from him.

With a trembling hand she attempted to spoon some fried rice and prawns on to her plate. 'It looks as though father did know best then!' she laughed.

He lightly curled his fingers round her wrist so that she was unable to move. 'You missed your vocation,' he said pleasantly. 'You should have been an actress.'

'Not in sex scenes,' she said flatly.

They ate the rest of the meal in silence.

Once in the car, Neal turned to look at her and his face was shuttered. 'You're mine,' he reminded her. 'You chose me of your own free will, and if that decision was made for the wrong reasons that's not my fault. You agreed to be my wife and as your husband I intend to take full advantage of what courts so quaintly term my conjugal rights.

'I'm tired of making efforts to get you to respond to me. I've had enough of your lacklustre performances. Starting from tonight we'll try playing by other rules, then at least one of us will be satisfied.'

'I don't know what you're talking about,' she lied.

'Don't think I'm not fully aware of the way you feel about Renato Bellini,' he continued. 'It's obvious that you're attracted to him, but you're wasting your time. Even he knows better than to try and take my wife away from me. You wouldn't get any encouragement from him if you threw yourself naked at his feet.'

'You're totally mad,' she said curtly. 'He's pleasant company and likes children, that's all. As for throwing myself naked at his feet, I can promise you the thought never crossed my mind.'

He chuckled. 'That I can believe. Mind you, after a few slightly more experimental nights you might be increasingly adventurous even in your daydreams!'

Once home Neal took hold of her still painful left wrist and pulled her up the stairs with him, almost pushing her into the bedroom before locking the door carefully behind him.

It seemed like hours before it was all over and as Lisa stood beneath the scalding spray of the shower, tears running down her face, she knew that Neal had nothing to worry about. No matter what happened to him she'd never want another man. Not after tonight. She realised that she could never be what men seemed to expect and that the resulting frustration always ended in violence.

The Italian wouldn't be any different, she thought fatalistically. No doubt he had images of her doing incredible things to him, performing sexual tricks she'd never even imagined, and he too would end up disappointed. Only the children made life bearable now.

She'd hoped that by the time she finished Neal would have gone to his own room but he was still lying on top of the bed. He watched her closely and saw the expression that crossed her face. He knew that tonight had been a shock. She'd learnt that he'd been the man her adoptive father had been saving her for, and she'd learnt that her body wasn't her own. He also knew that Naomi and Kay could have told her there were worse things, like learning that he'd tired of her, in which case she would have had every reason to feel afraid. But he hadn't.

He'd expected tears and hysterics tonight, not the screaming, white-hot rage that she'd demonstrated and he admired her for that. His admiration led to a continuing desire to have her accept him as her husband, responding to his touch as other women did. He was totally unaware that he'd now lost all the genuine affection and gratitude she'd once felt, leaving next morning under the misapprehension that from now on she would gradually come round. That since he'd demonstrated his darker side, she might appreciate a little more the way he usually treated her.

Lisa heard him drive away, and thought that if it weren't for the children she would probably kill herself, because the horror of that night was something she knew would never leave her. She felt totally betrayed.

* * *

332

The following Wednesday she was sitting in the small drawing-room, once Naomi's retreat and rapidly becoming hers. Gone was the previously insipid style of decoration. In its place were pale-apricot walls, warm peach-coloured damask curtains, a beige and white wool carpet and light beige chairs with deep cushions and high backs. It was a calm, restful room. She never invited Neal into it, and he never suggested joining her. It was as though, even for him, Naomi's ghost still lingered.

However, the children were often there. On this particular evening, since Neal was in town until late, Lisa had laid Alexi on the floor and Rebekah was watching *Dallas* while Jessica sat on her mother's lap with her thumb in her mouth, seemingly content. For a brief time, Lisa was happy.

'Do you want the news?' asked Rebekah, as the American soap ended.

'I suppose so. These days I don't read the papers and I ought to keep more up-to-date with the news. If your father ever does hold dinner parties again, I shan't have an opinion to offer on any subject except domesticity!'

'Can I watch it?'

'Only if you sit quietly. I don't want Jessica disturbed. Once it's finished I'll take you all up to bed. Your father won't want his house full of children when he gets back.'

'Two of us are his!' Rebekah was resentful of Neal's casual dismissal.

'Mind, Jessica! You nearly poked my eye out then!'

Jessica, busy exploring her mother's face, giggled. Alexi pulled off a sock with a shout of pleasure and rolled on to his stomach while Rebekah continued droning on about her father. As a result, Lisa missed the headlines and only began concentrating when Nicholas Witchell started giving the main story in depth.

'In what appears to be a carbon copy of a bullion robbery ten months ago, six masked men held up the unmarked van in the quiet solitude of the Surrey lanes. Tonight both driver and guard are in hospital with severe head and facial injuries but despite their courageous fight, the men escaped with over five million pounds' worth of gold bullion.

'The head of the bullion section of the firm, Express Delivery Co. Ltd., talked of his pride in his employees and explained his company's policy of not alerting the police when moving large amounts of gold round the country to our reporter ...'

'Boring!' declared Rebekah, standing up and moving in front of the screen. 'I think I'll go up now.'

'Sit down!' shouted Lisa. Jessica jumped and began to whimper but Lisa was unaware of anything but the grey-haired man in the dark suit talking earnestly to the reporter. A man with a small white scar on his left cheek. All at once the room seemed cramped and stuffy. She listened to the words coming from the man's mouth but her brain didn't register the sense of them. Her stomach was churning and she had a dull throbbing in her temples that presaged a bad headache.

The cameras returned to the newscaster. 'Most of the gold that was taken came from the London branch of the Italian bank owned by the Bellini family,' he said gravely. 'This is their second heavy loss and the London director, Giovanni Muti, said tonight that there would have to be an investigation into all aspects of their security. Renato Bellini, who is at present staying in England, was not available for comment.

'In America today, President Reagan said ...'

'Turn it off,' ordered Lisa.

Rebekah laughed. 'President Reagan said turn it off!'

'Very funny. Come on, it's late and you'll be too tired to get up in the morning.' Surprised by her sharpness, Rebekah hastily obeyed. 'Shall I send Janice down for Jessica?'

'Yes please, and tell Nanny I'll bring Alexi up in a moment.'

Aware that something was wrong but unable to decide quite what, Rebekah wrapped her arms round Lisa's neck. 'I love you!' she whispered as she kissed her goodnight, then with a quick smile she was gone. Lisa helped Jessica down to the floor and blinked back tears. She'd waited a long time to hear the words from Rebekah but they couldn't have come at a worse moment. She wished that she'd listened to her and never gone to the swimming pool, because then she wouldn't have known for sure. Now that she did she had to decide what to do.

'Jessica's been down here a long time,' said Janice as she came in. 'You must be pleased with her.'

'I am.'

'Say goodnight to Mummy,' said Jessica, standing on tiptoe to kiss Lisa. Would she ever understand the true meaning of words? thought Lisa as she returned the kiss. For the first time she wondered deep down if it even mattered.

The betrayal was only fleeting but instantly she felt ashamed, and she hated Neal for what he'd done to her. Night after night he was trying to educate her in the ways of some peculiar world of his own where she had no desire to go, and night after night she failed him. Sometimes she thought he'd carry on with his bizarre behaviour until one or the other of them dropped dead. If she could be granted one wish it would be for the ability to respond as he wanted and put an end to the nights that had long since ceased to have anything to do with love.

She held Alexi tightly against her and he squealed with surprise before beginning to laugh. 'It's all your fault!' she whispered, but he was such a happy, well-behaved child that she knew she would never be without him. 'What would Daddy say if he could see you up this late?' she laughed.

'He'd say that his son was up far too late!'

Lisa stood still and looked up the hallway to where her husband and Bishop were standing. 'I didn't hear your key,' she murmured.

'Obviously! Let's have a look at him since I'm here.' Bishop remained by the door, unusually silent even for him. Alexi smiled and snuggled against his father's shoulder while Neal glanced at his wife.

'You look tired. Why not take a bath and read for half an hour? I won't be long.' She hoped her expression didn't reveal her feelings. 'Bishop's had a nasty accident today,' he continued. 'He was crossing Harcourt Terrace when some stupid van driver drew away from the kerb and sent him flying. He's dislocated his shoulder. I brought him back here to recuperate. His head's had a nasty bang and if he should need a doctor in the night ...'

'Do you mean here and not in the annexe?'

'Yes.'

'Hadn't he better let Louise know? She is going to be his wife. If anyone's going to tend his fevered brow it ought to be her.'

'I'm not having that stupid bitch fussing over me,' said Bishop coldly.

'Same old Bishop. It seems the bang on the head wasn't severe enough!' snapped Lisa, horribly aware that he must have been hit during the bullion robbery and wishing he were lying dead in the quiet Surrey lane instead of sleeping under the same roof as her and her children.

'Lisa!'

'I'm going to bed, Neal. You can deal with Bishop.'

Neal handed over Alexi, his eyes thoughtful. 'Has something happened to annoy you?'

'I'm just tired.'

'Of course! Nine forty-five is very late! Please don't go to sleep yet.'

She turned on her heel and walked away from the men. The very thought of her husband's hands on her body made her flesh creep. It was one thing to suspect him of being less than a hundred per cent law-abiding but quite another to discover that he was involved in

335

multi-million pound robberies that involved bludgeoning innocent men round the head and face. As for Bellini, she couldn't let herself take in the full implications of his loss. He was an intelligent man, he must have had suspicions about Neal from the start. How would he react to this second attack on his bank?

'My, we're late,' said Nanny Thompson reproachfully.

'I wanted him to see his father,' lied Lisa, and the nanny's face cleared. Yes, she thought, his staff think he's wonderful. He only has to show himself in the nursery once a month and he's the perfect father. But then she too had been taken in by him, and there could no longer be any doubt that he was a very accomplished actor.

It was ten-thirty before he joined her in the bedroom and eleven-thirty when he finally rolled away from her with an exclamation of disgust. 'I'm not continuing with this farce! It's obvious you're totally frigid, and since I'm not into necrophilia don't blame me if I start taking my pleasure elsewhere.'

'As long as I don't know about it, you can do what you like,' she muttered.

Neal turned her to face him 'What sort of wife gives her husband that kind of freedom?' he shouted, his face darkening.

Lisa knew that if she didn't speak now she never would. For a second she hesitated. If she kept silent her life might continue along what many women would consider an acceptable path. She'd still have the money and position that marriage to Neal brought, and Jessica could continue with her treatment, but her husband would be away more and more and people would pity her as they'd once pitied Naomi. Suddenly she knew that she couldn't live like that. 'You're right,' she said slowly. 'I didn't mean it.'

'Good!'

'Because if you did start sleeping around, I might start discussing some of your business colleagues. Like the man with grey hair and a small scar on his face. You do remember him?'

'No.'

'But you must do. He's stayed here in the annexe at least twice.'

'A friend of Bishop's.'

'He told me most distinctly that he was your guest. That was the first time we met. The second time, I was in the pool and we didn't have an opportunity to speak. He seemed in a hurry to get away.'

'Why should you think he's of any importance, whoever he is?'

'He was on the news tonight.'

'Really?'

'That man is in charge of the Express Delivery security arrangements.'

'And?'

'They happen to have had one of their vans hijacked today with the resulting loss of five million pounds' worth of gold bullion.'

'I fail to see why this should interest either of us.'

'Most of that gold came from the Bellini bank!'

Neal laughed. 'That's why you're so incensed! Don't worry, he won't lose out. He probably only keeps his pocket money in that bank!'

'You were behind the robbery, Neal. You had that man here to gain inside information, and no doubt Bishop's injuries came from fighting one of the guards and not from any careless van driver in London.'

'You ought to write thrillers!' He smiled, putting out a hand to stroke back her hair.

Lisa flinched and moved out of his reach. 'Don't bloody patronise me!' she shouted. 'You know I'm right, why don't you admit it? I'm not stupid, and I'm not blind. It's screamingly obvious to anyone with any intelligence, and my brain works reasonably well.'

The amusement was gone from his face. 'Yes, indeed it does,' he commented softly. 'It's unfortunate I didn't realise what a hazard that would be when I began pursuing you. But what's done is done, and a wife can't testify against her husband however much she may want to!'

'You admit I'm right?'

'As you pointed out, I'd be sadly under-rating you if I continued denying it.'

'I don't know how you could do it!'

'I didn't use my own fair hands.'

'But you're in line for a knighthood! People think you're ...'

'Most people are either equally crooked, gullible or greedy. Providing I keep donating money to charity and have a legitimate business front, do you honestly think that many people are all that interested in this kind of crime?'

'Yes! Property counts for more than people in this country. Think of the train robbers. They got enormous sentences. The police ...'

'The police? My dear girl, if you've got sufficient money the police don't present any great threat. Most of them live way beyond their income.'

'I don't believe that. And what about those men today?'

'They're alive, aren't they? They'll get a pension and compensation if they can't return to work.'

'I can't believe this! How can you lie there talking so calmly about ...'

'I can't believe it either. In fact, I think it's rather important that I

337

make your position very clear to you before you say anything you'll regret. Put on your robe, we're going to take a little walk.

'Where are we going?' She was suddenly acutely aware that having ceased to please him either in bed or out of it, he had very little to lose by killing her. Despite herself her teeth began to chatter.

'Don't worry, my dear. For some unknown reason I still like having you as my wife. You're quite safe. This is just a visit we have to make so that you realise how important it is to keep all this exciting new knowledge to yourself.'

He bundled her into the ivory satin robe she'd received from him for her last birthday, a beautiful Bruce Oldfield creation she'd admired during the summer show, and then pushed her gently in front of him out on to the first landing and up the stairs. Up to the rooms where he never willingly went. The rooms where Jessica and Janice lived.

At the door of her daughter's bedroom, Lisa twisted free and tried to bar his way. 'Please, don't touch Jessica,' she begged. 'She's responding to the treatment now. Today she sat on my lap and watched television like any normal little girl. She's doing so well but she's very fragile.'

'I'm only here to show you how equally fragile my temper is when I'm blackmailed,' he snarled. 'I intend to remind you how much you gained by marrying me, and how quickly you can lose it all. Everything: my money, your social position, and − of course − your precious daughter. And I promise you this,' he added. 'If you *were* stupid enough to take your middle-class conscience to the police, Jessica would be killed long before they even got near me.'

'She hasn't got anything to do with this!' Lisa was frantic. 'I won't tell anyone, I promise, but don't go in there, Neal. She doesn't know you, she'll be petrified.'

Pushing her to one side he strode into the room and snatched the sleeping Jessica from her bed. Her eyes flew open and when she saw a strange face looming above her she turned into a scratching, screaming animal. With an exclamation of disgust, Neal caught hold of the back of her nightdress, walked to the beautiful bow window and flung it open.

'Look, Jessica!' he shouted in her ear. 'Look down there. It's a long way, isn't it? A long way for a little girl to fall.'

'Stop it!' sobbed Lisa, but she didn't dare approach him in case he accidentally dropped Jessica. Her daughter, reacting as usual quite inappropriately to the situation, began to giggle. Unaware that her laughter was meaningless, Neal's temper snapped and he held her further out, letting her dangle precariously above the thirty foot drop to the gravelled drive below.

338

'*Don't!*' Lisa's scream rang round the rooms and woke Janice who came sleepily in and then froze into terrified silence. Suddenly both women heard a ripping sound as Jessica's nightdress began to tear.

'Neal, please put her down,' pleaded Lisa.

'She's enjoying it!' he sneered. 'Listen to her, she can't stop laughing. Perhaps she wants to try and fly. Would you like to fly, Jessica?'

Lisa glanced at the nurse and signalled for her to leave the room. Once alone with her husband she took a deep breath and tried to speak calmly. 'Neal, I promise I'll never mention a word of what was said tonight to anyone.'

'You won't complain if I find myself a more interesting bed partner?'

'That's not fair! That's . . .'

He leant further out of the window.

'All right, I promise I won't complain. You can do what you like with anyone you choose, but please, please bring her back inside. I'll do anything you want but don't take it out on Jessica.'

Turning he dropped the child to the floor. 'How very generous of you, my dear. May I suggest that we now go back to bed and let Nurse Anthony cope with the brat?'

Jessica's eyes were wild as she began to whimper and shake, once again darting glances round the room, searching for a place of safety. 'Let me give her one cuddle. It's so important that she doesn't regress.'

'I don't think you heard me properly. I said, come back to bed.'

Lisa began to cry aloud. She cried for her daughter, and she cried because she knew that she was now totally under Neal's control and that the scene she'd witnessed tonight was his secret weapon. A weapon he wouldn't hesitate to use and against which she was helpless. She cried for herself, for her daughter, and for what she now knew was going to be a bleak and terrifying future.

As she left she glanced back into the bedroom. Janice was already trying to hold Jessica, but the little girl was stiff and her eyes were fixed on the nightlight over her bed. All the hours of therapy and progress had obviously been wiped out by this one terrifying half hour in which Lisa's life too had totally changed.

'I didn't realise you could still cry so well,' commented Neal. 'You've become quite hard lately.'

She wiped the tears away with the back of her hand. 'It won't happen again.'

'Why not? Perhaps you should play the weak little woman more often. It can be surprisingly effective.'

'It didn't get Naomi very far.'

'It kept her alive,' he said shortly as he climbed back into bed and snapped out his bedside light.

'There is such a thing as quality of life,' she muttered, keeping herself as far away from him as she could and trying to shut out the sounds of screaming from the top floor.

'I'm glad you realise it. Goodnight, my dear.'

In his first floor bedroom, Bishop, awake from the pain in his shoulder, had heard the child and the raised voices of the adults. Later on he'd picked out Lisa's sobbing and now he smiled to himself in the dark and wondered how much longer she would be allowed to live. Not too long if he had his way, and once he was Neal's son-in-law he would hold more influence in family affairs than he did at present. He was probably the only person to sleep well for the rest of the night.

When Lisa woke the next morning, Neal was gone. He hadn't left any word of when he'd return and Bishop, still convalescing, took blatant delight in her confusion as she tried to plan meals with the cook.

Louise, thrilled by Bishop's temporary inability to escape her attentions, hovered round him with cups of coffee, excited plans for their future and an excess of unwanted sympathy.

For three days Lisa waited nervously to hear from her husband. In the middle of the fourth afternoon he suddenly returned, kissed her warmly, congratulated Rebekah on her excellent school exam results and then linked his arm through Lisa's and went to the nursery to see their son.

Taut with tension she watched as he gently held Alexi in his hands, the same hands that had dangled her daughter out of the window, and knew that she hated him. She was afraid of him and she hated him but there was no possibility of escape.

'Coming along well, isn't he?' he said pleasantly. 'He'll soon be running around. Before I forget, we've got twelve people to dinner tomorrow night. Make sure you're looking your best. I don't want people to think there's any trouble between us. It could cost me my knighthood. Naturally you won't let me down?'

She lowered her eyes to hide her hatred. 'I won't let you down.'

'I thought not! How's Bishop's shoulder?'

'Ask Louise. She's been playing nurse to him.'

'In that case he's probably better. I don't imagine he enjoyed being the object of her tender ministrations!'

'When are they getting married?' asked Lisa, knowing that would cloud his infuriatingly jovial mood.

'Monday morning. We'll have to be there of course, plus Rebekah and Ruth. No one else.'

340

'Not even Mike and Steve?'

'Especially not those two. I don't want them chasing after Ruth.'

'I'd have thought it made sense to keep it all in the family!'

He gave her a hard look. 'Careful!'

'I'm going to speak to Cook,' she said hastily. 'I only hope you've given her enough notice.'

He hadn't, but once again it was Lisa who had to suffer the ill-humoured looks and petulant complaints. She didn't have enough emotional strength left to put the staff in their place any more; instead, she let their words wash over her until they fell silent in the face of her disinterest.

That evening, Neal insisted on a family game of snooker in the games room of the annexe. Lisa, who'd played on Simon's table, was quite useful but Louise was hopeless and Bishop's contempt finally reduced her to tears.

'You're like a bloody leaking tap!' he muttered as she sniffled into her handkerchief.

'So much for your weak and feeble little woman,' murmured Lisa to Neal.

'Louise overplays the role,' he said quietly. 'It needs to be done with discretion.'

'She could cry tears of blood and Bishop wouldn't care.'

'Possibly! Well, we won; obviously a good team!'

'Only if you intend making your living on the snooker circuit,' commented Bishop, annoyed by Lisa's apparent return to favour.

'It's because we understand each other,' said Neal calmly. For once Bishop didn't have an answer. He waited until he and Louise were alone and then smashed his cue down on the floor. 'Isn't he ever going to get rid of her?' he shouted, eyes dark with hatred.

Louise, still sobbing softly, shook her head. 'I don't think so. She must be good at something.'

'It's a pity I can't say the same for you,' retorted her husband-to-be, and when she began crying even louder, laughed unpleasantly.

Only when the first guests were arriving did Neal tell Lisa that Renato Bellini had been invited. Already dressed in a claret-coloured off-the-shoulder satin dress and wearing dark-red ruby ear-rings with a matching pendant, she hoped she didn't look too pale.

Despite careful makeup the signs of strain had been obvious to her when she'd looked in the mirror earlier and she didn't want the Italian to see them. Any sympathy from him would be her undoing in her present emotional state, and she resolved to stay as far away from him as possible.

Chapter Twenty-Seven

When they sat down to dinner she found that he'd been seated on her right. His greeting was markedly cooler than usual and despite her resolve she found herself admiring his blue ruffled evening shirt which accentuated his dark complexion and emphasised his size.

At first he talked to Louise, who was on his right and looking very pretty in a pale blue, empire-line dress. With her fair hair hanging in ringlets to her shoulders she looked young and innocent, a most inappropriate bride for the sharp-faced Bishop who sat further down the table, studiously ignoring the middle-aged women on either side of him.

Lisa felt exhausted. She made small talk with the man on her left and picked at each of the courses placed before her. Nothing about the evening felt real. It was as though she were outside herself, watching her own performance as a hostess. She was amazed that no one seemed to realise there was anything wrong. Only when the rich chocolate mousse was placed before him did Renato turn to her, but there was still no warmth in his eyes although his mouth smiled. 'Tell me, how is your daughter?'

Lisa remembered how Jessica had looked that very evening, rocking from one foot to the other and humming loudly, refusing to enter the everyday world for even a moment. 'Not very good, I'm afraid.'

'The treatment is not working?'

She pushed the mousse away. It was too rich and her stomach was already queasy. 'It did for a while. She's had ... setbacks.'

'You must not take it so much to heart. You look most unwell.'

'Thank you very much! Are all Italians so tactful?'

'Come now, you know it is true. You are still beautiful but not perhaps happy?

Glancing nervously down the table she was relieved to see Neal engrossed in conversation with a red-haired woman. 'Not right now,' she admitted quietly.

He looked carefully at her. 'I too am not happy right now. My family has lost a great deal of money due to a robbery. Since it is the second such robbery, our insurance company is also unhappy and there will be much paperwork and investigation before anything is done. It is most annoying.'

She felt the colour flooding her face and neck and tried to think of other things, to fix her mind on Jessica or Alexi, but all she could recall was her husband's part in the robbery and his casual dismissal of its effect on the Bellini family.

Renato watched her and realised with amazement that she knew something. Probably not everything, possibly nothing that he himself didn't know, but he was aware that any knowledge put her in a dangerous position. He flicked his eyes towards Neal and then turned back to Lisa. 'You heard about it?' The question was casual.

She'd never felt so hot before. The whole room was like a furnace and her skin was burning as she tried to think how she'd answer if she really were innocent of her husband's involvement. 'I saw it on the news.'

'It was an unnecessarily violent crime,' he continued, hating himself for what he was doing but compelled to press on because it was his duty to his family. 'Both the men who were guarding the bullion will be crippled for life. One is blind, the other may never walk again.'

'I suppose they'll get pensions,' she said feebly.

'I forget, but yes they will get pensions. How fortunate! No doubt they are in fact happy men and I am foolish to worry about them,' he retorted through clenched teeth.

'There's no need to be sarcastic!'

'You know something of this, do you not?'

'I've already told you I saw it ...'

'You realise,' he continued remorselessly, 'that your knowledge is dangerous. If you confide in me, I will help you.'

She looked down at Neal and saw that he was watching them both. Raising her chin she turned defiantly to Bellini. 'I don't think I need any help, and even if I did I wouldn't put my trust in you. I wouldn't put my trust in any man ever again.'

'Because you have married one who cheats and lies his way through life? Not all of us are the same.'

'Perhaps not, but my judgement appears at the very least to be unreliable. Besides, this is a stupid conversation. I don't know any more than the rest of the population about the robbery.'

'I think you do,' he said, smiling as though they were making small talk.

'Think what you like.'

'I would like to meet with you in London,' he murmured. 'We could talk further there.'

'I've nothing to say to you.'

Neal coughed slightly and she glanced at him. 'I was wondering how Jessica was tonight?' he asked gently. She realised that everyone at the table thought what a wonderful stepfather he was, showing such concern for a handicapped child. Only Lisa and Renato recognised the warning.

'I have to protect my daughter,' she murmured, and the Italian saw tears in her eyes as with a shaking hand she lifted her wine glass to her lips. 'I think it's time we ladies left you to your brandy,' she continued aloud, and rose swiftly to her feet. The gentlemen also stood and as she walked past Bellini, he murmured, 'If you want to see me, ask Mike. He will arrange it.'

By a supreme effort of will she managed not to falter and even Neal, who was watching her closely, didn't realise that the Italian had spoken. Instead he congratulated himself on his swift breakup of a potentially dangerous conversation.

Satisfied that his wife was thoroughly cowed he didn't visit their bed that night. Instead he took the red-haired woman to a room in the annexe and Bishop, who had been waiting for just such an occurrence, felt extremely happy.

Unaware of his betrayal, Lisa was relieved to find Neal in a good mood the next day. He congratulated her on the smooth running of the dinner party then suggested that she bought herself a new outfit for Louise's wedding. 'A loose fitting coat and dress would be nice,' he commented as he went to instruct Mike to take her to London.

'Why loose fitting?'

'Because it's time Alexi had a brother.'

She didn't argue but once she was safely on her way, opened the glass and after a few minutes general chatting plucked up the courage to ask Mike the all-important question, aware that if Renato were wrong she could be signing Jessica's death warrant.

'Mike, I want to meet with Renato Bellini.'

He glanced in the mirror and saw how pale she was. 'How soon?'

'As soon as possible, I suppose.'

'I'll see what I can arrange while you're looking round the shops. It would help if you chose something that needed altering. Then we could come back for another fitting in about a week's time.'

'That shouldn't be difficult.'

'One thing,' he added as he dropped her off outside Zandra Rhodes. 'Your husband's asked me to keep an eye on you.'

344

'You mean protection?'

'Not any more. I've had a change of job description! You're now under surveillance.'

Lisa stared at him. 'You won't . . .?'

'Of course not, but knowing your husband there'll be another tail too. We'll have to be very careful.'

She looked into his open, cheerful face and shuddered at the thought of what would happen to him if Neal discovered his betrayal. 'Why are you doing this for me?' she asked softly.

'Let's just say I think you deserve a better life.'

She didn't want that to be the reason. Two people had already died because of her, she couldn't take the responsibility for another. 'Surely Bellini's paying you, Mike?'

'Yeah, he's paying me.'

'Enough to make the risk worthwhile?'

He knew what was worrying her and sensed that a lie was necessary if she was ever to get free. 'Sure, enough to let me live out my days in the sun if I want!'

'I'm still grateful.'

'No need, it's only a job!'

She had a horrible feeling that he was lying but pretended to believe all he'd said and hurried into the shop. Mike glanced round him, saw the silver Renault parked across the road and knew that was the car he had to shake off. It wasn't difficult, and within twenty minutes he and Bellini were deep in conversation.

The staff at Zandra Rhodes had never before found the second Mrs Gueras anything but good humoured. Today was different; today nothing suited her as she niggled over hemlines or complained about the cut. Eventually she bought a bright orange and green silk dress with beading, the skirt slashed to the thigh on one side, and also requested that a lightweight coatdress with enormous scarlet pockets on a black and grey background be lengthened, even though it was obvious this would alter the entire balance of the garment.

'I'll call back in a week,' said Lisa, horribly uncomfortable with her behaviour and hoping that Mike had managed to set up a meeting for the right day. When he collected her and put her dress in the boot, he murmured, 'All set for next week. He'll meet you at Brown's at three. You'll go straight to his suite.' Lisa almost sagged with relief. 'Get in the car,' he added quickly. That silver Renault's been chasing me all the morning. It might look better if you told me I was late or something.'

Feeling ridiculous, Lisa made a small scene, complaining bitterly about the time Mike had taken doing her few errands. He looked suitably apologetic and they both got into the car. Then, totally exhausted by it all, she fell asleep. Mike, catching sight of her still frighteningly young and innocent face resting on the leather upholstery, prayed that for once in his life he was doing the right thing.

Lisa though it highly appropriate that Louise's wedding day was cold, wet and windy, more like March than July, and the heavy skies were reflected in the brooding features of the groom whose 'I do' sounded more as if he were reluctantly undertaking to die for his country than gaining a young, attractive and wealthy bride.

Even some of Louise's radiance dimmed in the presence of such obvious disinterest and when she left for their three day honeymoon, the longest time Bishop claimed he could spare, she clung briefly to her stepmother, her eyes perturbed.

'It will be all right,' Lisa murmured. 'You know how he hates formal occasions.'

'Yes, yes he does, doesn't he!' Louise's gratitude at the excuse for her husband's behaviour saddened Lisa intensely.

'Rather her than me!' exclaimed Ruth, still wearing the powder pink cotton dress despite the fact that it was intended for a warm summer's day.

'He never wanted you!' retorted Neal irritably. The entire day was abhorrent to him and only Louise's pregnancy had forced his permission, a fact he resented despite having used the same ploy to gain Lisa.

'Of course he didn't. He knew I'd be too much trouble. Lou's a born doormat.'

'I never noticed her bowing to authority when she lived here.'

'That's different, Daddy. She's so anxious to keep that revolting Bishop happy she lets him trample all over her. She'd be the same with any man she wanted to marry. It's probably because you never gave her any attention!' With that parting shot she went off to change.

'I imagine you wish your dresscoat had been fitted,' commented Neal as Lisa shivered in her bright but sleeveless silk dress.

'I'm still going to buy it. I'm due to have the final fitting next Wednesday,' she added casually. 'You did say I'd be needing loose clothes.'

He smiled approvingly. 'Of course! Don't forget to tell Mike you'll need him.'

'I won't. Why don't we all go out to dinner tonight? It would make a change for Rebekah and ...'

'I'm returning to London.'

'Can't you wait until morning?'

346

'No.'

'Then I'll take the children out.'

'Jessica as well?'

'Why do you always have to bring her into things? Of course I can't take her out, but Ruth and Rebekah will enjoy themselves.'

'I bring her into the conversation to remind you of your obligations,' he said pleasantly. 'One of which is to provide Alexi with a brother.'

'Even I can't manage that long-distance.'

'I thought we could go upstairs for an hour now.'

Inwardly feeling like a brood mare, Lisa shrugged. 'It crossed my mind that you might be saving yourself for someone else!'

'Even if you're correct, I'm quite capable of taking care of two women,' he assured her, his eyes now cold. Slowly she followed him to the bedroom.

After he'd finished and left, Lisa lay wondering if she'd been right about his having another woman. He no longer spent much time with her, and she didn't think their relationship could be satisying his deeper needs. Idly she wondered about the type of woman he'd take as a mistress. It didn't occur to her that he might have found one special woman, and the thought of an assortment of casual one-night stands wasn't unduly distressing. He was intelligent enough to protect himself against any undesirable consequences.

She thoroughly enjoyed her evening out with the girls, pleasantly surprised to discover that Ruth had a very quick wit and was an excellent mimic. 'When did you learn all these impersonations?' she asked in fascination.

'Mummy and I used to do them together watching television. Even towards the end, when the drinking got really bad, she did have good days and we'd have a few laughs together.'

'She never laughed with me!' objected Rebekah.

'That wasn't your fault. Daddy was in such a fury after you were born that I think he stopped all Mother's natural feelings towards you. She got terribly depressed around that time.'

Lisa realised that this was when she and Neal had met and wondered how much of his irritation had been caused by her. 'Do you still miss her, Ruth?'

'Not really; she wasn't with us in her mind much during the last year. I'm sure that nurse encouraged her drinking and pill popping because she got worse and worse with her. Also, she could be terribly embarrassing, coming down to meals late and drunk when Daddy was with us, and making scenes in front of the servants.

'It didn't stop me loving her, but somehow I guessed that she

347

wasn't going to live to an old age. How could she with that sort of self-abuse? Knowing that, I suppose I deliberately distanced myself emotionally. When you came along you were very nice, far nicer than Mummy had been for a long time and everything seemed so much better that it was difficult to miss her.'

'I suppose it was lucky she died in her sleep,' commented Lisa. 'It could have been worse. She might have had . . .'

'She died of fright,' interrupted Rebekah, her profiteroles stopping halfway to her mouth. 'I know she did. It was the spiders.'

'For goodness' sake eat those things up!' laughed Ruth. 'You look revolting with them falling off the spoon like that. And do stop talking about spiders. You aren't stupid. Where would a plague of spiders come from? And more to the point, where would they go?'

'I saw them!' insisted Rebekah, her voice muffled by the dessert. 'I know I did. It wasn't a dream. They were big and furry, real tarantulas.'

'Shut up!' Ruth's tone wasn't unkind but Lisa could see how furious Rebekah was at everyone's continuing disbelief of her story.

'Did your mother hate spiders, Ruth?'

'God, yes. Even a money spider sent her into a screaming fit. When I was really young I remember Daddy putting one in her iced soup at lunch time. It was titchy and couldn't possibly have hurt her but she went berserk. We laughed at first, but when she kept screaming we realised it wasn't funny at all.'

'Your father should have known that.'

'I expect he did but I don't suppose he felt guilty about laughing. He's always believed in making people face up to their fears. Like you and horse riding,' she added.

'That was horrid of him!' exclaimed Rebekah. 'I could see you shaking. That lovely Italian man looked ready to bop Daddy on the nose, he was so cross!'

'Fortunately the doctor's forbidden me to ride again now my arm's been broken twice. Even your father doesn't want a wife with a deformed arm, however satisfying he might find his treatment of my phobia.'

'I'm stuffed!' remarked Rebekah inelegantly, and Lisa could see that the girl's eyes were half closed.

'Time to go,' she responded, signing the bill automatically without even checking it.

'Is Mike taking us home? I like him,' said Rebekah sleepily.

'It's Steve,' said Ruth flatly. 'Anyway, you can't have Mike, he's in love with someone else.'

'Who?' demanded Rebekah, suddenly wide awake. 'Is it you?'

Ruth glanced at her stepmother and then away again. 'No, it's not me, although I agree he's nice. It isn't anyone you know,' she added.

Lisa, still pondering Rebekah's insistence of the reality of the tarantulas, didn't hear the conversation. She would have been amazed at her stepdaughter's intuition, and worried as well considering the risks she and the chauffeur were about to take. Fortunately it didn't matter. In both Ruth and Rebekah she had staunch allies.

Meanwhile, in the Scilly Isles, Louise – abruptly initiated into Bishop's true sexual tastes – lay weeping silently beside him, wishing with all her heart that she'd listened to her sister, her mother or even her stepmother before committing herself entirely to this man. A man who not only knew how to cause her pain but had also made clear his total contempt for her and all she represented.

Tonight he'd laughed at her tears before telling her exactly why he'd married her and how he intended to benefit from their union. As for the child she carried, she knew now that if she managed to carry it full term it wouldn't be because of Bishop. As far as he was concerned the growing foetus had served its purpose and with any luck would be miscarried. Unlike his father-in-law he had no desire for heirs. He was only interested in himself.

While his oldest daughter wept, Neal lay beside the auburn-haired socialite and wondered whether it would be safe to take her to the next film gala or if people might start to talk. Perhaps he should wait until he'd made Lisa pregnant, then there would be an excellent reason for her absence and the sight of a mature woman in her early forties at his side wouldn't arouse any controversy.

He rather regretted the fact that she was older, but he now knew that young flesh wasn't necessarily the most sensual and it was satisfying to feel a woman respond to his touch again. Yet deep down he wished that it was his wife beside him, sleeping soundly with the look of a woman who's well loved. Being a realist he also knew his wish could never come true. Not now. The time for that was past.

Jessica smiled broadly as her mother attempted to play pat-a-cake with her, their hands becoming hopelessly entangled every time. She was enjoying the game, actually accepting physical contact with pleasure, and Lisa felt that this could be the start of a big breakthrough. Finally she glanced at her watch. 'I have to go now,' she explained.

'I have to go now,' repeated Jessica, moving off in acknowledgement that the game was over.

'I'll be back soon.'

'Back soon ...' The echo sounded almost wistful. Tears pricked behind Lisa's eyelids but only when she was safely outside did she wipe her eyes and take a deep calming breath. She knew very well that it wasn't just Jessica's words that had upset her. It was the day's tension heightening every emotion, for today she was to meet Renato Bellini at Brown's.

She changed into a fuchsia pink, linen suit with a crisp white cotton blouse whose high collar hid the marks of Neal's aggressive lovemaking the previous night.

'Where are you going?' asked Louise, coming silently up the stairs.

'To town, I've got a dress to pick up.'

'I thought I might come with you. None of my clothes fit me now and there isn't a decent maternity shop for miles around.'

Lisa's heart thumped against her ribs. Although Louise's voice was innocent enough there was a look of challenge in her eyes, almost as though she knew her stepmother wouldn't want anyone going with her, which was ridiculous. Only Lisa, Mike and Bellini himself knew of the arrangement, and none of them would have told Louise. But of course there was Bishop. It was always impossible to be sure how much he knew.

'You'll have to take another car,' she said coolly. 'I'm hoping to call on Carol while I'm there and I might join some of the Red Cross Committee for tea later. I can't wait around for you all the time.'

All at once an expression of regret passed over Louise's features, to be quickly replaced by her more usual sullen pout. 'I'll go another day then,' she said indifferently. 'It isn't much fun shopping on my own. Actually, I wanted to use Daddy's charge cards.'

'Don't tell me your husband's keeping you short of money!'

'He doesn't understand about clothes. He seems to think I look all right in the ones I've got.'

'I never thought he was good husband material. Now, if you'll excuse me, I must go.'

'Try not to bump into Daddy,' said Louise spitefully. 'It might be embarrassing for you if you found him and his new woman having an intimate lunch.'

'What new woman?'

'I don't know her name, but I don't think you can complain. After all, he did the same to Mummy.'

'You're just a troublemaker,' retorted Lisa, but she thought that Louise had probably been speaking the truth. It made sense. Neal was in London a lot these days and rarely took her with him. He also behaved like a man with something on his conscience. No doubt it was a passing fancy. Only if Neal himself told her, or took the girl — she assumed it was a girl — to a public function would Lisa make a fuss.

'You're late,' remarked Mike with a frown.

350

'I was held up by Louise.'

'What did she want?'

'Firstly she wanted to come with us this morning.'

'Tricky!'

'And when I managed to wriggle out of that she told me that her father had a new girlfriend. Did you know about that?'

'No.'

'At least he's being discreet. God, I feel so nervous about this meeting.'

As well she might, thought Mike to himself. If her husband found out he wouldn't hesitate to have Mike killed and his wife would probably end up wishing he'd done the same to her. 'As long as we're careful, you've nothing to worry about,' he said casually, but his eyes constantly checked the driving mirror and he made sure that he dropped her off a long way from Brown's. 'Here's a sketch of the back streets you can walk through to get to the hotel. It should make life pretty difficult for anyone trying to follow you.'

Lisa took the piece of paper and then gasped as a tall, slim woman wearing a pink suit appeared from a shop doorway and climbed into the back of the car.

'Your double. I phoned on ahead with a description of the clothes.'

'You mean it's necessary to drive round London with someone impersonating me?'

'It's what's known in the trade as a sensible precaution. I'll get a call when you're to be picked up. You'd better go, he's waiting.'

When she realised how many steps were being taken to protect her, Lisa started to appreciate the enormity of what she was doing. Nervously she approached the receptionist at the hotel and took the key that was handed to her. She'd only just found his room when the door opened and Bellini was standing in front of her. Dressed in a dark silk suit with a brilliant white shirt and black and red silk tie he seemed more business-like than normal and her heart sank. This wasn't the man she'd imagined confiding in. This was a stranger. A man who belonged in her husband's world but not hers. Then he smiled and for a moment she felt better.

'I was worried for you.'

'I got held up at home.'

'You would like coffee?' he asked, ushering her in.

'I don't know. I ...' She felt sick with nerves and wasn't too sure if strong coffee was quite what her stomach needed.

'Try it,' he urged. 'And while you drink, tell me about Jessica.'

He was deliberately giving her a chance to compose herself, dismayed by her nervousness. He knew about Neal's current mistress,

351

and knew too that the marriage was in a bad way but he hadn't expected her to be quite so tense. Aware that his own physical size probably intimidated her he tried to make himself as small as possible in the huge armchair and was relieved to see her slowly unwind.

'Jessica's doing very well,' she said at last. 'I was playing with her this morning, really playing that is. She's learning to act out pat-a-cake, and although she can't get it right she's able to laugh instead of flying into a temper or giggling hysterically. She's talking more too, but she still can't cope with personal pronouns. Other people's raised voices upset her but not her own! On the whole I'd say she's better.'

'You should take her around more. Get her used to the outside world.'

'Neal doesn't like people to see her.'

'She cannot stay locked on the top floor for the rest of her life!'

'Of course not, and she does go into the garden every day, but ...'

'I understand. He is good to her, your husband?'

She thought of Neal dangling Jessica out of the bedroom window and closed her eyes for a moment. 'No,' she said shakily. 'He's not at all nice to her.'

'What does he do?'

'He doesn't hit her or anything like that, I wouldn't let him. Most of the time he simply pretends she doesn't exist, but these days when he wants to get at me he does it through Jessica. She's so vulnerable that ... I don't want to talk about it,' she finished quickly.

'You should talk about it. Please, tell me what he does that distresses you.'

'I can't.'

'I thought we were friends.'

Lisa looked carefully at him. His eyes looked very kind. She knew that he'd have compassion for Jessica and for her, but she also knew that he was a tough businessman in a tough world that was probably little different from her husband's, and she'd had enough of men like Neal to last her a lifetime.

'I don't have men friends any more,' she said tightly.

Renato's eyes moved away from hers. She'd been more badly damaged than he'd anticipated and he wished he could carry her off to Italy, leaving everything behind. He wanted to give her a new start in a land where she could be healed by sun, sea and constant, non-demanding love. Naturally it was impossible. She had children and responsibilities, and at the moment she was too fragile for him even to touch her, but one day he'd take her away, he promised himself. As soon as his business here was over ... providing Neal hadn't damaged her so much that she would no longer trust any man.

'Tell me what you know of the robbery,' he said abruptly, twisting round to face her.

'I don't . . .'

'You know something, do you not?'

'I've read about it and . . .'

'Was your husband behind it?'

'I think so,' she hedged.

'Have you asked him outright?'

She hated his staccato questions and arrogant demands, and her temper flared. 'Yes, if you must know I did ask him and he told me I was right. Then he dragged me along to Jessica's room and made me watch him hang her out of the window and threaten to drop her thirty feet to the front garden if I ever told anyone. Is that enough for you?'

'Yes,' he said gently. 'It is enough.'

'I knew because I'd seen the man in charge of the security firm at our house a couple of times.'

'The security people were themselves involved?'

'Not those poor drivers, but their boss certainly was.'

'I see. And you will still continue to live with your husband?'

'What choice have I got?' she demanded, her voice harsh with the effort of keeping back the tears. 'Can you imagine him letting me leave? Besides, he wants another son.'

Renato flinched. He didn't like imagining her in the arms of Neal Gueras. He'd been pleased to learn about his mistress, imagining this meant he no longer slept with his wife.

'You will let him give you another child?' He sounded almost contemptuous.

'How the hell can I stop him? I am his wife, and if I don't choose to give him a son willingly he'll get one by force. I don't enjoy violence so I let him get on with it. You're disgusted, aren't you? I can see it in your face but what else can I do?'

'I find it equally disgusting. There are times when I wonder how long I can live like this, but I chose it. Chose it of my own free will because I honestly thought that I could make him a good wife and that although I didn't love him I'd always respect him.'

'I don't respect him any more and I certainly don't love him, but there's still Jessica. Without Neal I couldn't have afforded the therapy that's made such a difference. And you see, Jessica will always be there. Who else would take her on?'

'I would,' he said softly.

Lisa shook her head. 'Don't say that. I can't get away from Neal and you'll only make my life more difficult if you tell me that things could be better.'

353

'But they could! I wouldn't keep Jessica shut away on her own, she'd be part of the family. How can you tell yourself that she's having the best treatment when you scarcely see her? And you don't do you? He hates you even to talk about her, I can see it in his eyes. She's his weapon against you, nothing more.'

'Stop it! I don't want to hear about all the wonderful things you'd do for her. You're not my husband, Neal is. And if I ever did get free of him, you don't honestly think I'd get involved with another man, do you?'

'Don't let him spoil your whole life, Lisa. It is true that to leave him will not be easy, but neither will it be impossible, providing it is done carefully and with good planning. If in time you could care for me, I would spend the rest of my life showing you what a good husband is like.'

'No you wouldn't!'

He smiled. 'Why so sure?'

She fiddled with her wedding ring, twisting it round and round on her finger. 'I'd be a disappointment to you.'

'In what way?'

'In the most important way, according to my husband.'

'You cannot cook!'

She hesitated. 'I'm no good in bed,' she admitted flatly, certain that this would silence him.

Renato wondered how much it had cost her to tell him that. 'That is a personal experience between two people who care for each other,' he said at last. 'There is no question of being either good or bad at it. You cannot be good on your own. It is always possible that you are not having the best of help!'

'I wasn't much good with my first husband either,' she said defiantly, determined to alienate him.

'There is more to married life than bed.'

'You wouldn't think so to listen to Neal these days. You can't imagine what it's like to hear a constant litany of your faults as a bed partner.'

'I think I can.'

'You wouldn't be any better!' she retorted, angry at him for what he'd made her reveal. 'According to my husband you wouldn't waste five minutes of your time on me if you knew what I was really like.'

'He tell you this?'

'Yes. I understand you're something of an expert, so I'd certainly be a terrible disappointment. It's lucky you'll never know, isn't it?'

'Do not do this to yourself. Naturally your husband wishes you to feel a failure as a woman, this is yet another way to keep you with

354

him. Now, listen carefully to me. As you know, he is a highly organised and efficient criminal. His entire organisation exists from the profits of crimes. Protection rackets, prostitution, drugs . . . these are the business commodities that really bring in the money. The rest is just a front.

'He is ruthless and clever, but over the past few years he has been over-reaching himself. My family in particular are incensed by his attacks on our banks. We . . .'

'You're all crooks too,' interrupted Lisa.

He raised his eyebrows in surprise. 'In what way, crooks?'

'You belong to some masonic lodge that goes round killing its own members.'

'You are thinking of the Banco Ambrosiano scandal. Possibly not all P2 members are blemish free, just as not all of your masons here are beyond reproach, but that is not the same as making a living from criminal activities, and for myself I know nothing of the Roberto Calvi affair.'

'I wouldn't expect you to admit it!'

He sighed. She was so much on the defensive it was impossible to reach her. He also sensed that she didn't want to be reached. That she was fighting to keep her hold on sanity and any interference from him could prove too much for her.

'Listen to me. You must naturally do what you think best for your children's safety, but should the time ever come when you need a safe place to hide then I can give you the key to such a house right now. Here, take it, the address is on the tag. Memorise it and I will tear up the tag before you go. That house will be empty day and night, and if you pick up the telephone in the hall you will immediately be put through to me, wherever I happen to be. Now, for my peace of mind, will you take it?'

'I think you're over-dramatising the situation, but since it seems to matter so much I suppose I should.'

Renato stood up and Lisa rose too, not wishing to have him towering over her. Taking her right hand in his, he gently caressed it with his thumb. 'I do not wish you to go back to your husband,' he murmured, 'but as you have pointed out there is no other option open right now. However, one day it will be different and then I will be free to tell you how I feel about you.'

She looked at his long, slender fingers and for once she didn't imagine them tightening round her wrist or twisting her arms as Neal's so frequently did. Instead she imagined them holding her safely, shutting out all the terror and deception that was her life, and without realising it she swayed towards him.

He put his hands lightly on her shoulders, his eyes taking in the small bruise on her throat and his brain registering the fragility of her bones beneath his hands. 'You know that I love you?' he asked.

'No!'

'You must have realised.'

She shook her head. 'Sometimes I wondered but I wasn't sure.'

'Then be sure. It will not always be like this. Eventually you will look back on this time as a bad memory, nothing more, but you must trust me. Do you trust me, Lisa?'

'I want to, but I've made too many mistakes to have any faith in my own judgement.'

'You do trust me enough to use the safe house if you need it? Promise me that.' His eyes spoke more clearly than his words and she felt a flicker of hope.

'I promise I'll go there if I need a place to hide.'

'You will not listen to your husband's destructive lies any more?'

'You don't understand. He's telling the truth!'

Renato sighed, realising she'd already accepted her husband's criticisms. 'Does he abuse you physically?' he demanded.

'He's too clever for that.'

'He is under pressure. Men do not always behave normally at such times. Now I think you must go and collect your lovely dress.'

As his hands left her shoulders she felt as though he was casting her away and had to suppress a whimper of fear. Renato touched her lightly beneath the chin. 'Don't worry. You are no longer alone.'

Before he could say more she turned on her heel and left the room. His fingers seemed to have left burning marks on her shoulders and she felt limp from the sudden release of tension. Yet despite what he'd said, she didn't believe she'd ever need his safe house, or consider sharing his life in the future because she couldn't imagine it would ever be feasible. What she did believe was that it might have been possible for her to be happy with him, and that was a bitter thing to accept.

Leaving Brown's by the back entrance she walked to Carol's old shop. The entire premises had been stripped, the windows daubed with white paint and a large 'For Sale' sign was suspended from the flat above. She wished that her friend had kept in touch; there was no way now in which she could contact her again.

When Mike drew up beside her she didn't hear him and he sat behind the wheel for a moment watching her. He was a straight-forward young man with excellent physical co-ordination, a quick brain and a low boredom threshold. Until the arrival of the second Mrs Gueras he'd never questioned the work into which he'd drifted, but now – watching this woman for whom he'd willingly die – he realised exactly how immoral his job was, and knew too the precise moment when he'd taken the wrong turning. It was when he met up with Bishop after a three year gap in their tenuous friendship, and agreed to help out by doing some chauffeuring for him.

The chauffeuring had paid well but the driving of get-away cars had paid better and he'd enjoyed the excitement, pitting his skills against those of police drivers. It had all seemed like a game then, but not any more. Since Lisa became involved it had changed. He wondered whether Bellini would succeed in getting her away. If he did, then Mike's own treachery would be justified. Finally he put his hand on the car horn. 'Finished your shopping, princess?'

'I wanted to see Carol.'

He'd seen Carol a few nights earlier and doubted if Lisa would like what her friend had become. 'Maybe she doesn't want to see you,' he commented. 'Perhaps she's making a fresh start somewhere.'

'Why?'

'Get in the car, it's time we got back!'

'Why should Carol want to lose touch with me?' she repeated once she was settled in the car.

'Perhaps she's done a bunk while owing your old man money?' It was possible, she realised, and had to be content with that. 'Meeting go all right?' he added, noticing that the silver Renault was three cars behind them.

'I suppose so.'

'You don't sound too sure.'

'I'm not sure of anyone anymore.'

No, he thought to himself. Nor would he be in her shoes. 'I think he's straight,' he assured her. 'He's a good bloke.'

'How do you know?'

'Word gets around. How a person treats his employees, the way he looks after his children, whether he's kind to dumb animals! Believe me, there isn't much you can't find out about rich people if you cultivate their staff. So far I haven't heard a bad word about the Italian.'

'Not even from his women?'

'Unfortunately he and I don't mix with the same ones!'

'I thought Neal was kind,' she murmured to herself. 'Why should Renato Bellini be any different?'

Mike, busy trying to work out exactly when the Renault had picked them up, was too distracted to answer, and in any case there really wasn't anything he could say. It was a judgement she had to make for herself.

Chapter Twenty-Eight

When Lisa arrived home she felt certain that her guilt at her secret meeting was written all over her face. Fortunately, Louise was in the middle of an enormous row with her husband which enabled Lisa to slip away unnoticed, change into beige pedalpushers and a cotton top, and then collect Alexi from the nursery. When Neal arrived, his wife was dutifully playing her maternal role and all his attention focused on Louise, now sobbing silently and alone in the room that had once been her mother's retreat.

'What's the matter with her?' he demanded.

'I've no idea.'

'I suppose I'd better find out. You come too; I can't stand weeping women.'

'I can't stand Louise!'

Neal took Alexi from her, deposited him on the rug in the hall and propelled her into the room ahead of him. Louise was slumped in an armchair, her head down on her knees and her shoulders shaking as she wept. For a moment Neal hesitated but finally he put a hand on his daughter's hair.

'What's the matter, Louise? We can hear you from the front of the house!'

'Go away,' she muttered, but without any conviction.

'If anyone goes it's you. You live in the annexe now, remember?'

Louise cried even harder. 'Very tactful!' commented Lisa.

Neal put a hand under his daughter's chin and tilted her face up. 'Either you ... what's happened to your face?'

Lisa glanced at her stepdaughter and saw that her jaw was swollen down the left side, while the skin around her left eye was puffy and discolouring. 'He hit me!' she sobbed. 'John hit me!'

'Why?' asked her father. Lisa noticed that he didn't sound shocked or annoyed, simply curious.

'Because I spent too much money this morning. I only went into town and bought some maternity clothes, but he'd said I didn't need any and ...'

'You promised to obey him. I was surprised you left that vow in, but as I recall it, you wanted to be the perfect, obedient wife. I'm afraid you'll have to live with the consequences.'

Louise's eyes widened in surprise. 'Daddy, he *hit* me! Aren't you going to speak to him?'

'I wouldn't dream of coming between a husband and wife. You chose him, you'll just have to put up with your choice.'

'Neal!' Lisa was truly shocked. Silly and shallow as Louise was, she couldn't believe Neal was going to let her be knocked around as though she no longer concerned him.

'It's all your fault!' shouted Louise, turning her pain at her father's betrayal into anger against her stepmother. 'If you'd let me come to town with you, I could have used Daddy's credit cards and none of this would have happened.'

'You're not using my credit cards any more,' retorted Neal. 'Let your husband keep you. Now go home, I want some time with my wife.'

'Why? Are you tired of Maria Phillips?' Louise's expression was spiteful.

'In a moment I shall strike you myself. Now get out.' With another sob, Louise ran from the room.

'Who's Maria Phillips?' asked Lisa slowly.

'Never mind her. Why didn't you let Louise come with you today?'

'I had several things to do and I didn't want her company.'

'I take it you collected your dress?'

'Yes.'

'What else did you do?'

'I tried to find Carol Blades.'

He frowned. 'Why on earth are you anxious to find her? She's gone out of business. I prefer you in other designs to be honest.'

'I liked her. Is that so strange?'

'I don't think you appreciate what she's really like, Lisa. I happen to know she's got a drug problem. That's probably why her business failed. If I'd known originally I'd never have invested money in the shop.'

'Don't be ridiculous! Out of all the people we know she's one of the few who won't touch them.'

'Are you calling me a liar?'

'Yes.' She waited to see what would happen, but after a short pause he gave a harsh laugh and put an arm round her. 'Your faith in human nature is quite touching! No doubt you'll run across Carol some time then you'll see for yourself what she's become. Did you enjoy looking round the Tate?' he addded casually.

'I didn't go to the Tate.'

'Someone told me they saw you going in. You were wearing a pink linen suit today?'

'Yes, but I didn't go to the Tate. I didn't have time.'

'They must have made a mistake. Let's go and see what young Alexi's up to, shall we?' He sounded relaxed but he'd learnt all he needed to know. Somehow, Lisa had given his man the slip today and he'd ended up following the wrong woman. Either Steve was incredibly incompetent or else Lisa had been very clever. If she'd been very clever then she'd had something to hide, and she couldn't have managed any deception alone. Mike would have had to be in it with her. All in all, he had a lot to think about that evening and Louise never crossed his mind again.

For the next week everything went comparatively smoothly. Neal stayed in London, Louise kept to the annexe and Lisa spent most of her time with the children. Mrs Honeywood came to visit Jessica and expressed delight at her progress.

'You and your husband must be very proud of her!' she exclaimed. 'Of course from now on her progress will be less dramatic, but providing you keep spending the time with her she should continue to improve, until she reaches her maximum potential.'

'You sound as though that might happen quite soon.'

'We aren't expecting her to take her place in ordinary society, are we? It's hard to tell what else she'll accomplish but ...'

'I expect her to take a place in society.'

Mrs Honeywood smiled indulgently. 'You mustn't get carried away by what's been achieved so far. Jessica is autistic and she'll always be autistic. What we have to do is ...'

'I don't believe it's incurable. I've read two case reports of children who went on to higher education, and they can remember how they felt when they were autistic. It's in a book by Nico Tinbergen and his wife. And in Japan ...'

'Those children were probably never autistic in the first place. I've told you what a difficult condition it is to diagnose.'

'Why should every child that recovers be assumed to have been incorrectly diagnosed? Aren't you interested in recovery? Don't you think it's something all parents should know about?'

'It would be most unfair to give parents unreasonable expectations. I'm surprised that an intelligent woman like you can't realise that.'

'Even if most parents will be disappointed, shouldn't the few that will succeed at least know there's a chance? Otherwise they might give up too soon.'

'Mrs Gueras, Jessica can now play quietly on her own, she doesn't hide from every stranger and has fewer rigid routines that she feels necessary for her security, but she's still a very disturbed little girl.' So would you be if you lived here, thought Lisa sourly. 'Your husband understands this. I had hoped to find him here today.'

'I told you, he isn't interested in Jessica.'

'You're wrong! He contacted me himself and said how well your little girl was doing. He was really more worried about you. He said you were becoming over-involved and pushing Jessica harder than you should. He did wonder if she might do better in a less demanding environment.'

Lisa stared at the woman she'd thought of as a friend and knew that once again she'd been deliberately cut off from a possible confidante. If she wasn't careful, Jessica was going to be moved 'for her own good', and doubtless she wouldn't be allowed to return until Lisa had obliged her husband with a second son. She wanted to scream aloud at his further betrayal but instead took a deep breath and looked the therapist straight in the eyes.

'Do you think I'm over-tiring her?'

'No, but I think you're building up false hopes for yourself. I'm against removing autistic children from their parents until the situation at home becomes intolerable and that isn't the case here. Obviously your husband's primary concern is for your mental health but I think I can assure him that after our little talk you won't be quite so ambitious in your plans for Jessica.'

'How much did he pay you?' asked Lisa quietly.

'He told you about the cheque, did he? Wasn't it kind of him! £10,000 for the National Society for Autistic Children. An absolute windfall because I'm afraid it isn't a fashionable charity and is desperately short of funds. The secretary will be writing herself but I had hoped to thank him in person.'

'He's in town.' Lisa wondered whether she should be flattered at the amount of money he was prepared to pay to get Jessica out of the way and leave her free for him.

'Would you pass on my thanks?'

'Of course.'

'Then I'll be off. Goodbye, Jessica!'

Jessica glanced up from her rag book and there was such a look of Toby about her that Lisa's breath caught in her throat. 'Goodbye, Jessica,' she repeated. Mrs Honeywood smiled. 'A strange phenomenon, isn't it? I never get used to hearing it.'

How could the woman be so stupid? wondered Lisa as she closed the front door. Presumably the sheer size of the cheque had prevented her from seeking any deeper motive behind the gift but once again Lisa had lost a friend. Mrs Honeywood's loyalty was no longer to Jessica, it was to all autistic children who could benefit from Neal's generosity.

No sooner had she closed the door behind the visitor than Rebekah came running out of the kitchen, throwing herself at Lisa with such force that she had a job to keep her balance. 'Don't listen to Lou! She's being nasty. Daddy doesn't know and . . .'

'I see the little sneak's got in first,' sneered Louise, walking out of the dining-room with a magazine held tightly in her hands.

'Don't you have a home of your own?' queried Lisa icily.

'I thought you'd like to have a look at this magazine of mine.'

'It's a silly old article!' cried Rebekah, trying to pull Lisa away. 'Come and push me on the swing.'

Louise held out the magazine. Lisa sighed. 'I assume I'm not going to like this?'

'If I don't show you, someone else will.'

'Really? How many enemies have I got?'

'A lot more than you realise,' said Louise venomously.

'Then I'd better read it now and get it over with. Thank you for bringing it round.' She took the copy of *Tatler* but Louise didn't move. 'I don't intend reading it with you standing over me. Please go,' said Lisa crisply.

'Suit yourself. And remember, my mother had to go through all this over you so it's no good feeling sorry for yourself.'

'I'm not in the habit of feeling sorry for myself — unlike some newlyweds I can think of!'

At this Louise turned and flounced away, leaving Lisa standing in the hall, an anxious Rebekah hovering beside her. 'Wait for me in the garden,' said Lisa quietly. 'You can take Alexi out if you like.'

'I don't want you to read it.' Rebekah's face was white and pinched. 'I remember how upset Mummy used to be when she read those magazine.'

'I'll be all right. Please, Rebekah, wait for me in the garden.'

Reluctantly the child gave in. Lisa walked into the dining-room and sat down at the table, dismissing one of the maids who was busy dusting. Slowly she turned to the society pages, and there, just as she'd expected, was a photo of her husband. Next to him, her arm linked possessively through his, was the red-haired woman who'd sat beside him at their last dinner party. She glanced at the words beneath it. 'Business tycoon Neal Gueras, pictured here with his constant companion Mrs Maria Phillips, widow of the late Gerald Phillips, head of the merchant bankers Phillips & Lyle. Mrs Phillips was wearing ...'

She never did see what Maria had been wearing. All she could see was her face at the dinner, the way she'd listened so attentively to Neal. She wondered how long it had been going on and why he'd chosen a woman older than herself. Strangely that hurt more than anything. She'd known he was being unfaithful but hadn't realised it was a serious affair, and she'd never dreamt that he'd be indiscreet enough to make it public knowledge.

She remained at the table for a long time. It was difficult to know how to react now that knowledge of the affair had been forced upon her. She was hurt that he cared so little for her feelings that he could make a fool of her in front of their friends. *His* friends, she corrected herself at once. None of them were hers. Except for Bellini, said a small voice in her head. He's your friend. She wondered if he knew about Maria Phillips. Almost certainly he must, and presumably had done when they met. That hurt too, that he should realise how little Neal valued her.

Yet he'd paid out £10,000 in order to keep her bound to him. That money, intended to get Jessica out of the house, was really being used to force Lisa into giving him another child, and she couldn't do that if he didn't want her as his wife. Apparently he did, but he also wanted a mistress to give him pleasure where his wife couldn't. The more she thought about his behaviour, the angrier she became. He must have known that eventually she'd find out but assumed that she'd keep quiet, or try even harder to please him. He was wrong on both counts. When he returned from London he was in for quite a surprise.

He came home the following night, a Friday evening, and found Lisa wearing a black silk dress with a draped effect and a hem that was just below the knee at the front, dipping to a fishtail at the back. The bodice sparkled with tiny diamanté and she wore large jet ear-rings in her ears. Her hair was swept back off her face and she looked tall, slim and elegant, everything he'd ever wanted her to be. He smiled his pleasure, but just as he reached for her she turned away to pour him a whisky.

'You're looking very attractive tonight!' His tone was jocular.

'Thank you.'

'And your hair's different.'

'Yes. Not red of course, but a different style.'

The first small warning bell sounded in his head. 'Are we going out or is all this glamour purely for me?'

363

'It's all for you.'

'I'm flattered.'

'I don't usually wear black but I thought perhaps I should change my image. Try a more mature look. You like the mature look, don't you?'

'I assume you mean sophisticated,' he said lightly, trying to hide his mounting unease.

'No, I mean mature. I'd call forty-three mature, wouldn't you?'

'I suppose so.'

'And that's how old Maria Phillips is.'

'How did you find that out?'

'Her age?'

'What else?'

'I thought you might be wondering how I found out about your affair, you bastard!' With surprising speed she hurled the contents of her wine glass straight in his face.

Neal didn't move. Lisa was quite frightened by his lack of response. He simply stood there, wine dripping from his face, and looked at her with a total lack of emotion.

'Say something!' she shouted when the silence became unbearable. He still didn't move. 'How could you do it?' she continued desperately. 'Don't you care what people think? I thought you were after a knighthood? I don't think the Queen approves of men who run a succession of wives and mistresses.'

'I've told people you're too involved with Jessica to leave here,' he said at last. There was still no flicker of emotion on his face.

'You like using her, don't you? I've heard all about your generous donation to the Autistic Society, you two-faced liar! You don't care about those children, all you care about is having sons of your own. You thought that by persuading Mrs Honeywood Jessica should go away you could force me into giving you more children. Well, you're wrong. After what I've read in *Tatler* I'm leaving you. I'm not Naomi. There's no way I'm going to have people laughing at me behind my back, or spend all my life here producing your bloody children while you ...'

'Shut up!' he snapped. 'I'm not listening to your hysterical rubbish. Naomi learnt to live with this situation and so will you. It's your own fault. You and I could have had a good life together but you had to keep meddling in my affairs and expending emotional energy on that idiot child of yours, so that in the end I didn't come very high on your list of priorities. All right, it's not what I wanted but that's the way it is. Maria is important to me for one reason only: sex. She'll never have any sort of status and she accepts that.'

'Bravo for Maria!'

'You, however, have the status of being my wife, and ...'

'That's about equal to knowing I was safely married to Al Capone!'

'... and,' he continued furiously, 'at least that ensures your physical safety.'

'It didn't ensure Naomi's.'

'Naomi died of a heart attack.'

'Liar!'

'Furthermore, you are the mother of my only son and that's something for which I'll always be grateful. You can have a perfectly good life here. Once you've produced another son then no doubt we can ensure that you do sometimes come to London with me, just as you used to, but not until then.'

'I'm not listening to any more of this!' shouted Lisa furiously. 'I'm leaving you, and taking Jessica and Alexi with me. You can threaten all you like but I won't stay here and be humiliated by you and that red-haired old crone in London.'

'Where do you think you'll go? Who do you imagine will take you in? You, a baby and a retarded four-year-old!'

'I'll find Carol; I'll ...'

'If you attempt to leave here with or without our son, I shall have you killed,' he said calmly.

She couldn't believe she'd heard him properly. 'You'll what?'

'You will die, just as Kay and Naomi died. Come now, you've kept telling me you knew they were murdered so why the pretence of shock? You were right, they were killed so that I could marry you. I still want you as my wife and you know far too much for me to allow you to leave and live.'

'You wouldn't get away with it again!'

'You underestimate me. It would look like an accident, and I'd be greatly pitied because everyone knows how devoted I am to you.'

Lisa looked into his eyes and wondered how she could ever have thought him understanding. He had dead eyes, incapable of any genuine emotion. 'You don't even love me any more do you?' she asked slowly.

'No.'

'But you won't let me go?'

'I can't, neither do I want to. I may not love you, but for some strange reason I still desire you. Perhaps because I've never felt I've truly managed to possess you.'

'I don't desire you,' she retorted. 'I've never desired you, but I did like you. I believed you cared for me and that in time I'd come to love you, but it didn't happen that way. It was all a sham, wasn't it?'

'I loved you once.'

'You didn't, not the real me. You liked the shell.'

'That's untrue. I cared for you, but unfortunately I underestimated your intelligence. I've never been drawn to clever women, and you are clever, aren't you, Lisa? Beneath the damage Toby inflicted, you're not in the least incapable. Perhaps it would have been better for both of us if you had been. If you knew less, I might have been able to let you go.'

He wouldn't have, she knew that. He'd never let anything of his go until he tired of it, and he hadn't yet tired of her physically. He also wanted more sons. Her knowledge of his business affairs certainly wasn't what kept him from letting her leave.

'I'm going to bed,' she said coldly. 'There's no point in continuing this argument. It obviously isn't going to lead anywhere.'

'You'll stay here,' he told her, and she realised that she'd been wrong. Now there was emotion in his eyes but it was an emotion she didn't like. Pure undisguised lust. As he stepped towards her, she slipped off her shoes and made a run for the door but he was there first, turning the key in the lock and then putting it in his pocket.

'I think I'd like to exercise my marital rights here and now,' he murmured. When she shook her head he simply laughed and reached for the neck of her dress. It was then that she began to fight him. When it was eventually over Neal looked down at her bruised skin with self-disgust, unable to meet her eyes. At one point there'd been a knocking on the door, caused no doubt by Lisa's screams of protest, but he'd shouted for the intruder to go away and after that they'd been left alone.

'I'm going straight back to London,' he muttered. 'Remember what I said, and perhaps after tonight you'll be a little more reasonable about your wifely duties. Once you're pregnant again you'll be left alone. I'd have thought that would make it all worth while.'

She lifted her head and the contempt on her face shook even him. 'All I'm asking for is another son!' he shouted furiously. 'It comes to something when I have to rape my own wife in order to get one!' With that he unlocked the door and within ten minutes was driving himself back to town.

Eventually Lisa forced herself to move. Her muscles ached and her bones felt stiff and sore but she knew that she couldn't delay any longer. Going into the hall, she found the house strangely silent. Obviously no one dared come and see what had happened, she realised, wondering what they must have thought when they heard her screaming. Not that it mattered any more because she was leaving. She had Bellini's key and she was going to use it.

366

She stood under a scalding shower until some of her aches had eased, then dressed in jeans, a sweatshirt and a bodywarmer because although the evening was mild she felt as though she'd never be warm again. After dressing she went into Alexi's room and wrapped him in a blanket then put him on his changing mat on the floor. That done she went and woke her daughter, deciding not to risk dressing her but only putting on a dressing gown and slippers before leading her down to the nursery. Finally, with Alexi under one arm and Jessica held firmly by the hand, she slipped outside, and keeping to the side of the house crept to where her own rarely used Fiesta was garaged.

She wished that she could have taken Rebekah with her but Rebekah was Neal's child and he would be entitled to come after her, possibly even accusing Lisa of kidnap. Much as it hurt, she had to leave Rebekah behind in order to get herself and her own children out of Neal's reach.

The car started at once and she drove slowly down the drive, her eyes anxiously scanning the grounds, but everything was quiet and no lights shone in the annexe. For a brief moment she thought it was going to be easy and then, as she reached the end of the drive, her heart sank as she saw that for the first time since she'd come here as Neal's wife, the wrought-iron gates were closed.

They were heavy but it wasn't beyond her strength to push them open. After one final glance into the surrounding darkness she stepped out of the car and began to fumble with the heavy latch. Just as she started to make progress she heard a sound more frightening than any human footsteps. It was a low growling noise coming from the bushes beside her. She'd always known that dogs patrolled the grounds at night but in her anxiety to get away had forgotten. Now her fingers tried to move more quickly and she cursed quietly as one hand slipped and tore a nail to the quick.

'Perhaps a little light might help you,' said a familiar voice. She turned sharply, immediately blinded by the glare of the torch Bishop was holding.

Narrowing her eyes she slowly made out where he was standing, realising at the same time that he wasn't alone. Beside him, tightly leashed but with their teeth showing as they pulled against the restraint, were two enormous Rotweillers.

'Going anywhere interesting?' he asked with a smile.

'That's none of your business.'

'On the contrary, I've been told to make certain you don't leave the grounds.'

She bit on her bottom lip, trying to work out her chances of escape. They weren't good but the latch on the gates had opened and as she stood with her back to them she pushed gently, relieved to find that they parted relatively easily. If the worst came to the worst she'd have to smash her way through. The children would be safe enough in the back of the car.

'I suggest you return to the house,' continued Bishop smoothly. 'I'll re-garage the car for you.'

'I'll drive it myself. The children are in the back seat.'

'Then take them out and carry them to the house.'

'All right.' Slowly she moved towards the car but at the last moment grabbed hold of the front door handle and wrenched at it. She wasn't quick enough. Bishop murmured 'Take' and she heard him slip the dogs free of their leads, and heard too the terrible growl deep in their throats as they bounded across the grass.

Automatically she turned to face them, then screamed in terror as the first one jumped directly for her throat. In an instinctive reaction she threw up her arms to protect her face, and then her screams echoed right through the grounds and into the house where Rebekah woke in terror at the terrible sound as the first dog's teeth sank deep into Lisa's right arm. It hung in mid-air, suspended by its grip, while its companion hurled itself like a thunderbolt into her stomach. She fell to the ground and lay there, still screaming, as the pair of dogs snapped and bit at her arms and hands.

She wondered how long it would take before one of them severed an artery and Bishop stood back watching while she bled to death on the drive. Despite the agonising pain in her arms she continued to protect her face, hearing the horrible sound of snapping teeth when the dogs missed their target.

Certain that she was going to die she suddenly heard Bishop call out an abrupt 'Leave!' and lay trembling, convinced that he was merely toying with her, intending to let them back after a brief respite. It was typical of his mentality and knowing that she didn't have any strength to protect herself further she simply lay there, waiting. Waiting for a death that didn't come.

'Get up!' he ordered, standing a bare six inches from her head. 'Stop that bloody noise and get your children back to the house.' She tried to stand but the pain from her arms made it difficult to move and she heard herself moaning quietly.

'And shut that child up,' he continued. Only then did she realise that Jessica had got out of the car and was standing in the middle of the drive, watching her mother and shrieking at the top of her voice, her eyes frantic with terror.

'You'll have to get me some help!' she implored him as her head began to swim.

'There'll be help back at the house. Move.'

'I can't take the children. Please get someone to fetch them.'

'And risk them seeing you like this? Not bloody likely. Either you take them or I do. Would you like me to carry Jessica!'

Lisa stumbled towards her daughter but fell before she reached her. For a moment Jessica continued to scream, then – abruptly – she stopped and stood staring into the distance, and even Bishop could see that the child had gone into shock. With a brief glance at Lisa, who was again trying to get to her feet, he reluctantly picked up the rigid child and put her beneath one arm. He left Alexi in the car with the two dogs standing guard and then, because he realised that she wasn't capable of doing it entirely alone, half-pushed Lisa to her feet. His left hand beneath her elbow helped keep her upright as far as the front door.

It was wide open and hall lights blazed down on the three figures as they walked into the house. Lisa, teeth chattering, limbs trembling and with blood pouring from her hands and arms; Jessica, stiff and totally silent; and Bishop himself, his mouth a thin, tight line of contempt as he looked Lisa up and down.

'You stupid bitch!' he muttered. 'I didn't expect you to be daft enough to try escaping after what went on here earlier, but you always know best, don't you? God save me from headstrong women.'

'Get me some help!' She knew that she was begging but was past caring. She'd have gone down on her knees to him if necessary because very soon she was going to pass out and then he could easily leave her to bleed to death right in front of Jessica.

'It's on its way. I'll fetch the precious son and heir once . . . Ah, the cavalry arrives! Dr Hughes, this is your patient. She had a small disagreement with our non-domesticated dogs and needs patching up. You'd better deal with her in the annexe, we don't want to wake the entire household.'

Everything was hazy now, a blurred picture spinning crazily round her, and she heard her own heart beating far too loudly. She tried to look up at the doctor, catching a glimpse of a small, dark-haired man whose eyes were shocked and compassionate, before she gave up and finally allowed herself to lose consciousness.

The doctor, staying overnight purely by chance, was relieved when she did. It made it much easier for him to treat her, and he was glad that she'd be spared some of the shock and pain from the dressing of her bites.

Lisa was lucky in one thing that night. Out of all the doctors who could have been called to her, Dr Hughes was easily the most compassionate and probably the most competent as well, but even he could only treat her physical symptoms. The psychological effects of the night's trauma she would have to deal with alone, and he wondered how any woman could come to terms with what must have happened to her.

As for the child, he knew her history and didn't doubt for one moment that what she'd witnessed that night had sent her back into herself for the rest of her life. Considering the setup in the house he thought that was the best possible thing. No child should have to see her mother suffer as this young woman had tonight. Not for the first time he wondered why it was that Bishop was so violently opposed to the second Mrs Gueras that he'd actually dared unleash two killer dogs on her.

'Still standing admiring her, are you?'

The doctor jumped. 'You're back quickly!'

'Thought I'd better get this young man back to his room before the nurse misses him. He's very important despite his size!'

'I'll need a hand carrying Mrs Gueras to the annexe.'

'Drag her!' he retorted, then carried Alexi upstairs leaving the doctor, his unconscious patient and the motionless Jessica in a huddle at the foot of the stairs. Only when he'd vanished from sight did Mike emerge from Neal's study. Together he and the doctor lifted Lisa carefully in their arms, carrying her through the secret door into the annexe and placing her carefully on the settee. Then Mike took Jessica up to her nurse, and when he returned Dr Hughes was already at work.

Mike – not easily disturbed by injuries – had to look away from the bloody mess of skin and bone that was Lisa's right arm. At that moment he could happily have killed Bishop himself. Instead, he got into his car and drove four miles to a public phone box. From there he made a short call then sped off to London, unable to stay in Berkshire and watch Lisa Gueras when she finally came round.

In his London apartment, Renato Bellini stood by the window and looked out over the Thames as he tried to keep himself under control. He knew that he mustn't act until he had thought it all through. To do anything now would be stupid, but soon, very soon, he'd take the greatest possible pleasure in killing Neal Gueras for what he'd allowed to happen that night.

At 6 a.m. the following morning, Neal's car screamed up the drive and before Mike had brought it to a halt his employer was out and running up the front steps. There had been no conversation on the journey home. Following Mike's description of what had happened at Beckett Lodge Neal remained totally silent, but from the look on his face, Bishop appeared to have badly over-reached himself.

Minutes later as Lisa murmured in a sedated sleep he looked at her white face, heavily bandaged arms and hands, and the dressing on her neck, and bit his lip. Although not blessed with a vivid imagination he could well picture the previous night's scene, and – like Bellini – he too felt the urge to kill, only his anger was directed at Bishop.

He laid a hand on his wife's hot forehead and smoothed back her hair. She seemed to quieten and her muttering ceased. Once she was more settled he quietly left, moving swiftly through to the annexe via his study. Bishop had heard a car arrive. Now, in the cold light of day, he realised that he'd made a mistake but decided to bluff it out. His chief reaction was anger against Lisa; anger that she should have caused him to make such an error of judgement.

When Neal walked into the gymnasium, Bishop was using the punch bag and turned casually to face him. There was no sign of apology on his face, merely slight surprise. 'I didn't expect you back today.'

'I didn't intend to come back. Unfortunately certain events called for a change in my plans.'

'Oh yes?'

'I'd like to know what the hell you thought you were doing when you let those killer dogs loose on my wife. She's lucky they didn't tear her throat out, although I don't suppose she feels very lucky. Perhaps you'd give me an explanation of your behaviour?'

Bishop stopped punching, picked up a towel and wiped non-existent sweat from his brow. 'She tried to get away. You told me to stop her at all costs.'

'I told you to stop her, not half-kill her.'

'At all costs, that's what you said.' Bishop's eyes glittered and there was a suggestion of a smile round his mouth that incensed Neal even further.

'All you had to do,' he said slowly, 'was point a gun at her daughter. Presumably you had your gun with you?'

'Sure.'

'And you knew Jessica was in the car?'

'I assumed she was.'

'Then why didn't you do that?'

'I didn't get the chance. Your wife was by the gates and ...'

'Standing alone by the gates?'

'Yes, trying to get them open so that she could drive her car out, taking Jessica and the precious Alexi with her. If I'd gone over to the car and threatened one of the children, she could have got away.'

Neal glared at his son-in-law. 'You knew she'd never have left the children. You set the dogs on her for your own personal satisfaction,

371

hoping to see them savage her, didn't you? It gave you some kind of twisted pleasure.'

'If I'd wanted them to kill her they would have done. I only gave the attack command.'

'How very generous! May I remind you that Lisa is my wife and should be treated as such. I suppose it made you feel very powerful, watching the dogs tearing her arms to pieces?'

'Probably not as powerful as if I'd raped her.'

Neal's face darkened. 'What the hell's that supposed to mean?'

'Come on! Louise heard what went on in the study before you left for London. You raped your own wife. Did that make you feel good?'

'Just who the hell do you think you are?' exploded Neal, taking a step towards Bishop. 'You're not indispensable, no one is. I could easily replace you if I wanted to.'

'I think not.'

'What is it about my wife that gets to you so badly?' Neal's voice was deceptively soft.

'She's ruined you. Clouded your judgement, pushed you into committing risky murders and kept you away from your work. Okay, so now the gilt's off the gingerbread and you're back in the swing of things, but you still come rushing home because she's hurt. It's pathetic. You wouldn't have come back here if Naomi had been savaged by a pack of wolves!'

'Then it isn't my wife you hate, it's what she's done to me?'

'Right! I'm not the only person to see it. Don't you realise that's why Bellini's here? They've heard that we're weak; ripe for a takeover or even elimination. They want our casinos, our contacts and ...'

'All they want is their gold back.'

'In that case they'd have picked up the phone and told you so. No, they want to make inroads into London and we're weak because of you. Bellini knows ...'

'Bellini isn't a crook!'

'He's a member of P2. His loyalty is to them.'

'Quite a number of important people in *this* country belong to P2. It doesn't mean they're all crooks. P2 is a divided lodge, and the Bellinis happen to belong to the law-abiding section.'

'It's an illegal lodge! Besides, you're hardly likely to say anything else!' sneered Bishop. 'I'm sorry to inform you that yours isn't the majority view. Quite a few of us think our entire organisation is at risk because of you and your precious wife. A wife who doesn't even enjoy having you as a husband!'

Neal's fist shot out and Bishop, entirely unprepared, took the blow

372

on the chin and fell heavily to the floor. 'Don't ever speak to me like that again,' said Neal quietly. 'As you pointed out, I've committed several murders lately. Yours wouldn't cause me any distress whatsoever. I find it quite exhausing trying to control a psychopath. Remember too that if you ever injure my wife again you'd better find somewhere safe to hide because next time I shan't hit you, I shall kill you. Is that clearly understood?'

'What if *she* needs killing one day?'

'You don't give up, do you! If she needs killing I'll do it myself. And another thing, please stop knocking my daughter around.'

'I'll do whatever's needed to control my wife. Perhaps you should have been firmer with her earlier,' he added insolently.

With a final glare, Neal walked out of the gym, past a weeping Louise sitting huddled on the stairs, and back into the house to talk to Dr Hughes.

At 8 a.m. Lisa woke. She wondered why her head hurt and why her arms were outside the duvet. Then, as she tried to sit up, pain shot from her fingertips to her shoulders and she had a sudden vivid picture of the two Rotweillers pinning her to the ground. She started to scream and was still screaming when Neal, closely followed by the doctor, burst into the room.

'It's all right,' he assured her, sitting carefully on the side of the bed and trying to put an arm round her shoulders. 'It's going to be all right.'

'Get away from me!' she sobbed. 'You let him do it. I hate you. Get out of here. Get out!'

'I did not let him do it. Lisa, I ...'

'I don't want him here,' she told the waiting doctor.

'Leave us alone,' instructed Neal, and naturally his order was obeyed.

She lay back exhausted and as the memories flooded back she began to shake. 'Leave me alone!' she implored him. 'I'm in such pain and I keep seeing ... What's happened to Jessica?' she added anxiously. 'Who took her back to Janice? I must go and see her.' And she tried to push the duvet off.

'She's fine. I've been to see Nurse Anthony and Jessica's safe.' That was true, but he didn't add that she'd been hitting her head against the wall in a steady rhythm. 'I'll get the doctor to give you something for the pain,' he added, seeing her wince. 'Thank God they didn't touch your face.'

'What did the doctor say about my hands?' she asked anxiously.

'You'll be scarred but there's no permanent damage to any ligaments. In time you'll regain full use of them.'

'No thanks to Bishop!' she muttered. 'How could you let him do that to me?'

'He acted on his own initiative, knowing full well that I would never have sanctioned such action. His orders were simply to keep you here. The dogs are for people trying to break in, not people trying to leave. I'd never have allowed anything like that to happen to you. You must believe me. Just the thought of it makes me feel sick.'

Lisa sighed. 'You live by a strange set of rules, Neal. Rape and physical abuse are acceptable; savaging by a dog isn't. Perhaps I ought to learn the code and save myself a lot of suffering.'

He wasn't surprised that she sounded bitter but was surprised by the grief that suddenly overwhelmed him. Grief at everything that had happened. 'I didn't mean it to be like this,' he said slowly. 'When we got married I wanted to look after you. To make up for the life you'd had with Toby. I just don't know how we've ended up as we have.'

'Neither do I,' she said softly. 'Somewhere along the way we must have taken the wrong turning.'

'But where?'

'I don't know.'

For a moment they sat in silence then Neal stood up. 'Well, it's probably little comfort now but I promise nothing like this will ever happen again. I'll let Dr Hughes come and make you more comfortable. We'll talk later.'

'Don't leave me alone here with Bishop.' There was panic in her voice.

'I won't. You have my word on that.'

She thought that for once she could believe him.

Chapter Twenty-Nine

It was another three weeks before Lisa plucked up enough courage to leave the safety of the house for even a short walk in the garden with the children. As soon as she set foot outside the door her chest would feel tight and the palms of her hands grow damp with fear. Every sound made her catch her breath, certain it was a Rotweiller lurking nearby. Everyone was very kind but she knew that only time and her own determination would get her better.

Neal stayed at home for two weeks, trying to repair some of the mental damage Bishop had inflicted, but was finally forced back to town by pressure of work. Once he was gone, Lisa found it easier to cope. He'd been very patient but in her mind he was still linked to Bishop and no matter how innocent he'd been she blamed him because he was ultimately responsible for everything Bishop did.

Finally on a misty September morning, she got straight up from breakfast, put on her Burberry and went out along the front drive. Rebekah was back at school and so Lisa walked alone. She assumed someone was watching her from the house but that didn't matter. As long as no one could witness her fear as she approached the wrought iron gates she didn't mind.

When she put her hand on the heavy latch her legs seemed too weak to support her but she forced herself to continue and finally walked slowly out into the country lane that led to the village. The clothes beneath her coat were drenched with sweat but once outside the boundaries of the house she started to feel better. There were no memories here, it was simply a quiet lane where she could wander without unseen eyes monitoring her every move.

She wandered along the grassy verge, relieved to find that the panic-induced weakness had passed. The mist was slowly lifting and she decided that if the sun came out she'd take Jessica into the garden later. Not that Jessica would show any pleasure. She no longer smiled and laughed, she didn't even rock or walk on tiptoe, instead she sat in the corner of the room pulling tufts of hair from her head and chewing on them for comfort, ignoring everything that went on around her. It was Jessica who'd been the most badly damaged by Bishop's cruelty and Lisa wasn't sure that the child would be able to cope when she herself felt strong enough to renew the holding therapy.

Lost in her thoughts she was suddenly aware of a car slowing as it approached her. It was an insignificant silver-blue Volvo but there was no doubt at all that the driver had recognised her and was stopping, though whether as a friend or an enemy she didn't know. Too late she realised the stupidity of straying away from the house.

Renato Bellini had been waiting day after day for an opportunity to see Lisa. He'd been staying at the local hotel under a false name, and when Mike's call had finally come through he could scarcely believe his luck because today was his last day in the area since Luciano was missing him. He also had to meet Neal for discussions concerning the second bullion robbery.

As he drew the car to a halt he noticed that Lisa was standing transfixed on the grass, her eyes huge in a face far thinner and sharper than when he'd last seen her. Hastily he got out of the car and walked round to the passenger side. 'It's all right, Lisa, it's me!'

The fear ebbed away but her relief at seeing him was so intense that a lump in her throat prevented her from speaking.

'How are you?' he asked urgently, glancing round to make sure they were unobserved.

She swallowed hard but the words simply wouldn't come. She'd kept her feelings to herself for so long now that she knew if she actually told him about the pain, the terror and the extent of her injuries, she'd start weeping and not be able to stop. She only shrugged.

Renato was shocked by her appearance. He'd expected to see a change, but she looked terrible and the dark rings under her eyes showed that she was sleeping very badly. Her wedding ring hung loosely on her finger and she fiddled nervously with it.

He stood as close to her as he thought she'd allow. 'Tell me the truth,' he urged. 'How are you feeling?'

She stared at him and her lips moved but no words came out. He realised that she couldn't tell him and unless he did something quickly she might never recover from what had happened to her. 'Listen to me, Lisa. There is talk in London about your husband and the Phillips woman. He is worried about this, because of the knighthood he so badly desires. Make yourself well enough to be shown in town. He is anxious to demonstrate to people that you are still a happily

376

married couple. You must do this soon.'

'I don't want to go to London with him,' she said tonelessly.

'It is your only chance to leave him. Choose a big occasion. A Ball perhaps? Then, early on, you will feel ill and tell him you must leave. This he will have to allow, especially if you talk loudly about your illness. Once you have left you must go to the safe house where I will join you. You understand?'

She understood very well and knew that he was right. Unless she left soon she was never going to get away. 'What about my children?' she whispered.

'I will have the children brought to you.'

'How?'

'It is enough that I say it will be done. I do not wish you to know too much.'

'I can't leave without the children. He'd kill Jessica.'

'You are not helping her living like this. You have to get away, and you must trust me.'

'I don't trust anyone any more,' she said sadly.

'Then you will die.'

Shocked by his brutality she lifted her head and found that his eyes were anguished. She realised he was right and for a third time she must put her trust in a man; only this time if she was wrong it wouldn't matter because she wouldn't be allowed to live long enough to realise her mistake. 'I'll do it,' she agreed softly.

Glancing down the road he saw a silver Renault pulling out from the drive. 'I have to go. Be brave, *cara*. Soon it will be over.'

She was amazed at how quickly he moved. Within seconds both he and the car were gone and as she turned back to the house she saw the Renault drawing out into the lane and realised that Steve hadn't recognised the Italian. In case he was suspicious she raised a bandaged hand in greeting as he passed and he sounded his horn in acknowledgement. She thought that they'd got away with it, but her relief was blunted by the realisation that now she had to act well enough to convince Neal she'd be fit to go to the Leukaemia Research Ball at the Grosvenor House in three weeks time. Hopefully, if he was as anxious as Renato had said to show her off in public, he'd accept her word for it. Even so, it wasn't going to be easy.

'I was wondering if I could come to the Ball next week,' she said casually, two weeks after her brief meeting with Bellini. 'I'm much better and beginning to feel I'd like to get dressed up again.'

'I'd love to take you but what about your arms?'

'I'll get a stunning new dress with long sleeves, and my hands don't

377

look too bad now. I could always get some plastic skin put on them for the one night.'

'There's still the risk of infection.'

'In that case I'll keep my gloves on.'

'Why the sudden urge to rejoin the social whirl?'

'I thought people might be beginning to talk,' she said lightly. Neal flushed. 'Well?'

'People always talk. I've explained that you had an accident, but probably some of them don't believe me.'

'They will once I've shown them the bandages!'

He considered the idea for a time and Lisa tried to look unconcerned as she waited for his verdict. 'I suppose you could do with some fun,' he conceded, but she knew full well that it was only the fact that her appearance was to his advantage that counted. 'I'll have a word with Dr Hughes.'

'Can I order a new dress?'

'I think someone should come here for the fittings. I don't want you wearing yourself out travelling to town all the time.'

'It's a pity Carol went out of business,' commented Lisa, but Neal pretended not to hear.

In the end she decided to make one trip to London and try to find something off the peg from one of the collections. The thought of having to display her arms in their present condition was too humiliating. Neither did she want strangers in the house.

As Mike was about to drive her there, Jessica and Janice came out of the front door. Jessica was wearing a pair of designer jeans with a Dash tracksuit top, and when she paused for a moment she looked absolutely beautiful. Her hair, so like her father's, shone with a blue-black sheen.

'Wait!' said Lisa quickly, watching from the car window as her daughter began descending the steps. Once she moved it became obvious she wasn't normal. Her brief moment of graceful beauty vanished as she lurched awkwardly before jumping down the last two steps and rolling around the gravel path like a tiny toddler. Then she set off across the immaculate front lawn, running on tiptoes with her hands held at eye level in front of her as she watched her fingers making intricate patterns in the air.

Lisa sighed. 'We'd better go.'

'Shame about the kid.' Mike's comment was casual but deeply felt.

'Sometimes I think she's lucky,' said Lisa bitterly. 'I wish I could shut out the world.'

'Self-pity won't get you anywhere.'

He was right but at times like this, when her arms were aching and

378

she was forced to face Jessica's regression, it was difficult not to allow herself the luxury.

Ironically, she found just what she wanted in Romeo Gigli's latest collection: a deceptively simple canary yellow silk sheath dress with a wide black satin belt and suitably long sleeves to hide her bandaged arms. At £3,000 it was expensive, but Neal wouldn't mind. He wanted her to shine for him at the Ball, and in this dress she couldn't fail to.

Feeling drained by her first outing she called in at Pamela Steven's for a massage and facial. They were pleased to see her again, expressing concern over her accident and the resulting tension in her upper back and neck. By the time they'd finished she felt much better and decided to have tea at Brown's before going back to Berkshire.

She'd just started a tiny cream cake when there was a stir of interest in the room and she looked up to see the large figure of Renato in the doorway. He had little Luciano with him, clutching a large Hamley's bag, his eyes shining with excitement.

Neither Renato nor Lisa knew how to react but then the Italian walked slowly to her table and gave a small bow. 'How nice to see you back in town, Mrs Gueras. I trust you're recovered from your accident?'

'Yes, thank you. In fact I've been buying myself a gown for next Thursday's Ball at the Grosvenor House.'

He let out a slow breath. 'I hope you enjoy it. For myself I am unfortunately engaged elsewhere that evening but no doubt I will see your photograph in the papers.'

'You might! What have you got in that bag, Luciano?'

The brown eyes were huge with excitement. 'It is a racing car with the remote control.'

'What have you done to deserve that?'

'Had the English 'flu!' he said indignantly.

She laughed. 'I'm afraid that's all part of visiting England. Still, it must have been worth it to get a remote controlled car!'

'*Si*!' His smile was as open and flashing as his father's. Lisa wanted to put her arms round his slight frame and hug him tightly. She knew that Renato doted on the boy but there was still an air of sadness about him and she sensed that what he needed was a mother. Unable to stop herself, she put out a hand and touched him gently on the cheek. 'I'm glad you're feeling better,' she said with a smile.

Luciano blushed bright red but wriggled with pleasure and glanced up to where his father towered over him, his eyes already straying to a spare table. 'Cannot we eat here, Papa?'

'I'm sorry,' said Lisa quickly. 'I'm just leaving.'

His face fell but it was plain that he was used to handling dis-

379

appointments for he instantly held out his hand. 'Then we will say goodbye!'

She rose, taking hold of the tiny fingers. 'Goodbye, enjoy your toy. Goodbye, Signor Bellini,' she added, and gave a brief nod as she left.

'She's a nice lady,' chattered Luciano, wriggling round on his chair.

'Yes, she is a nice lady.'

'Was my mama as nice as that?'

'Your mama was a very special person,' said Renato evasively and Luciano didn't pursue the matter. He was intelligent enough to realise that his mama quite obviously wasn't such a nice lady and spent the rest of his time daydreaming about his new car, and the tall dark-haired lady with the sad eyes.

'I thought you'd be out quickly!' commented Mike as she climbed into the car. 'Wasn't that Bellini with his lad?'

'Yes.'

'I hope you didn't spend long together. Bishop went in about three minutes after you.'

'I never saw him.'

'That's why he's so good at his job.'

'It doesn't matter. We only exchanged a few words and I talked to the little boy for a few minutes.'

'Good. We don't want anything going wrong again.' Lisa, her arms on the leather armrests, fervently agreed.

On the day of the gala she spent every single moment preparing herself for what was to be the most important evening of her life. First of all she took Rebekah to school, wishing she could explain why she would be leaving her alone with her father but knowing that all she could do was leave her with happy memories and hope that one day they'd have a chance to be together again, although under what circumstances she simply couldn't imagine.

Fortunately Rebekah, unaware of the imminent betrayal, chattered all the way and gave her stepmother a brief kiss and hug before getting out of the car. 'When will you come back?' she asked at the last moment.

'Tomorrow morning.'

'Good. I don't like it when you're not here. See you tomorrow.'

'Tomorrow,' she agreed, and wondered how Rebekah would cope with her deceit.

After that she gave Alexi his bath and played with him until he became grizzly and difficult, when she put him in his cot and settled him comfortably beneath the duvet. 'I'll see you again very soon,' she whispered, but his long lashes were already against his cheeks and he didn't see her leave.

Jessica proved even more difficult. She was in a strange, almost hysterical mood, and either ran away from her mother or clung like a limpet to her legs, screaming wildly when Janice pulled her loose. This time, Lisa ran out. Deep down she wasn't convinced she'd see her daughter again because she knew that it was against Jessica that Neal would make his first move once he realised she'd gone, yet it was for Jessica's sake that she had to break away, and the risk was an unavoidable one.

After that she lay on her bed trying to relax. She practised the breathing techniques she'd learnt for the birth of her children and then went through a series of exercises that were part of her recovery programme from Dr Hughes. Usually they worked well but not today. Today her neck remained obstinately stiff and it felt as though she had a steel rod down the middle of her back.

Her hairdresser arrived mid-afternoon and complained about the condition of Lisa's scalp. 'It's so dry!' he complained, flicking disparagingly at it with his comb.

'It's stress, and you're here to make me feel good not give adverse comments!' she snapped.

Startled by her unaccustomed irritation he quickly set about cutting and shaping her thick hair until he was satisfied with its shape, then he tried to correct the condition of her scalp with a protein cream that usually worked well. Three hours later they were both pleased with the result.

He'd cut her hair shorter at the sides, sweeping it back behind the ears and leaving only small tendrils on the cheeks. The top had been layered and highlighted, while that too was swept off the forehead leaving a lightly feathered fringe. The back was long with all the hair sweeping round towards it to create the impression of a french pleat down the middle.

'You look wonderful!' he enthused, thinking that she certainly looked a great deal better than when he'd arrived. There'd been a lot of rumours about the Gueras marriage; rumours that it was virtually over, her husband already tired of her. However, the dressings on her hands and lower arms showed that the reported accident was no lie, and when Neal Gueras arrived home before the hairdresser had quite finished, he gave his wife such a passionate kiss that André decided the gossips were wrong. He was pleased. He thought her a pleasant woman and wouldn't have envied her if she'd got on the wrong side of her far from pleasant husband.

Once alone with his wife, Neal's expansive good humour lessened slightly but he was still delighted with the way she looked. Just as she began to collect all her makeup he put a lightly restraining hand on her shoulder.

'I'd like to celebrate your return to society,' he commented. She knew immediately what he wanted and wondered if she could let him touch her. He no longer cared for her, he didn't even seem interested in Alexi, all he wanted was to reassure himself of his power over her. But much as she might hate the thought, she knew that today of all days she had to keep him off guard. She moved slowly over to the bed.

'Nice!' he murmured as he turned away and lit a cigarette. 'You've still got a wonderful body.'

'It probably is, especially compared to that of a forty-year-old.'

'And claws as well!'

'I ought to get dressed now,' she said briskly.

Neal gave her a quizzical look. 'When did you learn to become so detached? I remember how you used to cling to me, desperate for some kind of security. Now I can't reach you at all.'

'It's called the survival of the species. This is the only way I can live with you now.'

'I find it quite stimulating! By all means go off and get ready. We're due at Sir George Leonard's for drinks at seven-thirty.'

It took her a long time to do her face to her satisfaction but finally she was ready. She'd managed to look healthy, radiant and natural but was ruefully aware of how much time that look had taken to achieve.

'We must get you a maid!' commented Neal, handing over the grey silk cloak that he'd bought her while she was recovering. 'That way we might get out on time.'

'I prefer to look after myself.'

'You don't want your privacy invaded! I think a maid would be a good idea.'

Lisa enjoyed knowing that what he thought didn't matter because she would never have to return to the house again.

Sir George's London home was big and draughty. His wife, a small, washed-out woman in an over-frilled evening gown, spent all her time apologising for the state of the rooms while her husband drank glass after glass of whisky and kept calling Neal 'my good friend here', which Lisa took to mean that the unfortunate man owed her husband money and hoped he wasn't going to have his debt called in.

When introduced to Lisa, his tired eyes flickered with intelligence and he furrowed his brow in thought. 'Got it! You're Simon's girl, aren't you?'

'Yes.'

'Placed you now! My word, you certainly got what you wanted, Neal, my old friend.'

'I usually do,' said Neal pleasantly.

'What happened to your father, my dear?'

'He shot himself.'

'Don't believe it! Not the sort of thing he'd have done at all.'

'Well, someone shot him.' Neal's voice was cold and Sir George's eyes shifted to his guest.

'Very good, someone shot him! My word, yes!'

'What's funny about that?' demanded Lisa, unable to keep silent in spite of the fact that tonight nothing must ruffle their apparent domestic bliss.

'Sorry, my dear. Can't think why we're talking about Simon in the first place. A born loser. I blame his wife.'

'Wives have a lot to answer for.' Neal's smile was back in place and he put an affectionate arm round Lisa. She managed to smile back at him. After all, that was why she was there. An hour later the four of them moved on to the Ball.

After being in the country for so long, Lisa found the packed ballroom overpowering. Everyone seemed to be talking too loudly, the laughter either shrill and forced or deep and jarring. She saw that during her absence there had been several changes in partners. Older wives had vanished to be replaced by blonde-haired look-alikes with over developed busts and an apparent lack of material to cover them, while some of the wealthy older women were proudly holding on to the arm of their latest toy boy. Britt Ekland and Joan Collins had a lot to answer for, thought Lisa, seeing the desperation behind the older women's smiles as they gripped their young men over-tightly until their knuckles showed white while they pretended not to notice how their companions' eyes strayed again and again to the nubile blondes they couldn't yet afford.

People were constantly coming across to Neal and Lisa, welcoming her back to London. They glanced discreetly at her lightly bandaged hands, took in the obvious bulges beneath the sleeves of her dress, and then went away disappointed because obviously the tale of the accident was true and it was plain to them all that the Gueras marriage was still strong. Indeed, Neal seemed reluctant to relinquish his hold on his wife for even a second. He was constantly touching her with light gestures of affection, smiling as though only in her comapny could he truly be happy.

Lisa thought it a chillingly effective performance. Even she couldn't tell the difference between the way he was looking at her tonight and the way he'd looked at her when they'd been courting. That was frightening. If anything went wrong tonight, and confident as Bellini had sounded it was obvious that there were plenty of things that could go wrong, then Neal might settle for his one heir and have her murdered. No one, after seeing him here with her tonight, would have the slightest suspicion. All they'd remember was his devotion, and no doubt they'd feel even more sorry for him when he played the grieving widower for what he considered the necessary length of time.

During the meal he glanced continually up the table to where she sat between two immensely boring stockbrokers, and each time their eyes met he smiled encouragingly, as though he knew that like him she couldn't wait until they were together again.

When it was time for the dancing Neal danced only with Lisa, whispering softly in her ear as they moved gracefully round the floor, his hands firm and possessive on her body as his eyes caressed her.

It was the very skill of his performance that gave Lisa her opportunity to escape. Terrified by what he was doing, overwhelmed by the duplicity that lay behind it all and physically weakened by her accident, she finally succumbed to a genuine fit of panic as she found herself visualising her own death, probably at Bishop's hands, and suddenly she was gasping for air as all the blood drained from her face.

Neal immediately found her a chair and pushed the few over-bold photographers to one side to avoid pictures. There were beads of perspiration on his wife's forehead and her skin felt cold and clammy to his touch. He assumed he'd overtaxed her before she was fit, and having established their happiness in front of over a hundred guests didn't mind letting her return early to the Chelsea flat.

He'd have liked to go himself but, with a speech to make before the raffle was drawn, had to turn to the on-duty chauffeur of the evening to take her back. Naturally, given Bellini's careful planning, this was Mike.

As she stood shaking on the steps of the hotel, Lisa tried to draw in deep breaths of the fresh air, shuddering all the time and quite unable to control her trembling. 'I'll be back with you as soon as possible,' promised Neal. There was no trace of suspicion on his face because she was so obviously unwell. In any case, he would be putting her in one of his own cars and her own bodyguard would take her back to the apartment. All that worried him was that if he'd succeeded in making her pregnant recently, this outing might cause her to miscarry.

Lisa nodded, her teeth chattering as her terror increased. She didn't know what she'd do if it wasn't Mike at the wheel of the Rover, and when she finally saw him her mouth went dry. She knew now that it was all on, and if she failed then death would undoubtedly be a welcome release.

'Go straight to bed,' instructed Neal, bending down to the window. She nodded nervously. 'Hurry back to the flat,' he told Mike. 'No stopping for anything except red lights!'

'Understood.' As usual Mike's face was cheerful but alert. Neal had the utmost confidence in him and went back to the ballroom as content as possible under the circumstances.

After they'd been driving for a few minutes, Lisa tapped on the glass partition.

Mike pushed it back. 'You okay?'

'No, I . . . Mike, I'd like to walk for a few minutes. I need to clear my head.'

'You want to walk?'

'Yes.'

'I'd better stick close, make sure you're not accosted.'

'I'd rather you didn't. I'll just go round the block and then come back to the car.'

As they looked at each other, Lisa realised what she was asking of Mike. He was the man who'd been entrusted with taking her back home, and under no circumstances should he let her go for a walk on her own. She wondered how Renato could have been so stupid as to overlook the fact that if Mike did as she asked he was signing his own death warrant, and could have cried with frustration.

'Seems like a good idea,' he said casually as he got out to open her door.

For a second Lisa actually hesitated. She didn't know if she could make herself walk away from him, knowing what the result would be. 'Go on,' he murmured. 'Hurry!'

'Mike, I . . .'

'They know how to cherish princesses in Italy!' he said with a smile.

Lisa bit on her lip to stop the tears and lifted her head to look at him one last time. 'Perhaps you'll come out to join me. I expect English chauffeurs are highly fashionable.'

'Perhaps I will at that.'

They both knew that he wouldn't and as she turned away from him, her heels sounding sharply on the pavement, Mike got back into the car and looked resolutely in the other direction. It was one thing to help her go, but quite another actually to watch her walk out of his life forever. That was too much even for him.

* * *

She fumbled to get the key out of her satin evening bag where it had lain as heavy as lead all the evening. She felt a surge of relief when it fitted the lock and quickly slipped into the tiny terraced house, only to stand fighting for breath in the cramped hall.

It had been a long, nerve-racking walk. Time and time again she'd been certain that there were footsteps following her, and whenever a car slowed she'd had to fight down a desire to run, forcing herself to continue at a brisk but not ridiculous pace.

The house was almost bare of furniture and totally silent. On a small, hand-made shelf in the hall stood a modern telephone, and when she looked in the tiny front room she saw an old, badly scratched wooden table and two incongruously modern kitchen chairs. In the kitchen itself there was nothing except a kettle, a teapot and an opened box of tea bags. Several used bags were lying in the old sink, causing ugly brown stains, and there was mildew round the plughole.

A desolate, unused house, frightening in its impersonality. There was no hint of Renato Bellini here. No reminder that he would soon be bringing her the children. No indication that he'd ever been there. It could all so easily be a trap, she thought in panic, but caught back a sob. This was no moment to become hysterical. If she'd made a mistake she'd know soon enough. She picked up the phone as instructed, but nothing happened. After a few minutes she got the single, high-pitched note of a phone left off the hook. Slamming the receiver back she realised that Renato hadn't given her any number to call and suddenly she was convinced that the entire venture *was* a trap, set by either Bishop or Neal himself, and that Bellini had simply been helping them. Realising how stupid she'd been she suddenly had to rush to the bathroom where she brought back her entire dinner.

As she came down from the antique bathroom the telephone started to ring. She remained frozen on the stairs, unable to move even though she knew that the caller couldn't see her, and her heart beat sounded louder in her ears than the ringing itself.

At last it stopped but she still couldn't move as her mind raced round and round, trying to imagine who could have been at the other end of the line. If it was Renato checking to make sure she was safe then he'd now be worrying. But if it had been Neal, already aware of the address, then hopefully she'd diverted his attention elsewhere. When she'd finally convinced herself that it was some random caller who'd misdialled a digit she decided to make a cup of tea, but as she started to run the water, which came out a dingy yellow, the ringing began again.

This time she stood by the sink with her hands over her ears and waited for it to stop, her stomach tightening in apprehension when it continued far longer than before. Ridiculously it also sounded more aggressive, as though the caller was losing patience, and the fact that this could only be the product of her imagination didn't affect her conviction that it was Neal.

When she was drinking the bitter, black tea the bell rang yet again and her nerve broke. Sobbing aloud this time, she retreated to a small cupboard beneath the stairs, pulled the door as near closed as she could and huddled in the darkness, waiting for whoever it was finally to come to the house in person.

At the exact moment that she was retreating into the cupboard, Neal Gueras came smiling out of the Grosvenor House Hotel and walked briskly to his waiting car. Mike was already standing with the passenger door open, his face solemn. 'Not coming down with this 'flu, Mike?' he queried pleasantly, looking forward to a night in the flat with his wife.

'I've lost her,' muttered Mike, keeping his eyes down.

Neal stopped half-way in to the car. 'What the hell do you mean, you've lost her?'

'She felt ill and needed air. I stopped the car to let her out and when I next looked she'd vanished.'

'Into thin air? You can do better than that! What the bloody hell were you thinking of, letting her out of the car? If she needed air you should have opened all the windows. And if she was so bad she had to get out of the car, you should have got out too.'

'I'm sorry, I never thought . . .'

'Oh yes you did,' said Neal slowly. 'You thought about it very carefully and decided to let her go, isn't that right?'

Mike raised his eyes to his employer and they were totally innocent. 'Why should I "let her go" as you put it? She wasn't a prisoner, she was your wife. It never crossed my mind that she might be going to run off. Why should it? I thought you were both . . .'

'Get me back to the flat,' snarled Neal as he brushed the young man to one side. Mike obeyed, trying to work out if he had any chance at all of saving himself before Neal could move against him. When the car finally drew to a halt his employer hurried out, gesturing for Mike to follow. He started to obey and then as Neal turned his back on him, spun the wheel hard to the right, did a U-turn in the middle of the road and with a dramatic screaming of tyres was away, heading for the centre of London where he could ditch the car and try to hide among the unquestioning people who lived rough in the capital every night. Beneath a pile of newspapers one person looked very much like another, and if he could get through the next couple of days then it

387

might be safe for him to contact Bellini. At least he was going to try.

After two hours, Lisa began to think it was all a nightmare. For the past hour the phone had remained silent. A circular had been pushed through the letterbox but apart from that everything was quiet. Even so, she didn't dare emerge from her hiding place and as she cowered there waiting for some unknown horror she wondered if this was how Jessica felt all the time. If she did, it wasn't surprising that she hid in corners and kept her head averted. Lisa too felt safer shut away.

When her small, diamond-encrusted Patek Philippe watch showed 4 a.m. she heard the sound she'd been expecting, a key turning slowly in the front door. The hinges were well oiled, making it impossible to hear the door itself open, and only the gentle click of the latch told her that someone was now in the house with her.

She moved further back until she was touching the wall, trying to make her breathing shallow and silent. Until she actually heard Renato's voice she wasn't going to move. It was still possible that he and Neal were together and she'd finish up being murdered right here.

'Lisa?' Renato's voice was deep but tentative. 'Are you there? I tried to ring but the phone must have been out of order.'

She longed to move, wanting desperately to believe in him, but terror locked her limbs and her brain felt numb. Suddenly certain that he was the enemy as well, she gave a moan of fear, quickly stifled by her hand, but it was enough for the Italian. He spun round on his heel and dived for the cupboard, convinced that she was injured or being held against her will. As he flung the door open and stood with a gun held firmly in both hands, ready to shoot anyone who was harming her, she looked up, saw the weapon and knew that she'd been right. He was there to kill her. She began to scream.

Quickly he reached inside the cupboard and pulled her out, ignoring her cries as he checked with hands and eyes for recent injuries. Then, finding none, he simply wrapped his arms round her and held her closely against him, realising what a shock the sight of his gun must have been and also aware that the weeks of strain had finally caught up with her.

Lisa wasn't really aware of what was happening. All she knew was that he hadn't fired his gun and that she was at last being held by someone who seemed to understand that what she needed was a refuge. Simple, human contact unconnected with sexual feelings, so that she could relax and let herself cry until the tears finally dried up and she was sniffing and hiccuping in a most unattractive manner but feeling such an incredible release of tension that the dull headache that had plagued her for weeks was finally banished.

When the worst was over, Renato led her into the kitchen and produced a fold-down chair from the broom cupboard. He sat Lisa on this before making two mugs of strong, sweet coffee. She wrapped her fingers round the large, stained mug feeling tired but relaxed. She also felt rather foolish. 'I thought you were going to kill me,' she admitted at last. 'I'd been here so long with that wretched phone ringing and ringing and I'd finally convinced myself it was all some complicated plot that you and Neal had rigged up between you, so when I saw a gun pointed straight at me I just lost control!'

'I was ringing you! I wanted to be sure you were safely here.'

'I hoped it was you but I knew that if it wasn't and I picked up the phone, I'd have given myself away to Neal.'

'You were sensible,' he agreed. 'Stupidly I'd forgotten to give you my private number. Your gown is ruined,' he added, noticing a tear in the skirt and dirty marks down the sides and round the hem.

'That doesn't matter. I couldn't wear it again.'

'How are your arms?'

'Better than they were.'

'Still bandaged?'

'Not all the time, only for this evening. I didn't want my dress rubbing against the scabs.'

'We have to wait a while now until your children join us. There is nothing to fear, this house is unknown to your husband.'

'Are you sure?'

Renato wished he could do something to help her, to demonstrate that she had nothing to fear from him, but she was as jumpy and on edge as if he were keeping her a prisoner. His first instinct was to hold her again but wisely he kept his distance, talking instead of trivial things while her eyes continually moved to her watch as she waited for the children.

'Tell me about the dogs,' he said at last.

'The dogs?'

'Yes. Who set them on you? What were you doing when it happened?'

'I don't want to talk about any of that,' she said firmly.

'If you do not it will grow bigger and bigger in your mind until even a tiny terrier will be enough to frighten you.'

'I don't know if I can.'

'We have plenty of time,' he assured her. 'It does not matter how long you take.'

Very slowly she told him what had happened, and only the tightening of his lips and involuntary gestures of disgust gave any indication of the overwhelming rage he was experiencing.

When she'd finished she felt exhausted. 'What happens when the

389

children get here?' she asked quietly.

'We move to Giovanni Muti's house. It is well protected, with security cameras and guards in the grounds. You will all be safe there.' He didn't mention the dogs patrolling the grounds.

'But once Neal knows I'm gone, he isn't going to let you keep me away from him.'

'I have made my long-term plans, you must not worry about such things. It will all work out well, but as you rightly say your husband will make a great fuss and this will have to be dealt with before I can take you back to Italy with me. All of which will be accomplished in the fullness of time.'

'Back to Italy with you?'

His sudden smile was exactly like Luciano's when he showed Lisa his remote controlled car. 'But yes, we will spend the rest of our lives together, will we not?'

She wished it could be that easy but was aware of the fact that he didn't really know very much about her. He was attracted to her and liked her, but how long would that last after he'd taken her to his bed? One look at him was enough to confirm the stories she'd heard. He had the easy assurance of a man who'd known a lot of women, and by comparison with them she'd be a total disaster.

'I don't think that's a very good idea,' she said regretfully.

'I think it's an excellent idea; Luciano thinks so too.'

'Don't bring him into it, that isn't playing fair.'

He frowned. 'What do you mean? Surely you want to be my wife? I have not imagined the feelings that there are between us? You find me attractive and I find you attractive, yes?'

'Yes, I suppose so, but ...'

'I also admire you. You are a woman of spirit and a caring and compassionate mother. Together we will continue to heal Jessica, build up my little Luciano's confidence and raise our own children. All this part of your life will be as though it never existed. We will be happy together.'

'I'd disappoint you. I told you before ...'

'What?'

She heard the sound of a car outside, quickly followed by the unmistakable noise of Jessica yelling. Jumping off the chair, Lisa ran to the front door, only to find Renato there before her, his hand on the catch. 'I will go first. We have to be sure.'

'I want to see my children. Let me out!'

He grabbed her wrist then closed his eyes as she cried out in agony, doubling up and moving away from him as her injuries sent pain shooting up her arm. There was no time for Renato to apologise

390

because immediately there was a knocking on the door and he slid it open on the chain, saw Janice standing there with Alexi in her arms and a demented Jessica at her side, and swiftly let them in.

Jessica made a mad dash for the stairs and then rushed up them, banging her shoes on the uncarpeted steps and giggling at the noise echoing round the house. Alexi, his eyes alert but perfectly placid, gazed around him silently, but Lisa was still recovering from the pain in her wrist and couldn't welcome either of them properly.

'The children are safe!' exclaimed the nurse, putting her arms round Lisa. She nodded, trying to stand up as the pain slowly diminished.

'Were there any problems?' she asked anxiously.

'None at all. Bishop got called away and as soon as he'd gone, one of Mr Bellini's young men arrived. We piled the children and their clothes into the car and drove away.'

'When was all this arranged?'

'Several days ago. Mr Bellini thought it better that you didn't know.'

Still appalled by what he'd done, the tall Italian shrugged apologetically. 'It was safest. Suppose you'd been taken and questioned about the children? This way you had nothing to tell.'

'It's all right, you did marvellously. Where's Jessica gone?'

'Upstairs, clumping around enjoying all the noise. I'm sorry about your wrist, I forgot and ...'

'It doesn't matter! You've brought the children to me, and I'll never be able to thank you enough for that.'

'There is one thing,' said the nurse slowly. Renato and Lisa looked anxiously at her. 'That nice young driver, Mike, he's disappeared.'

The Italian muttered a quick prayer. 'We must hurry to Giovanni's house,' he said urgently. 'Come, we go out the back way. I have a Jaguar waiting there. Lisa, get Jessica and bring her with you. Janice and I will manage everything else.'

'It's my fault,' said Lisa hysterically. 'I've probably killed him. If I hadn't ...'

'He volunteered for the job,' snapped Renato, determined to stop her before she lost control. 'He knew the risk but wanted to do it. Even if he is dead, you are not to blame. Now get your daughter, and hurry!'

'Why would he take such a risk?' demanded Lisa as she ran up the stairs, but Renato didn't answer her. He knew only too well why Mike had done it and thought that Lisa would come to understand in her own time, but now wasn't the moment to burden her with such knowledge.

Chapter Thirty

They sped through London at eight in the morning. Twice Renato jumped the traffic lights to shake off any possible tail. Lisa had never been driven so fast before and yet she wasn't worried. Renato Bellini handled cars like he handled women, very efficiently indeed. By eight-thirty they were safely in the grounds of Giovanni Muti's mansion, and after that Lisa stumbled through a confused hour of settling the children and Janice while trying to listen to what the two men were discussing, although they had an irritating habit of lapsing into Italian when they didn't want her to understand them. Finally Eleanor took her quietly upstairs into a lovely lilac and white bedroom with adjoining bathroom.

'This is yours for as long as you wish to stay,' she said with a smile. 'Now I will send a maid to help you undress and then you must sleep. You are totally exhausted.'

'I don't have any clothes with me!'

'Signor Bellini has already thought of that. You will find day clothes in the wardrobe, and nightgowns and robes in the case beside the bed. Rest well, signora.'

The maid, who didn't speak a word of English, helped Lisa out of her filthy ballgown and into the bath she'd prepared for her. Then, as Lisa used the enormous box of Chanel talcum, she brought her a cream silk nightgown with capped sleeves. At last, with a sigh of relief, Lisa slipped beneath the goose-feather duvet and closed her eyes.

She'd expected to fall asleep immediately but her mind continued on its own mad whirl. She kept picturing Mike, wondering where he was and if he would manage to stay alive long enough to join them again. Annoyed at her wakefulness she tossed and turned, then jumped as her bedroom door opened. She sat up quickly as Renato came slowly into the room. 'Not asleep?'

'No, I . . .'

He saw the look of anxiety in her eyes and wondered just what kind of a husband Neal Gueras had been to reduce a woman of such obvious spirit as Lisa to a nervous wreck at the sight of a man in her bedroom. Surely she didn't believe he'd attempt to seduce her in her present condition? he thought, but from the look in her eyes she did. He smiled reassuringly. 'I bring you a pill. It will help to calm your mind and then sleep will come quickly, yes?'

'I hope so!'

'You are afraid of me.' He made the statement casually as he handed her the pill and a glass of water.

'Not exactly.'

'You look afraid of me.'

'I didn't mean to.'

'Listen to me.' He sat down on the side of the bed, keeping his voice very calm. 'I love you but I would never force myself upon any woman. Love is special. It is a gift too precious to abuse, and if you love me then eventually you will want us to make love together. It will be your decision, I promise you, so no more anxious looks every time I appear, yes?'

She gave a reluctant smile. 'I'm sorry, you must think me . . .' with a yawn, she lost track of what she'd been saying. 'I shan't ask you to make love to me,' she muttered, her lids already closing as she lay back on the pile of pillows.

'Why not?'

'Because then you'd know.'

'Know what?' He bent down to catch her murmured answer. She frowned, drifting away to sleep. 'Know what?' he repeated.

'That I'm frigid,' she sighed, and then her breathing became regular, her lashes lay motionless against her cheeks and he knew she was finally asleep. Her answer made him smile. If ever he'd seen a woman who was made for love it was Lisa and his judgement in such matters was never wrong. She'd lost confidence in herself but that didn't matter. Once she was willing to take him as her lover her fears would quickly be removed, but it was another mark against her husband.

While Lisa slept away the next twenty-four hours, Janice coped with Alexi and Renato himself sat with Jessica, letting her examine her room for as long as she needed, not even interfering when she wrenched down a shelf of books. Because he neither looked directly at her nor interfered with what she did, Jessica began to cast covert glances in his direction, intrigued by someone who ignored her presence so completely, and in consequence she settled relatively quickly.

At tea-time, when Lisa still hadn't woken, Renato went into town, collected Luciano from his music lesson and took him straight back to the new house. He didn't even stop to pick up any of his son's clothes or toys, knowing full well that his own apartment was bound to be watched. Fortunately, Luciano didn't mind. It was all a great adventure to him and he was looking forward to seeing Lisa again.

'Any word from Mike?' asked Renato when he arrived back at the Muti's.

'Not yet.'

'I wonder where he is?' mused the Italian.

Neal Gueras was wondering exactly the same thing.

'Find him!' shouted Neal. 'I don't care how long it takes or how many men are needed. Just find him and bring him here. He must know where she's gone.'

'Not necessarily,' said Bishop. 'He only let her go, he didn't have to have access to any further information.'

'We're not talking about a computer, we're talking about a human being. He was obviously besotted with my wife and would never have let her walk off into the night. He knew where she was going and I want to know as well. Yes?' he added as Steve came reluctantly into the Chelsea flat.

'I've had a call from Louise, sir.'

'Do you seriously think I'm interested in talking to my daughter at a time like this?'

'The children are gone.'

Every man in the room fell silent and only Bishop had the courage to look at Neal's face which went purple with fury while the veins in his temples bulged. 'Which children?' he barked.

'Jessica and ...'

'Yes?'

'Your son.'

'She's taken Alexi? How the hell did she manage that?'

'A black cab arrived at the house just after Bishop left on that wild goose chase. Louise didn't realise who'd gone from the house until much later. She ...'

'I'm not interested in what Louise thought, she's totally brainless. It's a pity you rushed off on that call, Bishop. If you'd checked with me first my son might still be at home.'

'If I'd checked every emergency call with you over the past two years we'd be a severely depleted organisation,' retorted Bishop, inwardly smiling at the way his employer had been out-manoeuvred.

'Find that damned chauffeur!' instructed Neal, and then slammed

394

off into the bedroom. They glanced at one another.

'Something wrong?' enquired Bishop.

'He's bound to be armed,' commented Steve.

'So?'

'We can't have a shoot-out in the middle of London. People might notice!'

'If any of you see him, just keep your distance and send for reinforcements. We should be able to take him quietly if there are enough of us. Now move!'

Murmuring and grumbling, they went out of the door. All of them liked Mike and resented the job they had to do. Once they'd gone, Bishop checked the silencer was on his gun, slipped out of the kitchen window and down the fire escape. Mike had been his choice for the organisation, and they went back a long way together. He had no intention of letting Neal find out the full extent of Mike's betrayal and the only way of stopping that from happening was to get to him before anyone else. Knowing him as well as Bishop did, he thought it should be relatively easy.

At 11 p.m. that night, Mike settled down on a bench near Marble Arch and covered himself with old newspapers. He'd spent the day dodging from doss houses to railway sidings, sighting operatives from the organisation several times but always managing to keep one move ahead of them. After tonight he thought he'd ring the number Bellini had given him. It was too early to be sure, but providing he got through this second night he would allow himself to consider the possibility of escape.

It never took him long to fall asleep and within ten minutes he was drifting pleasantly when he felt the round, hard end of a gun in his side and as he slowly sat up, Bishop removed the sheet of paper covering his face. 'Comfortable?' he asked politely.

'Very,' responded Mike. He noted the silencer and realised that Bishop was anxious to protect himself from any awkward questions should Mike reveal all he knew. He would therefore protect Mike from what would undoubtedly have been a highly painful and unpleasant final few hours on earth.

'You've been a bit stupid,' Bishop continued, his face very white in the light from a nearby lamp.

'A man's gotta do what a man's gotta do!'

'Why?' Bishop was genuinely puzzled.

'I didn't like the way she was treated.'

'You mean you threw it all away because of *her*? Not for money; not because you thought P2 offered the best prospect, but just because of one bloody woman?'

'I know, amazing isn't it! And I used to think girls were wet. Mind you, I was only ten at the time!'

'I wish to God he'd never set eyes on the stupid woman!' muttered Bishop. 'She's brought nothing but disaster to us all.'

'Me more than you, don't you think?'

Bishop's eyes narrowed. 'Yes, you more than me.'

'I take it I'm not to be questioned?'

For a moment a flicker of regret crossed Bishop's face. 'No, I wish you could be. You deserve it, playing the white knight of all things – I've no patience with that. Money, power ... I could have understood it then, but not this. Regrettably I recommended you, and the less they know about your misplaced gallantry the better for my reputation. So, as you correctly surmised, you won't be questioned.'

'You'll never take it all over,' cautioned Mike.

'Why not?'

'Because the Italian won't rest until there's nothing left to run.'

'Did he tell you that?'

'He didn't have to.'

'I see, you're psychic as well as soft in the head! Any last messages for anyone?'

'No.'

'Anyone you want told?'

'My mother ought to know.'

'Right. A case of "no flowers by request" I think, don't you?'

Mike gave a slight smile. 'Definitely no flowers by request.'

'That's it then. Remember who brought this about, won't you?'

And he did remember. The very last thing he pictured was the way Lisa Gueras had smiled at him the first time they met, and because Bishop was quick and efficient there was very little pain. Dying, reflected Bishop as he walked swiftly away, could be far easier than being born. Providing, of course, that you had someone like him to speed you on your way.

For three days, Lisa did little but eat and sleep, scarcely leaving her room even to see the children, and Renato removed the telephone from beside her bed once he realised how much she dreaded hearing it ring. Eventually, as they'd known he must, Neal located her.

His first move was to use Rebekah. Lisa went to the phone when Eleanor told her there was a little girl crying and asking for her. At the sound of her stepmother's voice, Rebekah burst into sobs, pleading with her to come home because she was so lonely.

'I can't,' explained Lisa, wishing her hands would stop trembling. 'I don't want to live with your father any more.'

396

'No one cares about me any more,' cried Rebekah. 'Daddy just tells me not to be a baby and that nasty Bishop keeps pulling my hair. He says I'm the plainest girl he's ever set eyes on and I ought to be put down. I'm not a dog! He can't make Daddy have me put down, can he?'

'He's just trying to upset you. Of course he can't make him do any such thing. Besides, your father loves you,' she added weakly.

'It isn't nice! I hate it here. Please come back, Lisa. Daddy promises he'll be nicer if you do.'

'I can't.' She could barely speak for the tears.

'When will I see you again? I don't even know where you are.'

'Your father knows, he gave you the telephone number. Ask him to let you come and see me.'

'I'm not allowed to come to you, but you can come here. Will you, Lisa? Just for a few hours?'

'I'm sorry, I can't,' she whispered, and replaced the receiver to shut out Rebekah's sobs. How could she tell the already terrified child that if she went back she would be murdered? Now Rebekah was even more upset, certain that all Lisa's affection had been false, and was once again alone in the large, uncaring household. Despite her tears, Lisa was angry. Angry with Neal for using his daughter and angry with Bishop and Louise for upsetting Rebekah with their teasing.

'You should not have let her take the call!' shouted an enraged Renato when he returned to find Lisa crying in her room, and heard about Rebekah.

'We thought she'd like to know the little girl was all right,' explained Eleanor.

'Apparently she wasn't!' he shouted. Luciano's eyes were like saucers, he'd never heard his father so angry before.

'It was a mistake,' she admitted.

'What is worse, it is only the beginning,' muttered Renato, taking the stairs two at a time and knocking on Lisa's door.

'Go away!' she called irritably. 'Just leave me alone.'

'Let me in. We have to talk.'

'No we don't! I don't want to talk to anyone.'

He was tempted to kick the door open, and only the memory of the violence in Lisa's past prevented him. 'I know you are feeling bad. Please, let me in so that we can talk about it. I want to help you.'

In the distance she could hear Jessica screaming. Reluctantly she got up, unlocked her door and glanced at Renato. 'I suppose you'd better come in. I'm afraid I haven't got dressed today. Every day I tell myself that I must make the effort, but when I try to get up I'm so afraid of what the day might bring that I retreat under the duvet again. It's pathetic!'

'I'm sorry about Rebekah,' he said, gently taking her left hand in his. 'But you must realise that however upset she was, your husband was behind it. He knows that she matters to you and is willing to use her as a weapon now that he no longer has Jessica.'

'He thought I'd go back.'

'No, he isn't that stupid. He thought it would cause you great distress, and it did.'

'I wish I could pull myself together,' she said ruefully.

'You have been under a period of great strain. This depression is to be expected.'

'Is it? How's Jessica coping?' she added.

'She is over-active and vocal! This is a difficult time for her too. When I was with her yesterday a dog barked in the grounds and she hid beneath the table.'

Lisa looked down at her hands. The scars were livid red marks, darker in colour where the incisors had sunk deep into the flesh, but the pain had eased. 'I'd probably have done the same thing!'

'Are you afraid that Neal will come here and take you back?' Renato asked, looking out into the grounds where blue-jacketed bodyguards patrolled the perimeter.

'Not really; it's as though I'm so used to being afraid that I can't switch off. I know this house is well protected and he isn't going to come in with a load of gunmen shooting everyone in sight just to get me back, so logically, no, I don't fear him coming. I'm just perpetually afraid.'

'Would you come down to dinner tonight? It will be pleasant to see you again and Luciano is allowed to eat with us because today is his saint's day, a second birthday in our country. He wants to eat with us because he thinks you will be there.'

'Now *you're* using a child to manipulate me.'

He shrugged his vast shoulders. 'Possibly, but for your own good!'

'I dislike being manipulated.' Her voice was tight.

'Would it help if I told you that I myself want to see you at dinner? That I take pleasure in your company, and miss you when you stay in your room?'

'If it's true then it's a better reason for coming down.'

'It is true. You must know that.'

She did, but she didn't want to think about it. Every time she saw Renato and felt herself drawn towards him she fought against her own emotions, knowing that if she allowed herself to become involved with him and then it went wrong she wouldn't be strong

398

enough to survive her third mistake. 'All right,' she conceded. 'I'll come down to dinner.'

He smiled at her, his expression so open and warm that for an instant she responded and smiled back, but almost immediately turned away, reminding herself of how she'd trusted Neal and what a disaster that had been. There were similarities between the Italian and her husband which confused her.

During the afternoon she washed her hair and was disconcerted to discover it was in need of a cut. The heavy layers at the back took ages to dry by hand. Then, when she put on one of the fitted Italian dresses Renato had bought for her, it hung loosely round her hips and bust, and she realised that she'd lost far too much weight. At the sound of the dinner bell she smoothed her dress nervously with her hands and wished that she looked better. She certainly wouldn't have met with Neal's approval tonight she reflected, hoping Renato wouldn't be too disappointed.

She needn't have worried. His delight at having her downstairs with them all was touching and he constantly checked that she felt all right, or that the wine was dry enough, or that Luciano wasn't exhausting her with his chatter.

It was Luciano who got her through the meal. From time to time she suffered surges of panic that made her want to dash from the room and out into the fresh air where breathing might be easier. She would break into a fine sweat, her heart racing until she could feel it in her throat. Only by fixing her attention on the chattering child could she force herself through the attacks, then as they gradually ebbed away she picked at her food, although swallowing it was difficult.

When Luciano finally went to bed at ten, Lisa took the opportunity to escape. She reached her room just as Renato came out of his son's and he raised his eyebrows. 'Bed so soon?'

'I'm tired.'

'Of course. How did you feel downstairs?'

'Not too bad.'

'No?'

'Why can't people believe what I say!'

'I do believe you. I also think that you are being brave. You did well tonight but inside the fear has not gone and this makes it difficult for you, does it not?'

'Since when were you a psychiatrist?'

'When a man is in love he does not need to be a psychiatrist to know how his woman feels. It is instinctive.'

'If you're so damned clever perhaps you'd like to tell me when I'm

399

going to feel better!' she shouted, her fingers tightening on the door handle.

He moved nearer to her. 'Tell me about it,' he suggested gently. 'Explain to me your fear.'

'I've already told you! It isn't a specific fear, it's just one huge general panic. Please tell your son I thoroughly enjoyed his saint's day feast. Now, goodnight.'

Renato put a foot in the door. He was beginning to realise that unless he forced the issue she was going to stay trapped with her terror until Neal finally made a move, by which time she would be unable to cope. He had to help her now so that they could carry out the final stage of his plan against the Gueras organisation.

'Get your foot away!' The panic was obvious.

He did as she asked but walked into her room behind her. 'I didn't mean that as an invitation. Please leave, Renato.'

Slowly he put his hands on her shoulders, his fingers moving gently over her collar bone, sharp beneath the silk dress. 'It is time for you to trust me,' he murmured, lowering his head and letting his mouth brush against the top of her hair. 'How can we ever learn to know one another while you shut me out all the time?'

'There's nothing for me to tell you. I'm sure you know everything that I do about my husband. Isn't that enough reason for me to be afraid?'

'Afraid of him? Yes! Of me also? I think not. I will never hurt you. What has happened to you in the past is over, and I will make up for it, but I need to know more about your fear. Is it that you no longer wish to be loved?'

'Loved? I've no idea what it's like to be loved. I'm an expert on being taken, with or without consent. I also know what men will do in the name of love, like raping you on the study floor with all the servants listening down the hall, or bringing in friends to liven you up, like Toby did. Then they lie, and cheat with other women, threaten small children and finally, when they've tried everything they can think of to ruin your life, they turn round and tell you you're frigid and that no other man would want you, implying you're lucky to have a husband of any sort. That's what happens in the name of love. And do you know what? In the end you believe it all.

'When I first met you I used to try and fantasise about what you'd be like as a lover. I thought you'd be different and tried to pretend my husband was you. Don't you think that's sick? And of course it didn't work, because I was so useless I ended up being grateful it wasn't you. Now, when you're really here, wanting me, I'm terrified that it's going to be like Neal said.'

'What did he say?'

'That you'd send me back to him when you found out what a fraud I was. He said you were used to real women and wouldn't have any time for someone like me. He's probably right. But if I fail with you there's nothing left, and so I'd rather not try.'

'It isn't a competition, *cara!* These other women your husband spoke of, they were all different and with them it was pleasant, but I do not compare. Besides, with you it is not the same because I love you, and one day I hope to make you my wife. We have all the time in the world to become used to one another. It is not an exam, there is no pass mark! All that I want for now is to hold you. Why should we rush through the enjoyable early stages of love?'

Lisa didn't answer. She turned away and half-stumbled so that he had to put out a hand to catch her. Immediately he drew her to him, holding her against his body, his hands gentle against her back.

She felt them moving rhythmically over her, one hand straying to the nape of her neck, lifting her hair and letting the fingers delicately roam over the sensitive skin. Gradually her breathing evened out and her body ceased to tremble. Even when he moved to the bed and they lay side by side on top of the duvet she didn't feel afraid because the only difference was that now he was able to kiss her forehead and eyelids; light, butterfly kisses that were tokens of love rather than forerunners of passion.

Eventually his mouth reached hers, but again the kisses were light, almost teasing as his lips brushed hers, lingering at the corner of her mouth and then moving away to the sensitive spots behind her ears as she felt the rough stubble of his chin grazing her lightly. She moved closer to him and he stopped, sitting up with his left hand resting beneath her body.

'Now you are tempting me!' he laughed.

'I didn't mean to,' she murmured contentedly.

'No? Just the same I should go. Remember, we have all the time in the world.'

'I've been stupid, haven't I?'

'You have been protecting yourself. Until now there has been no one else to do this. Now I will protect you against the world.'

'But not against you?'

'I think that I will be the one who needs protection!'

She laughed and he saw that the shadows had gone from her eyes. 'Sleep well,' he whispered as he left her, and for the first time since she'd left Neal, she did.

Next day she surprised her hosts by going down to breakfast, and surprised Janice even more by spending over two hours with Jessica.

She'd intended to take her outside but realising the risk involved, took her to the indoor pool instead where they both splashed around happily.

After lunch she played with Alexi. He was now walking and although sturdily built like his father and with his colouring, he was a placid affectionate child who enjoyed company.

Renato returned from London silent and grim-faced. He'd finally learnt of Mike's death and, knowing the delicate state of Lisa's emotional balance, didn't want to tell her but felt uncertain of his ability to disguise his own distress. It wasn't unexpected but it still hurt. Without Mike's help, Lisa could not have come to him, and it seemed wrong that it was Mike – his unquestionable love for the same woman totally unreciprocated – who should die.

The children were sent to bed early while the Mutis went to the opera, leaving Renato and Lisa alone downstairs. 'I too like the opera,' he announced as they waited for the coffee. 'One day we must go the open air performances at Verona and also to La Scala. Perhaps Carreras will sing in *La Bohème*. That is well worth waiting for.'

'Not Carreras,' she said quickly.

'No? Perhaps he is not to everyone's liking but for myself I find him exciting. There is such passion there!'

'I saw him at Covent Garden in *Andrea Chenier*. It made me cry. He was too realistic and I felt unbearably sad.'

'You are afraid of your emotions. There is nothing wrong in being moved by a performer. It is part of the beauty of the arts.'

'I don't think . . .'

'Then we will not go. Perhaps we will . . .'

'What's wrong?' she asked abruptly. 'Why are you talking about opera when you're really upset about something? Is it because you don't want me to know? Have you heard from Neal?'

He reached out and touched her lightly on the face. 'No, I have not heard from your husband and I do not expect to. But, yes, there is something that has distressed me. You look so much better today that I don't want to destroy your mood.'

'I'd rather know than live in a fool's paradise.'

'Mike is dead.'

'How?' she whispered, her eyes filling with tears.

'It was quick, which surprises me. He would have known little about it.'

'What did they do to him?'

'He was shot. He'd been living rough, sleeping under newspapers until they slowed down their hunt for him. He was found and shot through the chest but no one realised for twenty-four hours since he

402

was concealed beneath a pile of newspapers.'

'Why didn't they question him to find out where I was?'

'I understand that this was your husband's intention. However, someone got there first and silenced him.'

'Someone from your side?'

'No! That is not our way. He had helped us and would have been rewarded if he had managed to leave this country.'

'Then who was responsible?'

'Perhaps the man who had promoted him to a position of such importance that he was able to help us. The man who never suspected that his friend was a double agent.'

'Bishop?'

'I myself think it was Bishop. Your husband, like you, believes that I had him killed.'

'He was such a nice man,' said Lisa quietly. 'Always cheerful and helpful. It isn't fair.'

'He knew he would probably die. It was his choice. He had become disillusioned with his life. For him it was a way of making amends.'

'I shouldn't have asked him to let me out of the car.'

'We had arranged it many weeks before, without your knowledge. If you'd lost your courage he would have suggested the walk himself. No, if anyone is to blame it is I, not you.'

Sitting at his feet she rested her head on his knees. 'You're not just saying that to make me feel better?'

'No,' he lied. 'He wanted to come over to our side and this was his way of showing his loyalty.'

For a time they sat in silence until Renato slowly stood up and put a hand on Lisa's shoulder. 'Shall we go upstairs?'

She nodded, needing to be close to him tonight to blot out the memory of Mike and the fact that her freedom had cost him his life.

They went straight past Lisa's room and along the corridor to Renato's. Once inside she hesitated for a moment, unsure of what to do or how to act, but then he was carefully undoing her zip and tenderly slipping the sleeves away from her arms, his fingers lingering over the scars on her forearms as he uttered a small exclamation of shock at the extent of her injuries.

When she was in her camisole and panties he quickly took off his own clothes and drew her on to his bed, again contenting himself with holding her closely, murmuring gently as he felt her beginning to tremble. She was startled by the power of him. He had the body of a sportsman with big shoulders and arm muscles, a narrow waist and legs that were solid without an ounce of spare flesh. There were even muscles running down his chest and she wondered when he found the time to keep so fit.

Lightly he traced a line down her neck and beneath the straps of the camisole top. When she seemed quite relaxed he carefully slipped both straps from her shoulders and eased it off over her head. Again he stopped, telling her of his love before he allowed his hands to touch her breasts, and even now, when all that he wanted to do was possess her, he was careful to keep his touch gentle.

He made love to her body with his fingers, his lips and his tongue until she was nearly crying with desire for him and once he was quite sure that she was as anxious as he was, he eased the satin pants down her legs, allowing his hands to roam lightly over the smooth skin of her inner thighs.

He was the first man to touch her so tenderly, to bring her whole body to life so that it tingled and quivered with the sensations, and he was the first man to bring her to a climax before he even entered her. When he was poised above her he sensed a brief moment of resistance and hesitated, so that she looked up and saw the question in his eyes.

'Yes,' she murmured. 'Please, don't stop now.' Then, finally, he allowed himself to become lost in his own pleasure rather than hers, but he was still careful not to frighten her with too much passion this first time. It was obvious that once she was used to him, her passion would soon match his.

It was several minutes before he realised that she was crying against his shoulder, and he wiped the tears from her cheeks. 'What's the matter?' he whispered. 'Did I hurt you?'

'No, you were wonderful! It's just that ... He was right, wasn't he? I'm not very good at this and I did so want it to be good for you.'

He frowned. 'What makes you think anything was wrong?'

'We weren't together.'

Renato couldn't help laughing, and his laugh was deep and infectious. 'We are not in the Olympic ice dancing! I can see that you are a puritan who feels guilty about pleasure. This I will certainly change!'

She moved nearer to him, her arms resting against the dark hair that covered his chest and abdomen. 'I love you,' she whispered. 'Even when you laugh at me, I love you!'

'I will never love anyone as I love you,' he promised. 'You are the only woman I have ever loved and there will never be anyone else.' He spoke the truth but wasn't sure that she believed him.

When Lisa finally fell asleep, he lay working out how he could get rid of her husband, leaving the way clear for them to become man and wife. After tonight the very thought of another man having the slightest claim to her was unbearable. Now that she had shown she

404

returned his love, he was free to move against the Gueras organisation. This time he'd use all the power and contacts he could because it was vital to stamp them out in one attack. There must be nothing left behind from which the organisation could reform.

This meant that Bishop too must die. Remembering Lisa's arms, the thought gave Renato intense satisfaction.

Chapter Thirty-One

During the next few days, Lisa felt as though she was slowly coming alive again. Each night, under Renato's expert and loving tuition, her natural sexuality was released until it nearly matched his. During the days she found herself free of all the restraints marriage to Neal had cast over her right from the very beginning, long before it all went wrong. She'd been so anxious to do everything he considered right, to compensate for the fact that she didn't love him. Now there was no right or wrong way for anything. She could act instinctively, and with that freedom she also regained her sense of humour and love for life.

Her days were mostly filled by Jessica. No longer confined to one small area, it was difficult for the child to understand her freedom but once she realised that most doors were open to her she began to explore, using her hands and mouth to touch and taste all the new things she found.

Again it was wonderful to find that neither Renato nor their hosts minded. They put away the more valuable pieces of porcelain, moved expensive clocks to higher shelves and then accepted any breakages as part of Jessica's rehabilitation. The were patient, calm and understanding about her autism and Lisa discovered that not all the progress she'd made over the past year had been destroyed. Jessica was cautiously returning to the point she'd reached before her mother was attacked. In Renato's presence she seemed more stable than ever before.

Such idyllic peace wasn't destined to last. On the Saturday after she'd moved into the Muti household, Lisa received a brown package through the post. Renato refused to allow her to open it before checking for wires, and insisted on being with her when she took off the inner wrapping. She recognised the distinctive green box at once and appreciated the irony of what Neal had sent her. A large, dark, cut-glass bottle of her favourite perfume, Poison.

'No message?' Renato asked.

'I think it's in the name!' Although she laughed she felt uneasy.

'What's in the carton?'

'Probably a gun so that I can shoot myself!' she quipped as she opened it, only to hurl it across the room with a scream before running for the door. Renato was about to follow her when he saw something crawling out of the carton. Something large, tan-coloured and furry. Taking off one of his leather shoes he threw it with great force and total accuracy, knocking the creature flat to the floor, but its legs still waved menacingly in the air and he had to force himself to crush it beneath his other shoe, hearing a soft squelching sound as its large body finally crumpled beneath the pressure.

Looking down at the spider he shivered. It could easily have bitten Lisa the moment it was released from its over-small prison. Quickly he wrapped its mangled remains in a large handkerchief before taking it to the nearest dustbin. Then he went looking for Lisa.

He found her in his room, which had become theirs over the past few nights. She was by the window with her arms wrapped round her chest and the terrible tension had returned to her body. 'It's dead,' he assured her.

'That's how he murdered Naomi,' she said quietly.

'No one mentioned any bite marks on her, darling.'

'I don't suppose she was bitten. Rebekah said her mother was terrified of money spiders, so just imagine how she'd have felt with a mass of those revolting things on her bed. Ugh!'

'You cannot be sure that ...'

'Rebekah saw them! At first she thought it was a dream, then later she kept bringing the subject up again and again until Bishop got quite ... Bishop! He must have done it while we were in Paris. Suppose he finds out that Rebekah knows?'

'She doesn't know. You said yourself she thinks it's a nightmare, and she isn't likely to let on if she realises the truth.'

'I suppose not.' Lisa's face crumpled. 'When's it going to end, Renato?'

'Very soon.' His voice was grim. 'After this I don't think we can delay any longer. I'd hoped to wait until you were stronger but he isn't giving us the luxury of time. This could easily be the start of a whole campaign of fear. We have to move first.'

'Why did you want to wait until I was stronger?'

He sat on the bed, pulling her on to his lap. '*Cara,* you are part of the plan. I do not wish it to be so but there is no other way. You are going to have to see your husband one last time.'

He hated watching all the newfound confidence drain out of her but forced himself to go on. 'I will make an appointment with your husband. Once we are talking I shall tell him that you do not interest me any longer. He will believe this because he is ignorant of love. Then I shall offer to return you to him in exchange for something that he knows I badly want: my bank's gold.'

'You mean I'll actually have to go back?'

'In a way. That part I will explain later, once your husband has taken the bait.'

There was doubt in Lisa's eyes now and he took her face in both hands. 'Do you doubt me? Is it possible that you still have no trust in my love for you? You are the first woman I have ever told that I loved, and that is because you *are* the first. Once this is over I shall take you home to Italy and you will become strong again. We will never have to worry about your husband. We will grow old together and watch our grandchildren playing on the beach. It sounds idyllic, does it not?'

'I can't imagine you old!' she said with a shaky laugh.

'Perhaps neither of us will age. We will be like Dorian Grey and leave ageing portraits in the attic of our palazzo!'

'I do trust you,' she murmured, kissing him on the corner of the mouth. 'But I'm so afraid of Neal and Bishop.'

'If my plan works neither of them will worry us for much longer. Now, since you seem determined to keep kissing me, I shall have to let myself be seduced.'

'On a Saturday morning?'

'What time could be better!' He laughed and they fell back on the bed their bodies already moving perfectly together, and when it was over the memory of the morning's post was easier to bear. At least she had someone to keep guard over her, Lisa thought as she watched Renato pulling on a dark blue sweatshirt. Poor Naomi had been quite alone.

The three men met on Sunday night in the top floor of a small Italian restaurant where Bellini had made certain they wouldn't be disturbed. He ordered for them all and when the food arrived, dismissed the waiter. No one must be around while they talked.

'You've come alone,' said Neal, staring with disinterest at his risotto.

'Of course. This is a meeting strictly between we three.'

'You didn't feel the need for protection?'

The Italian's smile was threatening. 'I think not. Unlike you, I am young and fit enough to take care of myself.'

'And my wife!' snapped Neal, annoyed by the larger man's composure.

'Yes, your wife . . .' Bellini let his voice tail off.

'I want her back,' said Neal quickly.

'That, I think, is probably best. She is not – how would you say? – quite to my taste.'

The older man laughed unpleasantly. 'I thought not! You Italians are used to hot-blooded women. Lisa's the typical English wife, cold and unwelcoming.'

'Yet you desire her back?'

'She's my wife, that's reason enough.'

'Of course, a matter of honour! This I *can* understand.'

Bishop moved restlessly in his chair. He wasn't interested in listening to them discuss Lisa; he wanted to hear what the Italian would demand in return for the woman. Renato turned to Bishop. His eyes were no longer soft but hard and dark, and his face was tighter than ever before. 'You are bored, Bishop? Why not play with your pet spiders while you wait?'

'What makes you think they belong to me?'

'Let us say that you suit each other.'

'In what way?'

'You are both poisonous insects that I wish to crush!' Now he was smiling again but even the normally imperturbable Bishop felt uneasy.

'I take it you want something in return?' said Neal, worried in case his son-in-law lost his temper and ruined the entire meeting.

'No one gets something for nothing in our line of work! I want our gold back.'

Neal and Bishop glanced at each other. 'All of it?' asked Neal.

'All of it.'

'That's three million pounds, taking both robberies into account.'

'It is four million,' said Renato flatly.

'Not according to your bank's accounts.'

'Come, my friend, surely you have heard of creative accounting? There was gold taken that was surplus to the stated amount and I want it back. It is not as though I am asking for much; only what is mine.'

Neal picked up his wine glass and stared into the clear liquid. 'You'll leave the country once this is cleared up?'

'Yes.'

'And you won't attempt to contact my wife again?'

'She no longer interests me,' Renato said indifferently.

'I suppose it's too much to hope that you might keep her daughter as a token hostage or something until the transaction's complete?'

'If you speak of Jessica, her mother would not leave her.'

409

'A pity, but you're right.'

'Then we are agreed on the terms?'

Neal looked at Bishop who shook his head. He didn't believe a word the Italian had spoken. Although untouched by it himself, he knew very well the lengths to which people would go when they thought themselves in love, and he was certain that Bellini was still in love with Neal's wife. In which case he was undoubtedly going to pull some kind of double-cross on them, but at that moment Bishop couldn't think how.

'What's wrong?' demanded Neal.

'I'm not sure I believe Signor Bellini.'

Renato looked at him much as he'd looked at the spider. 'You now run the organisation?'

Neal flushed. 'No, the decision's mine and I agree to the terms. We ought to get down to details of how the swap will be carried out.'

Bishop saw the Italian's face lighten as he leant across the table and knew that he was right to distrust him. He'd let his father-in-law set everything up and then keep his eyes open. No one was going to make a fool of him, particularly not when Lisa Gueras was involved. He had no intention of becoming yet another victim of her inexplicable effect upon powerful men.

'How did it go?' asked Lisa, hurrying to greet Renato when he returned. He lifted her off the ground and kissed her forcefully, knowing full well that she wasn't going to like what he had to say and wishing there was some other way.

'It went well. We came to an agreement.'

'What was it?'

'That I get back all my bank's gold in exchange for returning you to your husband.'

'You're sending me back to him?'

'He thinks that I am.'

'What will really happen?'

Renato swallowed hard, put an arm round her waist and guided her into the deserted drawing-room. 'Tomorrow evening at six o'clock I will receive a telephone call from my Swiss banker, telling me that the money has been deposited in our company's account but that it will only be available for use the following morning after a telephone call from your husband.'

'The next morning he will come to this house and find you waiting with a suitcase, then he will telephone from here to release my money. After I have made a call to check this, he will leave with you.'

'What about the children?'

'I have decided that they must have the mumps. Most men are nervous of mumps and usually unsure whether or not they have had it! This will enable me to keep the children behind.'

'And what happens to me once we've left you?'

'On the journey home, at a time decided between us, you will say that you are feeling ill.'

'He isn't likely to believe that one, not after I used it to get away the first time.'

'This he will want to believe because you will say that you are nauseous due to carrying his child. Perhaps you should cry a little, saying that this is why I did not want to keep you. His vanity will make him believe.'

'Then what?'

'Then you make the driver pull over to the side of the road and stumble away to a field. We will already have picked a suitable spot. Make sure that you get as far from the car as you can because it will be set to explode.'

'What about the driver?'

'I hope the driver will be Bishop!'

Lisa's hands clenched in her lap as she considered possible flaws. 'Suppose Neal doesn't let me get out?'

'He *has* to let you out. There will be no way I can stop the car from exploding.'

'But he might not!' She was almost in tears. 'Suppose he keeps me with him? Am I supposed to sit there and die?'

Renato sighed heavily. 'It is difficult. Should you be unable to leave the car, then at the last moment you must tell him what is going to happen. Then he will leave the car very quickly!'

'Yes, and probably leave me behind.'

'Not if he believes you are pregnant.'

'By then I doubt if he'll believe a word I say!'

'Lisa, this *has* to work. If you play your part properly there is no reason why it shouldn't. Negative thinking is not helpful to our cause. You must believe that you can do it. I believe you can do it, isn't that enough?'

'Not when I'm the one waiting to be blown to kingdom come! Please, don't make me do this. I don't think I'm up to it and I don't want to leave the children behind.'

'You think they would be allowed out of the car because you were suffering from morning sickness?'

'Of course not!'

'Then it is not possible!'

'He'll know I'm nervous. He always knew when I was nervous.'

'It is what he would expect. You are after all the returned wife, despoiled by an Italian gigolo, not knowing what he plans to do with you once you reach home again. Of course you will be nervous.'

'How can you ask me to do this?' she asked in despair.

'Because it is the only way. Do you think I want you to go away with him? Can't you imagine what it will be like for me waiting here, knowing nothing? But it has to happen so that we can be truly free of him.'

'It's not much better than making me sit on that horse!' she said resentfully.

Renato flinched. 'That was barbaric, he was being sadistic and I felt sick to see it. Do you truly think that what I am asking of you is the same?'

She shook her head. 'No, but I'm tired of fighting him. We've been so happy these last few days. I can't imagine sitting next to Neal while he plays the loving husband. It was bad enough before, but after what we've had together I don't know if I can bear it.'

Renato shut his eyes for a moment. 'Very well, if you truly cannot do it I will try and think of something else, but ...'

'I'll do it.' Suddenly she sounded confident.

'Why do you change your mind?'

'Because you offered to let me off! It wasn't just the thought of being with Neal that terrified me, it was the horrible sensation of being used again.'

The harsh planes of his face softened. 'I forget that winning your trust will take a long time. Also, I know that what I ask is almost too much but I look ahead and then it is worth it, yes?'

'Yes,' she agreed. 'We can't build a life for ourselves until he's dead. The only thing is, aren't we just as bad as him? Sitting here talking casually of two murders.'

'It is necessary,' he said shortly.

She knew he was right but for the first time since they'd become lovers she turned away from him that night, frightened that he wasn't so very different from her husband after all. Renato knew what was wrong and regretted it but he was careful to remain affectionate, pleased that she still chose to fall asleep at his side rather than return to her own room.

He understood her fears and accepted that in a way they were justified but he didn't make his living from robbery and blackmail. If murder was more familiar to him than to Lisa, well, he'd been born in a country where the Mafia was an accepted part of life. When it came to removing Neal Gueras from the earth, he felt no compunction at all.

* * *

'Where are the children?' asked Neal, picking up Lisa's small suitcase and looking around him.

'They're ill.' She was so upset at leaving them that she sounded totally convincing. 'They've both got mumps. I suppose they could come but I thought you might not . . .'

'No thank you!' he said quickly. 'I've never had it and I certainly don't want it at my age.'

'They'll have to come later,' she murmured, her voice shaking.

'Is Alexi bad?'

'No, but Jessica . . .'

'We'd better be going. Where's your ex-lover?'

'Making a telephone call to Switzerland,' she said bitterly.

Neal laughed. 'What an insult, finding he preferred gold to your body! I did warn you but you wouldn't listen. I suppose you imagined a Latin lover would make all the difference?'

'I don't want to talk about it.'

'I don't suppose you do! Everything all right?' he added as Renato came out of the study, a cordless phone in his hand. He nodded. 'Nothing to say to him, Lisa?' he asked with amusement. 'No fond farewells?'

'Just take her away,' snapped Renato. 'All I got from her was the return of my money. For the rest, you're welcome to her.'

'I find her equally unrewarding,' commented Neal, 'but useful on occasions.'

'Her usefulness to me is over. If you would care to leave now?'

Neal pushed Lisa ahead of him and turned round in the doorway. 'Perhaps you'll stick to your own women from now on!'

'Perhaps I will.'

'You know, it's almost been worth it to see the look of disenchantment on your face today, Bellini. I hope your father isn't too annoyed that you wasted so much time pursuing her.'

'*Basta!*' exclaimed the Italian and Neal left, well content.

Inside the car, Bishop sat watching as Lisa and her husband approached. She looked fitter than when he'd last seen her and she'd put on weight. That didn't tie in with a disastrous love affair culminating in her return to a husband she disliked. He was also instinctively alarmed by the absence of the children. Somehow they were going to be double-crossed but he couldn't work out where.

After five minutes, Neal put a hand on his wife's knee. 'I'm looking forward to welcoming you home,' he said menacingly. 'Perhaps the Italian taught you a trick or two to liven things up?' She tried to move her legs away and he laughed. 'Still the ice maiden? What a pity his hot Italian blood didn't prove enough to melt you. Never mind, we've

413

got our whole lives ahead of us. I'm sure I can think of something to make you more responsive.'

She knew he was deliberately provoking her, hoping for some reaction, preferably tears, but she was too nervous to cry. A quick glance at her watch told her that she didn't have much time and she put a hand to her mouth. 'I'm sorry, I don't feel well,' she gasped.

'I think you said the same thing to Mike!'

'I feel sick.'

'Then be sick.'

'You'll have to ask Bishop to pull up. Neal, I'm pregnant. If you must know, that's why Renato went off me so quickly. He soon realised that I was carrying your child and said he didn't have any intention of bring up a bastard in his household.'

'He's got more sense than I had! But I'm glad you're still good for something. Pull over here, Bishop, by that gate.'

Lisa caught a glimpse of Bishop's eyes in the driving mirror. They were fixed on her and smouldering with hatred, presumably because he believed her story and didn't want Neal to have more sons. 'Hurry up!' she begged, so white and with such genuine urgency that Neal's last doubts vanished.

'I'll go along too,' said Bishop, watching her run towards the field.

'She can't get away from us here!'

'I'd still prefer to keep her within arm's length.'

'Suit yourself. I'll wait here.'

Bishop walked briskly down the farm track, put a hand on the five-bar gate and leapt lithely over it. He didn't know why he was following Lisa, he only knew that there was going to be trouble somewhere and this incident could well be connected with it.

Lisa was being sick as he approached. Her nerves had affected her even more badly than she'd feared and as she retched violently she shivered, but at least she knew that the worst was over and in a few seconds she'd be free.

The explosion was so-loud that for a moment she went deaf, and when her sense of hearing began to return there was a ringing in her ears. Smoke billowed from the roadside and she saw pieces of metal in the field, propelled over the gate by the force of the explosion.

Sighing with relief she straightened up and looked straight into Bishop's eyes. 'Well, well!' he said softly. 'Who's a clever girl then?'

Any fear that Lisa wouldn't be able to display sufficient shock after the car bomb was ended by Bishop's disastrously unplanned survival. The sight of him standing in front of her, eyes narrowed and mouth thin-lipped with rage, was sufficient to start her screaming. She hadn't stopped when the first police car arrived on the scene quickly followed by a fire engine and an ambulance.

Not that the ambulance was needed. There wasn't enough of Neal Gueras for them to carry away on a stretcher and formal identification was only possible through his dental records.

'I assume I was meant to have been despatched with him?' murmured Bishop, under the guise of whispering words of comfort. Lisa shivered at the touch of his hand on her arm.

'She's in shock, mate,' said an ambulance man. 'She ought to go to hospital.'

'No!' cried Lisa, terrified of losing touch with Renato.

'I'll call the family doctor,' Bishop assured him. 'She'll be better off with her family.'

The police were busy taking notes from passers-by and one unfortunate family whose car had been damaged, causing the wife to go temporarily deaf and reducing their two young children to total panic.

Lisa was so confused by Bishop's presence that she couldn't concentrate on what the police said to her. They gave up, informing Bishop they'd call at Beckett Lodge later, once the bomb experts had given their opinion. 'Any idea who might be responsible?' the senior officer asked Bishop.

'None at all.'

'No business enemies?'

'Of course he had business enemies! Tell me any self-made millionaire who hasn't.'

'Not everyone has the kind of enemies who blow you sky-high.'

'Mistaken identity, I imagine.'

Noting down where the car had been parked overnight and the address from which they'd collected Lisa, the policemen left. After a short wait, Steve arrived with another car and at last Bishop was able to take Lisa away from the charred wreck of the Daimler and the terrible smell of death that hung over the area, as tangible as the smoke that had now cleared.

She sat shivering in the back as far away from him as possible, wishing she'd brought a cardigan to put on over her light summer dress but most of her clothes had been left behind. Neal hadn't wanted any reminders of her time with the Italian.

'*Are* you pregnant?' Bishop's tone was deceptively indifferent.

'No.'

'Clever!'

'Not that clever or you'd be dead too.'

Back at the house, Lisa stared up at the redbrick walls, remembering her first visit and how hard she'd worked to make the girls like

415

her. If she'd known the truth she wouldn't have bothered. How naive she'd been, and what amusement that must have given everyone, especially the man standing at her elbow.

'Just think, it's all yours!' he said harshly.

'I don't want it.'

'That's the difference between us – I do.'

'Then you should have married Neal, not Louise.'

'Sharp-tongued to the last. I never knew what he saw in you. We'd better go in, people are watching.'

Before her eyes had adjusted to the gloom of the hall, Lisa was nearly knocked over as Rebekah came flying into her arms, sobbing loudly. 'They said on the television that Daddy was dead. Is it true?'

She swallowed hard and put a hand on the child's silky hair. 'I'm afraid it is. He had a car accident.'

'Your precious stepmother and her lover planted a bomb in the car,' said Bishop, his voice cutting like a knife through the child's distress. Rebekah's eyes widened.

'Lisa wouldn't kill Daddy. You're a rotten liar!'

Bishop's hand shot out and hit her round the ear. 'Mind what you say. I'm not the one who tells lies around here. Now go away. Lisa and I have a lot to talk about.'

Rebekah set her mouth like her father's and drew herself up as tall as possible. 'You *do* tell lies. You killed Mummy. I saw you.'

'Run away.' He was suddenly bored with her, anxious to get down to the important business.

'I'll tell!' she shouted. Lisa tried to quieten her but Bishop held her back.

'Tell what, Rebekah?'

'About the spiders. It wasn't a dream at all. You frightened Mummy to death with those horrible tarantulas. They were crawling all over her bed and she was sobbing and trying to keep still. I saw them and I heard you laugh.'

'I'll deal with you later,' he said menacingly. Lisa's eyes closed as she realised she was powerless to help anyone unless Renato managed to get to her quickly.

He must have heard what had happened by now. The police would have visited the Muti's house and he'd know that Bishop was alive. If she could only play for time he'd get her away, but how much time could she get?

'Come into the study,' ordered Bishop. 'I don't want anyone over-hearing our little discussion. A sex romp on the floor's one thing, a business discussion quite another!' Sitting in Neal's chair he gestured for her to take the seat opposite him. 'Presumably you've already

416

worked out that your son's going to inherit everything of value,' he said slowly.

'I hadn't thought about it at all.'

'I'm inclined to believe that. You've always been stupid about the business. I can assure you that he does, but at less than two years old I don't think he's going to put up much of a fight if I take over as regent, do you?'

'You can have it all,' said Lisa bitterly. 'I don't want my son growing up to be a high-powered criminal.'

'I intend to have it all. I've waited a long time for this. Working all the hours God made while Neal chased around after you like a stupid schoolboy, making excuses when he didn't turn up at meetings, then watching while you steadily destroyed his lifetime's work. You and your Italian gigolo did me a great favour today. I don't need your permission to take everything because it's mine by right. And that includes you.'

'You don't need me. You've got a wife who's willing to be the doormat your sexual inclinations seem to crave, and I'm not going to try and take anything that you count as important so I don't see the need for me to be included in this unsavoury package.'

'I want to destroy you, just as you destroyed your husband. That's why you're part of the package. You're the icing on the cake; the ultimate pinnacle of pleasure that I'll achieve when you're on your knees, begging me to let you die.'

She'd never imagined it possible to see such hatred on another human face as Bishop's reflected then and her hair prickled with fear. 'I'm afraid you can't have me,' she said, but to her annoyance her voice was trembling.

'Why's that?'

'Renato won't let you.'

Bishop laughed. 'You don't believe he's going to come rushing in here like a knight in shining armour and whisk you off to his homeland where you'll live happily ever after, do you? Won't you ever learn, you stupid bitch!

'Perhaps he does like you. Perhaps he even enjoyed bedding you, although from what I've heard he'd be the first one who did, but even so he won't lift a finger to help you now. He can't. His father's one of the most influential men in P2, and to them business comes first. Peace is what they want – peace to get on with their job, just as we want to get on with ours.'

'Renato isn't ruled by what his father wants.'

'Of course he is! If he makes a move against me his Papa will click his fingers and summon him back to Rome, and believe me your lover boy will go.'

'The Bellinis aren't mixed up in anything crooked. P2 is just another masonic lodge.'

'Like the Krays were just a couple of businessmen!'

'You think everyone's the same as you, don't you? Well they're not. He explained about P2 to me and ...'

'He's another crook!' shouted Bishop, losing his temper. 'I suppose you'd have believed him if he'd told you the moon was made of blue cheese. Watch my lips, Lisa. *Renato Bellini is a crook.* His family have a long history of criminal connections. They were friends of the Calvis. You were part of his game plan. Rattle the Gueras organisation; make out with his wife; get them quarrelling among themselves. He was very good at it too. But the bottom line was that he finally swapped you for a van of gold bullion!'

'He didn't! That was all part of the plan.'

'Are you sure?' he asked softly. 'Why do you think I didn't stay in my driving seat? I don't usually bother to follow pregnant women around. The truth is he'd tipped me off. He didn't want you back.'

She stared into his eyes and to her horror found that she was beginning to have doubts. It made a kind of sense. Why had Bishop got out of the car? It wasn't his usual style. And why wasn't Renato here now, helping her?

All the fears and insecurities from her time with Toby and Neal swept back, and suddenly she couldn't even picture Renato's face clearly. She could still feel the way he touched her, remember the kindness he'd shown as he'd taught her how to love again, but she couldn't visualise his face. It seemed like a bad omen.

Bishop saw the doubt creeping up on her and smiled to himself. He'd guessed it would be easy to get her distrusting the Italian. Despite Neal's initial adoration and two years of financial security, he knew she hadn't gained in self-confidence. It was almost too easy, but still intensely pleasurable. He continued staring at her until her eyes dropped and she bit hard on her bottom lip to stop herself from crying aloud.

'Naturally Jessica will have to go away,' he continued brusquely. 'I'm not listening to her tantrums or having scenes in front of guests once I'm in control. I don't think she needs a private home, either. Our national health institutions are wonderfully caring!'

Lisa's brief moment of despair was banished as his words sunk in. To his amazement, she suddenly launched herself at him, fingers extended as she went for his eyes. His reactions were quick but not quick enough for him totally to evade her, and her long nails made deep scratches down the left side of his face. She was screaming at him now, cursing him with words he'd never imagined she knew, and

418

when she began kicking as well he drew back his right hand and slapped her with an open palm, more in self-defence than anything else since for the moment he wanted her in one piece.

The blow sent her stumbling away to her right and as she knocked her hip painfully against the window ledge, she saw two men moving stealthily across the gravel drive. Quickly she remained with her back to the window, totally blocking Bishop's view.

'Don't ever do that again,' he ordered, dabbing at the blood trickling down his face.

'I hate you!' she spat at him. 'You're despicable, taking out your spite on a handicapped child. No real man would behave like that.'

'Your husband used her too,' he muttered, sitting down again. 'He used her to get you to marry him.'

'He promised to look after her and he kept that promise,' she protested, trying to continue talking to prevent Bishop hearing any sound from the intruders.

'By shutting her away on the top floor? Very generous, I must say!'

'All right, he wasn't perfect but next to you he looks like a saint.'

'I'll break you,' he promised. 'I'll break you for what you did to your husband, and for Mike.'

Mike. At the sound of his name she felt the despair threatening again, and in that brief moment of silence both she and Bishop heard the creak of the front door opening. He was instantly out of his chair, walking swiftly to the door, his hand moving towards his inside pocket, but he wasn't quite quick enough. The door was abruptly kicked in and in the entrance stood the large figure of Renato Bellini, gun in hand, while two equally powerful men stood solidly behind him.

'I've come for Lisa,' he said calmly, taking in the red mark that discoloured one side of her face and the streaks down her cheeks where a few tears had made a path through the dust of the explosion.

'She can't leave,' protested Bishop, moving slowly backwards as the Italian advanced into the room. 'The police want to interview her.'

'Then they'll have to come to Italy to do it.'

'She isn't worth this!' he sneered. 'I doubt if even P2 can cope with the havoc she creates.'

'I'm not interested in what you think. She's coming, and what's more we're taking Rebekah with us.'

'I think the courts would feel she should stay with her sister and brother-in-law.'

'I'm surprised her brother-in-law wants her when she's the only witness to what he probably once considered the perfect murder!'

419

'That's precisely why she has to stay!' snarled Bishop, totally impotent as one of Renato's heavies skimmed their hands over his body, removing both his gun and the stiletto-style knife concealed inside the sleeve of his jacket.

'If she comes to Italy with us, she'll stay silent.'

'She'll stay silent if she stays with me! Even if I let the child go you're not having Mrs Gueras. I've waited a long time for this moment, and just because you lust after her it doesn't mean that I'm going to give her up. Find yourself another tart; there are plenty around, most of them more accomplished than her.'

Renato's smile was the most sinister sight Lisa had ever seen, and even Bishop was startled. His body tensed for what he assumed was going to be a physical attack and he silently cursed Steve's ineptitude in letting the men get into the house unobserved.

'I will now make myself clear,' said Renato, the smile never faltering. 'It is true that my family are masons, and as such we do have contacts here that are possibly not known to you.'

'I know every P2 member there is and you can call yourselves masons if you like. I prefer the term criminal.'

'No doubt it is a more familiar word in your vocabulary. As I was saying, we have enough contacts to make sure that within twelve months – the time it will certainly take you to sort out your late employer's affairs – there will be nothing left for you to take over. Not a casino, not a prostitute, not even one of your favourite sado-masochistic blue movies. We will move in on them all and there will be nothing you can do about it. Nothing!'

The blue stubble on Bishop's chin stood out against the ivory white of his skin as he took in the information. 'And if I let her go?' he asked at last.

'Then naturally you have it all. There is nothing of yours that we want. The only reason I came was to reclaim what was mine.'

'I told Neal to leave your bank's gold alone but he was too busy chasing after your fancy piece to listen.'

'At least you have the satisfaction of knowing you were right. Doubtless your own record will be totally unblemished. Emotional entanglements are unlikely to affect your judgement!'

For a few seconds they all waited while Bishop turned over possible ways of retaliating in his mind and was forced to reject them one by one. 'Take her!' he shouted at last. 'Take them both and get the hell out of here.'

As his bodyguards kept their guns trained on Bishop, Renato finally crossed to Lisa and put an arm round her. 'Come,' he urged. 'It is over now. We will leave here and you need never return to this country again. Rebekah is already in the car, and back at Giovanni's both Alexi and Jessica are ready to go. We will be in Italy by tonight.'

'The police want to talk to me.'

'The police will not make any trouble. They have been seen to.'

'Very law-abiding!' commented Bishop, then grunted as one of the men pushed the muzzle of his gun into his solar plexus.

'He said you didn't love me,' she muttered incoherently. 'I thought ...'

'Please, come with me. It is time we left.'

Very slowly, like an old woman, she allowed him to lead her from the room. In the doorway he paused to look back at Bishop. 'If I ever set eyes on you in Italy,' he said bitterly, 'I will kill you.' Bishop stared back, his face expressionless, but just as Lisa turned away she accidentally caught his eye and knew that for him this wasn't the end.

She climbed into the waiting Ferrari and sat shivering while Renato wrapped a wool rug round her knees and put his jacket around her shoulders. Then Rebekah uncurled from the corner of the back seat and cuddled close to her stepmother, offering the emotional warmth Lisa so desperately needed.

Renato sat on the other side of the little girl, his arm resting along the back of the seat with his fingers just touching Lisa's shoulder, and slowly they pulled away from the house. At the curve in the drive she glanced back and saw Bishop staring out of the front window. He was too far away for her to see his expression but she could imagine it, and despite everything Renato had said, and the knowledge that there was no logical reason why she should ever set eyes on Bishop again, she knew with bone-chilling certainty that she would. She knew too that until that moment she would never be entirely free of fear.

Chapter Thirty-Two

Nearly a year to the day after Neal's death, Lisa sat in the sun-drenched courtyard of Renato's villa in Portofino watching Jessica and Rebekah playing in the swimming pool. Behind her there was the soothing sound of a tiny fountain falling into the shell-shaped pond where Alexi was busy dabbling his hands, splashing at the surface of the water and laughing as the droplets splattered over the stone slabs and on to his mother's tanned back.

Dressed in a backless sundress with her hair long and loose on her shoulders, she looked years younger than the tense young woman who'd been welcomed so warmly into the heart of the Bellini family on her arrival from England.

Renato's mother had exclaimed with horror over her lack of curves, and spent several months trying to rectify the situation while his father – a man to whom love and marriage did not necessarily go hand-in-hand – seemed to accept her at once as his son's future wife, and treated her with touching old world courtesy.

Even now, when they were living in their own villa, she saw his parents at least once a week, and his mother more often because she was a doting grandmother, continually bringing presents for Luciano and Lisa's own children.

Once, when Lisa expressed surprise that she treated the children alike, the woman's eyes had widened in astonishment. 'They are all *bambini!*' she exclaimed, and that was explanation enough.

Lisa knew she'd never tire of the beautiful countryside. The clear blue creeks wandering among the olive trees, yews and sea pines; and her favourite walk to the tiny Church of San Giorgio with its wonderful view from the terrace where she could sit for hours soaking up the sun.

Jessica had improved so much in the year that people didn't always realise she was any different from other highly-strung children.

Renato had accomplished much of this himself. His patience was never-ending, and when Lisa despaired he assured her that eventually her daughter would find a place in life.

He had given Jessica the holding therapy himself for the first few weeks of their life in Italy, when Lisa had been too exhausted and emotional to manage herself, and his steady, unflappable presence gave her the first sense of security in her tense, ever-changing life. She responded at first with hesitant gestures of affection, and then – when they were never rebuffed – with more open signs of trust. On her bad days it was still Renato who could soothe her quickest. The only thing that really set Jessica back these days was her own mother.

When Lisa's mind refused to stop dwelling on her last image of Bishop, or after a night of disturbed sleep when she'd dreamt that Neal had returned for her, Jessica became hyperactive and difficult, reverting to rocking and banging her head against the walls of the villa. She was the barometer by which Renato judged Lisa's state of mind because she'd become expert at hiding her fears from him.

Her love for the Italian had deepened over the past year. He was the kindest man she'd ever met and when she lay in his arms, relaxing as his hands and mouth worked their usual magic on her, it was difficult to believe that he was the same man who'd held a gun to Bishop and cold-bloodedly murdered her husband. But he was, and this memory intruded on her contentment.

She loved him mentally and physically and she couldn't imagine life without him yet there was still something holding her back from total happiness. She felt that she was simply marking time; waiting for something to happen; something inevitable, arising from her past. Somehow she knew that she was going to pay a price for what had happened in England and for the happiness she was experiencing here in Italy. Until that moment was reached she refused to consider marrying Renato, turning his proposal aside with gentle humour as she tried to prepare herself for this unknown ordeal that lay ahead. An ordeal she felt sure she would have to face alone.

'Mama!' said Alexi, tugging at her cotton skirt. 'We go to the beach today?' She looked at his sturdy figure, his skin tanned by the Italian sun, eyes shining with an innocence never seen in Jessica's, and she marvelled again that he bore so little resemblance to his father. If she tried hard enough it was possible to see a similarity in the set of the mouth but generally there was nothing in him to remind her of Neal.

His disposition was a different matter. Since he was usually over-indulged by everyone it was easy for him to be sunny-tempered and he bestowed his smiles upon them all, already aware of his ability to charm. But when he was crossed, when Lisa or Renato disciplined him, then it was a different matter. He didn't scream or cry as most toddlers do; instead he turned his face away from whichever adult was opposing him and appeared to give in gracefully while inevitably managing to find a way round the restrictions, even if it took him two or three days.

He most certainly had his father's determination to get his own way, but at the moment he did it with charm and it was impossible to be angry with him for long because he was a tremendously affectionate boy. Renato asserted that their best hope of disciplining him when he was older lay in establishing such a loving relationship now that Alexi would do as they asked because he didn't want to upset them. Lisa hoped he was right.

'Why not swim in the pool with the girls?' she asked lazily, picking him up and kissing his soft skin.

'Beach!' he insisted. 'I want Papa. Papa likes the beach.'

'Papa's away on business,' she said regretfully. She hated the times when his work took him away from the villa.

All the children called Renato 'Papa'. At first Lisa was worried that Luciano would mind, but he'd been delighted with his instant brother and sisters. All that worried him was that his father was living in mortal sin. He was terrified that Renato would die before he married Lisa. He listened to his father's assurances about God being understanding but knew that the priests and his grandparents didn't think him quite so benevolent.

I ought to take them to the beach, thought Lisa. It was easy to become lazy these days. She could sit in the sun and let her mind wander back, re-living her mistakes for hour after hour if she wasn't careful, and nothing was changed except possibly her present happiness. Sometimes she wondered if she'd be better if they weren't so rich and she didn't have servants doing everything for her. 'All right,' she conceded. 'After lunch we'll go to the beach.'

At that moment a small cloud passed over the sun and she gave a quick shiver but almost immediately it was warm again and she went inside to ask the cook for a picnic tea.

After their siesta, Rebekah, Jessica, Luciano and Alexi set off with Lisa for their private stretch of beach that was a mere three minute walk from the gates of the villa. She smiled at one of the guards who stood on duty twenty-four hours a day both here and in Milan. In Italy to be rich was to be a target for kidnapping and security had to be tight. It didn't give her the assurance it should have done. She knew that all the guards and cameras money could buy wouldn't be enough to stop whatever it was that she had to face.

The sand was light and silky beneath their feet, not like the sand of her holidays in England as a child, but the children didn't know anything different. Luciano and Alexi ganged up together and annoyed the girls as soon as they reached the beach. Rebekah secretly enjoyed it when Luciano chased her and threatened her with death from sea monsters or giant jellyfish because she knew that really he was very fond of her. Just the same, she pretended to be annoyed and a little frightened before taking Jessica's hand and leading her away to sit in the shade where they could pour sand into tiny cups and hold a pretend tea-party just as Luciano's grandparents did on feast days.

Lisa lay back on her sand mat and began to relax. The children were safe here and their privacy wouldn't be invaded because there were large signs all round the perimeter of the beach telling people in Italian, French and English that it was private property. She closed her eyes, listening to the chatter of the boys and the occasional giggle from Jessica.

'Mama, money quick!' cried Alexi a little later, hurrying up and accidentally kicking sand in her face.

'What do you want money for?' she asked lazily.

'Ice cream!'

'Where ...?'

'There's a man by the sign and he's selling ice cream. It's all right, he knows us. He told me to ask my mummy for the money.'

'That doesn't mean he knows us!'

'He said he knew me when I was a baby. He said, "Hello, Alexi," and gave a funny smile!'

Slowly she sat up, pushing her sunglasses into her hair and staring down the beach to where a man stood waiting in the heat of the afternoon sun. 'I'll go and get the ice creams,' she said quietly. 'You fetch Luciano and the girls and tell them all to wait here on the mat.'

'No! I want to come. I want ...'

'*Do as I say*!' She'd never sounded so angry with him before and his bottom lip trembled but he did as she'd asked and trotted off to round up the others.

It was a very small beach yet the walk to the water's edge seemed to take forever. She'd known who it was all along but only when she got within a few yards could she make out his face beneath the straw hat perched on top of the dark brown hair, now flecked with the odd strand of grey. He'd aged a great deal, she realised, far more than she or Renato.

'Surprised?' His voice was still as clipped as she'd remembered in her nightmares.

'No, I think I always knew that one day you'd come. You could say I've been waiting for you.'

'I hear you haven't married him.'

'My previous experiences of marriage didn't make me over-enamoured of the state! Speaking of which, how's Louise?'

'Dead.'

She remembered Louise's adoration of this man. Her golden beauty that she'd chosen to waste on him. 'How did she die?'

'She killed herself.' He could have been speaking of a stranger.

'Really?'

He gave a thin smile. 'Yes, she really did. She left the house one night just before Christmas and threw herself under a train. I'd say that was a pretty determined way to commit suicide, wouldn't you?'

'I'm sorry.'

'For her or for me?'

'For Louise. She must have been very unhappy.'

He shrugged. 'I suppose so. She'd had two miscarriages and for some reason that changed her. I didn't mind. I never wanted children but she did.'

'And what happened to Ruth?' Again he glanced out to sea, his eyes narrowing as he looked across the empty ocean. Lisa risked turning to the children and saw Rebekah standing tensely on the sand. She gestured towards the cliff path, hoping she'd get all the children away while Lisa kept Bishop talking.

'I've no idea,' he responded, now checking the cliffs behind them. 'I never heard from her after Neal died. She packed her things, walked out of her school and vanished. The police searched for a time but now she's just another missing person.'

'Didn't Louise worry about her?'

'She never mentioned her to me.'

'Why have you come?' she asked at last, seeing the children moving very slowly up the beach, pretending to play with their ball as they went.

He looked her straight in the face. 'For you, of course. I've come to kill you.'

'Any particular reason?' She was pleased by how calm she sounded but didn't dare turn round any more and prayed that Rebekah was getting them all away.

'Yes. Your handsome Italian lover doesn't keep his word. He and his fellow masons shopped us all along the line. Our drug ring's smashed, our casinos all closed. To cap everything they've arrested Steve and three other men for an armed robbery, and Steve's singing like the proverbial canary to save his skin. I had a fucking awful time getting out of the country.'

'Perhaps it's gone wrong because you didn't know how to run it.'

426

'I knew how to run it. I could run the entire operation with my eyes shut. I'd been doing it all the time you and Neal were married. No, it wasn't that. P2 didn't keep their word. As soon as you were safely away they systematically destroyed us. Fair enough. If they can't keep their word, I don't intend to keep mine.'

Her mouth was dry and her skin felt damp and cold with terror but she continued to keep her eyes locked on his, knowing he wouldn't want to be the first to look away.

'Don't you understand?' he repeated quietly. 'I've come to kill you.'

'I understand.'

'Why don't you try and get away?'

'I don't think I'd stand much chance!'

'Or talk me out of it?'

'There's no point. I've always known you wouldn't rest until I was dead. You'll get enough satisfaction out of the killing. I'm not going to add to it by going down on my knees and begging for mercy. And that's what you really want, isn't it, to see me crawl?'

'I'll see you beg anyway,' he snarled. 'Where's that son of yours?' And for the first time he looked back up the beach. Unable to stand the suspense any longer, Lisa turned too and at the sight of the deserted sand she gave a cry of relief, quickly stifled by the look on Bishop's face. 'Where did he go?' he asked, catching hold of her left wrist and twisting it painfully.

'Home, where you can't get him. They've all gone home, Bishop. I'm the only one left.'

Already some of the excited anticipation had left his face and she knew that even in death she would have cheated him. That knowledge gave her more strength to face whatever was in store for her. 'It looks as though I'll have to settle for you then,' he said slowly. 'Just think what your rich lover will go through when he discovers that he didn't manage to protect you, after all. He'll never forgive himself. Imagine it, thirty years or more left to remember how he failed, and to mourn the love of his life. It's enough to make a strong man weep!' And he laughed aloud.

At that moment she accepted that he was quite mad. Everything he'd wanted had turned to ashes in his hands and he'd finally lost his precarious hold on normality so that now killing and death were all that were left to him. Let it be quick, she prayed fervently. A gun perhaps, or even one fatal stab with a knife, but not a slow death. If that was what he had planned she didn't know if her courage would stand up to it.

'Any last words, Mrs Gueras?'

'No.'

'You know what they say, "it's better to have loved and lost ..."'
And he began to pull her the last few yards to the water's edge.

It wasn't true, she thought despairingly. She didn't want to die
after such a short time with Renato. A short time that she'd allowed
to be spoilt by her precognition of this moment. It took every ounce
of willpower that she possessed to stop herself from weeping.

When she understood that he was going to drown her, she thought
that it wouldn't be too hard to get it over quickly. She'd simply give
herself up to the water and let her lungs fill as speedily as possible, but
the moment he pushed her head beneath the cobalt blue sea she
instinctively began to fight, kicking out with her legs and hitting him
repeatedly with her one free arm as her body refused to accept what
her mind had decided.

The struggle was intense and silent except for the occasional gasp
when Lisa's head surfaced for a few vital seconds, or Bishop's rasping
breaths as he tried to keep her immersed despite the nauseating pain
in his groin where she'd kicked him.

To Lisa the struggle didn't seem silent at all. There was a continual
rushing in her ears and her heartbeats were thunderously loud. At
first, while Bishop was recovering from her initial attack, she'd
thought it might be possible to break away from him, but her hopes
faded as his strength returned.

Coughing and retching, she surfaced for what she thought was
about the fourth time and could no longer see anything except a red
mist that was darkening all the time. She could feel her body weaken-
ing, her limbs growing heavy and sluggish, and suddenly she was
incredibly tired.

Bishop, glancing anxiously up the beach in case the children had
raised the alarm, felt her body going limp and directed all his energy
into one final attempt at finishing her off. They were both over waist
deep in the water now and it was easier for him to immerse her head.
When his hands pressed down on the long, sun-streaked hair there
was no resistance and he bared his teeth in an expression of triumph,
knowing that this time when she came to the surface she'd be dead
and out of his life forever.

He'd waited so long for this moment that he became lost in the
sheer pleasure of watching the tiny bubbles, their surfacing slowing
down as Lisa ceased breathing. This was a mistake because, involved
in the intense almost sexual pleasure that her dying moments were
giving him, he ceased listening to anything but the sighing escape of
the bubbles and only heard the sound of the motor boat when it was
nearly on him.

Renato, who was standing in the front of the boat, launched himself straight at the startled Bishop before it had even cut its engine, his shout of rage reverberating round the cove.

Swearing furiously Bishop pushed harder on Lisa's head but then the Italian's hands were on him and he had to release her. Out of the corner of his eye he saw her drift to the surface, and noting that there was no sign of life in her body he laughed as the giant Italian grabbed him by the collar, lifting him clear of the water.

'Too late, Renato!' he gloated. 'For once the cavalry didn't arrive on time! She's dead. See for yourself.'

Renato's grip didn't loosen but he glanced to where his men were pulling Lisa aboard, turning her face down and trying to clear her lungs of water. Bishop stayed motionless in the huge hands, knowing full well that he was going to die but totally uncaring because at last he'd achieved his five-year ambition to kill the woman who'd ruined his entire world.

'The signora lives!' shouted one of the bodyguards.

Suddenly it was Renato's turn to smile. 'Poor Bishop! You will go to your death knowing that once again you failed, as you have been failing ever since Neal Gueras died.'

Bishop twisted and turned, his face contorted with disbelief. 'She can't be alive! Not after all that time!'

Renato turned the smaller man to face the stationary boat. There was the sound of coughing and retching and then, before Bishop's disbelieving eyes, Lisa was slowly assisted to a sitting position by one of the men. She stared across the water at him, shaking her head to clear her vision.

'See, she lives, but now it is your turn!' snarled Renato, and with amazing ease held Bishop away from him with his left hand before landing a crushing right-handed blow to his chin that knocked him unconscious. Then, with almost insulting casualness, he held the body under the water until he knew that any struggle for life must be over.

He pulled the dead body to the surface, looking down at the features that even in death were hard and uncompromising, and a great weight was lifted from his shoulders. One of the bodyguards surfaced next to him and swam gently away, towing the body behind him.

Renato swam powerfully to the boat then climbed aboard and folded the trembling Lisa in his arms. 'It is truly over,' he murmured, wiping her face with a towel. 'He will never trouble us again.' The boat edged its way to the beach and he climbed out with Lisa in his arms before sending it back to collect the other bodyguard and his dead companion.

'Dispose of it in the cross-currents,' he instructed in Italian. They nodded, moving away until finally there was no one left but Renato and Lisa. He carried her up the beach and laid her on the sand mat where she'd been before Bishop arrived. For a time she kept her eyes closed, but when she opened them she looked up at him with such an expression of love that the breath caught in his throat.

'I thought you were going to die,' he muttered, his hands holding hers as he rubbed them absent-mindedly. 'When the children told their nanny she thought it was a game. That's why we took so long.'

'At first I thought I was going to die too. It was strange. I wanted to live but it seemed more important that the children escaped. After all, I've had twenty-five years, and a fine mess I've made of most of them! The children are only just beginning.'

He traced her jawline with a finger and eased some of her wet hair back off her forehead. 'Weren't you afraid?'

'Terrified, yet it was something I'd been waiting for. I didn't know that Bishop would come to the beach today but for the past year I've been expecting something to happen. I always knew that it wasn't over.'

'It should never have happened! Our security was lax.'

'It had to happen one day. You couldn't keep me in a glass case, even if that was what you wanted. Do you know the worst thing about it all?'

'Tell me.'

'I kept thinking that we hadn't had enough time. That was what upset me most, not the prospect of dying but the loss of what we've shared. When I realised I was never going to see you again, I . . . That was when I nearly broke down. It would have been such a waste.'

And now she did begin to cry. He bent closer to her, kissing the tears from her cheeks as she sobbed against his chest, and when she started moving against him he knew that finally she wanted him as passionately as he had always wanted her.

She was no longer passive but instead making her need obvious, whispering to him to love her and as he covered her body with his own and gently slid his hand up her leg, she cried out with desire; arching her body against his, trying to hurry his slow movements so that she could be utterly possessed and lose herself in the safety and pleasure of his love.

Afterwards, lying with her head on his shoulder, Lisa turned her head and studied this man who'd finally given her the courage to become a woman. She still found if difficult to believe that anyone so handsome should be totally selfless, taking pleasure from the happiness of those he loved rather than expecting them to make him happy, as was usual with highly attractive men.

Sensing that her eyes were on him he slowly lifted his heavy lids and smiled into her face, only inches from his own. 'What is the matter? I am looking old perhaps, because my young girlfriend is wearing me out?'

'Don't fish for compliments.'

'What is this "fish for compliments"?'

'You know perfectly well you look disgracefully young and attractive, and you're trying to make me tell you as much!'

He grinned. 'Perhaps I like to hear it because I cannot believe that you are still here with me, despite my grey hairs!'

'I like your grey hairs, they're very distinguished.'

'My father was grey before he was thirty. I am doing better than that.'

'He's still attractive.'

'Ah, it is my father you really love!'

'You've guessed it! Renato ...'

He sat up, leaning on one elbow. '*Si?*'

'I don't know how you'll feel about this but ... I'm pregnant.'

His liquid eyes widened and he looked questioningly at her. 'You're sure?'

'Absolutely sure.'

His face lit up. 'Then I am the happiest man in the world! How can I ever tell you what this means to me. Luciano is a lovely boy and will always be special because he was my first child, but for his mother I felt very little. The marriage was arranged and we were not well suited. To have a child by the woman one loves − this, I think, is the greatest miracle that can happen.'

'I'm glad you're pleased.'

'You are not?'

She flushed. 'Of course I am. I'd begun to wonder if there was something wrong with me. We've been together over a year and I've never taken any precautions.'

'You too wanted a child of our own?'

'Yes. It will be the first time I've loved the father of my child. That's terrible, isn't it? I wonder what kind of a woman it makes me?'

'More honest than many, that's all!'

'Will you still love me when I'm fat?'

'Even more than I do now, because there will be more of you to love! I ask only one thing,' he added quietly, 'but it is important to me.'

Conditions, she thought despairingly. There always seemed to be conditions. 'What's that?' she asked as lightly as she could.

431

'It is nothing so terrible! All I ask is that you never change.'

A huge wave of relief swept over her. He truly did accept her as she was and loved her without demanding anything more than she could give, enough to let her feel free. It was the first time in her entire life that anyone had loved her solely for what she was and as Renato stood up and shook the sand from his body she thought back to her childhood.

For the first time it didn't hurt so much. She could even understand Simon and Stephanie a little more. In their own way they too had been victims of the Gueras organisation, and under such intense pressure she could understand how Simon might have hoped to achieve a measure of freedom through her marriage.

'We'll go back to the house now,' he said gently. 'It is time for us to change for dinner. The children will want to talk about their exciting adventure when they escaped from the bad man on the beach! Alexi and Jessica think it was one of Luciano's games. Naturally he and Rebekah understand more and they will need assurances that the man has gone forever.'

'What will we tell them?'

'That he drowned,' said Renato briefly and turned away, walking briskly up the path to the villa, obviously wanting to leave the memories of this final murder behind him.

In the early hours of the morning, after the children had been calmed, congratulated and allowed to have dinner with the adults, Lisa and Renato lay awake in the king-size bed, fingers loosely intertwined after their lovemaking.

'Will I ever forget it all?' she asked quietly. 'Can I possibly wipe it from my mind? Those years with Toby and Neal. The way Toby drank and what he did to me. The fear that seemed to grow the longer Neal and I were married, and silly little incidents that still terrify me, like the time he made me ride a horse in front of you. When am I going to be free of all that?'

He thought carefully for a moment. 'Perhaps you will not forget. There are some things that one always has to live with, but it does not matter. All that has happened to you in the past has made you the woman you are, the woman I love and want to marry. I think that if you accept everything in this way, positively, realising what you have learnt from your mistakes, then it will not matter so much. Eventually you will, I think, come to terms with it. That in itself is a kind of freedom.'

'Also you have grown stronger and accomplished much during these years. There is Jessica, scarcely recognisable as the terrified creature I saw at the dinner party so long ago; Alexi, growing into a

432

fine little boy; Rebekah who is happy and bright; and my own son who adores you. All these children are better for what you have done. They will grow up undamaged because even in the midst of your worst times you cared for them and their needs.'

'Yes,' she murmured. 'There have been good times with the children.'

'And now I will ask you properly, because it is something you never took seriously before. Will you become my wife, Lisa?' To his intense disappointment she still hesitated, her eyes clouded with uncertainty. 'There is nothing more I can offer to assure you of my love. If you do not trust me now then I think you never will, but since you are not sure . . .'

Moved by the misery in his voice she looked at his bewildered expression and her eyes cleared as she moved closer to his body. 'Of course I trust you, Renato. I trust and love you more than I'd ever have believed possible.'

'But still you hesitate.'

'Only because I don't know how I can ever make you as happy as you've made me.'

'If you marry me there is nothing more I could wish for. You are all I have ever wanted.'

At last she believed him. 'Yes,' she murmured, her breath warm against his neck, 'I'll marry you. Will we live happily ever after?'

'But of course! That is the way it is for Bellini wives!' he laughed.

She fell alseep lying in his arms and never dreamt of Toby, Neal or Bishop again.

It was different for Renato. From time to time in the years to come he would look back, although he never mentioned this to his radiant and self-confident wife. He looked back to his time in England and reminded himself that he'd killed twice in order to secure the safety of the woman at his side; but although the deaths lay heavily on his conscience, never to be mentioned until his final death-bed confession, he knew that there was nothing he would wish to change because no price had been too high in order to secure his life with Lisa.

Murder was wrong, he accepted that, but he was strong enough to cope with his memories, and such was the happiness that Lisa and the family brought him that the times when he actually remembered were few and fleeting. Despite everything he considered himself a most fortunate and privileged man.

433

Epilogue

Every year, on the anniversary of his death, Lisa ordered a bunch of red roses to be placed on the grave of Mike Brooks. Mike, who had sacrificed his life so that she and the children could be free to live theirs. She only hoped that somehow he knew what happiness he'd allowed into their lives.

Out of all the deaths during her years in England, his was the greatest tragedy but with her newfound maturity she finally understood and accepted that he had been content to die for a love that would never be returned.

When she and Renato named their youngest son Michael, they did it in honour of the young man who'd made it all possible, a tangible gesture of their gratitude.

Even if Mike didn't know, the roses brought comfort in the early years to his mother who had never understood why her son died but studied the unsigned card that bore the same inscription every year and was happy, believing that there had been a special girl in his life. A worthy girl who kept his memory alive.

It was such a lovely inscription on every card, beautiful in its simplicity. It read:

'Your love was the greatest love of all'.